The Glorious Adventures of

Tyl Ulenspiegl

by Charles de Coster

Reformation ⑤

This is the first complete

English translation by Allan Ross Macdougall;

introduced to the English-speaking world

by Camille Huysmans; *illustrated with*

one hundred woodcuts by the author's

compatriot Frans Masereel; *and published*

A.D. MCMXLIV *in New York by*

PANTHEON BOOKS · INC.

Designer: Ernst Reichl

MANUFACTURED IN THE U. S. A. BY H. WOLFF, NEW YORK

Contents

Translator's Note

It is a fine thing that this mighty book—this "popular epic, unique in our time," as Romain Rolland calls it—is at last being brought out in a popular edition. A fine thing, too, that it is being published at a moment when the free peoples of the whole world are united in another episode of the eternal struggle against the evil powers of darkness and oppression. For the magnificent masterpiece of Charles de Coster depicts with epic force one of the earlier victories of freemen over those who fear Freedom for any but themselves.

When I began this translation in the fall of 1929 in the tranquil Berkshire farmhouse of Edna St. Vincent Millay, I was already looking forward to seeing it being read by many thousands who would savor, as I myself had done, its poetry, its humor, its drama, the deep passion and the sweeping power of it. The popular edition projected by my publishers, however, never appeared; instead the book was handsomely issued to a limited number of readers.

Now it comes forth in its new popular dress, the translation revised and the text decorated with superb woodcuts by Frans Masereel. This Flemish artist, according to Romain Rolland, "has allied within him the two opposing elements which are so characteristic of Tyl Ulenspiegl: the enormous buffoonery and the dark demons of the soul: violence and melancholy." Seldom has an author been so well served by his illustrator.

And now as to the original prose of De Coster. In the admirable Introduction which follows, Camille Huysmans speaks of Tyl Ulenspiegl as being written "in an archaic and strongly rhythmic language that is not easy of translation into another tongue." The translator's task indeed is not easy. He is confronted with the following problem: Shall he carry over into his English version that artificially archaic language, and imitate the style, say, which Sir Thomas Urquhart created for his inimitable translation of the first three books of Gargantua; or, on the other hand, shall he let all the inversions, the Thees, the Thous and the Gadzooks, go by the board and write simply in unfrilled, yet rhythmic English, taking care that none of the essential vigor of the original be lost in the process.

I chose the second course, with what success the reader must judge for himself. But as Roger Ascham said, almost four hundred years ago: "Even the best Translation is for mere Necessity but an evil imped Wing to fly withal, or a heavy Stump Leg of Wood to go withal. Such the higher they fly, the sooner they falter and fail; the faster they run, the oftener they stumble, and sorer they fall." I hope my falterings and failings, my stumblings and fallings have not been so many that they will spoil the pleasure of the reader in this truly great book. And I hope that he may find pleasure and profit in more than one reading of it, as I myself have done.

ALLAN ROSS MACDOUGALL

New York City, June, 1943.

Introduction

WHEN Charles de Coster's epic novel, ULENSPIEGL, was published in 1869, only thirty years had elapsed since the emergence of Belgium as an independent nation. De Coster and Belgium are thus of the same age, and, through the genius of the writer, Belgian literature made its start full-grown, in the shape of a masterpiece that equals the DON QUIXOTE of Spain and the PANTAGRUEL of France. Of ULENSPIEGL, Romain Rolland has written: "In the creation of this epic it seems that the destiny of a race had more to do than the will of a man, and that the genius of the man had been to make himself the instrument of that destiny."

Ulenspiegl's story is the history of his country, for De Coster chose as subject the revolution of seven Low Country provinces, in the sixteenth century, against the power of Spain represented by King Philip II and the Duke of Alba, his governor and hangman in Flanders. In this tale of love of liberty and fight for liberation, the popular hero is Ulenspiegl, the noble hero is William the Silent.

It is significant that, although ULENSPIEGL has never been unread or forgotten, it has always been vigorously revived in times of war. The reason is not far to seek: like all truly great books, it mirrors the passions and struggles that belong to all ages, all places, all men driven to fight for liberty. Innumerable parallels to our time strike the present-day reader, who relives in this book the history of today.

But there are other reasons for reading ULENSPIEGL. It is masterly in construction. It is well written, in an archaic and strongly rhythmic language that is not easy of translation into another tongue. The work has an epic quality, not only because of its impressive presentation of historical fact and background, but because of the fascinating central character.

De Coster's Ulenspiegl is more than the traditional figure of farce as it is familiar in the folk literature of the Flemish, Dutch and Lower-German provinces. The conventional prankster has already accumulated in his person, by the well-known process of epic concentration, popular, legendary jest and buffoonery, just as to Charlemagne were attributed the heroic deeds of both his predecessors and his contemporaries. This frolicsome character of tradition was already popular before De Coster built a novel around him, but the importance of De Coster's book is that he put Ulenspiegl into a setting of history, fitted him into a great revolutionary adventure. Thus the comic hero becomes also the valiant and patriotic defender of his country, and of liberty; his life, like that of all mankind, is a mingling of comedy and tragedy.

The legendary Ulenspiegl farces were legion, and De Coster's problem was to organize this vast material. He solved this by a kind of literary geometry. His story is constructed with the architectural pattern of a cathedral, beginning with two parallel lines representing Ulenspiegl on the one side and Philip II on the other. The lives of these two from childhood follow parallel but contrasting lines of development, one committed to the salvation of man, the other to his damnation.

As a foil to Ulenspiegl there is an additional element, borrowed from Cervantes. Sancho Panza is the alter-ego to the Knight of the Rueful Countenance; Lamme Goedzak is the companion to Ulenspiegl. Lamme is as fat as Sancho, and Ulenspiegl is as thin as Don Quixote. Yet there is no contrasting character to set off Philip II. There cannot be, for Philip is alone and he will remain alone. He loves no one; he is aware of no one but himself. He is the one who gives commands. He is the only one of his kind and he has all the vices of the solitary.

Associated with Ulenspiegl is a whole series of other characters, arranged on different planes. There is his father, Claes, the honest charcoal-burner, tainted with heresy like his preacher-brother. There is Ulenspiegl's good mother, Soetkin. And there is Katheline, the mad-woman, mother of Ulenspiegl's sweetheart, Nele. Katheline is the link between the real and the unreal, between historical happenings and the fantasies of the wandering, unlimited imagination, a role which the society of her time judged to be that of a witch. The magic and witchcraft that played a part in so many trials of the sixteenth century, and of the seventeenth, may even be taken seriously, in certain places, in the twentieth. And, finally, there is the idyll of Ulenspiegl's and Nele's love, dramatic relief to the violence of other scenes. Tenderness, chastity, faithfulness, long trials borne with stout heart, all this is Nele, "the heart of Flanders."

On the historical plane, appear the rebels, William the Silent, Louis of Nassau, Brederode, all the great lords of the Low Countries—Flanders and the Netherlands. Rebels on land, rebels on the sea. Here, too, are those who understood too late, like Egmont, like the unthinking men of today—like all those who want to live without a struggle. And on Philip's side are the

Book One

—

1 AT DAMME, in Flanders, when May was unfolding the hawthorn blossoms, Ulenspiegl, son of Claes, was born. A gossipy mid-wife named Katheline wrapped him in warm swaddling-clothes and, looking at his head, saw a piece of skin hanging therefrom.

'Born with a caul,' she cried joyfully, 'born under a lucky star!' But, the moment after, she moaned as she pointed to a tiny black mole on the babe's shoulder.

'Woe! Woe!' she wept, ' 'tis the black fingerprint of the Devil.'

'Master Satan,' replied Claes, 'must have risen early if he has had time to set his mark on my son.'

'He hasn't even been to bed,' cried Katheline, 'for there crows Chantecleer only just awakening the hens.' And, placing the child in the arms of Claes, she ran from the room.

Then the dawn came bursting through nocturnal clouds, the yammering swallows dipped and skimmed over the fields, while the red sun showed his dazzling face on the horizon.

Pushing the window open, Claes spoke to Ulenspiegl, saying:

'Boy with a caul, there is our Lord the Sun who comes to greet the land of Flanders. Gaze on him whenever you can and when, in other years, you may be caught in any doubt, not knowing the right thing to do, ask counsel of him. He is bright and warm. Be sincere as he is bright, and kind as he is warm!'

'Claes, goodman,' said Soetkin, 'you are preaching to the deaf. Come, drink, my son.'

And the mother offered to her newly-born nature's fair flagons.

2 WHILE ULENSPIEGL lipped them, all the birds of the countryside began to awaken. Claes, who was bundling faggots, watched his goodwife suckle their child.

'Wife,' said he, 'have you laid in good store of that fine milk?'

'The pitchers are full,' she answered, 'but not enough for my content.'

'You speak very lightly of so great a joy.'

15

'I was thinking,' she said, 'that there is not so much as a pennypiece in the leathern wallet hanging there on the wall.'

Claes took it down and vainly shook it; no silver music fell on his ears. Quite crestfallen, yet hoping to comfort his wife, he said:

'Why do you worry yourself? Have we not in the bin the cake that Katheline gave us yesterday? And do I not see a great piece of beef that should make good milk for the babe for three days at least? Does that well-filled bean sack in the corner foretell famine? Is that tub of butter a phantom? Are they but spectres, those flags and banners of apples, ranged warlike in the loft in ranks of eleven? Is there not promise of good drinking in that paunchy cask of *cuyte of Bruges* whose belly holds refreshment for us?'

'When we take the child to the christening,' said Soetkin, 'we shall have need of two patards for the priest and a florin for the feasting.'

Thereüpon Katheline, carrying a great bunch of herbs, entered and said:

'For the child born with a caul, I bring *angelica* that preserves man from lust; *fennel* that drives away Satan . . .'

'Have you none of that herb,' broke in Claes, 'that conjures forth florins?'

'No!' she answered.

'Then I will go and see if there be not any growing by the canal.'

So out he went, carrying his line and net, knowing well that he would be unlikely to meet anyone, since it still lacked an hour before the *oosterzon*, which is, in Flanders, the six-o'clock-in-the-morning sun.

3 CLAES CAME to the Bruges Canal, not far from the sea. There, having baited his line, he cast it into the water and lowered his net. On the opposite bank, sleeping like a log on a clump of mussels, lay a well-dressed little boy. The noise made by Claes awoke him, and he was about to run away, fearing that some village constable had come to pick him up and carry him before the *steen* as a vagabond.

But when he recognised Claes he was no longer afraid. 'Would you like to earn six liards?' Claes called over to him. 'Drive the fish this way.'

At these words the boy entered the water, his little belly puffed out, and, arming himself with a reed switch, he drove the fish toward Claes.

When the fishing was over, Claes drew in his net and line and, having crossed the lockgate, came to the boy.

'You are the little fellow whose Christian name is Lamme, but you are called Goedzak because of your gentle nature; you live in the Heron

16

Street behind the Church of Our Lady. How comes it that, young and well-dressed as you are, you sleep here in the open?'

'La, Mr. Charcoal-burner,' replied the boy, 'I have a sister at home who is a year younger than I and who beats me at the least quarrel. But I dare not strike her back, for I would hurt her, sir. Last night at supper I was very hungry and was cleaning out the bottom of a dish of beef and bean stew with my fingers. She wanted a share, sir, but there was only enough for me. When she saw me lick my fingers because the sauce tasted so good, she became furious and struck out at me with such force that I fled from the house all bruised.'

'And what were your parents doing during this scene?' Claes asked him.

'My father struck me on one shoulder and my mother on the other, crying "Avenge yourself, coward!" But I, not wanting to strike a girl, ran away.'

All at once Lamme went pale and began to tremble and Claes saw a tall woman approaching with a little, thin and fierce-looking girl walking at her side.

'Oh,' cried Lamme, clutching at Claes's breeches, 'here come my mother and sister to find me! Protect me, Mr. Charcoal-burner!'

'Here, take first these seven liards you have earned,' said Claes, 'and let us go to meet them fearlessly.'

When the two women saw Lamme, they ran forward ready to beat him, the mother because of the anxiety he had caused her and the sister because it was her habit to do so. Lamme hid behind Claes, crying:

'I've earned seven liards! I've earned seven liards! Don't beat me!'

His mother was already hugging him however, while the sister was trying to force open his fingers to take the money away from him. But Lamme cried:

'It's mine! You shan't have it!'

And he clenched his fists tightly. Then Claes shook the girl roughly by the ears, saying:

'If ever again you pick a quarrel with your brother, who is good and gentle as a lamb, I shall throw you into my charcoal-pit, and there your ears won't be pulled by me but by the red devil from Hell who'll tear you to pieces with his great claws and his forked teeth.'

At this threat the girl, not daring to look at Claes or go near her brother, hid behind her mother's skirts, but when she re-entered the town she cried aloud everywhere:

'The charcoal-man beat me! He keeps the devil in his cellar!'

But she never struck Lamme again, though being the bigger of the

18

two she made him do her work for her. And he, the gentle simpleton, did it willingly.

On his way home, Claes sold all his catch to a farmer who usually bought fish from him and, when he reached the house, he said to Soetkin:

'Here's what I found in the bellies of four pike, nine carp and a basketful of eels.' And on the table he threw two florins and a patard.

'Why don't you go fishing every day, good man?' asked Soetkin.

'For fear I might turn fish and be caught in the village constable's net,' he replied.

4 IN DAMME, the father of Ulenspiegl was known as Claes the *Kooldraeger* or charcoal-burner. He was black-haired, bright-eyed, and his skin was the colour of his wares except on Sundays and holidays, when there was lots of soap in his cottage. He was short, thick-set and strong, with a happy countenance.

If, at the end of the day when evening fell, he went to any tavern on the road to Bruges to lave his coal-dusty gullet with *cuyt*, all the women standing in their doorways taking the evening air would call out a friendly greeting to him:

'Good even and good beer to you, Charcoal-man!'

'Good even, and a watchful husband!' would answer Claes.

The girls returning in bands from the fields would plant themselves in front of him to stop his passage and demand:

'What will you pay us for the right of way? Scarlet ribbon? Buckles of gold? Velvet shoon? Or a florin-piece for alms?'

But Claes, catching hold of one of them by the waist, would kiss her cheek or her neck, depending on which cool skin was nearest his mouth. Then he would say:

'Ask, my sweets, ask your lovers for the rest.'

19

And they would go their way, bursting with laughter.

The children knew Claes by his loud voice and the noise his clogs made. Running to him they would say:

'Good even, Charcoal-burner!'

'God give you the same, my little cherubs,' he would answer, 'but come no closer or I'll turn you into blackamoors.'

But, being bold, the children would go closer just the same. Then Claes would seize one of them by the doublet and, rubbing his grimy hands over the little one's clean nose, would send him off all smudged, but laughing just the same, to the great delight of the others.

Soetkin, the wife of Claes, was a good helpmeet, early as the dawn, diligent as the ant. She and Claes tilled their field together, yoked like oxen to the plough. Hard though it was dragging the plough along, it was even harder pulling the harrow, when that rustic implement had to tear up the stony earth with its wooden teeth. Yet they laboured with light hearts, singing some old ballad all the while.

In vain was the earth stony-hard; in vain did the sun hurl down on them his scorching beams; in vain did the tugging at the harrow force them to bend their knees and cruelly strain their loins; if they but stopped for a moment and Soetkin turned her gentle face to Claes and he kissed that mirror of her tender heart, they both forgot their great weariness.

5   THE NIGHT BEFORE, the town crier had given notice before the Town Hall that Madame, the wife of the Emperor Charles, being heavy with child, it behoved the people to pray for her speedy deliverance.

Katheline ran to the house of Claes, all trembling.

'What ails you, woman?'

'Alas!' she replied, speaking jerkily, 'last night spectres, mowing men down like grass—young girls buried alive—on the bodies danced the hangman—stone that sweated blood for nine months broken last night!'

'Mercy on us,' groaned Soetkin, 'Lord God have mercy on us! 'Tis a black omen for Flanders.'

'Saw you these things with your own eyes or in a dream?' demanded Claes.

'With my own eyes,' said Katheline. Then she continued, all pale and weeping: 'Two babes are born—the one in Spain, the Infante Philip; the other in Flanders, the son of Claes, who shall later be called Ulenspiegl. Philip will grow up an executioner, being engendered by

20

Charles V, the destroyer of our country. Ulenspiegl will be a great master of jolly words and youthful pranks but good-hearted withal, having had for father Claes the valiant labourer, who knows how to earn his bread bravely, honestly and simply. Charles the Emperor and Philip the King will ride rough-shod through life, doing ill by battles, extortions and other crimes. Claes, toiling all the week, living righteously and lawfully, laughing rather than weeping over his heavy

labours, will be the model of all good toilers of Flanders. Ulenspiegl, ever young and deathless, will roam the world, settling nowhere. He will be peasant, noble, painter, sculptor —all in one. And throughout the world he will go praising all good and lovely things and flouting loudly all stupidities. Claes is your courage, oh, noble Flanders folk; Soetkin your valiant mother; Ulenspiegl your soul. A sweet and gentle girl, lover of Ulenspiegl, and like him immortal, shall be your heart; and Lamme Goedzak, a great puff-belly, shall be your stomach. Above shall be the devourers of the people; below, their victims; above shall be the thieving hornets; below, the busy bees: and in the skies shall bleed the wounds of Christ!'

And having said all this, Katheline, the kindly mid-wife, fell asleep.

6 THEY CARRIED Ulenspiegl to the christening; suddenly there fell a shower that soaked him through. So was he christened for the first time. When they entered the church, the god-father and godmother, father and mother, were told by the school-master-beadle where they were to stand about the baptismal font, and they took their places.

But in the roof above the font there was a hole, made by a mason who was to hang up a star-shaped lamp of gilded wood. This mason, after watching from above the godfather and godmother standing stiffly about the uncovered font, poured through the hole a treacherous bucket of water that fell between them on the lid of the font and made a great splash. Ulenspiegl received most of it, however, and so was he christened for the second time.

The dean arrived and they complained to him, but he told them to make haste, that it was only an accident. Ulenspiegl squirmed because of the water that had fallen on him. The dean gave him the salt and water and named him *Tylbert*, which means 'rich in movements'. So was he christened for the third time.

Leaving the Church of Our Lady, they crossed the Long Street to the 'Rosary of Bottles,' whose credo is a pitcher. They drank seventeen bottles of *dobble cuyt*, and more. For the true Flanders way of drying drenched folk is to light a fire of beer in their bellies. Ulenspiegl was christened in this way for the fourth time.

Staggering home along the road, the head heavier than the body, they came to a plank bridge thrown across a pond. Katheline, who was the godmother and carried the child, made a mis-step and fell into the mud with Ulenspiegl, who was thus christened for the fifth time.

But they pulled him out of the pond and washed him in warm water at the house of Claes, and that was his sixth christening.

7 THAT SAME DAY, His Sacred Majesty Charles resolved to celebrate with much festivity the birth of his son. He decided, like Claes, to go fishing, not in the canal however, but in the pockets and wallets of his people. It is from such places as these that the royal lines draw forth crusadoes, silver daelders, gold lions and all the marvellous fish that change at the fisher's desire into velvet robes, precious jewels, exquisite wines and fine foods. For the best stocked rivers are not always those with most water.

Having called his council about him, His Sacred Majesty resolved that the fishing should be done in the following manner:

The Lordly Infante would be borne to the christening about nine or ten o'clock. The inhabitants of Valladolid, to show their joy, should revel and feast all night—at their own expense—and should scatter their silver for the poor in the town square.

At five crossings there should be great fountains from which would flow, till dawn, strong wine paid for by the city. At five other crossings should be set out, in wooden booths, sausages, saveloys, botargoes, chitterlings, ox-tongues and other meats—also at the city's expense.

The townsfolk should set up—at their own expense—along the route of the procession, triumphal arches representing Peace, Felicity, Abundance, Fortune, propitious and emblematic of all the divers gifts

22

showered down on them from the heavens under the reign of His Sacred Majesty.

Finally, beside these pacific arches, there should be placed several others on which should be painted, in bright colours, less benignant attributes, such as eagles, lions, lances, halberds, pikes with flamboyant blades, serrated hackbuts, cannon, falconets, mortars with great mugs, and other weapons pictorially showing the strength and war-like power of His Sacred Majesty.

As for the lighting of the church, the Guild of Candlemakers should be permitted to make, freely and for nothing, more than twenty thousand candles whose unburned ends would revert to the chapter.

For all other expenses the Emperor would willingly pay, thereby showing his kindly desire not to overburden his people too much.

As the town was about to carry out these orders, lamentable news came from Rome. The Emperor's captains—Orange, Alençon and Frundsberg—had entered the Holy City and, having sacked and pillaged the churches, chapels, and houses, had spared no one, neither the priests, nuns, women, nor children. The Holy Father had been made prisoner. For a week the pillage went on and *reiters* and *landsknechts* wandered about Rome stuffed with food, drunk with wine, brandishing their arms, seeking out cardinals, saying they would carve the hides of them deep enough to prevent their ever being popes. Others, having already executed that threat, went proudly about the town, wearing on their breasts rosaries of twenty-eight or more beads, large as nuts and all bloody. Certain streets were red streams, wherein lay the rifled bodies of the dead.

Some said that the Emperor, having need of money, had decided to fish for it in the blood of the Church, and that, having taken cognizance of the treaty imposed by his commanders on the captive pontiff, he forced him to cede all the strongholds of his state, pay 400,000 ducats and remain a prisoner until all this was carried out.

Yet the grief of His Majesty was so great that he countermanded all the joyful preparations, feasts and rejoicings, and ordered all the lords and ladies of his household to put on robes of mourning.

And the child was baptised in his white robes—the robes of royal mourning. And this was interpreted by the lords and ladies as a sinister omen.

Nevertheless, Madame the Nurse presented the child to the lords and ladies of the palace so that they might, according to custom, offer their good wishes and gifts.

Madame de la Coena placed about his neck a black stone against poison; it was shaped and sized like a hazel nut and had a shell of

23

gold. Madame de la Chauffade fastened on him a silken cord bearing a filbert that dangled down to his stomach and was precipitative of good digestion of all nourishment. Messer van de Steen of Flanders, presenting a Ghent sausage, five ells long and half an ell thick, humbly wished that His Highness but smelling it would thirst for *clauwert* in the Ghentish way; he added that he who loves the beer of a town can never hate the brewers. Messer Squire Jacque-Christopher of Castille begged the Lordly Infante to wear green jasper on his dear little feet to make them run well. Jan de Paepe, the Jester, who was present, said:

'Sire, give him rather the trumpet of Joshua, at whose sound all the towns ran at a great trot before him, going to plant themselves elsewhere with all their inhabitants, men, women and children. For our Lord must not learn to run but to make others run.'

The tearful widow of Floris van Borsele, who was Lord of Veere in Zeeland, gave my Lord Philip a stone which, she said, made men loving and women inconsolable.

But the Infante whimpered like a calf.

And at the same time Claes put a wicker rattle with bells in his son's hands and said, as he made Ulenspiegl dance on his broad palm, 'Bells, bells, tinkling bells: may you always have them on your cap, my little man. For only the fools shall inherit the Kingdom of Good Times.'

And Ulenspiegl laughed.

8   CLAES, HAVING CAUGHT a large salmon, it was eaten on Sunday by himself and Soetkin and Katheline and little Ulenspiegl.

But Katheline ate no more than would a bird. 'Goodwife,' said Claes, 'is the air of Flanders now so solid that it is enough for you to breathe it to be fed as with a plate of meat? When may we live this way? The rains shall be good soups, it shall hail beans, and the snows, changed to celestial fricassees, shall cheer poor travellers!'

Katheline, nodding her head, said not a word.

'Look now, she's in the dumps. What can be grieving her?' demanded Claes.

But Katheline, speaking with a voice that was a whisper, said: 'The wicked one! Night falls black—I hear him foretelling his coming—screaming like a sea-bird—trembling, I pray our Lady the Virgin—in vain—for him neither walls nor hedges, doors nor windows. Entering everywhere like a spirit—creaking ladder. Seizing me in his cold arms, hard as marble—frozen face, kisses damp like snow—cottage tossed on the earth, moving like a bark on a stormy sea . . .'

'You must go each morning to Mass,' said Claes, 'so that our Lord

24

Jesus may give you strength to drive away this phantom come from
Hell.'

'He is so beautiful,' she said.

9 ULENSPIEGL, being weaned, grew like a young poplar. Claes no
longer kissed him often, yet he loved him with a rough air,
so as not to soften him.

When Ulenspiegl would come home, complaining of having been
beaten in some set-to, Claes would give him a drubbing because he had
not beaten the others and, educated in this way, Ulenspiegl grew up
valiant as a young lion.

If Claes were absent and Ulenspiegl asked Soetkin for a liard to go
and play, Soetkin, becoming angry, would say:

'What need have you to go and play? It were better you stayed here
to bundle these faggots.'

Seeing that she gave nothing, Ulenspiegl would scream like an eagle,
but Soetkin clattered the pots and pans she was washing in the wooden
tub, pretending not to hear. Ulenspiegl would weep then and the gentle
mother would no longer feign harshness and, coming to him, would
kiss him and say: 'Will a denier be enough for you?' (Note that the
denier was worth six liards!)

So did she love him overmuch, and when Claes was not at home
Ulenspiegl was king of the house.

10 ONE MORNING Soetkin saw Claes with bent head, wandering
about the kitchen like a man lost in thought. 'What's trou-
bling you, man?' she asked. 'You are pale, angry and distraught.'

With a low voice, as of a growling dog, Claes replied: 'They are
going to renew the cruel edicts of the Emperor. Once more Death is
going to fly low over the Land of Flanders. Informers are to have one-
half of the victims' goods, if such goods do not exceed a hundred
florins.'

'We are poor,' she said.

'Not poor enough,' he replied. 'There are those vile enough—ravens,
and corpse-devouring vultures—who would denounce us as much to
share a bag of charcoal as a sack of florins. What had poor Tanneken,
the widow of Sis the Tailor, who was buried alive at Heyst? A Latin
bible, three golden florins, and a few household utensils of English
pewter which her neighbour coveted. Johannah Martens was burned

for a witch after she had been thrown into the water, where her body floated—bewitched, they said. She had some miserable furnishings and seven gold florins in a wallet, and the informer wanted half of them. I could speak of these things till it be morrow, but come, mother, life's no longer worth living in Flanders because of these edicts. Soon each night the chariot of Death will pass through the town, and we will hear the dry rattle of bones as the skeleton shakes.'

'You mustn't frighten me, my man,' said Soetkin. 'The Emperor is the father of Flanders and Brabant and, as such, is endowed with fore-bearance, kindness, patience and pity.'

'He would lose much by all that,' replied Claes, 'for he inherits the confiscated goods.'

Suddenly the town heralds' trumpets sounded and the cymbals clashed. Claes and Soetkin, each in turn carrying Ulenspiegl in their arms, ran with the crowd to the place where the sound came from. They came to the Town Hall, before which stood the mounted heralds, sounding their trumpets and clanging their cymbals, the Provost hold-ing the Rod of Justice, and the town Proctor on horseback, holding in both hands an Imperial edict which he was about to read to the assem-bled multitude.

Claes heard that from thenceforward it was forbidden to all and sundry to print, read, have or support the writings, books or doctrines of Martin Luther, John Wyclif, John Huss, Mercilius of Padua, Æco-lampadius, Ulricus Zwynglius, Philippus Melanchthon, Franciscus Lambertus, Joannes Pomeranus, Otto Brunselsius, Justus Jonas, Joannes Puperis and Gorcianus: likewise the New Testament printed by Adrien de Berges, Christophe de Remona, and Joannes Zel, full of Lutheran and other heresies condemned and reproved by the Theo-logical Faculty of the University of Louvain.

Neither, in a like manner to paint or portray, nor cause to be painted or portrayed any opprobrious paintings or figures of God, or the Blessed Virgin Mary, or His Saints; nor to break, destroy or efface the images or portrayals that might be made in the honour, memory or remembrance of God, the Virgin Mary, or the Saints approved by the Church.

Moreover, continued the edict, let no one, no matter what his station, presume to discuss or dispute the Holy Writ, even in doubtful matters, if he be not a theologian renowned and approved by a well-known University.

His Sacred Majesty decreed, among other penalties, that the suspect might never hold honourable estate. As for those fallen again in their errors or who were obstinate in them, they would be condemned to

26

burn by slow or fast fire, in a straw covering, or else bound to the stake, according to the judges' discretion. Other men, if they were nobles or good burghers, would perish by the sword, commoners would be hanged, and women buried alive. Their heads would be fixed on pikes as a warning to all others. The goods of all these people, if they lived in places subject to confiscation, would go to the Emperor.

His Sacred Majesty accorded to all informers one-half of all the property of those executed, provided such property did not exceed one hundred pounds of Flanders money. As for the Emperor's part, he reserved it for works of piety and mercy, as he did at the sack of Rome.

And Claes went off sadly with Soetkin and Ulenspiegl.

11 THE YEAR having been good, Claes bought himself a donkey and nine measures of peas for seven florins. And one morning he mounted the beast, with Ulenspiegl holding on to the crupper behind him. In this way they went to greet their uncle and elder brother Josse Claes, who lived not far from Meyborg in Germany.

Josse, who had been simple and kind-hearted in his youth, was now crotchety, having suffered divers wrongs; his blood had turned to bile; to him all men were hateful, and he lived alone.

It was now his pleasure to set two so-called faithful friends fighting each other, and he would give three patards to the one who gave the other the bitterest beating.

He also loved to bring together in a well-heated room a great many old wives—the oldest and most crabbed—and set before them toasted bread and hypocras. To those who were more than sixty years, he gave wool so that they might knit in the corner, and he always recommended them to let their nails grow long. And it was wonderful to hear all the gurgling, tongue-clacking, mischievous babblings, coughings and sour spittings of these old hags who sat with their knitting-needles under their arms, nibbling together at their neighbours' honour.

When he saw them all quite lively, Josse would throw some hair into the fire and, as it burned, the air would suddenly become foul-smelling.

The old wives then, all talking together, would accuse each other of causing the stink. All would deny it and soon they would have each other by the hair, while Josse threw more foul-smelling stuff in the fire and scattered clipped horse-hair on the floor. When he could no longer see because of the furious struggle, the thick smoke and the up-raised dust, he went to get two of his men, dressed as constables. With sound blows from switches, they would chase from the room the old women, who resembled a flock of furious geese.

27

And Josse, looking over the battle-field, would find bits of skirts, shoes, blouses and old teeth.

And very sadly he would say to himself:

'A wasted day; not one of them lost her tongue in the fray!'

12 CLAES, BEING in the bailiwick of Meyborg, traversed a wood. As it walked, the donkey nibbled at the thistles; Ulenspiegl threw out his cap after butterflies and picked it up without leaving the donkey's back. Claes munched a slice of bread, thinking to wash it down at the next tavern. From afar he heard a bell ringing and the noise made by a great crowd of men when they speak together.

'It's a pilgrimage,' said he, 'and the pilgrims are doubtless many. Hold on well to the donkey, son, so that you won't be knocked over. Let's go and see. Come on, donkey, to heel!'

And off the beast ran.

Leaving the edge of the wood, they came to a large plain bordered on its west side by a river. On the eastern side there was a little chapel whose gable was surmounted by the image of Our Lady, having at her feet two figurines each representing a bull. Upon the chapel steps stood a laughing hermit ringing his bell; fifty footmen holding lighted candles; players, blowers, beaters of drums, clarions, fifes, shawms and bagpipes; and a bunch of jolly companions, holding in both hands iron boxes full of old iron, but all silent at that moment.

Five thousand, and even more, pilgrims walked along, seven by seven, helmets on their heads and staffs of green wood in their hands. If others arrived, helmeted and armed in like manner, they ranged themselves noisily behind the others. Then, passing seven by seven before the chapel, they had their staffs blessed and received, each one from the hands of the footmen, a candle for which they paid half a florin to the hermit.

The procession was so long that the candles of the first pilgrims were burned down to the wick, while those of the latest comers burned with difficulty from the excess of tallow.

Claes, Ulenspiegl and the donkey, all astonished, thus saw passing before them a great variety of bellies, fat, high, long, pointed, proud, firm or falling ignobly on their natural props. And all the pilgrims wore helmets.

Some of these helmets had come from Troy and were like Phrygian bonnets, or were surmounted with aigrettes of red horsehair; other pilgrims, although puffy-faced and paunchy, wore helmets with outspread wings that had no thought for flight; then came those crowned with salads scorned by snails for their lack of greenery.

But the majority wore helmets so old and rusty that they seemed to date back to Gambrinus, the King of Flanders and Beer, who lived nine hundred years before our Lord and always wore a quart beer-pot as a hat so as never to go thirsty for want of a mug to drink from.

All at once rang, groaned, thundered, thumped, yelped, brayed, clattered bells, bagpipes, shawms, drums and scrap iron.

At the sound of this tumult, which was a signal for the pilgrims, they all turned about, placing themselves face to face by bands of seven and, by way of provocation, every man thrust his lighted candle in the face of the man before him. This caused great sneezing. Then the staffs began to fall and the pilgrims fought each other with foot, head, heel and everything else. Some rushed at their foes like rams, with downed heads that were forced into their shoulders by the impact, and so caused them to fall back blindly into a group of others who did not receive them at all kindly.

Others, whiners and cowards, moaned because of the blows, but while they murmured their doleful prayers two groups of fighting pilgrims rushed over them like lightning, knocking them to earth and trampling on them mercilessly.

And the hermit laughed.

Other groups of seven, clustered like grapes, rolled from the plain into the river, where they still kept pounding at each other without any dampened ardour.

And the hermit laughed.

Those who stayed on the plain were blacking each other's eyes, knocking out teeth, pulling out hair and tearing off each other's doublets and hose.

And the hermit laughed and cried out:

'Courage, friends, he who strikes well but loves better! To the hard-

29

est fighters the loves of their ladies! Our Lady of Rindisbels, here's where you see males!'

And the pilgrims went at it with happy hearts.

In the meantime, Claes had drawn nearer to the hermit, while Ulenspiegl laughed and cried, cheering the blows.

'Father,' asked Claes, 'what crime have these poor fellows done, to be forced to strike each other so cruelly?'

But the hermit, heedless, cried:

'Loafers! You're losing your courage! If the fists are weary, what of the feet? Living God! Some of you have legs to flee like hares! What makes the spark fly from the flint? The iron that strikes it. What enlivens old men's virility, if not a good dish of blows well seasoned with manly rage?'

At these words the pilgrims continued to fight each other with helmets, hands and feet. It was a furious melée wherein Argus with the hundred eyes would have seen nothing but uplifted dust and the tip of some helmet.

Suddenly the hermit rang his bell. Fifes, drums, trumpets, bagpipes, shawms and scrap iron ceased their noise. And that was the signal for peace.

The pilgrims picked up their wounded. Among them were seen several tongues swollen with anger and protruding from the mouths of the combatants. But they returned of themselves to their accustomed palates. The most difficult task was to pry off the helmets that had been forced down to the necks of some who tried to shake them off but succeeded no more than had they been unripened plums.

And, after all this, the hermit said to them:

'Each of you recite an *Ave* and go back to your good wives. In nine months there will be as many more children in the bailiwick as there have been valiant champions in the battle today.'

And the hermit sang an *Ave*, and they all joined in with him. And the bell rang.

The hermit then blessed them in the name of Our Lady of Rindisbels and said:

'Go in peace.'

And off they went shouting, jostling and singing all the way back to Meyborg. All the wives, old and young, awaited them on the thresholds of their houses, wherein the men entered like troopers into a captured city.

The bells of Meyborg rang wildly; the boys whistled, shouted and played the *rommel-pot*.

30

The stoups, tankards, goblets, glasses, flagons and pint-pots clinked wondrously. And wine flowed down the gullets.

During the ringing and while gusts of wind brought to Claes from the town the songs of the men, women and children, he spoke again to the hermit and asked him what heavenly grace these fellows thought to obtain by their rough devotions.

The smiling hermit replied:

'Do you see two sculptured figures representing two bulls on this chapel? They were placed there in memory of the miracle of Saint Martin, who changed two oxen into bulls by making them fight each other with their horns. Then he rubbed their muzzles with a candle and green-wood for an hour or more.

'Knowing of this miracle and provided with a brief from His Holiness—for which I paid well—I came and established myself here. Since then all the old coughers and pot-bellies of Meyborg and the surrounding country, persuaded by me, have been certain that after being strongly beaten once by the candle, which is unction, and the green-wood staff, which is strength, they gain favour with Our Lady. The wives send their old men here. The children born by virtue of this pilgrimage are violent, bold, fierce, nimble, and make perfect troopers.'

Suddenly the hermit said to Claes:

'Don't you know me?'

'Yes,' replied Claes, 'you are my brother Josse.'

'That I am,' said the hermit, 'but who is the little man making faces at me?'

'He's your nephew,' said Claes.

'What difference do you think there is between me and the Emperor Charles?'

'He is great,' answered Claes.

'He is small,' retorted Josse, 'for we are both alike in that he causes men to slay one another and I cause them to beat one another for our profit and pleasure.'

Then he brought them to his hermitage, where they feasted and revelled for eleven days without respite.

13   WHEN CLAES left his brother, he mounted his donkey once more, taking Ulenspiegl on the crupper behind him. He passed through the town square of Meyborg and noticed a great number of pilgrims standing about in groups who, when they saw him, became enraged and, brandishing their staffs, suddenly cried out: 'You good-for-nothing, you!' This was because Ulenspiegl had

downed his breeches, lifted his shirt and was showing them his back-side.

Claes, seeing that it was his son they were menacing, said to him:

'What have you done to make them so angry with you?'

'Dear father,' replied Ulenspiegl, 'I'm sitting on the donkey not speaking to anybody and yet they say I'm a good-for-nothing!'

Then Claes set him in front.

In this position Ulenspiegl stuck out his tongue at the pilgrims who, vociferously, shook their fists at him and lifted their staffs to strike Claes and the donkey.

But Claes dug his heels into the donkey to flee from their wrath and, while they pursued him losing their breath, he said to his son:

' 'Twas a most unlucky day when you were born. Here you are sitting in front of me doing no harm to anyone and they want to hammer at you.'

Ulenspiegl laughed.

Passing by Liége, Claes learned that the poor people of Rivage were starving and that they had been placed under the jurisdiction of the Official, a tribunal composed of ecclesiastical judges. They had rioted, demanding bread and lay judges. Several were beheaded, or hanged, and the rest were banished from the countryside, so great at that time was the clemency of Monseigneur de la Marck, the gentle archbishop.

Going on his way, Claes saw the banished ones fleeing the pleasant valley of Liége and on the trees near the town he saw the bodies of the men hanged for having been hungry. And he wept over them.

14 WHEN HE CAME home on his donkey, bearing a sack full of patards, the gift of his brother Josse, and a fine tankard of English pewter, there were junkets in his cottage on Sunday and daily feasts, for every day they had beef and beans to eat.

Claes filled himself with *dobble cuyt* and often emptied the great tankard of English pewter. Ulenspiegl ate enough for three and strutted among the plates like a sparrow on a mound of grain.

'Look!' said Claes. 'He's eating the salt cellar, too!'

Ulenspiegl answered: 'When, as with us, the salt cellar is but a piece of hollowed bread, it must be eaten now and then so that in ageing it breed no worms!'

'Why do you wipe your greasy hands on your breeches?' asked Soetkin.

'So that my thighs may never be wet,' replied Ulenspiegl.

Whereat Claes drank a deep draught of beer from his tankard, and Ulenspiegl said to him:

'Why have you such a great big cup when I have such a poor little goblet?'

'Because I am your father and the *baes* herein,' answered Claes.

Ulenspiegl retorted: 'You have been drinking for forty years and I for nine only; your time to drink is past, mine is come; it is for me, therefore, to take the tankard and for you to take the goblet.'

'Son,' said Claes, 'he would be throwing his beer in the gutter who tried to pour a hogshead into a keg.'

'You would be wise then to pour your keg into my hogshead, for I am larger than your tankard,' replied Ulenspiegl.

And Claes, delighted, passed him the tankard to down. And so Ulenspiegl learned to speak up for his drink.

15 SOETKIN CARRIED under her girdle the signs of renewed maternity. Katheline was also *enceinte* but, being fearful, did not dare leave her house. 'Ah,' said the doleful, fattened one, when Soetkin went to visit her, 'what shall I do with the poor fruit of my womb? Shall I smother it? I would rather die! But if the sergeants take me for having a child without being married, they will make me pay twenty florins like a loose woman, and I will be whipped in the Market Place.'

Soetkin would then console her with some soothing words and, having left her, would go home pondering. Then one day she said to Claes:

'If I had two children instead of one, would you beat me, husband?'

'I know not,' answered Claes.

'But, if the second were not really mine, but like that of Katheline, the offspring of someone unknown—the Devil maybe?'

'Devils,' replied Claes, 'engender fire, death, and smoke; children, no. I will hold Katheline's child as mine.'

'You will do this?' she asked.

'I have said it,' he answered.

Soetkin went to carry the good news to Katheline.

Hearing it, the latter, unable to contain herself, cried out with joy:

'He has spoken, the good man, spoken for the salvation of my poor body. He shall be blessed by God, blessed by the Devil, if it is,' said she, all trembling, 'a devil that engendered you, poor little one that stirs within me.'

Soetkin and Katheline brought into the world, the one a little boy, the other a little girl. Both were carried to the christening as the son and daughter of Claes. Soetkin's son was named Hans and did not live; Katheline's daughter was named Nele and throve well.

She drank the liquor of life from four flagons; two were Katheline's and two were Soetkin's. And they both would dispute tenderly as to who was to give the child drink. But, against her will, Katheline was forced to let her milk dry up, lest she be asked by someone how it came about so, and she not a mother.

When little Nele, her daughter, was weaned, she took her home with her and only let her go back to Soetkin when the child called for 'Mother'.

The neighbours said it was good of Katheline, who was well-off, to look after the child of Claes, who customarily lived a poor and laborious life.

16 ONE MORNING Ulenspiegl found himself alone in the house and bored with everything; he began to whittle down one of his father's clogs to make a little boat. He had already planted the mainmast in the sole and bored the toe-cap to place the bowsprit, when he saw at the half-door the bust of a rider and the head of a horse.

'Is there anyone within?' asked the rider.

'There is,' said Ulenspiegl; 'a man and a half and a horse's head.'

'How is that?' demanded the rider.

'Because,' replied Ulenspiegl, 'I see a whole man, myself; the half of a man, your bust; and a horse's head, that of your mount.'

'Where are your father and mother?' asked the man.

'My father's gone to make bad worse,' replied Ulenspiegl, 'and my mother is working to bring us shame or loss.'

'Explain yourself,' said the rider.

'At this very moment,' replied Ulenspiegl, 'my father is busy deepening the holes that will bring from bad to worse the hunters who trample down his corn. My mother has gone to borrow money. If she repays too little, she will shame us; if she repays too much, it will be our loss.'

The man then asked which way he should go.

'There where the geese are,' Ulenspiegl told him.

Off he went, but returned just as Ulenspiegl was making an oared galley out of the other clog.

'You misled me,' he said. 'Where the geese are, there is nothing but mud and a swamp wherein they waddle.'

'I never told you to go where the geese waddle but where they walk,' Ulenspiegl replied.

'Show me, at least,' said the man, 'a road that goes to Heyst.'

'In Flanders, it's the travellers who go and not the roads,' replied Ulenspiegl.

17 ONE DAY Soetkin said to Claes: 'Husband, I'm heartbroken. It's three days now since Tyl left the house; don't you know where he is?'

Claes replied sadly:

'He is where the homeless dogs are, on some highway, with several other good-for-nothings like himself. God was cruel to give us such a son. When he was born, I saw in him the joy of our old age, one tool more in the house. I thought to make him a craftsman, and wicked fate has made him a thief and a loafer.'

'Be not so hard, my man,' said Soetkin. 'Our son, being but nine years old, is full of childish folly. Must he not let his bud-sheaths fall on the ground before he puts forth the leaves which for the human tree are honesty and virtue? He is full of malice, I know, but his malice will turn later to his profit, if, instead of using it for mean tricks, he applies it to some useful trade. He is ready to mock his neighbour but later also he will be able to hold his own in some gay brotherhood. He's always laughing, yes. But faces that are sour before being ripe are ill omens of the faces to come. If he runs, 'tis because he has need to grow; if he doesn't work, it is because he is not of an age when one feels that labour is a duty; and if he sometimes stays out day and night for half a week, it is because he does not know with what pain he afflicts us, for he is good-hearted and loves us.'

Claes shook his head and made no answer and, when he slept, Soetkin wept alone. And in the morning, thinking that her son was sick at some highway corner, she went to the doorway to see if he was in sight. But she saw nothing and went in again to sit by the window and watch the road from there. And many a time her heart danced in her breast at the sound of the light step of some lad; but when he passed and she saw it was not Ulenspiegl she wept, the sorrowful mother.

In the meantime Ulenspiegl and his good-for-nothing comrades were at Bruges, at the Saturday market.

There might be seen cobblers and shoemakers in booths apart; tailors selling clothes; Antwerp *miesevangers* who, with an owl, catch tomtits at night; poultry merchants; dog-thieves; sellers of catskins for gloves, waistcoats and doublets; and buyers of all sorts; burghers,

36

menservants and maidservants, pantrymen and butlers, cooks; and altogether merchants and buyers, according to their quality, cried and decried, vaunted and disparaged the merchandise.

In one corner of the market-place there was a fine canvas tent mounted on four poles. At the entrance to the tent a peasant from the lowlands of Alost, accompanied by two monks out for the profits, showed for a patard, to the curious faithful, a morsel of the shoulderblade of Mary of Egypt. He brayed with a broken voice the merits of the saint and did not omit to tell in his ballad how, for want of money, she paid a young ferryman with her body, rather than sin against the Holy Ghost by refusing the labourer his hire.

And the two monks nodded their heads as much as to say that the peasant was telling the truth. Beside them a great ruddy wench, lascivious as Astarte, inflated a mean bagpipe violently, while beside her a sweet little girl sang like a bird, but no one heard her. Above the entrance to the tent there was a bucket, hanging by its two handles to cords which were attached to a couple of poles. It was filled with holy water, blessed in Rome, according to the fat woman's song, which was approved by the nodding heads of the two monks. Ulenspiegl, watching the bucket, became pensive.

Attached to one of the poles that supported the tent was a donkey nourished more on grass than oats. With lowered head it was staring at the ground, without any hope of ever seeing thistles spring up.

'Comrades,' said Ulenspiegl, pointing to the fat woman, the two monks and the melancholy donkey, 'since its masters sing so well, we must make the donkey dance.'

And having said this, he went off to a nearby booth, bought six liardsworth of pepper, came back and, lifting the donkey's tail, placed the pepper there.

The donkey, feeling the pepper, looked round at its tail to see where the unaccustomed heat was coming from. Thinking there was a fiery devil behind, he started to run away to escape him and began to bray, rear and shake the pole with all his might. At this first shock, the bucket hanging between the two poles spilled all its holy water over the tent and those who were within. Then the tent soon collapsed and covered with a moist mantle those who were listening to the story of Mary of Egypt. And from under the tent Ulenspiegl and his comrades heard a great noise of groans and lamentations, for the devout who were there were accusing each other of having tipped the bucket and, wild with anger, were exchanging furious blows. The canvas was uplifted with the struggling of the combatants. Each time that Ulenspiegl

38

saw a roundness showing, he jabbed a needle into it. There were louder cries from under the canvas and a greater distribution of blows.

And he was overjoyed, but more so when he saw the donkey flee, dragging behind it canvas, bucket, and poles, while the *baes* of the tent with his wife and daughter clung to the baggage. The donkey, unable to run any more, lifted his muzzle in the air and only stopped his singing to turn and see if the fire beneath his tail wouldn't soon be out.

All this while the devout continued their battle and the monks, without paying any attention to them, gathered up the money that had fallen from the collection plates. And Ulenspiegl devoutly helped them, not without profit to himself.

18 As THE WORTHLESS SON of the charcoal-burner grew up in happy mischief, the doleful offspring of the sublime Emperor vegetated in lean melancholy. Lords and ladies saw the miserable child dragging through the rooms and corridors of Valladolid his frail body and tottering legs that wearily bore the weight of his big head covered with fair, stiff hair.

Ceaselessly seeking out the dark passages, he would sit there for hours on end with sprawling legs. If some servant trod on him by accident, he would have him flogged and, delighted to hear him cry out under the lashes, he never even smiled.

Next day, going elsewhere to set the same traps, he would sit in some other corridor with his legs out. The lords, ladies, and pages passing along—quickly or otherwise—would trip over him, fall and hurt themselves. This pleased him also; but he never smiled.

When one of them, having run into him, did not fall, he screamed as though he had been beaten by that one, and he was happy seeing all fearful; but he never smiled.

His Sacred Majesty, being informed of these goings-on, gave orders that no notice was to be taken of the child, saying that if he did not want his legs to be tripped over he should not place them in the way of people's feet.

This displeased Philip, who said nothing, but no one saw him after that save when, on a clear summer's day, he went out in the courtyard to warm his shivering body in the sun.

One day, returning from the wars, Charles saw him steeped in melancholy.

'Son,' he said to him, 'how different you are from me! At your age I loved climbing trees to hunt squirrels; with the aid of a rope I would go down some steep cliff to birdnest for eaglets. At that sort of game I might have left my bones, but they only became the hardier for it. In the chase, the animals fled to their dens when they saw me coming with my bow!'

'Oh,' sighed the boy, 'I have a pain in my belly!'

'The wine of Paxaretos is a sovereign remedy,' said Charles.

'I do not care for wine; my head aches, my Lord and Father.'

'My boy,' said Charles, 'you must run, leap and romp as other children of your age do.'

'My legs are stiff, my Lord and Father.'

'How could they be otherwise,' said Charles, 'if you do not use them any more than if they were wooden legs? I will have you attached behind some active steed.'

The boy wept.

'Do not attach me, my Lord and Father, my back aches.'

'But,' said Charles, 'you ache all over then?'

'I would suffer no more, if they left me in peace,' replied the boy.

'Think you to pass your royal life dreaming like a writer?' retorted the Emperor impatiently. 'To them, if needs must be, to spot their parchments with ink, silence, solitude, and retirement; you, son of the sword, have need of hot blood, the eye of a lynx, the cunning of a fox, the strength of Hercules. Why do you cross yourself? God's blood! 'Tis not for a lion's cub to ape female tellers of beads.'

'The Angelus, my Lord and Father,' replied the boy.

19 THE MONTHS OF May and June were true flowery months that year. Never had there been seen in Flanders such fragrant hawthorn, never in the gardens so many roses, jasmines and honeysuckles. When the wind blew up out of England and drove the mists of the flowering land towards the east, everybody, and especially in Antwerp, would joyfully lift their noses in the air, saying:

40

'Do you smell the good wind that comes out of Flanders?'

And so the bees were busy in sucking the honey from the flowers, making wax, and laying eggs in hives too small to house their swarms. What a music of labour under the blue sky that brightly covered the rich earth!

Hives were made of rushes, of straw, of wicker, of tressed hay. Basket-makers, coopers, barrellers, all wore out their tools. As for the hive-makers, they were no longer equal to their task.

The swarms were of thirty thousand bees and two thousand seven hundred drones. The honeycombs were so exquisite that because of their rare quality the Dean of Damme sent eleven to the Emperor Charles to thank him for having, by his new edicts, re-instituted the Holy Inquisition. Philip it was who ate them, but they did him no good.

Tramps, beggars, vagabonds and a whole rag-tag and bobtail of worthless loafers, dragging their idleness along the highways and pre-ferring to hang rather than work, enticed by the honey, came to get their share of it. And they prowled about in bands at night.

Claes had made hives to attract the swarms; some of these were well-filled, others empty, awaiting the bees. Claes watched all the night to guard this sweet wealth. When he was tired he would ask Ulen-spiegl to take his place, which he did with a right good will.

Now one night Ulenspiegl, to keep out of the cold, curled himself up in one of the empty hives and kept his watch through the two holes at the top.

Just as he was about to fall asleep, he heard the hedge bushes being rustled and then heard the voices of two men whom he took to be thieves. He looked through the opening of the hive and saw that they both had long hair and long beards, although the wearing of a beard was a sign of high rank.

They went from hive to hive and then came to his, which they lifted, saying:

'Let's take this one; it's the heaviest.'

Then, putting their sticks under it, they carried it off.

It did not amuse Ulenspiegl at all to be carted away in a hive. The night was clear and the two thieves walked along without saying a word. At every fifty paces or so they stopped to catch breath and then went forward again. The man in front grumbled furiously at having to carry such a heavy load; the man behind whined in a melan-choly way. For in this world there are two sorts of loafing cowards: those who become angry with work and those who whine when they have to work.

Ulenspiegl, having nothing else to do, pulled the long hair of the thief who marched first and tugged the beard of the other who walked behind.

This to such purpose that the furious one said to the whiner:

'Stop pulling my hair or I'll land you such a whack on your bean that it'll be smashed inside you and you'll be able to look out through your ribs like a thief through prison bars.'

'I wouldn't dare pull your hair, my friend,' replied the whiner, 'but it's you rather who's tugging at my beard.'

'I never hunt for lice in lepers' hair,' retorted the angry one.

'Oh, sir,' said the whiner, 'don't shake the hive about so much. My poor arms won't be able to hold out.'

'I'll rip them off altogether,' replied the angry one.

Then, unshouldering his strap, he laid the hive down on the ground and leaped on his companion. And so they fought together, the one cursing, the other crying out for mercy.

Ulenspiegl, hearing the blows raining down, came out of the hive and dragged it with him to the wood nearby, where he could find it again, and then returned home.

And so it is in quarrels that the crafty profit.

20 WHEN ULENSPIEGL was fifteen, he set up a tent on four poles in the town of Damme. To all who passed he cried out that they might now see their past and future shown in a handsome frame of hay. When there came a man of law, most haughty and puffed up with his own importance, Ulenspiegl, sticking his own head in the frame and making a face like an old monkey, would say:

'An old mug may rot, but flower—never! Am I not your very mirror, Sir Doctoral Phiz?'

If he had as a client a sturdy soldier, Ulenspiegl would hide and, instead of showing his own face, he would hold up within the frame a dog's dish of meat and bread, saying:

'Battle will make a hash of you. What will you give me for my prophecy, O trooper, beloved of the big-mouthed guns?'

When an old man bearing his hoary head ingloriously would bring his young wife to Ulenspiegl, the latter, hiding himself as he had done for the soldier, would show in the frame a little tree to whose branches were attached knife-handles, caskets, combs, inkholders, all made of horn, and would shout:

'Where do all these fine knick-knacks come from, Mister? Is it not

42

from the hornbeam that grows in the gardens of old husbands? Who shall now say that cuckolds are useless folk in a republic?'

And Ulenspiegl would show in the frame his young face alongside the tree.

The old man hearing him would cough with manly rage, but his sweet would soothe him with her hand and, smiling, would come to Ulenspiegl:

'And my mirror,' she would say, 'will you show it me?'

'Come closer,' Ulenspiegl would reply.

She would obey and he then would kiss her where he could, saying: 'Your mirror is stark youth staying with upstanding cod-piece.'

And off the sweet one would go also, but not without giving him a florin or two.

To the fat and thick-lipped monk who would ask to see his present and future set forth, Ulenspiegl would reply:

'You are a cupboard for ham and you will also be a cellar for beer; for salt calls forth drinking, doesn't it, pot-belly? Give me a patard for not having lied.'

'My son,' replied the monk, 'we never carry money about.'

'Then money carries you about,' retorted Ulenspiegl, 'for I know that you place it between the two soles under your feet. Give me your sandal.'

'My son, it belongs to the convent. However, I'll take out two patards, if I must, for your trouble.'

The monk gave them; Ulenspiegl received them graciously.

And so he showed their mirror to the folk of Damme, Bruges, Blankenberghe and even Ostend.

And instead of saying to them in

his Flemish speech: *Ik ben u lieden spiegel* (I am your mirror), he shortened it to *Ik ben ulen spiegel,* even as they still say it in East and West Flanders.

And that was how he came by the surname of Ulenspiegl.

21 As HE GREW UP, Ulenspiegl began to like to wander through fairs and markets. If he saw a player of the oboe, the rebeck or the bagpipes, he would, for a patard, have them teach him how to make these instruments sing.

He became especially skilful in the manner of playing the rommel-pot; an instrument made of a pot, a bladder and a stiff straw. This is how he did it. In the evening he stretched the dampened bladder over the pot, fixed with a cord the centre of the bladder about the joint of the straw that touched the bottom of the pot, about whose top he finally stretched the bladder almost to the bursting point. In the morning the bladder, being dry, sounded like a tambourine when it was tapped; and if the straw was rubbed it hummed better than a viola. And Ulenspiegl, with his pot that hummed and bayed like a mastiff, went about singing carols from door to door in company with other children, one of whom carried a shining paper star on Twelfth Night.

If any master painter came to Damme to portray, on their knees on canvas, the companions of some *gilde*, Ulenspiegl, desiring to see how he worked, asked to be allowed to grind the colours. All he wanted for pay was a slice of bread, three liards and a pint of cervoise ale.

While grinding away, he would watch his master's manner of painting. And when he was absent, Ulenspiegl would try to paint as he did, but he laid on too much scarlet. He tried to portray Claes, Soetkin, Katheline and Nele, as well as pots and pans. Looking over his efforts, Claes predicted that if he worked boldly, he might one day earn florins by the dozen in painting the inscriptions on the *speel-wagens*—the pleasure carts of Flanders and Zeeland.

He learned also from a master mason how to carve wood and stone when the man came to carve a stall in the choir of the Church of Our Lady; a stall so constructed that, when it was necessary, the aged Dean could sit down in it and yet have the appearance of standing up.

It was Ulenspiegl who first carved the handle of the knife used by Zeeland folk. He made this handle in the form of a cage. Inside, a death's head rolled about; above it, a crouching dog. These emblems together meant: Blade faithful unto death.

And in this way it was that Ulenspiegl began to fulfill the prediction of Katheline and show himself to be painter, sculptor, peasant, noble, all in one. For from father to son, the arms of the Claes were three steins *argent au naturel* on a field of *bruinbier*.

But Ulenspiegl stuck to no trade, and Claes told him that if he kept on at this game, he would turn him out of the house.

44

22 THE EMPEROR, having returned from the war, demanded to know why his son Philip had not come to salute him. The Archbishop-Governor of the child replied that he had not wanted to come, for he only loved, he said, his books and solitude.

The Emperor enquired where he was keeping himself at that moment.

The Governor replied that they had better seek him out in the dark-est places. This they did.

Having passed through a great many rooms, they came finally to a kind of closet, unpaved and lit only by a skylight. There they saw a stake stuck in the ground and to this a monkey was attached by the waist (a female monkey, very little and darling, that had been sent from the Indies to amuse His Highness with her youthful antics). At the foot of the stake there were smoking faggots, still glowing, and the closet was filled with a foul odour of burned fur.

The little beast had suffered so in dying by this fire that its tiny body seemed to be not that of an animal having lived, but rather a fragment of a wrinkled and twisted root; and in its mouth, opened as though crying on death, was seen a bloody froth; and the face was all wet with tears.

'Who has done this?' demanded the Emperor.

The Governor did not dare answer, and they both stood there speech-less, angry and sad.

Suddenly in this silence was heard a feeble sound of coughing that came from a corner in the shadow behind them. His Majesty, turning about, saw his son Philip all dressed in black and sucking a lemon.

'Don Philip,' he said, 'come and salute me.'

The child, never moving, looked at him out of fearful eyes, in which there was no love.

'Was it you who burned this little beast in that fire?' demanded the Emperor.

The child hung his head.

But the Emperor continued: 'If you were cruel enough to do it, be brave enough to avow it.'

The child made no answer.

His Majesty snatched the lemon from his hands and threw it to the ground and was about to beat his son, who was pissing with fright, when the Archbishop stopped him by whispering in his ear:

'His Highness will be a great burner of heretics one day.'

The Emperor smiled, and the two men went away, leaving the Prince alone with his monkey.

But there were others, and not monkeys either, who were to die by fire.

46

23 NOVEMBER, the month of hail-storms, came, when coughers give themselves up whole-heartedly to the music of phlegm; the month also when the small boys descend in bands on the turnip fields, snatching whatever they can to the great anger of the peasants, who chase them vainly with sticks and pitchforks.

Now, one evening, as Ulenspiegl was returning home from one of these raids, he heard a groan in the corner of a nearby hedge. When he bent down, he saw a dog lying on some stones.

'Ho, wee timorous beastie,' said he, 'what are you doing there so late?'

Caressing the dog, he felt that its back was wet and thought that someone must have tried to drown it. He took it up in his arms to warm it.

When he reached home, he said:

'I have brought back someone wounded; what shall we do?'

'Bind up his wounds!' replied Claes.

Ulenspiegl then laid the dog on the table, and Claes and Soetkin saw, by the light of the lamp, that it was a little red Luxemburg terrier, wounded in the back. Soetkin sponged the wounds, covered them with healing balm, and bound them up with linen. Then Ulenspiegl bore the animal to his bed; albeit Soetkin wanted to take it to her own, saying she was afraid that Ulenspiegl, who rolled about his bed like the devil in a holy-water stoup, would hurt the terrier as he slept.

But Ulenspiegl had his own way, and cared for the wounded animal so well that after six days it ran about like other dogs and gave itself great airs.

And the *school-meester* named it Titus Bibulus Schnouffius: Titus, in memory of a certain good Roman Emperor, who willingly gathered

47

in lost dogs; Bibulus, because the dog loved beer dearly, with a drunkard's love; and Schnouffius, because of his sniff-sniffing and his ceaseless nose-thrusting in rat-holes and mole-holes.

24 AT THE END OF Our Lady's Street, two willows were planted, facing each other, at the edge of a deep pond. Between the two willows, Ulenspiegl stretched a rope on which he danced one Sunday after vespers. He did it well enough to be applauded with hand and voice by all the vagabonds who crowded about. Then he descended from the tight-rope and held out to all of them a little bowl that was soon filled with coppers, and he emptied it into Soetkin's apron and kept eleven liards for himself.

The following Sunday, he wished to dance again on the tight-rope, but some worthless little boys, jealous of his agility, had made a nick in the rope, so that after he had made a few jumps, the rope broke and he fell into the water.

As he swam toward the edge, the little rope-cutting fellows shouted:

'How's your nimble health, Ulenspiegl? Are you going down to the bottom to teach the carps to dance, priceless dancer?'

Ulenspiegl, coming out of the water and shaking himself, cried after them, for they had removed themselves for fear of blows:

'Don't be frightened. Return next Sunday and I'll show you some tricks on the rope, and you'll all have your share of the proceeds.'

On Sunday the boys did not touch the rope and kept watch about it to see that no one else touched it, for there was a great crowd of people.

Ulenspiegl said to them:

'Each of you give me one of your shoes, and I'll wager that, big or little as they may be, I will dance with all of them.'

'What'll you pay if you lose?' they demanded.

'Forty quarts of *bruinbier*,' replied Ulenspiegl, 'and you will pay me three patards if I win.'

'Yes,' they said, and each one of them gave him one of his shoes. Ulenspiegl placed them in the apron he was wearing and, so loaded, he danced on the rope but not without trouble.

The rope-cutters called up from below:

'You said you'd dance with each of our shoes. Put them on and stick to your wager!'

'I didn't say I would put on your shoes but that I would dance with them. Now I dance and everything in my apron dances with me. Don't you see with your staring frog's eyes? Pay me the three patards.'

48

But they booed him and shouted that he should give them back their shoes.

Ulenspiegl threw them down, one after another, in a heap. This caused a furious fight, for no one could distinguish clearly, or take without contest from the heap, the shoe that belonged to him. Then Ulenspiegl came down from the rope and watered the combatants— but not with fresh water.

25   THE INFANTE, being fifteen years of age, wandered as usual along the corridors, up and down the stairs and in the rooms of the castle. But most often he was seen hanging about the rooms of the ladies in order to pick quarrels with the pages, who like himself were as cats on the hunt along the corridors. Other pages stayed in the courtyard, noses in the air, singing some tender ballads.

The Infante, hearing them, would show his face at the window and so frighten the poor pages, who saw this pale phiz instead of the soft eyes of their ladies.

Among the ladies of the court there was a Flemish gentlewoman from Dudzeele near Damme. Plump, a fine ripe fruit and marvellously beautiful, for she had green eyes and crinkled red hair that shone like gold. Of a gay humour and a fiery temperament, she never hid from anyone her liking for the fortunate lord to whom she allowed the heavenly privilege of love's right of way over her comely lands. At that moment there was one, handsome and proud, whom she loved. Every day at a certain hour she went to meet him, and this Philip discovered.

Seating himself on a bench placed against a window, he watched for her. As she passed in front of him, eyes sparkling, lips parted, complacent, fresh from her bath, and making her yellow brocaded skirts

49

rustle about her, she saw the Infante who, without getting up from his bench, said to her:

'Madame, can you not stay for a moment?'

Impatient as a filly held back in her career, at the moment when she rushes to the splendid stallion neighing in the field, she answered:

'Your Highness, each one here must obey your princely will.'

'Sit down beside me,' he said.

Then looking at her lecherously, stonily and craftily, he said:

'Repeat the *Pater* to me in Flemish; they taught it to me but I have forgotten it.'

The poor lady must needs then say a *Pater*, and he needs must ask her to say it more slowly.

And so he forced the poor thing to say ten of them, she who had thought the time was come to say other orisons.

Then, praising them, he spoke of her lovely hair, her bright colour, her shining eyes; but he did not dare speak to her of her shapely shoulders, her rounded breasts, nor of any other thing.

When she thought she could slip away and was already looking out into the courtyard where her lord awaited, the prince asked her if she really knew what the womanly virtues are.

As she made no reply, for fear she might say the wrong thing, he replied for her and in a preachy voice said:

'The womanly virtues be chastity, regard for her honour, and modesty in her ways.'

He counselled her, therefore, to go and clothe herself decently and hide closely all that she had to hide.

And she nodded assent with her head, saying that for his Hyperborean Highness she would rather cover herself with ten bearskins than an ell of muslin.

Having shamed him with this answer, she fled from him joyously.

But in the heart of the Infante the fire of youth was thus lit—not the glowing fire that drives the strong souls to high deeds nor the sweet flame that makes tender hearts weep, but rather a sombre fire come from Hell and doubtless lit by Satan. And it flamed in his grey eyes like a winter moon shining down on a charnel house. And it burned him cruelly.

Feeling himself without love for others, the poor crafty one did not dare offer himself to women. He went then to an out of the way corner in a little white-washed room that was lit by narrow windows where he usually devoured pastries whose crumbs attracted flies. There, caressing himself, he would crush their heads against the window panes, killing hundreds of them until his hands trembled so much that he

50

could not continue his bloody business. And he took a mean delight in this cruel recreation, for lechery and cruelty are infamous twin sisters. He would leave this room sadder than ever and everyone fled from the face of this prince, pale as though nourished on the fungi of wounds.

And the doleful prince suffered, for evil heart is suffering.

26 THE LOVELY gentlewoman left Valladolid one day to go to her castle in Dudzeele in Flanders. Passing by Damme, her fat attendant following on behind, she saw, sitting by a cottage wall, a young lad of fifteen, blowing a bagpipe. Before him stood a red terrier who, not liking the music, was howling dismally. The sun shone brightly. Beside the lad stood a pretty girl, bursting with laughter at each piteous howl from the dog.

The lovely lady and her fat attendant, passing before the cottage, watched Ulenspiegl blowing, Nele laughing, and Titus Bibulus Schnouffius howling.

'You naughty boy,' said the lady, speaking to Ulenspiegl, 'can you not stop making the poor terrier howl that way?'

But Ulenspiegl, looking at her, blew more stoutly into his bagpipe. And Bibulus Schnouffius howled more dismally, and Nele laughed harder than ever.

The servant, becoming angry, said to the lady as he pointed to Ulenspiegl:

'Were I to beat this poor man's spawn with my scabbard he would cease this insolent row.'

Ulenspiegl looked at the servant, called him *Jan Papzak* because of his big belly, and continued to blow his pipe. The servant went up to him with a threatening fist, but Bibulus Schnouffius jumped at him and nipped his leg. The servant fell with fright, crying: 'Help!'

The lady, smiling, said to Ulenspiegl:

'Can you not tell me, Bagpiper, if the road that goes from Damme to Dudzeele is still the same?'

Ulenspiegl, without stopping to play, threw back his head and stared at the lady.

'Why do you stare at me so fixedly?' she demanded.

But he still played on and opened wide his eyes as though transported in an ecstasy of admiration.

She said to him:

'Are you not ashamed, young as you are, to look at ladies in that manner?'

Ulenspiegl blushed a little, still blew and stared harder.

52

'I asked you,' she repeated, 'if the road that runs from Damme to Dudzeele is still the same?'

"It greens no more since you deprived it of the joy of bearing you,' returned Ulenspiegl.

'Will you show me the way?' said the lady.

But Ulenspiegl still sat where he was, still staring. And she, seeing him so roguish, and knowing it all for the gameness of youth, willingly forgave him. He got up and was about to enter the house.

'Where are you going?' she demanded.

'To dress myself in my best,' he replied.

'Go,' she said.

And she sat down then on the bench near the door-step. The servant did likewise. She wanted to talk to Nele, but Nele would not answer her, for she was jealous.

Ulenspiegl came back all washed and dressed in fustian. The little man looked well in his Sunday clothes.

'Are you really going with that fine lady?' asked Nele.

'I will soon be back,' replied Ulenspiegl.

'Shall I go instead?' asked Nele.

'No, the roads are muddy.'

'Why,' said the lady, who was also annoyed and jealous, 'why are you trying to prevent him coming with me, little girl?'

Nele did not reply, but great tears started from her eyes and she looked sadly and angrily at the lovely lady.

The four of them set off; the lady seated like a queen on her white hackney, caparisoned with the black velvet; the servant whose belly shook at each step; Ulenspiegl, who held the bridle of the lady's horse; and Bibulus Schnouffius, who walked alongside him with his tail proudly in the air.

So they rode and walked for a while, but Ulenspiegl was not at ease; dumb as a fish, he breathed in the fine scent of benjamine wafted from the lady and looked out of the corner of his eye at all her beautiful gear, rare jewels and trinkets, and also at her sweet expression, her shining eyes, her bare neck, and her hair which the sun made to shine like a hood of gold.

'Why are you so quiet, my little man?' she asked.

He made no answer.

'Your tongue is not so deep in your boots that it couldn't carry a message for me, is it?'

'We'll see,' said Ulenspiegl.

'You must,' said the lady, 'leave me here and go to Koolkercke, at the other side of the wind. There you will find a gentleman dressed in

53

a black and red motley. Tell him he must not wait for me today but come Sunday at ten o'clock at night to my castle by the postern gate.'

'I will not go,' said Ulenspiegl.

The lady said to him:

'What is it, little ruffled cock, that inspires you with this fierce will?'

'I will not go!' said Ulenspiegl.

'But, if I gave you a florin?'

'No!' he said.

'A ducat?'

'No!'

'A carolus?'

'No!' repeated Ulenspiegl. 'And yet,' he sighed, 'I would rather see it than a mussel-shell in the maternal wallet.'

The lady smiled and suddenly cried:

'I have lost my rare and lovely purse that was made of silken cloth all broidered with pearls. It was still hanging from my belt at Damme.'

Ulenspiegl did not move, but the servant advanced toward the lady.

'Madame,' he said, 'do not send this young thief off to search for it or you will never see it again.'

'And who will go then?' she demanded.

'I will,' he replied, 'in spite of my great age.'

And off he went.

When midday rang out the heat was great and the solitude profound. Ulenspiegl said not a word, but took off his new doublet and laid it down so that the lady could sit under a lime tree without fearing the damp ground. He remained standing nearby, sighing.

She looked at him and felt sorry for the timid little man and asked him if he were not tired standing upright in that way on his young legs. He said not a word and as he slid down beside her she caught him and drew him to her bare bosom, where he remained so willingly that she would have thought herself guilty of the sin of cruelty had she asked him to seek out another pillow.

After a while the servant returned, saying that he could not find the purse.

'I found it myself,' replied the lady, 'when I got off my horse. When it unfastened, it had become caught in the stirrup. Now, take us straight to Dudzeele,' she said to Ulenspiegl, 'and tell me your name.'

'My patron is Master Saint Tylbert, a name that means *light i' the foot to run after good things*. My name is Claes and my surname is Ulenspiegl. If you will look at yourself in my mirror, you will see that there is not in all this land of Flanders a flower as dazzling in its beauty as your fragrant grace.'

The lady blushed with pleasure and was in no way angry with Ulen-spiegl.

And Soetkin and Nele wept during his long absence.

27 WHEN ULENSPIEGL returned from Dudzeele, he saw Nele at the entrance of the town, leaning against a barrier. She held a bunch of black grapes in her hand. Eating the grapes one by one, she was doubtless refreshed and delighted but she showed no pleasure. On the contrary she seemed annoyed, and tore the grapes

from the stem angrily. She was so doleful and showed a countenance so grieved and sweetly sad that Ulenspiegl was seized with a loving pity and advancing toward her gave her a kiss on the neck.

But she, in return, landed him a great smack.

'I don't see any clearer for that,' retorted Ulenspiegl.

She wept and sobbed.

'Nele,' said he, 'are they now going to place the fountains at the village entrance?'

'Go away!' she said.

'But I can't go away if you weep like that, my sweet.'

'I'm not sweet and I'm not weeping,' said Nele. 'Will you please go away?'

'No, you're not weeping, but just the same there's water coming out of your eyes.'

'Won't you go away?' said she.

'No!' he said.

And all the while she held her pinafore in her little trembling hands and tugged at it with spasms, while her tears ran down wetting it.

'Nele,' asked Ulenspiegl, 'will it be fine soon?'

And he looked on her, smiling lovingly.

'Why do you ask me that?' said she.

'Because when it's fine it doesn't weep,' replied Ulenspiegl.

'Go back to your lovely lady with the brocaded gown; you made that one laugh enough,' she said.

Ulenspiegl then sang:

> 'When I see my darling weep
> My heart is torn in twain.
> 'Tis honey when she smiles at me
> And pearl when she weeps.
> But always I will love my dear.
> And I'll buy drinks for both of us
> The good wine of Louvain;
> And I'll buy drinks for both of us
> When my Nele smiles again.'

'Low fellow,' she said, 'you are still mocking me.'

'Nele,' said Ulenspiegl, 'I am a fellow but not low, for our noble family, a family of aldermen, bears three steins *argent* on a field of *bruinbier*. Nele, is it true that in the country of Flanders, when one sows kisses one reaps smacks?'

'I don't want to speak to you,' she said.

'Then why do you open your mouth to say so?'

'I am annoyed,' she said.

Ulenspiegl gave her a very light blow on the back with his fist and said:

'Kiss a mean girl, she'll slap you; slap a mean girl, she'll anoint you. Anoint me then, my sweet, since I have slapped you.'

Nele turned around. He opened wide his arms and she threw herself into them, weeping and saying:

'You won't go there again, will you, Tyl?'

But he made no answer, for he was too busy clasping her poor trembling fingers and wiping away with his lips the warm tears that fell from Nele's eyes like the heavy drops of a stormy rain.

28 IN THESE DAYS the noble town of Ghent refused to pay her quota of financial aid, which her son, the Emperor Charles, demanded. She could not pay, being, by the fault of this same Charles, quite drained of money. It was a great crime and he himself resolved to go and punish the town.

For a son's stick is more painful than any other to a mother's back.

Francis of the Long Nose, his enemy, offered him the right of way through France. And Charles accepted the offer, so that, instead of being held prisoner, he was feted and cherished most imperially.

'Tis a sovereign bond between princes to aid each other against the people.

For a long time Charles stayed at Valenciennes and gave no sign of his wrath. Mother Ghent lived then without fear in the belief that the Emperor, her son, was going to pardon her for having acted within her rights.

Charles arrived under the walls of the town with four thousand horsemen. The Duke of Alba accompanied him, as did also the Prince of Orange. The common people and the petty tradesmen had wanted to prevent this filial entry and called out eighty thousand men of the town and the surrounding lowlands, but the burghers, known as *hoogh-poorters,* opposed this for fear of the predominance of the people. Yet, had this happened, Ghent could have easily made mince-meat of her son and his four thousand horsemen. But she loved him too well, and the petty tradesmen themselves regained confidence. Charles also loved the city, but only for the sake of the money he had of hers in his coffers, and the further monies which he still hoped to get from her.

Having become master of the town, he established everywhere military posts, set day and night patrols wandering about, and then with great pomp and ceremony pronounced sentence on the town.

The most notable burghers were to come before his throne, ropes about their necks, to make public apology. Ghent was declared guilty of the most costly crimes, to wit: disloyalty, the breaking of treaties, disobedience, sedition, rebellion and high treason. The Emperor declared that each and every privilege, right, franchise, custom and usage was null and void. And he stipulated and engaged also for the future, as though he were God Himself, that thenceforward none of his successors on coming to the throne should ever observe any one of these things that he had voided, excepting the Caroline Concession of slavery granted by him to the town.

He razed the Abbey of Saint Bavo to erect a fortress from which he might easily pierce his mother-town's breast with bullets. Like a good son, eager for his heritage, he confiscated all the wealth of Ghent, her revenues, houses, artillery and munitions.

Finding it still too well guarded, he destroyed the Red Tower, the Toad's Hole Tower, the Braampoort, the Steenpoort, the Waalpoort, the Ketelpoort and many others that were wrought and carved like jewels of stone.

58

When strangers came thereafter to Ghent, they said to themselves:
'What is this flat and desolate town of which we had heard wonders sung?'

And the people of Ghent replied:

'The Emperor Charles took her precious girdle from the town.'

And, saying this, they were shamed and angry. And from the ruins of her town gates, the Emperor took the bricks for his fortress.

He desired that Ghent be poor, for in this way she could not, by labour, industry or silver, oppose his proud designs; therefore he condemned her to pay the part she refused before—400,000 golden florins, to which was added 150,000 down and 6,000 more every year in perpetuity. She had once lent him money on which he owed her annual interest of 150 pounds gross. But by force he took possession of the deeds recording his debt and, in repaying in this way, he actually enriched himself.

Many times before Ghent had loved and succoured him, but now he struck at her breast with a dagger, seeking for blood because there was not milk enough.

Finally he looked on *Roelandt*, the great bell, and to its clapper he ordered to be bound and hanged the man who had sounded the alarm which called forth the people to defend their rights. He had no pity for *Roelandt*, the very tongue of his mother, the tongue by which she spoke to Flanders; *Roelandt* the proud bell that sang of herself:

> *Als men my slaet dan is't brandt,*
> *Als men my luyt dan is't storm in Vlaenderlandt.*

> When I ring there's a burning brand,
> When I peal a storm's up in Flanders land.

And, finding that his mother spoke out too loud and free, he carried away the bell. And the lowland folk said that Ghent died because her son had torn out her tongue with pincers of iron.

29 IN THESE DAYS, which were bright and clear spring days, when all the earth is full of love, Soetkin was talking by the open window. Claes hummed a tune, while Ulenspiegl tied a judge's high hat to the head of Titus Bibulus Schnouffius. The dog wagged his forepaws as though he were passing judgment, but in reality he was trying to rid himself of the hat.

Suddenly Ulenspiegl closed the window, ran into the room, jumped on the tables and chairs, his hands stretched toward the ceiling. Soetkin and Claes saw that he was carrying on in this way in order to try and catch a darling, wee bird who with quivering wings chirruped with fear and cowered against a beam in the corner of the ceiling.

Ulenspiegl was just about to seize it when Claes sharply spoke to him, saying:

'Why are you jumping about in that way?'

'To catch it,' replied Ulenspiegl, 'and put it in a cage and give it seeds and make it sing for me.'

Meanwhile the bird, crying with anguish, fluttered about the room, knocking its head against the window panes.

Ulenspiegl continued jumping about after it, till Claes laid a heavy hand on his shoulder.

'Catch it,' he said, 'put it in a cage and make it sing for you. But I will also put you in a cage closed about with good iron bars, and I will make you sing. You love to run about; you will no longer be able to. You will be in the shade when you are cold and in the sun when you are hot. Then one Sunday, we'll go out, forgetting to leave food for you, and coming back Thursday we will find Tyl dead from hunger and all stark.'

Soetkin wept and Ulenspiegl darted forward.

'Where are you going?' demanded Claes.

'To open the window for the bird,' replied Ulenspiegl.

And the bird, a goldfinch, with a joyful cry went out through the window, shot up like an arrow through the air and then alighted on a neighbouring apple-tree. There it smoothed its wings with its beak, ruffled its plumage, and then becoming angry sang in its bird language a thousand insults to Ulenspiegl.

Then Claes said to him:

'Oh, my son, never take away from man or beast his freedom, for freedom is the greatest thing in the world. Let each man go in the sun when he is cold and in the shade when he is hot. And may God judge His Sacred Majesty who, having enchained free thought in the land of Flanders, has now put the noble Ghent in a cage of slavery.'

30 PHILIP, HAVING married Marie of Portugal, whose possessions he added to the Spanish crown, had by her a son, Don Carlos the Mad and Cruel. But he loved not his wife.

Suffering from the after-effects of the birth, the Queen stayed in bed and kept about her many ladies of honour, among whom was the Duchess of Alba.

Philip often left her alone to go and see the burning of the heretics. And all the lords and ladies of the court followed him. Even also the Duchess of Alba, the noble Keeper of the Queen's Bedchamber.

Now at this time the Ecclesiastical Judges had seized a certain Flemish sculptor, a Roman Catholic, who, having been refused the price promised him by a monk for his wooden statue of Our Lady, had struck the face of the work with his chisel, saying that he would rather destroy his work than give it away for a low fee.

He was denounced by the aforesaid monk as an iconoclast, mercilessly tortured and condemned to be burned alive.

During the torture they had burned the soles of his feet and, as he walked from the prison to the stake, covered with the *Sanbenito*, he screamed:

'Cut off my feet! Cut off my feet!'

And from afar Philip heard these cries and was pleased; but he did not smile.

Queen Marie's ladies of honour all left her to assist at the burning and after them went the Duchess of Alba who, hearing the sculptor's cries, wished also to see the spectacle; and so the Queen was left alone.

Philip, his noble servitors, princes, counts, esquires and ladies being present, the sculptor was fastened by a long chain to a stake that was set in the middle of a flaming circle composed of bales of straw and faggots. These were to roast him slowly if he hugged his stake and did not want to be burned by the quick fire.

And they all watched him curiously, naked or almost naked as he was, trying to stiffen his soul's strength against the heat of the fire.

At the same moment, Queen Marie thirsted on her child-bed. She saw the half of a melon on a plate and, dragging herself out of bed, she seized it and left nothing of it.

Then because of the coldness of the melon, she began to sweat and shiver and lay there on the floor unable to move.

'Ah!' she said, 'I could get warm again if someone would carry me back to bed.'

Then she heard the poor sculptor screaming out:

'Cut off my feet!'

'Ah,' said Queen Marie, 'is it a dog howling at my death?'

61

At that moment the sculptor, seeing about him only the faces of his Spanish enemies, thought of Flanders, the land of men, then crossed his arms and, trailing his long chain after him, walked to the flaming straw and faggots and, standing on them with his arms still folded, called out:

'Here is how the men of Flanders die in the face of their Spanish butchers! Cut off their feet, not mine, so that they may no longer run to murder! Long live Flanders! Flanders for ever!'

And the ladies applauded, crying for mercy as they saw his proud countenance.

And he died.

And Queen Marie, shaking all over, her teeth chattering with the cold of approaching death, said, as her arms and legs stiffened:

'Put me to bed that I may be warm.'

And she died.

And so, following the prediction of Katheline, the good witch, Philip sowed everywhere death, blood and tears.

31 But Ulenspiegl and Nele loved each other with a great love. It was now the end of April with every tree in bloom and all the plants bursting with sap, awaiting May who descends to earth accompanied by a peacock, flowered like a nosegay, and makes the nightingales sing in the trees.

Often Ulenspiegl and Nele walked together along the highways. Nele took Ulenspiegl's arm, clinging to it with her two hands clasped.

Ulenspiegl liked this and sometimes put his arm about the waist of Nele, the better to hold her up, he said. She was happy, but she never spoke.

The wind rolled the scents of the fields softly along the roads. Far away the sea boomed lazily to the sun. Ulenspiegl was like a young devil, all proud, and Nele like a little saint of Paradise, quite shamed with her pleasure.

She laid her head against the shoulder of Ulenspiegl and he took her hands in his and, walking along, he would kiss her brow and her cheeks and her sweet little mouth. But she never spoke.

After some hours, when they grew hot and thirsty, they drank some milk at a peasant's house, but they were not refreshed.

Then they sat down on the grass by the side of a ditch. Nele, all pale, was pensive. Alarmed, Ulenspiegl looked at her.

'Are you sad?' she asked him.

'Yes,' he answered.

'Why?' she demanded.

'I know not,' he replied, 'but these flowering apple-trees and cherry-trees; this air, warm and as though charged with fire and thunder; these daisies that open blushing in the field; the hawthorn there close to us in the hedge, so white . . .

'Will no one tell me why I feel troubled and always ready to die or fall asleep? And my heart beats so quickly when I hear the birds awake in the trees and I see the returned swallows. Then I want to go beyond the sun and the moon. And sometimes I'm cold and sometimes I'm hot. Oh, Nele, I would I were no longer of this low world or that I could give a thousand lives to the one who would love me.'

But she made no answer and, smiling happily, looked on Ulenspiegl.

32 On All Souls' Day Ulenspiegl went from the church of Our Lady with certain other scamps of his own age. Lamme Goedzak had wandered among them like a lamb among wolves. Lamme stood them all drinks, for his mother gave him three patards each Sunday and each Feast-day.

With these comrades he went then to *In den rooden schildt* (At the Sign of the Red Shield), where Jan van Liebeke served them *dobble knollaert* from Courtrai.

Warmed with the drink, they began to talk of prayers, and Ulenspiegl declared right out that he thought the prayers for the dead were only advantageous to the priests.

But there was a Judas in the company and he denounced Ulenspiegl as an heretic. Despite the tears of Soetkin and the pleading of Claes, Ulenspiegl was taken and put in prison. He was kept in a barred cave during a month and three days without seeing anyone. The jailer ate three-quarters of his rations. During that time enquiries were made about his good or bad renown. It was only found that he was a mocker, always railing against his neighbours but never speaking ill of the Lord God, or Madame the Virgin, or any of the Saints. Therefore the sentence passed on him was light, for he might have been branded on the face with a red-hot iron or flogged till his blood ran.

In consideration of his youth, the judges condemned him to walk behind the priests, with only his shirt on and with head and feet bare and holding a candle, in the first procession leaving the church.

That was on Ascension Day.

When the procession was on the point of entering, he had to stop beneath the porch of the church of Our Lady and there cry out:

'Thanks be to our Lord Jesus! Thanks be to Messers the priests! Their prayers are sweet to the souls in purgatory, yea, refreshing, for every *Ave* is a bucket of water that falls on their backs and every *Pater* a tub!'

And the people listened with great devotion, but not without smiling.

At the Feast of Pentecost he had again to follow the procession wearing his shirt and, head bare and feet bare, carrying a candle. As they were about to re-enter, he stood under the porch, and holding his candle quite respectfully, not without making a few waggish faces, he said, in a high, clear voice:

'If the prayers of the Christians are a great solace to the souls in purgatory, those of the Dean of Our Lady, saintly man and perfect in the practice of all the virtues, calm so well the pains of fire that these are transformed into sherbets quite suddenly. But the tormenting devils get not a crumb of them.'

And the people listened as before with great devotion, not without smiling, and the Dean, pleased, smiled ecclesiastically.

Then Ulenspiegl was banished from the country of Flanders for three years on condition that he make a pilgrimage to Rome and return with absolution from the Pope.

Claes had to pay three florins for this sentence: but over and above that, he gave one to his son and furnished him with the pilgrim garb.

Ulenspiegl was heart-broken when the day of departure came as he embraced Claes and his unhappy mother, Soetkin, who wept. They, with several townsfolk, accompanied him far on his way.

When they returned to the house, Claes said to his wife:

'Wife, it's very hard to condemn so young a boy in this way to that stiff sentence for such silly words.'

'You're weeping, husband,' said Soetkin. 'You loved him more than you ever showed, for now you shake with manly sobs which are as lion's tears.'

But he did not reply.

Nele had hidden herself in the barn so that no one might see that she also was weeping for Ulenspiegl. She had followed far behind Soetkin and Claes and the townsfolk and, when she saw Ulenspiegl going on his way alone, she had run up to him and thrown her arms about his neck.

'You'll be finding many beautiful ladies where you're going,' she said.

'Beautiful? I don't know,' replied Ulenspiegl. 'But fresh as you, never. For they are all parched by the sun.'

64

For a long time they walked together; Ulenspiegl was pensive and would say every now and then:

'I'll make them pay their masses for the dead!'

'What masses? And who's to pay?' asked Nele.

'All the deans, priests, clerks, beadles and the rest of them, high and low, who feed us their windy humbug. Had I been a strong working man they would have robbed me of the fruit of three years' toil. But it's poor Claes who pays. They shall repay me my three years a hundredfold. And I, too, will say the mass for the dead for them, in their own coin.'

'Alas, Tyl, be prudent! They will burn you alive,' replied Nele.

'I am fireproof!' he answered.

And so they parted, she all in tears and he heart-broken and angry.

33 PASSING BY BRUGES on the Wednesday market, he saw a woman being led along by the executioner and his men, and there was a great mob of other women about her shouting and screaming a thousand vile insults.

Ulenspiegl, seeing that the top of her dress was sewn with bits of red stuff and that she bore about her neck the stone of justice with its iron chains, knew that she was a woman who had sold for money the young, fresh bodies of her daughters. He was informed that her name was Barbe, that she was married to Jason Darue and that she was to be walked in this costume from place to place till she finally arrived back at the Great Market Place, where she would be put on the scaffold already set up for her. Ulenspiegl followed with the great mass of shouting people. When they arrived back again at the Great Market Place, the woman was placed upon the scaffold and tied to the stake, and the executioner laid before her a bunch of grass and a morsel of earth signifying the grave-pit.

Ulenspiegl was also informed that she had been already whipped in the prison.

As he left the place, he met Henri Marechal, a swashbuckling rogue who had been hanged in the county of West Ypres and could still show the marks of the rope about his neck. It was said that he had been delivered after being strung up by merely saying a good prayer to Our Lady of Hal; by a real miracle the bailiffs and the judges were already gone, the rope that no longer choked him broke, and he fell safely to the ground.

But Ulenspiegl learned later that this rogue, delivered from the gallows, was a false Henri Marechal whom they allowed to go about

65

telling his lying tale because the Dean of Our Lady of Hal had given
him a signed parchment, for the Dean saw that because of the story told
by Henri Marechal all those who smelled the gallows from near or far
would flock to his church and pay well. And for a long time afterwards
the church of Our Lady of Hal was known as the church of Our Lady
of the Hanged.

34 ABOUT THIS TIME the inquisitors and the theologians made,
for the second time, representations to the Emperor Charles.
They said that the Church was lost; that its authority was
scorned; that if he had won so many illustrious victories, he owed them
to the prayers of Catholicism which maintained his imperial power
high upon the throne.

A Spanish archbishop demanded of him that he cut off six thousand
heads or burn as many bodies, so that the malignant Lutheran heresy
be rooted out of the Netherlands. His Sacred Majesty deemed that this
was not enough.

And so everywhere that the poor, terrified Ulenspiegl went he saw
nothing but heads on stakes, young girls stuffed into sacks and thrown
alive into the river, men stretched naked on the rack and beaten with
great blows from iron bars, women thrown into pits and the earth over
them and the executioner dancing on their chests to break them. And
their confessors and those to whom they had repented beforehand
gained twelve sols each time.

At Louvain he saw the executioners burn thirty Lutherans at once,
lighting the wood about them with gunpowder. At Limburg he saw
a whole family, men and women, daughters and sons-in-law, march
straight to the torture singing psalms. The man who was old cried out
while they burned him.

And Ulenspiegl, with fear and grief, journeyed over the poor earth.

35 IN THE FIELDS he shook himself like a bird, like a freed dog,
and his heart was cheered by the trees, the meadows and the
bright sun. Having walked for three days he came to the outskirts of Brussels, to the powerful township of Uccle. Passing before
the hostelry of The Trumpet, he was allured by the heavenly odour of
fricassees. He asked a little urchin who, with nose in the air, sniffed
the delectable perfume of the sauces, in whose honour this incense
of festivity arose to the heavens. The boy replied that the Brothers
of the Goodly Phiz were to meet after vespers to celebrate the

66

deliverance of the township by the women and girls of other days.

Seeing in the distance a pole surmounted by a popinjay and all about it women armed with bows, Ulenspiegl asked if women were becoming archers nowadays.

The urchin, sniffing the odour of the sauces, replied that in the days of the Good Duke these very bows, in the hands of the women of Uccle, had made more than a hundred brigands slide from life to death.

Ulenspiegl wanted to learn more, but the urchin said he couldn't say any more, since he was both hungry and thirsty, unless he received a patard to enable him to eat and drink. And out of pity Ulenspiegl gave it to him.

As soon as the urchin received the coin he entered the hostelry of The Trumpet like a fox in a henhouse and came out again triumphantly holding half a sausage and a large loaf of bread.

Suddenly Ulenspiegl heard a sweet sound of tabors and violas and saw a great troop of dancing women, and in the midst of them one lovely woman wearing a golden chain about her neck.

The urchin, who smiled happily for having eaten, told Ulenspiegl that the young and beautiful woman was the Queen of the Archers. She was named Mietje and was married to Messer Renonckel, one of the town's aldermen. Then he asked Ulenspiegl for six liards for a drink; Ulenspiegl gave them to him. So, having eaten and quenched his thirst, the urchin sat on his beam ends in the sun and picked his teeth with his nails.

When the women archers caught sight of Ulenspiegl in his pilgrim's garb, they began dancing around him, saying:

'Good morrow, fair pilgrim! Come you from afar, youthful pilgrim?'

Ulenspiegl replied:

'I come from Flanders, a lovely country rich in loving girls.'

And he thought sadly of Nele.

'What was your crime?' they asked, stopping their round.

'I do not dare confess it, so great it is,' he said. 'But I have other things about me that aren't any smaller.'

They smiled at this and then demanded to know why he was forced to journey about with the staff, the wallet and the cockleshell.

'For having said,' he answered, lying a little, 'that the masses for the dead are advantageous for the priests.'

'They bring in ringing coin to the priests,' they replied, 'but they are also of advantage to the souls in purgatory.'

'I have never been there,' answered Ulenspiegl.

'Would you like to eat with us, pilgrim?' said the nicest archer to him.

'I would like to eat with you and at you,' he replied, 'and all the others in turn, for you are morsels fit for a king and more delicious to nibble at than ortolans, thrushes or woodcocks.'

'God feed you,' they said, 'it's priceless game.'

'So are you all, my dears,' he answered.

'Yes, but we are not for sale.'

'Given away?' he asked.

'Yes, with blows to the overbold!' they answered. 'And if needs be we'll flail you like wheat.'

'I give up!' he said.

'Come eat,' said they.

He followed them into the courtyard of the tavern, happy to see these fresh faces about him. Suddenly he saw coming into the court-yard, with great ceremony and banner, trumpet, flute and tabor, the Brothers of the Goodly Phiz wearing fatly the jolly name of their brotherhood. As they observed him curiously the women told them that he was a pilgrim that they had met on the road and that finding he also had a goodly phiz, like their husbands and sweethearts, they wanted him to share in the festivity.

The men approved the women's story and one of them said:

'Pilgrim pilgriming, will you make a pilgrimage over these sauces and fricassees?'

'I'll put on my seven league boots!' answered Ulenspiegl.

As they were about to go into the festal hall, he saw twelve blind men walking along on the Paris highway. As they passed before him making moan of their hunger and thirst, Ulenspiegl said to himself that they would sup that evening like kings at the expense of the Dean of Uccle and in memory of the mass for the dead.

He went up to them and said:

'Here are nine florins, come and eat. Do you smell the odour of the fricassees?'

'La, since half-a-league,' they answered, 'but without hope.'

'You shall eat, having now nine florins,' said Ulenspiegl. But he made no move to give them the money.

'Blessings on you!' they said.

And led by Ulenspiegl they sat themselves about a little table while the Brothers of the Goodly Phiz seated themselves with their wives and sweethearts at the largest table.

Speaking with the assurance of nine florins, the blind men said proudly:

'Mine host, give us to eat and drink of your best!'

The host, having heard speak of nine florins and thinking they were in the tin-cups, asked what they desired.

All of them, speaking at once, called out:

'Peas and bacon; a hotchpotch of beef, veal, mutton and fowl.' 'Are sausages meant for the dogs?' 'Who nosed the black and white puddings as they went by without snatching at them? I used to see them, alas, when my poor eyes served me as candles.' 'Where are the *koeke-bakken* with the Anderlecht butter? They sang i' the pan, succulent, crisp; mothers to downed quarts.' 'Who'll stick ham and eggs or eggs and ham under my nose, these tender friendly brothers to the mouth?' 'Where are your heavenly *choesels* swimming, proud meats in the midst of kidneys, cock's combs, sweet-breads, ox-tails, sheep's trotters, and many onions, peppers, cloves and nutmegs, all stewed together and three quarts of white wine for the sauce?' 'Who will bring you before me, divine chitterlings, so good that they don't say a word when they're swallowed? They come straight from *Luy-leckerland,* the great land of famous loafers and lickers of everlasting sauces. But where are you, dried leaves of past autumns?' 'I want a leg o' mutton with haricot beans.' 'I want pig's plumes—their ears!' 'Me for a rosary of ortolans with a *Pater* made of woodcocks and a fat capon as the *Credo.*'

The host answered quietly:

'You shall have an omelette of sixty eggs and, as signposts to guide your spoons, fifty black puddings stuck all reeking hot on that mountain of nourishment. You'll have *dobble peterman* over and above all that: that shall be the river.'

The mouths of the poor blind men watered, and they said:

'Bring on the mountain, the signposts and the river.'

And the Brothers of the Goodly Phiz and their women already seated at the table with Ulenspiegl said that this day was one of invisible feasting for the blind men and that the poor men were losing half their pleasure.

When the omelette came in, all dressed with parsley and nasturtium and carried on high by the host and four cooks, the blind men would fain have thrown themselves in it and were already quarrelling over it. But the host served each man his part in their tins, though not without difficulty.

The women archers were touched to see the blind men stuffing themselves and sighing contentedly; they were so starved that they downed the black puddings like oysters. And the *dobble peterman* ran into their bellies like cascades falling from mountain heights.

When they had cleaned out their bowls they again demanded *koeke-bakken,* ortolans and new fricassees. The host only served them a great dish of beef, veal and mutton bones all swimming in a goodly sauce; but he did not serve it out.

When they dipped their bread and hands up to the elbow in the sauce and only caught hold of rib-bones and leg-bones and some even the jaw-bones of an ox, each man imagined that his neighbour had taken the meat, and they began to fight among themselves, beating each other furiously about the face with the bones.

The Brothers of the Goodly Phiz, having laughed their fill, most charitably placed a part of their feast on the plates of the poor men and whoever among the latter sought for a bone-weapon found under his hand a thrush, or a chicken, or a lark or two; the goodwives, holding the blind men's heads back, poured Brussels wine down their throats, and the men feeling to see where these streams of ambrosia came from caught at skirts which they tried to hold on to. But the women quickly made off.

So they all laughed, drank, ate and sang. Several of them, scenting out the sweet goodwives there, ran maddened about the room, bewitched by love. But the teasing girls dodged them, then hiding behind some Brother of the Goodly Phiz they would cry out: 'Kiss me!' which the blind men tried to do only to find that instead of a woman they were embracing some bearded phiz, and not without rebuffs.

The Brothers of the Goodly Phiz sang and the blind men did likewise, and the merry goodwives smiled with tender pleasure seeing them all so happy.

But when these succulent hours had passed the *baes* said to the blind men:

'You have eaten well and drunk well; you owe seven florins.'

Each one of them swore that he had not the purse and accused his neighbour. This started another battle, in which they all tried to strike at each other with foot, fist and head; but they did not succeed except to strike out wildly, for the Brothers of the Goodly Phiz, seeing what they were about, kept them back one from the other. And so their blows fell on the air, all except one that unluckily fell across the face of the *baes* who, becoming angry, had them all searched and only found on them an old scapular, seven liards, three breeches buttons and their rosaries.

He wanted them cast into the pig-pen and left there with bread and water until such time as they paid what they owed.

'Would you like me to go surety for them?' asked Ulenspiegl.

'Yes,' replied the *baes*, 'if someone will go surety for you.'

The Brothers were about to do so, but Ulenspiegl stopped them, saying:

70

'The Dean will go surety; I will go find him.'

Thinking of the Masses for the Dead, he went to the Dean and told him a story of the host of The Trumpet Inn who, being possessed of a devil, could only speak of pigs and blind men, pigs eating blind men and blind men eating pigs in divers impious forms such as roasts and fricassees. During this fit the *baes*, said he, broke up everything in the place. He therefore begged the Dean to come and deliver the poor man from the wicked demon.

The Dean promised he would but could not do so right away, for he was at the moment in the middle of making up the accounts of the Chapter and trying to make something out of them for himself.

Seeing his impatience, Ulenspiegl said that he would return with the wife of the innkeeper so that the Dean might speak to her himself.

'Come both of you,' said the Dean.

Ulenspiegl then returned to the *baes* and said:

'I have just seen the Dean and he will go surety for the blind men. While you watch over them let the *baesinne* come with me to the Dean's and he will repeat to her what I just told you.'

'Go, goodwife!' said the *baes*.

Off the *baesinne* went with Ulenspiegl to the Deanery, where the Dean was still figuring out how he could make something for himself. When she entered with Ulenspiegl he impatiently waved her away with his hand, saying:

'Be at ease. I shall come to your husband's aid in a day or two.'

And Ulenspiegl, walking back to The Trumpet, said to himself:

'He will pay seven florins and that will be my first mass for the dead.' And off he went and the blind men likewise.

36 THE FOLLOWING DAY, finding himself on the highway in the middle of a great crowd of men, Ulenspiegl followed them and soon learned that it was the day of the pilgrimage to Alsemberg. He saw poor old women walking backwards, barefooted, for a florin and the expiation of the sins of certain great ladies. By the roadside, to the sound of rebecks, violas and bagpipes, more than one pilgrim was having a frying feast and a junket of *bruinbier*. And the smoke of delicious stews arose to heaven like a suave incense of nourishment. But there were other pilgrims, mean-looking, needy starvelings, who walked backwards for six sols paid by the Church.

One little fellow, quite bald, with staring eyes and a fierce air, skipped along behind them reciting paternosters.

Ulenspiegl, desiring to know why he imitated a crayfish in that way, placed himself before the little fellow and smiling, skipped along. The rebecks, fifes, violas and bagpipes, and the pilgrims' groans, made the music of the dance.

'Jan van den Duivel,' said Ulenspiegl, 'is it to fall more surely that you run in this way?'

The man made no reply but continued to murmur his paternosters.

'Maybe you want to know how many trees there are along the road? But don't you also count the leaves?'

The man who was reciting a *Credo* made a sign to Ulenspiegl to be silent.

'Maybe,' continued the latter, still skipping in imitation before him, 'maybe it's as a result of some sudden madness that you go contrariwise to everybody else. But he who would draw from a fool a wise answer is not very wise himself. Isn't it true, mister peeled poll?'

Still the man did not reply, and Ulenspiegl continued to skip, making such a noise with the tapping of his soles on the road that it resounded like a wooden box.

'Maybe you're dumb, sir?' said Ulenspiegl.

'*Ave Maria*,' recited the man, '*gratia plena et benedictus fructus ventris tui Jesu.*'

'Maybe you're also deaf?' said Ulenspiegl. 'We shall see. They say the dumb hear neither praise nor insults. Let's see whether your eardrums are made of skin or iron. Do you think, O, candleless lamp, imitation walker, that you resemble a man? You will only do so when they have all become rags. Where has one seen that jaundiced phiz, that peeled head save on the gallows-field? Were you not hanged once?'

And Ulenspiegl danced and the man began to get angry and ran backwards, cholerically mumbling his paternosters with a secret fury.

'Maybe,' continued Ulenspiegl, 'you don't understand High Flemish; I will speak to you in Low. If you're not a glutton, you're a drunkard; if you're not a drunken water-drinker, you're badly constipated somewhere; if you're not constipated, you're loose-boweled; if you're not a lecher, you're an eunuch; if there is temperance, it was not that which filled the tun of your belly; and if out of the thousand million men who people this earth there were but one cuckold, that one would be you.'

At these words Ulenspiegl fell on his beam ends, legs in the air, for the man had landed him such a blow on the nose that he saw more than a hundred stars. Then, cunningly falling on him in spite of the weight of his belly, he struck everywhere, and the blows fell like hail on Ulenspiegl's thin body. And his staff fell to the ground.

'Learn by this lesson,' said the man to him, 'not to pester honest folk going on a pilgrimage. For, mark me well, I am going in this way to Alsemberg, according to the custom, to pray Madame Saint Mary to cause the miscarriage of the child which my wife conceived when I was on my travels. To obtain such a great boon one needs must walk and dance backwards without speaking from the twentieth step outside one's house to the bottom of the church steps. La, I must begin all over again.'

Ulenspiegl, having picked up his staff, said:

'I'm going to help you, you good-for-nothing, who would have Our Lady kill the babes in their mothers' wombs.'

And he fell to beating the nasty cuckold so cruelly that he left him for dead on the road.

While up to the heavens still arose the pilgrims' groans, the sound of fifes, violas, rebecks and bagpipes; and, like a pure incense, the savour of frying.

37 CLAES, SOETKIN and Nele sat together by the fire and talked of the pilgrim pilgriming. 'Daughter,' said Soetkin, 'why cannot you by the force of your youthful charm keep him always with us?'

'Alas,' said Nele, 'I cannot.'

' 'Tis because,' said Claes, 'he has a countercharm that forces him to run on without ever resting, except to fill his•mouth.'

'The ugly, cruel one,' sighed Nele.

'Cruel, I grant you,' said Soetkin, 'but ugly, no. If my son has not a Greek or Roman countenance, he's all the better for that. For they are of Flanders his agile feet, and of the freemen of Bruges his fine brown eyes, and his nose and mouth made by two foxy experts in the science of cunning and carving.'

'And who then,' demanded Claes, 'made his lazy arms and his legs too prompt to run after pleasure?'

'His over-young heart,' replied Soetkin.

38 IN THESE DAYS Katheline cured by simples an ox, three sheep, and a pig belonging to Speelman, but she could not cure a cow belonging to Jan Beloen. He accused her of witchcraft; he said she had cast a spell over the animal, inasmuch as, when she was giving it the simples, she caressed and talked to it, doubtless in a devilish language, for an honest Christian should not speak to an animal.

The aforesaid Jan Beloen added that he was the neighbour of Speelman whose ox, sheep and pig she had cured, and that if she killed *his* cow it was done no doubt at the instigation of Speelman, who was jealous of seeing Beloen's lands so well tilled and more profitable than his own. On the testimony of Pieter Meulemeester, a man of good life and conduct, and also that of Jan Beloen, certifying that Katheline was a well-known witch in Damme and had no doubt killed the cow, she was arrested and condemned to be tortured until she confessed her crimes and misdeeds.

She was questioned by a sheriff who was always in a rage, for he drank brandy all day long. He had Katheline placed upon the first torture-bench before him and the men of the *Vierschare*.

The torturer stripped her naked, then shaved her head and all her body, looking everywhere to see that she had no concealed charm about her.

Not having found anything, he bound her with ropes to the torture-bench. Then she said:

'I am ashamed, being so naked before these men. Madame Saint Mary, let me die.'

The torturer placed wet cloths on her breast, her belly and her legs, and then, lifting up the bench, he poured such a quantity of hot water in her stomach that she seemed all swollen up. Then he let the bench drop.

The sheriff asked Katheline if she wished to confess her crime. She made a sign that she would not. The torturer poured in more hot water but she spewed it all out.

Then at the surgeon's bidding she was untied. She did not speak but beat her breast to show that the hot water had burned her. When the sheriff saw that she was rested from that first torture, he said to her:

'Confess that you are a witch and that you cast a spell over the cow.'

'I will not confess,' she said. 'I love all animals, and while it is in the power of my feeble heart I will rather do myself ill than harm those who cannot defend themselves. I used the needful simples to cure the cow.'

'You gave it poison,' said the sheriff, 'for the cow is dead.'

'Sir sheriff,' replied Katheline, 'I am here before you in your power, yet I will dare to say to you that an animal may die of disease like a man, in spite of the assistance of doctors. And I swear by the Lord Christ who died on the cross for our sins that I wished no ill to that cow but rather sought to cure it by herbal remedies.'

Furious, the sheriff cried:

'This devil's monkey will not deny forever. Let her be put upon another torture-bench.'

And then he drank a great glass of brandy.

The torturer dumped Katheline on the cover of an oaken coffin set on trestles. This cover, roof-shaped, was sharp as a blade. A great fire burned in the fireplace, for it was already the month of November.

Katheline, seated on the coffin and a spit of pointed wood, was shod with tight shoes of new leather and placed before the fire. When she felt the cutting wood of the coffin and the pointed spit entering into her flesh, and the heat of the fire tightening the leather of the shoes, she cried out:

'I suffer a thousand pains! Who will give me black poison?'

'Put her nearer the flames,' said the sheriff.

Then, questioning Katheline:

'How many times,' said he to her, 'have you ridden astride a broomstick to go to the Witches' Sabbath? How many times have you caused the wheat to wither in the ear, the fruit on the tree, the child in its mother's womb? How many times have you caused two brothers to become sworn enemies and made of two sisters rivals full of hate?'

Katheline wanted to speak but she could not and she waved her arms as though to say no. Then the sheriff said:

'She will not speak until she feels all her witch's fat melting before the fire. Push her closer.'

Katheline screamed. The sheriff said to her:

'Pray Satan that he cool you.'

And she made a sign that she wished to take off her shoes which smoked before the heat of the fire.

'Pray Satan to un-shoe you,' said the sheriff.

Ten o'clock sounded and that was the hour of the raging one's dinner. He went off with the torturer and the clerk, leaving Katheline alone before the fire in the torture-chamber.

At eleven they returned to find Katheline stiff and immobile. The clerk said:

'She's dead, I think.'

The sheriff ordered the torturer to take Katheline from the coffin and the shoes from her feet. Unable to take them off, he cut at them and the feet of Katheline were seen all red and bloody.

And the sheriff, thinking of his meal, watched her without a word. And soon she recovered her senses and, falling on the floor without being able to rise again, despite her efforts, she said to the sheriff:

'Long ago you wanted me to wife, but now you shall not have me. Four times three is the sacred number and the thirteenth is the husband.'

Then, as the sheriff was about to speak, she said to him:

76

'Stay silent! He has hearing finer than the archangel who counts in heaven the heart-beats of the just. Why come you so late? Four times three is the sacred number; he kills those who desire me.'

The sheriff said:

'She receives the devil in her bed.'

'She is mad with the pain of the torture,' said the clerk.

Katheline was taken back to prison. Three days later, the sheriff's court being assembled in the *Vierschare*, Katheline was condemned, after they had deliberated, to the penalty of the fire.

She was taken to the Great Market Place of Damme by the executioner and his men, where the scaffold had been erected and on which she mounted. In the market place stood the provost, the herald and the judges.

The herald's trumpet sounded three times; then, turning to the people, he said:

'The magistrate of Damme, having had compassion on the woman Katheline, has not wished to punish her with the extreme rigour of the law of the town, but in order to bear witness that she is a witch her hair will be burned, she will pay a fine of twenty gold carolus and be banished from the territory of Damme under pain of losing one limb.'

And the people applauded this harsh leniency.

The executioner then attached Katheline to the stake, set a wig of tow upon her head and fired it. And for a long time the tow burned and Katheline screamed and wept. Then she was detached and carried out of the territory of Damme in a cart, for her feet were burned.

39 ULENSPIEGL being now at Bois-le-Duc in Brabant, the men of the town wanted to have him appointed their jester but he refused this dignity. 'A pilgrim pilgriming cannot play the fool in one place steadily, but only at inns and on highways.'

At this same time Philip, who was King of England, came to visit the countries of his future inheritance—Flanders, Brabant, Hainaut, Holland and Zeeland. He was then in his twenty-ninth year; in his gray eyes dwelt sour melancholy, fierce dissimulation and cruel resolution. Cold his countenance, stiff his head, covered with wild hair; stiff also his thin body and his feeble legs. His speech was slow and thick as though he had wool in his mouth.

In the midst of tourneys, jousts and feastings, he visited the happy Duchy of Brabant, the county of Flanders and his other seignories. Everywhere he swore to guard the privileges; but when, at Brussels, he swore on the Testament to observe the Golden Bull of Brabant, his hand contracted so strongly that he had to take it from the Holy Book.

He went to Antwerp, where they set up twenty-three triumphal arches to receive him. The town spent one hundred and eighty-seven thousand florins to pay for these arches, and also for the costumes of eighteen hundred seventy-nine merchants who were all dressed in crimson velvet, and for the rich livery of four hundred and seventeen lackeys, and the brilliant silk trappings of four thousand burghers, all dressed alike. Many feasts were given by the rhetoricians of all the Lowland towns—or nearly all.

There were seen, with their male and female jesters, the Prince of Love of Tournai, mounted on a sow that was called Astarte; the King of the Foolish, of Lille, who led a horse by the tail and walked behind; the Prince of Pleasure, of Valenciennes, who amused himself by counting his donkey's farts; the Abbot of Mirth, of Arras, who drank Brussels wine from a flask shaped like a breviary, and jolly reading it was; the Abbot of the Ill-Provided, of Ath, who only had holey linen and down-at-the-heel boots, but he had a sausage with which he filled his belly; the Provost of the Madcaps, a young lad mounted on a frightened goat that ran into the crowd and who, because of this, received many a blow; the Abbot of the Silver Dish from Quesnoy who, mounted on his horse, pretended to be sitting in a dish, saying: 'There is no beast so big that it can't be cooked by fire.'

And they played all sorts of innocent follies; but the King remained sad and severe.

That same evening the Margrave of Antwerp, the burgomasters, captains, and deans, came together to try and find play that might make King Philip smile.

The Margrave said:

'Have you not heard tell of a certain Pierkin Jaconsen, town jester of Bois-le-Duc, and well renowned for his merry tricks?'

'Yes,' they said.

'Well,' said the Margrave, 'let us summon him hither, and may he do some nimble trick, since our own jester has lead in his boots.'

'Let us summon him hither,' they said.

When the messenger from Antwerp arrived at Bois-le-Duc, they told him that the jester Pierkin had burst from too much laughing but that there was in town another visiting jester named Ulenspiegl. The messenger sought him out in a tavern where he was eating a fricassee of mussels and making a skirt for a little girl out of the shells.

Ulenspiegl was delighted when he learned that it was for him that the town messenger of Antwerp, mounted on a fine *Veurne-Ambacht* horse and leading another by the reins, had come all that way.

Without setting foot on the ground, the messenger asked him if he knew where to find a new·trick to make King Philip smile.

'I have a mine of them under my hair,' replied Ulenspiegl.

Off they went together. The two horses, galloping loose-reined, brought Ulenspiegl and the messenger to Antwerp.

Ulenspiegl came before the Margrave, the two burgomasters, and the townsmen.

'What do you intend to do?' the Margrave asked of him.

'Fly i' the air!' replied Ulenspiegl.

'How will you set about this?' asked the Margrave.

'Do you know,' asked Ulenspiegl, 'what is worth less than a pricked bladder?'

'I do not,' said the Margrave.

'A secret let out,' replied Ulenspiegl.

Meanwhile the heralds of the games, mounted on their fine horses, caparisoned with crimson velvet, rode through all the main streets, places and crossways of the town, sounding their trumpets and beating their drums. In this way they announced to the *signorkes* and *signorinnekes* that Ulenspiegl, the jester from Damme, was going to fly in the air over the Quay, there being present upon a stage King Philip and his high, illustrious and distinguished company.

Facing the stage there was a house built in the Italian style, along whose roof ran a gutter. An attic-window opened out on this gutter.

Ulenspiegl, mounted on a donkey, traversed the town that day. A footman ran alongside him. Ulenspiegl had donned the fine robe of crimson silk which the townsmen had given him. His head-dress was a hood, also of crimson, which had two asses' ears with a bell at the end of each ear. He wore a collar of copper medals, each embossed with the arms of Antwerp. The sleeves of his robe hung down pointed and each had a gilded bell. He had shoes with gilt soles and a bell at the pointed toe of each.

His donkey was caparisoned in crimson silk, which had the arms of Antwerp embroidered on it in fine gold at each thigh.

The footman brandished in one hand an ass's head and in the other a branch at whose end tinkled the bell of a woodland cow.

Ulenspiegl, leaving his footman and donkey in the street, climbed up to the roof-gutter.

There, shaking his bells, he opened wide his arms, as though he was about to fly. Then, leaning down towards King Philip, he said:

'I thought I was the only fool in Antwerp, but I see the town is full of them. If you had told me you were going to fly I would not have believed you; but let a jester come and say he will do it and you believe him. How would you have me fly, since I have no wings?'

Some laughed, others swore, but all said:

'It's quite true what the fool says.'

But King Philip sat stiff as a king of stone.

And the townsmen whispered among themselves:

'No need to have made such great festivity for such a sour phiz.'

And they gave three florins to Ulenspiegl, who departed, after having been forced to return the robe of crimson silk.

'What are three florins in a young man's pocket but a snowball before a fire; a full bottle before you, large-throated drinkers? Three florins! The leaves fall from the trees and sprout upon them again, but florins come out of pockets and never re-enter. The butterflies flutter off with the summer and the florins too, although they weigh more.'

And so saying, Ulenspiegl looked well at his three florins.

'What a proud mien,' he murmured, 'has the Emperor Charles on this side, all cuirassed and helmeted, holding a sword in one hand and in the other the globe of this poor world. He is, by the grace of God, Emperor of the Romans, King of Spain, and so forth, and he is right gracious for our countries, this mailed Emperor. And here on the other side is a shield graven with the arms of duke, count and so forth of his different possessions, with the fine device: *Da mihi virtutem contra hostes tuos: Give me strength against thine enemies.* Strong he was, indeed, against the Reformists who had goods to confiscate so that he might inherit them. Ah, if I were the Emperor Charles, I would have florins made for everybody, and everybody being rich, no one should work any more.'

But Ulenspiegl looked in vain at the lovely coins; off they went to the land of ruin, to the tune of the clinking of quart pots and the clanking of bottles.

40 WHILE HE HAD stood up in the roof-gutter dressed in crimson silk, Ulenspiegl had not seen Nele in the crowd, who looked up at him smilingly. At this time she was living at Borgerhout near Antwerp and had thought that if any jester was to fly before King Philip it could be none other than her friend Ulenspiegl.

As he walked dreamily along the highway, he did not hear the sound of hastening steps behind him, but he felt the two hands that were laid flatly on his eyes. Scenting Nele, he said:

'Are you here?'

'Yes,' she said. 'I've been running behind you ever since you left the town. Come with me.'

'But,' he said, 'where is Katheline?'

'Do you not know,' she asked, 'that she was unjustly tortured as a witch, then banished from Damme for three years? That they burned her feet and a tow wig upon her head? I tell you this so that you may not be afraid of her, for she is witless because of her great suffering. Often she spends whole hours looking at her feet, and saying: "Hanske, my sweet devil, see what they have done to your dear." And her poor feet are like two wounds! Then she weeps, saying: "Other women have husbands or lovers, while I live on earth like a widow." Then I tell her that Hanske will hate her if she speaks of him before anyone else but me. And she obeys me like a child except when she sees a cow or an ox, the cause of her torture. Then she flees away, running swiftly, and nothing will stop her, fences, streams or ditches, until she falls from very weariness by some highway corner or the wall of a farm, where I go to pick her up and bind her bleeding feet. And I think that in burning the hank of tow on her head they also burned the brain within her head.'

And both of them were grieved thinking of Katheline.

They drew near to her and saw that she was sitting in the sun, on a bench against the wall of her house. Ulenspiegl said to her:

'Do you know me?'

'Four times three,' said she, 'is the sacred number and the thirteenth is Thereb. Who are you, child of this wicked world?'

'I am Ulenspiegl,' he answered, 'son of Soetkin and Claes.'

She nodded her head and recognized him. Then, beckoning him with her finger and bending to his ear:

'If you see him whose kisses are as snow, tell him to return, Ulenspiegl.'

Then, pointing to her burned hair:

'I am ill,' she said. 'They have taken my wits away, but when he

81

comes back again he will refill my head that is now quite empty. Do you hear? It rings like a bell; that is my soul knocking at the door to depart because it is burning. If Hanske comes and will not fill my head I will tell him to make a hole with his knife; the soul that is there, always knocking to get out, grieves me cruelly; yes. And I sleep no more, and I always wait, and he must fill my head; yes.'

And, sinking down, she groaned.

And the peasants returning from the fields for dinner, while the church bell called them, passed before Katheline, saying:

'There's the madwife.'

And they crossed themselves.

And Nele and Ulenspiegl wept together, for Ulenspiegl had to continue his pilgrimage.

41 As HE PILGRIMAGED at this time, he entered into the service of a certain Josse, surnamed *Kwaebakker*, the angry baker, because of his sour face. The *Kwaebakker* gave him three stale loaves each week and lodged him in a loft under the roof, where it rained and breezed wonderfully.

Seeing himself so badly treated, he played several tricks on the baker and among them this one. When they bake in the early morning they must, at night, sift the flour. One night, as the moon was shining, Ulenspiegl asked for a candle to see what he was doing. And from his master he received this reply:

'Sift the flour in the light of the moon.'

Obediently Ulenspiegl sifted the flour on the floor where the moon shone.

In the morning the *Kwaebakker*, going to see what sort of a job Ulenspiegl was doing, found him still sifting, and said:

'Does flour no longer cost anything that you must sift it on the ground?'

'I sifted the flour in the moonlight as you ordered me to,' answered Ulenspiegl.

Said the baker: 'Ignorant donkey! 'Twas in a sieve you should have done it.'

'I thought the moon was a new kind of sieve,' replied Ulenspiegl, 'but there will be no great loss. I will gather up the flour.'

'It is too late to make the dough and bake it,' said the *Kwaebakker*.

82

'*Baes*,' retorted Ulenspiegl, 'our neighbour's dough is ready in the mill. Shall I go and take it?'

'To the gallows with you and seek what's there.'

'I go, *baes*,' replied Ulenspiegl.

He ran off to the gallows-field and there found a dried hand of a thief, which he carried back to the *Kwaebakker*, saying:

'Here is a hand of Fame that makes invisible all those who carry it. Do you wish to hide your nasty character from now on?'

'I'm going to complain to the court about you,' replied the *Kwaebakker*, 'and you will learn that you have infringed the rights of the master.'

When they were both before the burgomaster, the *Kwaebakker*, wishing to string off the misdeeds of Ulenspiegl, saw that he opened his eyes staring wide. This made him so angry that, interrupting his testimony, he said:

'What do you want?'

Ulenspiegl replied:

'You said to me that you would accuse me in such a way that I would see. I want to see and that's why I'm looking.'

'Out of my sight!' shouted the baker.

'If I was in your sight,' replied Ulenspiegl, 'I could not help, when you closed your eyes, but come out through your nostrils.'

The burgomaster, seeing that this was their day for jokes, would listen no more.

Ulenspiegl and the *Kwaebakker* walked out together. The *Kwaebakker* raised his stick, but Ulenspiegl dodged it, saying:

'*Baes*, since it is with blows that you sift my flour, take the chaff; that's your anger. I'll keep the white; that's my gaiety.'

Then, showing his backside:

'And this is the mouth of the oven if you want to bake.'

42 ULENSPIEGL, as he pilgrimaged, would gladly have become a highway robber, but he found the stones too heavy to carry.

He was walking by chance on the road to Audenaerde, where there was then a garrison of Flemish *reiters* charged with the defence of the town against the French bands who were ravaging the countryside like locusts.

The *reiters* were commanded by a certain captain, Frisian born, named Kornjuin. They ran over the Lowlands, pillaging the populace who were, as usual, eaten from both sides.

Everything was good for them: hens, chickens, ducks, pigeons, calves, pigs. One day, as they were returning laden with plunder, Kornjuin and his lieutenants saw Ulenspiegl lying at the foot of a tree, fast asleep and dreaming of fricassees.

'What do you do for a living?' demanded Kornjuin.

'I die of hunger,' answered Ulenspiegl.

'What is your trade?'

'To go on a pilgrimage for my sins, watch the others labour, dance on the tight-rope, portray pretty faces, carve knife-handles, play on the *rommel-pot*, and sound the trumpet.'

If Ulenspiegl spoke so bravely of the trumpet, it was because he had learned that the post of watchman at Audenaerde Castle was now vacant following the death of the old man who occupied it.

Kornjuin said to him:

'You shall be the town trumpeter.'

Ulenspiegl followed him and was placed on the highest tower of the ramparts, in a sentry-box that was well ventilated by the four winds, though the south wind fanned it with only one wing.

He was enjoined to sound the trumpet as soon as he spied the enemies coming, and to keep his head clear and his eyes always open; and for these ends not to give himself over too much to eating or drinking.

The captain and his troopers stayed within the tower and there feasted all day long at the expense of the Lowlands. More than one capon, whose only crime was being plump, was killed and eaten. Ulenspiegl, continually forgotten and having to content himself with his thin soup, was not at all amused by the odour of the sauces. When the French came and carried off many cattle, Ulenspiegl gave never a sound out of the trumpet.

Kornjuin climbed up to where he was, and said:

'Why did you not sound?'

Ulenspiegl answered:

'I return you no thanks for your food.'

The following day, the captain commanded a great feast for himself

84

and his troopers, and Ulenspiegl was again forgotten. They were just about to stuff themselves when Ulenspiegl blew on his trumpet.

Kornjuin and his men, thinking the French had come, left wine and viands and jumped to their horses. Out of the town they rode in haste, but in the open country they found nothing but an ox chewing the cud, and this they dragged back with them.

During their absence Ulenspiegl had filled himself with their wines and edibles. When the captain entered, he found him standing, smilingly and with shaking legs, by the door of the banquet hall. He said: 'It's traitor's work to sound the alarm when you see no enemy, and not to sound it when you do.'

'Sir Captain,' answered Ulenspiegl, 'in my tower I am so puffed up with the four winds that I might have floated away had I not blown into the trumpet to relieve myself. Hang me now, or another time, when you need a donkey's skin for your drums.'

Kornjuin went off without a word.

Meanwhile news came to Audenaerde that His Gracious Majesty, the Emperor Charles, was about to come to town right nobly accompanied. On this occasion the sheriffs gave to Ulenspiegl a pair of glasses so that he might see better the coming of His Sacred Majesty. Ulenspiegl was to sound the trumpet three times when he saw the Emperor march on Luppeghem, which is about a quarter of a league from the Borg-poort.

In this way the townsfolk would have time to ring the bells, prepare the fireworks, put the meats in the oven and the spigots in the barrels.

One day toward noon, the wind coming from Brabant and the sky being clear, Ulenspiegl saw on the road that leads to Luppeghem a great band of horsemen mounted on prancing steeds, the plumes of their toques fluttering in the wind. Several carried banners. He who rode ahead proudly bore a cap of cloth of gold with long plumes. He was dressed in brown velvet embroidered with gold and silver threads.

Ulenspiegl, putting on the glasses, saw that it was the Emperor Charles-Quint, who was coming to allow the folk of Audenaerde to serve him their finest wines and their tastiest meats.

All the band ambled along, sniffing in the fresh air to give them an appetite; but Ulenspiegl thought that they usually dined well enough to go hungry this one day without passing out. So he watched them come and did not blow on his trumpet.

They advanced laughing and talking while His Sacred Majesty looked down into his stomach to see if there was room enough for the dinner that the Audenaerde folk were to give him. He seemed surprised and displeased when no bell rang to announce his coming.

At that moment a peasant entered the town, running to announce

85

that he had seen, riding in the outskirts, a French band marching on the town to eat and plunder everything.

When he heard these words, the porter closed the gate and sent a servant of the town to warn the other porters. And the *reiters* feasted on, ignorant of all this.

His Majesty drew nearer, annoyed not to hear the bells, cannon and arquebuses, ringing, booming and snapping. Vainly straining his ear, he heard nothing but the chimes marking the half-hour. Arriving before the gate and finding it closed, he beat upon it with his fist to make it open.

The lords of his suite, as angry as he was, growled sour words. The keeper of the gate, who was up on the ramparts, shouted down to them that if they did not cease their noise he would spray them with shot to cool their impatience.

But His Majesty, raging:

'Blind swine, do you not know your Emperor?'

The keeper of the gate replied: That the least swinish are not always the most gilded; that he knew that the French were good mockers by nature, seeing that the Emperor Charles, warring at that moment in Italy, could not be before the gates of Audenaerde.

Thereupon Charles and his lords shouted louder, saying:

'If you don't open we'll roast you on the point of a lance. And you'll eat your keys beforehand.'

At the noise they were making, an old trooper came out from the artillery-room and, showing his nose above the wall, said:

'You're wrong, Keeper. That's our Emperor there. I know him well although he has grown older since he took Marie Van der Gheynst from here to the Castle of Lallaing.'

The gate-keeper fell down stiff as death with terror, and the trooper took his keys and went to open the great gate.

The Emperor demanded to know why they had kept him waiting so long. The trooper having told him, His Majesty ordered that the gates be locked and that the *reiters* of Kornjuin be brought before him, and these he ordered to march past him beating their drums and playing their fifes.

Soon the bells awoke one by one to peal with all their might. So preceded, His Majesty came with an imperial din to the Great Market Place. The burgomasters and the aldermen were there assembled; the sheriff Jan Guigelaer came out at the noise, and then returned to the council chamber, crying:

'*Keyser Karel is alhier!*—The Emperor Charles is here!'

Sore afraid on learning this news, the burgomasters, sheriffs and

86

councillors came out from the town hall to go in a body and greet the Emperor, while their servants ran through the town to make ready the fireworks, set the fowls to roasting and stick the spigots in the barrels.

Men, women and children scurried about, shouting:

'*Keyser Karel is op 't groot marckt!*—The Emperor Charles is up at the Great Market Place!'

Soon there was a great crowd in the place.

The Emperor, very angry, demanded to know of the two burgomasters if they did not merit hanging for having so lacked the respect due their sovereign.

The burgomasters replied that they did indeed merit it but that Ulenspiegl merited it more, since, at the rumour of His Majesty's coming, he had been placed there equipped with a good pair of glasses, with express instructions to sound the trumpet three times as soon as he saw the imperial procession coming toward the town. But he had done no such thing.

The Emperor, still angry, demanded that Ulenspiegl be brought before him.

'Why,' said he to him, 'having glasses so clear, did you not sound the trumpet at my coming?'

So saying, he passed his hand over his eyes because of the sun and looked at Ulenspiegl.

The latter also passed his hand over his eyes and replied that, since having seen His Sacred Majesty look from between his fingers, he had no longer any desire to use glasses.

The Emperor told him that he was going to be hanged; the gatekeeper said that it were well done; and the burgomasters were so terrified with this sentence that they said not a word either to approve or disapprove.

The executioner and his assistants were sent for. They came bearing a ladder and a new rope, seized Ulenspiegl by the collar and marched him off before the hundred *reiters* of Kornjuin who mocked him bitterly.

The people who followed said:

'It is really a great cruelty to put such a poor young lad to death for so light a fault.'

And the weavers were there in great numbers and armed. They said:

'We shall not let Ulenspiegl be hanged. It's against the law of Audenaerde.'

But now they were come to the gallows-field and Ulenspiegl was hoisted up the ladder and the executioner put the rope about him. The weavers flocked about the gallows. The provost was there on

88

horseback, resting on the animal's shoulder the rod of justice wherewith he was, on a sign from the Emperor, to give the signal for the
hanging.

All the assembled people cried out:

'Pardon! Pardon for Ulenspiegl!'

Ulenspiegl, up on his ladder, said:

'Pity! Gracious Emperor!'

The Emperor raised his hand and said:

'If this rascal asks me to do something I cannot do, his life shall be
saved.'

'Speak, Ulenspiegl!' cried the people.

The women wept and said:

'There's nothing he can ask, the little man, for the Emperor can do
everything.'

And all of them said:

'Speak, Ulenspiegl!'

'Sacred Majesty,' spoke Ulenspiegl, 'I shall not ask you for silver,
nor lands, nor life, but only for one thing for which you must not, if
I dare say it, have me flogged, nor laid on the rack, before I go to the
land of spirits.'

'I promise you,' said the Emperor.

'Majesty,' said Ulenspiegl, 'I ask that before I am hanged you come
and kiss the mouth by which I speak no Flemish.'

The Emperor, laughing like every one else, replied:

'I cannot do that which you ask me to, and you will not be hanged,
Ulenspiegl.'

But he condemned the burgomasters and sheriffs to wear, for six
months, glasses at the back of their heads, so that, he said, if the
Audenaerde folk could not see before, they might at least see behind.

And by imperial decree these glasses are still seen on the arms of
the town.

And Ulenspiegl went away modestly, with a little bag of silver that
the women had given him.

43 ULENSPIEGL being at Liége, at the fish market, followed a fat
youth who, with one net-bag under his arm, filled with all
kinds of poultry, was filling another with haddocks, trout,
eels and pike.

Ulenspiegl recognised Lamme Goedzak.

'What are you doing here, Lamme?' he asked.

'You know how welcome Flanders folk are in this pleasant land of Liége; well, I follow my loves. And you?'

'I'm on the look out for a master to serve for my daily bread,' replied Ulenspiegl.

'Pretty dry nourishment,' said Lamme. 'You would do better to pass from the dish to the mouth a rosary of ortolans with a thrush for the *Credo*.'

'Are you rich?' Ulenspiegl asked him.

'I have lost my father, my mother and my young sister who used to beat me so. I shall inherit all their goods, and for the moment I'm living with a one-eyed servant who is a mistress of the arts in the making of fricassees.'

'Would you like me to carry your fish and your poultry?' asked Ulenspiegl.

'Yes,' said Lamme.

And the two of them wandered about the market.

Suddenly Lamme said:

'Do you know why you are mad?'

'No,' answered Ulenspiegl.

'Because you carry your fish and poultry in your hands, instead of carrying them in your stomach.'

'You said it, Lamme!' answered Ulenspiegl. 'Since I've been without bread the ortolans won't look at me any more.'

'You shall eat them, Ulenspiegl,' said Lamme, 'and work for me, if my cook will have you.'

As they walked along, Lamme pointed out to Ulenspiegl a lovely, nice and winsome girl, who, clad in silk, tripped through the market and looked at Lamme with soft eyes.

An old man, her father, walked behind her bearing two net-bags, one with fish and the other with game.

'That one,' said Lamme, pointing to her, 'I am going to make my wife.'

'Yes,' said Ulenspiegl, 'I know her. She's Flemish, from Zotteghem, and lives in Vinave-d'Isle Street. The neighbours say that her mother sweeps the street in front of their house instead of her and that her father irons her shirts for her.'

But Lamme made no answer to this and said joyfully:

'She looked at me!'

Together they came to Lamme's house near the Pont-des-Arches and knocked on the door. A one-eyed servant came to let them in. Ulenspiegl saw that she was old, tall, flat and fierce.

90

'La Sanginne,' said Lamme to her, 'would you like this boy to help you with your work?'

'I'll give him a trial,' said she.

'Take him then,' he said, 'and let him try out the delights of your cooking.'

La Sanginne then placed on the table three black puddings, a stein of cervoise ale and a great loaf of bread.

While Ulenspiegl ate, Lamme also nibbled at a black pudding.

'Do you know,' said he, 'where our souls dwell?'

'No, Lamme,' answered Ulenspiegl.

'In our stomachs,' shot back Lamme. 'There they dig without ceasing, forever to renew in our bodies the force of life. And what are the best companions? They are the good and choice eatables and, over and above them, the wine of the Meuse.'

'Yes,' said Ulenspiegl, 'puddings are agreeable company for a lonely soul.'

'He wants some more; give them to him, Sanginne,' said Lamme.

This time La Sanginne gave white puddings to Ulenspiegl.

While he stuffed them into him, Lamme, grown pensive, said:

'When I die my belly will die with me and, there below in purgatory, they will leave me fasting, carrying my flabby and empty belly about with me.'

'The black ones seem better to me,' said Ulenspiegl.

'You've already eaten six,' replied La Sanginne, 'and you'll get no more!'

'You know that you will be well treated here,' said Lamme, 'and that you will eat what I do.'

'I will remember these words,' answered Ulenspiegl.

Ulenspiegl, seeing that he ate the same as Lamme, was happy. The puddings that he had downed gave him such a great courage that he made the cauldrons, pots and pans to shine like suns that day.

Living well in that house, he willingly haunted the kitchen and the wine-cellar, leaving the garret to the cats. One day La Sanginne, having two chickens to roast, told Ulenspiegl to turn the spit while she went off to the market to get some herbs for the seasoning.

The two chickens being finally done, Ulenspiegl ate one of them.

When La Sanginne returned she said:

'There were two chickens; I see but one now.'

'Open your other eye and you'll see them both,' retorted Ulenspiegl.

In a rage, she went to tell Lamme Goedzak what had happened and he, descending to the kitchen, said to Ulenspiegl:

'Why do you mock my servant? There were two chickens.'

'There were indeed, Lamme,' said Ulenspiegl, 'but when I came here you told me that I was to eat and drink like yourself. There were two chickens; I ate one; you shall eat the other. My joy is past; yours is yet to come. Are you not happier than I?'

'Yes,' said Lamme, smiling, 'but do what La Sanginne bids you and you'll have but half to do.'

'I shall be careful to do so,' replied Ulenspiegl.

Thus, each time that La Sanginne asked him to do something, he did but the half. If she asked him to bring in two pails of water, he brought in but one. If she asked him to go fill a pitcher of ale at the barrel, he would pour half of it down his gullet on the way back; and so on, and so on.

In the end La Sanginne, weary of his carryings-on, said to Lamme:

'If that good-for-nothing stays any longer in the house, I am leaving right away.'

Lamme went down to where Ulenspiegl was and said to him:

'You must go, my boy, in spite of the fact that you're looking well since you've been here. Listen to the cock crowing! It's two o'clock in the afternoon. That means there's going to be rain. I would rather not send you out in the bad weather there's going to be, but think, my boy, that La Sanginne by her fricassees is the keeper of my life. I could not, without risking sudden death, let her leave me. Go then, my boy, with God's grace, and take these three florins and this string of saveloys to enliven your way.'

And Ulenspiegl went away, quite crestfallen, regretting Lamme and his kitchen.

44 NOVEMBER CAME to Damme and elsewhere, but the winter was tardy. There was neither rain nor snow, nor any cold weather; the sun shone undimmed from morning until night. The children rolled about in the dust of the streets and highways. At the hour of repose after supper, the merchants, shopkeepers, goldsmiths, cartwrights and artisans came out on their stoups to look on the everlastingly blue sky, on the trees whose leaves fell not, on the storks that stood up on the ridges of the roofs, and on the swallows that had not yet flown away. The roses had flowered three times and for the fourth time they were in bud; the nights were warm and the nightingales continued singing.

The folk of Damme said:

'Winter's dead; let's burn Winter.'

And they made a tremendous mannekin with a face like a bear's, a long beard of shavings, and thick hair of flax. They dressed it up in white clothes and then burned it with high ceremony.

Claes was steeped in melancholy; he had no blessing for the ever-blue sky nor for the swallows that would not depart. For no one in Damme burned charcoal, save in the kitchen, and everybody having enough for that bought none from Claes, who had spent all his savings paying for his stock.

Therefore if, as he stood on his doorstep, he felt a breath of sharp air chill the tip of his nose, he would say:

'Ah, that's my bread coming to me!'

But the sharp wind did not continue blowing; the sky stayed always blue; and the leaves would not fall from the trees. And Claes refused to sell his winter stock for half-price to the miserly Grypstuiver, the dean of the fishmongers. And soon there was no more bread in the cottage.

45 BUT KING PHILIP hungered not and ate pastries beside his wife, Ugly Mary of the Royal House of the Tudors. He had no love for her but hoped, in begetting a child by this wretched woman, to give the English nation a Spanish monarch. Little good did this union do him; it was that of a cobble-stone and a fire-brand. Still they were sufficiently united to drown the poor protestants and burn them by the hundreds.

When Philip was not absent from London, or out disguised, sporting in some low haunt, the bed-time hour re-united the two spouses.

Then Queen Mary, attired in fine Tournay linen and Irish lace, would lie back on the nuptial couch while Philip stood up straight as a post before her and looked to see if he could not detect some sign of maternity in his wife. But seeing nothing he would grow angry, say not a word and stare at his nails.

Then the barren ghoul spoke tenderly, and with her eyes that she tried to make soft, begged the glacial Philip for love. Tears, cries, supplications, she spared nothing to obtain a warm caress from him who loved her not at all.

Vainly, joining her hands, she dragged herself to his feet; in vain like a mad woman she laughed and wept together to make him yield; neither the laugh nor the tears melted away the stone of the hard heart.

In vain, like an amorous snake, she wound her thin arms about him and clasped to her flat breast the narrow cage where lived the stunted soul of the king of the blood. But he did not budge any more than a post.

She tried, the poor ugly one, to make herself gracious; she called him all the sweet names that women wild with love give to the lovers of their choice. Philip stared at his nails.

Sometimes he replied:

'Are you not going to have children?'

At these words, Mary's head would fall forward on her breast.

'Is it my fault,' she would say, 'that I am barren? Have pity on me. I live as a widow.'

'Why have you no children?' Philip would say.

Then the queen would fall on the carpet like one smitten by death. And in her eyes there were but tears: she would have wept blood, if she could have, the poor ghoul.

And thus God avenged upon their murderers the victims with which they had strewn the soil of England.

46 THERE WAS A RUMOR running among the people that the Emperor Charles was going to take away from the monks the right of inheriting freely the goods and chattels of those who died in their monasteries; and this greatly displeased the Pope. Ulenspiegl, being then by the banks of the Meuse, thought to himself that the Emperor would profit both ways, for he would inherit that which the families would not. So he sat down on the river-bank and cast into the water a well-baited line. Then, nibbling at a bit of old brown bread, he regretted having no Romagna wine to wash it down; but, thought he, one cannot always have everything just right.

Yet he threw bits of his bread into the water, saying that he who eats without sharing his repast with his neighbour is not worthy of having anything to eat.

At this, up came a gudgeon that nosed a crumb, licked it with its lips and opened its innocent mouth wide, thinking doubtless that the bread would just fall into it. Gaping this way in the air, it was suddenly swallowed by a treacherous pike that shot out at it like an arrow.

The pike did the same thing to a carp that was catching flies in their flight, quite heedless of danger. Thus well-filled, it remained motionless below the water's surface, scorning the lesser fry who, to tell the truth, swam swiftly away from it, all fins working. While it was taking its ease in this way, there came rapidly on the scene a hungry and voracious pike whose mouth hung open. With a bound it was on the other pike, and a furious combat began between them. Immortal jaw strokes were exchanged that day; the water was red with blood. The pike that had eaten defended itself badly against the hungry one. The latter backed up; then, gathering force, shot out at its opponent that was awaiting it with open mouth, and disappeared halfway down its throat. Then, trying to free itself, found it could not because of the incurving teeth. And both of them thrashed about sadly.

So interlocked, they did not see a strong hook attached to a silken cord that came up from the bottom of the water and embedded itself in the gills of the pike that had dined, drew him and his adversary out of the water and threw them both on the grass without any ceremony.

Ulenspiegl, as he killed them, said:

'Pikes, my dears, might you not be the Pope and the Emperor devouring each other, and might I not be the people who in God's own good time hook you up in the midst of your battle?'

47 MEANWHILE KATHELINE, who had not left Borgerhout, wandered endlessly about the outskirts of the town, continually saying: 'Hanske, my man, they made a fire on my head; make you a hole that my soul may come out. Alas! It is always knocking and each knock is a stinging pain.'

And Nele tended her in her folly; and, seated by her, thought dolefully of her friend Ulenspiegl.

And at Damme Claes tied up his faggots, sold his charcoal and often fell into melancholy, thinking that the banished Ulenspiegl could not return to the cottage for so long a time.

Soetkin stayed all day long by the window, watching to see if her son Ulenspiegl were coming back.

He, having arrived at the outskirts of Cologne, thought that at that moment he had a taste for gardening.

So he went and offered himself as a lad to Jan de Zuursmoel who, being captain of the *landsknechte,* had narrowly escaped hanging for want of a ransom and held hemp in horror; hemp, in Flemish, was then known as *hennep.*

One day Jan de Zuursmoel, wishing to show Ulenspiegl what he had to do, took him to the bottom of his property and there they saw a field adjoining the property, all sown with green *hennep.*

Jan de Zuursmoel said to Ulenspiegl:

'Each time that you see this ugly plant you must vilify it shamefully, for it serves the rack and the gallows.'

'I will vilify it,' replied Ulenspiegl.

Jan de Zuursmoel being seated at table one day with several good eating friends of his, the cook said to Ulenspiegl:

'Go down into the cellar and get some *zennip* (which is mustard).'

96

Ulenspiegl, maliciously taking in *hennep* for *zennip*, shamefully vilified the pot of *zennip* in the cellar and brought it up to the table, not without laughing.

'Why are you laughing?' asked Jan de Zuursmoel. 'Think you that our nostrils are of iron? Eat this *zennip*, since you yourself prepared it.'

'I like things better grilled with cinnamon,' replied Ulenspiegl.

Jan de Zuursmoel arose to beat him.

'There is, said he, 'vilification in this mustard-pot.'

'*Baes*,' said Ulenspiegl, 'do you not remember the day I followed you down to the end of your property? There, you said to me, pointing out the *zennip*, "Wherever you see that plant vilify it shamefully, for it serves the rack and the gallows." I will vilify it, *baes*, I will vilify it to its face. Do not beat me for my obedience.'

'I said *hennep* and not *zennip*,' shouted Jan de Zuursmoel, in a rage.

'*Baes*, you said *zennip* and not *hennep*,' retorted Ulenspiegl.

So they argued for a long time, Ulenspiegl speaking humbly, Jan de Zuursmoel screaming like an eagle and mixing up zennip, hennep, hemp, zemp, semp, hemp, zemp, like a skein of ravelled silk.

And the guests laughed like devils eating chops of Dominicans' and Inquisitors' kidneys.

But Ulenspiegl had to leave Jan de Zuursmoel.

48 ULENSPIEGL hired himself out to a tailor, who said to him: 'When you sew, sew closely, so that I won't be able to see it.' Ulenspiegl went and sat under a barrel and there began to sew.

'That's not what I mean,' cried the tailor.

'I'm in a barrel; how do you think anyone can see?' replied Ulenspiegl.

'Come, seat yourself there on the table and sew your stitches closely to each other, and make the coat like this wolf.' (Wolf was the name for a peasant's jerkin.)

Ulenspiegl took the jerkin, cut it in several pieces and then sewed them together to make them resemble a wolf.

The tailor, seeing this, cried:

'What in the devil's name have you made?'

'A wolf,' replied Ulenspiegl.

'Evil mocker,' retorted the tailor, ' 'tis true I said a wolf, but you know that that is what they call a peasant's jerkin.'

A while later he said to him:

'Boy, throw these sleeves on this doublet before you go to bed.'
(Throw means to baste, in tailors' language.)

Ulenspiegl hung the doublet on a nail and passed the night throwing the sleeves at it.

At the noise he made, the tailor came.

'Good-for-nothing,' said he, 'what new and nasty trick are you playing me there?'

'Is it a nasty trick?' asked Ulenspiegl. 'You see these sleeves? I've been throwing them all night at the doublet and they haven't stuck yet!'

'That goes without saying,' answered the tailor, 'and that's why I'm throwing you out into the street. See if you'll stay there any better.'

49 NELE WAS STILL very miserable about herself and her poor mad mother. In the meanwhile, when Katheline was with some kind neighbour and well guarded, Nele wandered far, far afield, quite alone, as far as Antwerp, along by the Scheldt, or elsewhere, always searching on the river boats, or the dusty roads, to see if she could not see her friend Ulenspiegl.

He, finding himself at Hamburg one fair-day, saw all about him merchants and old Jews living off money-lending and the sale of old clothes.

Ulenspiegl, desiring to be a merchant too, saw some horse turds lying on the ground and carried them back to his lodging, which was a bastion of the ramparts. There he dried them. Then he bought some red and green silk, made little sachets, placed the horse dung in them and tied them up with ribbons as though they were full of musk.

Then with several boards he made himself a tray, which he suspended from his neck with old cords, and off he went to the market-place carrying before him the tray filled with sachets. In the evening, to light them up, he set a little candle in the midst of them.

When anyone came to ask what it was he was selling, he would reply mysteriously:

'I'll tell you, but let us not speak too loudly.'

'What is it then?' the customers would ask.

'These are prophetic seeds, come straight out of Arabia into Flanders and prepared with great art by the Master, Abdul-Medil, of the tribe of the great Mahomet.'

Certain customers would whisper among themselves:

'He's a Turk.'

But others said:

'He's a pilgrim, come from Flanders; don't you hear his accent?'

98

And the ragged, miserable, lousy folk would come to Ulenspiegl and say:

'Give us some of these prophetic seeds.'

'I'll give them when you have florins to buy them,' replied Ulenspiegl.

And the poor miserable, ragged, lousy ones would go away crestfallen, saying:

'There is no joy in this world but for the rich.'

The rumour of these seeds for sale soon spread through the market-place. The burghers said one to the other:

'There is a Fleming there who has prophetic seeds blessed at Jerusalem on the tomb of our Lord Jesus; but they say he will not sell them.'

And all the burghers would come to Ulenspiegl and ask him for the seeds.

But he, wishing to have large profits, replied that they were not ripe enough; and he had his eye on two rich Jews who were wandering about the market-place.

'I would really like to know,' said one burgher, 'what's to become of my ship that's on the sea?'

'It will go up to heaven, if the waves are high enough,' replied Ulenspiegl.

Another said, showing off his sweet daughter, all blushing:

'This one will doubtless turn out well?'

'Everything turns out as Nature wishes,' replied Ulenspiegl, who had just seen the girl give a key to a young fellow, all puffed up with contentment, who said to Ulenspiegl:

'Master merchant, give me one of your prophetic bags so that I may see whether I sleep alone to-night.'

'It is written,' replied Ulenspiegl, 'that he who sows the wind of seduction reaps the whirlwind of cuckoldry.'

The young man became angry:

'Who told you that?'

'The seeds say,' continued Ulenspiegl, 'that they wish you a happy marriage and a wife that will not cover you with Vulcan's hat. Do you know that head-gear?'

Then, preaching:

'For she who gives an advance on the marriage bargain afterwards gives to others all the merchandise for nothing.'

At this the girl, wishing to put on an air of self-possession, said:

'Do you see all that in the prophetic sachets?'

'I also see a key,' whispered Ulenspiegl in her ear.

But the young lad had already gone off with the key.

100

Suddenly Ulenspiegl saw a thief snatching from a pork butcher's stall a long sausage, which he hid under his cloak. The merchant, however, did not see this. Quite happy, the thief came to Ulenspiegl and said to him:

'What are you selling there, prophet of bad-luck?'

'Sachets wherein you may see that you will be hanged for having loved sausages too well,' replied Ulenspiegl.

At these words the thief fled swiftly away, while the merchant from whom he had stolen shouted:

'Stop thief! Stop thief!'

But it was too late.

While Ulenspiegl was speaking, the two rich Jews, who had been listening with great attention, came up to him and said:

'What are you selling there, Fleming?'

'Sachets,' replied Ulenspiegl.

'What can one see,' they asked, 'by means of your prophetic seeds?'

'Future happenings, if you suck them,' said Ulenspiegl.

The two Jews consulted together and the elder said to the other:

'We might see in this way when our Messiah is to come; that would be a great consolation for us. Let us buy one of these sachets. How much do you sell them for?' said they to Ulenspiegl.

'Fifty florins,' replied Ulenspiegl. 'If you don't want to pay me that, off with you. He that does not buy the field must leave the dung where it is.'

Seeing Ulenspiegl so determined, they counted out the sum and carried away one of the sachets and went off to their meeting-place, where soon flocked all the Jews, knowing that one of the old men had bought a secret by which he could learn and announce the coming of the Messiah.

Knowing this, they all wanted to suck the prophetic sachet without paying. But the oldest, who had bought the thing and whose name was Jehu, intended doing this himself.

'Sons of Israel,' said he, holding in his hand the sachet, 'the Christians mock at us and drive us from among our fellow-men and they shout after us as they do after thieves. The Philistines would like to abase us lower than the earth; they spit in our faces, for God has unstrung our bows and shaken the bridle before us. How long, O Lord, God of Abraham, Isaac and Jacob, must the evil come to us while we await the good and the darkness cover us when we hope for light? Wilt thou soon come down to earth, Divine Messiah? When shall the Christians hide themselves in the caverns and the holes of the earth because of the terror they shall have of Thee and Thy magnificent glory when Thou shalt rise up to chastise them?'

And the Jews cried out:

'Come, Messiah! Suck, Jehu!'

Jehu sucked and then spewed, exclaiming piteously:

'I tell you truly, this is nothing but dung and the pilgrim from Flanders is a thief!'

Then all the Jews rushed at him, tore open the sachet, saw what it contained and went off in a great rage to the fair to find Ulenspiegl, who had not waited their coming.

50 A DAMME MAN, being unable to pay Claes for his charcoal, gave him his most valued possession: a cross-bow with twelve well-pointed quarrels to serve as missiles. At times when he had no work to do, Claes went shooting with the bow: more than one hare, for having loved the cabbage patch too well, was killed by him and turned into a fricassee.

Then Claes ate greedily and Soetkin would say, looking out at the deserted highway:

'Tyl, my son, don't you smell at all the scent of the sauce? He is hungry now, no doubt.' And all pensive she fain would have kept him his part of the feast.

'If he is hungry,' said Claes, 'it's his own fault. Let him come home and he'll eat as we do.'

Claes kept pigeons; he also liked to hear about him the singing and chirruping of the warblers, goldfinches, sparrows and other birds that sing and chatter. And so he willingly shot down buzzards and hawks, royal eaters of these poor birds. Now once, when he was measuring charcoal in the yard, Soetkin pointed out to him a great bird that hovered high in the air above the dove-cot.

Claes took up his bow and said:

'May the devil save His Hawkship!'

Having armed the cross-bow, he took his stand in the yard, following every movement of the bird so as not to miss it. The light in the sky was between daylight and dark. Claes could only see a black speck. He let fly the arrow and then saw a stork come falling into the yard.

Claes was sorely grieved; but Soetkin was more so, and cried:

'Oh, cruel! You have slain the bird of God!'

Then she took up the stork, saw that it was merely wounded in the wing, and went to fetch a healing balm. And while she dressed the wound she said:

'Stork, my friend, it was not clever of you, whom we love, to hover in the sky like the hawk we all hate. And so poor folks' arrows fly to the wrong address. Does your poor wing hurt you, stork, that you submit so patiently, knowing that our hands are friendly hands?'

When the stork was healed she had everything she wanted to eat; but she preferred to eat the fish that Claes fished for her out of the canal. And each time that the bird of God saw him coming she opened wide her great beak.

She followed Claes about like a dog but liked best to stay in the kitchen, where she warmed her stomach before the fire and tapped with her beak the belly of Soetkin who was preparing the meal, as much as to say: 'Is there nothing for me?'

And it was pleasant to see this grave messenger of good-luck wandering about on her long legs in the cottage.

51 Now THE BAD DAYS had returned and Claes worked on the land alone and sad, for there was not work enough for two. Soetkin stayed alone in the cottage, cooking in all sorts of ways the beans that were their daily fare, in order to make them more tempting. And she sang and laughed so that he might not suffer to see her sad. The stork stayed beside her, standing on one leg and with its beak buried in its feathers.

A man on horseback stopped before the cottage; he was dressed all in black, very thin and with a most sad air.

'Is there anyone within?' he asked.

'God bless your melancholy,' said Soetkin, 'but am I a phantom that, seeing me here, you ask if there is anyone within?'

'Where is your father?' asked the horseman.

'If my father's name is Claes,' replied Soetkin, 'he is over there and you can see him sowing corn.'

The horseman went off and Soetkin also, quite doleful, for she had to go, for the sixth time, and seek bread from the baker without paying for it. When she came home empty-handed, she was astonished to see Claes coming towards the house, all triumphant and glorious, riding the horse of the man in black, while he walked alongside on foot holding the bridle rein. Claes held proudly against his thigh a leather bag that seemed well-filled.

Dismounting, he embraced the man, slapped him joyously, then, shaking the bag, he cried:

'Long live my brother Josse, the good hermit! God keep him in joy, in fat, in mirth and in good health! He's the Josse of Benediction! The Josse of Abundance! The Josse of Rich Soups! The stork has not lied!' And he placed the bag on the table.

Whereat Soetkin said, lamentingly:

'My man, we shall not eat to-day; the baker has refused me bread.'

'Bread?' said Claes, opening the bag and letting a stream of gold run on the table, 'bread? There's bread, butter, meat, wine, beer! There's hams, marrow-bones, heron pies, ortolans, pullets, such as the great lords have! There's beer in hogsheads and wine in barrels! Right mad is the baker who will refuse us bread; we'll buy no more from him!'

'But, my man,' said Soetkin in a daze.

'Now listen,' said Claes, 'and be gay. Katheline, instead of ending her term of banishment in the marquisate of Antwerp, went on foot, under Nele's guidance, as far as Meyborg. There Nele told my brother Josse that we lived in misery in spite of our hard toiling. According to what this good messenger told me,' here Claes pointed to the horseman dressed in black, 'Josse has left the holy Roman religion to adhere to the heresy of Luther.'

The man dressed in black replied:

'They are heretics who follow the cult of the Great Harlot. For the Pope is a prevaricator and a seller of holy things.'

'Oh,' said Soetkin, 'do not speak so loud, sir. You will have all three of us burned.'

'And so,' said Claes, 'Josse said to this good messenger that since he was going to fight in the ranks of Frederick of Saxony and was taking with him fifty well-equipped men-at-arms, he had no need, going to war, of so much money to leave to some worthless *landsknecht*. Take these seven hundred golden florins then, he said, to my brother with my blessing; tell him to live in comfort and think on his soul's salvation.'

'Yes,' said the horseman, 'it's time, for God will render unto man according to his works and treat each man according to the merits of his life.'

'Sir,' replied Claes, 'it will not be forbidden me in the meantime to

104

rejoice at this good news. Deign to stay with us, for we are going to celebrate it with good tripes, many carbonadoes, and a little ham that I lately saw at the pork butcher's, so plump and appetising that it made my teeth come a foot long out of my jaws!'

'Alas,' said the man, 'the unfeeling rejoice while the eyes of God are upon their ways.'

'Come, now, messenger,' replied Claes, 'will you or won't you eat and drink with us?'

'It will be time enough for the faithful to give their souls up to earthly joys when the mighty Babylon has fallen low.'

Soetkin and Claes made the sign of the cross, and the man turned to go. Claes said to him:

'Since it pleases you to leave us without being entertained, give my brother Josse the kiss of peace and watch over him in battle.'

'That I will do,' said the man.

And away he went, while Soetkin left to seek out something wherewith to celebrate their propitious fortune. For supper that day, the stork had two gudgeons and a cod's head.

The news soon spread through Damme that the poor Claes had become the rich Claes by the act of his brother Josse, and the Dean said that Katheline had doubtless cast a spell on Josse, since Claes had received from him a very large sum of money and had not given the tiniest vestment to Our Lady.

Claes and Soetkin were happy, Claes working in the fields and selling his charcoal and Soetkin working right bravely in her house.

Yet Soetkin, still sad at heart, sought endlessly with her eyes on the highway for a sign of her boy Ulenspiegl.

And the three of them—Claes, Soetkin, and the stork—tasted the happiness that had come to them from God while they awaited that which would come to them from men.

52 THE EMPEROR CHARLES had received that day a letter from England in which his son said:

Sir and Father:

It displeases me to have to live in this country where the accursed heretics swarm like fleas, worms and locusts. Fire and the sword would not be enough to remove them from the trunk of the life-giving tree that is our Holy Mother, the Church. As though this were not grief enough for me, still must they look on me, not as their King, but as the husband of their Queen, having no authority. They mock me, saying, in vile pamphlets whose authors and printers cannot be found, that the Pope pays me to trouble and harm the realm by hangings and impious burnings; and when I wish to levy some urgent tax on them— for out of sheer malice they often leave me without money—they reply in evil lampoons that I have only to ask it from Satan whose work I do. Parliament makes excuses and hunches its back lest I should bite, but it gives nothing.

All the while the walls of London are covered with lampoons which show me as a parricide ready to strike down Your Majesty in order to inherit from you.

But you know, my Lord and Father, notwithstanding all ambition and legitimate pride, I wish for Your Majesty a long and glorious reign.

They also circulate through the town a design, most cunningly engraved on copper, showing me playing a harpsichord by the paws of cats, locked in the box of the instrument and whose tails protrude through holes, where they are clamped with iron pins. A man— that is me—is shown burning the tails with red-hot irons, thus making them strike the keys with their paws and mew furiously. I am made out so ugly that I do not wish to see myself. And I am shown laughing. Yet you know, Sir and Father, if I ever indulged in this profane pleasure. I have tried, no doubt, to distract myself by making these cats mew, but I never laughed at it. In their rebel talk they make a crime out of what they call the novelty and cruelty of this harpsichord, though animals have no souls and all men, and notably royalty, may use them up to the point of death for their diversion. But in this English country the people are so fond of animals that they treat them better than their own servants; the stables and kennels here are palaces, and there are lords who sleep with their horses on the same litter.

Moreover, my noble wife and Queen is barren; they say, as a bloody affront, that the fault is mine and not hers, she who is jealous, fierce, and gluttonous for love out of all measure. Sir and Father, I pray the Lord God every day that He keep me in His grace, hoping for another

106

throne, even though it be the Turkish one, awaiting that which I will be called to through the honour of being the son of your Most Glorious and Most Victorious Majesty.

(Signed) Philip

The Emperor replied to this letter, saying:

Sir and Son:

That your troubles are great I do not dispute, but try to endure with patience your wait for a more brilliant crown. I have already made known to several people my intention of retiring from the Netherlands and my other dominions, for I know that, old and gouty as I become, I cannot stand out against Henry of France, second of that name, for fortune favours the young. Think also that, as master of England, you wound by your power France, our enemy.

I was villainously defeated before Metz and lost forty thousand men. I was forced to flee before the King of Saxony. If God, by a stroke of His good and divine will, does not re-establish me in my full force and vigour, I am minded, Sir and Son, to quit my realms and leave them to you.

Have patience, therefore, and in the meantime, do your duty fully against the heretics, sparing none of them, men, women, girls nor children; for word has come to me—not without causing me great pain—that Madame your Queen has often been minded to show them mercy.

Your affectionate father,
(Signed) Charles

53 HAVING TRAMPED a long time Ulenspiegl, whose feet bled, met in the bishopric of Mayence a cart full of pilgrims who took him with them to Rome. As he entered that town and jumped down from the cart, he noticed by the door of an inn a sweet-looking woman, who smiled when she saw that he was looking at her.

Encouraged by this good humour he said:

'Hostess, will you give shelter to a pilgrim pilgriming? For I am come to my time and am about to be delivered of my sins.'

'We give shelter to all who pay.'

'I have a hundred ducats in my purse,' replied Ulenspiegl, who really had only one, 'and I want to spend the first one drinking a bottle of old Roman wine.'

'Wine is not dear in this holy city,' she replied. 'Come on in and drink a soldo's worth.'

They drank together so long, and emptied so many flasks as they talked together, that the hostess was forced to tell the servant to serve the clients in her stead while she and Ulenspiegl retired to a back-room all in marble and cold as winter.

Leaning her head on his shoulder, she asked him who he was. Ulenspiegl replied:

'I am the Sire of Geeland, Count of Gavergeeten, Baron Tuchtendeel, and I have at Damme, my birth-place, twenty-five *bonniers* of moonlight.'

'What sort of land is that?' asked the hostess, drinking from Ulenspiegl's tankard.

'It is,' said he, 'a land where they sew the seed of illusions, wild hopes and airy promises. But you were not born in the moonlight, sweet hostess of the amber skin and eyes that glisten like pearls. Of the colour of the sun is the burnished gold of your hair; it was Venus, without jealousy, who made these well-fleshed shoulders, these bouncing breasts, these rounded arms, these darling hands. Shall we sup together this evening?'

'Handsome pilgrim from Flanders,' said she, 'why have you come here?'

'To speak to the Pope,' answered Ulenspiegl.

'La!' said she, clasping her hands, 'speak to the Pope! I who belong here have never been able to do so.'

'I will do it,' said Ulenspiegl.

'But,' said she, 'do you know where he goes, what he looks like, what his habits are and his ways of living?'

'They told me as I came along,' said Ulenspiegl, 'that he is called Julius the Third, that he is lecherous, jolly and dissolute, a good talker and subtle in repartee. They also told me that he had taken an extraordinary friendship for a little beggar-fellow who used to go about black, muddy and forbidding, begging with a monkey, and that when he was raised to the pontifical throne he made a Cardinal of this fellow and that he becomes ill now if a day passes without his seeing him.'

'Drink,' said she, 'and don't speak so loud.'

'They also told me,' continued Ulenspiegl, 'that he swore like a trooper: *Al dispetto di Dio, potta di Dio*, one day at supper when he could not find a cold peacock that he had asked them to save for him, saying, "As the Vicar of God I can certainly swear for a peacock, since my Master became angry over an apple!" You see, my dear, that I know the Pope and what he is.'

'La!' she said, 'but don't speak about this to anyone else. In any case you'll never see him.'

'I shall speak to him,' said Ulenspiegl.

'If you do I'll give you a hundred florins.'

'They're won!' said Ulenspiegl.

The following day, although leg-weary, he ran about the town and learned that the Pope would say Mass that day in St. John Lateran. Ulenspiegl entered and placed himself as near to, and as much in view of, the Pope as he could. And each time that the Pope elevated the chalice or the Host, Ulenspiegl turned his back to the altar.

Beside the Pope there was an assisting Cardinal—brown-skinned, cunning and portly—who, carrying a monkey on his shoulder, served the sacrament to the people with many wanton gestures. He noticed what Ulenspiegl was doing and told the Pope. The latter, when the Mass was ended, sent for four hefty soldiers—such as they have in these war-like countries—who laid hold of the pilgrim.

'What is your faith?' asked the Pope of him.

'Most Holy Father,' replied Ulenspiegl, 'I have the same faith as my hostess.'

The Pope had the woman brought before him.

'What is your belief?' said he.

'The same as that of Your Holiness,' she replied.

'And mine too!' said Ulenspiegl.

The Pope asked him why he had turned his back on the Holy Sacrament.

'I felt myself unworthy to face it,' replied Ulenspiegl.

'You are a pilgrim?' asked the Pope.

'Yes,' he answered, 'and I have come from Flanders to ask for the remission of my sins.'

The Pope blessed him, and Ulenspiegl went off with the hostess who counted out to him a hundred florins. So ballasted, he left Rome to return to the land of Flanders.

But he had to pay seven ducats for his pardon, all inscribed on parchment.

54 IN THOSE DAYS there came to Damme two Premonstratensian friars with indulgences to sell. They were dressed in beautiful lace-trimmed vestments which covered their monkish robes. Standing at the church door when it was fair and under the porch when it was raining, they showed their tariff wherein they gave for six liards, for a patard, for half-a-sovereign, for seven or twelve florins, a

hundred, two hundred, three hundred, four hundred years indulgences and, according to the price, semi-plenary or full plenary indulgence and pardon for the most heinous crimes—even that of wanting to violate Madame the Virgin. But that one cost seventeen florins.

They delivered to their clients, who paid them, little bits of parchment whereon was written the number of years of indulgence. Above could be read this inscription:

He that does not wish to be
Stewed, roasted, fricasseed
A thousand years in Purgatory,
Burning eternally in Hell,
Let him buy these indulgences,
Pardons and forgivenesses
For a little money.
God will repay him.

And buyers came to them from six leagues around. One of the good friars often preached to the people; he had a rosy phiz and carried his three chins and his pot-belly without any embarrassment.

'Miserable men!' he would say, fixing his eyes on one or another of his listeners. 'Miserable men! There you are in Hell! The fire is burning you cruelly; they are boiling you in the cauldron full of oil where they prepare the *olie-koekjes* of Astarte. You are nothing but a sausage on Lucifer's frying-pan. A leg o' mutton on Guilguiroth's, the great devil, for you are cut into pieces beforehand. Look at that great sinner there who scorned indulgences; look at that plate of stew; 'tis he! 'tis he! His impious body, his damned body so reduced. And with what sauce! Brimstone, pitch and tar! And all these poor sinners are thus eaten, to be born again to endless pain. And down there, verily, there is weeping and wailing and gnashing of teeth. Have pity, O merciful God! Yes, there you are in Hell, poor damned soul suffering all these torments. But let them give a denier for you and straightway the pain in your right hand would be eased; let them give a half more and then your two hands are out of the flames. But the rest of the body? A florin, and over it falls the dew of indulgence. Oh delicious coolness! And during ten days, a hundred days, a thousand years—according to the payment—no more roast, no more

110

olie-koekje, no more fricassee! And even if it be not for yourself, sinner, is there no one down there in the secret depths of the flames, some poor souls, relations, a dear wife maybe, or a sweet girl with whom you once delighted to sin?'

And so saying the monk nudged with his elbow the brother who stood beside him holding a silver basin. And the brother, lowering his eyes at this signal, shook the basin unctuously to call forth contributions.

'Have you not,' pursued the preacher, 'have you not in that horrible fire a son, a daughter, some beloved wee infant? They cry, they weep, they call upon you. Can you remain deaf to these lamenting voices? Oh no, you cannot: your icy heart is about to melt, but it will cost you a carolus. And see! At the sound of the carolus on this base metal' (the companion monk shook again his basin) 'a space opens in the midst of the flames and the poor soul mounts up to the mouth of some volcano. And now he is in the cool air, the free air! Where are the torments of the fire? The sea is near and in he plunges. He swims on his back and on his belly, on the waves and under them. Listen to the joyful cries; see how he rolls in the water! The angels look down and are happy. They await, but he has not had enough yet; he would fain become a fish. He does not know that on high there are delicious baths, all perfumed and with morsels of white sugar candy, cool as ice, floating about in them. A shark appears; the soul fears it not. He mounts it and it does not feel him there. He wants to go with it to the depths of the sea. He is going to greet the angels of the waters who feed on *waterzoey* from coral cauldrons, and fresh oysters on mother-of-pearl plates. And how well-received he is; how cherished and fêted! But still the angels call him on high. At length, most refreshed and happy, do you not see him mount and sing like a lark right to the very highest heaven, where God is enthroned in glory? There he finds his earthly relations and friends excepting those who, having slighted these indulgences and our Holy Mother the Church, still burn in the depths of Hell. And so forever, and forever, and forever, century after century, through all-consuming eternity. But the other soul is close to God, cooling himself in the suave baths and crunching the sugar candy. Buy these indulgences, my brothers: we give them for crusados, for golden florins, for English sovereigns! Even copper coins are not refused. Buy! Buy! This is the holy shop. There is here for the rich and the poor. Most unhappily we cannot give credit, my brothers, for to buy and not pay ready money is a crime in the eyes of the Lord.'

The brother who did no preaching shook his plate. The florins, crusados, ducats, patards, sols and deniers fell into it thick as hail.

111

Claes, feeling himself rich, paid a florin for ten thousand years of indulgences. The monks gave him a piece of parchment in exchange.

Soon, seeing that there was nobody in Damme except the misers who had not bought indulgences, the two monks went on to Heyst.

55 DRESSED IN HIS pilgrim's robe and well absolved of all his sins, Ulenspiegl left Rome and, walking straight ahead, came to Bamberg, where the best vegetables in the world are. He went into an inn, where there was a jolly hostess who said to him:

'Young master, do you want to eat for your money?'

'Yes,' said Ulenspiegl. 'But for what sum does one eat here?'

The hostess replied:

'You may eat at the lords' table for six florins; at the burghers' table for four; and at the family table for two.'

'The more money the better for me,' replied Ulenspiegl.

He went and sat down at the lords' table. When he was well filled and had washed down his dinner with *Rhyn-wyn*, he said to the hostess:

'Goodwife, I have eaten well for my money: give me the six florins.'

The hostess said to him: 'Are you mocking me? Pay your score.'

'Dear *baesinne*,' said Ulenspiegl to her, 'you don't have the face of a bad debtor. I see in it, on the contrary, such good faith, so much loyalty and love of your neighbour, that you would sooner pay me eighteen than refuse me the six that you owe me. These lovely eyes! They're the sun shining on me, making my amorous madness rise higher than weeds in a forsaken garden.'

The hostess replied: 'I have nothing to do with your madness or your weeds; pay and go.'

'Go,' said Ulenspiegl, 'and not see you any more? I would rather give up the ghost right away. *Baesinne*, sweet *baesinne*, I have not the habit of eating for six florins; I, the poor little fellow that wanders o'er hill and dale. I am stuffed full and soon my tongue will be hanging out like a dog in the sun. Be so good as to pay me, for I earned well the six florins by the hard labour of my jaw-bones. Give them to me and I will caress you, kiss you, embrace you, with such a great warmth of gratitude that twenty-seven lovers could not together suffice for such a task.'

'You are talking for money,' she said.

'Would you have me eat for nothing?' said he.

'No,' she answered, defending herself against him.

'Ah,' he sighed as he pursued her, 'your skin is like cream, your hair is like the pheasant browned on the spit, your lips like cherries! Is there anyone more dainty than you?'

113

'It suits you well, nasty villain,' said she, smiling, to come still demanding the six florins from me. Be happy that I fed you freely and asked for nothing more.'

'If you only knew,' said Ulenspiegl, 'how much space there still is!'

'Go!' said the hostess, 'before my husband comes.'

'I will be a gentle creditor,' answered Ulenspiegl. 'Give me but one florin for my future thirst.'

'Here,' she said, 'bad boy.'

And she handed it to him.

'But will you let me return again?' Ulenspiegl asked her.

'Will you kindly go!' she said.

'To go kindly,' said Ulenspiegl, 'would be to go toward you, my dear; but it's going unkindly, leaving your lovely eyes. If you would deign to keep me I would eat no more than for a florin a day.'

'Must I take a stick?' said she.

'Take mine!' replied Ulenspiegl

She laughed, but he had to go, just the same.

56 LAMME GOEDZAK, in these days, came to live again at Damme, the Liége country not being very peaceful because of the heresies. His wife followed him quite willingly, for the folk of Liége, good mockers by nature, made game of her husband's meekness.

Lamme often went to see Claes, who, since his inheritance, haunted the *Blauwe-Torre* tavern and had chosen a table there for himself and his companions. At the next table, meanly drinking his pint of beer, would sit Josse Grypstuiver, the miserly dean of the fish-mongers, stingy, parsimonious, living on salt herrings, and more in love with money than his soul's salvation.

Claes had placed in his pouch the piece of parchment on which was marked his ten thousand years of indulgence. One night, when he was at the *Blauwe-Torre* in the company of Lamme Goedzak, Jan van Roose-bekke, Mathys van Assche, Josse Grypstuiver was also present. Claes had been imbibing freely, and Jan Roosebekke said to him:

'It's a sin to drink so much.'

Claes replied:

'One only burns half a day for a quart too much. And I have ten thousand years indulgence in my pouch. Who wants a hundred, so's he can drown his stomach without fear of the consequences?'

All cried:

'What are you selling them for?'

'A quart,' replied Claes. 'But I'll give a hundred and fifty for a *muske conyn*'—that's a portion of rabbit.

Some of the drinkers gave Claes a stoupe of beer, others some ham, and for all of them he cut off a strip of parchment. It was not Claes, however, who ate and drank the price of these years of indulgence. It was Lamme Goedzak who ate so much that he swelled visibly, while Claes came and went about the tavern selling his merchandise.

Grypstuiver, turning his sour phiz toward him, said:

'Have you a piece for ten days?'

'No,' replied Claes, 'that's too difficult to clip.'

And everybody laughed while Grypstuiver swallowed his rage.

Then Claes went off to his cottage, followed by Lamme, who staggered along as though his legs were made of wool.

57 TOWARDS THE END of the third year of her banishment, Kathe-line returned to her home in Damme. And ceaselessly she said: 'Fire on my head. The soul knocks. Make a hole, it wants to get out.' And she always fled away if she saw sheep or oxen. And she would sit on a bench under the lime trees behind her cottage, shaking her head without knowing them, while she watched the Damme folk who passed before her, saying: 'There's the mad wife.'

Meanwhile Ulenspiegl, wandering along paths and by-paths, saw on the highway a donkey that was harnessed in leather studded with copper nails, its head adorned with tufts and tassels of red wool.

Several old women stood about the donkey, all speaking at once, saying: 'No one can catch hold of it, it's the horrific steed of the Baron de Raix who was burned alive for having sacrificed eight children to the devil. . . It fled so quickly, my dears, that no one could catch it. Satan protects it. . . Yes, when it was weary and stopped by the roadside, the village constables came to carry it off but it kicked out and brayed so terribly that they didn't dare approach. . . Yes, and it wasn't the bray of an ass but the bray of a demon. . . So they let it eat thistles without bringing it before the court or burning it alive as a sorcerer. . . These men have no courage.'

In spite of all these fine speeches, as soon as the donkey lifted its ears or whisked its flanks with its tail, they ran off screaming, only to come back again chattering and jabbering, and then run off again when the donkey made the slightest movement.

But Ulenspiegl laughed as he watched them.

'Ah,' he said, 'endless curiosity and eternal talk that flows like a stream from the mouths of women, especially the old, for in the young the flow is less frequent because of their amorous occupations.'

Then, considering the donkey, he said:

'This bewitched beast is alert and doubtless trots well. I can ride it or sell it.'

Off he went without a word to find a pack of oats, which he gave to the ass to eat. While it ate he jumped lightly on its back and, grasping the reins, turned its head to the north, to the west, to the east; and from afar he blessed the old women. They, almost swooning with fear, knelt on the ground, and it was told that night by the fireside how an angel, in a felt hat with a pheasant's feather stuck in it, had come by a special favour of God, blessed them all, and then taken away the sorcerer's donkey.

And Ulenspiegl went off astride his donkey in the midst of rich fields, where horses ran about freely, where cows and heifers grazed and lay in the sun lazily. And he named his donkey Jef.

The donkey had stopped and quite joyfully ate a meal of thistles. Sometimes it shivered all over its skin, however, and with its tail it lashed its sides to drive away the voracious horseflies that wanted, like it, to eat, but of its flesh.

Ulenspiegl, whose stomach rumbled with hunger, was melancholy.

'You would be right happy, Mister Ass,' said he, 'dining as you do on ripe thistles, if no one came to disturb your ease and recall to you that you are mortal, that is to say, born to endure all sorts of villainies.'

'Like yourself,' he pursued, gripping it with his legs, 'He of the Holy Slipper has his gadfly—Master Luther. And His High Majesty has his also—Messire Francis, first of that name, the king with the very long nose and the sword longer still. It is then quite allowed me to have my gadfly also, Mister Ass. La, all my pockets are holey and by the holes run out all my fine ducats, florins and daelders, like a legion of mice running from the jaws of a cat. I don't know why money will have none

116

of me, I who want money so badly. Fortune is *not* a woman, no matter what they say, for she only loves the stingy misers who coffer, bag and lock her up with twenty locks and never let her show at the window even a tiny bit of her golden nose. There's the gadfly that bites me and makes me itch and tickles me without making me laugh. You're not listening to me, Master Donkey, you're only thinking of grazing. Ah, belly-lover, fill your paunch, your long ears are deaf to the cry of an empty stomach. Listen to me, I insist.'

And he whipped it bitterly, so that it began to bray.

'Let us go on now that you've sung,' said Ulenspiegl.

But the donkey didn't move any more than a milestone and seemed to have formed the project of eating every last thistle on the road. And he didn't miss one.

Seeing this, Ulenspiegl jumped to the ground and gathered a bunch of thistles. Then he straddled the donkey again and placed the bunch under its nose and so led it to the country of the Landgrave of Hesse.

'Mister Ass,' he said as he went along, 'you run after my bunch of thistles, thin fare, and leave behind you a lovely road all covered with these dainty plants. So do all men, some scenting the bouquet of Fame, which Fortune sticks under their noses, others the bouquet of Gain, others the bouquet of Love. At the end of the road they perceive, like you, that they have left behind them that which amounts to something —health, work, repose and well-being in the home.'

So conversing with his donkey, Ulenspiegl arrived in front of the Landgrave's palace.

Two captains of the musketeers were playing dice on the palace steps.

One of them, who was red of head and gigantic in size, noticed Ulenspiegl sitting modestly on Jef, watching the mplay.

'What do you want,' he asked, 'pilgrim with the famished face?'

'I am famished, as you say,' replied Ulenspiegl, 'and pilgrim 'gainst my will.'

'If you are hungry,' retorted the captain, 'eat with your neck the rope that hangs from the next gallows destined for vagabonds.'

'Messire Captain,' said Ulenspiegl, 'if you will give me the fine golden cord that you wear about your hat I will go and hang myself by the teeth to the fat ham that balances over there at the rôtisserie.'

'Where do you come from?' asked the captain.

'From Flanders,' answered Ulenspiegl.

'What do you want?'

'To show His Landgravial Highness a painting of my doing.

'If you are a painter and from Flanders,' said the captain, 'enter within, and I will lead you to my master.'

117

Coming to where the Landgrave was, Ulenspiegl saluted him three times or more.

'May Your Highness deign to excuse my insolence in daring to come and lay before his feet a painting which I did for him and in which I have the honour to show Madame the Virgin in imperial attire.'

'This painting,' he continued, 'he may like, perhaps, and in that case I may presume sufficiently to hope that I may hoist my seat as far as that fine crimson velvet chair where, during his life, the ever-lamented painter of Your Magnanimity had his seat.'

The Landgrave, having considered the painting, which was beautiful, said:

'You shall be our painter. Sit you in the chair.

And he kissed him joyously on both cheeks. Ulenspiegl sat down.

'You are very miserable looking,' said the Landgrave, considering him.

Ulenspiegl replied:

'I am indeed, my Lord. Jef, my donkey, has been dining on thistles, but I, for three days, have lived on misery and nourished myself with the fumes of hope.'

'You will sup soon on better meat,' said the Landgrave. 'But where is your donkey?'

Ulenspiegl replied:

'I left him on the Great Place facing the palace of Your Goodness. I shall be more at ease if I know that Jef is to have shelter for the night, litter and fodder.'

The Landgrave immediately ordered one of his pages to treat Ulenspiegl's donkey like one of his own.

Soon came the supper-hour and the meal was like a revel and a feast. And the meats smoked and the wines rained down their gullets.

Ulenspiegl and the Landgrave were both red as braziers; Ulenspiegl became jolly while the Landgrave remained pensive.

'Our painter,' he said suddenly, 'you must portray me, for it is indeed a great satisfaction to a prince who is mortal, to bequeath to his descendants the memory of his face.'

'Sir Landgrave,' replied Ulenspiegl, 'your pleasure is my will, but it seems to my poor self that, portrayed all alone, Your Lordship will not have much joy in the centuries to come. You must be accompanied by your noble spouse, Madame the Landgravine, by your lords and ladies, your captains and most war-like officers, in whose midst Your Lordship and Madame will shine like two suns among lanterns.'

'You are right, painter,' said the Landgrave, 'but how much shall I have to pay you for this great work?'

118

'A hundred florins, either now or later,' replied Ulenspiegl.

'Here they are now,' said the Landgrave.

'Compassionate lord,' retorted Ulenspiegl, 'you have oiled my lamp, it shall burn in your honour.'

The following day he asked the Landgrave to make those who were to have the honour of being portrayed pass before him.

Among them came the Duke of Lunebourg, commander of the Landgrave's infantry. He was a big man carrying with difficulty his paunch, swollen with food. He approached Ulenspiegl and whispered these words in his ear:

'If in portraying me you do not take off the half of my fat, I'll have you hanged by my troopers.'

The Duke passed on.

Then came a noble dame who had a hump on her back and a breast as flat as the blade of the sword of Justice.

'Messire Painter,' she said, 'if you do not give me two lumps instead of the one you'll take away, and if you do not place these two before instead of behind, I shall have you quartered like a poisoner.'

The lady passed on.

Then came a young maid of honour, fair, fresh and darling, but lacking three upper teeth.

'Messire Painter,' said she, 'if you do not make me smile and show thirty-two teeth, I'll have you chopped up by my lover over there.'

And she pointed to the captain of the musketeers, who had been playing dice on the palace steps; then she passed on.

The procession contiued and Ulenspiegl was left alone with the Landgrave.

'If,' said the Landgrave, 'you have the ill-luck to falsify any one of their traits in portraying all these physiognomies, I will cut off your head as I would a hen's.'

'Deprived of my head,' thought Ulenspiegl, 'quartered, chopped up, or at least hanged, it were easier to portray nothing at all. I will think me of this.'

'And where is the chamber which I must decorate with all these paintings?' he asked the Landgrave.

'Follow me,' said the Landgrave.

And, showing him a great chamber with large, bare walls, he said: 'This is the room.'

'I should be very pleased,' said Ulenspiegl, 'if large curtains were hung before these walls, so that my paintings may be spared the affronts of flies and kept free from dust.'

'That shall be done,' said the Landgrave.

The curtains being hung, Ulenspiegl asked for three apprentices in order, so he said, to mix his colours.

During thirty days Ulenspiegl and his apprentices feasted and enjoyed themselves, sparing neither the fine foods nor the old wines. The Landgrave saw that they were provided for.

However, on the thirty-first day he came to push his nose in at the door of the room where Ulenspiegl had given orders that no one was to be admitted.

'Well, Tyl, where are the portraits?'

'Not quite ready, yet,' replied Ulenspiegl.

'May we not see them?'

'Not yet.'

The thirty-sixth day he again put his nose in at the door.

'Well, Tyl?' he questioned.

'Hey, Sir Landgrave, they're working towards the end.'

The sixtieth day the Landgrave became angry and, entering the room, said:

'You are going to show me these paintings at once.'

'Yes, dread Lord,' replied Ulenspiegl, 'but deign not to open the curtains until you have called within all the lords, captains and ladies of your court.'

'I consent,' said the Landgrave.

And everyone came at his call.

Ulenspiegl stood before the well-closed curtain.

'My Lord Landgrave,' said he, 'and you, Madame the Landgravine, and you, My Lord of Lunebourg, and all you other lovely ladies and valiant captains, I have pictured to the best of my ability, behind this curtain, your faces, sweet or war-like. It should be easy for each one of you to recognize yourselves. You are curious to see yourselves and that is no more than right, but deign to be patient and let me say a word or six. Lovely ladies and valiant captains, who are all of noble blood, you may see and admire my painting; but if there is one among you who is of low birth he will see but the blank wall. And now, deign to open your noble eyes.'

Ulenspiegl pulled back the curtain.

'The noblemen alone see; only the noble dames see. Soon they will be saying: "Blind to painting as a knave, clear-seeing as a nobleman"!'

All of them opened wide their eyes, pretending to see, showing off to each other, pointing out and recognizing but really only seeing the bare wall, which left them secretly ashamed.

Suddenly the Fool, who was there, leaped three feet into the air and rattled his bells:

120

'Let them call me low-bred, low-bred breeding lower-bred, but I shall say and I shall shout with trumpets and fanfares that I see there a bare wall, a blank wall, a naked wall. So help me God and all his saints!"

Ulenspiegl replied:

'When fools enter the conversation, it is time for wise men to go.'

He was about to leave the palace when the Landgrave stopped him:

'Follying fool,' he said, 'who goes through the world praising things lovely and good, and mocking stupidities with loud mouth, who dares —before so many high dames and more high and great lords—vulgarly mock their armorial and lordly pride, you will be hanged one day for your too free speech.'

'If the cord be of gold,' replied Ulenspiegl, 'it will break with fright when it sees me coming.'

'Here,' said the Landgrave, giving him fifteen florins, 'here is the first bit of it.'

'Much thanks, my Lord,' answered Ulenspiegl, 'each inn by the way shall have a strand, one of the golden strands that makes Croesuses of all these thieving innkeepers.'

And off he went on his donkey, wearing his hat high joyfully, its plume flying in the wind.

58 THE LEAVES YELLOWED on the trees and the autumnal wind began to blow. Katheline was sometimes in her right mind for an hour or two. And Claes would then say that the spirit of God in His sweet compassion had come to pay her a visit. In these moments she had the power to cast, by a sign or a word, a spell over Nele which caused her to see what was going on in the places, streets or houses a hundred leagues away.

Therefore on this day, in the company of Claes, Soetkin and Nele, Katheline, being in her right mind, ate *olie-koekjes*, well washed down with *dobble-cuyt*.

Claes said:

'Today is the day the Emperor Charles-Quint is going to abdicate. Nele, my dear, could you see as far as Brussels in Brabant?'

'I could, if Katheline wishes it,' replied Nele.

Katheline then made the girl sit on a bench and by her words and gestures, which acted as a charm, Nele sank into a trance.

Katheline said to her:

'Enter into the little house in the Park which is the favourite place of the Emperor Charles-Quint.'

'I am in,' said Nele in a low voice that sounded as though she were

121

suffocating. 'I am in a small room painted with green oil-paint. There is a man there, about fifty-four years old, bald and gray, with a blond beard on a prominent chin, with a mean look in his gray eyes that are full of cunning, cruelty and feigned good nature. And this man they call Sacred Majesty. He has catarrh and coughs much. Beside him is another man, young, with an ugly snout like that of a hydrocephalous monkey; I saw him at Antwerp; it's King Philip. At this moment His Sacred Majesty is reproaching him with having slept out the night before; no doubt, he says, to be with some trumpet in one of the dens of the lower quarter of the town. He tells him that his hair stinks of the tavern; that it is not a royal pleasure, seeing he has only to choose dainty bodies, satiny skins freshly bathed and the hands of great ladies, most loving, which are better far than a mad sow just come, scarcely washed, from the arms of some drunken trooper. There is not, he tells him, any virgin, married or widow woman who would resist him, among the noblest and loveliest who light their loves with perfumed tapers and not by the greasy glimmers of stinking tallow-candles.

'The King replies that he will obey His Sacred Majesty in all things.

'Then His Sacred Majesty coughs and drinks a few mouthfuls of hypocras.

' "You will presently see," he says, addressing Philip, "the States-General, prelates, nobles and burghers; Orange the Silent, Egmont the Vain, Hoorn the Unpopular, Brederode the Lion; and also all those of the Golden Fleece of whom I will make you the sovereign. You will see there a hundred wearers of baubles who would all cut off their noses if they could only wear a golden chain about their necks as a sign of the highest nobility."

'Then, changing his tone, and quite sorrowfully, His Sacred Majesty says to King Philip:

' "You know that I am about to abdicate in your favour, my son, making a great show before the world and speaking before a great crowd although I cough and hiccup—for all my life I have eaten too much, my son—and you must have a very hard heart if, after hearing me, you do not shed a few tears."

' "I shall weep, Father," replies King Philip.

'Then His Sacred Majesty speaks to a valet by the name of Dubois:

' "Dubois," says he, "give me a morsel of Madeira sugar, I have the hiccups. I hope they do not come upon me when I am about to speak to the crowd. Will that goose I ate yesterday never go down? Shall I drink a tankard of Orleans wine? No, it's too harsh! Shall I eat a few anchovies? They are very oily. Dubois, give me some Romagna wine."

'Dubois gives to his Sacred Majesty that which he asked for, then

122

puts upon him a robe of crimson velvet and over that throws a mantle of gold, girds on his sword, places in his hand the sceptre and the globe, and on his head the crown.

'Now His Sacred Majesty leaves the Park House mounted on a little mule and followed by King Philip and many high personages. They go thus to a great building which they call a palace and there they find in a room a very tall, thin man, richly dressed, whom they call Orange.

'His Sacred Majesty speaks to this man and says to him:

' "Do I look well, cousin William?"

'The man makes no answer.

'His Sacred Majesty then says to him, half smiling, half angry:

' "Are you always going to be dumb then, cousin, even when it comes to putting old fogies in their places? Shall I continue to reign or shall I abdicate, Silent One?"

' "Sacred Majesty," replies the thin man, "when Winter comes even the strongest oaks let fall their leaves."

'Three o'clock strikes.

' "Silent One, lend me your shoulder that I may lean on it."

'And so he enters with Orange and his suite into a great room, and seats himself on a daïs under a canopy of crimson silks and tapestry. There are three seats: His Sacred Majesty sits on the one in the middle, more ornate than the others and surmounted by an imperial crown; King Philip sits on the second; and the third is for a woman who is doubtless a queen. To the right and the left, seated on tapestried benches, are men dressed in red and wearing about their necks golden sheep. Behind them stand several personages who are no doubt princes and lords. Facing them, at the bottom of the daïs, seated on uncushioned benches, are men dressed in plain-cloth. I hear it said that these men are seated and dressed so modestly because it is they alone who will have to pay the bills. Every one had risen when His Sacred Majesty had entered, but as soon as he was seated he made a sign to the others to do likewise.

'An old man then speaks for a long time about gout, and then the woman who seems to be a queen hands to His Sacred Majesty a roll of parchment, whereon there are things written that His Sacred Majesty reads, coughing, and with a low, hollow voice. And speaking of himself he says:

' "I have made many journeys through Spain, Italy, the Netherlands, in England and in Africa, and all for the glory of God, the renown of my arms, and the good of my peoples."

'Then having spoken for a long time, he says that he is weak and

124

weary and wishes to place the crown of Spain, the counties, marquisates, duchies, of these countries in the hands of his son.

'Then he weeps, and all weep with him.

'King Philip then rises from his chair and falls to his knees:

' "Sacred Majesty," he says, "am I permitted to receive this crown from your hands when you are still capable of wearing it?"

'Then His Sacred Majesty whispers in his ear to speak kindly to the men who are seated on the cushioned benches.

'King Philip, turning towards them, says to them in a sour tone and without rising:

' "I understand French fairly well, but not well enough to speak to you in that tongue. You will hear what the Bishop of Arras, Master Granvela, has to say to you in my behalf."

' "You speak ill, my son," says His Sacred Majesty.

'And indeed the assembly murmurs, seeing the young king so haughty and supercilious. The woman, who is a queen, also speaks his praises and then comes the turn of an old doctor who, when he has ended, receives a wave of the hand from His Sacred Majesty by way of thanks. These ceremonies and harangues ended, His Sacred Majesty declares that his subjects are free from their oath of fidelity, signs the acts drawn up to ratify all this, and rising from his throne sets his son thereon. And everybody in the room weeps. Then they go out and away to the Park House.

'There, being once more in the green chamber, all alone and all doors shut, His Sacred Majesty laughs loudly, and speaking to King Philip who does not laugh, says:

' "Did you see," he says, speaking, hiccuping and laughing all at once, "how little it needs to move these good people? What a deluge of tears! And that fat Maes who, when he finished his long speech, wept like a calf. You yourself seemed moved, but not enough. These are really the sort of spectacles the populace needs. My son, we men cherish most those mistresses who cost us most. So with the people. The more we make them pay, the more they love us. I have tolerated in Germany the reformed religion that I punish so severely in the Netherlands. If the German princes had been Catholics, I would have become a Lutheran and confiscated their goods. They believe in the integrity of my zeal for the Roman faith and they regret to see me go. By my doing there have perished in the Netherlands, because of heresy, fifty thousand of their most valiant men and their dearest girls. I am going now; they lament me. Without counting the confiscations, I have raised from them in taxes more than the Indies and Peru; and they are sorry to lose me. I tore up the peace of Cadzant, subdued Ghent, suppressed

125

all that might annoy me; liberties, franchises, privileges, and placed them under the direction of the officers of the prince. These good folk still think they are free because I allow them to shoot with the crossbow and carry their corporation banners in processions. They feel my masterful hand; placed in a cage, they find themselves at ease singing and weeping for me. My son, be with them as I was—gentle in words and harsh in deeds; lick only so long as there is no need for you to bite. Swear, always swear to their liberties, franchises and privileges but, should they become a danger to you, destroy them. They are of iron when touched by a timid hand, of glass when crushed by a strong arm. Strike at heresy not because of its difference with the Roman religion, but because in the Netherlands it would ruin our authority; those that attack the Pope who wears three crowns will soon have done with the princes who wear but one. Make, as I did, freedom of conscience a treason with confiscation of goods, and you shall inherit as I have done all my life. And when you go to abdicate or die they will say: 'Oh, the good prince!' And they will weep."

'And I hear nothing more,' continued Nele, 'for His Sacred Majesty has laid him down on a bed to sleep, and King Philip, supercilious and haughty, watches him without any love in his eyes.'

Having said all this, Nele was awakened by Katheline.

And Claes, pensive, watched the flame on the hearth light up the chimney.

59 ULENSPIEGL, on leaving the Landgrave of Hesse, mounted on his donkey and crossing the Great Place, saw several wrathful looking lords and ladies, but he heeded them not. Soon he arrived in the lands of the Duke of Luneburg and there fell in with a troop of *Smaedelyke broeders,* joyous Flemings from Sluys who set aside a certain sum of money each Saturday to be able to go once a year into Germany.

They went along, singing, in an open wagon drawn by a vigorous *Veurne-Ambacht* horse which brought them romping along the highways and through marshes of the duchy of Luneburg. There were those among them who played on the fife, the rebeck, the viola and the bagpipes with great racket. Alongside the wagon, at frequent intervals, a *dikzak* playing the *rommel-pot* walked in the hope of reducing his great belly.

As they were down to their last florin they saw Ulenspiegl come to them laden with clinking coin, and went into an inn and paid a round of drinks for him. Ulenspiegl accepted willingly. Yet, noticing that the

Smaedelyke broeders winked as they looked on him and smiled as they poured out his drink, he scented a trick, and going outside he stood by the door to hear what they might say. He heard the *dikzak* speaking of him:

'He's the painter of the Landgrave who handed him more than a thousand florins for a picture. Let's feast him with beer and wine and he'll pay us back double.'

'Amen!' said the others.

Ulenspiegl went and tied up his donkey, all saddled, at a farmer's place about a thousand paces away, gave a girl two patards to watch it, returned to the room at the inn and sat down at the table of the *Smaedelyke broeders* without saying a word. They poured out a drink for him and paid for it. Ulenspiegl rattled the Landgrave's florins in his pouch and said that he had just sold his donkey to a peasant for seventeen silver daelders.

They travelled on, eating, drinking, playing the fife, the bagpipes and the *rommel-pot* and picking up by the way the goodwives they thought prepossessing. In this way they begot foundlings. Ulenspiegl and his goodwife had a child later which she named *Eulenspiegelken*, which means little mirror and owl in high German, for the goodwife did not very well understand the meaning of her casual man's name, or it may be perhaps in memory of the hour in which the little one was conceived. And it is of this Eulenspiegelken that it is falsely said that he was born at Knittingen in the country of Saxony.

Letting themselves be drawn by their stout horse, they went along a road by the side of which was a village and an inn with the sign: *In den Ketele* (In the Kettle). From this inn there came a goodly smell of fricassee.

The *dikzak* playing the *rommel-pot* went to the *baes* and said to him, speaking of Ulenspiegl:

'He is the Landgrave's painter; he will pay everything.'

127

The *baes,* considering Ulenspiegl's looks, which were good, and hearing the sound of the florins and daelders, brought out to the table the wherewithal to eat and drink. Ulenspiegl was not found wanting, and always jingled the coins in his pouch. Many times he struck his hat, saying that there was his greatest treasure. The revels having lasted two days and one night, the *Smaeldelyke broeders* said to Ulenspiegl:

'Let's drink up here and pay up the bill.'

Ulenspiegl replied:

'When the rat is in the cheese, does it ask to go?'

'No,' they said.

'And when a man eats and drinks well, does he seek the dust of the road and the water of springs full of leeches?'

'No,' they said.

'Then,' said Ulenspiegl, 'let us stay here as long as my florins and daelders last to serve as funnels to pour down our gullets the drinks that engender laughter.'

And he commanded the host to bring on still more wine and sausage.

While they drank and ate, Ulenspiegl said:

'I'll foot the bill; I'm the Landgrave for the nonce. If my pouch were empty, what would you do, comrades? You might take my soft felt hat and find it full of florins, in the bottom as well as round the brim.'

'Let's feel it,' they all said together. And, sighing, they felt between their fingers great coins having the size of golden florins. One of them fingered the hat with so much love that Ulenspiegl took it back, saying:

'Impetuous milker, you must learn to await the milking-hour.'

'Give me the half of your hat,' said this *Smaedelyke broeder.*

'No,' replied Ulenspiegl, 'I don't want you to have a madman's brain, one half in the shadow, the other half in the sun.'

Then, giving his hat to the *baes,* he said:

'You keep this in any case, for it is warm. As for me, I'm going to empty myself outside.'

And out he went and the host kept the hat.

As soon as he was outside the inn he went off to the farmer's place, mounted his donkey and hastened off full speed along the road that leads to Embden.

The *Smaedelyke broeders,* seeing that he did not come back, said among themselves:

'Has he gone? Who's to foot the bill?'

The *baes,* seized with fear, cut open Ulenspiegl's hat with a knife. But instead of finding the florins between the felt and the lining, he found but mean copper counters.

Becoming furious, then, against the *Smaedelyke broeders*, he said to them:

'Brothers in roguery, you'll not get out of here until you've all left me your clothes, shirts excepted.'

And all of them had to strip themselves to pay their shot.

So they went in their shirt-tails over hill and dale, for they would not sell their horse nor their wagon.

And everybody seeing them in such a pitiful plight gave them freely of bread to eat and wine to drink, and sometimes they also gave them meat, for they went about saying that they had been despoiled by robbers.

And among them all they had but one pair of breeches.

And in this way they came back again to Sluys in their shirt-tails, dancing in their wagon and playing the *rommel-pot*.

60 IN THE MEANTIME Ulenspiegl, astride the back of Jef, rode through the lands and the marshes of the Duke of Luneburg. The Flemings called this duke *Water-Signorke*, because it was always damp in his country. Jef obeyed Ulenspiegl like a dog, drank *bruinbier*, danced better than a Hungarian master in the arts of suppleness, played dead, and lay down on his back at the least sign.

Ulenspiegl knew that the Duke of Luneburg, annoyed and angry with him for having mocked him at Darmstadt in the presence of the Landgrave of Hesse, had forbidden him entrance to his lands under pain of the halter. Suddenly he saw His Ducal Highness in person, and as he knew that the noble was of a violent temper, he was seized with fright. Speaking to his donkey, he said:

'Jef, here is my Lord of Luneburg coming this way. I have at my neck a great itch of the rope; but may it not be the hangman that scratches me! Jef, I don't mind being scratched, but not hanged. Think that we are brothers in misery and long ears; think also what a good friend you would lose in losing me.'

And Ulenspiegl wiped his eyes, and Jef began to bray.

Continuing his discourse:

'We live together joyfully, or sadly, according to circumstances; do you remember, Jef?' The ass continued to bray, for he was hungry. 'And you can never forget me,' said his master, 'for what friendship is strong if not that which laughs at the same joys and weeps over the same sorrows? Jef, you must lie on your back.'

The gentle ass obeyed and was seen by the Duke with its four hooves in the air. Ulenspiegl sat lightly on its belly. The Duke came up to him:

129

'What are you doing there?' he said. 'Do you not know that in my last edict I forbade you, under penalty of the rope, to set your dusty foot on my lands?'

Ulenspiegl replied:

'Gracious Lord, have pity on me.'

Then, pointing to his donkey:

'You know well,' said he, 'that by right and law a man is always free who lives between his four posts.'

The Duke answered:

'Get out of my country or you shall die.'

'My Lord,' replied Ulenspiegl, 'I could get out so quickly mounted on a florin or two!'

'Scamp,' said the Duke, 'not content with disobedience, are you going to ask money of me besides?'

'I needs must, my Lord, since I cannot take it away from you.'

The Duke gave him a florin.

Then Ulenspiegl said, speaking to his donkey:

'Jef, arise and salute my lord.'

The ass arose and began to bray. Then both of them went off together.

61 SOETKIN AND Nele were seated by one of the windows of their cottage that looked into the street. Soetkin said to Nele: 'Dear, do you not see my son Ulenspiegl coming?'

'No,' said Nele, 'we shall never see him again, the nasty vagabond.'

'Nele,' said Soetkin, 'you must not be angry with him; you must be sorry for him, for he is away from home, the little man.'

'I know very well,' said Nele, 'he has another house quite far from here, richer than his own, where some lovely lady doubtless gives him lodging.'

'That will be all the better for him,' said Soetkin, 'he is perhaps fed on ortolans.'

'Why don't they give him stones to eat, he would soon be here, the glutton!' said Nele.

Soetkin laughed then and said:

'Where does this great anger come from, dear?'

But Claes, who bound up faggots in a corner of the room, very pensive, said:

'Do you not see that she is infatuated with him?'

'Look you now,' said Soetkin, 'the crafty, cunning one that never let fall a word to me! Is't true, darling, that you long for him?'

'Do not believe it,' said Nele.

130

'You'll have there,' said Claes, 'a brave spouse with a great mug, an empty belly, and a long tongue, making liards of florins and never a sou for his labour, always beating the road and measuring the highway with the yard-stick of vagabondage.'

But Nele replied, all red and angry:

'Why don't you make something else out of him?'

'There,' said Soetkin, 'she's crying now; hold your peace, my man.'

62 ULENSPIEGL came one day to Nürnberg and passed himself off as a great doctor, victor of sicknesses, most illustrious purger, famous tamer of fevers, renowned sweeper away of plagues and invincible scourge of the itch. There were so many sick people in the hospital that they did not know where to put them. The master hospitaller, having heard of Ulenspiegl's coming, went to see him and asked him if it were true that he could cure all these ailments.

'Excepting the last,' replied Ulenspiegl; 'but promise me two hundred florins for the curing of all the others and I will not take a liard until all your patients say they are cured and are outside the hospital.'

He went the next day to the hospital, with a confident look, and put on a solemn doctoral phiz. In the rooms he took each patient aside and said to him:

'Swear not to confide in anyone that which I am about to whisper in your ear. What is your sickness?'

The patient would tell him and swear by his great God to hold his tongue.

'Know,' said Ulenspiegl, 'that I must reduce one of you to dust by fire and I will make of this dust a marvellous mixture to be given to all the patients to drink. The one that cannot walk will be burned. To-morrow I will come here and, standing in the street with the master hospitaller, I will summon you all by crying: "Let him that is not sick pack up his bag and come!" '

In the morning Ulenspiegl came and called out as he said he would. All the sick, the lame, the catarrhal, rheumy, feverish attempted to get out together. All were in the street and even some that had not left their beds for ten years.

The master hospitaller asked them if they were cured and could walk.

'Yes,' they all replied, thinking that there was one who was being burned in the courtyard.

Ulenspiegl then said to the master hospitaller:

'Pay me, since they are all out and declare themselves cured.'

The master paid him the two hundred florins. And Ulenspiegl went off.

But on the second day the master saw his patients coming back to him in a worse state than they had been before, all save one who, being cured by the fresh air, was found drunk and singing in the streets: 'Glory be to the great doctor Ulenspiegl!'

63 THE TWO HUNDRED florins having flown away, Ulenspiegl came to Vienna and hired himself out to a wheelwright who was always scolding his workmen because they did not make the bellows work strong enough. 'Keep in time,' he always shouted, 'follow with the bellows!'

One day when the *baes* went into the garden, Ulenspiegl detached the bellows and, carrying them on his shoulders, followed his master. The latter was astonished to see him so strangely burdened, and Ulenspiegl said to him:

'*Baes*, you commanded me to follow with the bellows, where must I place this one while I go get the other?'

'Dear lad,' replied the *baes*, 'that was not what I said; go put the bellows back in their place.'

He bethought himself however how to repay this trick. And from then on he got up every day at midnight and awakened his workers and set them to work.

The workers said to him:

'*Baes*, why do you awaken us in the middle of the night?'

'It's a custom of mine,' replied the *baes*, 'not to let my workers stay in bed more than half a night during the first seven days.'

The following night he again awoke his workers at midnight. Ulenspiegl, who slept in the garret, placed his bed on his back and, so burdened, descended to the forge.

The *baes* said to him:

'Are you mad? Why don't you leave your bed in its place?'

'It's a custom of mine,' replied Ulenspiegl, 'to pass the first seven days one half of the night on my bed and the other half under it.'

'Well, it's a second custom of mine,' replied the master, 'to throw my impudent workers out in the street with leave to pass the first week on the pavement and the second under it.'

'In your cellar, *baes*, if you will, by your barrels of *bruinbier*,' replied Ulenspiegl.

133

64 HAVING LEFT the wheelwright and returned to Flanders, he must needs hire himself out as apprentice to a shoemaker who stayed more willingly in the streets than at his last in the workshop. Ulenspiegl, seeing him getting ready for the hundredth time to go out, asked him in what way he wanted the uppers cut.

'Cut them,' answered the *baes*, 'for big and medium feet, so that all who lead big and little cattle may enter them easily.'

'So it shall be, *baes*,' replied Ulenspiegl.

When the cobbler had left, Ulenspiegl cut the uppers good only for mares, asses, heifers, sows and ewes.

Returning to the workshop and seeing his leather in pieces, he cried: 'What have you done there, worthless botcher?'

'What you told me to do,' replied Ulenspiegl.

'I ordered you to cut me shoes wherein might easily go all that lead the oxen, swine, sheep, and you make me shoes for the feet of these animals.'

'*Baes*, who then leads the boar if not the sow, the jackass if not the ass, the bull if not the heifer, the ram if not the ewe in the season when all the beasts are in heat?'

Then he went out and had to stay out.

65 IT WAS THEN April and the air that had been soft suddenly froze hard and the sky was as gray as a sky on All Souls' day. The third year of Ulenspiegl's banishment had long since run out and Nele awaited her friend every day.

'La,' she said, 'it is going to snow on the pear-trees and on the jasmines in flower, and on all the poor plants that opened with confidence in the warmth of a precocious renaissance. Already tiny flakes fall from the sky on the roads. And it snows also in my poor heart.

'Where are the clear rays that played over the happy faces and on the roofs which they made ruddier and on the window-panes which they made to flame? Where are they, warming the earth and the sky, the birds and the insects? La, by night and by day I am now chilled with sadness and the long wait. Where are you, Ulenspiegl, my dear?'

66 ULENSPIEGL, approaching Renaix in Flanders, was hungry and thirsty but he would make no moan, and tried to make people laugh so that they would give him bread. But he joked badly and the people passed him by and gave him nothing.

It was cold: turn about, it snowed, rained, and hailed on the back

134

of the poor vagabond. If he passed through the villages, his mouth watered even in seeing a dog gnawing at a bone in a corner. He fain would have earned a florin but did not know how a florin might fall into his pouch.

Looking upwards, he saw pigeons who, from the roof of a dove-cot, let drop on the roadway white pieces; but they were not florins. He sought on the ground, but the florins did not flower between the cobble-stones.

Looking to the right, he saw clearly a wicked cloud that came over the sky like a large watering-pot, but he knew that if anything were bound to drop from the cloud it would not be a rain of florins. Looking to the left, he saw a great idle horse-chestnut tree, living without doing anything. 'Ah,' he said to himself, 'why are there not florin trees? They would be quite lovely ones!'

Suddenly the great cloud burst and the hailstones rained thick on Ulenspiegl's back like pebbles. 'La,' he said, 'I sense it well enough, stones are never thrown save at wandering dogs.' Then he began to run. 'It's not my fault if I have never a palace nor yet a tent to shelter my thin body. Oh, the nasty hail-stones; they're hard as bullets. No, it's not my fault if I drag my tatters about the world; it's only because it pleased me to do so. Why am I not an Emperor? These hail-stones want to enter by force into my ears, like bad words.' And he ran. 'Poor nose,' he added, 'you'll soon be pierced through and then you can serve as a pepper-shaker in the festivals of the great of the earth on whom it does not hail.' Then, wiping his cheeks, 'These,' he said, 'will do well for ladles for cooks who are too hot by their fires. Ah, far-off memory of sauces of other days! I am hungry. Empty belly, do not complain; doleful guts, rumble no more. Propitious fortune, where are you hiding? Lead me towards the place where the pasture is.'

As he spoke in this way to himself the sky brightened up with a shining sun; the hail ceased to fall, and Ulenspiegl said:

'Good day to you, sun, my only friend, coming to dry me!'

But he kept on running, being cold. Suddenly he saw coming toward him, from far along the road, a black and white dog running straight ahead, his tongue hanging out and his eyes jumping out of his head.

'That beast,' said Ulenspiegl, 'has madness in his belly.' He hurriedly picked up a large stone and climbed a tree. As he got to the first branch the dog passed and Ulenspiegl cast the stone, which caught him on the head. The dog stopped and sadly and stiffly tried to climb the tree and snap at Ulenspiegl, but it could not and fell down dead.

Ulenspiegl was not happy, and less so when, having come down from the tree, he saw that the dog had not the parched mouth usual in attacks of hydrophobia. Then, considering the skin and seeing that it was fine and worth selling, he stripped it off, washed it, hung it on his staff, let it dry for a while in the sun, and then placed it in his pouch.

Hunger and thirst still tormenting him, he entered several farms but did not dare sell the skin for fear it might be that of a dog having belonged to the farmer. He asked for bread and they refused him. Night came. His legs were weak and he entered a little inn. He saw an old *baesinne* who caressed an ancient wheezy dog whose skin was like that of the dead one.

'Where do you come from, traveller?' the old *baesinne* asked him.

Ulenspiegl replied:

'I come from Rome where I cured the Pope's dog of an inflammation that troubled him extraordinarily.'

'You have seen the Pope, then?' she said to him, as she drew him a glass of beer.

'Alas,' said Ulenspiegl, emptying his glass, 'I was only allowed to kiss his sacred foot and his holy slipper.'

Meanwhile the old dog of the *baesinne* coughed without spitting.

'When did you do this?' asked the old woman.

'The month before last,' replied Ulenspiegl. 'I arrived, being awaited, and knocked at the door. "Who is there?" asked the chamberlain arch-cardinal, arch-privy, arch-extraordinary to His Most Holy Holiness. I answered: "It is I, my Lord Cardinal, come from Flanders expressly to kiss the Pope's toe and cure his dog of the phlegm." "Ah, it's you, Ulenspiegl!" said the Pope, speaking from the other side of a little door. "I would gladly see you but it is impossible for me to do so at this moment. I am forbidden by the Holy Decretals to show my face to strangers while the holy razor is being passed over it." "Alas!" said I, "I am most unlucky, I who have come from such distant lands to kiss the toe of Your Holiness and cure your dog of its phlegm. Must I return without being satisfied?" "No!" said the Holy Father. Then I heard

136

him crying: "Arch-chamberlain, push my chair as far as the door and open the wicket at the bottom of it." This was done and I saw a foot shod with a golden slipper pushed through the wicket-hole, and I heard a voice rolling like thunder, saying: "This is the dreaded foot of the Prince of Princes, the King of Kings, the Emperor of Emperors. Kiss, Christian, kiss the holy slipper." And I kissed the holy slipper, and my nose was all embalmed with the heavenly perfume exhaled by the foot. Then the wicket closed and the same dreadful voice bade me wait. The wicket re-opened and there came out, saving your grace, a hairless dog, blear-eyed, coughing, swollen like a wine-skin and forced to walk with its legs askew because of the largeness of its belly.

'The Holy Father deigned to speak to me again. "Ulenspiegl," said he, "you see my dog? He was taken with the phlegm and other maladies while gnawing the bones of heretics that had been broken. Cure him, my son; much good will come to you." '

'Drink!' said the old woman.

'Pour!' replied Ulenspiegl. Continuing his talk, he said: 'I purged the dog with a marvellous draught that I had composed. This made him piss for three days and three nights without stopping and he was cured thereby.'

'*Jesus God en Maria!*' said the old woman. 'Let me kiss you, glorious pilgrim, who has seen the Pope and may also cure my dog.'

But Ulenspiegl, not caring much for the kisses of the old woman, said to her: 'Those whose lips have touched the holy slipper may not, within two years, receive the kisses of any woman. First give me for supper some good carbonades, a black-pudding or two, and a sufficiency of beer, and I will give your dog a voice so clear that he'll be able to sing the top notes of the *aves* in the choir-loft of the High Church.'

'May what you say be true,' whined the old woman, 'and I'll give you a florin.'

'It shall be done,' said Ulenspiegl, 'but only after supper.'

She laid before him all that he asked for. He ate and drank his fill and would have, out of belly gratitude, kissed the old woman were it not that he had already told her he could not.

As he ate, the old dog placed his fore-paws on Ulenspiegl's knees to beg for a bone. He gave him several, then said to his hostess:

'If someone ate here and did not pay, what would you do?'

'I would lift from the back of such a thief his best garment,' replied the old woman.

'Right!' retorted Ulenspiegl. Then he put the dog under his arm and went out to the stable. There he shut it up with a bone and, taking the dead dog's skin out of his pouch, he went in again to the old woman and asked her if she had really said that she would lift the best garment off the back of anyone that didn't pay for what they ate.

'Yes,' replied the old woman.

'Well, your dog dined with me and didn't pay. Therefore, following your own precept, I have taken off his best and only garment.'

And he showed her the skin of the dead dog.

'Ah,' said the old woman, weeping, 'it was cruel of you, doctor! Poor little doggie! To me, a widow, he was my child. Oh, why did you take from me the only friend I had in the world? I might as well die now.'

'I will bring him back to life again,' said Ulenspiegl.

'Bring him to life!' said she. 'And he will caress me again, and he will watch me again, and he will lick me again, and watching me he will wag his poor old stump of a tail! Do this, sir doctor, and you'll have dined here for nothing on a most costly dinner; and I'll give you more than a florin into the bargain.'

'I will bring him to life again,' said Ulenspiegl, 'but I must have hot water, syrup to stick the joints, a needle and thread, and some of the sauce of the carbonades; and I wish to be alone during the operation.'

The old woman gave him all that he asked for and, picking up the skin of the dead dog, he went to the stable.

He smeared the sauce on the muzzle of the old dog who let it be done right joyfully. Then he traced a stripe of syrup along the belly, placed some on each of the paws, and put some sauce on the tail.

Giving a great shout three times, he then said: *'Staet op! Staet op! ik be veel het vuile hond!'*

Then, quickly placing the skin of the dead dog in his pouch, he landed the living one a great kick and so sent it flying into the parlour of the inn.

The old woman, seeing her dog alive and licking himself, was eager to embrace it; but Ulenspiegl would not allow this.

'You may not,' said he, 'caress the dog until he has laved with his tongue all the syrup with which he is covered; then only will the seams in his skin be closed. Count me out now my ten florins.'

'I said one,' answered the old woman.

'One for the operation, nine for the resurrection,' replied Ulenspiegl.

She counted them out. And off Ulenspiegl went, throwing back in the parlour the skin of the dead dog, saying: 'Here, woman, keep his old skin, it will serve to piece the new when that becomes holey.'

67 On that Sunday in Bruges the procession of the Holy Blood was held. Claes told his wife and Nele to go and see it and perhaps they would find Ulenspiegl there in town. As for himself, he said, he would stay in the cottage and await the return of the pilgrim.

The women went off together; Claes stayed at Damme, sitting by the doorway, and he found the town quite deserted. He heard nothing save the crystalline chimes of some village bell, while from Bruges there came to him, by gusts, the music of the carillons and the great noise of the guns and the fireworks being shot off in honour of the Holy Blood.

Claes, looking pensively for Ulenspiegl on the roads, saw nothing save the clear sky, all blue and cloudless, some sleeping dogs lying with their tongues out in the sun, some unconstrained sparrows fluttering and twittering in the dust, a cat spying on them, and the sunlight entering friendly-wise in all the houses, making the copper kettles and pewter tankards on every dresser to shine.

But Claes was sad in the midst of that joy and, looking for his son, he sought to see him behind the gray mists of the fields, to hear him in the glad rustling of the leaves and the gay concert of the birds in the trees. Suddenly he saw on the road from Maldeghem a man of great stature and knew that it was not Ulenspiegl. He saw him stop by a carrot-field and eat greedily of some of these vegetables.

'There's a man who is mighty hungry,' said Claes.

Having lost sight of him for a moment, he saw him re-appear at the corner of the Heron street and recognized him as the messenger of Josse who had brought him the seven hundred golden carolus. He went out to the road to meet him and said:

'Come into my house.'

The man replied:

'Blessed are they that are kind to an errant traveller.'

On the outside window-sill were some crumbs which Soetkin had placed there for the birds of the neighbourhood. They came there in the winter to seek their nourishment. The man took some of the crumbs and ate them.

'You are hungry and thirsty,' said Claes.

The man replied:

'Since I was stripped by robbers eight days ago, I have fed myself on carrots from the fields and roots in the woods.'

'Then,' said Claes, 'it is now the hour for feasting. And here,' he said, opening the cupboard, 'is a bowl full of peas, eggs, black-puddings, hams, Ghent sausages, *waterzoey* (a hotchpotch of fish). Downstairs in

139

the cellar sleeps a bottle of Louvain wine made after the Burgundy manner, red and clear as a ruby; it asks but awakening in the glasses. Come now, let us throw a log on the fire. Do you hear these black-puddings sing on the grill? That's the song of good cheer.'

Claes, turning and re-turning them, said to the man:

'Have you not seen my son Ulenspiegl?'

'No,' he answered.

'Do you bring me news of my brother Josse?' said Claes, setting the grilled puddings on the table along with an omelette of fat ham, cheese, great tankards, and the wine of Louvain, red and clear, sparkling in the flasks.

The man replied:

'Your brother Josse died on the rack at Sippenaken, near Aix. And that for having—being a heretic—borne arms against the Emperor.'

Claes was like one beside himself and, trembling all over so great was his anger, he cried:

'Vile butchers! Josse! My poor brother!'

The man then said, ungently:

'Our joys and sorrows are not of this world.'

And he began to eat. After a while, he said:

'I aided your brother in his prison in passing myself off as a relation of his, a peasant from Nieswieler. I have come here because he said to me: "If you do not die for the faith as I do, go to my brother Claes; enjoin him to live in the peace of the Lord, practising works of mercy, bringing up his son in secret in the laws of Christ. The money I gave him was taken from poor, ignorant people, let him use it in bringing up Tyl in the science of God and His word."'

And having said this the messenger gave Claes the kiss of peace.

And Claes lamented, saying:

'Dead on the rack, my poor brother!'

And he could not overcome his great sorrow. Still, as he saw that the man was thirsty and held out his glass, he poured out wine for him; but he himself ate and drank without joy.

Soetkin and Nele were gone for seven days; during that time the messenger of Josse stayed under Claes's roof.

Every night they heard Katheline screaming in her cottage:

'Fire! Fire! Make a hole; the soul would out!'

And Claes would go to her and calm her with gentle words, and then he would return to his own home.

At the end of seven days, the man left and would not take from Claes but two carolus to pay for nourishment and shelter on his way.

68 NELE AND SOETKIN having returned from Bruges, Claes, seated on the kitchen floor after the manner of tailors, was sewing buttons on an old pair of breeches. Nele was beside him, egging on Titus Bibulus Schnouffius against the stork. The dog would rush at the bird and back away again, screaming with his shrillest voice. The stork, standing on one leg, grave and pensive, watched him and withdrew its long neck into the feathers of its breast. Titus Bibulus Schnouffius, seeing the stork so peaceful, screamed all the louder. But suddenly the bird, weary of this music, shot its bill like an arrow on the back of the dog, who ran away yelping:

'Help!'

Claes laughed, as did Nele, and Soetkin did not cease looking out into the street to see if she could not see Ulenspiegl coming.

Suddenly she said:

'Here is the provost and four constables. It's surely not us they want. Two of them are turning about the cottage.'

Claes raised his nose above his work.

'And two have stopped in front,' continued Soetkin.

Claes arose.

'Who are they going to arrest in this street?' said she. 'Jesus God, my man, they're coming here!'

Claes leapt from the kitchen into the garden, followed by Nele:

'Save the carolus, they are behind the chimney-back.'

Nele understood. Then, seeing that he passed over the hedge and that the constables grabbed him by the collar, and that he was struggling to free himself from them, she cried and wept:

'He is innocent! He is innocent! Don't harm my father Claes! Ulenspiegl, where are you? You would kill both of them!'

And she threw herself on one of the constables and tore his face with her nails. Then, crying: 'They will kill him!' she fell on the grass and rolled about distracted.

Katheline had come out at the noise and, standing straight and motionless, she watched the sight, saying as she shook her head: 'Fire! Fire! Make a hole; the soul wants out!'

Soetkin, seeing nothing of all this, spoke to the constables who entered the cottage:

'Sirs, what do you seek in our poor home? If it is my son, he is far away. Are your legs very long?'

Saying this, she was gay.

At that moment Nele cried for help and Soetkin, running to the garden, saw her man held by the collar and struggling in the road by the hedge.

142

'Strike!' she shouted. 'Kill! Ulenspiegl, where are you?'

And she tried to succour her man, but one of the constables carried her off bodily, not without danger.

Claes struggled and fought so hard that he might have escaped if the two constables to whom Soetkin had spoken had not come to the aid of the two who held Claes.

They brought him, with his two hands tied, to the kitchen where Soetkin and Nele wept and sobbed.

'Messer Provost,' said Soetkin, 'what has my poor man done that you must tie him up with cords in this way?'

'Heretic!' said one of the constables.

'Heretic?' retorted Soetkin. 'Heretic yourself! These demons have lied.'

Claes replied:

'I place myself in God's keeping.'

He went out; Nele and Soetkin followed him, weeping and thinking that they also were to be brought before the judge. Men and women came up to them; when they learned that Claes walked shackled in that manner because he was suspected of heresy, they were so frightened that they all rushed back into their houses, shutting all the doors behind them. Only a few little girls dared to come up to Claes and say to him:

'Where are you going tied up that way, charcoal-man?'

'To the grace of God, little girls,' he replied.

They took him to the town prison. Soetkin and Nele sat down on the door-step. Towards evening, Soetkin told Nele to leave her and go see if Ulenspiegl had not yet returned.

69 THE NEWS SOON ran through the neighbouring villages that they had imprisoned a man for heresy and that the inquisitor Titleman, Dean of Renaix, named the Pitiless Inquisitor, would direct the questioning. Ulenspiegl was then living at Koolkercke, in the intimate favour of a darling farmeress, a gentle widow who refused him nothing of what belonged to her. He was very happy, cared for and caressed until the day when a traitorous rival, a sheriff of the town, awaited him one morning when he came out of the tavern and sought to rub him with a cudgel. But Ulenspiegl, to cool his anger, threw him into the pond; from whence the sheriff scrambled out as best he could, green as a paddock and soaked like a sponge.

For this doughty deed Ulenspiegl had to quit Koolkercke and go as fast as his legs would carry him to Damme, fearing the vengeance of the sheriff.

The evening falling cool, Ulenspiegl ran swiftly; he was longing to be home again and already, in his mind's eye, he saw Nele sewing, Soetkin getting supper ready, Claes bundling faggots, Schnouffius gnawing a bone, and the stork tapping the housewife's stomach with her bill to ask for a few crumbs of food.

A pedlar tramp said to him as he passed:

'Where are you going in such a rush?'

'To Damme, to my home,' said Ulenspiegl.

The tramp said:

'The town is no longer safe because of the reformers being arrested there.'

And he passed on his way.

Coming to the Inn of the *Roode-Schildt,* Ulenspiegl entered to drink a glass of *dobble cuyt.* The *baes* said to him:

'Are you not the son of Claes?'

'I am that,' answered Ulenspiegl.

'Haste you, then,' said the *baes,* 'for an evil hour has struck for your father.'

Ulenspiegl asked him what he meant by that.

The *baes* replied that he would learn soon enough.

And Ulenspiegl continued to run on his way.

As he came to the entrance of Damme the dogs that sat by the doors jumped about his legs barking and yelping. The goodwives came out at the noise and said to him, all talking at once:

'Where have you come from? Have you news of your father? Where's your mother? Is she also with him in prison? La, if only they don't burn him!'

And Ulenspiegl ran faster.

He ran into Nele, who said to him:

'Tyl, do not go to the house. The town council have set a guard there on behalf of His Majesty.'

Ulenspiegl stopped:

'Nele,' he said, 'is it true that Claes, my father, is in prison?'

'Yes,' said Nele, 'and Soetkin sits weeping on the doorstep.'

Then the heart of the prodigal son was bursting-full of sorrow, and he said to Nele:

'I am going to see them.'

'That is not what you must do,' she said. 'Rather do what Claes wants; he told me before he was taken: "Save the carolus; they are behind the chimney-back." Those you must save first for they are the heritage of Soetkin, the poor woman.'

But Ulenspiegl paid no attention and ran right to the prison. There he saw Soetkin sitting on the doorstep; she embraced him tearfully and they wept together.

The populace assembling in a crowd before the prison, the sergeants came and told Soetkin and Ulenspiegl to get out as quickly as they knew how.

The mother and son went off to the cottage of Nele, hard by their own, before which they saw one of the foot-soldiers, summoned from Bruges for fear of the troubles that might arise during the trial and the execution. For the Damme folk loved Claes greatly.

The trooper was sitting on the edge of the road before the door, occupied in draining the last drop from a bottle of brandy. Finding no more in the bottle, he threw it from him and, drawing his dagger, amused himself by digging up the cobble-stones.

Soetkin entered Katheline's house all in tears.

And Katheline, shaking her head, said: 'Fire! Make a hole; the soul wants out!'

70 THE BELL CALLED *borgstorm* (town storm) having summoned the judges to the court, they united in the *Vierschare*, as the clock struck four, under the lime-tree of justice.

Claes was brought before them and saw, sitting on the daïs, the bailiff of Damme and beside him and facing him the Mayor, the sheriffs and the clerk of the court.

The populace came running at the sound of the bell, a great multitude, saying:

'Many of the judges are not there to do the work of justice, but that of imperial bondage.'

The clerk declared that the court, having first met in the *Vierschare* under the lime-tree, had decided that, in view of the denunciations and testimonies brought before it, it thought fit to arrest Claes, charcoal-burner, native of Damme, spouse of Soetkin, Joosten's daughter. They would now, he added, proceed with the hearing of the witnesses.

Hans Barvier, neighbour of Claes, was first heard. Having taken the oath, he said: 'Upon my soul's salvation I do affirm and swear that Claes, present before this court, has been known to me for over seventeen years, that he has always lived honestly and followed the laws of our Holy Mother the Church and has never spoken of her opprobriously, nor housed, to my knowledge, any heretic, nor hidden Luther's

145

book, nor yet spoken of the aforesaid book, nor ever done anything that might make him be suspected of ever having forgotten the laws and ordinances of the Empire. So help me God and all His Saints.'

Jan van Roosebekke was then heard and said: that during the absence of Soetkin, wife of Claes, he had thought he heard many times, coming from the accused's house, two men's voices, and that often in the evening, after the curfew, he had seen a light in the little room under the roof, and two men, one of them Claes, talking together. As to whether the other man was or was not a heretic he could not say, having only seen him from afar. 'As far as Claes is concerned,' he added, 'I will say, speaking the whole truth, that since I have known him he has always kept Easter regularly, taken communion at the principal feast days, gone to Mass each Sunday except that of the Holy Blood and the Sunday following it. And I know nothing more. So help me God and all His Saints.'

Questioned if he had not seen Claes selling indulgences and mocking Purgatory in the Tavern of the *Blauwe-Torre*, Jan van Roosebekke answered that Claes had indeed sold the indulgences but without scorn or mockery, and that he himself had bought, even as Josse Grypstuiver —the Dean of the Fishmongers, who was in the crowd—had wanted to do also.

The bailiff then said that he would make known the acts and gestures for which Claes had been brought before the court of the *Vierschare*.

Said he: 'The informer, having by chance stayed at Damme—so as not to go to Bruges and spend all his money in feasting and revelling as is too often done on these sacred occasions—was soberly taking the air by his own door-step. Being there, he saw a man who walked along the Heron Street. Claes, seeing the man, went towards him and greeted him. The man was dressed in black-cloth. He entered Claes's cottage and the door was left ajar. Curious to know who this man was, the informer entered the porch, heard Claes speaking in the kitchen with the stranger about a certain Josse, his brother, who, having been made a prisoner among the Reformation troops, was, because of this, broken alive on the rack, not far from Aix. The stranger told Claes that the money he had received from his brother was money gotten through the ignorance of the poor people, and that he must use it to bring up his son in the Reformed Religion. He also enjoined Claes to leave the bosom of our Holy Mother the Church, and pronounced many other impious words to which Claes only replied by saying: "Cruel butchers! My poor brother!" And the accused thus blasphemed our Holy Father the Pope and His Royal Majesty in accusing them of cruelty because

146

they had justly punished heresy as a crime of divine and human treason. When the man had finished eating, the informer heard Claes cry out: "Poor Josse—may God keep you in His glory—they were cruel to you." He thus accused God even of impiety in judging Him capable of receiving heretics in His heaven. And Claes kept on saying: "My poor brother!" The stranger, entering into a fury like a predicator at his preaching, cried out: "She will fall, the Great Babylon, the Roman Whore, and she will become the abode of demons and the haunt of all execrable birds!" Claes said: "Cruel butchers! My poor brother!" The stranger, continuing his discourse, said: "For the angel will take up the stone that is large as a mill-stone, and cast it into the sea, and he shall say: 'So will be cast the great Babylon, and she will be found no more'." "Sir," said Claes, "Your mouth is full of anger; but tell me, when shall come the reign when those who are meek in heart may live in peace on earth?" "Never," replied the stranger, "as long as reigns the Anti-Christ who is the Pope and the enemy of all truth." "Ah," said Claes, "you speak disrespectfully of our Holy Father. He surely does not know the cruel tortures with which they punish the poor reformists." The stranger replied: "He does indeed know, for he it is who sends out the edicts and causes them to be executed by the Emperor, and now by the King, who both reap the benefits of the confiscations, inherit from the defunct, and willingly bring suit for heresy against the rich". Claes answered: "They tell of these things in the land of Flanders, I must believe them; the flesh of man is weak, even when it's royal flesh. My poor Josse!" And Claes thus gave out that it was by a vile desire for lucre that His Majesty punished the heretics. The stranger wishing to speak further, Claes interrupted him, saying: "Deign, sir, to speak no more; such speeches which if they were heard would stir up some nasty suit against me".

'Claes arose to go to the cellar and, re-mounting with a pot of beer, he then said: "I am going to close the door". And the informer could hear no more, for he had to get out of the house quickly. The closed door was nevertheless reopened as night fell. The stranger came out but soon returned again and knocked, saying: "Claes, I'm cold; I don't know where to go; give me shelter; no one saw me come in, the town is deserted." Claes let him in, lighted the lantern, and was seen preceding the heretic up the stairs and leading him to the little room under the roof, whose window opens on the country-side—'

'Who then,' cried Claes, 'could have told all this if not you, vile fish-monger? I saw you Sunday, standing straight as a post by your door-way, hypocritically watching the swallows wheel in the air.'

147

And he pointed with his finger to Josse Grypstuiver, Dean of the Fishmongers, who showed his ugly phiz in the midst of the people.

The fishmonger smiled nastily, seeing Claes betray himself in this way. And all the populace, men, women and girls, said among themselves:

'Poor man, his words will be the cause of his death, no doubt.'

But the clerk of the court continued his declaration:

'The heretic and Claes talked that night together for a long time, and also during six other nights, during which one could see the stranger make many gestures of threats or of benediction, lifting his arms to the heavens as do his fellows in heresy. Claes seemed to approve his words.

"Most certainly during these days, evenings and nights, they talked opprobiously of the mass, of confession, of indulgences and of His Royal Majesty—'

'No one heard me,' said Claes, 'and you cannot accuse me thus, without proof.'

The clerk went on:

'Something else was heard. When the stranger left your house on the seventh day at ten o'clock, night having already fallen, you walked with him almost to the boundary-line of Katheline's fields. There he asked you what you had done with the wicked idols'—here the bailiff crossed himself—'of Madame the Virgin, of Master Saint Nicholas, and of Master Saint Martin. You answered that you had broken them and thrown them into the well the night before; the pieces are now in the torture chamber.'

At these words Claes seemed overwhelmed. The bailiff asked him if he had any reply to make. Claes made a sign that he had nothing to say.

The bailiff then asked if he did not wish to retract the damned thought that led him to break the images and the impious error by virtue of which he had pronounced opprobrious words against His Divine Majesty and His Royal Majesty.

Claes replied that his body belonged to His Royal Majesty but that his conscience was in Christ's keeping and that he would follow His law. The bailiff demanded to know if this law were that of our Holy Mother the Church. Claes replied:

'It is in the Holy Gospel.'

Summoned to reply to a question which asked if the Pope was God's representative on earth, he answered:

'No.'

Questioned if he believed it was forbidden to adore the images of Madame the Virgin and Masters the Saints, he answered that it was

148

idolatry. Questioned on the point of whether auricular confession is a good and salutary thing, he answered:

'Christ said: "Confess yourselves one to the other".'

He was brave in his replies, although he appeared sorely troubled and frightened to the bottom of his heart.

Eight o'clock having sounded and eventide come, the gentlemen of the court retired, deferring until the morrow their final judgment.

71 In KATHELINE's cottage Soetkin, distraught with sorrow, wept, and continued to repeat: 'My man! My poor man!' Ulenspiegl and Nele embraced her with a great welling-up of tenderness. She, drawing them together in her arms, wept silently. Then she made a sign to them to leave her alone. Nele said to Ulenspiegl:

'Let us leave her; she wants us to. Let us go and save the carolus.'

Off they went together; and Katheline circled about Soetkin, saying:

'Make a hole; the soul wants to go!'

And Soetkin, with fixed eyes, stared at her without seeing her.

The cottages of Claes and Katheline adjoined each other; that of Claes was set back with a garden before the house, while Katheline's had a bean-patch that bordered the street. This patch was surrounded by a green hedge, in which Ulenspiegl, to get to Nele and Nele to get to Ulenspiegl, had in their youth made a great hole.

Ulenspiegl and Nele entered the patch and from there they could see the trooper-guard who, with wagging head, spat into the air, but the spittle fell back on his doublet. A wicker-covered flask lay beside him.

'Nele,' said Ulenspiegl, in a whisper, 'this drunken trooper has not drunk away his thirst; he must drink more. We will then be masters. Let's take the flask.'

At the sound of the voices, the soldier turned his heavy head towards them, sought his flask and, not finding it, continued to spit in the air and try to watch his spittle fall by the light of the moon.

'He's filled to the teeth with brandy,' said Ulenspiegl. 'Do you hear how hard it is for him to spit?'

Meanwhile the trooper, having spit many times and looked into the air, stretched out his arm again to put his hand on the flask. He found it, put the neck to his mouth, threw back his head, turned up the flask, slapped its bottom to get out the last drop and sucked like a child at its mother's breast. Finding not a drop, he resigned himself, set down the flask beside him, swore a little in High German, spat again, wagged his head from left to right, and fell asleep, mumbling unintelligible paternosters.

Ulenspiegl, knowing that this sleep would not last long, and that he must be made more sleepy, slid through the hole in the hedge, took the trooper's flask and passed it to Nele, who filled it with brandy.

The trooper kept on snoring; Ulenspiegl re-passed through the hole in the hedge, placed the flask between the sleeping man's legs, re-entered Katheline's bean-patch and waited with Nele behind the hedge.

Because of the coolness of the freshly drawn liquor, the trooper awoke a little, and his first move was to seek out that which made him cold under his doublet.

Judging with drunken intuition that it might well be a full flask, he placed his hand on it. Ulenspiegl and Nele, by the glimmer of the moon-light, saw him shake the flask to hear the sound of the liquor, then taste it and laugh, marvel that it was so full, drink a sip, then a mouthful, lay the flask on the ground, take it up again and drink once more.

Then he sang:

> 'When Seigneur Maan shall come
> To say good-night to Lady Zee . . .'

To the High Germans, Lady Zee is the Sea and the wife of Seigneur Maan, the Moon and the master of women. So he sang:

> 'When Seigneur Maan shall come
> To say good-night to Lady Zee,
> The Lady Zee shall set him down
> A mighty stoup of spicèd wine
> When Seigneur Maan shall come.
>
> Then with him she will sup that night
> And with her kisses be quite free,

And when they'll both have supped
Then in her bed they both shall lie,
When Seigneur Maan shall come.

So may my true love be with me;
Rich supper and some spicèd wine;
So may my true love be with me
When Seigneur Maan shall come.'

Then, turn about, drinking and singing a quatrain, he fell asleep. And
he could not hear Nele saying: 'They're in a pot behind the chimney-
back.' Nor could he see Ulenspiegl enter by the stable to the kitchen of
Claes's house, find there the pot of gold, re-enter the bean-patch of
Katheline, hide the carolus beside the wall of the well, knowing that if
they sought for them, it would be within the well and not without.

Then they returned to Soetkin and found the sorrowful spouse weeping and saying:

'My man! My poor man!'

And Nele and Ulenspiegl watched over her until morning came.

72 THE FOLLOWING DAY, with great peals the *borgstorm* summoned the judges to the court of the *Vierschare*. When they
were seated on the four benches about the tree of justice, they
again interrogated Claes and asked him if he was willing to recant his
errors.

Claes raised his hand toward heaven.

'The Lord Christ sees me from on high,' he said. 'I looked upon His
sun when my boy Ulenspiegl was born. Where is he now, the vagabond?
Soetkin, my gentle wife, will you be brave in the face of misfortune?'

Then, looking at the lime-tree, he said, cursing it:

'Harsh winds and drought, make all the trees of the land of my fathers
to perish rather than let freedom of thought be condemned to death
under their shade! Where are you, my son Ulenspiegl? I was hard on
you. Sirs, have pity on me and judge me as would our Merciful Lord.'

All that heard him wept, save the judges.

Then he asked if there was no pardon for him, saying:

'I toiled always, earning little; I was good to the poor and gentle to
everybody. I left the Roman Church obeying the spirit of God who spoke
to me. I implore no grace other than that of having the penalty of burning commuted to the sentence of perpetual banishment from the Land
of Flanders during my life—a heavy enough penalty, as it is.'

151

And all those who were present cried out:

'Pity, sirs! Mercy!'

But Josse Grypstuiver did not join in the cry.

The bailiff made a sign to the people to be silent and said that the edicts expressly forbade the demanding of grace for heretics; but that if Claes would abjure his error, he would be executed by the rope instead of by the fire.

Among the people it was said:

'Fire or rope, it's death.'

And the women wept and the men growled sullenly.

Claes then said:

'I will not abjure. Do with my body as your mercy pleases.'

The Dean of Renaix, Titelman, cried out:

'It is intolerable to see such heretical vermin lift their heads before their judges. Burning their bodies is a passing pain, we must save their souls and force them by torture to renounce their errors, so that they may not give to the people the dangerous spectacle of heretics dying in final impenitence.'

At these words the women wept more and the men said:

'When a confession has been made, there may be penalty, but no torture.'

The court decided that, torture not being prescribed by the ordinances, there was no ground for torturing Claes. Summoned once more to abjure, he answered:

'I cannot.'

He was then, by virtue of the edicts, declared guilty of simony because of the sale of the indulgences; heretic and harbourer of heretics; and, as such, condemned to be burned alive until death ensued, before the Town Hall.

His body would be left two days, attached to a stake, to serve as a warning. Then it would be buried in the place usua.ly reserved for such executed criminals.

The court awarded to the informer, Josse Grypstuiver, who was not named, fifty florins of the first hundred of the inheritance, and a tenth of all over that.

Having heard this sentence, Claes said to the dean of the fishmongers:

'You will die an evil death, vile man, who for a paltry sum makes a widow of a happy spouse and of a joyous son a grieving orphan.'

The judges had allowed Claes to speak, for they also, excepting Titelman, held the denunciation of the dean of the fishmongers in great scorn.

And the dean appeared all livid with shame and anger.

And Claes was taken back to prison.

152

73 ON THE MORROW—the day before the execution of Claes—the sentence was made known to Nele, to Ulenspiegl, and to Soetkin. They asked to be allowed to enter the prison and were permitted to do so, Nele excepted.

When they entered, they saw Claes attached to the wall with a long chain. A little log fire burned in the chimney because of the dampness. For it is commanded by justice and law in Flanders to be kind to those about to die, and give them bread, meat or cheese, and wine. But the greedy jailers often violate the law, and there were many of them who ate the greatest part and the best bits of the poor prisoner's fare.

With tears Claes embraced Ulenspiegl and Soetkin, but he was the first to have dry eyes, because he willed it so, being a man and the head of a family.

Soetkin wept, and Ulenspiegl said:

'I want to break these ugly irons.'

Soetkin wept, saying:

'I will go to King Philip; he will pardon you.'

Claes answered:

'The King inherits the goods of the martyrs.' Then he added: 'Beloved wife and son, I go sadly and with sorrow from this world. If I have some apprehension of suffering in my body, I am also troubled in thinking that when I am no more you will both be poor and miserable, for the King will take your goods.'

Ulenspiegl answered, speaking in a low voice:

'Nele saved all with me, last night.'

'I am most happy,' replied Claes. 'The informer will not laugh over my spoils.'

'May he die first,' said Soetkin, her eyes tearless and burning with hate.

But Claes, thinking of the carolus, said:

'How clever you were, Tylken, my dear boy; she will not then go hungry in her old age, my widow Soetkin.'

And Claes embraced her, pressing her strongly to his breast, and she wept all the more, thinking that soon she would lose this gentle protection.

Claes looked at Ulenspiegl and said:

'Son, you often sinned in running off along the highways as wicked lads do; you must not do it any more, my child, nor ever leave the afflicted widow alone in the house, for you owe her defence and protection, you, the male.'

'Father, I will protect her,' said Ulenspiegl.

'Oh, my poor man!' said Soetkin, embracing him. 'What great crime have we committed? We lived together an honest and simple life, peacefully; we loved each other well, as the Lord God knows. We rose early to work and, in the evening, giving Him thanks, we ate our daily bread. I will go to the King and tear him with my nails. Lord God, we were not guilty!'

But the jailer entered and said that they must part.

Soetkin asked to be allowed to stay. Claes felt her poor face burn against his own and the tears of Soetkin fell in floods wetting his cheeks, and her poor body shook and trembled in his arms. He asked that she be allowed to stay with him. The jailer said again that she must go, and took Soetkin from the arms of Claes.

Claes said to Ulenspiegl:

'Watch over her.'

He replied that he would. And Ulenspiegl and Soetkin went off together, the son supporting his mother.

74 THE DAY FOLLOWING being the day of the execution, the neighbours came and, out of pity, locked Ulenspiegl, Soetkin and Nele up together in Katheline's house. But they did not think that they might hear from afar the cries of the burning man and from the windows see the flames of the pyre.

Katheline wandered about the town nodding her head and saying: 'Make a hole; the soul wants out!'

At nine o'clock Claes, with nothing but his shirt on and his hands tied behind his back, was taken from his prison. In accordance with the sentence, the pyre was set about a stake in Our Lady's Street before the Town Hall. The executioner and his aides had not yet finished piling up the wood.

Claes, in the midst of his jailers, waited patiently until this task was done, while the provost on horseback, the officers of the bailiwick, and the nine soldiers from Bruges had great trouble keeping order among the murmuring people.

All were saying that it was a cruelty to murder thus unjustly in his old age a poor man who was so gentle, compassionate and stout of heart at toil.

Suddenly they all fell on their knees and began to pray. The bells of the Church of Our Lady tolled for the dead.

Katheline, still out of her wits, was also in the crowd of people, in the first row. Watching Claes and the pyre, she said, wagging her head: 'Fire! Fire! Make a hole; the soul wants out!'

Soetkin and Nele, hearing the sound of the tolling bells, both crossed themselves. But Ulenspiegl would not do so, saying that he did not

154

wish to adore God after the manner of the executioners. And he ran about the cottage, trying to break open the doors and jump out of the windows; but they were all guarded.

Suddenly Soetkin cried, hiding her face with her apron:

'The smoke!'

The three afflicted ones saw that the sky was indeed a great whirl of black smoke. It came from the pyre whereon Claes stood attached to the stake. The executioner had just lit the pile in three places, in the name of God the Father and of God the Son and of God the Holy Ghost.

Claes looked about him and, not seeing Soetkin and Ulenspiegel in the crowd, was happy, thinking that they would not see him suffer.

No other sound was heard save the voice of Claes, praying; the crackling wood; the growling men; the women weeping; Katheline saying: 'Take away the fire! Make a hole; the soul wants out!'

All at once Soetkin went white as snow, her whole body shaking; and tearless, she pointed a finger to the sky. A long straight flame had shot up from the pile and at times rose above the roofs of the lower houses. It was a cruel and scorching flame to Claes for, following the wind's caprice, it ran up his legs, touched his beard, making it to smoke, and licking his hair and singeing it.

Ulenspiegel held Soetkin in his arms and tried to drag her away from the window. They heard a piercing scream; it came from Claes, whose body was only being burned on one side. But after that he was silent and only wept. And his breast was wet with his tears.

Then Soetkin heard a great sound as of many voices. It was the burghers, the women and children shouting:

'Claes was not condemned to be burned by slow fire but by a quick fire. Stir up the fire, executioner!'

This the executioner did, but the fire did not take very well.

'Strangle him!' they shouted.

And they threw stones at the provost.

'The flame! The great flame!' cried Soetkin.

And indeed, mounting to the sky in the midst of smoke, there was a great red flame.

'He is about to die,' said the widow. 'Lord God, have pity on the soul of this innocent man. Where is the King, that I may tear out his heart with my nails?'

The bells of the Church of Our Lady tolled for the dead.

Soetkin again heard Claes give a great cry, but she did not see his body writhe because of the great pain of the fire, nor its contractions, nor his head that turned from side to side and vainly knocked itself against the stake. The people continued to shout and whistle, the

156

women and the boys threw stones, when suddenly the whole pyre went up in a blaze and they all heard, out of the flame and the smoke, the voice of Claes, saying:

'Soetkin! Tyl!'

And his head fell forward on his breast as though it were made of lead.

And a lamentable and piercing cry was heard coming from the cottage of Katheline. Then no one heard anything more save the poor madwoman, wagging her head and saying:

'The soul wants out!'

Claes was dead. The pyre, having burned out, fell about the bottom of the stake. And the poor blackened corpse remained hanging by the neck.

And the bells of the Church of Our Lady tolled for the dead.

75 SOETKIN STOOD in Katheline's house against the wall, her head hanging down and her hands joined together. She held Ulenspiegl in her embrace, speechless and tearless. Ulenspiegl also stayed silent; he was terrified to feel the feverish fire that burned through his mother's body.

The neighbours who had returned from the execution place said that the sufferings of Claes were over.

'He is in glory,' said the widow.

'Pray,' said Nele to Ulenspiegl; and she gave him her rosary. But he would not make use of it, for the beads had been blessed by the Pope.

Night having fallen, Ulenspiegl said to the widow:

'Mother, you must go to bed; I will watch over you.'

But Soetkin said: 'I have no need for you to watch over me; sleep is good for young men.'

Nele made a bed for each of them in the kitchen and then retired.

They both stayed together as long as the fire of the tree-roots burned in the chimney.

Soetkin then went to bed. Ulenspiegl followed suit and heard her weeping underneath the covers.

Outside, in the silence of the night, the wind was making the trees along the canal murmur like the sea and, precursor of Autumn, was whirling sprays of dust up against the window.

Ulenspiegl thought he saw a man going and coming; he heard, it seemed, a noise of footsteps in the kitchen. Watching carefully, he saw no man; listening, he no longer heard anything but the wind soughing in the chimney and Soetkin weeping under her covers.

Then he heard footsteps again, and behind him, close to his head, a sigh. 'Who's there?' he said.

No one answered, but three knocks were made on the table. Ulenspiegl was frightened and, trembling, he said again: 'Who's there?' No answer came, but three knocks were made on the table and he felt two arms clasped about him, and over his face there leaned a body whose skin was all wrinkled and which had a hole in its breast, and there was about it an odour of burned flesh.

'Father,' said Ulenspiegl, 'is it your poor body that weighs over me so?'

There was no answer and, despite the fact that the shadow was close to him, he heard a cry from outside, saying: 'Tyl! Tyl!' Suddenly Soetkin rose from her bed and came to Ulenspiegl: 'Do you hear anything?' said she.

'Yes,' he said, 'my father is calling me.'

'I,' said Soetkin, 'I felt a cold body beside me, in my bed; and the mattresses moved and the curtains shook, and I heard a voice saying, "Soetkin"; a low voice like a breath, and a step as light as the sound of a gnat's wing.' Then, speaking to the spirit of Claes:

'You must, my man,' she said, 'if you desire anything in heaven where God keeps you in his glory, you must tell us what it is, so that we may accomplish your will.'

Suddenly a gust of wind opened the door impetuously and filled the room with dust, and Ulenspiegl and Soetkin heard the far-off croakings of ravens.

They went out together and came to the stake.

The night was black save when the clouds—chased by the bitter north wind and coursing across the sky like stags—let the stars shine through.

A sergeant walked up and down, keeping watch over the stake. Ulenspiegl and Soetkin heard on the hardened ground the noise of his steps, and the voice of a raven, calling the others, no doubt, for they heard answering croakings.

Ulenspiegl and Soetkin had approached close to the stake; the raven flew down on the shoulder of Claes; they heard its beak pecking at the body; and soon other ravens came.

Ulenspiegl wanted to rush to the stake and strike the ravens; the sergeant said to him:

"Sorcerer, do you seek these famous hands? Know that the hands of those burned do not render one invisible; that is done only by the hands of someone hanged, as you shall be one day.'

'Messire Sergeant,' replied Ulenspiegl, 'I am not a sorcerer, but the orphan son of the man tied there, and this woman is his wife. We

158

would but kiss him again and take some of his ashes for a memory of him. Give us leave to do this, sir, you who are certainly no foreign trooper but a son of this land.'

'Be it as you wish,' replied the sergeant.

The orphan and the widow, walking over the charred wood, came to the body; in tears they both kissed the face of Claes.

Ulenspiegl took from the place where the heart had been, where the flames had hollowed out a great hole, a few of the ashes of the dead man. Then, kneeling, he and Soetkin prayed. When the dawn came, paling the sky, they were both still there; but the sergeant made them go, for fear of being punished because of his kindness.

Returned home again, Soetkin took a piece of red silk and a piece of black silk; of these she made a sachet and in it she placed the ashes. To the sachet she attached two ribbons, so that Ulenspiegl might always wear it about his neck. And, in giving him the sachet, she said:

'May these ashes that were the heart of my man, this red that is his blood and this black that is our sorrow, stay always on your breast as the fire of vengeance against the murderers.'

'So be it,' said Ulenspiegl.

And the widow embraced the orphan, and the sun rose.

76 THE FOLLOWING DAY the sergeants and the town crier came to the house of Claes to cast the furnishings into the street, and there they proceeded with a judicial sale. Soetkin, looking out from Katheline's place, saw them throw out the cradle of iron and brass which had, from father to son, always been in the Claes family. The poor dead man had been rocked in it and Ulenspiegl also had been rocked in it. Then they brought out the bed where Soetkin had conceived her child and wherein she had passed such pleasant nights by her man's side.

159

Then came the trough wherein she had kneaded her bread, the cupboard where, in days of fortune, the meats were kept; the kettles and pots no longer shining as they did in happier times but now soiled with the dust of abandon. They recalled to her the family feasts when the neighbours called, drawn there by the savour.

Then came also a tun of *simpel* and a keg of *dobble cuyt* and, in a basket, flasks of wine, of which there were at least thirty; and all this was cast into the road, even to the last nail that the poor widow heard being dragged noisily from the wall.

Seated, she watched—without crying out or complaining, but quite brokenhearted—all these humble riches go. The crier having lighted a candle, the furnishings were sold by auction. The candle having almost burned out, the dean of the fishmongers had bought almost everything at a low price to sell it again; and he seemed to be as happy as a weasel sucking out a hen's brain. Deep in his heart, Ulenspiegl said: 'You'll not laugh long, murderer.'

Meanwhile the sale ended, and the sergeants, who searched everything, found no carolus. The fishmonger exclaimed:

'You search badly. I know that Claes had seven hundred, only six months ago.'

Deep in his heart Ulenspiegl said: 'You shall not inherit, murderer.'

Suddenly, Soetkin turned to him:

'The informer!' said she, pointing to the fishmonger.

'I know,' said he.

'Do you want him,' said she, 'to inherit the blood of your father?'

'I would rather suffer a whole day on the torture bench,' answered Ulenspiegl.

Soetkin said:

'I, also, but do not give me away out of pity, no matter what agony you see me suffering.'

'Alas, you are a woman,' said Ulenspiegl.

'Poor boy,' said she, 'I brought you into the world and I know how to suffer. But you, if I saw you—' Then growing pale, 'I shall pray to Madame the Virgin who saw her Son on the cross.'

And she wept, caressing Ulenspiegl.

And so between them was made this pact of hate and strength.

77 THE FISHMONGER had to pay only half of the purchase price, the other half serving to pay him for his denunciation until such time as the seven hundred which had led him into the foul deed were found. Soetkin passed her nights in weeping and her days

in doing the household tasks. Often Ulenspiegl heard her talking to herself, saying:

'If he inherits, I shall kill myself.'

Knowing well that she would do as she said, he and Nele tried their best to persuade Soetkin to go to Walcheren, where she had some relatives. Soetkin would not go, saying that there was no need for her to run away from the worms that would soon be eating her widowed bones.

In the meanwhile, the fishmonger had gone to the bailiff and told him that the defunct had inherited, only a few months before, seven hundred carolus, and that, being a niggardly man who lived on very little, he certainly had not spent that great sum which was undoubtedly hidden somewhere, in some corner.

The bailiff wanted to know what harm Ulenspiegl and Soetkin had done him that even after taking from the one his father and from the other her man, he still bethought himself of other means to harass them cruelly.

The fishmonger replied that, being a leading burgher of Damme, he wished to see that the laws of the Empire were respected and so deserve the clemency of His Majesty.

Having said this, he placed in the hands of the bailiff a written accusation and produced witnesses who, speaking the whole truth, certified in spite of themselves that the fishmonger was not lying.

The men of the sheriffs' chamber, having heard the witnesses, declared that the indications of culpability were sufficient to call for torture. As a consequence of this, they sent the sergeants to search the house; the men were also empowered to bring back the mother and son to the town prison, where they would be held until the executioner, whom they had sent for, should arrive from Bruges.

When Ulenspiegl and Soetkin passed down the street, their hands tied behind their backs, the fishmonger stood by the threshold of his house watching them.

And the burghers of Damme and their wives were also standing at their door-ways. Maythyssen, a close neighbour of the fishmonger, heard Ulenspiegl say to the informer:

'God curse you, tormentor of widows!'

And Soetkin said to him:

'You'll die an evil death, persecutor of orphans!'

The Damme folk, having thus learned that it was on a second denunciation of Grypstuiver that the widow and orphan were being taken to prison, hooted the fishmonger and at night threw stones through his windows. And his door was covered with excrement.

And he did not dare go out from his house any more.

161

78 Towards ten o'clock in the morning, Ulenspiegl and Soetkin were taken to the hall of torture. There they saw the bailiff, the clerk of the court, the sheriffs, the executioner from Bruges, his helper and a surgeon-barber.

The bailiff demanded of Soetkin if she did not hold any wealth belonging by rights to the Emperor. She replied that, having nothing, she could hold back nothing.

'And you?' demanded the bailiff, speaking to Ulenspiegl.

'About seven months ago,' he answered, 'we inherited seven hundred carolus; we used some of them. As for the others I do not know where they are: just the same I think that the traveller who stayed with us, for our undoing, took what remained, for I have not seen them since.'

The bailiff wanted to know again if they both persisted in declaring themselves innocent.

They answered that they held no wealth that belonged to the Emperor.

The bailiff then said, gravely and sadly:

'The charges against you being heavy and the accusation motivated, you must, if you do not confess, undergo torture.'

'Spare the widow,' said Ulenspiegl. 'The fishmonger bought up everything.'

'Poor boy!' said Soetkin. 'Men do not know how to endure pain as women do.'

Seeing Ulenspiegl pale as a corpse because of her, she said again:

'I have hate and strength.'

'Spare the widow,' said Ulenspiegl.

'Take me in his stead,' said Soetkin.

The bailiff asked the torturer if he had made ready the instruments necessary to draw forth the truth.

The torturer replied:

'They are all here.'

The judges, having conferred, decided that, to get at the truth, it were best to begin with the woman.

'For,' said one of the sheriffs, 'there is no son cruel enough to stand by and see his mother suffer, without delivering her by confessing the crime; by the same token so would a mother act to save her offspring, even though she were a tigress at heart.'

Speaking to the torturer, the bailiff said:

'Set the woman in the chair and place the baguettes on her hands and feet.'

The torturer obeyed.

'Oh! Do not do that, Master Judges,' cried Ulenspiegl. 'Put me in her

162

place, break the fingers of my hands and the toes of my feet, but spare the widow!'

'The fishmonger!' said Soetkin. 'I have hate and strength!'

Ulenspiegl seemed pale, trembling, beside himself, and he kept silent.

The baguettes were little rods of box-wood, placed between each finger, touching the bones, and united by cords to an instrument so cunningly designed that the torturer, at the judges' will, could squeeze all the fingers together, strip the flesh from the bones, crush them, or just give the victim a slight pain.

He placed the baguettes on the feet and hands of Soetkin.

'Tighter,' said the bailiff to him.

He did so, cruelly.

Then the bailiff, speaking to Soetkin:

'Describe to me,' he said, 'the place where the carolus are hidden.'

'I do not know it,' she replied, groaning.

'Make it tighter,' he said.

Ulenspiegl tried to shake free his hands, which were tied behind his back, and come to Soetkin's aid.

'Do not tighten any more, Master Judges,' he said, 'these are a woman's bones, thin and brittle. A bird could break them in his beak. Do not tighten any more, master torturer, I do not speak to you, for you must obey the orders of these gentlemen. Do not tighten any more; have pity!'

'The fishmonger!' said Soetkin.

And Ulenspiegl was silent.

However, seeing that the torturer screwed the baguettes more tightly, he cried out once more:

'Pity, sirs! You are breaking a widow's fingers which she has need of for her work. La, her feet! She will never walk again now! Pity, sirs!'

'You'll die an evil death, fishmonger!' cried Soetkin.

And her bones cracked and the blood from her feet fell in tiny drops.

Ulenspiegl watched all this, and, trembling with anguish and anger, cried:

'A woman's bones, do not break them, Master Judges.'

'The fishmonger!' groaned Soetkin.

And her voice was low and muffled, like the voice of a phantom.

Ulenspiegl trembled and cried:

'Master Judges, the hands are bleeding and the feet, too. They have broken a widow's bones.'

The surgeon-barber touched them with his finger and Soetkin gave a loud scream.

163

'Confess for her,' said the bailiff to Ulenspiegl.

But Soetkin looked at him with eyes staring wide open as of one just dead. And he understood that he might not speak, and wept in silence.

The bailiff then said:

'Since this woman is endowed with the resolution of a man, we must try her courage before the torture of her son.'

Soetkin heard nothing of this, for she was senseless because of the great pain she had suffered.

They brought her back to herself with much vinegar. Then Ulenspiegl was stripped of his clothes and set naked before the widow's eyes. The torturer shaved his head and all the hair about his body so as to see if he did not have about him any sorcery. He noticed on his back the little black mark which Ulenspiegl had had there since his birth. He stabbed it several times with a long needle but, blood having flowed, he judged that there was no sorcery in the mark. By an order from the bailiff, Ulenspiegl's hands were tied to two ropes which went over a pulley, fixed to the ceiling, so that the torturer might, as the judges willed, pull the victim up and down with brutal jerks; and this he did nine times, after having attached to each leg a twenty-five pound weight.

At the ninth jerk the skin about the wrist and the ankles was torn and the bones of the legs began to come out of their sockets.

'Confess,' said the bailiff.

'No!' said Ulenspiegl.

Soetkin watched her son and could not find within her the strength to cry out or speak; she only put her arms before her, fluttering her bleeding hands to show by this gesture that they must stop the torture.

The torturer made Ulenspiegl go up and down with a jerk once more. And the skin of the wrists and the ankles were torn much more; the bones of the legs came out more from their sockets; but he did not cry aloud. Soetkin wept and fluttered her bleeding hands.

'Confess the concealment,' said the bailiff, 'and you will be pardoned.'

'The fishmonger has need of pardon,' answered Ulenspiegl.

'Are you mocking your judges?' said one of the sheriffs.

'Me, mock? La!' replied Ulenspiegl, 'I am but feigning, believe me.'

Soetkin then saw the torturer, at the command of the bailiff, blowing up a brazier of red coals, while his helper lit two candles.

She tried to rise to her feet, but fell back again in her chair, and cried out:

'Take away that fire! Ah, Master Judges, spare his poor youth. Take away the fire!'

'The fishmonger!' shouted Ulenspiegl, seeing her weaken.

'Raise Ulenspiegl to about a foot from the floor,' said the bailiff; 'put the brazier under his feet and a lighted candle under each armpit.'

The torturer obeyed. The hairs that remained under the arm-pits fizzled and smoked in the flame.

Ulenspiegl cried and Soetkin, weeping, said:

'Take away the fire!'

The bailiff said:

'Confess the concealment and you will be taken down. Confess for him, woman.'

And Ulenspiegl said:

'Who wants to throw the fishmonger in the ever-burning fire?'

Soetkin made a sign with her head that she had nothing to say. Ulenspiegl gnashed his teeth, and Soetkin looked at him with haggard and tear-filled eyes.

Yet, when the torturer, having snuffed the candles, set the brazier under Ulenspiegl's feet, she cried out:

'Master Judges, have pity on him: he knows not what he says.'

'Why does he not know what he says?' demanded the bailiff craftily.

'Do not question her, Master Judges; you can see that she is out of her mind with pain. The fishmonger lied,' said Ulenspiegl.

'Will you speak like him, woman?' demanded the bailiff. Soetkin nodded her head in answer.

'Burn the fishmonger!' shouted Ulenspiegl.

Soetkin was silent and brandished her arm in the air as though to curse.

Yet, seeing the flame of the brazier rise higher under her son's feet, she cried out:

'Oh, Lord God! Madame Marie, who art in Heaven, make this torture to cease! Have pity! Take away the brazier!'

'The fishmonger!' groaned Ulenspiegl again.

And he vomited blood in great gushes through his mouth and nose and, with head fallen forward, remained suspended above the live coals.

Then Soetkin cried:

'He's dead, my poor orphan! They've killed him! Take away the

165

brazier, Master Judges! Let me take him in my arms so that I too may die close to him! You know that I cannot run away on my broken feet.'

'Give her son to the widow,' said the bailiff.

Then the judges deliberated among themselves.

The torturer untied Ulenspiegl and placed him naked and all covered with blood over Soetkin's knees while the surgeon re-set the bones in their sockets.

And Soetkin kissed her son and said, weeping:

'Son, poor martyr! If the judges wish, I shall heal you. But wake up, Tyl, my son! Master Judges, if you have killed him I shall go to His Majesty; for you have gone against all right and justice, and you shall see what a poor woman can do against the wicked. But, sirs, let us go free together. We have only each other in all the world, poor folk on whom the hand of God has fallen heavily.'

Having deliberated, the judges rendered the following sentence:

'Inasmuch as you, Soetkin, widowed wife of Claes, and you, Tyl, son of Claes, surnamed Ulenspiegl, having been accused of frustrating the wealth which by confiscation belonged to His Majesty, notwithstanding all privileges to the contrary, and having, in spite of cruel torture and adequate ordeal, confessed nothing:

'The court, considering the lack of sufficient proofs, and in you, woman, the pitiful state of your members, and in you, man, the severe torture you have suffered, hereby declares you freed and permits you to live with him or her of the town who may be pleased to give you lodging, notwithstanding your poverty.

'Thus decreed at Damme, the third and twentieth day of October, in the year of our Lord 1558.'

'Thanks be unto you, Master Judges,' said Soetkin.

'The fishmonger!' moaned Ulenspiegl.

And the mother and the son were carried in a cart to Katheline's house.

166

79 IN THAT YEAR, which was the fifty-eighth of the century, Katheline came to where Soetkin was, and said: 'Last night, having anointed myself with balm, I was transported to the tower of Our Lady, and I saw the elementary spirits carrying the prayers of men to the angels who, flying to the highest heavens, bore them to the throne. And the sky was strewn with radiant stars. Suddenly there arose from a pyre a figure that seemed black to me and mounted to take its place beside me on the tower. I recognized Claes as he was in life, dressed in his charcoal-burner's clothes. "What are you doing on the tower of Our Lady?" he said to me. "But you, yourself," I said to him, "where are you going, flying through the air like a bird?" "I'm going to the judgment; do you not hear the angel's trumpet?" I found myself quite close to him and felt that his spirit-body was not hard like the body of living folk; but so subtle that in going against him I entered as into a warm vapour. At my feet, over all the land of Flanders, shone several lights, and I said to myself: "They who rise early and work late are blessed of God."

'And all through the night I heard the angel's trumpet. And I saw another shade that arose, coming from Spain; this one was old and decrepit, having a chin like a slipper and quince-jelly on the lips. It wore over its back a mantle of crimson velvet lined with ermine, on the head an imperial crown, in one of the hands an anchovy at which it was nibbling, and in the other a tankard full of beer.

'It came, through weariness, no doubt, to sit on the tower of Our Lady. Going down on my knees, I said to it:

'"Crowned Majesty, I venerate you, but I do not know you. Where do you come from, and what do you do in the world?" "I come," it said, "from Saint Just in Estramadura and I was the Emperor Charles-Quint." "But," said I, "whither do you go now on this cold night, through these clouds charged with hail?" "I am going," it said, "to the judgment." As the Emperor was about to finish his anchovy and down the beer in his tankard, the clarion of the angel sounded. The spirit of the Emperor rose in the air, grumbling at being interrupted at its repast. I followed His Sacred Majesty's shade. It swept through space, hiccuping with fatigue, wheezing asthmatically, and sometimes vomiting, for death had taken him during an attack of indigestion. We continued mounting, like arrows sped from a bow. The stars glided beside us, tracing lines of fire in the sky; we saw them break loose and fall down. The angel's clarion sounded. What a piercing and powerful sound! As each fanfare struck the vapours of the air, they opened up as though a nearby hurricane had blown through them. And so the way was traced for us. Having risen a thousand leagues or

167

more, we saw Christ in His Glory, seated on a starry throne, having on His right the recording angel, who sets down on his brazen register the deeds of men, and on His left Mary His Mother, ceaselessly imploring mercy for the sinners.

'Claes and the Emperor knelt down before the throne.

'An angel cast the crown from the Emperor's head. "There is but one Emperor here, Christ."

'His Sacred Majesty seemed annoyed; yet, speaking, quite humbly, he said: "May I not keep this anchovy and this tankard of beer, for the long journey has made me hungry?"

' "As you were all your life," retorted the angel, "but eat and drink as you will."

'The Emperor emptied the tankard and nibbled at the anchovy.

'Christ then said:

' "Do you come to judgment with a clean soul?"

' "I hope so, my gentle Lord, for I confessed my sins," answered the Emperor Charles.

' "And you, Claes?" asked Christ. "You do not tremble like this Emperor."

' "My Lord Jesus," answered Claes, "there is no soul that is clean and therefore I have no fear of You who are the Sovereign Good and the Sovereign Justice. Nevertheless I am afraid for my sins, for they were many."

' "Speak carrion!" said the angel, addressing the Emperor.

' "I, Lord," answered Charles, in an embarrassed tone of voice, "being anointed by the hands of your priests, was crowned King of Castile, Emperor of Germany and King of the Romans. I had always close to my heart the conservation of the power that came from you and to that end I wrought by the rope, by steel, pit and fire against all the Protestants."

'But the angel said:

' "Dyspeptic liar, you seek to deceive us. You tolerated in Germany the Reformers, for you were afraid of them, but you beheaded, burned, hanged and buried alive those of the Netherlands, where you feared naught save the possibility of not inheriting enough from those laborious bees, rich in so much honey. A hundred thousand souls perished by your work, not because you loved Christ our Lord, but because you were despotic, tyrannic and a waster of your country, loving only yourself, and after that meats, fish, wines and beers; for you were gutsy as a dog and thirsty as a sponge."

' "And you, Claes, speak," said Christ.

' "This man has nothing to say. He was good and laborious as are

168

the poor people of Flanders. He worked willingly and laughed freely. He kept the faith he owed his princes and thought that they would keep the faith they owed to him. He had money, he was accused; and as he had given shelter to a Reformer, he was burned alive."

' "Ah," said Mary, "poor martyr! But there are in Heaven cool springs, fountains of milk, and exquisite wine that will refresh you; and I will lead you to them myself, charcoal-burner."

'The angel's clarion sounded once more and I saw, arising from the depths of the abyss, a beautiful and naked man crowned with an iron crown. And on the rim of the crown were written these words:

SORROWFUL UNTIL THE DAY OF DOOM

'He approached the throne and said to Christ:

' "I am your slave until that day when I shall be your master."

' "Satan," said Mary, "a day is coming when there will be neither slaves nor masters; when Christ who is Love and Satan who is Pride shall mean: Might and Knowledge."

' "Woman, you are all goodness and beauty," said Satan.

'Then, speaking to Christ and pointing to the Emperor, he said:

' "What is to be done with this one?"

'Christ answered:

' "You will place this crowned worm in a chamber wherein you will gather together all the instruments of torture in use during his reign. Each time that an innocent wretch endures the torture of water which causes men to swell up like bladders; that of the candles which burns the soles of their feet and their arm-pits; that of the *strappado* which breaks their limbs; or that of the four galleys racking them asunder; each time that a free soul gives up its last breath on the stake, he must endure in turn these deaths, these tortures, so that he may learn the wrong an unjust man may do who has power over millions of others. Let him rot in prison, die on the scaffold, groan in exile far from his country; let him be dishonoured, vilified, flogged; let him be rich and see the tax-collectors devour his wealth, the informers accuse him, the confiscation ruin him. You will make him a donkey, so that, being gentle, he shall be ill-treated and under-nourished; you will make him poverty-stricken, so that, demanding alms, he shall receive only insults; a workman, so that he labours long and eats little. Then, when he has suffered much with his body and in his man-soul, you will make him a dog, so that, being good, he shall receive blows; a slave in India, so that he shall be sold at auction; a soldier, so that, fighting for another, he shall be killed without knowing why or wherefore. And when, at the end of three hundred years, he shall have drained the dregs of all

170

suffering and all misery, you will make him a free man; and if in that state he is good as Claes was good, you will give his body a corner of the earth that is shaded at noon, visited by the morning sun, and there, under a lovely tree, covered by a cool greensward, he shall find eternal rest. And his friends shall come to his tomb and weep their bitter tears and plant violets there, the flowers of remembrance."

' "Have mercy, my Son," said Mary, "he knew not what he did. Power hardens the heart."

' "There is no mercy," said Christ.

' "Ah," said His Sacred Majesty, "if I only had a glass of Andalusian wine!"

' "Come," said Satan, "the time for wine, and meats, and fowl, is past."

'And he carried away to the deepest depths of Hell the soul of the poor Emperor still nibbling at a bit of anchovy.

'Satan let him do this out of pity. Then I saw Madame the Virgin lead Claes to the highest Heaven, where the stars hung like grapes to the vaulted roof. And there the angels laved him and he became young and fair. Then they gave him *rystpap* to eat from a silver spoon. And the heavens closed again.'

'He is in glory,' said the widow.

'His ashes beat against my heart,' said Ulenspiegl.

80 DURING THE twenty-three days that followed, Katheline became white, thin, and dried up as though she were devoured by a fire within, more consuming than the fire of folly. She no longer said: 'Fire! Make a hole; the soul wants out!' She seemed to be always in a transport of ecstasy and, speaking to Nele, would say:

'Spouse I am; spouse you should be. Handsome; long hair; warm love; cold knees and arms cold!'

And Soetkin looked at her sadly, thinking some new madness was on her.

Katheline continued her talk:

'Three times three make nine, the sacred number. He, who at night has shining eyes like a cat, alone sees the mystery.'

One night Soetkin, listening to her, made a sign of doubt. But Katheline said:

'Four and three, misfortune under Saturn; under Venus the marriage number. Cold arms! Cold knees! Heart of fire!'

Soetkin retorted:

'You must not speak of these wicked pagan idols.'

Hearing which, Katheline crossed herself and said:

'Blessed be the grey horseman. Nele must have a husband, a fine husband wearing a sword, dark husband with a shining face.'

'Yes,' said Ulenspiegl, 'a fricassee of husbands for whom I shall make a sauce with my knife.'

Nele looked at her friend through eyes all moist with the pleasure of seeing him so jealous.

'I want no husband,' she said.

Katheline replied:

'When will he come, the grey-clad one, all booted and spurred, another way?'

Soetkin said:

'Let us pray God for the mad-wife.'

'Ulenspiegl,' said Katheline, 'go fetch us four litres of *dobble cuyt* while I make ready the *heete-koeken*' (pancakes in the French style).

Soetkin asked why she feted on Saturday, like the Jews.

Katheline replied:

'Because the batter is ready.'

Ulenspiegl was standing, holding an English pewter pot that held just four litres.

'Mother, what shall I do?' he asked.

'Go,' said Katheline.

Soetkin did not wish to say anything, not being mistress of the house; she said to Ulenspiegl:

'Go, my son.'

Ulenspiegl ran all the way to the *Scaek* and from there he brought back four litres of *dobble cuyt*.

Soon the smell of *heete-koeken* spread throughout the kitchen and made them all hungry, even the poor afflicted one.

Ulenspiegl ate well. Katheline had given him a great tankard, saying that, being the only male and head of the house, he should drink more than the others and sing afterwards.

And saying this she had a malicious look; but Ulenspiegl drank and did not sing. Nele wept watching Soetkin, all pale and huddled up; Katheline alone was gay.

After the meal, Soetkin and Ulenspiegl went up to the garret to their beds; Katheline and Nele stayed in the kitchen where their beds had been made up.

Towards two in the morning—Ulenspiegl had been asleep for a long time because of the heavy drink—Soetkin lying wide-awake, as she did every evening, prayed Madame the Virgin to give her sleep, but Madame heeded not her prayer.

Suddenly she heard the cry of a sea-eagle and from the kitchen a

172

like cry came in answer; then from afar other cries resounded and always, it seemed, answering cries came from the kitchen.

Thinking it was only night-birds, she paid no attention. She heard the neighing of horses and the sound of iron-shod hoofs striking the cobble-stones; she opened the garret window and saw that there were two horses, saddled, pawing the ground and eating the grass by the roadside. She then heard a woman's voice crying, a man's voice threatening, blows struck, more cries, a door being noisily banged, and agonized steps rushing up the stairs.

Ulenspiegl snored and heard nothing; the garret door opened; Nele entered, almost nude, out of breath, weeping and sobbing, and began to pile hastily against the door a table, chairs, an old stove and all the furniture she could find. The last stars were dimming, the cocks were crowing.

Ulenspiegl, at the noise made by Nele, turned about in his bed and continued to sleep.

Nele threw her arms about Soetkin's neck. 'Soetkin,' she said, 'I'm frightened, light a candle.'

Soetkin did so; and Nele continued to moan.

The candle being lit, Soetkin, looking at Nele, saw that the girl's chemise was torn at the shoulder and that on her brow, cheek, and neck were bloody marks such as are left by scratches from finger-nails.

'Nele,' said Soetkin, embracing her, 'where have you come from, scratched in this way?'

The girl, trembling and still moaning, said: 'Don't have us burned, Soetkin.'

In the meantime Ulenspiegl had awakened and was blinking in the candle-light. Soetkin said:

'Who is below?' Nele replied: 'Quiet! It is the husband they want me to have.'

Soetkin and Nele suddenly heard Katheline scream, and their legs gave way under them.

'He is beating her! He is beating her because of me!' said Nele.

'Who's in the house?' cried Ulenspiegl, leaping from his bed. Then, rubbing his eyes, he wandered about the room until he got his hand on a heavy poker that lay in a corner.

'No one,' said Nele, 'no one; don't go down, Ulenspiegl!'

But he paid no heed and rushed to the door, casting aside the chairs, tables and stove. Katheline continued to scream downstairs; Nele and Soetkin held Ulenspiegl back on the landing, the one with her arms about his body, the other holding on to his legs, crying: 'Don't go, Ulenspiegl; they are devils.'

173

'Yes,' he answered, 'devil-husband of Nele. I'm going to join him in wedlock with this poker. Marriage of iron and flesh! Let me go down!'

But they would not let him go, for they were strengthened by holding on to the banister. He dragged them down the stairs and they were afraid to approach any closer to the devils. But they could do nothing with Ulenspiegl. Going down the stairs by leaps and bounds, like a snow-ball down a mountain-side, he entered the kitchen. There he saw Katheline worn out and pale in the light of the dawn, and heard her say: 'Hanske, why do you leave me alone? It isn't my fault if Nele's wicked.'

Ulenspiegl, without listening to her, opened the stable door. Finding no one there he ran out to the garden and from there to the roadway; from where he stood he saw two horsemen galloping away until they were lost in the mists of the morning. He ran after them to try and catch up with them, but they galloped ahead like the storm-wind that swirls up withered leaves.

Troubled by anger and despair, he returned, saying between his teeth: 'They violated her! They violated her!' And he looked on Nele with an ugly glow burning in his eyes, while she, all quivering, stood before the window; and Katheline said:

'No, Tyl, my dearest! No!'

And as she said this, she looked him in the eyes so sadly and so frankly that Ulenspiegl saw that she was really telling the truth. Then questioning her:

'Where did these cries come from?' he asked. 'Where did these men go? Why is your chemise torn at the shoulder and the back? Why does your brow and cheek bear the marks of nail-scratches?'

'Listen,' she said, 'but do not have us burned, Ulenspiegl. Katheline —whom God save from Hell—has had, for twenty-three days, as her lover a devil dressed in black, booted and spurred. He has a face that shines with a flame that is seen on the waves in summer when it is hot.'

'Why did you go, Hanske, my dear?' said Katheline. 'Nele's wicked.'

But Nele, continuing, said:

'He screams like a sea-eagle to announce his presence. Mother sees him in the kitchen every Saturday. She says that his kisses are cold and that his body is like snow. He beats her when she does not do what he wants her to. He brought her several florins once, but he took from her all her others.'

During this tale Soetkin, her hands clasped, prayed for Katheline; Katheline, most happy, said:

'My body is no longer mine, mine no longer my spirit; they are his. Hanske, my dear, take me again to the Witches' Sabbath. It's only Nele who doesn't want to go; Nele's wicked.'

174

'They leave at dawn,' continued the girl; 'the following day mother tells me a hundred most strange things. . . But you must not look at me with these mean eyes, Ulenspiegl. Last night she told me that a handsome lord, dressed in grey and named Hilbert, wanted to marry me and would come here to show himself to me. I told her I wanted no husband, either handsome or ugly. By her maternal authority, she forced me to stay up to await him, for she does not lose her wits where her love affairs are concerned. We were half undressed, ready to go to bed; I was asleep on the chair over there. When they came in I did not wake up. Suddenly I felt someone embrace me and kiss me on the neck. And there, by the light of the shining moon, I saw a face clear as the crests of the sea-waves in July when it's about to thunder, and I heard someone say: "I am Hilbert, your husband; be mine, and I will make you rich." The face of the one who spoke had a fishy smell. I pushed him away from me; he tried to take me by violence, but I had the strength of ten men like him. Just the same he tore my chemise, scratched my face, and kept on saying: "Be mine, I will make you rich." "Yes," I said, "like my mother, from whom you have taken her last liard." Then he redoubled his violence, but he could do nothing against me. As he was uglier than a corpse I dug my nails in his eyes so deeply that he screamed in pain and I managed to escape and go up to Soetkin.'

Katheline continued to say:

'Nele's wicked. Why did you leave so quickly, Hanske, my dear?'

'Where were you, bad mother,' said Soetkin, 'while they tried to dishonour your child?'

'Nele's wicked,' said Katheline. 'I was close to my black lord when the grey devil came with bleeding face and said: "Let's go from here, lad; this is an evil house; the men would beat us to death and the women have knives at their finger-tips." Then they ran to their horses and disappeared in the mist. Nele's wicked!'

81   NEXT MORNING, as they were drinking hot milk, Soetkin said to Katheline: 'You see that grief is driving me from this world; do you want to send me fleeing from it by your damned witcheries?'

But Katheline continued to say:

'Nele's wicked. Come back, Hanske, my dear.'

The following Wednesday, the two devils returned together. Since Saturday Nele had been sleeping at the house of the widow Van den Houte, having said that she could not continue staying with Katheline because of the presence of the young fellow, Ulenspiegl.

Katheline received her black lord and his friend in the *keet*—the washhouse and bakery adjoining the main dwelling. And they feasted and revelled with the old wine and smoked oxtongue that always awaited them. The black devil said to Katheline:

'For an important work we have to do, we have need of a large sum of money. Give us as much as you can.'

As Katheline was unwilling to give them more than a florin, they threatened to kill her. But they called it quits for two carolus of gold and seven deniers.

'Come no more on Saturday,' she said to them, 'for Ulenspiegl knows the day and will await you, armed to strike you down. And I would die after you.'

'We will come next Tuesday,' they said.

On that day Ulenspiegl and Nele slept without fearing the devils, for they thought they would only come on Saturday.

Katheline arose and went to see if her friends were already in the *keet*. She was very impatient for, since she had seen Hanske again, the madness she suffered had greatly lessened; folk said she had love-folly now.

Not seeing them there, she was distressed. Then, when she heard the sea-eagle's cry coming from the direction of Sluys, she walked towards the cry. Going along in the field at the bottom of a dyke of faggots and turf, she heard on the other side of the dyke the two devils talking together. One said:

'I shall have half of it.'

The other answered:

'You shall have none of it; what's Katheline's is mine.'

Then they blasphemed furiously, discussing between them which one should have to himself the love and the wealth of both Katheline and Nele together. Transfixed with fear, not daring to speak or budge, Katheline soon heard them battling together, and then one of them saying:

'This is cold steel.' Then there was a croak and the fall of a heavy body.

Fearful, she walked straight to her cottage. At two o'clock in the morning she again heard the cry of the sea-eagle; this time in her garden. She went to open and saw her devil friend, alone, standing before the door. She asked him:

'What have you done with the other?'

'He will come no more,' he replied.

Then he embraced and caressed her. And he seemed colder than usual.

176

And Katheline's wits were well awakened. When he left, he demanded twenty florins, all that she had; she gave him seventeen. In the morning, curious, she went the length of the dyke; but she saw nothing save a spot as large as a man's coffin, where there was blood upon the turf that was softer under-foot. But in the evening the rain washed away the blood.

The following Wednesday she again heard in her garden the cry of the sea-eagle.

82 EACH TIME that he had need of money to pay their share of the expenses, Ulenspiegl would go at night and lift the stone that covered the hole beside the well, and take out a carolus. One evening the three women were spinning; Ulenspiegl was carving with a knife a box that the bailiff had ordered from him and on which he was skilfully cutting out a fine hunt with a pack of Hainaut dogs; Cretan mastiffs, very ferocious beasts; Brabant dogs, going in pairs, called ear-eaters; and other dogs, straight, bandy, skinny, fat, and greyhounds.

Katheline being present, Nele asked Soetkin if she had hidden her treasure well. Trustingly the widow replied that it could not be better than by the wall of the well.

Towards midnight of Thursday Soetkin was awakened by Bibulus Schnouffius, who bayed shrilly, but not for long. Judging that it was a false alarm, she fell asleep again.

Friday morning at daybreak, Soetkin and Ulenspiegl, having arisen, saw no sign of Katheline in the kitchen as was usual; nor was the fire lit or the milk heating on the hearth. They were astonished and looked out into the garden to see if by chance she were there. There they saw her, despite a drizzling rain, dishevelled, in her night-gown, soaked and chilled, but not daring to enter.

Ulenspiegl went out to her and said:

'What are you doing there, half-naked, when it's raining?'

'Ah,' she said, 'yes, yes, a great portent!'

And she showed him the dog with its throat cut, lying stiff.

Ulenspiegl immediately thought of the treasure. He ran to the spot. The hole was empty and the earth was all strewn about.

Jumping at Katheline and beating her, he cried:

'Where are the carolus?'

'Yes, yes, a great portent!' replied Katheline.

Nele, defending her mother, cried:

177

'Mercy and pity, Ulenspiegl!'

He ceased striking her. Soetkin then came out and wanted to know what was happening.

Ulenspiegl showed her the slain dog and the empty treasure-hole. Soetkin paled and said:

'You smite me heavily, Lord God. My poor feet!'

And this she said because of the pain she had gone through and the torture vainly suffered for the golden carolus. Nele, seeing Soetkin so gentle, despaired and wept. Katheline, waving a bit of parchment, said:

'Yes, a great portent. Last night he came, good and lovely. He no longer had on his face the pale glow that caused me so much fear. He spoke to me with a great tenderness. I was ravished, my heart melted away. He said to me: "I am rich now and will soon bring you a thousand golden florins." "I am more pleased for you than for myself, Hanske, my dear." "But is there no other person here," he asked, "that you love and that I might enrich?" "No," I answered, "those who are here have no need of you." "You are proud," said he; "Soetkin and Ulenspiegl are rich then?" "They live off their neighbours' help," I replied. "In spite of the confiscation?" said he. To that I answered that you had suffered torture rather than let your wealth be taken. "I knew that," said he. And he began, laughing quietly and very low, to jeer at the bailiff and the sheriffs for not having been able to make you confess. I also laughed as he did. "They wouldn't have been so silly," he said, "as to hide their treasure in the house?" I laughed. "Nor in the cellar of it?" "Nay, nay," said I. "Nor in the garden?" I made no answer. "Ah," said he, "that would be a great imprudence." "A little one," said I, "for neither the water nor its wall will ever speak." And he continued laughing.

'Last night he left earlier than usual, after having given me a powder by which I would be enabled to go to the finest Witches' Sabbath. I saw him to the garden gate in my night-gown and I was all sleepy. I went, as he said, to the Sabbath, and I did not return until dawn, when I found myself here and saw the dog with its throat cut and the treasure-hole empty. It's a very heavy blow for me, who loved him so tenderly and gave him my soul. But you shall have all that I have and I'll work my hands and feet off to support you.'

'I am as the corn under the mill-stone. God and a devil-thief grind me at once,' said Soetkin.

'Thief! Speak not so!' retorted Katheline. 'He is a devil, a devil. And to prove it, I will show you the parchment he left in the courtyard. On it is written: "Never forget to serve me. In three times two weeks and

178

five days I will return you the treasure two-fold. Doubt not, else you die." And he will keep his word, I'm sure.'

'Poor mad one!' said Soetkin.

And that was her last reproach.

83 THE TWO WEEKS had passed three times and the five days likewise, but the devil-friend came not. Yet Katheline lived on without despairing. Soetkin no longer worked but sat eternally before the fire, bent and coughing. Nele gave her the best and most fragrant herbs, but there was no remedy for her. Ulenspiegl no longer left the cottage, fearing that Soetkin might die when he was not there.

It then came about that the widow could no longer eat or drink without vomiting. The surgeon-barber came to bleed her. After the bleeding, she was so weak that she could not leave her bench. Then finally, withered up with grief, she said one evening:

'Claes, my man! Tyl, my boy! Thanks, God, who takes me!'

And, sighing, she died.

Katheline not daring to keep watch by the corpse, Ulenspiegl and Nele did so together, and all night long prayed for the dead one.

At dawn a swallow entered by the open window.

Nele said:

'The bird of souls; it's a good omen. Soetkin is in heaven.'

The swallow flew three times around the room and left with a cry.

Then a second swallow entered, larger and blacker than the first. It flew about Ulenspiegl, and he said:

'Father and Mother, the ashes beat against my breast; I will do what you ask of me.'

And the second went off crying like the first. The day showed brighter. Ulenspiegl saw thousands of swallows skimming over the fields, and the sun arose.

And Soetkin was buried in Potters' Field.

84 AFTER SOETKIN'S DEATH, Ulenspiegl wandered about the kitchen, dreamy, mournful or angry, hearing nothing, taking what nourishment or drink was given to him, without choosing. And often he arose in the night. In vain did Nele, with her softest voice, exhort him to hope; vainly did Katheline tell him that she knew Soetkin was in paradise by the side of Claes. To everything Ulenspiegl answered:

'The ashes beat.'

And he was like a man out of his mind, and Nele wept, seeing him so.

Meanwhile the fishmonger lived in his house, alone like a parricide, and only dared to go out in the evening, for the men and women passing him by would boo him and call him murderer, and the little children fled before him, for they had been told that he was the executioner. He wandered alone and did not dare enter into any of the three taverns of Damme; for they pointed at him and, if he stood there but a minute, the other drinkers all left.

So it came about that the *baesen* did not wish him for a customer and, if he came, they closed the door in his face. Then the fishmonger would make a humble protest; the tavern-keepers would reply that it was their right and not their duty to sell.

Weary of this sort of treatment, the fishmonger went to drink at the *In't Roode Valck* (The Red Falcon), a little tavern far from the town, on the banks of the Sluys canal.

There they served him with drink; for they were hard-working folk who received all money with a welcome. But the *baes* of the *Roode Valck* never spoke to him, neither did the wife. They had two children and a dog. When the fishmonger tried to caress the children, they fled, and when he called the dog to him, it tried to bite him.

One evening Ulenspiegl stood by the threshold. Mathyssen, the cooper, seeing him so dreamy, said:

'You must work with your hands and forget the sorrowful blow.'

Ulenspiegl answered:

'The ashes of Claes beat against my breast.'

'Ah!' said Mathyssen. 'He leads a sadder life than you, the doleful fishmonger. No one speaks to him and everyone flees from him, so much so that he is forced to go to the poor beggars of the *Roode Valck* to drink his stein of *bruinbier* alone. It's a great punishment.'

'The ashes beat!' said Ulenspiegl again.

That same evening, while the bell of the church of Our Lady sounded the ninth hour, Ulenspiegl walked toward the *Roode Valck* and, seeing that the fishmonger was not there, wandered along under the trees that bordered the canal. The moon shone bright.

He saw the murderer coming.

As he passed before him, he could see him closely and hear him say, speaking aloud as men who live alone do:

'Where have they hidden the carolus?'

'Where the devil found them,' answered Ulenspiegl, striking him in the face with his fist.

'La!' said the fishmonger, 'I know you, you are the son. Have pity

180

on me, I am old and without strength. That which I did was not done through hatred, but to serve His Majesty. I crave your pardon. I will give you back the furniture that I bought, you won't have to pay me a sou. Isn't that enough? I bought them for seven golden florins. You shall have them all and a half florin besides, for I am not rich, you must not think I am.'

And he tried to go on his knees before him.

Ulenspiegl, seeing him so ugly, so trembling, and so cowardly, threw him into the canal.

And off he went.

85 THE FAT OF the victims smoked on the stakes. Ulenspiegl, thinking of Claes and Soetkin, wept alone. He went one evening to find Katheline to ask her for a remedy and vengeance.

She was alone with Nele, sewing beside the lamp. At the sound he made in coming in, Katheline lifted her head heavily like a woman awakened from a deep sleep.

He said to her:

'The ashes of Claes beat against my breast. I want to save the land of Flanders. I have asked the great God of Heaven and Earth, but he has made me no answer.'

Katheline said:

'The great God could not hear you; for you must first speak to the spirits of the elemental world, which having both celestial and terrestrial natures, receive the complaints of poor men and transmit them to the angels, who afterwards bear them to the throne.'

'Help me,' he said, 'with my project; I shall repay you in blood, if necessary.'

Katheline answered:

'I will help you, if a girl who loves you wishes to take you with her to the Sabbath of the Spirits of Spring, the re-awakening of the sap.'

'I will take him,' said Nele.

Katheline poured a grey mixture into a crystal tankard which she gave both of them to drink; with this mixture she rubbed their temples, nostrils, the palms of their hands, and their wrists, made them swallow a pinch of white powder and told them to look at each other, so that their souls would be as one.

Ulenspiegl looked at Nele, and the soft eyes of the young girl lit a great fire within him; then, because of the mixture, he felt as though a thousand crabs were nipping him.

Then they undressed, and they were very lovely thus lit by the lamp,

182

he in his proud strength, she in her sweet grace; but they could not see each other, for they were already as though asleep. Then Katheline placed the arm of Ulenspiegl around Nele's neck and, taking his hand, placed it on the heart of the young girl.

And so they stayed naked, the one lying by the other.

It seemed to both of them that their bodies, in touching, made a soft fire like the sun in the month of roses.

They arose, as they told later on, climbed on the window sill, and from there went off into space, and felt the air bearing them, as the sea bears ships.

Then they saw nothing more, neither of the earth where slept poor men, nor of the sky where lately their feet had rolled the clouds. And they set foot upon Sirius, the cold star. Then from there they were cast down upon the Pole.

There they saw, not without fear, a new giant, the giant Winter, with wild hair, seated on bergs against a wall of ice. In pools of water bears and seals moved about him, a noisy troop. With a hoarse voice, he called hail, snow, the cold blasts, the grey clouds, the red and foul-smelling fogs, and the winds, among which blows strongest the biting North wind, and all of them came at once in that deadly place.

Smiling at these disasters, the giant lay on flowers that his hand had withered, on leaves that his breath had dried. Then, leaning over and scratching the earth with his nails and biting it with his teeth, he made a hole to seek out the heart of the earth, devour it and also place the black charcoal where there were shady forests, straw where there was wheat, sand instead of the fruitful earth. But, the heart of the earth being of fire, he did not dare touch it and recoiled affrighted.

He was enthroned as a king, draining his cup of oil, in the midst of all his bears and his seals, and the skeletons of all those whom he had killed on sea, on land, and in the cottages of poor folk. He listened joyfully to the growling of the bears, the barking of the seals, the rattling of the bones of skeletons of men and animals under the claws of vultures and ravens, seeking out a last morsel of flesh, and the noise of icebergs being pushed against each other by the gloomy water.

And the voice of the giant was like the roaring of hurricanes, the noise of winter tempests, and the wind soughing in the chimneys.

'I am cold and afraid,' said Ulenspiegl.

'He can do nothing against the spirits,' answered Nele.

Suddenly there was a great stir among the animals; the seals hastily re-entered the water; the bears, lowering their ears with fright, growled plaintively; and the ravens, croaking with anguish, flew up and were lost in the clouds.

183

And now Nele and Ulenspiegl heard the dull sounds of a battering ram against the icy walls which served as a support to the giant Winter. And the wall broke and quivered under the blows of the ram.

But the giant Winter heard nothing and he howled and shouted joyfully, filling and emptying his cup of oil; and he sought out the heart of the earth, to freeze it, but did not dare touch it.

Meanwhile the blows resounded louder and the wall cracked more, and a rain of broken icicles ceaselessly fell about him.

And the bears continued to growl plaintively and the seals complained in the gloomy waters.

The wall fell and there was daybreak in the sky; a man descended, naked and lovely, supporting himself with one hand on a golden axe. And this man was Lucifer, the King of Spring.

When the giant saw him, he threw away his cup of oil and begged not to be killed.

And with the warm breath of the King of Spring, the giant Winter lost all his strength. The King then took chains of diamonds, bound him and attached him to the Pole.

Then, stopping, he called out—but tenderly and lovingly—and from the skies came down a fair woman, naked and beautiful. Placing herself beside the King, she said to him:

'You are my conqueror, strong man.'

He replied:

'If you are hungry, eat; if you are thirsty, drink; if you are afraid, come close to me. I am your male.'

'I am not,' she said, 'hungry or thirsty, save for you.'

The King cried aloud again, seven times, terribly. And there was a great noise of thunder and lightning and behind him was formed a dais of suns and stars. And they sat upon the thrones.

Then the King and his wife, without their noble countenances moving or without making any gesture contrary to their strength or calm majesty, cried out.

At these cries there was an undulating movement in the earth, the hard stone, and the icebergs. And Nele and Ulenspiegl heard a noise such as gigantic birds might make in trying to break the shells of enormous eggs with their beaks.

And in this great movement of the soil, rising and falling, like the waves of the sea, were shapes like those of eggs.

Suddenly, from everywhere, trees came forth with their dry branches entwined, while their trunks moved and swayed like drunken men. Then they parted, leaving between them a vast empty space. From the agitated soil came forth the genii of the earth; from the depths of

184

the forest, the spirits of the woods; from the neighbouring sea, the genii of the water.

Ulenspiegl and Nele saw there the dwarf guardians of treasures— hunchbacked, splay-footed, hairy, ugly and grimacing; princes of stones; men of the woods living like trees and bearing, in place of mouth and stomach, a bunch of roots on the lower part of their faces, through which they sucked in their nourishment from the breast of the earth; the emperors of mines, who do not know how to speak, having neither heart nor guts and moving like brilliant automatons. There were dwarfs of flesh and blood, having lizards' tails and paddocks' heads with lanterns on them; at night these dwarfs leap on the shoulders of drunken pedestrians or frightened travellers, then, leaping down again and shaking their lanterns, lead into bogs and holes the poor wretches who think the lanterns are the candles shining from the windows of their homes.

There, also, were flower-maidens, flowers of strength and feminine health, naked and not at all blushing, proud of their beauty, and having only their hair for mantle.

Their eyes shone moistly like mother of pearl in water; the flesh of their bodies was firm, white and gilded by the light; from their red half-opened mouths came a breath more fragrant than jasmine.

These are they who wander in the evening in parks and gardens, or in the depths of woods by the shady lanes, amorous and seeking to enjoy some man's soul. As soon as any young boy and girl pass before them, they try to kill the girl, but being unable to do so, they breathe into the dear one's ear, she still withholding herself, a desire for love so that she will finally give herself to the lover; for then the flower-maiden has half of the kisses.

Ulenspiegl and Nele also saw, descending from the highest heavens, the protecting spirits of the stars, the genii of wind, breezes and rain, winged young men who fecundate the earth.

Then from all points of the heavens appeared the birds of souls, the dear swallows. When they were come, the light seemed more vibrant. Flower-maidens, princes of stones, emperors of mines, men of the woods, spirits of the water, of fire and of earth, cried out together: 'Light! Sap! Glory to the King of Spring!'

Although the noise of their unanimous clamour was more powerful than the furious sea, than the pealing thunder and the unchained tempest, it sounded like grave music to the ears of Nele and Ulenspiegl, who, motionless and dumb, shrank back behind the rugged trunk of an oak-tree.

But they were more frightened yet when the spirits, by thousands,

185

took their places on seats that were enormous spiders, frogs with elephants' trunks, interlaced serpents, crocodiles standing on their tails and holding a group of spirits in their jaws, serpents carrying more than thirty male and female dwarfs on their undulating bodies, and well over a hundred thousand insects larger than Goliaths, armed with swords, with lances, serrated scythes, forks with seven prongs and all other kinds of murderous weapons. They fought together with a great din, the strong eating the weak, battening on them and showing thus that Death is made of Life and that Life is made of Death.

And there came out of all this crowd of spirits, swarming, dense, confused, a noise like to that of a low thunder and a hundred weavers' looms, fullers and locksmiths all working together.

Suddenly appeared the Spirits of the Sap, short, thick-set, having loins as big as the great tun of Heidelberg, thighs as big as hogsheads of wine, and muscles so strangely strong and powerful that one would have said that their bodies were made of great and small eggs joined one to another, and covered with a red greasy skin, glowing like their sparse beards and their red hair; and they carried large tankards filled with a strange liquor.

When the spirits saw them come, a great tremor of joy ran through them; the trees and plants began to shake and the earth cracked open to drink.

The Spirits of the Sap poured out their wine; all things thereupon began to bud, grow green, and flower; the grass was full of insects murmuring and the sky filled with birds and butterflies; the spirits continued to pour and those who were below them received the wine as best they could; the flower-maidens opened wide their mouths or leaped upon the red cup-bearers, kissing them to have more; some joined their hands together in sign of prayer; others, in ecstasy, let it rain over them; but all, avid or thirsty, flying, standing, running or motionless, sought to have the wine, and became more intensely alive with each drop they could get. And there were no elders there; but all, ugly or fair, were full of vernal strength and quick youth.

And they laughed, cried out, sang, as they pursued each other on the trees like the squirrels, in the air like the birds, each male seeking his female and falling to the holy work of nature under God's sky.

And the Spirits of the Sap carried a great cup of their wine to the King and the Queen. And the King and the Queen drank of it and embraced each other.

Then the King, holding the Queen close to him, cast upon the trees, the flowers, the spirits, the dregs of his cup, and cried out:

'Glory to Life! Glory to the Free Air! Glory to Strength!'

186

And they all cried out:

'Glory to Nature! Glory to Strength!'

And Ulenspiegl took Nele in his arms. So enlaced, a dance began; a swirling dance like the leaves brought together by a whirlwind, where all was in movement—trees, plants, insects, butterflies, heaven and earth, King and Queen, flower-maidens, emperors of mines, water-spirits, hunchback dwarfs, princes and stones, men of the woods, lantern-bearers, protecting spirits of the stars, and the hundred thousand horrific insects, intermingling their lances, their serrated scythes, their seven-pronged forks; a frenzied dance that swayed about in space and quite filled it, a dance in which the sun, the moon, the planets, the stars, the wind, and the clouds all took part.

And the oak-tree, to which Ulenspiegl and Nele were holding on, rolled into the vortex, and Ulenspiegl said to Nele:

'Dear one, we are about to die.'

A spirit heard them and saw that they were mortal:

'Humans!' he screamed. 'There are humans in the place!'

And he tore them from the tree and threw them into the crowd.

And Ulenspiegl and Nele fell limply on the backs of the spirits, who sent them bouncing from one back to another, saying:

'Greetings, humans! Welcome, earth-worms! Who wants the little boy or the little girl? They have come to visit us, the poor things!'

And Ulenspiegl and Nele, bouncing from one back to another, cried: 'Pardon!'

But the spirits heard them not, and they both continued to fly through the air, feet up, heads down, turning like feathers in a winter wind; and the spirits said:

'Glory to the little man and the little woman who dance as we do!'

The flower-maidens, wishing to separate Nele from Ulenspiegl, struck at her and would have killed her if the King of Spring, stopping the dance with a sign, had not called out:

'Bring these two lice before me!'

And they were separated one from the other; and each flower-maiden, in trying to tear Ulenspiegl away from her rivals, said:

'Tyl, would you not die for me?'

'I will do so soon,' answered Ulenspiegl.

And the dwarf spirits of the woods, who were carrying Nele, said:

'Why are you not as we are, so that we might take you?'

Nele answered: 'Have patience.'

So they were brought before the throne of the King; and they trembled sorely, when they saw his golden axe and his iron crown.

And he said to them:

187

'What have you come to do here, poor things?'

They made no answer.

'I know you, witch's bud,' added the King, 'and you also, offspring of the charcoal-burner. But having, by the strength of witchcraft, penetrated this laboratory of Nature, why have you now your beaks closed, like capons stuffed with crumbs?'

Nele trembled as she looked on the terrible devil; but Ulenspiegl, recovering his manly self-possession, answered:

'The ashes of Claes beat upon my heart, Divine Highness. Death goes through Flanders mowing down, in the name of the Pope, the strongest men and the dearest women; the privileges of the country are broken, its charters wiped out; famine gnaws at her; the weavers and the drapers abandon her to go to foreign parts, seeking freedom to work. She will soon die if someone does not help her. Your Highnesses, I am but a poor little fellow, born into the world like anyone else, having lived as I could, imperfect, limited, ignorant, not virtuous, and neither chaste nor worthy of any human or divine mercy. Soetkin died, following her torture and as a result of her grief, but Claes burned in a terrible fire, and I would avenge them, and did so once; I would also like to see the poor soil, where their bones are laid, more happy; and I asked God for the death of the persecutors, but he heard me not. Weary of making complaint, I invoked you by the power of a spell of Katheline, and we have come to kneel at your feet, I and my trembling companion, to ask you, Divine Highnesses, to save this poor land.'

The Emperor and his spouse answered together:

'By war and by fire,
By death and by sword,
Seek the Seven.

In death and in blood,
In ruins and in tears,
Find the Seven.

Ugly, cruel, mean, deformed,
Real plagues for this poor earth,
Burn the Seven.

Await, and hear, and see,
Say, wretch, are you not glad?
Find the Seven.'

And all the spirits sang together:

> 'In death and in blood,
> In ruins and in tears,
> Find the Seven.

> Await, and hear, and see,
> Say, wretch, are you not glad?
> Find the Seven.'

'But, Highnesses,' said Ulenspiegl, 'and you, spirits, I understand naught of your language. You are mocking me, no doubt.'

But, without listening to him, they said:

> 'When the North
> Shall kiss the West,
> Then shall ruin end,
> Find the Seven,
> The Girdle find!'

And this with such a great ensemble and such a fearful strength of sonority that the earth trembled and the heavens shook. And the birds whistling, the owls hooting, the sparrows twittering with fear, and the sea-eagles complaining, all fluttered about in dismay. And the beasts of the earth—lions, serpents, bears, stags, bucks, wolves, dogs and cats —roared, hissed, growled, howled, barked and mewed terribly.

And the spirits sang:

> 'Await, and hear, and see,
> Love the Seven
> The Girdle love.'

And the cocks crowed, and all the spirits vanished, save one mean emperor of mines, who, taking Ulenspiegl and Nele each by an arm, brutally hurled them into the void.

They found themselves lying close to one another as though for sleep, and they shivered in the cool morning breeze.

And Ulenspiegl looked upon the sweet body of Nele, made golden by the rising sun.

Book Two

ON THAT MORNING, which was in September, Ulenspiegl took
his staff, three florins that Katheline gave him, a piece of pig's
liver, and a slice of bread, and started out from Damme towards
Antwerp, seeking the Seven. Nele slept. As he walked along, he was
followed by a dog that came sniffing after him because of the liver; it
jumped up about his legs. Ulenspiegl tried to shoo it away but, seeing
that it persisted in following him, he spoke to it as follows:

'Puppy, my dear, you are ill-advised to leave the home where good
stews, delicious scraps and bones full of marrow await you, to follow
along the highway of adventure a vagabond who will not always have
even roots to feed you with. Believe me, imprudent little dog, and
return to your *baes*. Avoid the rains, snows, hails, drizzles, fogs, hoar-
frosts and other lean soups that fall on vagabond backs. Stay by the
chimney-corner, warming yourself, rolled up in a ball, before the jolly
fire; leave me to walk in the mud, the dust, the cold, the heat, cooked
today, congealed tomorrow, stuffed on Friday and famished on Sunday. You would be doing a sensible thing in thinking where you're
going, inexperienced little dog.'

The animal did not seem to hear Ulenspiegl. Wagging its tail and
jumping as high as it could, it barked hungrily. Ulenspiegl imagined
it was a friendly bark, for he had no thought of the liver he was carrying in his pouch.

He walked on, the dog followed. Having thus covered a league, they
came to a wagon standing by the side of the road; to it was harnessed
a donkey that stood with a lowered head. On the roadside, between two
clumps of thistles, there sat a fat man holding in one hand a knuckle-
bone of mutton, at which he gnawed, and in the other a flask whose
juice he sucked in. When he was not either eating or drinking, he was
moaning and weeping.

Ulenspiegl having stopped, the dog also stopped. Scenting the mutton and the liver, he mounted upon the bank. There, sitting on his haunches by the man, he pawed at the man's doublet that he might have a part of the feast. But the man, shoving him away with his elbow and holding high in the air his mutton-bone, moaned miserably. The dog imitated him out of covetousness. The donkey, angry at being harnessed to the wagon and so unable to get at the thistles, began to bray.

'What do you want, Jan?' the man asked the donkey.

'Nothing,' answered Ulenspiegl, 'save that it would like to lunch off these thistles that flower at your sides as they do on the rood-screen of Tessenderloo, beside and above our Lord Christ. That dog, also, wouldn't be at all annoyed to marry its jaws to the bone you hold in your hand. In the meantime I'm going to give it this piece of liver I have here.'

The liver having been eaten by the dog, the man looked at his bone, gnawed at it to get off any more meat that remained, then he gave it so stripped clean to the dog, who, holding it with its forepaws, began to crunch it on the grass.

Then the man looked at Ulenspiegl, who recognized him as Lamme Goedzak of Damme.

'Lamme,' he said, 'what are you doing here, drinking, eating and snivelling? What trooper unceremoniously rubbed down your ears?'

'La, my wife!' said Lamme.

He was about to empty his flask of wine, when Ulenspiegl placed a hands on his arm.

'Don't drink so,' said he, 'for drinking precipitately is of no profit save to the kidneys. It were better that it profited someone who has no bottle.'

'You speak well,' answered Lamme, 'but could you drink better?'

And he handed him the flask.

Ulenspiegl took it, raised his arm, then returned the flask.

'Call me a Spaniard,' said he, 'if there's enough left in it to intoxicate a sparrow.'

Lamme looked at the flask and, without ceasing to moan, groped in his bag and brought out another flask and another piece of sausage which he set about cutting in slices and munching sadly.

'Do you eat continually, Lamme?' asked Ulenspiegl.

'Often, my boy,' answered Lamme, 'but only to drive away my sad thoughts. Where are you, wife?' he said, drying a tear.

And he cut six slices of sausage.

'Lamme,' said Ulenspiegl, 'don't eat with so much haste and so little pity for a poor pilgrim.'

194

Weeping, Lamme handed him four slices, and Ulenspiegl, in eating them, was touched by their good flavour.

But Lamme, still weeping and eating, said:

'My wife, my good wife! How gentle she was and how well-formed was her body; light as a butterfly, quick as lightning, singing like a lark! Yet she loved too well to deck herself out in finery. La! they suited her so well. But flowers also are richly garbed. If you had seen

her, my boy, her little hands so light at caressing, you would never have allowed her to touch a frying-pan or a pot. The kitchen fire would have darkened her complexion that was as clear as daylight. And what eyes! I melted away with tenderness merely in looking at them. (Take a swallow of wine, I'll drink after you.) Ah, if only she isn't dead! Tyl, I kept all the work of the house for myself, so as to spare her the least task; I swept the house, I made the nuptial bed whereon she lay in the evening weary with comfort; I washed the dishes, and also the linen which I ironed myself. (Eat, Tyl, this sausage comes from Ghent.) Often, having gone out walking, she

returned to dinner too late, but it was such a great joy for me to see her that I did not dare chide her, very happy when at night she did not turn her back on me, pouting. I have lost everything. (Drink this wine; it is Brussels-made in the Burgundy manner.)'

'Why did she leave you?' asked Ulenspiegl.

'Do I know?' retorted Lamme Goedzak. 'Where are the days when, going to her house, in the hope of wedding her, she ran from me in fear and in love? If her arms were bare, lovely white and round arms, and she saw that I looked upon them, she suddenly let down her sleeves. At other times, she gave way to my caresses and I could kiss her lovely eyes which she closed, and her large and firm neck; then she would quiver, uttering little cries and, throwing her head back, would hit me on the nose with it. And laughed when I cried: "Ouch!" and I beat her amorously and there was nothing between us but games and laughter. (Tyl, is there any wine left in the flask?)'

'Yes,' answered Ulenspiegl.

Lamme drank, and continued his discourse:

'At other times, more amorous, she would throw her two arms about my neck and say to me: "You are handsome!" and she would kiss me madly a hundred times on the cheek and on the brow, but never on the mouth, and when I asked her the cause of this great reserve in that otherwise great liberty, she would run and take, from a tankard sitting on the cupboard, a baby doll dressed in silk and pearls and would say as she dandled and cradled it: "I do not wish this." No doubt her mother, to keep her virtuous, had told her that children were made by the mouth. Ah, sweet moments! Tender caresses! (Tyl, see if you cannot find a little ham in that bag?)'

'A half of one,' answered Ulenspiegl, giving it to Lamme, who ate it all.

Ulenspiegl, watching him do it, said:

'That little ham does great good to my stomach.'

'To mine also,' said Lamme, picking his teeth with his nails. 'But I shall never see my dear again, she has flown from Damme! Would you like to search for her with me in my wagon?'

'I would,' replied Ulenspiegl.

'But,' said Lamme, 'is there nothing left in the flask?'

'Nothing,' answered Ulenspiegl.

And they both got into the wagon that was drawn by the donkey, which gave a melancholy bray as a departing signal.

As for the dog, it had gone, well filled, without a sound.

2 As THE WAGON rolled along on the dyke, between a pond and a canal, Ulenspiegl, very pensive, stroked the ashes of Claes on his breast. He asked himself if the vision he had seen were false or true, if these spirits had mocked him or if they had, by riddles, told him what was really necessary to find, to make the land of his fathers happy.

Seeking vainly the meaning of it all, he could not find what the Seven or the Girdle signified.

Thinking of the dead Emperor, of the living King, of the Vice-Regent, of the Pope of Rome, of the Grand Inquisitor, of the General of the Jesuits, he found there six great executioners of the country that he would have liked to burn on the spot. But he thought it could not be they, for they were too easy to burn, so the Seven must be in some other place.

And he kept saying over in his mind:

'When the North
Shall kiss the West,

> Then shall ruin end,
> Love the Seven,
> The Girdle love.'

'La!' he said to himself. 'In death, blood and tears, find Seven, burn
Seven, love Seven! My poor mind is all confused, for who then burns
that which he loves?'

The wagon, having already eaten up much of the highway, they
heard a noise of footsteps on the sand and a voice that sang:

> 'You who pass by, say, have you seen
> The wild young lover I have lost?
> All aimless goes he on his way;
> Say, have you seen?
>
> Even as the eagle takes a lamb
> He took my heart all unawares.
> He's now a man though beardless yet.
> Say, have you seen?
>
> Oh, if you find him say that Nele
> Is weary searching everywhere.
> Beloved Tyl, where are you then?
> Say, have you seen?
>
> Knows he how languishes the dove
> When she has lost her only mate?
> And so 'tis with a faithful heart.
> Say, have you seen?

Ulenspiegl smote the stomach of Lamme and said to him:
'Hold your breath, great pot-belly.'
'La,' answered Lamme, 'that is very hard for a fat man like me.'
But Ulenspiegl, without listening to him, hid himself behind the
canvas of the wagon and, imitating the voice of an asthmatic old man
singing after a drink, he sang:

> 'Your wild young lover I have seen
> Within a rickety, tottering cart,
> Beside a gluttonous great fat man
> I saw him well.'

'Tyl,' said Lamme, 'you have a nasty tongue this morning.'
Ulenspiegl, without listening to him, stuck his head through a hole
in the canvas, and said:

197

'Nele, don't you recognize me?'

She, seized with fright, weeping and laughing at the same time, so that her cheeks were wet, said:

'I see you, traitorous villain!'

'Nele,' said Ulenspiegl, 'if you want to beat me I have a stick here. It is heavy enough to hurt and knotty enough to leave a mark.'

'Tyl,' said Nele, 'are you going toward the Seven?'

'Yes,' answered Ulenspiegl.

Nele carried a bag which seemed ready to burst, so well stuffed it was.

'Tyl,' she said, handing it to him, 'I thought that it was unhealthy for a man to go travelling without taking with him a good fat goose, a ham and Ghent sausages. And you must eat this in memory of me.'

As Ulenspiegl looked at Nele and had no thought at all of taking the bag, Lamme, pushing his head through another hole in the canvas, said:

'Provident damsel, if he does not accept, it is through forgetfulness; but hand me that ham, give me that goose, pass me those sausages; I will keep them for him.'

'Whose is that goodly phiz?' said Nele.

'It belongs,' answered Ulenspiegl, 'to a victim of marriage who, devoured by sorrow, would dry up like an apple in an oven, if he did not recuperate his strength with incessant nourishment.'

'That's right, my boy,' answered Lamme, with a sigh.

The sun shining down fell hotly on Nele's head. She covered it with her apron. Wishing to be alone with her, Ulenspiegl said to Lamme:

'Do you see that woman wandering there in the fields?'

'I see her,' said Lamme.

'Do you recognize her?'

'La!' said Lamme. 'Could that be my wife? She is not dressed like a townswoman.'

'Do you still doubt, blind mole?' said Ulenspiegl.

'If it be not she?' said Lamme.

'You shall lose nothing, for there on the left toward the north is a *kaberdoesje* where you will find good *bruinbier*. We shall come and join you. And here is the ham to salt your natural thirst.'

Lamme, jumping from the wagon, ran with great steps toward the woman in the fields.

Ulenspiegl said to Nele:

'Why do you not come up beside me?'

Then, helping her up on the wagon, he seated her beside him, took the apron from her head and the mantle from her shoulder; then giving her a hundred kisses, he said:

198

'Where were you going, beloved?'

She made no reply but seemed ravished with ecstasy. And Ulenspiegl, as transported as she was, said to her:

'Here you are, then! The roses that flower in the sweetbriar hedges are not so softly pink as your fresh skin. You are not a queen, but let me crown you with kisses. Dear arms, so soft, so pink, meant by love for kisses alone. Oh, beloved girl, shall not my rugged male hands crush and wither that shoulder? The fluttering butterfly settles on the crimson carnation, but can I, heavy lout, rest on your vivid whiteness without withering it? God's in His heaven, the King on his throne, and the sun triumphant on high; but am I God, King, or Light to be so close to you? Oh hair, softer than silken floss: Nele, I strike, I rend, I break in pieces! But be not afraid, my love. Your darling little foot! How comes it to be so white? Has it been bathed in milk?'

She wanted to rise up.

'What are you afraid of?' said Ulenspiegl to her. 'It is not the sun shining down on us that paints you all in gold. Don't lower your eyes. See what a lovely flame he has lighted in mine. Listen, beloved; hearken, dear; it is now the silent mid-day hour; the labourer is home before his soup, shall we not feed on love? Why have I not a thousand years to count one by one at your knees, like pearls from the Indies?'

'Golden tongue!' said she.

And Master Sun shone through the white canvas of the wagon, and a lark sang up over the clover, and Nele laid her head on Ulenspiegl's shoulder.

3 MEANWHILE, Lamme came back sweating great drops and blowing like a dolphin. 'La,' said he, 'I was born under an unlucky star. After having to run hard to get up to that woman, who was not mine and who was old—I saw from her face that she was at least forty-five, and from her coif that she had never been married—she asked me tartly what I was doing with my pot-belly in the clover.'

' "I am looking for my wife who has left me," I answered gently, "and thinking you were she, I ran toward you."

'At these words, the old maid said to me that all I had to do was to go back where I came from and if my wife had left me she had done well, seeing that all men were thieves, scoundrels, heretics, disloyal, poisoners, wronging maids despite their maturity, and that in any case she would set her dog on me, if I did not pack up and get out quicker than that.

'And that was what I did, not without fear, for I saw a great mastiff

199

crouching and growling at her feet. When I got over the boundary of her field, I sat down and, to restore myself, I bit into your piece of ham. I was sitting then between two pieces of clover, when suddenly I heard a noise behind me and, turning around, I saw the old maid's great mastiff, no longer menacing, but wagging his tail with gentleness and appetite. He wanted my ham. I gave him several thin pieces, when his mistress appeared, crying:

'"Snap that man! Snap your teeth in him, son!"'

'And off I ran with the great mastiff at my heels; he bit a piece of my leg through my trousers. But, becoming angry because of the pain, I turned around and handed him such a whack on his front paws with my stick that I broke at least one of them. He fell down crying, in his dog language, "Mercy!" which I granted him. In the meantime his mistress threw clods at me for want of stones, and I continued running.

'La! is it not cruel and unjust that because an old maid has not enough beauty to find a husband she should avenge herself on poor innocents like me?

'Nevertheless I went off all melancholy to the *kaberdoesje* that you told me of, hoping to find there the *bruinbier* of consolation. But I was wrong, for as I went in, I saw a man and a woman fighting. I asked them if they would kindly interrupt their battle to give me a pot of *bruinbier,* were it a quart or six; but the woman, a real *stokfisch,* answered me furiously that if I did not get out quicker than that, she would make me swallow the clog with which she was banging her husband's head. And here I am, my friend, very sweaty and very weary; have you nothing to eat?'

'Yes,' said Ulenspiegl.

'At last!' said Lamme.

4 So REUNITED, they went on their way together. The donkey, with lowered ears, pulled the cart. 'Lamme,' said Ulenspiegl, 'here we are four good companions: the ass, beast of the good God, feeding by chance on the thistles in the fields; you, good potbelly, seeking her who is fled from you; Nele, gentle, beloved, with a tender heart, finding the unworthy, I mean myself, the fourth.

'Now then, children, courage! The leaves are yellowing and the sky is more brilliant. Soon Master Sun shall set in autumnal mists, winter shall come, image of death, covering with snowy winding-sheets those who sleep under our feet, and I shall march on for the happiness of the land of my fathers. Poor dead ones; Soetkin, who died of grief; Claes, who died at the stake; oak of goodness and ivy of love; I, your offspring, suffer greatly and shall avenge you, beloved ashes that beat against my breast.'

Lamme said:

'You must not weep for those who died for justice's sake.'

But Ulenspiegl remained pensive; suddenly he said:

'This hour, Nele, is that of farewells; for a long time—and maybe never—I shall not see your sweet face.'

Nele looked at him with her eyes shining like bright stars:

'Why do you not leave this cart,' said she, 'and come with me into the forest, where you will find choice nourishment, for I know the herbs and how to call birds?'

'Damsel,' said Lamme, 'it's wrong of you to try to stop Ulenspiegl on his way to seek the Seven and help me find my wife.'

'Not yet,' said Nele; and she wept and smiled tenderly through her tears at her friend Ulenspiegl.

Seeing this, Ulenspiegl said to Lamme:

'You have time enough to find your wife, when you want to find a new sorrow.'

'Tyl,' said Lamme, 'are you going to leave me alone in this way in my cart for that damsel? You make no answer to me and think only of the forest where the Seven are not, nor my wife either. Let us rather seek them on this stony road whereon the carts roll along so well.'

'Lamme,' said Ulenspiegl, 'you have a full satchel in the cart, therefore you'll not die of hunger, if you go without me from here to *Koelkerke*, where I shall rejoin you. You must be alone, for there you shall know towards which cardinal point you must go to find your wife. Listen and attend. You will go with your cart three leagues from here to *Koelkerke*, the Cool Church as it is called, because it is blown upon by the four winds at once, like many others. On the steeple is a vane, shaped like a cock, turning to all the winds on its rusty axis. It is the screeching of this vane that shows poor men who have lost their lovers the road they must follow to find them. But beforehand you must strike each wall seven times with a hazel wand. If the vane creaks when the wind blows from the north, it is toward that side that you must go, but prudently, for the north wind is the war wind; if from the south, go gaily; that's the wind of love; if from the east, run with great strides, that's gaiety and light; if from the west, go gently, that's the wind of rain and of tears. Go, Lamme, go to *Koelkerke* and await me.'

'I go,' said Lamme.

And he left in the cart.

As Lamme rumbled toward *Koelkerke*, the wind that was strong and warm chased, like a flock of sheep, the grey clouds wandering in the sky. The trees soughed like the waves of a swelling sea. Ulenspiegl and Nele had been alone in the forest for a long time. Ulenspiegl was hungry and Nele sought out the choice roots and found only kisses, which her love gave to her, and acorns.

Ulenspiegl, having set the snares, whistled to call the birds in order to cook those that came. A nightingale settled on a branch near Nele.

She did not touch it, wishing to let it sing; a warbler came, and she had pity on it because it was so prettily proud; then came a lark, but Nele said that it would do better to go and sing a hymn to nature in the highest heavens than to come carelessly and to struggle against the murderous point of a spit.

And she said truly, for in the meantime Ulenspiegl had lighted a fire and whittled a spit that only awaited its victims.

But the birds came no more, save a few nasty ravens that croaked very high above their heads.

And so Ulenspiegl had nothing to eat.

However, the time came for Nele to go back again to Katheline. And she walked away weeping, and Ulenspiegl watched her from afar.

But she came back again and threw her arms about his neck:

'I am going,' said she.

Then she walked several steps and came back again, saying once more: 'I am going.'

And this went on for twenty times or more.

Then she went away, and Ulenspiegl stayed alone. After a while, he took to the road to go and find Lamme.

When he came close to him he found him seated at the foot of the tower with a great pot of *bruinbier* between his legs and nibbling most sadly at a hazel wand.

'Ulenspiegl,' said he, 'I think that you sent me here so as to be alone with the maiden; I tapped as you told me to, seven times on each wall

202

with the hazel wand, and even though the wind blew like the very devil, the vane did not screech.'

'That's because they have had it oiled, no doubt,' answered Ulenspiegl.

Then they both went off toward the Duchy of Brabant.

5 KING PHILIP gloomily and endlessly worked among documents all day and sometimes into the night, and scribbled on papers and parchments. It was on these that he poured out the secrets of his hard heart. Loving no man in this life, knowing that no one loved him, wishing to carry alone, a dolorous Atlas, his immense empire, he bowed beneath the burden. He was phlegmatic and melancholy; this excess of work devoured his weak body. Detesting all happy faces, he had conceived a hatred for our country because of its gaiety; a hatred for our merchants because of their luxury and their wealth; a hatred for our nobles because of their free speech, their frankness of manner and the full-blooded dash of their brave joviality. He knew, for he had already been told, that long before the Cardinal Cusanus, towards the year 1380, had pointed out the abuses of the Church and had preached the necessity for reform; the revolt against the Pope and the Roman Church, manifesting itself in our country under different kinds of sects, was in all our heads, like boiling water in a closed kettle.

Obstinate mule, he thought that his will, like that of God, should weigh upon the whole world; he wanted our country, unaccustomed to obedience, to bow under the ancient yoke without obtaining any reform. He wanted his Holy Mother Church, Apostolic and Roman, one, indivisible, universal, without modifications or changes, for no other reason save that he wanted it. In this he acted like an unreasonable woman, tossing about at night on his bed as on a bed of thorns, ceaselessly tormented by his thoughts.

'Yes, Master Saint Philip, yes, Lord God, even if I have to make of the Netherlands a Potters' Field and throw therein all the inhabitants, they shall return to you, my Blessed Patron Saint, to you also, Madame Virgin Mary, and to you, Masters and Mistresses, Saints of Paradise.'

And he tried to do as he said and in this way was more Roman than the Pope and more Catholic than the Councils.

And Ulenspiegl and Lamme, and the peoples of Flanders and the Netherlands, full of anguish, thought they could see, afar in the Palace of the Escurial, that crowned spider with his long legs, claws open, spinning his web to envelop them and suck the purest of their blood.

Although the Papal Inquisition, under the reign of Charles, had by

the stake, the pit and the rope killed a hundred thousand Christians; although the wealth of the poor condemned ones had entered the coffers of the Emperor and King, like rain in a gutter, Philip judged that this was not enough; he imposed on the country new bishops and claimed to introduce the Spanish Inquisition.

And the heralds of the towns, to the sound of trumpets and drums, read everywhere edicts decreeing that for all heretics, men, women and children, there should be death by fire for those who would not abjure their error, and by rope for those who abjured it. Women and girls would be buried alive, and the executioner would dance on their bodies.

And the fire of resistance ran through the whole country.

6   THE FIFTH OF APRIL, before Easter, the Lords, Count Louis of Nassau, Culemburg, Brederode, the drinking Hercules, entered with three hundred other gentlemen in the Court of Brussels, where Madame, the Duchess of Parma, reigned as Vice-Regent. Going in ranks of four, they mounted in this way the great stairway of the palace.

Having come into the hall where Madame sat, they presented her with a request in which they asked her to seek to obtain from King Philip the abolition of the edicts touching upon religion and also the Spanish Inquisition, declaring that in our discontented country these could only result in troubles, ruin and general misery.

And this request was known as *The Compromise*.

Berlaymont, who was later so traitorous and cruel to the land of his fathers, was standing beside Her Highness and said to her, jeering at the poverty of several of the confederated nobles:

'Fear nothing, Madame. These are but beggars.'

Signifying, thus, that these nobles had ruined themselves in the serv-

205

ice of the king, or else in trying to match the luxury of the Spanish lords.

To turn to scorn the words of the Sieur of Berlaymont, the lords declared afterwards that they 'held it an honour to be esteemed and named beggars for the service of the king and the good of the country.'

They began to wear a golden medal about their necks; on one side it had the king's head, and on the other two hands clasped over a wallet with these words: 'Faithful to the king even unto the wallet.' They also wore on their hats and bonnets golden brooches in the form of beggars' cups and beggars' hats.

In the meantime, Lamme carried his pot-belly throughout the whole town, seeking his wife and finding her not.

7 ULENSPIEGL said to him one morning: 'Follow me; we are going to greet a high, noble, powerful and much feared personage.' 'Will he tell me where my wife is?' asked Lamme. 'If he knows,' answered Ulenspiegl. And off they went to Brederode, the drinking Hercules.

He was in the courtyard of his house.

'What do you want of me?' he demanded of Ulenspiegl.

'To speak to you, my lord,' answered Ulenspiegl.

'Speak,' said Brederode.

'You are,' said Ulenspiegl, 'a fine, valiant and mighty lord. Long ago you crushed a Frenchman in his armour like a mussel in its shell. But if you are mighty and valiant, you are also well-advised. Why then do you wear that medal, whereon I read: "Faithful to the king even unto the wallet?" '

'Yes,' asked Lamme, 'why, my lord?'

But Brederode made no answer and looked at Ulenspiegl. The latter continued his discourse.

'Why do you noble lords wish to be faithful to the king even unto the wallet? Is it because of the great good he wishes you or for the good friendship he bears you? Why, instead of being faithful even unto the wallet, do you not make it so that the executioner, despoiled of his country, shall be always faithful to the wallet?'

And Lamme nodded his head as a sign of agreement.

Brederode watched Ulenspiegl with his keen eye, smiled and, seeing his good countenance, said:

'If you are not one of King Philip's spies you are a good Fleming; in both cases I am going to reward you.'

He led him, Lamme following, into his office. There, twisting his ear until it bled, he said:

'That's for the spy.'

Ulenspiegl did not cry out.

'Bring me,' said Brederode to his cellarer, 'bring me that boiler of wine spiced with cinnamon.'

The cellarer brought in a boiler and a great tankard of mulled wine that perfumed the air.

'Drink,' said Brederode to Ulenspiegl. 'This is for the good Fleming.'

'Oh, good Flemish,' said Ulenspiegl, 'lovely cinnamon tongue, the saints speak not its like.'

Then, having downed the half of his wine, he passed the other half to Lamme.

'Who is that pot-bellied papzak,' said Brederode, 'who is rewarded without having done anything?'

'He's my friend, Lamme,' said Ulenspiegl; 'he thinks that each time he drinks mulled wine he's going to find his wife.'

'Yes,' gurgled Lamme, as he drained the wine from the tankard with great devotion.

'Where are you going now?' asked Brederode.

'We are going to seek the Seven,' answered Ulenspiegl, 'who shall save the land of Flanders.'

'What Seven?' asked Brederode.

'When I have found them, I shall tell you who they are,' answered Ulenspiegl.

But Lamme, very lively after his drink, said:

'Supposing we go to the moon to seek my wife, Tyl?'

'Order the ladder,' answered Ulenspiegl.

In May, the vernal month, Ulenspiegl said to Lamme:

'Here is the lovely month of May! Oh, the clear blue sky, the happy swallows; here are the branches of the trees ruddy with sap; the earth is in love. Now's the time to hang and burn for the Faith. There they are, the good little inquisitors. What noble faces! They have full power to correct, punish, degrade, turn over to lay judges, and they have their own prisons. (Oh, the lovely month of May!) They can arrest, judge without following the ordinary processes of justice, burn, hang, behead, and dig for women and girls the pit of premature death. The finches sing in the trees. The good inquisitors have their eye on the rich. And the king shall inherit. Away, maidens, dance in the fields to the sound of pipes and shawns. (Oh, the lovely month of May!)'

The ashes of Claes beat upon the breast of Ulenspiegl.

'Let us go on,' said he to Lamme. 'Happy are they who, in the dark days to come, shall keep their hearts up and their swords aloft!'

8 ONE DAY in the month of August, in Flanders Street in Brussels, Ulenspiegl passed before the house of Jean Sapermillemente. He was so called because his paternal grandfather, when angry, swore in that way so as not to blaspheme the most Holy Name of God. The afore-mentioned Sapermillemente was a master broiderer by trade but, having become deaf and blind from too much drinking, his wife, an old gossip with a sour phiz, broidered in his place the coats, doublets, mantles and shoes of the lords. Her pretty daughter helped her in this well-paid labor.

Passing before the house in the last daylit hours, Ulenspiegl saw the daughter at the window and heard her crying:

> 'August, August,
> Tell me, sweet month,
> Who'll take me to wife,
> Tell me, sweet month?'

'I will,' said Ulenspiegl, 'if you like.'

'You?' said she. 'Come closer and let me see you.'

But he said: 'How comes it that you cry out in August what the Brabant girls cry out on the Eve of March?'

'They have only one month,' she said, 'to give them a husband; I have a dozen, and on the eve of each of them, not at midnight but during six hours until midnight, I leap from my bed, I make three backward steps to the window and call out what you have just heard. Then, turning about, I take three backward steps to the bed, and at midnight, getting into bed, I fall asleep, dreaming of the husband I shall have. But the months, sweet months, being mockers by nature, it is not any longer of one husband that I dream but of a dozen at once; you shall be the thirteenth if you will.'

'The others would be jealous,' answered Ulenspiegl. 'You also cry "Deliverance".'

The blushing girl answered:

'I cry "Deliverance" and know what I ask for.'

'I also know and bring it to you,' replied Ulenspiegl.

'You must wait,' said she, smiling and showing her white teeth.

'Wait?' said Ulenspiegl. 'Oh, no! A house might fall about my head, a gust of wind blow me into a pit, a hydrophobic tyke bite me in the leg; I shall not wait.'

'I am too young,' said she. 'I only cry out the saying for custom's sake.'

And Ulenspiegl became suspicious, remembering that it is on the Eve of March and not the month of corn that the Brabant girls cry out the saying for a husband.

208

She repeated smilingly:

'I am too young, and only cry out the saying for custom's sake.'

'Are you going to wait until you're too old?' asked Ulenspiegl. 'That's bad arithmetic. I never saw neck so round nor breasts so white; Flemish breasts full of the good milk that makes men.'

'Full?' said she; 'not yet, impatient traveller.'

'Wait?' repeated Ulenspiegl. 'Must I have no more teeth to eat you raw with, dear? You do not answer; you smile with your clear brown eyes and your cherry-red lips.'

The girl, looking at him cunningly, said:

'Why do you love me so quickly? What is your trade? Are you a beggar or are you rich?'

'Beggar I am,' he said, 'and rich at the same time, if you give me your sweet body.'

She answered:

'That's not what I wish to know. Do you go to Mass? Are you a good Christian? Where do you live? Will you dare to say that you are a beggar, a real beggar who resists the Edicts and the Inquisition?'

The ashes of Claes beat upon the breast of Ulenspiegl.

'I am a beggar,' he said; 'I would like to see the oppressors of the Netherlands dead and worm-eaten. You look at me astonished. This fire of love that burns for you is the fire of youth, dear. God lighted it and it will flame like the sun until it goes out. But the fire of vengeance that smoulders in my heart, God also lit. It shall be the avenging sword, fire, rope, conflagration, devastation, war and ruin for the oppressors.'

'You are handsome,' she said sadly, kissing him on both cheeks, 'but hold your peace.'

'Why do you weep?' he asked.

'You must always watch,' she said, 'both here and elsewhere, wherever you are.'

'Have these walls ears?' asked Ulenspiegl.

'None but mine,' said she.

'Carved by love, they'll be stopped by my kiss.'

'Foolish friend, listen to me when I speak.'

'Why? What have you to say to me?'

'Listen to me,' she said impatiently. 'Here comes my mother. . . . Be quiet, be quiet, above all, before her. . .'

The old woman Sapermillemente entered. Ulenspiegl looked at her.

'She has a muzzle as full of holes as a strainer,' said he to himself, 'eyes with a hard and false look, and a mouth that would fain laugh and grimace; she makes me curious.'

'God be with you, master,' said the old one, 'be with you eternally. I received moneys, daughter, good moneys, from Master Egmont, when I took to him the mantle on which I broidered the fool's bauble. Yes, master, the fool's bauble against the Red Dog.'

'Cardinal Granvelle?' asked Ulenspiegl.

'Yes,' said she, 'against the Red Dog. They say he informs the King of their doings; he would fain have them perish. They are right, are they not?'

Ulenspiegl said not a word.

'Have you not seen them in the streets in grey doublets and *opperst-kleed*, such as the common folk wear, with long sleeves hanging down and monkish hoods, and on all the *opperst-kleederen* the fool's bauble embroidered? I sewed twenty-seven at least, and my daughter fifteen. It makes the Red Dog angry to see these fool's baubles.'

Then, whispering in Ulenspiegl's ear:

'I know that the lords have decided to replace the fool's bauble by a wheat sheaf in sign of unity. Yes, yes, they are going to fight against the King and the Inquisition. That's fine of them, is it not, master?'

Ulenspiegl said not a word.

'The stranger's air brews melancholy,' said the old woman; 'his beak's shut all of a sudden.'

Not a word came from Ulenspiegl, and he went out.

He soon entered into a *musico*, so as not to forget how to drink. It was full of drinkers, speaking most imprudently of the King, of the

210

detested Edicts, of the Inquisition, and of the Red Dog who must be forced to leave the country. He saw the old woman, dressed in rags, and seeming to doze by a pint of brandy. She stayed thus for a long time; then, taking a little saucer from her pocket, she was seen by Ulenspiegl to go begging among the groups, demanding alms especially from those who spoke the most imprudently.

And the good fellows freely gave her florins, deniers and patards.

Ulenspiegl, hoping to find out from the daughter what the old wife Sapermillemente had not told him, passed before the house again; he saw the girl, no longer crying, but smiling to him and winking a sweet promise.

The old woman re-entered quite suddenly after him.

Ulenspiegl, quite annoyed at seeing her, ran like a hart into the street, crying: ''T brandt! 'T brandt!' (Fire! Fire!) until he came to the house of Jacob Pietersen, the baker. The German-style windows were flaming with the reflection of the setting sun. A thick smoke from the branches, turning to live coals in the furnace, issued forth from the chimney of the bakery. Ulenspiegl continued to cry as he ran: ''T brandt! 'T brandt!' The watchman of Our Lady of the Chapel sounded the trumpet, while the beadle made the *Wacharm* bell peal out for all he was worth. And the boys and girls swarmed to the place, singing and whistling.

The bell and the trumpet still sounding, the old wife Sapermillemente left everything and ran. Ulenspiegl was watching her. When she was well away, he entered the house.

'You here?' said the young girl. 'Is there no fire there, then?'

'There? No,' answered Ulenspiegl.

'But that bell that peals out so sadly?'

'It doesn't know what it's doing,' replied Ulenspiegl.

'And that doleful trumpet? And all the people running?'

'The number of fools is infinite.'

'What's burning, then?' said she.

'Your eyes and my flaming heart,' answered Ulenspiegl.

And he leapt to her mouth.

'You're biting me,' said she.

She looked on him, smiling and distressed. Suddenly weeping:

'Never return here again,' she said. 'You are a beggar, enemy of the Pope; never return. . .'

'Your mother!' said he.

'Yes,' she answered, blushing. 'Do you know where she is at this moment? She's listening there where the crowd thinks there's a fire.

Do you know where she will go presently? To the palace of the Red Dog to tell all she knows and prepare the way for the Duke who is to come. Fly, Ulenspiegl, I'm saving you, fly! One more kiss, but never return again; one more, you are beautiful; I weep, but begone!'

'Brave damsel,' said Ulenspiegl, holding her in his embrace.

'I was not always so,' said she. 'I, too, like her . . .'

'Those songs,' said he, 'those mute appeals of beauty to amorous men?'

'Yes,' she said, 'my mother wished it so. I saved you because of my love for you. I shall save the others in remembrance of you, beloved. When you are far away, shall your heart be drawn towards the repentant girl? Kiss me, darling. Never again for money will she hand over victims to the stake. Be off; no, stay yet awhile. How soft your hand is! There, I kiss your hand as a sign of enslavement; you are my master. Listen, come closer, hush. Men, scoundrels and thieves and among them an Italian, came here last night, one after the other. My mother brought them to this room where you now are, ordered me to leave, then closed the door. I heard these words: "Stone crucifix . . . Borgerhout Gate . . . Procession . . . Antwerp . . . Our Lady . . ." There was smothered laughter and florins counted out on the table . . . Be off, they're coming, be off, my love. Keep a sweet memory of me; be off . . .'

Ulenspiegl ran as she bade him and came to the Old Cock (*In den ouden Haen*) and there found Lamme steeped in melancholy, biting into a sausage and draining his seventh stein of Louvain *peterman*.

And he forced him to run off like himself, in spite of his pot-belly.

9   RUNNING ALONG thus at full speed, followed by Lamme, he found in the Eikenstraat a savage lampoon directed against Brederode. This he took to him directly. 'I am, my lord,' said he, 'that good Fleming and that King's spy whose ears you twisted so well and to whom you gave such a fine mulled wine to drink. I have brought you a dear little pamphlet wherein you are accused, among other things, of calling yourself the Earl of Holland, like the King. It comes hot from the press of Jan a Calumnia, who lives by the Rogue's Quay, in the alley of the Thieves of Honour.'

Smiling, Brederode answered:

'I shall have you flogged for two hours if you do not tell me the real name of the writer of this.'

'My lord,' replied Ulenspiegl, 'you may have me flogged for two years, if you care to, but you'll never be able to make my back tell what my mouth knows not.'

And away he went, not without having received a florin for his trouble.

213

10 Since June, the month of roses, conventicles had begun in the country of Flanders. And the apostles of the Primitive Christian Church preached everywhere, in all sorts of places; in fields and gardens; on the hillocks which in times of flood served to keep the cattle from drowning; on rivers, in barks.

On land they were entrenched as though in a camp, surrounding themselves with their wagons. On the rivers and in the ports, barks full of armed men kept guard about them.

And in the camps, musketeers and archers kept them from the surprises of the enemy.

And thus was the word of Freedom heard everywhere in the land of our fathers.

11 Ulenspiegl and Lamme, being at Bruges with their cart, which they left in a neighbouring courtyard, went into the Church of the Redeemer instead of going into a tavern, for no longer in their pouches was there any happy tinkle of money. Father Cornelis Adriaensen, a minor friar, dirty, shameless, and a furious and bellowing preacher, bustled about that day in the pulpit of truth.

Young and beautiful devout women thronged about the pulpit.

Father Cornelis was speaking of the Passion. When he came to the passage of the Holy Gospel where the Jews cry to Pilate, referring to our Lord Jesus: 'Crucify him! Crucify him! for we have our law, and by that law he must die,' Broer Cornelis exclaimed:

'You have just heard, good folk, if our Lord Jesus Christ suffered a horrible and shameful death, it is because there have always been laws to punish heretics. He was justly condemned because he disobeyed the law. And yet they would count as nothing the Edicts! Ah, Jesus! What malediction would you let fall on this country? Honoured Mother of God! If only the Emperor Charles were still alive to see the scandal of these confederated nobles who dared present a request to the Vice-Regent against the Inquisition and the Edicts which were made with

214

such a good end in view, which were so ripely thought out and pro-
claimed after such long and prudent reflections, to destroy all sects and
all heresies! And they would fain reduce them to nothing when they
are as necessary as bread and cheese. Into what stinking, loathsome,
abominable abyss do they tumble us now? Luther, that filthy Luther,
that mad ox, triumphs in Saxony, in Brunswick, in Lüneburg, in Meck-
lenburg; Brentius, that dungy Brentius who lived in Germany on
acorns that even the swine wouldn't touch, Brentius triumphs in Würt-
temberg; Servet, the moon-struck, who has a quarter of the moon in
his head, Servet, the Trinitarian, reigns in Pomerania, in Denmark and
in Sweden, and there he dares to blaspheme the sacred, glorious and
puissant Trinity. Yes! But they tell me he has been burned alive by
Calvin, who was good only for that; yes, by the foul-smelling Calvin,
who stinks rancidly; yes, with his long bottle-shaped muzzle; cheese-
face with teeth like gardener's shovels. Yes, these wolves devour each
other; yes, that ox of a Luther, that mad ox, armed the princess of
Germany against the Anabaptist Munzer, who was a good man, they
say, and lived according to the Gospel. And all through Germany the
bellowings of this ox have been heard. Yes!

'Yes, and what do we see in Flanders, Guelders, Frisia, Holland,
Zeeland? Adamites running naked in the streets; yes, my good folk,
quite naked in the streets, shamelessly showing off their lean meat to
the passers-by. There was but one, you say; yes, let it pass, one is as
good as a hundred, a hundred as good as one. And he was burned, you
say, burned alive at the request of the Calvinists and the Lutherans.
These wolves devour each other, I tell you!

'Yes, what do we see in Flanders, Guelders, Frisia, Holland, Zeeland?
Libertines teaching that all servitude is contrary to the word of God.
They lie, the stinking heretics; we must submit to our Mother, the Holy
Roman Church. And there, in that cursed town of Antwerp, the meeting-place for all the bastardly heretics of the world, they have dared to
preach that we cook the Host with dog's fat. Another said—he's that
beggar seated on a piss-pot at that street corner—there is no God, nor
life eternal, nor resurrection of the body, nor eternal damnation! Says
another, over there, with a whining voice: "We can baptise without
salt, or lard, or spittle, without exorcism or candle." "There is no Purgatory," says another. No Purgatory, good folk! Ah, it were better for you
to have lain with your mothers, your sisters, your daughters, than to
harbour even a doubt about Purgatory.

'Yes, and they turn up their noses at the Inquisitor, the holy man, yes.
There came to Belem, near here, four thousand Calvinists with armed
men, banners and tabors. Yes! And you can smell from here the smoke

215

of their kitchens. They took the Church of Saint Catholyne to dishonour, profane and desecrate it by their damned preachifying.

'What is this impious and scandalous tolerance? By the thousand devils of Hell, flabby Catholics, why do you not also arm yourselves? You have, like these damned Calvinists, armour, lances, halberds, swords, daggers, arbalests, knives, staffs, pikes, the town cannon.

'They are peaceful, you say; they only want in all freedom and tranquillity to hear the word of God. That's all the same to me. Out of Bruges! Hunt, kill, blow up for me all these Calvinists outside the Church. What, you are not yet gone? Fie on you! You are nothing but hens trembling with fright on your dung-heaps! I see at this moment where these damned Calvinists are beating a tattoo on your wives' and daughters' bellies, and you let them do it, men of tow and putty. Don't go over there, don't go. . . You'll get your socks wet in the battle. Fie on you, Brugeois! Fie on you, Catholics! You are indeed quite catholicised, oh, cowardly poltroons! Shame on you, ducks and drakes, geese and turkeys that you are!

'Are these not good-looking preachers that you should go in crowds to listen to the lies they spew out; that the young maidens should go at night to their sermons; yes, in order that the town, after nine months, should be filled with little beggar-boys and beggar-girls? There were four there, four scandalous good-for-nothings, who preached in the cemetery of the church. The first of these good-for-nothings, skinny and pale, the ugly craven, was capped with a filthy hat. Thanks to that his ears were not seen. Which of you have seen the ears of a preacher? He was shirtless, for his bare arms, showing no linen, came out through his doublet. I saw that all right, although he tried to cover it up with a filthy little mantle; and I saw clearly also in his black canvas breeches, open as the spire of the Church of Our Lady, the swinging of his bells and clapper. The other preached in a doublet and no shoes. No one saw his ears. And he stopped short in the middle of his preaching, and the boys and girls hooted him, crying: "Ya! Ya! He doesn't know his lesson." The third of these scandalous good-for-nothings was capped with a filthy, nasty little hat with a little feather on it. And no one saw his ears either. The fourth good-for-nothing, Hermanus, better dressed than the others, must have been marked twice on the shoulder by the executioner; yes!

'They all wore, under their hats, greasy silk caps that cover their ears. Did you ever see a preacher's ears? Which of these good-for-nothings would dare to show his ears? Ears! Ah! yes, show his ears; they've been cut off. Yes, the executioner has cut off all their ears.

'And yet it is about these scandalous good-for-nothings, these cut-purses, these cobblers escaped from their lasts, these tatterdemalion

216

preachers, that all the populace cried: "Up with the Beggars!" as though they were all mad, drunk or foolish.

'Ah, it only remains for us poor Roman Catholics to quit the Netherlands, since they allow them to bray out the cry of: "Up with the Beggars! Up with the Beggars!" What mill-stone of malediction has then fallen upon this bewitched and stupid people, Oh, Jesus? Everywhere, rich and poor, noble and base, young and old, men and women, all cry out: "Up with the Beggars!"

'And who are all these lords, all these peeled leather-bottoms who have come to us from Germany? All they owned went to harlots, or was spent on gaming, lechery, nights out, drawn-out debauchery, villainies, abominations of dice, and triumph of outward display. They haven't even a rusty nail to scratch themselves where they itch. They needs must have now the wealth of the churches and the convents.

'And there at their banquet with that worthless Culemburg, with that other worthless Brederode, they drank from wooden bowls to scorn Messer Berlaymont and Madame the Vice-Regent. Yes, and they cried: "Up with the Beggars!" Ah, if I had been the good God (with all respect), I would have turned their drinks, whether beer or wine, into dirty, loathsome dish-water; yes, into filthy, abominable, stinking suds in which they should have washed their shirts and their foul sheets.

'Yes, bray, asses that you are, bray: "Up with the Beggars." Yes, and I am a prophet. And all the maledictions, miseries, fevers, plagues, conflagrations, ruins, desolations, cankers, English sweats and Black Plagues shall fall upon the Netherlands. Yes, and God shall be revenged for your filthy braying of: "Up with the Beggars!" And there shall be no stone of your houses left standing upon another one, and not a morsel of bone in your damned legs that run after this accursed Calvinism and preachifying. And so be, be, be, be, be it. Amen.'

'Let us go, my boy,' said Ulenspiegl to Lamme.

'In a moment,' said Lamme.

And he looked over the young and fair devout women present at the sermon, but he did not find his wife.

12 ULENSPIEGL and Lamme came to the place called *Minne-Water* (Love Water); the great doctors, however, and the *Wysneusen* (pedants) say that it is *Minre-Water*, or *Minim-Water*. Ulenspiegl and Lamme sat down by its banks and watched pass under the trees, all leafy right down to their very heads, like a low roof, men, women, young men and maidens, hand in hand, wreaths of flowers about their brows, walking hip to hip, gazing tenderly into

217

each other's eyes, without seeing anything in the world but themselves.

Ulenspiegl, thinking of Nele, watched them. In his melancholy remembrance, he said:

'Let's go and drink.'

But Lamme, heedless of Ulenspiegl, was also watching the loving couples.

'In olden days my wife and I passed here, loving each other under the nose of those who, as we are now, lay stretched out on the banks, alone and loverless.

'Come and drink,' said Ulenspiegl, 'we shall find the Seven at the bottom of a stein.'

'Drinkers' words,' answered Lamme. 'You know that the Seven are giants who couldn't even stand up under the great vaulted roof of the Church of The Redeemer.'

Ulenspiegl, thinking sadly on Nele, and also thinking that maybe he could find, in some hostelry, good lodging, good supper and a comely hostess, again said:

'Let's go and drink.'

But Lamme heeded not and said, as he looked at the tower of the Church of Our Lady:

'Madame Saint Mary, patron saint of lawful loves, grant that I may see again her white bosom, soft pillow.'

'Come and drink,' said Ulenspiegl, 'you'll find her showing it to the drinkers in a tavern.'

'Dare you think so badly of her?' said Lamme.

'Come and drink,' answered Ulenspiegl, 'she's a *baesinne* somewhere, no doubt.'

'Thirsty speech,' said Lamme.

Ulenspiegl continued:

'Maybe she holds in reserve for poor travellers a plate of stewed beef whose spices embalm the air, not too rich, but tender, succulent as rose leaves and all the pieces floating like Shrove Tuesday fish amid cloves, nutmeg, cocks' combs, sweet-breads and other heavenly dainties.'

'Cruel!' said Lamme. 'You doubtless want to kill me. Don't you know that for two days we have been living on dry bread and small beer?'

'Hungry speech,' answered Ulenspiegl. 'You are weeping with appetite. Come on and eat and drink. I have here a fine half-florin that will pay the costs of our feasting.'

Lamme laughed. They went to seek out their cart and go through the town searching for the best inn. But, seeing several muzzles of crabbed *baes* and unpleasing *baesinnes,* they passed on their way, thinking that a sour phiz is a bad signboard for a hospitable kitchen.

They came to the Saturday Market and entered the hostelry named *de Blauwe Lanteern* (The Blue Lantern). There the *baes* had a goodly countenance.

They put up the cart and led the ass to the stable, where it had a peck of oats for company. They ordered supper to be served, ate their fill, slept well, and arose to eat again. Lamme, bursting with pleasure, said:

'I hear heavenly music in my stomach.'

When it came the time to pay, the *baes* came to Lamme, and said:

'I must have ten patards.'

'He has them,' said Lamme, pointing to Ulenspiegl, who answered:

'I have not got them.'

'And the half-florin?'

'I haven't got it,' answered Ulenspiegl.

'This talk is all very well,' said the *baes;* 'but I'm going to take the doublet and shirt from both of you.'

Suddenly Lamme, plucking up drunken courage.

'And if I wish to eat and drink,' he shouted, 'eat and drink, yes, drink for twenty-seven florins or more, I shall do it. Think you there's not a pretty penny in this belly? Living God! Until now it was fed only on ortolans. You will never have one like it under your greasy, leather belt. For like the nasty one you are, you have your tallow on the collar of your doublet and not like me, three inches of dainty fat on your belly!'

The *baes* had fallen into an ecstasy of rage. A stutterer by nature, he wanted to speak fast; the faster he tried, the more he sneezed like a dog coming from the sea. Ulenspiegl threw bread-pellets at his nose. And Lamme, becoming more lively, continued:

'Yes, I have the wherewithal to pay for your three scraggy hens and

219

your four mangy chickens, and that great silly peacock that drags its filthy tail about your yard. And if your skin were not drier than an old cock's, if your bones were not crumbling to dust in your breast, I would still have enough to eat you, your snotty man-servant, your one-eyed maid, and your cook, whose arms, if he had the itch, would be too short to scratch himself.

'Look you,' he continued, 'look you at this fine bird who for half a florin would fain strip our shirts and doublets from us. Tell me what your wardrobe is worth, tattered impertinence, and I'll give you three liards.'

But the *baes*, becoming more and more angry, blew and puffed more than ever.

And Ulenspiegl threw bread-pellets in his face.

Lamme, like a lion, said:

'How much do you think, scrawny phiz, a good donkey's worth, with fine muzzle, long ears, wide chest and legs of iron? Eighteen florins at least, isn't that true, miserable *baes*? How many old nails have you in your coffers to pay for such a fine beast?'

The *baes* kept on puffing and blowing still more, but did not dare to budge.

Lamme said:

'How much do you think a fine cart of ashwood, all painted purple, and covered over with Courtrai canvas, as a protection against sun and showers, is worth? Twenty-four florins at least, eh? And how much do twenty-four florins and eighteen florins make? Answer, leprous, bad counter. And as to-day is market day, and as there are peasants in your cheap hostelry, I am going to sell them the ass and the cart right away.'

And this was done, for Lamme was known to all of them. And from the sale of his ass and cart he had forty-four florins and ten patards. Then, jingling the gold under the nose of the *baes*, he said to him:

'Do you scent the savour of feastings to come?'

'Yes,' answered the host.

And he said under his breath:

'When you sell your skin I shall buy a liard's worth to make a bracelet-charm against prodigality.'

Meanwhile, a darling and pretty woman who was out in the dark yard often came to the window to look at Lamme, then drew away each time he might see her pretty face.

That evening, on the stairway, as he was going up without any light, staggering a little because of the wine he had downed, he felt a woman hug him, kiss him on the cheek, the mouth, and even on the nose, hungrily, wetting his face with amorous tears, then leave him.

And Lamme, sleepy from his drink, went to bed, slept, and next day went off to Ghent with Ulenspiegl.

13 THERE HE SOUGHT out his wife in all the *kaberdoesjen, tafelhooren, musicos* and taverns. In the evening he rejoined Ulenspiegl *in de Zingende Zwaan* (At the Singing Swan). Ulenspiegl went about wherever he could, spreading the alarm and rousing the people against the executioners of the land of his fathers.

Finding himself at the Friday Market near the *Dulle Griet* (the Big Gun), Ulenspiegl lay down flat on his stomach on the pavement.

A charcoal-man came and said to him:

'What are you doing there?'

'I'm wetting my nose to see which way the wind's blowing,' answered Ulenspiegl.

A carpenter came up.

'Do you take this pavement for a mattress?' said he.

'There are those who'll soon be taking it for a blanket,' answered Ulenspiegl.

A monk stopped.

'What's this calf doing there?' he asked.

'He's flat on his belly asking your benediction, father,' answered Ulenspiegl.

The monk, having bestowed his blessing, went on his way.

Ulenspiegl then lay with his ear to the ground. A peasant came.

'Do you hear any noise there below?' he said to him.

'Yes,' answered Ulenspiegl, 'I hear the trees pushing up through the earth, the trees whose branches will later serve as faggots to burn the poor heretics.'

'Do you hear anything else?' a town sergeant asked him.

'I hear the gendarmerie coming from Spain; if you have anything worth keeping, bury it, for soon the towns will no longer be safe because of robbers.'

'He's mad,' said the town sergeant.

'He's mad,' repeated the burghers.

14 MEANWHILE LAMME, thinking of the sweet vision of the stairway in the Blue Lantern, ate nothing. His heart was drawn towards Bruges, but Ulenspiegl led him by force to Antwerp, where he continued his sad searching. Ulenspiegl, being in the taverns

among good Protestant Flemings or even Catholics who were friends of Freedom, spoke to them on the subject of the Edicts, saying: 'They bring us the Inquisition on the pretext of purging us of heresy, but that kind of rhubarb will serve only to purge our purses. We have no love of being physicked unless it please us; we'll get angry; we'll revolt and arm ourselves. The King knows this well in advance. Seeing that we don't want his rhubarb, he'll send on the syringes, in other words the great and small cannon, the artillery, the big-mugged mortars. A royal enema. There will not be a single rich Fleming left in all Flanders so physicked. Happy our country to have so royal a physician.'

But the burghers laughed.

Ulenspiegl said: 'Laugh to-day, but flee or arm yourselves the day they break something in the Church of Our Lady.'

15 ON THE FIFTEENTH of August, the great feast of Mary and of the blessing of herbs and roots, when, stuffed with grain, the hens are deaf to the clarion of the cock imploring love, a great stone crucifix was broken at one of the gates of Antwerp by an Italian in the pay of the Cardinal Granvelle; on this day also the procession of the Virgin, preceded by red, green and yellow fools, came forth from the Church of Our Lady.

But the statue of the Virgin, insulted along the route of the procession, was hurriedly replaced in the choir of the church, the wrought-iron work doors of which were then closed.

Ulenspiegl and Lamme entered the Church of Our Lady. Wretched young ragamuffins, and several men among them, strangers to everybody, stood before the choir making certain signs and grimaces to each other. With their feet and their tongues they made a great din. Nobody had ever seen them in Antwerp, nobody ever saw them again. One of them, with a face like a burned onion, asked if Mieke—meaning Our Lady—had been frightened that she had so hurriedly re-entered the church.

'It wasn't of you that she was afraid, low blackamoor,' said Ulenspiegl.

The young fellow to whom he spoke came up to him to strike him, but Ulenspiegl, grasping him by the collar, said:

'Strike me and I'll make you spew out your tongue.'

Then, turning to several Antwerp men who were there, he said, pointing to the young rag-tags:

'*Signorkes* and *pagaders*, beware, these are false Flemings, traitors paid to bring us to trouble, misery and ruin.'

Then, speaking to the strangers, he said:

223

'Hey, donkey snouts, all withered up with misery, who gave you the money we hear clinking in your pouches to-day? Have you sold your skins in advance for drum-skins?'

'Look at the preacher!' said the strangers.

Then they began to shout together, speaking of Our Lady:

'Mieke has a lovely robe! Mieke has a lovely crown! I'll give them to my slut!'

They went out while one of them climbed into the pulpit to make some stupid remarks; then they returned, shouting:

'Come down, Mieke, come down before we come and get you. Perform a miracle so that we can see if you know how to walk as well as be carried, Mieke the sluggard!'

But in vain Ulenspiegl shouted: 'Workers of ruin, cease your vile talk; all pillage is criminal!' They did not cease their remarks, and several of them even spoke of breaking into the choir to make Mieke come down.

Hearing this, an old woman who sold the candles in the church threw in their faces the charcoal ashes from her foot-warmer; but she was beaten and cast to the ground, and then the uproar began.

The Markgrave came to the church with his sergeants. Seeing the populace assembled, he exhorted them to leave the church, but he spoke so feebly that only a few left; the others said:

'We first want to hear the canons sing Vespers in honour of Mieke.'

The Markgrave replied:

'There shall be no singing.'

'We ourselves shall sing,' answered the ragged strangers.

And they did sing, in the naves and by the porch of the church. Some of them played at *krikee-steenen* (cherry-stones) and said: 'Mieke, you never play in Paradise and you're bored there: play with us.'

And continually insulting the statue, they shouted, booed and whistled.

The Markgrave pretended to be afraid and went off. By his order all the doors of the church, but one, were closed.

Without being joined by the populace, the rag-tag and bobtailed crew of strangers became more daring and shouted all the more.

And the vaulted roofs re-echoed as though to the noise of a hundred cannon.

One of them, the one with the face like a burned onion, who seemed to have some authority, went up into the pulpit, waved his hand over them and began to preach:

'In the name of the Father, and of the Son, and of the Holy Ghost,' said he, 'the Three making but One and the One making Three, may

224

God save us from an arithmetical Paradise. This day, the twenty-ninth of August, Mieke went forth with a great and triumphant get-up to show her wooden face to the *signorkes* and *pagaders* of Antwerp. But Mieke met the devil Satanas in the procession and Satanas mockingly said to her: "There you are, quite proud, prinked up like a queen, Mieke, and borne aloft by four *signorkes*, and you don't care to look at the poor *pagader* Satanas walking along on foot." And Mieke answered: "On your way, Satanas, or I will crush your head harder than ever, foul serpent!" "Mieke," said Satanas, "that's the job you've been spending your time doing for fifteen hundred years, but the Spirit of the Lord your Master delivered me. I am stronger than you are, and you'll no longer stamp on my head, and I'm going to make you dance now." Satanas took a great whip, very cutting, and began to strike at Mieke, who did not dare scream out for fear of showing her terror; and so she began to run with great steps, forcing the *signorkes* who bore her to run also, so as they wouldn't let her fall with her golden crown and her jewels in the midst of the poor common people. And now Mieke stays stiff and still with fear in her niche, watching Satanas, who is there at the top of the pillar under the dome, and who, holding his whip and chuckling, says to her: "I will make you pay for the blood and tears that flow in your name! How is your virginal bearing? It's time to get out. You'll be cut in two, nasty wooden statue, for all the statues of flesh and blood who were pitilessly burned, hanged and buried alive in your name." So spoke Satanas; and 'twas well spoken. And you must come down from your niche, bloody Mieke, cruel Mieke, who was not at all like your Son Christus.'

And all the mob of strangers, booing and crying, shouted: 'Mieke, the time has come to get out. Are you wetting your linen out of fear in your niche? At them, Brabant of the good Duke! Remove the wooden saints! Who'll take a bath in the Scheldt? Wood swims better than fish!'

The populace listened to them in silence.

But Ulenspiegl, going up into the pulpit, kicked the one who was speaking down the stairs.

'Fools fit for tying,' he said, speaking to the populace, 'moonstruck fools, idiot fools, who see no farther than the ends of your snotty noses, don't you understand that all this is the work of traitors? They want to make you commit sacrilege and pillage so that you may be declared rebels, have your coffers emptied, your heads cut off, or have you burned alive! And the King will inherit. *Signorkes* and *pagaders*, put no faith in the words of these workers for evil: leave Our Lady in her niche, live steadfastly, labour gladly, spending your earnings and your profits. The black demon of ruin has his eye on you; by sackings and

225

destruction he will call up the enemy horde to treat you as rebels and make the Duke of Alba to reign over you with dictatorship, inquisition, confiscation, and death!'

'And he will inherit!'

'La,' said Lamme, 'don't pillage, *signorkes* and *pagaders*, the King is already quite angry. The broiderer's daughter told my friend Ulenspiegl so. Don't pillage, sirs!'

But the populace could not hear.

The strangers shouted:

'Sack and out with them! Sack Brabant for the good Duke! To the water with the wooden saints! They swim better than fish!'

Ulenspiegl, still in the pulpit, cried out in vain:

'*Signorkes* and *pagaders*, don't allow this pillage! Don't bring down ruin on the town!'

He was dragged down from there and his face, doublet, and hose all torn, despite the fact that he used his hands and feet well. And, all bleeding, he kept on shouting:

'Don't allow this pillage!'

But it was all in vain.

The strangers and the rag-tag and bobtail of the town rushed at the gates of the choir, which gave way before them, shouting:

'Up with the Beggars!'

All of them began to break, sack and destroy. Before midnight that great church, wherein there were seventy altars, all sorts of beautiful paintings and precious things, was emptied like a nut. The altars were broken, the images cast down, and all the locks smashed.

This being done, the same strangers started out to treat, as they had done Our Lady, the Minor Brothers, the Franciscans, Saint Peter, Saint Andrew, Saint Peter-in-the-pot, the Bourg, the Fawkens, the White Sisters, the Grey Sisters, the Third Order, the Preachers, and all the churches and chapels of the town. They took the candles and the torches and ran about everywhere in this way.

There was neither quarrel nor dispute among them; not one of them was hurt in this great breaking of stone, wood and other materials.

They went on to The Hague, there to proceed with the clearing away of statues and altars, without being aided there, or elsewhere, by the Reformists.

At The Hague, the magistrate asked them where their commission was.

'Here it is,' said one of them, 'tapping on his heart.'

'Their commission, do you hear, *signorkes* and *pagaders?*' said Ulenspiegl, having learned of this. 'There is then someone who sends them

about this business of sacrilege. If some thieving plunderer comes to my cottage, I shall do as the magistrate of The Hague did. I shall say, lifting my hat: "Nice thief, gracious good-for-nothing, venerable rogue, show me your commission." He will tell me that it is in his heart which is hungry for my goods. And I shall give him the keys to everything. Seek, seek out who it is that profits by this pillage. Beware of the Red Dog; the crime has been committed; now for the punishment. Beware of the Red Dog! The great stone crucifix has been cast down. Beware of the Red Dog!'

The Great Sovereign Council of Malines having sent out word by the organ of its president, Viglius, that nothing was to be put in the way of the image-breakers, Ulenspiegl said: 'La, the harvest is ripe for the Spanish reapers. The Duke! The Duke marches upon us. Flemings, the sea rises, the sea of vengeance. Poor women and girls, flee the pit! Poor men, flee the gallows, the fire, the sword! Philip would fain finish the bloody work of Charles. The father sowed death and exile; the son has sworn that he would much rather reign over a cemetery than over a race of heretics. Flee from the executioner and the grave diggers.'

The populace listened to Ulenspiegl and the families left the cities by the hundreds, and the roads were encumbered by carts laden with the household goods of those going off into exile.

And Ulenspiegl went about everywhere followed by the doleful Lamme, searching for his love.

And at Damme, Nele wept beside Katheline the madwoman.

16 ULENSPIEGL, being at Ghent during the barley month, which is October, saw Egmont returning from feasting and revelling in the noble company of the Abbot of Saint Bavon. Being in a singing humour, Egmont dreamily allowed his horse to amble along. Suddenly he noticed a man, holding a lighted lantern, marching along with him.

'What do you want of me?' demanded Egmont.

'Good,' replied Ulenspiegl, 'the good of a lantern when it is lit.'

'Be off and leave me,' answered the Count.

'I will not be off,' retorted Ulenspiegl.

'Do you want a blow from my whip, then?'

'I would take ten if I could place in your head such a lantern as would make you see clear from here to the Escurial.'

'I am not interested either in your lantern or in the Escurial,' answered the Count.

228

'Well, for my part,' replied Ulenspiegl, 'I am aching to give you some good advice.'

Then, taking hold of the bridle of the Count's horse, which reared and kicked, he said:

'My lord, think that you are now dancing well on your horse and that your head also dances very well on your shoulders; but the King wishes, they say, to interrupt this fine dance, leaving you your body, but taking your head and making it dance in countries so far away that you would never be able to catch it again. Give me a florin, I have earned it.

'The whip, if you do not retire, evil news-giver.'

'My lord, I am Ulenspiegl, son of Claes, burned alive for his faith, and Soetkin, who died of grief. The ashes beat against my breast, telling me that Egmont, the brave soldier, might, with the gendarmerie under his command, oppose the Duke of Alba with his thrice victorious troops.'

'Be off,' answered Egmont, 'I am no traitor.'

'Save the country; you alone can do so,' said Ulenspiegl.

The Count would have lashed Ulenspiegl; but the latter did not wait for this, and flew off, crying:

'Eat lanterns! Eat lanterns, master Count! Save the country!'

Another day, Egmont, being thirsty, stopped in front of the Inn of *In't Bont Verken* (The Piebald Pig). It was kept by a woman from Courtrai, a darling wench named *Muizeken* (Mousiekins).

The Count, rising up in his stirrups, called out:

'Drink!'

Ulenspiegl, who was in *Muizeken's* service, came out to the Count with a pewter tankard in one hand and a flask of red wine in the other.

The Count, seeing him, said:

'There you are, dark-omened raven.'

'My lord,' answered Ulenspiegl, 'if my omen is dark, it is because it is badly washed; but will you tell me which is redder, the wine that flows down the gullet or the blood that spurts from the neck? That's what my lantern wants to know.'

The Count made no answer, drank, paid and departed.

17 ULENSPIEGL and Lamme, each mounted on an ass that had been given to them by Simon Simonsen, one of the followers of the Prince of Orange, went everywhere warning the burghers of the black designs of the King and always keeping on the watch for news that came out of Spain.

They sold vegetables, being dressed like peasants and frequenting all the markets.

Returning from the Brussels market, they passed a stone house on the Brick Wharf, and in one of its low rooms they saw a lovely lady dressed in satin. She had a high complexion, a fine bosom, and a lively eye.

She was saying to a young and fresh cook:

'Scour me this pan, I don't like rusty sauce.'

Ulenspiegl stuck his nose in at the window.

'I like all sauces,' he said, 'for a famished belly can't be a chooser of fricassees.'

The lady turned about.

'Who is this little fellow,' she said, 'who meddles with my soup?'

'Alas, lovely lady,' answered Ulenspiegl, 'if you would only make a little in my company, I would teach you of travellers' stews unknown to fair ladies who sit at home.'

Then, smacking his lips, he said:

'I'm thirsty.'

'For what?' said she.

'For you,' he said.

'He's a nice-looking fellow,' said the cook to the lady. 'Let him come in and he'll tell us his adventures.'

'But there are two of them,' said the lady.

'I'll take care of one,' retorted the cook.

'Madame,' said Ulenspiegl, 'we are two, it is true, myself and my poor Lamme, who cannot carry a hundred pounds on his back but carries willingly five hundred pounds of meat and drink in his belly.'

'My boy,' said Lamme, 'mock not unfortunate me, whose belly costs so much to fill.'

'It shall not cost you a liard to-day,' said the lady. 'Enter within, both of you.'

230

'But,' said Lamme, 'there are also two donkeys on whose backs we are.'

'Fodder,' answered the lady, 'is not lacking in the stables of the Count of Meghem.'

The cook left her pans and led Ulenspiegl and Lamme into the yard on their donkeys, which began to bray brazenly.

'That's the fanfare for nourishment near at hand,' said Ulenspiegl. 'They're trumpeting their joy, the poor donkeys.'

And, both of them having dismounted, Ulenspiegl said to the cook:

'If you were an ass, would you like to have me for a jackass?'

'If I were a woman,' she answered, 'I would like a fellow with a happy face.'

'What are you then, being neither woman nor ass?' asked Ulenspiegl.

'I'm a virgin,' she said, 'and a virgin is not a woman any more than she's an ass; do you understand, big belly?'

Ulenspiegl said to Lamme:

'Don't you believe her, she's half a wild-maid and the quarter of two she-devils. Her carnal tricks have already bespoken a place for her on a couch in Hell to fondle Beelzebub.'

'Nasty mocker,' said the cook, 'if your hair were horse-hair I wouldn't even want it to walk over.'

'I should like to eat all your hair,' said Ulenspiegl.

'Golden tongue,' said the lady, 'must you have it all?'

'No,' answered Ulenspiegl, 'it would be sufficient for me to have a thousand strands melted into one like you.'

The lady said:

'Drink first a stein of *bruinbier*, eat a piece of ham, cut into this leg of mutton, disembowel this pasty, swallow this salad.'

Ulenspiegl clasped his hands together.

'The ham,' he said, 'is good meat; the *bruinbier* is heavenly beer; the leg of mutton, flesh divine; a pasty disemboweled makes the tongue to quiver in the mouth with pleasure; a rich salad is princely swallowing. But blessed shall be the man who is allowed by you to sup of your beauty.'

'See how he runs on,' she said. 'Eat first, scamp!'

Ulenspiegl answered:

'Shall we not say the blessing before the grace?'

'No,' said she.

Then Lamme, moaning, said:

'I'm hungry.'

'You shall eat,' said the lovely lady, 'since you have no other care than to eat cooked meats.'

231

'And fresh, also, as was my wife,' said Lamme.

The cook became sullen at these words. Nevertheless they ate plenty and drank like fish. And the lady gave Ulenspiegl his supper that night, and also the next night and the days that followed.

The donkeys had double oats and Lamme double rations. During a week he did not leave the kitchen, trying conclusions with the dishes but not with the cook, for the thought of his wife.

This annoyed the girl, who said that it wasn't worth his trouble encumbering the world, if he was only going to think of his belly.

In the meantime Ulenspiegl and the lady lived amicably. And she said to him one day:

'Tyl, you have no manners; who are you?'

'I am,' said he, 'the son that Lucky Chance had one day by Good Adventure.'

'You don't speak ill of yourself!' said she.

'That's for fear that the others won't praise me,' answered Ulenspiegl.

'Would you take up the defence of your brothers who are being persecuted?'

'The ashes of Claes beat upon my heart,' answered Ulenspiegl.

'How splendid you are!' she said. 'Who is this Claes?'

Ulenspiegl answered:

'My father, burned for his faith.'

'The Count of Meghem is not as you are,' said she. 'He would fain bleed the country that I love, for I was born at Antwerp, the glorious town. Know then that he has made an agreement with Scheyf, the Councillor of Brabant, to let him into Antwerp with his ten companies of infantry.'

'I shall denounce him to the burghers,' said Ulenspiegl, 'and I'm off at once, light as a phantom.'

Off he went, and the following day the burghers were up in arms.

Ulenspiegl and Lamme, however, having left their asses with a farmer of Simon Simonsen, had to hide themselves for fear of being caught by the Count of Meghem, who was seeking them everywhere in order to hang them, for he had been told that two heretics had drunk his wine and eaten his meat.

He was jealous, and said so to his lovely lady, who gnashed her teeth in anger, wept, and swooned away seventeen times. The cook did likewise, though not so many times, and declared upon her share of Paradise and the eternal salvation of her soul that neither she nor her lady had done anything except give the leavings of a dinner to two poor pilgrims who, astride two miserable asses, had stopped before the kitchen window.

232

And that day there were so many tears shed that the floor was all damp. And, seeing this, Master Meghem was assured that they were not lying.

Lamme did not dare show his face at Meghem's house, for the cook always called him: 'My wife!'

And he was very doleful, thinking on the nourishment. But Ulenspiegl always brought some good dish to him, for he entered the house by Saint Catherine Street and hid himself in the garret.

The following day, at Vespers, the Count Meghem confessed to his lovely goodwife that he had resolved to lead the gendarmerie he commanded into Bois-le-Duc before daybreak. Then he fell asleep. The lovely goodwife went to the garret to tell this news to Ulenspiegl.

18 ULENSPIEGL, dressed as a pilgrim, started off immediately, without provisions of money, in order to warn the burghers of Bois-le-Duc. He counted on picking up a horse en route at Jeroen Praet's, the brother of Simon, for whom he had letters from the Prince. From there he would go at full speed by short cuts to Bois-le-Duc.

Crossing the road, he saw a troop of soldiers coming. He was very much afraid because of the letters.

But, being resolved to set a good face against misadventure, he boldly awaited the troopers and stopped dead, muttering his paternosters. As they passed him, he fell in with them and, marching along, learned that they were on their way to Bois-le-Duc.

A company of Walloons headed the column. It was led by Captain Lamotte and his guard of six halberdiers; then, according to their rank the ensign with a lesser guard, the provost, his halberdiers, two bailiffs, the chief watchman, the baggage-keepers, the executioner and his helper, and fifes and drums, making a great din.

Then came a Flemish company of two hundred men, with its captain and its ensign-bearer. It was divided into two centuries commanded by troop-sergeants, and into decuries commanded by *rot-meesters*. The provost and the *stocks-knechten*, staff-aides, were likewise preceded by fifes and drums beating and squealing.

Behind them, in two open carts, bursting with laughter, twittering like birds, singing like nightingales, eating, drinking, dancing, standing up, lying down, or riding, came their women, rare and wild wenches.

Some of them were dressed like foot-soldiers but with fine white linen, low-necked, slashed at the arms, the legs, the doublet, showing their sweet flesh; they were coifed with fine linen bonnets edged with

gold and surmounted with fine ostrich plumes waving in the wind. At
their belts of cloth-of-gold, crimped with red satin, hung the cloth-of-
gold scabbards for their daggers. And their shoes, their stockings, their
breeches, their doublets, shoulder-knots and trappings were all made
of gold and of white silk.

Others were dressed as *landsknechts*, but in blue, in green, in scarlet,
in azure, in crimson, slashed, broidered and blazoned, according to their
fancy. And all of them had about their arms the coloured armlets that
indicated their profession.

A *hoer-wyfel*, their sergeant, tried to make them be silent; but by
their darling grimaces and words they forced him to laugh and did not
obey him at all.

Ulenspiegl, dressed as a pilgrim, walked alongside the two troops,
like a small boat beside a great ship. And he murmured his paternosters.

Suddenly Lamotte said to him:

'Where are you going in this way, pilgrim?'

'Master Captain,' answered Ulenspiegl, who was hungry, 'I once committed a great sin and was condemned by the Chapter of Our Lady to
go to Rome on foot and demand pardon from the Holy Father, who
gave it to me. I returned to this country, cleansed of my sins on condition that I preach of the Sacred Mysteries to all and every trooper I
might meet on the way; they in return for my sermons owe me bread
and meat. And so, preaching, I sustain my poor life. Will you grant me
permission to keep my vow at the next halt?'

'Yes,' said Master Lamotte.

Ulenspiegl, mixing fraternally with the Walloons and the Flemings,
felt for his letters underneath his doublet.

The wenches called out to him:

'Pilgrim, handsome pilgrim, come here and show us the power of
your scallop.'

Ulenspiegl, coming up to them, said modestly:

'My sisters in God, mock not a poor pilgrim who goes by hill and
dale preaching the holy faith to troopers.'

And he ate up their darling graces with his eyes. But the wild wenches,
thrusting their lively faces through the canvas, said:

'You are too young to be preaching to troopers. Come on up in the
cart and we'll teach you sweeter discourses than that.'

Ulenspiegl would have obeyed willingly, but he could not because
of his letters; already two of the girls had passed their white, rounded
arms out of the cart and were trying to hoist him up into it beside them,
when the *hoer-wy fel*, jealous, said to Ulenspiegl: 'If you don't move on,
off goes your head.'

And Ulenspiegl moved on ahead, turning to watch on the sly the gay wenches gilded by the sun that shone brightly on the highway.

They came to Berchem. Philip de Lannoy, Sieur of Beauvoir, who commanded the Flemings, ordered a halt.

At that place there was an oak tree of medium height, bereft of all its branches save one large one, broken in the middle, from which they had hanged an Anabaptist by the neck the month before.

The troops stopped and the canteen-keepers came to sell them bread, wine, beer, and all sorts of meats. To the wild wenches they sold sugar, *castrelins*, almonds, tartlets; and seeing all this, Ulenspiegl became more hungry than ever.

Suddenly, climbing the tree like a monkey, he seated himself astride the large branch, which was seven feet from the ground. There he lashed himself with his scourge, while the troopers and the wenches made a circle about him.

'In the name of the Father, and of the Son, and of the Holy Ghost, Amen,' said he. 'It is written: "He that gives to the poor, lends to God." Troopers, and you, lovely ladies, sweet comrades in love to these valiant warriors, lend to the Lord; that is to say, give me bread, meat, wine, beer, if you like, tartlets, if it please you, and the Lord, who is rich, shall repay you with heaps of ortolans, rivers of malmsey wine, mountains of sugar-candy, with *rystpap* that you shall eat out of silver spoons in paradise.'

Then, lamenting:

'Do you not see by what cruel tortures I am trying to merit the pardon of my sins? Will you not ease the sharp anguish of this scourge that wounds my back and makes it bleed?'

'Who is this fool?' said the troopers.

'My friends,' answered Ulenspiegl, 'I am no fool but am repentant and famished; for while my spirit weeps for my sins, my stomach bemoans the absence of meat. Blessed troopers, and you, fair maidens, I see there among you fat ham, goose, sausages, wine, beer, tartlets. Will you not give something to the pilgrim?'

'Yes, yes,' said the Flemish troopers, 'he has a goodly mug, the preacher.'

And all of them began to throw morsels of food at him like balls. Ulenspiegl kept on talking and ate as he sat astride the branch.

'Hunger,' he said, 'renders a man hard and unused to prayer, but ham takes away at once that bad humour.'

'Beware of a split head!' shouted a troop-sergeant, as he threw a half-filled bottle at him.

235

Ulenspiegl seized the bottle in mid-air and drank a few gulps from it, saying:

'If hunger, furiously sharpened, is a thing harmful to the poor body of man, there is another thing more pernicious; and that is the anguish of a poor pilgrim to whom generous troopers have given, one a slice of ham and the other a bottle of beer. For the pilgrim is customarily sober, and if he drank with such slight nourishment in the stomach, he would get drunk right away.'

As he spoke he caught once again in the air the leg of a goose.

'This is a miraculous thing,' said he, 'to catch in the air a fish of the field. But it has disappeared, bone and all! What is more voracious than dry sand? A barren woman and a famished belly.'

Suddenly he felt the point of a halberd prick his backside. And he heard an ensign say:

'Do pilgrims now scorn legs of mutton?'

Ulenspiegl saw, spitted on the blade of the halberd, a great shoulder of mutton. Taking it, he said:

'Shoulder for shoulder, I like this better between my teeth than the other in my doublet. I'll make a marrow flute to sing your praises, compassionate halberdier. Yet, what is a meal without dessert,' he said, as he gnawed at the meat, 'what is a leg o' mutton, be it ever so succulent, if after it the pilgrim does not see coming up to him the blessed face of a tartlet?'

So saying, he put his hand to his face, for two tartlets, coming up from the group of wenches, had flattened themselves one against his eye and the other against his cheek.

And the wenches laughed and Ulenspiegl answered them, saying:

'Many thanks, pretty damsels, for giving me this jammy kiss.'

But the tartlets had fallen to the ground.

Suddenly the drums were beaten, the fifes squealed, and the troops resumed their march.

Master de Beauvoir told Ulenspiegl to come down from his tree and walk alongside the troops, from whose side he was wishing he were a hundred leagues away, for, from some words he had heard being spoken by a few sour-faced troopers, he scented that he was suspected and that he would soon be taken for a spy, and that they would search him and hang him if they found the missives on him.

So he tumbled into a ditch and called out:

'Pity, soldiers, my leg is broken, I won't be able to walk any farther. let me get into the wenches' cart.'

But he knew that the jealous *hoer-wyfel* would not allow this.

They, from their cart, called out to him:

'Come on, nice pilgrim, come on. We'll love you, caress you, feast you, heal you in a day.'

'I know it,' he said, 'women's hands are heavenly balm for every wound.'

But the jealous *hoer-wyfel*, speaking to Master Lamotte, said:

'Sir, I think that the pilgrim is mocking us with his broken leg in order that he may get into the wenches' cart. Order him to be left on the road.'

'Very well,' said Master Lamotte.

And Ulenspiegl was left in the ditch.

Several troopers, thinking that he had really broken his leg, were sorry because he was so gay. They left him meat and wine enough for two days. The wenches would have liked to have gone to his aid but, being unable to do so, they threw to him all that remained of their *castrelins*.

The troops being far away, Ulenspiegl took to the fields in his pilgrim's garb, bought a horse, and by roads and lanes entered Bois-le-Duc like the wind.

At the news of the coming of Messires Beauvoir and Lamotte, the townsfolk, to the number of eight hundred, shouldered arms, chose captains, and sent Ulenspiegl, dressed as a charcoal-burner, to Antwerp to ask for help from the drinking Hercules, Brederode.

And the troopers of Messires Lamotte and Beauvoir were unable to enter Bois-le-Duc, vigilant city, ready for a stout defence.

19 THE FOLLOWING MONTH a certain doctor, Agileus, gave Ulenspiegl two florins and letters which he was to carry to Simon Praet, who would then tell him what he had to do. At Praet's, Ulenspiegl found food and shelter. He slept well and his countenance bloomed youthfully; Praet, on the contrary, was miserable and of

piteous mien and always seemed to be closed about with sad thoughts. And Ulenspiegl was astonished to hear at night, if by chance he awoke, the sounds of hammering.

No matter how early he arose, Simon Praet was up before him, with more piteous mien, and a sadder look in his eyes, that shone like those of a man preparing for death or battle.

Often Praet sighed, joining his hands to pray, and always he seemed filled with indignation. His fingers were blackened and greasy, as were his arms and his shirt.

Ulenspiegl determined to know the reason for the hammerings, the blackened arms and the melancholy of Praet. One evening, after having been to the *Blauwe Gans*, the tavern of the Blue Goose, in company with Simon, who was there against his will, he feigned to be so drunk and so full in the head that he must immediately bear it to his pillow.

And Praet brought him sadly to the house.

Ulenspiegl slept in the garret, near the cats; Simon's bed was downstairs near the cellar.

Ulenspiegl, continuing to sham his drunkenness, staggered up the stairs, pretending to be about to fall down and holding on to the rope. Simon aided him with the tender care of a brother. Then, having put him to bed, condoling with him for his drunken state and praying God to forgive him, he went downstairs and soon Ulenspiegl heard the same sound of hammering that had so many times awakened him.

Arising noiselessly, he went with bare feet down the narrow stairs so that, after two and seventy steps, he came to a low doorway through the chink of which filtered a thread of light.

Simon was printing broadsides on the antique type of the time of Laurent Coster, the great propagator of the noble art of printing.

'What are you doing there?' demanded Ulenspiegl.

Frightened, Simon answered him:

'If you are on the devil's side, denounce me that I may die; but if you are on God's side, let your mouth be the prison of your tongue.'

238

'I am on God's side,' answered Ulenspiegl, 'and I wish you no evil. What are you doing there?'

'I am printing Bibles,' answered Simon, 'for if by day, in order to keep my wife and children, I publish the cruel and wicked edicts of His Majesty, by night I sow the true werd of God and so repair the evil I have done during the day.'

'You are brave,' said Ulenspiegl.

'I have the faith,' answered Simon.

And in this way, it was from this holy printing press that the Flemish Bibles were issued and scattered through the countries of Brabant, Flanders, Holland, Zeeland, Utrecht, North Brabant, Over-Yssel, Guelderland, until the day when Simon was condemned to have his head cut off, ending thus his life for Christ and Justice.

20 SIMON SAID one day to Ulenspiegl: 'Listen, brother, have you courage?' 'I have,' answered Ulenspiegl, 'enough to flog a Spaniard till he dies, kill an assassin, destroy a murderer.' 'Would you know how to sit patiently in a chimney,' demanded the printer, 'and listen to what was being said in a room?'

Ulenspiegl answered:

'Having by the grace of God a strong back and supple knees, I could stay as long as I cared to, like a cat.'

'Have you patience and a good memory?' demanded Simon.

'The ashes of Claes beat upon my breast,' answered Ulenspiegl.

'Listen, then,' said the printer, 'you will take this playingcard folded so, and you will go to Dendermonde and there knock twice loudly and once softly on the door of the house, the design of which is here sketched. Someone will open and ask if you are the chimney-sweep; you will answer that you are thin and that you have not lost the card. You will show it to him. After that, Tyl, you must do the best you can. Great woes are hovering over the land of Flanders.

'They will show you a chimney, prepared and swept in advance; you will find good clamps to climb by and a little wooden plank, firmly supported for you to sit on. When he who opened the door for you tells you to go up the chimney, do so, and there you will stay quite quiet. Illustrious lords will meet in the room, before the chimney where you'll be. These lords are William the Silent, Prince of Orange, the Counts Egmont, Hoorn, Hoogstraeten, and Ludwig of Nassau, the valiant brother of the Silent One. We Reformists wish to know what these lords will and can undertake to save the country.'

Now on the first of April, Ulenspiegl did as he had been told and

239

posted himself in the chimney. He was satisfied to see that there was no fire burning and thought that, there being no smoke, he would hear all the better.

Soon the door of the room opened and he was pierced by a gust of wind that went right through him. But he took this wind quite patiently, saying that it would freshen his attention.

Then he heard my lords of Orange and Egmont, and the others, come into the room. They began to speak of their fears, of the King's anger, and the maladministration of the revenues and the finances. One of them spoke with a sharp, clear and haughty tone; that was Egmont. Ulenspiegl recognized him, as he also recognized Hoogstraeten by his hoarse voice; Hoorn by his loud voice; the Count Ludwig of Nassau by his firm and soldierly speech; and the Silent One by the slow manner in which he pronounced all his words, as though he had weighed each one in the balance.

Count Egmont demanded to know why they were meeting for a second time, when at Hellegat they had had the leisure to decide what they wished to do.

Hoorn answered:

'The hours go swiftly by, the King grows angry, let us beware of temporizing.'

The Silent One then said:

'The country is in danger; we must defend it against the attack of a foreign army.'

Egmont answered angrily that he thought it astonishing that the King, his master, thought it necessary to send an army when all had been pacified by the efforts of the lords and notably his own.

But the Silent One said:

'Philip has in the Netherlands fourteen bands of regulars whose troops are devoted to the man who commanded them at Gravelines and Saint-Quentin.'

'I do not understand,' said Egmont.

The Prince continued:

'I do not wish to say more, but you are about to have read to you, you and the other lords met here, certain letters, beginning with those of the poor prisoner, Montigny.'

In these letters Messer Montigny wrote:

'The King is extremely angry with what has happened in the Netherlands, and he will punish, when the time comes, those who caused all the trouble.'

At this the Count Egmont said he was cold and that it might be a
240

good thing to light the great log fire. This was done while two lords spoke of the letters.

The fire did not draw because of the great stoppage in the chimney, and the room was soon full of smoke.

The Count Hoogstraeten then read, coughing, the intercepted letters which had been addressed to the Vice-Regent by the Duke of Alba.

'The ambassador,' said Hoogstraeten, 'writes that all the evil that has come to the Netherlands is the fault of three; to wit: Messires Orange, Egmont, and Hoorn. We must, says the ambassador, show fair face to these three lords and tell them that the King recognizes that he only holds these lands in fee through their services. As for the two single ones—Montigny and Berghes—they are where they should be.'

'Ah,' said Ulenspiegl, 'I'd rather be in a smoky chimney in the country of Flanders than in a cool prison in Spain; for there garrotes sprout between damp walls.'

'The aforesaid ambassador adds that the King said in the town of Madrid:

' "By all that has happened in the Netherlands, our Royal reputation has been diminished, the service of God is debased, and we shall abandon all our other lands rather than let such a rebellion go unpunished. We have decided to go in person to the Netherlands, and have requested assistance from the Pope and the Emperor. Under the present evil lies the future good. We shall reduce the Netherlands under our absolute obedience and modify, according to our own will, the state, religion and government." '

'Ah, Philip the King,' said Ulenspiegl to himself, 'if I could modify you after my own will you should submit, under my Flemish stick, to a great modification of your thighs, arms and legs. I would nail your head to your back with two nails to see if in that state, looking back at the graveyard you leave behind you, you would sing in your own way your song of tyrannical modification.'

Wine was brought in. Hoogstraeten arose and said: 'I drink to the country!' All of them did likewise, and he, setting down his tankard on the table, added: 'An evil hour rings out for the Belgian nobility. We must take thought of the means whereby to defend ourselves.'

Waiting for a reply, he watched Egmont, who said not a word.

But the Silent One spoke: 'We shall resist,' said he, 'if Egmont who, twice, at Saint-Quentin and Gravelines, made France tremble; who has all the authority over the Flemish troopers, wishes to come to our aid and prevent the Spaniard from entering our country.'

Messer Egmont answered: 'I have too respectful an opinion of the King to think that we must take arms against him as rebels. Let those

242

who fear his anger retire. I shall stay, having no means of livelihood without his help.'

'Philip can avenge himself cruelly,' said the Silent One.

'I have confidence,' answered Egmont.

'Your head included?' demanded Ludwig of Nassau.

'Included,' answered Egmont. 'Head, body, devotion, all are his.'

'Beloved and trusty friend, I will follow you,' said Hoorn.

The Silent One said: 'We must foresee and not wait.'

Then Messer Egmont spoke with vehemence: 'I had twenty-two Reformists hanged at Grammont. If the preaching ceased, if we punished the image-breakers, the King's anger would be appeased.'

The Silent One answered: 'These are uncertain hopes.'

'Let us arm ourselves with confidence,' said Egmont.

'Let us arm ourselves with confidence,' repeated Hoorn.

'It is with steel and not with confidence that we must arm ourselves,' retorted Hoogstraeten.

At this, the Silent One made a motion that he wished to leave.

'Adieu! Landless Prince,' said Egmont.

'Adieu! Headless Count,' answered the Silent One.

Ludwig of Nassau then said: 'The stake is for the sheep and glory for the soldier-saviour of his country!'

'I cannot and will not,' said Egmont.

'The blood of the victims falls upon the head of the courtier!' said Ulenspiegl.

The lords withdrew.

Then Ulenspiegl came down from his chimney and immediately went to bear the news to Praet. And the latter said: 'Egmont is a traitor, God is with the Prince.'

The Duke! The Duke in Brussels! Where are the winged strongboxes?

Book Three

1 THE SILENT ONE goes on, God guiding him. The two counts are already captured; and Alba has promised the Silent One leniency and pardon if he will appear before him. When he heard of this, Ulenspiegl said to Lamme:

'*Heuque de m'amie*, the Duke has summoned to appear before him within thrice fourteen days—at the instance of Dubois, the Procurator-General—the Prince of Orange, his brother Ludwig, Hoogstraeten, Van den Bergh, Culemburg, de Brederode and other friends of the Prince, promising them good justice and mercy. Listen, Lamme: One day an Amster-

dam Jew summoned one of his enemies to come down into the street; the summoner was on the pavement and the one summoned was up at a window. "Come down here," said the summoner to the summoned, "and I will give you such a whack on the head that it will be smashed down into your breast and you'll be looking through your ribs like a thief through his prison bars." The summoned one answered: "Were you to promise me a hundred-fold more than that I would not come down." And so may Orange and the others answer the Duke.'

And they did, refusing to appear. But Egmont and de Hoorn did not follow their example. And weakness in duty calls forth the fated hour.

2 AT THIS TIME there were beheaded in the Horse Market in Brussels the sires of Andelot, the sons of Battembourg, and other illustrious and valiant knights who had tried to take Amsterdam by surprise. And as they walked to their execution—there were eighteen of them, singing hymns as they marched along—the kettle-drums beat before and behind them the whole length of the way.

And the Spanish troopers, escorting them and carrying flaming torches, burned them on all parts of the body. And, when they writhed with pain, the troopers would say: 'How now, Lutherans, does it hurt you so much to be burned so soon?'

And the man who betrayed them was named Dierick Slosse; he

brought them to Enckhuysen, still Catholic, where they were handed over to the Duke's torturers. And they died bravely.

And the King inherited.

3   'DID YOU SEE HIM PASS?' asked Ulenspiegl, dressed as a woodsman, to Lamme, dressed likewise. 'Did you see the wicked Duke with his forehead flat as an eagle's and his long beard hanging down like a gallows' cord? God strangle him! Did you see that spider with his long hairy legs that Satan in his vomiting spewed out on our country? Come, Lamme; come. We'll go cast stones in his web.'

'La!' said Lamme, 'we'll be burned alive.'

'Come to Groenendael, my good friend; come to Groenendael, there's a lovely cloister there, where his spiderish dukality goes to pray God for peace to finish his work, that is, to let his black wits wallow in carrion. We are in Lent and it is only from blood that the Duke has no mind to fast. Come, Lamme, there are five hundred armed horsemen about the house of Ohain; three hundred footmen have departed in little bands to enter the forest of Soignes.

'Soon, when Alba is saying his prayers, we shall run at him and, having taken him, we'll place him in a fine iron cage and send him to the Prince.'

But Lamme, quivering with anguish, said to Ulenspiegl:

'A great risk, my boy! A great risk! I would follow you in this enterprise if my legs were not so weak and my belly so bloated with that sour beer they drink in this town of Brussels.'

These words were spoken in a hole in the woods, dug in the ground in the midst of a thicket. Suddenly, looking out through the leaves as out of a burrow, they saw the yellow and red uniforms of the Duke's troopers, whose weapons glistened in the sun as they walked through the woods.

'We're betrayed,' said Ulenspiegl.

When he could see no more troopers, he ran with great speed to Ohain. The soldiers let him pass without a word, because of his woodsman's clothes and the load of wood he carried on his back. At Ohain he found horsemen waiting; he spread the news among them and they all dispersed and escaped, all save the Sire de Beausart, who was taken. As for the footmen coming from Brussels, not even one was found.

And it was the cowardly traitor of the regiment of Sieur de Likes who betrayed them all.

The Sire de Beausart paid cruelly for the others.

248

Ulenspiegl, his heart thumping with anguish, went to the Cattle Market in Brussels to see his terrible torture.

And poor Armentieres, tied on the rack, received thirty-seven blows from an iron bar on his legs, his arms, his hands and his feet; which were in turn broken to pieces, for the executioners wanted to see him suffer cruelly.

The thirty-seventh blow he received on the chest, and of that one he died.

4 ON A JUNE DAY, bright and soft, there was set up at Brussels, in the Market Place before the Town Hall, a scaffold covered with black cloth; alongside it were two tall stakes with iron points. On the scaffold there were two black cushions and a little table on which was laid a silver cross. And on this scaffold were put to death, by the sword, the noble counts of Egmont and Hoorn. And the King inherited.

And the ambassador of François, first of that name, speaking of Egmont, said:

'I have just seen beheaded the man who caused France to tremble twice.'

And the heads of the counts were set up on the iron-spiked stakes.

And Ulenspiegl said to Lamme:

'The bodies and the blood are covered with black cloth. Blessed are they who hold their hearts high and keep aloft their sword in the black days that are to come!'

5 IN THESE DAYS the Silent One gathered together an army and invaded the Netherlands from three sides. And Ulenspiegl said, at a meeting of Wild Beggars in Marenhout:

'On the advice of the Inquisitors, Philip the King has declared each and every inhabitant of the Netherlands guilty of treason through heresy, as much for having adhered to it as for not having set obstacles in its way and, considering this execrable crime, condemns them all, regardless of sex or age—with the exception of those noted by name—to the penalties reserved for such misdemeanours; and this without any hope of pardon.

'The King inherits.   •

'Death reaps in the rich and vast lands that border the North Sea, the County of Emden, the river Amise, the countries of Westphalia, Cleves, Juliers and Liége, the Bishopric of Cologne and that of Treves, the countries of Lorraine and France.

'Death reaps over a soil of three hundred and forty leagues, in two hundred walled towns, in a hundred and fifty villages having town rights, in the country-places, the boroughs and the plains. The King inherits.

'And it is not enough that eleven thousand executioners do the work,' he continued. 'Alba calls them soldiers. And the land of our fathers has become a charnel-house from whence the arts take flight, that the trades quit, that the industries abandon to go and enrich the foreigners who allow them to worship the God of Free Conscience. Death and ruin reap. The King inherits.

'These countries had conquered their privileges through the money given to these needy princes; these privileges are confiscated. They had hoped, after the contracts passed between them and their sovereigns, to enjoy the riches which were the fruits of their labour. They were wrong; the mason built for the fire, the labourer worked for the robber. The King inherits.

'Blood and tears! Death reaps at the stake, on the trees that serve as gallows along the highway, in the open pits where poor young girls are thrown alive, in the drownings in prison, in the circle of flaming faggots in whose midst the victims are burned by slow fire, in the huts of blazing straw within which the victims die in flames and smoke. The King inherits.

'So has willed the Pope of Rome.

'The towns are teeming with spies awaiting their share of the victims' goods. The richer you are, the more guilty you are. The King inherits.

'But the brave men of the land will not let themselves be slain like lambs. Among those who have fled there are some armed ones who have taken refuge in the woods. The monks have denounced them so that they might be killed and thus have their goods confiscated. And so by night, by day, going about in bands like wild beasts, they rush in on the cloisters and re-take, in the form of candelabras, gold and silver

250

reliquaries, pyxes, patens and precious vases, the money stolen from the poor. Is that not so, goodmen? They drink the wine which the monks keep for themselves alone. The vases, melted down or pawned, serve to provide money for the holy war. Up with the Beggars!

'They harass the soldiers of the King, killing and despoiling them, and then flee back to their dens. One can see in the woods, day and night, fires lighted and extinguished, continually changing place; these are the fires for our feasts. For us the furred and feathered game. We are lords. The peasants give us bread and bacon when we want it. Look at them, Lamme. Raggle-taggled, fierce, resolute and proud-eyed, they wander in the woods with their hatchets, halberds, longswords, daggers, pikes, lances, crossbows, muskets; for any weapon is good for them, and they will never march under officers. Up with the Beggars!'

And Ulenspiegl sang:

> *Slaet op den trommele van dirre dom deyne,*
> *Slaet op den trommele van dirre dom dom.*
> Beat the drums! *van dirre dom deyne,*
>   Beat the drums of war.
> Let us tear from the Duke his guts
>   And slap them in his face!
> *Slaet op den trommele,* beat the drums.
> Cursed be the Duke! To the killer, death!
>
> Let him be thrown to the dogs! To the butcher,
>   death! And up with the Beggars!
>   Hang him by the tongue,
> And by the arm; by the tongue that commands
> And the arm that signs the warrant of death.
>   *Slaet op den trommele.*
> Beat the drums of war. And up with the Beggars!
>
> Let the Duke be locked up alive with his victims' corpses,
>   That in the rotting stink
>   He may die there of the plague!
> Beat the drums of war. And up with the Beggars!
>
>   Christ, from on high, look down on us,
>   Thy soldiers risking fire, the rope,
>   The sword, for Thy Word's sake.
> We fight to deliver our father's land.
> *Slaet op den trommele van dirre dom deyne,*
> Beat the drums of war. And up with the Beggars!

And they all drank and shouted:

'Up with the Beggars!'

And Ulenspiegl, drinking from a gilt tankard, looked with pride on the valiant faces of the Wild Beggars.

'Wild men,' said he, 'you are wolves, lions, tigers. Eat up the dogs of this king of the blood.'

'Up with the Beggars!' said they singing:

> *Slaet op den trommele van dirre dom deyne,*
> *Slaet op den trommele van dirre dom dom.*
> Beat the drums of war. And up with the Beggars!

6   ULENSPIEGL, being at Ypres, recruited soldiers for the Prince. Pursued by the Duke's men, he presented himself as beadle to the provost of Saint Martin. There he had for a companion a bell-ringer named Pompilius Numan, a low coward, who at night took his shadow for the devil and his shirt for a ghost.

The provost was stout and plump as a capon fattened•and ready for the spit. Ulenspiegl soon saw on what grass he grazed, to make him so fat. According to what the bell-ringer told him and what he saw with his own eyes, the provost lunched at nine o'clock and dined at four. He stayed in bed until eight-thirty; then, before lunching, he would go for a walk in his church to see if the poor-boxes were well filled. And half of their contents he put in his own purse. At nine he lunched on a bowl of milk, half a leg of mutton, a little heron patty, and downed five tankards of Brussels wine. At ten o'clock, sucking a few plums and then washing them down with Orleans wine, he prayed God never to lead him into the ways of gluttony. At noon, to pass the time, he munched at a wing and a leg of fowl. At one o'clock, thinking of his dinner, he downed a great draught of Spanish wine; then, stretching out on his bed, he refreshed himself with a little nap.

On waking up, he ate a little smoked salmon to tickle his appetite, and emptied a large tankard of Antwerp *dobble knol*. Then, going down to the kitchen, he seated himself before the fireplace where an enormous log-fire was blazing. He watched, being roasted and browned for the monks of the abbey, a great side of veal or well-scalded little pig, which he would rather have eaten than a hunk of bread. But his appetite seemed to be lacking. And he would contemplate the spit, which turned by itself marvellously. It was the handiwork of Pieter van Steenkiste, the blacksmith, who lived in the castellany of Courtrai. The provost paid him fifteen Paris pounds for one of these spits.

Then he went up again to bed, there to drowse because of his weariness; at two he would awaken to gulp a little pig-jelly which he washed down with Romagna wine worth two hundred and forty florins the barrel. At three o'clock he would eat a fledgling in Madeira sugar and empty two glasses of Malvoisie worth seventeen florins the keg. At three thirty he took the half of a jar of jam and washed it down with hydromel. Now wide awake, he would take one of his feet in his hands and remain thus quite thoughtful.

The dinner hour being come, the vicar of St. John's sometimes happened along to visit him at that succulent hour. They often debated as to who would eat the most fish, fowl, game and meat. The one who was soonest full had to pay the other a dish of carbonades with three hot wines, four spices and seven vegetables.

So eating and drinking, they talked together of heretics, both being of the opinion that there could not be too many of them destroyed. Thus they never quarrelled, except when they discussed the thirty-nine ways of making good beer soup.

Then, drooping their venerable heads on their sacerdotal paunches, they would snore. Sometimes, half waking, one of them would say that life in this world is a very sweet thing and that poor folk are wrong in complaining about it.

It was for this saintly man that Ulenspiegl became the beadle. He helped him very well at mass, not without filling the flagons three times—twice for himself and once for the provost. The bell-ringer, Pompilius Numan, sometimes aided him at this.

Ulenspiegl, who saw Pompilius so flourishing, paunchy and puffed out, asked him if it was in the service of the provost that he had laid up his treasure of enviable health.

'Yes, my boy,' replied Pompilius, 'but shut the door for fear someone might hear us.'

Then, speaking in a whisper:

'You know that our master, the provost,' he said, 'loves all wines and beers, all meats and fowls, with a tender love. Therefore he locks up his meats in a cupboard and his wines in a cellar the keys of which he continually carries about with him in his pouch. And he sleeps with his hands over them . . . At night, when he's sleeping, I go and take the keys from off his paunch and then put them back again, not without trembling, my boy, for if he knew of my crime he would have me boiled alive.'

'Pompilius,' said Ulenspiegl, 'you mustn't take so much trouble; get the keys once and I'll make models of them, and we'll leave the originals on the belly of the good provost.'

'Do so, my boy,' said Pompilius.

Ulenspiegl made the keys and, towards eight o'clock at night, as soon as they judged that the good provost was sound asleep, they went down to make their choice of edibles and bottles. Ulenspiegl carried the bottles and Pompilius the meats, because Pompilius always trembled like a leaf and the hams and legs of mutton would not break if they fell. Sometimes they took uncooked poultry, and many cats in the neighbourhood were blamed for this and done to death for the crime.

Armed with their booty, they would then go to the *Ketel-Straat*—the street of the wild women. There they kept back nothing, but donated liberally to their darlings smoked beef and ham, saveloys and poultry, and gave them to drink of Orleans and Romagna wines, and *Ingelsche Bier* which is called *ale* at the other side of the North Sea, and which they poured in floods down the cool throats of the fair ones. And they were re-paid with caresses.

It came to pass one morning after lunch that the provost sent for both of them. He had a terrible look as he sucked—not without anger—at a marrow-bone from his soup.

Pompilius trembled in his breeches and his belly quivered with fright. Ulenspiegl, standing quite still, fingered agreeably in his pocket the keys of the cellar.

The provost, speaking to him, said:

'There's someone been drinking my wine and eating my poultry. Is it you, my son?'

'No,' answered Ulenspiegl.

'And that bell-ringer,' said the provost, pointing to Pompilius, 'have not his fingers been dipped in the crime? For he is white as a dying man, as he may well be with the stolen wine, that will act as poison to him.'

'La! Messire,' said Ulenspiegl, 'you wrongfully accuse your bell-ringer. For if he is white, it is not from having drunk wine but rather because he does not drink enough of it, and from this he is so loosed that if something is not done to stop it, his soul will be running out in a stream in his breeches.'

'The poor we have always with us,' said the provost, as he drank a deep draught of wine from his tankard. 'But tell me, my son, if you, with your lynx-eyes, have not seen the thieves?'

'I will keep on the watch for them, Messire Provost,' answered Ulenspiegl.

'May God keep you both in His joy, my children,' said the provost, 'and live soberly. For it is from intemperance that all evils come in this valley of tears. Go in peace.'

And he blessed them.

And he still sucked at the marrow-bone from the soup, and he drank another great draught of wine.

Ulenspiegl and Pompilius both went out.

'The filthy miser,' said Ulenspiegl, 'wouldn't even give you a drop of his wine to drink. It will be worth while stealing more from him. But why are you trembling so?'

'My breeches are all wet,' said Pompilius.

'Water dries quickly, my boy,' said Ulenspiegl. 'But be gay; to-night there will be music of flagons in the *Ketel-Straat*. And we'll fill up the three night-watchmen who, with snores, shall guard the town.'

And this they did.

And now they were close to Saint Martin's Day. The church was all decked for the feast. Ulenspiegl and Pompilius entered it at night and closed all the doors, lighted all the candles, took a viola and bagpipes and played them as best they could. And the candles blazed like suns. But that was not all. Their job being done, they went to the provost, whom they found still on his feet in spite of the lateness of the hour, nibbling at a thrush, drinking Rhine wine, and staring wide-eyed at the windows of the church all lit up.

'Messire Provost,' said Ulenspiegl to him, 'would you know who eats your meats and drinks your wines?'

'And that illumination?' said the provost, pointing to the church windows. 'Ah, Lord God, do you permit Master Saint Martin to burn the candles of the poor monks in this way, at night, without paying?'

'He's doing something else as well, Messire Provost,' said Ulenspiegl, 'but come and see.'

The provost took his crosier and followed them. They entered the church.

There he saw, in the middle of the great nave, all the saints come down from their niches and, standing in a circle, seemingly commanded by Saint Martin, who stood a head above them and held in the index finger of his hand, raised to bless, a roast turkey. The others held in their hands or lifted towards their mouths bits of chicken or goose, sausages, hams, raw fish or cooked fish, and among others a pike that weighed at least fourteen pounds. And each one had a flask of wine at his feet.

At this spectacle the provost, in controlling his anger, became so red and his face so swollen that Pompilius and Ulenspiegl thought he was going to burst. But the provost, without paying any attention to them, marched straight up to Saint Martin—menacing him as though he would accuse him of the crime of the others—snatched the turkey from his finger and struck at him with such great blows that he broke the saint's arm, nose, crosier and mitre.

As for the others, he did not spare them his whacks, and more than one left under his blows their arms, hands, mitres, crosiers, scythes, axes, gridirons, saws and other emblems of dignity and martyrdom. Then the provost, his belly quivering, went himself to snuff out the candles with fury and celerity.

He carried off all that he could of hams, poultry and sausages and, bowed down under the load, he re-entered his bedroom, so grieved and angry that he drank, draught for draught, three great flagons of wine.

Ulenspiegl, being assured that he was asleep, bore off to the *Ketel-Straat* all that the provost thought he had saved and also all that remained in the church, not without having first supped off the best bits. And the debris was laid at the feet of the saints.

Next morning, as Pompilius was ringing the matin bell, Ulenspiegl went up to the bedroom of the provost and asked him to come down to the church.

There, showing him the debris of saints and poultry, he said:

'Messire Provost, your efforts were in vain; they are just the same.'

'Yes,' answered the provost, 'they came right to my bedroom like robbers, to take back what I saved. Ah, master saints, I shall complain to the Pope.'

'Yes,' replied Ulenspiegl, 'but the day after to-morrow is the procession, and the workmen will soon be coming to the church. If they see all these poor mutilated saints, don't you fear you'll be accused of iconoclasm?'

'Oh, Master Saint Martin,' said the provost, 'spare me the fire, I knew not what I did.'

Then, turning to Ulenspiegl, while the frightened bell-ringer pulled the bell-ropes, he said:

'They'll never be able to repair Saint Martin between now and Sunday. What am I going to do, and what will the people say?'

'Messire,' answered Ulenspiegl, 'you must use an innocent subterfuge. We will stick a beard on the face of Pompilius, who is quite respectable, being always melancholy; we will dress him up with the mitre, alb, amice, and the saint's great cloak of cloth of gold; we will tell him to hold himself still on his pedestal and the people will take him for the wooden Saint Martin.'

The provost went toward Pompilius, who was swinging on the bell-ropes:

'Stop ringing,' said he, 'and listen to me. Do you want to earn fifteen ducats? Sunday, the day of the procession, you will be Saint Martin.

256

Ulenspiegl will dress you up in the right way and if, borne by four men, you make a move or say a word I'll have you boiled alive in the oil of the great cauldron that the executioner has just had set up in the market place.'

'I thank you, Monseigneur,' said Pompilius, 'but you know that I hold in my water with great difficulty.'

'You must obey,' retorted the provost.

'I shall obey, Monseigneur,' said Pompilius, quite piteously.

7 THE FOLLOWING DAY, under a bright sun, the procession left the church. Ulenspiegl had repaired as best he could the twelve saints that swayed on their pedestals between the banners of the corporation; then came the statue of Our Lady; then the young girls of the Virgin, all dressed in white and singing canticles; then the archers and musketeers; then, nearest to the daïs and swaying more than the others, Pompilius bending under the heavy vestments of Master Saint Martin.

Ulenspiegl, having provided himself with itching powder, had himself dressed Pompilius in his episcopal costume, put on his gloves and crosier, and showed him the Latin way of blessing the people. He had also helped the priests to clothe themselves. On the ones he placed the stole, on the others the amice, and on the deacons the alb. He ran hither and yon about the church, arranging the folds of this doublet or these breeches. He admired and praised the well-polished weapons of the musketeers and the dreaded bows of the brotherhood of archers. And to each one he gave on the ruff, or the back or the wrist, a pinch of itching powder. But the dean and the four bearers of Saint Martin were among those who received the most. As for the young girls of the Virgin he spared them, considering their darling grace.

The procession went out with banners in the wind, ensigns showing, in fine order. Men and women crossed themselves as it passed. And the sun shone down brightly.

The dean was the first to feel the effects of the powder, and scratched himself a little behind the ear. All of them, priests, archers, bow-men, scratched their necks, legs, wrists, without daring to do so overtly. The four bearers scratched themselves also, but the bell-ringer—more itchy than the others for he was more exposed to the blazing sun—did not dare move for fear of being boiled alive. Pinching his nose, he made an ugly grimace and trembled on his shaky legs, for each time that his bearers scratched themselves he almost tumbled down.

But he did not dare budge and, through fright, passed water, and the bearers said:

'Great Saint Martin, is it going to rain now?'

The priests sang a hymn to Our Lady,

Si de coe . . . coe . . . coe . . . lo descenderes
O sanc . . . ta . . . ta . . . ta . . . Ma . . . ma . . . ria

with voices that trembled because of their itching, which became excessive; but they scratched themselves modestly. Just the same the dean and the four bearers of Saint Martin had their wrists and necks scratched to pieces. Pompilius kept very quiet, shaking on his poor legs that itched more and more.

But suddenly all the crossbow-men, archers, deacons, priests, dean and the bearers of Saint Martin stopped dead to scratch themselves. The powder was itching at the soles of Pompilius's feet but he did not dare move for fear of toppling.

And the onlookers said that Saint Martin rolled very fierce eyes and made a very menacing face at the poor people.

Then the dean started the procession on its way again.

Soon the hot sun, shining straight down on all these processional backs and bellies, made the effects of the powder quite intolerable.

And then the priests, archers, crossbow-men, deacons, and the dean were all seen to stop and scratch themselves shamelessly all over where they itched like a band of monkeys.

The young girls of the Virgin sang their hymn and it was like the song of the angels, all these sweet clear voices mounting up to heaven.

All, in the end, went off as they could; the dean, as he scratched himself, saved the Holy Sacrament; the pious people carried the relics into the church; the four bearers of Saint Martin threw Pompilius roughly to the ground. There, not daring to scratch himself, nor either speak or move, the poor bell-ringer closed his eyes devoutly.

Two young lads would have carried him away but they found him too heavy, so they stood him up against the wall and there Pompilius wept great tears.

The people assembled about him; the women went off to fetch fine white linen kerchiefs with which they wiped his face so that they could preserve the tears as relics; and they said to him:

'Monseigneur, how hot you are!'

The bell-ringer looked at them ruefully and in spite of himself wriggled his nose.

But, as the tears poured from his eyes, the women said:

'Great Saint Martin, are you weeping over the sins of the town of

258

Ypres? Is not your noble nose moving? Yet we have followed the counsel of Louis Vives, and the poor of Ypres shall have the wherewithal to work and eat. Oh, the great tears! They are pearls. Our salvation is here.'

The men said:

'Great Saint Martin, must we tear down the *Ketel-Straat*? But teach us, above all, the way to keep the poor girls from going out at night and thus run into a thousand adventures.'

Suddenly the people cried: 'Here's the beadle!'

Ulenspiegl then came and, taking up Pompilius by the middle, carried him off on his shoulder, followed by a crowd of the faithful.

'La!' whispered the poor bell-ringer in his ear, 'I'm going to itch to death, my boy.'

'Hold yourself stiff,' answered Ulenspiegl, 'are you forgetting that you're a wooden saint?'

He ran with great strides and set down Pompilius before the provost, who was currying himself with his nails until the blood ran.

'Bell-ringer,' said the provost, 'did *you* scratch yourself as we all did?'

'No, Messire,' answered Pompilius.

'Did you speak or make any move?'

'No, Messire,' answered Pompilius.

'Then you shall have your fifteen ducats,' said the provost. 'Go and scratch yourself now.'

8 THE FOLLOWING DAY the people, having learned the facts from Ulenspiegl, said that it was a nasty mockery to have made them adore as a saint a whiner who let his water run from him. And many became heretics. And, leaving with their goods, they fled to join the prince's army.

Ulenspiegl returned toward Liége.

Being alone in the woods, he sat himself down and mused. Looking up at the clear sky, he said:

'War, always war, for the Spanish enemy kills the poor people, pillages our goods, violates our wives and daughters. And all the time our fair money goes, and our blood runs in the gutter, profiting no one except that royal bumpkin who wishes to place one more flower of authority in his crown. A flower that he thinks glorious; flower of blood, flower of smoke. Ah, if I could only flower you as I would like to, there would be none but flies that would want to keep you company.'

As he thought of these things, he saw passing before him a whole herd of stags. There were among them old ones and tall, having still

260

their dowcets and proudly carrying their antlers with nine points. Pretty brockets, which are their squires, trotted alongside them, seeming quite ready to come to their aid with their pointed horns. Ulenspiegl did not know where they were going but he judged that it must be to their lair.

'Ah!' said he, 'old stags and pretty brockets, you are going gay and proud to your lair in the depths of the woods, eating young sprouts, scenting out the embalmed fragrances, happy until the hunter-executioner comes. So is it with us, old stags and brockets!'

And the ashes of Claes beat upon the breast of Ulenspiegl.

9 IN SEPTEMBER, when the gnats no longer bite, the Silent One, with six field-guns and four large cannon speaking for him, and fourteen thousand Flemings, Walloons and Germans, crossed the Rhine at Saint Vyt. Under the yellow and red ensigns of the knotty staff of Burgundy—staff that so long bruised our country, staff of the beginning of the servitude exercised by Alba, the bloody duke—marched twenty-six thousand and five hundred men, rumbled along seventeen field guns and nine great cannon.

But the Silent One was not to have any great success in that war, for Alba continually refused to battle with him.

And the Silent One's brother, Ludwig, the Bayard of Flanders, after many towns won and many boats ransomed on the Rhine, lost at Jemmingen, in Frisia, to the son of the duke, sixteen cannon, fifteen hundred horses and twenty ensigns, because of the cowardly mercenary troopers who demanded money when they should have fought. And through ruins, blood and tears, Ulenspiegl vainly sought the salvation of the land of his fathers.

And the executioners throughout the country hanged, beheaded, burned the poor innocent victims.

And the King inherited.

261

10 WALKING THROUGH the Walloon country, Ulenspiegl saw that the prince had no hope of aid from there; and so he came close to the town of Bouillon. Little by little he saw the road filled with hunchbacks of every age, sex and condition. All had great rosaries, whose beads they were telling devoutly.

And their prayers were as the croakings of frogs in a pond at night in warm weather.

There were hunchback mothers carrying hunchback children, while other little ones of the same brood clung to their skirts. And there were hunchbacks on the hills and hunchbacks in the plains. And everywhere against the clear sky Ulenspiegl saw their thin silhouettes outlined.

He went up to one of them, and said:

'Where are they going, all these poor men, women and children?'

The man answered:

'We are going to the tomb of Master Saint Remacle, to pray him to give us our heart's desire and take from our backs this hump of humiliation.'

Ulenspiegl retorted:

'Could Master Saint Remacle also give me what my heart desires and take from off the back of the poor towns the duke of the blood who weighs on them like a hump of lead?'

'He has no power to remove the humps of penance,' answered the pilgrim.

'And does he remove any others?' asked Ulenspiegl.

'Yes, when the humps are young. If the miracle of healing occurs then, we revel and feast all over the town. And each pilgrim gives a silver piece, and many times a golden florin to the fortunate healed one, who, through his cure, has become a saint and may with efficacy pray for others.'

Ulenspiegl said:

'Why does the rich Master Saint Remacle, like any perfidious apothecary, make folk pay for his cures?'

'Impious tramp, he punishes blasphemers!' answered the pilgrim, shaking his hump furiously.

'La!' moaned Ulenspiegl.

And he fell down, all doubled up at the foot of a tree.

The pilgrim, gazing at him, said:

'Master Saint Remacle strikes hard those whom he strikes.'

Ulenspiegl, hunching his back and scratching it, moaned:

'Glorious saint, have mercy. It's the punishment. I feel between my shoulders a stinging pain. La! Ay! Pardon, Master Saint Remacle. Go,

262

pilgrim, go, and leave me alone here, as a parricide, to weep and repent.'

But the pilgrim had already flown to the great square of Bouillon, where all the hunchbacks were assembled.

There, shivering with fright, he said to them, speaking jerkily:

'Met a pilgrim straight as a poplar . . . blaspheming pilgrim . . . hump on the back . . . flaming hump!'

Hearing this, the pilgrims gave vent to a thousand happy shouts, saying:

'Master Saint Remacle, if you give humps, you can take them away. Take away our humps, Master Saint Remacle!'

In the meantime, Ulenspiegl left his tree. Passing through a deserted suburb he saw, hanging by the low door of a tavern, two bladders swinging from a pole—pigs' bladders hung up in this way are a sign of a black-pudding kermesse, *panch kermis,* as they say in the Brabant country.

Ulenspiegl took one of these bladders, picked up from the ground the backbone of a *schol* (dried plaice), pricked himself and let the blood flow into the bladder, blew it up, closed it, placed it on his back and above it set the sharp bone of the *schol.* So equipped, with his back bent, his head wagging, and his legs tottering like an old hunchback, he came to the square.

The pilgrim who had witnessed his fall saw him and shouted:

'There's the blasphemer!'

And he pointed his finger at him. And everybody ran to see the afflicted one.

Ulenspiegl nodded his head piteously.

'Ah,' said he, 'I merit neither grace nor pity; slay me like a mad dog.'

And the hunchbacks, rubbing their hands together, said:

'One more in our confraternity.'

Ulenspiegl—muttering between his teeth: 'I will make you pay for this, evil ones'—seemed to bear all patiently, and said:

'I will neither eat nor drink, even to strengthen my hump, until Master Saint Remacle has deigned to cure me, even as he smote me.'

At the rumour of the miracle, the dean came out of the church. He was a tall, paunchy and majestic man. Nose in the air, he plowed through the sea of hunchbacks like a ship.

They showed him Ulenspiegl, to whom he said:

'Is it you, my good little man, who has been smitten by the scourge of Saint Remacle?'

'Yes, Messire Dean,' answered Ulenspiegl, 'I am indeed the humble worshipper who would fain be cured of his new hump if it so please the saint.'

The dean, scenting some trick behind these words, said:

'Let me feel that hump.'

'Feel it, Messire,' said Ulenspiegl.

Having done this, the dean said:

'It is of recent date, and wet. I hope, however, that Master Saint Remacle will be pleased to act mercifully. Follow me.'

Ulenspiegl followed the dean and entered the church. The hunchbacks walked behind him, shouting: 'There's the accursed one! There's the blasphemer! How much does your new hump weigh? Will you make a bag of it to put your coins in? All your life you've jeered at us because you were straight; it's our turn now. Glory to Master Saint Remacle!'

Ulenspiegl, without saying a word, his head lowered, still followed the dean, and entered a little chapel where there was a tomb all done in marble. It was covered with a table, likewise in marble. Between the tomb and the wall of the chapel there was a space of only about the width of a large hand spread out. A crowd of hunchbacked pilgrims followed one another in file, passing between the wall and the table of the tomb, against which they rubbed their humps silently. And they hoped in this way to be delivered of them. And those who rubbed their humps would not make room for those who had not yet rubbed theirs, and so they fought each other, but noiselessly, not daring to strike any but sly blows, or jabs with their humps, because of the holiness of the place.

The dean told Ulenspiegl to get up on the top of the table of the tomb, so that all the pilgrims might see him. Ulenspiegl said:

'I cannot do so alone.'

The dean helped him up and stood beside him, commanding him to kneel. This Ulenspiegl did, and remained in this posture, with his head lowered.

The dean then, having meditated, preached in a sonorous voice, and said:

'Sons and brothers in Jesus Christ, you see here at my feet the greatest, most impious, worthless blasphemer that Master Saint Remacle in his anger ever smote.'

And Ulenspiegl, striking his breast, said: '*Confiteor.*'

'Once,' pursued the dean, 'he was straight as a halberd staff and gloried in it. Look at him now, humped and bowed under the stroke of the heavenly malediction.'

'*Confiteor*, take away my hump,' said Ulenspiegl.

264

'Yes,' continued the dean, 'yes, great Saint, Master Saint Remacle, you who since your glorious death have performed thirty and nine miracles, lift from his shoulders the weight that bears him down. And may we, for this, sing your praises for centuries and centuries, *in sœcula sœculorum*. And peace on earth to hunchbacks of goodwill.'

And the hunchbacks in chorus said:

'Yes, yes, peace on earth to hunchbacks of goodwill; peace from humps, truce for the deformed, amnesty from humiliations. Take away our humps, Master Saint Remacle!'

The dean commanded Ulenspiegl to come down from the table and rub his hump against the edge of it. Ulenspiegl did this, continuing to say: '*mea culpa, confiteor,* take away my hump.' And he rubbed it thoroughly in the sight and knowledge of all who stood about.

And they all cried:

'Look at the hump, it bends! Look you, it's giving way! It's going to melt on the right.—No, it will enter the chest; the humps don't melt, they go down into the intestines, and from thence out.—No, they enter the stomach wherein they serve as nourishment for eighty days.—That's the Saint's gift to the cured hunchbacks.—Where do the old humps go?'

Suddenly all the hunchbacks gave a great yell, for Ulenspiegl had just burst his hump by leaning heavily against the edge of the table of the tomb. All the blood that was within it ran out over his doublet and fell in large drops on the stone floor. And he shouted, straightening himself up and spreading out his arms:

'I am rid of it!'

And all the hunchbacks shouted together:

'Master Saint Remacle the blessed, it's kind for him but hard for us!—Master, take away our humps!—I will give you a calf.—I will give you seven sheep.—I, the produce of the year's hunting.—I, six hams.—I give my cottage to the church.—Take away our humps, Master Saint Remacle!'

And they looked on Ulenspiegl with envy and respect. There was one who wanted to feel under his doublet, but the dean said to him:

'There is a wound that may not see the light.'

'I shall pray for you,' said Ulenspiegl.

'Yes, pilgrim,' said the hunchbacks, all speaking at once, 'yes, Master Made-straight, we jeered at you; forgive us, for we knew not what we were doing. Our Lord Christ gave pardon from the cross, give us pardon also.'

'I pardon you,' said Ulenspiegl benevolently.

'Then,' said they, 'take this *patard,* accept this florin, permit us to

265

give this *real* to Your Straightness, offer him this *crusado,* place in his hands these *carolus* . . .'

'Hide your carolus,' said Ulenspiegl, in a whisper to them. 'Let not your left hand know what your right hand giveth.'

And he spoke in this way because of the dean, who was devouring with his eyes the money of the hunchbacks, without knowing whither it was of gold or silver.

'Grace be unto you, sanctified sir,' said the hunchbacks to Ulenspiegl.

And he proudly accepted their gifts like a miracle-man.

But the misers rubbed their humps at the tomb without saying a word.

And in the evening Ulenspiegl went to the tavern, where he revelled and feasted.

Before going to bed, thinking that the dean would certainly want his part, if not all, of the booty, he counted up his gains and found that he had more gold than silver, for there were almost three hundred *carolus.* He noticed a dry bay-tree in a pot and, taking the plant by its branches, pulled out the roots and the earth and placed the gold at the bottom of the pot. All the half-florins, *patards,* and *patacoons* he scattered out on the table.

The dean came to the tavern and went up to Ulenspiegl's room.

Seeing him, the latter said:

'Messire Dean, what do you want of my wretched person?'

'Nothing but your good, my son,' he answered.

'La,' groaned Ulenspiegl, 'does that mean what you see on the table?'

'Just that,' retorted the dean.

Then, stretching out his hand, he cleared the table of all the money on it and dropped it into a bag brought for that end.

And he gave a florin to Ulenspiegl, who pretended to groan.

And he demanded the instruments of the miracle.

Ulenspiegl showed him the bone of the *schol* and the bladder.

The dean took them while Ulenspiegl lamented, begging him to leave a little more money, for the way was long from Bouillon to Damme for a poor pedestrian such as he was, and he would no doubt die of hunger.

The dean went off without saying a word.

Being alone, Ulenspiegl fell asleep with one eye on the bay-tree. Next morning at dawn, having gathered up his booty, he left Bouillon and went to the camp of the Silent One, to whom he gave the money and told his story, saying that therein was the real way to levy war-taxes on the enemy.

And the prince gave him ten florins.

As for the bone of the *schol*, it was enshrined in a crystal box and placed between the arms of the cross on the high altar at Bouillon.

And everyone in the town knows what the cross encloses—the hump of the blasphemer who was straightened out.

11 THE SILENT ONE, in the neighbourhood of Liége, before crossing the Meuse, marched and counter-marched his men and in this way baffled the duke's vigilance. Ulenspiegl, attending to his duties as a soldier, handled with dexterity the wheel-locked musket and kept his eyes and ears wide open.

About this time there came to the camp Flemish and Brabant gentlemen who lived on good terms with the lords, colonels and captains of the Silent One's retinue.

Soon there were formed in the camp two parties ceaselessly quarrelling with each other, the one saying: 'The prince is a traitor,' the others answering that they lied in their throats and that they would be made to eat their words. Distrust spread like a spot of oil. Groups of six or eight or a dozen men came to blows and fought with every weapon of single combat, even muskets.

One day the prince came out at the noise and walked between the two parties. A bullet carried away his sword from his side. He made them stop their fight and visited the whole camp to show himself, so that they would not say: 'The Silent One is dead; dead the war.'

The following day, about midnight, in misty weather, Ulenspiegl, getting ready to leave a house where he had been singing a Flemish love song to a Walloon girl, heard at the door of the nearest cottage to the house the croaking of a raven three times repeated. Other croakings came in answer from afar, three times by three times. A peasant came to the threshold of the cottage. Ulenspiegl heard footsteps on the road.

Two men, speaking Spanish, came to the peasant, who asked them in the same language:

'What have you done?'

'Good work, in lying for the king,' they said. 'Thanks to us, distrustful captains and troopers say among themselves:

' "It is only by low ambition that the prince resists the king. He is waiting to be feared and to receive as a pledge of peace towns and lordships. For five hundred thousand florins he would abandon the brave lords fighting for their country. The duke offered him complete amnesty with promise on oath to restore their estates to him and all the high chiefs of the army if they would place themselves in obedience to the king. Orange is going to negotiate with him alone."

267

'The faithful followers of the duke answered us:

'"Offers from the duke, a treacherous trap, into which he will not enter, remembering what happened to Egmont and Hoorn. They well know that the Cardinal Granvela, being at Rome when the counts were captured, said: 'They take the two gudgeons but leave the pike; they have taken nothing, since the Silent One remains to be captured.'"'

'Is there great variance in the camp?' asked the peasant.

'There is great variance,' said they, 'and it grows every day. Where are the letters?'

They entered the cottage, where a lantern was lit. Ulenspiegl, looking through a skylight, saw them unseal two missives which they read with much pleasure, drink some hydromel, and then depart, saying to the peasant in Spanish:

'Camp divided. Orange taken. That will be a good drink.'

'These men,' said Ulenspiegl to himself, 'cannot be allowed to live.'

They went out into the heavy mist. Ulenspiegl saw the peasant bring them a lantern, which they took. The light of the lantern being often intercepted by a form, he supposed that they were walking one behind the other.

He loaded his musket and fired at the dark shape. He then saw the lantern lowered and raised several times and judged that one of the two having fallen, the other sought to see what sort of a wound he had received. He loaded his musket again. Then at the lantern going alone quickly and swinging, in the direction of the camp, he fired again. The lantern wavered, then fell and went out, and there was darkness.

Running then towards the camp, he saw the provost coming out with a crowd of troopers wakened by the noise of the musket-shots. Ulenspiegl, accosting them, said:

'I am the hunter, go and pick up the game.'

'Jolly Fleming,' said the provost, 'you speak otherwise than with your tongue.'

'Tongue talk blows away,' answered Ulenspiegl, 'while leaden talk stays in the bodies of the traitors. But follow me.'

He led them, they carrying their lanterns, to the place where the two had fallen. And there indeed they saw them, the one dead, the other in the throes of death holding his hand on his breast, where was found a letter crumpled up in the last conscious effort.

They carried away the bodies, which they recognized from their uniform as belonging to the gentlemen's corps, and came with them and their lanterns to the prince, who had been interrupted in a council with Frederick of Hollenhausen, the Markgrave of Hesse and other lords.

Followed by *landsknechts, reiter,* green-coats and yellow-coats, they stopped before the tent of the Silent One and demanded with shouts that he receive them.

He came from the tent. Then, taking the word from the tongue of the provost who was coughing in preparation to accusing him, Ulenspiegl said:

'My lord, I have killed, instead of two ravens, two traitorous nobles of your retinue.'

Then he told of what he had seen, heard and done.

The Silent One did not say a word. The two bodies were searched, there being present himself, William of Orange the Silent, Frederick of Hollenhausen, the Markgrave of Hesse, Diederich of Schoonenbergh, the Count Albert of Nassau, the Count Hoogstraeten, Antoine de Lalaing, governor of Malines, the troopers and Lamme Goedzak, whose belly trembled. Sealed letters from Granvela and Noircarmes were found on the gentleman; these letters enjoined them to sow dissension in the retinue of the prince and thereby diminish by that much his strength, force him to give in, and deliver him to the duke to be beheaded according to his merits. It was necessary, said the letters, to proceed subtly and by veiled speech in order that the men in the army might think that the Silent One had already—for his own profit— made a personal agreement with the duke. His captains and troopers being angry at this would make him a prisoner. For recompense there was sent to both of them a draft for five hundred ducats on the Fuggers of Antwerp; there would be a thousand more as soon as the four hundred thousand they were expecting arrived in Zeeland from Spain.

This plot being discovered, the prince, without a word, turned to the gentlemen, lords and troopers, among whom were many who suspected him. He pointed to the two dead bodies in silence, wishing by that gesture to reproach them of their distrust. All of them clamoured in a great tumult:

'Long life to Orange! Orange is faithful to the countries!'

Out of contempt they wanted to throw the corpses to the dogs; but the Silent One said:

'It is not the dead bodies that must be thrown to the dogs, but the faintness of spirit that makes you doubt high intentions.'

And the lords and the troopers shouted:

'Long live the Prince! Long live Orange, the countries' friend!'

And their voices rose like thunder threatening injustice.

And the prince, pointing to the bodies:

'Give them Christian burial,' said he.

'And me?' Ulenspiegl demanded. 'What are they going to do with my faithful carcass? If I have done wrong, let them beat me; if I have done right, let them accord me my recompense.'

The Silent One then spoke and said:

'This musketeer shall have in my presence fifty blows with a green-wood stick for having without orders, and with great contempt for all discipline, slain two gentlemen. He shall also receive thirty florins for having seen and heard well.'

'My lord,' answered Ulenspiegl, 'if they were to give me first the thirty florins I could bear with patience the blows from the green-wood stick.'

'Yes, yes,' groaned Lamme Goedzak, 'give him first the thirty florins and he will bear the rest with patience.'

'And besides,' said Ulenspiegl, 'having a clean conscience I have no need to be washed with oak nor rinsed with cornel.'

'Yes,' groaned Lamme Goedzak again, 'Ulenspiegl has no need to be either washed or rinsed. He has a clean conscience. Don't wash him, my lords, don't wash him.'

Ulenspiegl having received the thirty florins, the provost ordered the *stock-meester* (assistant batoner) to seize him.

'See, my lords, how pitiable he looks. He loves wood not at all, my friend Ulenspiegl.'

'I love to see a beautiful leafy ash-tree, growing in the sun in its native verdure; but I hate to the death those ugly wooden sticks still dripping their sap, debranched, bereft of their leaves and twigs and of fierce look and harsh acquaintance.'

'Are you ready?' demanded the provost.

'Ready?' repeated Ulenspiegl. 'Ready for what? To be beaten? No, I am not, and I do not wish to be, master *stock-meester*. Your beard is red and your air most dreadful; but I am sure you have a kind heart and don't like to break the back of a poor man like me. I must tell you that I neither like to do it or see it done, for a Christian's back is a

270

sacred temple even like to the breast, holding in the lungs through which we breathe the good God's air. What piercing remorse would gnaw at you if I were to break in pieces by a brutal blow from your stick!'

'Make haste,' said the *stock-meester*.

'My lord,' said Ulenspiegl, speaking to the prince, 'believe me, there is no hurry; first this stick should be dried, for they say that green wood entering the living flesh imparts to it a deadly poison. Would Your Highness want to see me die of that foul death? My lord, I hold my faithful back at Your Highness's service; have it beaten with rods, lashed with the whip; but if you don't want to see me dead, spare me, if it please you, the green-wood stick.'

'Pardon him, prince,' said Messires Hoogstraeten and Diederich de Schoonenbergh together. The others smiled compassionately.

Lamme also said:

'My lord, my lord, pardon him; green wood is pure poison.'

The prince then said: 'I pardon him.'

Ulenspiegl, leaping into the air several times, slapped Lamme's belly and forced him to dance, saying:

'Praise with me our Lord who spared me the green-wood stick.'

And Lamme tried to dance but could not because of his belly.

And Ulenspiegl treated him to food and drink.

12 UNWILLING TO GIVE BATTLE, the duke ceaselessly harried the Silent One as he wandered about the flat lands between Juliers and the Meuse, sounding the river at Hondt, Malines, Elsen, Meersen, and everywhere finding it filled with snares and caltrops to wound the men and horses that tried to pass over it by fording.

At Stocken, the sounders found no traps and the prince ordered the crossing. The *reiters* traversed the Meuse and held themselves in battle formation on the other bank so as to protect the crossing from the side of the bishopric of Liége. Then, lined up from one bank to the other, breaking in this way the current of the stream, were ten rows of archers and musketeers, among whom was Ulenspiegl.

He was in water up to his thighs and often some treacherous wave would lift him up, him and his horse.

He saw the foot soldiers pass over, bearing sacks of powder on their heads and holding their muskets up in the air. Then came the wagons, the hooked hackbuts, the manœuvre troops, linstocks, culverins, double-culverins, falcons, falconets, serpentines, demi-serpentines, double-serpentines, mortars, double-mortars, cannon, demi-

271

cannon, double-cannon, *sacres*, little field-pieces mounted on carriages drawn by two horses and able to manœuvre at a gallop, in all ways quite like those nicknamed the Emperor's Pistols; behind them, protecting the rear, came *landsknechts*, and *reiters* from Flanders.

Ulenspiegl sought some warming drink. The archer Riesencraft, a High German, lean, cruel, gigantic fellow, snored as he sat on his charger beside him, and with each snore he breathed out the scent of brandy. Ulenspiegl, seeking for the flask on the crupper of his horse, found it hung like a shoulder-belt by means of a cord which he cut; and he took the flask and drank from it joyfully. The archer's companions said:

'Hand us over some.'

Which he did. The brandy being all drunk, he knotted the cord of the flask and was about to put it back again where it belonged. As he lifted the arm to pass it over, Riesencraft awoke. Taking hold of the flask, he wished to milk his accustomed cow. Finding that she gave no more milk, he fell into a great rage.

'Robber,' said he, 'what did you do with my brandy?'

Ulenspiegl answered:

'I drank it. Among soaked horsemen the brandy of one is the brandy of everyone. Wicked is the miser.'

'To-morrow I'll carve your flesh in the lists,' replied Riesencraft.

'We'll carve each other,' said Ulenspiegl, 'heads, arms, legs and all. But aren't you constipated, that you have such a sour phiz?'

'I am,' answered Riesencraft.

'You must purge yourself then,' retorted Ulenspiegl, 'and not fight.'

It was agreed between them that they should meet next day, mounted and accoutred, each after his fancy, to carve each other's fat with a short, stiff sword.

Ulenspiegl asked that he be allowed to replace the sword with a stick, and this was permitted.

In the meantime, all the troops having crossed the river and fallen into order at the voice of their colonels and captains, the ten ranks of archers also crossed over.

And the Silent One said:

'Let us march on Liége!'

This made Ulenspiegl glad, and with all the Flemings he shouted:

'Long life to Orange! Let us march on Liége!'

But the foreigners, and notably the High Germans, said they were too washed and rinsed to march on. Vainly did the prince assure them that they were going on to certain victory in a friendly town. They

272

would not listen and lighted great bonfires and warmed themselves in front of them, with their horses unharnessed.

The attack on the town was put off until the morrow, when Alba, greatly astonished at the bold crossing, learned from his spies that the troops of the Silent One were not yet ready for the attack.

Thereupon he threatened Liége and all the surrounding country-side to put them to fire and the sword, if the partisans of the prince made any movement. Gerard de Groesbeke, the bishop's catchpoll, armed his troops against the prince, who arrived too late, through the fault of the High Germans who had been afraid of a little water in their breeches.

13   ULENSPIEGL and Riesencraft having taken seconds, these said that the two troopers were to fight on foot until death ensued, for such were the conditions laid down by Riesencraft. The place of the combat was a little heath. In the early morning Riesencraft put on his archer's dress. He put on his *salad* (helmet) with the throat-piece and without visor, and his sleeveless shirt of mail. His other shirt being all tattered, he stuffed it in the *salad* in case he had need of lint. He armed himself with an arbalest of good Ardennes wood, with a quiver of thirty arrows; with a long dagger; but not with the two-handed sword which is the archer's sword. And he came to the field of combat mounted on his charger, carrying his war saddle and the plumed chamfron, and all barded with iron.

Ulenspiegl made up an armament for a gentleman at arms. His charger was a donkey; his saddle was a wench's petticoats; his plumed chamfron was of osier garnished above with fine fluttering shavings. His barde was of bacon for, said he, iron is too costly, steel is beyond price and, as for bronze, they have made so many cannons of it in these latter days that there isn't enough left to arm a rabbit for battle. In place of headgear, he set on his head a fine salad that the snails had not yet devoured; the salad was surmounted by a swan's feather, to make him sing in case he passed out.

His sword, stiff and light, was a good, long, thick pine-stick, at the end of which there was a broom of branches of the same wood. At the left-hand side of his saddle there hung his knife, also of wood; on the right-hand side swung a good mace—elderwood with a turnip on the end of it. His cuirass was full of flaws.

When he came thus accoutred on the field of combat, Riesencraft's seconds burst out laughing, but he himself preserved his sour phiz.

Ulenspiegl's seconds then asked those of Riesencraft that the German
274

remove his armaments of mail and iron, seeing that Ulenspiegl was only armed in tatters. To this Riesencraft consented. Then his seconds wanted to know from those of Ulenspiegl why he was armed with a broom.

'You granted me the stick but you did not forbid me to enliven it with foliage.'

'Do as you like,' said the four seconds.

Riesencraft said never a word and cropped down with little sword strokes the meagre plants of the heath.

His seconds requested him to replace his sword with a broom like Ulenspiegl.

He answered:

'If that scoundrel has chosen of his own free will such an unusual weapon, it is because he thinks he can defend his life with it.'

Ulenspiegl having said again that he wanted to use his broom, the four seconds agreed that everything was all right.

They both faced each other, Riesencraft on his horse barded with iron, Ulenspiegl on his jackass barded with bacon.

Ulenspiegl advanced to the middle of the field. There, holding out his broom like a lance, he said:

'I find more stinking than plague, leprosy and death, those lice of ill-natured fellows who, in a camp of troops and boon companions, having nothing else to do, go about showing off everywhere their sour mugs and their mouths slavering anger. Where they are laughter dares not show itself and songs are stilled. They must always be grumbling or fighting, introducing thus, alongside the legitimate combat for the fatherland, single combat that is the ruination of the army and the delight of the enemy. Riesencraft here present, for mere innocent words, has killed one and twenty men without ever having in any battle or skirmish performed one act of striking bravery nor merited by his courage the slightest recompense. Now it pleases me to-day to brush the wrong way the bare hide of this crabbed cur.'

Riesencraft answered:

'That drunkard has dreamed fine things about the abuse of single combats; it will please me to-day to crack open his skull to show everybody that there's nothing but hay where his brains should be.'

The seconds made them dismount from their chargers. In jumping off Ulenspiegl let the salad fall from his head and this the ass quietly ate; but it was interrupted at the job by a kick which one of the seconds landed it to make it get off the field of combat. The horse also was made to move. And they both went off together to graze in company.

Then the seconds carrying the broom—Ulenspiegl's men—and the others carrying the sword—Riesencraft's—whistled the signal for the combat to begin.

And Riesencraft and Ulenspiegl fought each other furiously; Riesencraft striking out with his sword, Ulenspiegl parrying with his broom; Riesencraft swearing by all the devils, Ulenspiegl fleeing before him, wandering over the heath obliquely and roundabout, zigzagging, sticking out his tongue and making a thousand other grimaces at Riesencraft, who got out of breath and struck into the air with his sword like a maddened trooper. Ulenspiegl, feeling him close on his heels, turned

about suddenly and landed him a great whack on the nose with the broom. Riesencraft fell down with his arms and legs outstretched like a dying frog.

Ulenspiegl jumped on him and pitilessly scrubbed his face this way and that, saying:

'Cry mercy, or I'll make you swallow my broom!'

And he scrubbed and re-scrubbed without stopping, to the great joy of the assistants, continually saying:

'Cry mercy, or I'll make you swallow it!'

But Riesencraft could not cry out, for he had died of black rage.

'God have your soul, poor madman,' said Ulenspiegl.

And off he went, steeped in melancholy.

14 THEY WERE THEN at the end of October. The prince lacked money and his army was hungry. With muttering troops he marched towards France and offered battle to the duke, who would not accept it. Leaving Quesnoy-le-Comte to go on towards Cambresis, he met ten companies of Germans, eight ensigns of Spaniards, and three cornets of light horse, commanded by the duke's son, Don Ruffele Henricis, who was in the midst of the fight, crying out in Spanish:

'Kill! Kill! No quarter! Long live the Pope!'

Don Henricis was then face to face with a company of musketeers in which Ulenspiegl was *dizenier,* and with his men he launched out at them. Ulenspiegl said to the sergeant of the troop:

'I'm going to cut this butcher's tongue!'

'Cut away,' said the sergeant.

And Ulenspiegl, with a well-aimed bullet, smashed to pieces the tongue and the jaw of Don Ruffele Henricis, the duke's son.

Ulenspiegl also brought down from his horse the son of the Marquis Delmares.

The eight ensigns and the three cornets were beaten.

After that victory, Ulenspiegl sought for Lamme in the camp but could not find him.

'La,' said he, 'now he's gone, my friend Lamme, my fat friend. In his warlike ardour, forgetting the weight of his belly, he must have pursued the fleeing Spaniards. Breathless he has fallen like a sack on the road. And they'll have picked him up to hold him for ransom, ransom of Christian fat. My friend Lamme, where are you then, where are you, my fat friend?'

Ulenspiegl sought him everywhere and, not finding him, became most melancholy.

15 In NOVEMBER, the month of snowy tempests, the Silent One sent for Ulenspiegl to come before him. The prince gnawed at the cord of his shirt of mail. 'Listen and understand,' said he. Ulenspiegl answered: 'My ears are the gates of a prison; one gets in with facility but to get out is no easy affair.'

The Silent One said: 'Go through Namur, Flanders, Hainaut, South Brabant, Antwerp, North Brabant, Guelder, Overyssel, North Holland, announcing everywhere that if fortune betrays our holy and Christian cause on land we shall continue on sea the fight against unrighteous violences. God directs this affair in all grace whether in good or evil fortune. When you arrive in Amsterdam, you will give an accounting to my trusty friend, Paul Buys, of all you have done and performed. Here are three passes signed by Alba himself and found on bodies at Quesnoy-le-Comte. My secretary has filled them in. Maybe on the way you will find some boon companion whom you can trust. They are worthy who answer to the lark's song with the warlike clarion-cry of the cock. Here are fifty florins. You will be brave and faithful.'

'The ashes beat against my heart,' answered Ulenspiegl.

And off he went.

16 By the hand of the king and the duke he had power to carry all arms at his own convenience. He took his wheel-lock musket, cartridges and dry powder. Then, clad in a ragged cloak, a tattered doublet, and breeches slashed in the Spanish style, wearing a toque with feather flying in the wind, and carrying a sword, he left the army near the French border and walked towards Maestricht.

Wrens, those heralds of the cold, flew about the houses, asking shelter. The third day it snowed.

Many times along the way Ulenspiegl had to show his safe-conduct. They allowed him to go on. He walked towards Liége.

He had just entered on a plain; a great wind drove swirling flakes in his face. He saw before him the plain, that stretched out all white, and the snowy swirls driven by the blast. Three wolves followed him but, after he had shot down one with his musket, the others threw themselves on the stricken one and then took to the woods, each bearing a piece of the carcass.

Ulenspiegl being thus delivered and looking to see if there was not another band in the country, saw at the far end of the plain specks that were like grey statues moving amid the swirling eddies, and behind them dark forms of mounted troops. He climbed a tree. The wind brought to him a distant murmur of lamentation.

'These are perhaps pilgrims dressed in white robes,' said he to himself, 'I can barely see their bodies in the snow.' Then he distinguished men running naked and saw two *reiters* all in black, mounted on great chargers, driving the poor troop before them with great blows from their whips. He loaded his musket. He saw amongst these afflicted ones, young men, old men, naked, shivering, frozen, huddled up, and running to escape the whips of the two troopers who took pleasure, being well-clad, flushed with brandy and good feeding, in lashing the bodies of the naked men to make them run faster.

Ulenspiegl said: 'You shall be avenged, ashes of Claes.' And, with a bullet in the face, he killed one of the *reiters*, who fell from his horse. The other, not knowing where the unexpected bullet had come from, took fright. Thinking that there were enemy troops hidden in the woods, he sought to flee with his companion's horse. While he had taken hold of the bridle-rein and had dismounted to rifle the dead man, he was struck with another bullet in the neck and likewise fell.

The naked men, thinking that an angel from heaven, a good musketeer, had come to their defence, fell on their knees. Ulenspiegl then came down from his tree and was recognized by those of the band who had, like him, served in the armies of the prince. They said to him:

'Ulenspiegl, we are from France, sent in this pitiful state to Maestricht

278

where the duke is, there to be treated as rebel prisoners, being unable to pay ransom and condemned beforehand to be tortured, beheaded, or to row like rogues and robbers in the king's galleys.'

Ulenspiegl, giving his *opperst-kleed* to the eldest of the band, answered:

'Come, I will lead you as far as Mezières, but first we must strip these two troopers and take their horses with us.'

The doublets, breeches, boots and headgear, and cuirasses were divided among the weakest and most ailing, and Ulenspiegl said:

'We'll go into the woods where the air is thicker and kinder. Run, brothers.'

Suddenly a man fell and said:

'I am hungry and cold, and I am going before God to bear witness that the Pope is the anti-Christ on earth.'

And he died. And the others wished to carry him away so that he might have a Christian burial.

As they were journeying along the highway, they saw a peasant leading a canvas-covered wagon. Seeing the naked men, he had pity on them and let them climb into the wagon. There they found hay to lie down on and sacks to cover themselves with. Being warm, they thanked God. Ulenspiegl, riding alongside the wagon on one of the *reiters'* horses, held the other by the bridle-rein.

At Mezières they all got down; there they were handed out good soup, beer, bread, cheese, with meat for the old men and the women. They were housed, clad and armed, also at the expense of the town. And they all gave the kiss of benediction to Ulenspiegl, who received it joyfully.

He sold the horses of the two *reiters* for forty-eight florins, thirty of which he gave to the French.

Walking on his way alone, he said to himself: 'I go through ruins, blood and tears, finding nothing. The devils lied, without a doubt. Where is Lamme? Where is Nele? Where are the Seven?'

And the ashes of Claes beat against his breast.

He heard a voice, like a whisper, saying:

'In death, ruins and tears, seek.'

And he went on his way.

17 ULENSPIEGL arrived at Namur in March. There he saw Lamme who, having been taken with a great passion for the fish of the Meuse and notably the trout, had rented a boat and fished in the stream with permission from the town. But he had paid fifty florins to the fishmongers' corporations. He sold and ate the fish he

caught and gained at this trade a larger belly and a little sack of *carolus*.

Seeing his friend and companion walking along the banks of the Meuse in order to enter the town, he was very glad. He rowed his little boat to the bank and, climbing the bluff, not without puffing, he came to Ulenspiegl. Stuttering with joy:

'Here you are then,' said he, 'my boy, my boy in God; for my belly-ark could carry two like you. Where are you going? What do you want?

You're not dead, doubtless? Have you seen my wife? You shall eat fish from the Meuse, the best there is in this world below; they do sauces in this country that make you want to eat your fingers right up to the shoulder. You are proud and superb, your cheeks bronzed with battles. Here you are then, my boy, my friend Ulenspiegl, the jolly vagabond.'

Then, in a low voice:

'How many Spaniards did you kill? Did you ever see my wife in their wagons full of sluts? And the wine of the Meuse that's so delicious for constipated folk, you'll drink some? Are you wounded, my boy? You'll stay here then, fresh, nimble, alert as a young eagle. And the eels, you'll taste them? Not a taste of swamps about them. Kiss me, my belly-boy. Glory to God, how happy I am!'

And Lamme danced, leaped, puffed and forced Ulenspiegl to dance.

Then they walked towards Namur. At the city-gates, Ulenspiegl showed his pass signed by the duke. And Lamme led him to his house.

As he cooked the meal, he made Ulenspiegl tell his adventures and recounted his own. He had left the army, he said, to follow a girl that he thought was his wife. In pursuit of her he had come right to Namur. And endlessly he said:

'Didn't you see her?'

'I saw others, very lovely,' answered Ulenspiegl, 'and especially in this town where they are all amorous.'

'That's a fact,' said Lamme, 'they wanted to have me a hundred times. But I remained faithful, for my sorrowful heart is big with one single memory.'

'As your belly is big with numerous platesfull,' answered Ulenspiegl.
Lamme replied:
'When I am afflicted, I must eat.'
'There's no truce to your grief?' asked Ulenspiegl.
'La, yes!' said Lamme.
And, pulling a trout from a basin, he said:
'See how fine and firm it is. This flesh is as pink as that of my wife.
To-morrow we'll quit Namur—I have a sack full of florins—we'll each
buy a donkey and, riding them, we'll go towards the land of Flanders.'
'You'll lose a lot,' said Ulenspiegl.
'My heart draws me to Damme, the place where she loved me well;
maybe she has returned there.'
'We shall leave to-morrow,' said Ulenspiegl, 'since that is what you
want.'
And indeed they left, each sitting on a donkey and straddling along,
side by side.

18 A SHARP WIND was blowing. The sun, bright as youth in the
morning, had become grey as an old man. A hailing rain was
falling. The rain having stopped, Ulenspiegl shook himself,
saying: 'The sky which drinks up so many vapours must relieve itself
sometime.'

Another rain, more haily than the first, beat down on the two com-
panions. Lamme groaned:
'We were well washed; must we now be rinsed?'
The sun reappeared and they straddled along light-heartedly.
A third rain fell, so full of hail-stones and so deadly that it cut up,
as though with a bunch of knives, the dry twigs of the trees.
Lamme said:
'Ho! A roof! My poor wife! Where are you, good fire, soft kisses and
thick soups?'
And he wept, the fat man.
But Ulenspiegl said:
'We are lamenting. But still, is it not from ourselves that our ills
come? It rains on our backs; but this December rain will make the
clovers in May. And the cows will low with pleasure. We are shelterless;
but why didn't we mary? I mean myself, with little Nele, so lovely and
kind, who would be making for me now a stew of beef and beans. We
are thirsty in spite of the water that falls; why did we not become
workmen steady in one place? Those who are received as masters have
full barrels of *bruinbier* in their cellars.'

The ashes of Claes beat upon his heart, the sky cleared up, the sun shone, and Ulenspiegl said:

'Master Sun, thanks be to you, you warm backs again; ashes of Claes, you warm our hearts again and tell us that they who wander about for the deliverance of the land of their fathers are blessed.'

'I'm hungry,' said Lamme.

19 THEY ENTERED an inn, where they were given supper in an upper chamber. Ulenspiegl, opening the window, saw a garden wherein walked a comely girl, plump, full-breasted, golden-haired, and dressed only in a petticoat, a white linen jacket and a holey apron of black linen.

Chemises and other women's linens were bleaching on the lines; the young girl, always turning to Ulenspiegl, took down the chemises and put them back again, smiling and still looking at him, sat down on linen bands, then swung on two knotted ends of rope.

In the neighbourhood Ulenspiegl heard a cock crow and saw a nurse playing with a child, whose face she turned towards a man standing up, saying:

'Smile to papa, Boelkin.'

The child wept.

And the pretty girl continued to walk about the garden, putting up and taking down the linen.

'She's a spy,' said Lamme.

The girl placed her hands over her eyes and, smiling through her fingers, looked at Ulenspiegl.

Then, with both hands, she lifted her two breasts and let them down again, then swung once more without letting her feet touch the ground. And the linens, in unwinding themselves, made her spin like a top; while Ulenspiegl watched her arms bare to the shoulders, and round and white in the pale sunlight. Turning and smiling, she continued looking at him. He went out to go and find her. Lamme followed him. He sought an opening in the garden hedge to pass through but could find none.

The girl, watching what was going on, looked once more smilingly through her fingers.

Ulenspiegl tried to climb over the hedge while Lamme held him back, saying to him:

'Don't go, she's a spy. We'll be burned.'

Then the girl walked about the garden, covering up her face with

282

her apron and looking through the holes to see if her chance friend was not coming soon.

Ulenspiegl was about to leap over the hedge with one bound but he was stopped by Lamme who, taking hold of his leg, made him sprawl, and said:

'Rope, sword and gallows, she's a spy, don't go.'

Sitting on the ground, Ulenspiegl struggled against the hold of Lamme. The girl, pushing her head above the hedge, cried:

'Adieu, sir, may love keep your longanimity hanging.'

And he heard a peal of mocking laughter.

'Ah,' said he, 'it's in my ear like a pack of pins!'

Then a door was closed noisily.

And he was sad.

Lamme said to him, still holding on:

'You are counting over the sweet treasures of beauty lost thus to your shame. She's a spy. You fall well when you do fall. I am going to burst with laughing.'

Ulenspiegl said never a word, and they both remounted their donkeys.

20 THEY CONTINUED on their way, each one having one leg this way and one leg that way on his donkey. Lamme, chewing the cud of his last meal, sniffed the cool air joyfully. Suddenly Ulenspiegl with his whip landed him a great stinging lash on the beam-end that was like a pad on his saddle.

'What are you doing?' cried Lamme, piteously.

'What?' asked Ulenspiegl.

'That lash with your whip?' said Lamme.

'What lash?'

'The one you just landed me,' retorted Lamme.

'From the left side?' asked Ulenspiegl.

'Yes, from the left side and on my behind. Why did you do that, scandalous rogue?'

'I did it through ignorance,' answered Ulenspiegl. 'I know quite well what a whip is, quite well also what a behind is, well-seated on a saddle. But seeing that one, large, puffed out, tight and overflowing the saddle, I said to myself: "Since I cannot pinch it with my finger and thumb, a whip stroke could never pinch it either with its lash. I was wrong."'

Lamme smiling at these words, Ulenspiegl continued, in these terms:

'But I am not the only one in this world to sin through ignorance, and there is more than one master idiot displaying his fat on a donkey's saddle who could give me points. If my whip sinned on your behind,

283

you sinned more heavily on my legs in preventing them from running after the girl who flirted in the garden.'

'Crow's meat!' said Lamme, 'It was a revenge then?'

'Just a little one,' replied Ulenspiegl.

21 AT DAMME, Nele the afflicted one lived alone with Katheline, who still called with love the cold devil that never came.

'Ah,' she said, 'you are rich, Hanske, my darling, and might bring back to me the seven hundred carolus. Then Soetkin would return alive to the earth from limbo, and Claes would laugh in heaven; you can well do it. Take away the fire, the soul would out, make a hole, the soul would out!'

And endlessly she pointed her finger to the place where the tow had been.

Katheline was very poor, but the neighbours helped her by giving beans, bread and meat, according to their means. The town gave her a little money. And Nele sewed dresses for the rich women of the town, went to their homes to do ironing, and in this way earned a florin each week.

And Katheline continually said:

'Make a hole, take out my soul. It knocks to get out. He will bring back the seven hundred carolus.'

And Nele wept as she listened to her.

22 MEANWHILE ULENSPIEGL and Lamme, armed with their passes, went into a little inn backed against the Sambre rocks, which in some places are covered with trees. On the sign-board of the inn was written *Chez Marlaire*. Having downed many flagons of Meuse wine, made the Burgundy way, and eaten much jerked fish, they gossiped with their host, a papist of the deepest dye but gabby as a magpie because of the wine he had drunk, and continually winking his eye, cunningly. Ulenspiegl, divining some mystery under this winking, plied him with more drink, so much so, that mine host began to dance and burst out laughing; then, sitting down again at the table:

'Good Catholics,' said he. 'I drink to you.'

'To you we drink,' answered Lamme and Ulenspiegl together.

'To the extinction of every plague of rebellion and heresy.'

'We drink,' replied Lamme and Ulenspiegl, who kept on refilling the goblet that the host could never see full.

'You are good fellows,' said he. 'I drink to your generosities; I profit on wine drunk. Where are your passes?'

'Here they are,' said Ulenspiegl.

'Signed by the duke,' said the host. 'I drink to the duke.'

'To the duke we drink,' answered Lamme and Ulenspiegl.

The host continued:

'How do we catch rats, mice and field-mice? In rat-traps, snares and mouse-traps. Who is the field-mouse? The great heretic, Orange as hell-fire. God is with us. They are coming. Hey, hey, drink! Pour; I roast, I burn. Drink! Three fine little reformed preachers. . . I said little . . . fine little brave, stout troopers, oaks. . . Drink! Don't you want to go with them to the camp of the great heretic? I have passes signed by him. . . You'll see what their business is.'

'We shall go to the camp,' replied Ulenspiegl.

'They'll get there, and at night, if the occasion offers' (and the host, with a whistle, made the gesture of one man cutting another's throat). 'Steel-wind shall stop the blackbird Nassau from whistling any more. How now, drink, here!'

'You are gay, despite the fact that you are married,' said Ulenspiegl.

'I am not, nor ever was. I keep the secrets of princes. Drink! My wife would steal them from under the pillow in order to have me hanged and be a widow sooner than Nature meant. Living God! They're going to come. . . Where are the new passes? On my Christian heart. Let's drink! They are there, there, at three hundred paces along the road, near Marche-les-Dames. Do you see them? Let's drink!'

'Drink,' said Ulenspiegl to him, 'drink; I drink to the king, to the duke, to the preachers, to steel-wind. I drink to you, to me; I drink to the wine and to the bottle. You're not drinking.' And at each health they drank, Ulenspiegl filled up his glass and the host emptied it.

Ulenspiegl considered him for a while; then, rising, he said:

'He sleeps; let us get out, Lamme.'

When they were outside:

'He has no wife to betray us. . . It is dusk. . . You clearly heard what that rogue said, and you know who the three preachers are?'

'Yes,' said Lamme.

'You know that they are coming from Marche-les-Dames in skirting the Meuse and that it will be better to wait for them on the road before the steel-wind blows.'

'Yes,' said Lamme.

'We must save the prince's life,' said Ulenspiegl.

'Yes,' said Lamme.

'Here,' Ulenspiegl said, 'take my musket, go there in the thicket between the rocks; load it with two bullets and shoot when I croak like a raven.'

'That I will,' said Lamme.

And he disappeared in the thicket. And Ulenspiegl soon heard the creaking of the musket-lock.

'Do you see them coming?' said he.

'I see them,' replied Lamme. 'There's three of them walking like troopers, and one of them is a head taller than the others.'

Ulenspiegl sat down by the roadside, legs out, mumbling prayers over a rosary, as beggars do. And his hat was between his knees.

When the three preachers passed, he held out his hat but they dropped nothing therein.

Ulenspiegl, getting up then, said piteously:

'My good sire, don't refuse a patard to a poor quarry worker who lately strained his back in falling down a mine. They are very hard in this place and would give me nothing to ease my wretched misery. La, give me a patard and I'll pray for you. And God will hold your magnanimities in joy all the rest of your days.'

'My son,' said one of the preachers, a robust fellow, 'there shall be no more joy for us in this world as long as the Pope and the Inquisition reign.'

Ulenspiegl sighed as he did, saying:

'La, what are you saying, my masters? Speak lower, if it please your Graces. But give me a patard.'

'My son,' said a little preacher with a warrior-like face, 'we others, poor martyrs, we have only enough patards to keep us in sustenance along our route.'

Ulenspiegl threw himself down on his knees.

'Bless me,' said he.

The three preachers held out their hands over Ulenspiegl's head without any devotion.

Noticing that they were lean men and yet had powerful paunches, he arose, made as to fall and as he struck with his head the belly of the tallest preacher he heard a jolly jingling of money.

Standing up straight then and pulling out his dagger:

'My fine fathers,' said he, 'it's getting cold, I'm badly clad and you are too well. Give me of your wool so that I may cut myself a cloak. I am a beggar. Up with the Beggars!'

The tall preacher replied:

'Cox-combed beggar, you carry your comb high; we're going to cut it for you.'

'Cut it!' said Ulenspiegl, stepping backwards. 'But steel-wind shall

blow for you before it blows for the prince. Beggar I am, up with the Beggars!'

Astounded, the three preachers said to each other:

'How did he get the news? We have been betrayed. Kill! Long live the Mass!'

And they drew from above their leggings fine daggers, well-sharpened.

But Ulenspiegl, without waiting for them, stepped back to the thicket where Lamme was hidden. Judging that the preachers were within range of the musket, he said:

'Ravens, black ravens, lead-wind is about to blow. I sing your blow-out.'

And he croaked.

A musket-shot, from out of the thicket, knocked over the tall preacher and laid him with his face to the ground; and this was followed by another one that threw the second down.

And Ulenspiegl saw in the brushwood the goodly face of Lamme and his arm raised to re-charge his musket hastily.

And a bluish smoke rose from the dark brushwood.

The third preacher, furious with manly rage, wanted at all costs to strike down Ulenspiegl, who said:

'Steel-wind or lead-wind, you are about to pass from this world to the next, infamous worker of murders!'

And he attacked him, and defended himself bravely.

And they stood stiffly face to face on the road delivering and parrying blows. Ulenspiegl was all bloody, for his adversary, skilful trooper, had wounded him in the head and the leg. But he attacked and defended himself like a lion. The blood that ran from his head blinded him, yet he moved about with great strides and wiped his face with his left hand; he grew weaker. He would have been killed if Lamme had not shot the preacher and brought him down.

And Ulenspiegl saw and heard him spew forth blasphemies, blood and death-froth.

And the bluish smoke rose above the dark brushwood among which Lamme again showed his goodly face.

'Is that all?' said he.

'Yes, my boy,' answered Ulenspiegl. 'But come here. . .'

Lamme, coming from out of his niche, saw Ulenspiegl all covered with blood. Running then like a stag in spite of his belly, he came to Ulenspiegl, who was sitting on the ground near the slain men.

'He's wounded, my sweet friend,' said he, 'wounded by that murderous rogue.' And with a blow from his heel he smashed the teeth of the nearest preacher. 'You don't answer, Ulenspiegl! Are you going to

288

die, my boy? Where is the balsam? Ha, in the bottom of his sack under the sausages. Ulenspiegl, don't you hear me? La, I've no warm water to clean your wound, and no way of getting any. But the water of the Sambre will suffice. Speak to me, my friend. You are not so severely wounded, in any case. A little water. There, very cold, isn't it? He's waking. It's me, my boy, your friend; they are dead! Linen! Linen to bind up his wounds. There isn't any. My shirt, then.' He undressed himself and continued talking: 'In bits the shirt! The blood's stopped. My friend won't die.'

'Ha,' said he, 'how cold that nipping air is on the bare back. Let us dress ourselves again. He won't die. It's me, Ulenspiegl, me, your friend, Lamme.' He smiled. 'I'm going to rifle the murderers. They have bellies of florins. Golden guts, carolus, florins, daelders, patards and letters! We are rich. More than three hundred carolus to share. Let us take the weapons and the money. Steel-wind shall not blow yet for my lord.'

Ulenspiegl, his teeth chattering because of the cold, got up.

'There you are, upstanding,' said Lamme.

'It's the strength of the balsam,' said Ulenspiegl.

'Balsam of the brave,' replied Lamme.

Then, taking the bodies of the three preachers one by one, he threw them into a hole among the rocks, leaving on them their weapons and their clothes except their cloaks.

And all about them, overhead in the sky, croaked the ravens awaiting their prey.

And the Sambre flowed on like a stream of steel under the grey sky.

And the snow fell, washing away the blood.

Nevertheless they were troubled. And Lamme said:

'I'd rather kill a chicken than a man.'

And they remounted their donkeys.

At the gates of Huy, Ulenspiegl's blood was still flowing; so they feigned to fall into a quarrel together, and fenced about with their daggers, apparently very cruelly. Then, having ceased the combat, they remounted and entered Huy after having shown their passes at the town gates.

The women, seeing Ulenspiegl wounded and bleeding, and Lamme on his donkey playing at being the victor, looked on Ulenspiegl with tender pity and shook their fists at Lamme, saying: 'That's the scoundrel who wounded his friend.'

Lamme, uneasy, only sought among them to see if he could not see his wife.

But in vain, and he was plunged in melancholy.

23 'WHERE ARE WE GOING?' asked Lamme. 'To Maestricht,' replied Ulenspiegl. 'But, my boy, they say that the duke's army surrounds it and that he himself is in the town. Our passes will not be sufficient. Even if the Spanish troops think they are good, we'll nevertheless be held in the town and questioned. In the meantime they'll have learned of the death of the preachers and we shall have ceased to live.'

Ulenspiegl answered:

'The ravens, the owls and the vultures will soon have finished with their flesh; already, no doubt, their faces are unrecognizable. As for our passes, they may be good; but if they learn of the murder, we shall be, as you say, taken prisoners. Just the same, we must go to Maestricht in passing by Landen.'

'They'll hang us,' said Lamme.

'We shall pass,' replied Ulenspiegl.

So conversing, they arrived at the Magpie Inn, where they found good food, good lodgings and hay for their donkeys.

The following morning they set out for Landen.

Having arrived at a large farm near the town, Ulenspiegl whistled like a skylark, and right away, from the inside of the farm, came the answering, war-like crow of the cock. A farmer with a goodly face appeared on the sill of the farm house and said to them:

'Friends, as freemen, up with the Beggars! Come within!'

'Who is this?' asked Lamme.

Ulenspiegl answered:

'Thomas Utenhove, the brave Reformist; all his maid-servants and men-servants on the farm work like him for the freedom of conscience.'

Utenhove then said:

'You are the prince's envoys. Eat and drink.'

And the ham began to crackle in the frying-pan and the black-

290

puddings likewise, and the wines to trot about, and the glasses to be filled. And Lamme drank in like the dry sands and ate well.

The lads and lasses of the farm came, turn about, to stick their noses in at the half-open door to watch him make his jaw-bones work. And the lads, jealous of him, said that they could do as well as he could.

At the end of the meal Thomas Utenhove said:

'A hundred peasants leave here next week on a pretence of going to work on the dykes at Bruges and the surrounding country. They will go in bands of five and six and by different roads. There will be barks at Bruges to transport them by sea to Emden.'

'Will they be provided with arms and money?' asked Ulenspiegl.

'Each one will have ten florins and big cutlasses.'

'God and the prince will repay you,' said Ulenspiegl.

'I do not work for payment,' answered Thomas Utenhove.

'What do you do?' asked Lamme, as he lustily devoured the fat black-pudding, 'What do you do, Master Host, to get a dish so savory, so succulent and with such fine grease?'

'We put in cinnamon and cat-nip,' said the host.

Then, speaking to Ulenspiegl:

'Is Edzard, Count of Frisia, still the prince's friend?'

Ulenspiegl replied:

'He doesn't show it, while at the same time harbouring the prince's ships at Emden.'

And he added:

'We must go to Maestricht.'

'You won't be able to,' said the host; 'the duke's army is before the town and all about it.'

Then, taking him up to the garret, he showed him in the distance the ensigns and guidons of the cavalry and infantry, riding and marching about the country-side.

'I'll pass through them if you, who are powerful in this country, grant me permission to marry. As for the woman, she must be sweet, gentle and lovely, and wishful to marry me, if not for always at least for a week.'

Lamme sighed and said:

'Don't do it, my boy; she'll leave you alone, burning up with the fire of love. Your bed, where you sleep so quietly, will become as mattress of holly to you, taking away your soft sleep.'

'I will take me a wife,' answered Ulenspiegl.

And Lamme, finding nothing else on the table, was quite grieved. However, having discovered a bowl of *castrelins*, he crunched them most sadly.

Ulenspiegl said to Thomas Utenhove:

'How now, let's drink! Give me a wife, rich or poor. I shall go with her to the church and have the marriage blessed by the priest. He will give us a marriage certificate which will not be valid since it is of a papist inquisitor; we'll have it set down that we are all good Christians, having been confessed and received communion, living apostolically according to the precepts of our Holy Mother the Roman Church—who burns her children—and calling down upon us the benediction of our Holy Father the Pope, the celestial and terrestrial armies, the saints, the deans, the vicars, monks, troopers, catchpolls and other scoundrels. Armed with the aforementioned certificate, we shall make preparations for the usual journey of wedding festivities.'

'But the woman?' said Thomas Utenhove.

'You will find her for me,' answered Ulenspiegl. 'I will then take two wagons, I will deck them with wreaths made of pine branches, holly and paper flowers; I will fill them with several good fellows whom you want to send to the prince.'

'But the woman?' said Thomas Utenhove.

'She is here, no doubt,' answered Ulenspiegl.

And, continuing what he was saying:

'I will harness two of your horses to one of the wagons and our two donkeys to the other. I will place in the first wagon my wife and myself; in the second the drummers, the fife-players, and those who play the shawm. Then, bearing the gay wedding banners, drumming, singing, drinking, we shall pass at a trot along the highway that leads us to *Galgen-Veld* (the Gallows Field) or Liberty.

'I will help you,' said Thomas Utenhove. 'But the women and girls will want to follow their men.'

'We shall go, by the grace of God,' said a sweet young girl, sticking her head in at the half-open door.

'There shall be, if there's need for them, four wagons,' said Thomas Utenhove; 'thus we can pass more than twenty-five men.'

'The duke will be abashed,' said Ulenspiegl.

'And the prince's fleet served by several good troopers the more,' said Thomas Utenhove.

Having summoned all his serving men and women by the ringing of a bell, he said to them:

'All of you who come from Zeeland, hearken: Ulenspiegl, the Fleming here present, wants you to pass through the duke's army in wedding array.'

The men and women of Zeeland shouted together:

'Danger of death! We are willing!'

And the men said among themselves:

292

'It's joy for us to leave this land of servitude to go towards the open sea. If God be with us, who can be against us?'

And the women and girls said:

'Let us follow our husbands and lovers. We are from Zeeland and we'll find shelter there.'

Ulenspiegl noticed a sweet young girl, and said to her jestingly:

'I want to marry you.'

But she, blushing, replied:

'I am willing you should—but in church only.'

The women, laughing, said to each other:

'Her heart is drawn to Hans Utenhove, the son of the *baes*. He will go with her, no doubt.'

'Yes,' said Hans.

And his father said to him:

'You may.'

The men dressed themselves in their festal garb: doublet and breeches of velvet and over them the great *opperst-kleed* and on their heads wide-brimmed hats to keep off the sun and the rain. The women had on black stockings and pinked shoes; on their foreheads they wore the big gilt jewel, to the left for the girls and to the right for the married women; about their necks the white ruff; the breast-plate all broidered in gold, scarlet and azure; the petticoat of black wool with the large stripes of velvet of the same colour; black woollen stockings and velvet shoon with silver buckles.

Then Thomas Utenhove went to the church to beg the priest to marry without more ado, and for two *rycksdaelders* which he slipped into his hand, Thylbert, son of Claes—that was Ulenspiegl—and Tannekin Pieters. And to this the priest consented.

Ulenspiegl then went to the church, followed by all the wedding-party and there, before the priest, he married Tannekin, so lovely and sweet, so gracious and well-formed that he would have liked to have bitten her cheeks as he would a love-apple. And he told her so, not daring to do it out of the respect he had for her sweet loveliness. But she, pouting, said to him:

'Leave me alone; there's Hans casting murderous glances at you.'

One of the girls, who was jealous, said to him:

'Seek elsewhere; can't you see that she's afraid of her lover?'

Lamme, rubbing his hands together, cried:

'You shan't have all of them, rascal.'

And he was delighted.

Ulenspiegl, accepting his hardship with patience, returned to the

293

farm with the party. And there he drank, sang and was gay, clinking glasses with the girl who was jealous. This made Hans happy, but not Tannekin any more than the lover of the girl.

At noon, under a bright sun and a cool wind, the flowered and verdant wagons started off, all banners flying, to the sound of the tabors, the shawms, the fifes and the bagpipes.

At the camp of Alba there was another sort of party. The advanced outposts and sentinels, having sounded the alarm, returned one after the other, saying:

'The enemy is close; we have heard the noise of tabors and fifes and have seen the banners. They're a strong body of cavalry come here to attract you into some sort of ambush. The rest of the army is farther off, no doubt.'

The duke at once informed his camp-masters, colonels and captains, and ordered them to get the army into battle formation and send out to reconnoitre the enemy.

Suddenly appeared the four wagons advancing towards the musketeers. In the wagons the men and women danced, the bottles went around, and gaily piped the flutes, moaned the shawms, beat the tabors, and droned the bagpipes.

The wedding-party having halted, Alba himself came out at the noise and saw the bride on one of the wagons; Ulenspiegl, her spouse, all beflowered, beside her, and all the peasants, having come down from the wagons, dancing about and offering drinks to the troopers.

Alba and his followers marvelled greatly at the simplicity of these peasants who feasted and sang while all were in arms about them.

And those who were in the wagons gave all their wine to the troops.

And by them they were greatly applauded and made much of.

The wine having given out in the wagons, the peasants went on their way to the sound of the tabors, fifes and bagpipes, and were not interfered with.

And the troops gaily fired a salvo of musket-shots in their honour.

And so they entered Maestricht, where Ulenspiegl made arrangements with the Reformist agents to send arms and munitions by boat to the Silent One's fleet.

And they did the same at Landen.

And they went about in this way everywhere, dressed as workers.

The duke learned of the stratagem; and there was a song made up about it whose refrain ran:

> Duke of the blood, Oh ninny duke,
> At the newlywed did you have a look?

And every time he made a false manœuvre the troops sang:

> The duke can't see beyond his nose:
> He saw the bride in her wedding-clothes.

24 IN THE MEANTIME, King Philip was steeped in sullen melancholy. In his woeful pride he prayed God to give the power to vanquish England, conquer France, take Milan, Genoa, Venice and so, as great dominator of the seas, reign over the whole of Europe. Dreaming of this triumph, he never smiled at all.

He was continually cold; wine did not warm him up, neither did the fire of scented wood that burned in the room where he was. There, always writing, seated amidst as many letters as would have filled a hundred casks, he dreamed of the universal domination of the world, such as the Roman Emperors exercised; of his jealous hatred for his son Don Carlos, ever since he wanted to go to the Netherlands instead of the Duke of Alba, to try to reign there no doubt, he thought. And seeing him so ugly, deformed, mad, fierce and mean, he hated him the more. But he never spoke of this.

Those who served King Philip and his son Don Carlos knew not which one of the two was more to be feared: the son, agile, murderous, tearing at his servants with his nails; or the father, cowardly and crafty, striking through others and, like a hyena, living on corpses.

The servants were terrified, seeing them prowling one after the other. And they said that before long there would be someone dead in the the Escurial.

Then they soon learned that Don Carlos had been imprisoned for the crime of high treason. And they knew that he was eating his heart out with black vexation; that he had wounded himself in the face trying to escape through the bars of his prison; and that Madame Isabella of France, his step-mother, wept without ceasing.

But King Philip did not weep.

The rumour came to them that Don Carlos had been given green figs and that he had died the following day as though he had fallen asleep. The doctors said: 'As soon as he had eaten the figs the heart ceased beating, the functions of life, such as Nature wills them, were interrupted; he could no longer spit, nor vomit, nor pass anything out of his body. His belly swelled when he died.'

King Philip heard the mass for the dead for Don Carlos, had him buried in the chapel of his royal residence, and set up a stone over his grave. But he did not weep.

And the servants said among themselves, mocking the princely epitaph that was found on the tombstone:

**HERE LIES HE WHO, EATING GREEN FIGS,
DIED WITHOUT HAVING BEEN SICK**

*Aqui yace quien para, decir verdad,
Murió sin infirmidad.*

And King Philip looked with lecherous eye on the Princess of Eboli, who was married. He besought her love and she yielded to him.

Madame Isabella of France—of whom it was said that she favoured the designs of Don Carlos on the Netherlands—grew haggard and mournful. And her hair fell out in great handfuls at a time. She vomited often and her finger-nails and toe-nails fell off. And she died.

And Philip wept not.

The Prince of Eboli's hair likewise fell out. He became sad and complained all the time. Then his toe-nails and finger-nails also fell off.

And King Philip had him buried.

And he paid for the widow's mourning and wept not.

25 AT THIS TIME several of the women and girls of Damme came to ask Nele if she would not be the May bride and hide in the brushwood with the groom they would find for her; for, said the women, not without jealousy, there is not a single young man in all Damme or round about who would not like to be betrothed to you, you who stay so lovely, good and blooming: a witch's gift, no doubt.

'Goodwives,' answered Nele, 'tell the young men who seek me out: "The heart of Nele is not here, but with him who wanders to deliver the land of our fathers! And if I am blooming, as you put it, it is not a witch's gift, but that of good health."'

The goodwives answered:

'Katheline is suspected, just the same.'

'Do not believe what vile folk say,' replied Nele; 'Katheline is not a witch. The men-at-law burned tow on her head and God smote her with madness.'

And Katheline, nodding her head, in the corner where she was crouching, said:

'Take away the fire, he'll come back again, Hanske, my sweet.'

The goodwives having asked who this Hanske was, Nele answered:

'He's the son of Claes, my foster-brother, whom she thinks she has lost ever since she was stricken by God.'

And the kind goodwives gave silver coins to Katheline. And when they were new she showed them to some invisible person, saying:

'I am rich, rich with shining silver. Come, Hanske, my sweet; I will pay for my love.'

And when the goodwives were gone, Nele wept in the lonely cottage. And she thought of Ulenspiegl wandering about in far-off countries without her being able to follow him; and of Katheline who moaned: 'Take away the fire!' and often held her two hands on her breast, showing thereby that the fire of folly burned feverishly in her head and body.

And in the meantime the bride and the groom of May hid themselves in the grass.

He or she who found one or the other of them, according to the sex of the one found, was King or Queen of the feast.

Nele heard the joyous cries of the boys and girls when the bride of May was found at the edge of a ditch, hidden in the tall grass.

And she wept, dreaming of the sweet time when they sought for her and her friend Ulenspiegl.

26 MEANWHILE LAMME and he straddled along on their donkeys, one leg this way, the other leg that way. 'Listen, now, Lamme,' said Ulenspiegl, 'the nobles of the Netherlands, through jealousy of Orange, have betrayed the Confederates' cause, the holy alliance, brave covenant signed for the good of the land of our fathers. Egmont and Hoorn were likewise traitors without any profit for themselves; Brederode is dead, and there remains nothing for us in this war but the poor populace of Brabant and Flanders, who but await loyal leaders to go forward. And then, my boy, the isles, the isles of Zeeland, and North Holland, too, over which the prince is governor; and farther still, on the sea, Edzard Count of Emden and East Frisia.'

'La,' said Lamme, 'I see clearly, we perambulate between the rope, the rack and the stake, dying of hunger, gaping with thirst, and without any hope of rest.'

'We are only at the beginning,' replied Ulenspiegl. 'Deign to consider that all this is a pleasure for us, killing our enemies, making a mock of them, having our pouches filled with florins; well-laden with meat, beer, wine and brandy. What more do you want, a feather-bed? Do you want that we should sell our donkeys and buy horses?'

'My boy,' said Lamme, 'a horse's trot is very hard on a man of my corpulence.'

'You'll sit on your steed the way the peasants do,' answered Ulenspiegl, 'and nobody will mock at you, since you are dressed like a peasant and carry a pike-staff and not a sword as I do.'

'Are you sure, my boy,' said Lamme, 'that our two passes will be of any use in the small towns?'

'Have I not the priest's certificate,' said Ulenspiegl, 'with the great red-wax seal of the church hanging by two tails from the parchment; and our confession cards? The troops and the catchpolls of the duke can do nothing against two men so well armed. And the black pater-nosters we have to sell? We are both *reiters*, you Fleming and I German, going about at the express orders of the duke to win the heretics of these countries to the Catholic faith by the sale of articles that have been blessed. We will be able to enter everywhere in this way—in the houses of the noble lords and the rich abbeys. And they will give us an unctuous hospitality. And we'll surprise their secrets. Lick your chops, my gentle friend.'

'My boy,' said Lamme, 'we'll be doing the work of spies.'

'By right and law of war,' replied Ulenspiegl.

'If they learn of what happened to the three preachers, we shall doubtless die,' said Lamme.

Ulenspiegl sang:

> 'My banner bears the words *Live On,*
> Live on forever in the light;
> Of leather is my first skin made,
> My second skin of strongest steel.'

But Lamme sighed:

'I have but one very soft skin, the slightest stroke of a dagger would immediately make a hole in it. It would be better for us to settle down at some useful trade rather than gad about over hill and dale working for these great princes who, with feet in velvet hose, eat ortolans from gilt tables. For us the blows, dangers, battles, rain, hail, snow, and vaga-bond's watery soups. For them the fine sausages, fat capons, odorous thrushes, succulent pullets.'

'Is your mouth watering, my sweet friend?' said Ulenspiegl.

'Where are you, fresh bread, golden *koeke-bakken,* delicious creams? But where are you, my wife?'

Ulenspiegl answered:

'The ashes beat upon my heart and drive me into battle. But you, gentle lamb, who have neither the death of your father nor that of your mother to avenge, nor the grief of those whom you love, nor your present poverty, leave me alone to go where I must, if the war's weari-nesses terrify you.'

299

'Alone?' said Lamme.

And he pulled up his donkey, which began to nibble at a bunch of thistles, of which there were many on that road. Ulenspiegl's donkey stopped and likewise began to eat.

'Alone?' said Lamme. 'You would not leave me alone, my boy? That would be an arrant cruelty. To have lost my wife and then lose my friend, cannot be. I won't whine any more, I promise you. And since it must be,' and he raised his head proudly, 'I'll go through a rain of bullets, yes! And in the midst of swords, yes! Right in the face of these nasty troops that drink blood like wolves. And if one day I fall at your feet, bloody and stricken to death, bury me; and if you see my wife, tell her I died because I did not know how to live without being loved by someone in this world. No, I could not, Ulenspiegl, my boy.'

And Lamme wept. And Ulenspiegl was touched, seeing his mild courage.

27 AT THIS TIME the duke, dividing his army in two corps, sent one marching towards the Duchy of Luxemburg and the other towards the Marquisate of Namur. 'This is some military resolution unknown to me,' said Ulenspiegl; 'it's all the same to me, let us go towards Maestricht with confidence.'

As they skirted the Meuse near the town, Lamme saw Ulenspiegl look attentively at all the boats that moved on the river and light on one of them that bore a siren on the prow. And this siren held a scutcheon whereon was marked in letters of gold, on a sable ground, the sign I. H. S., which is that of our Lord Jesus Christ.

Ulenspiegl signed to Lamme to stop, and began to whistle like a lark, merrily.

A man came out on the boat, crowed like a cock, and then—at a sign from Ulenspiegl, who brayed like an ass and pointed to the populace assembled on the quay—began to bray terribly. The two donkeys of Ulenspiegl and Lamme laid back their ears and sang their natural song.

Women passed, and men also, seated on towing-horses, and Ulenspiegl said to Lamme:

'That bargeman is mocking us and our steeds. Supposing we go and attack him on his boat?'

'Let him come here, rather,' answered Lamme.

A woman then spoke and said:

'If you want to return with your arms broken, your back sprained, your snouts in pieces, let Sterke Pier bray as he pleases.'

'Hee haw! Hee haw! Hee haw!" cried the bargeman.

'Let him sing,' said the goodwife. 'We saw him lift up on his shoulders, the other day, a cart loaded with heavy casks of beer, and stop another cart that was pulled by a vigorous horse. There,' she said, pointing to the Inn of the *Blauwe Toren* (The Blue Tower), 'he pierced with his knife, thrown from twenty paces away, an oak plank that was a foot thick.'

'Hee haw! Hee haw! Hee haw!' cried the bargeman, while a boy of twelve came up on the deck of the barge and likewise began to bray.

Ulenspiegl replied:

'He doesn't frighten us, your Strong Peter! However Sterke Pier he is, we are stronger; and there's my friend Lamme, who could eat two like him without even a hiccough.'

'What are you saying, my boy?' demanded Lamme.

'The truth,' said Ulenspiegl; 'do not contradict me through modesty. Yes, good folk, goodwives and workers, soon you will see him work his arms and reduce to nothing this famous Sterke Pier.'

'Shut up!' said Lamme.

'Your strength is known,' replied Ulenspiegl, 'you could never hide it.'

'Hee haw!' brayed the bargeman. 'Hee, haw!' brayed the boy.

Suddenly Ulenspiegl whistled again most melodiously, like the lark. And the men, women and workers, ravished with delight, asked him where he had learned that divine whistle.

'In paradise, from whence I came straight here,' answered Ulenspiegl.

Then, speaking to the man, who kept on braying and mockingly pointing a finger at him:

'Why do you stay on your barge, scoundrel? Don't you dare come on land to mock at us and our steeds?'

'Don't you dare?' said Lamme.

'Hee haw! Hee haw!' brayed the bargeman. 'Master donkeys donkeying, come on my boat.'

'Do as I do,' whispered Ulenspiegl to Lamme.

And, speaking to the bargeman:

'If you are Sterke Pier, I am Tyl Ulenspiegl. And these two here are our donkeys, Jef and Jan, who know better than you how to bray, for that's their natural way of speaking. As for coming on your badly joined planks, we don't care to. Your boat is like a tub; each time a wave pushes it, it goes backwards and it can only go, like the crabs, sideways.'

'Yes, like the crabs!' said Lamme.

The bargeman, speaking then to Lamme:

'What are you muttering there between your teeth, block of lard?'

Lamme, getting into a rage, said:

'Wicked Christian who reproaches me with my infirmity, know that

my lard is my own and comes from my good food; while you, old rusty
nail, you only live on old red-herrings, candle-wicks, stockfish skins,
judging by your skinny flesh that can be seen through the holes of your
breeches.'

'They're going to pitch into each other, toughly,' said the men, women
and workers, delighted and curious.

'Hee haw! Hee haw!' brayed the bargeman.

Lamme wanted to get down off his donkey to pick up stones to throw
at him.

'Don't throw any stones,' said Ulenspiegl.

The bargeman whispered in the ear of the boy hee-hawing alongside
him on the barge. He detached a little boat from the side of the barge
and, with the aid of a boat-hook which he handled cleverly, came close
to the shore. When he was quite close, he said, standing up most proudly:

'My *baes* asks you if you dare come on the boat and fight him with
fist and foot. These goodmen and goodwomen will be witnesses.'

'We want to,' said Ulenspiegl, with much dignity.

'We accept the fight,' said Lamme, with great pride.

It was noon; the dyke-builders, the pavers, ship-builders, women
carrying their husbands' mid-day meal, the children who had come to
see their fathers restore themselves with beans and boiled beef, all
laughed and clapped their hands at the idea of the battle soon to take
place, and they gaily hoped that one or the other of the fighters would
have his head broken or fall in bits in the river for their amusement.

'My boy,' said Lamme in a whisper, 'he's going to cast us into the
water.'

'Let yourself be cast in,' said Ulenspiegl.

'The big man is frightened,' said the crowd of workers.

Lamme, still seated on his donkey, turned on them and looked angrily
at them, but they booed him.

'Let's go on the boat,' said Lamme, 'they'll see if I'm frightened.'

At these words they booed him again, and Ulenspiegl said:

'Let's go on the boat.'

Getting off their donkeys, they threw the reins to the boy, who caressed the animals amicably and led them to where he saw some thistles.

Then Ulenspiegl took the boat-hook, made Lamme get into the little boat and rowed out to the barge where, by the aid of a rope, he climbed on to it, preceded by Lamme, sweating and puffing.

When he was on the deck, Ulenspiegl bent down as though he wanted to lace his boots, and said a few words to the bargeman, who smiled and looked at Lamme. Then he vociferated against him a thousand insults, calling him scoundrel, puffed up with criminal fat, jail-seed, *pap-eter*, and ended by saying: 'Great whale, how many barrels of oil do you give when you're bled!'

Suddenly, without saying a word, Lamme shot out at him like an enraged steer, knocked him down, and struck at him with all his might; but did not hurt him much because of the fatty weakness of his arms. The bargeman, pretending all the while to struggle, let him strike, and Ulenspiegl said: 'That rascal will pay for the drinks.'

The men, women and workmen, watching the battle from the river bank, said: 'Who would have thought that the big man was so impetuous?'

And they both fought with their hands while Lamme struck out hard. But the bargeman took no other care than to protect his face. Suddenly Lamme was seen with his knee on the chest of Sterke Pier, while one hand held him by the throat and the other was raised to strike.

'Cry mercy,' said he furiously, 'or I'll push you through the planks of your tub!'

The bargeman, coughing to show that he could not cry out, asked for mercy with a sign of the hand.

Then Lamme was seen generously helping his enemy to his feet who, when he was standing, turned his back on the crowd and stuck out his tongue at Ulenspiegl, who burst out laughing to see Lamme shaking proudly the feather of his beret and walking about in great triumph on the deck.

And the men, women, boys and girls who were on the bank applauded as best they could, saying: 'Long live the conqueror of Sterke Pier! He's a man of iron. Did you see how he punched him with his fist and how with a head-blow he knocked him on his back? There, they are going to drink now, to make peace. Sterke Pier has come up from the hold with wine and sausages.'

And indeed Sterke Pier had come up on deck with two tankards and a great quart of white wine of the Meuse. And Lamme and he made peace. And Lamme, very gay because of his triumph, because of the wine and the sausages, asked him, as he pointed to an iron chimney that was belching forth a thick black smoke, what fricassees were being done down there in the hold.

'War cooking,' replied Sterke Pier with a smile.

The crowd of workers, women and children, having moved away to return to their work or their houses, the rumour went from mouth to mouth that a big man, riding on a donkey and accompanied by a little pilgrim also mounted on a donkey, was stronger than Samson and that one must take care not to offend him.

Lamme drank, and watched the bargeman victoriously.

The latter suddenly said:

'Your donkeys are bored over there.'

Then, taking the barge over to the quay, he landed, took hold of one of the donkeys by the fore-legs and the hind-legs and, carrying it as Jesus did the little lamb, he set it down on the deck of the boat. Then, having done the same with the other, without losing a breath, he said:

'Let's drink.'

The boy leapt on deck.

And they drank. Lamme, amazed, did not know any more if it was he himself, native of Damme, who had beaten that robust man, and he did not dare look at him except on the sly, without any triumph, fearing that he might take it into his head to lift him up as he had lifted the donkeys and cast him alive in the Meuse out of spite for his defeat.

But the bargeman, smiling, gaily invited him to drink again, and Lamme, recovered from his fright, looked at him again with victorious assurance.

And the bargeman and Ulenspiegl laughed.

In the meantime the donkeys, astonished to find themselves standing on a wooden floor, had lowered their heads and laid back their ears, and dared not drink for fear. The bargeman went to seek out one of the pecks of corn that were given to the horses which towed his boat; this he bought himself so as not to be cheated by the drivers in the price of fodder.

When the donkeys saw the oats, they muttered paternosters of the jaw while staring at the deck of the boat sadly and not daring, for fear of slipping, to move a hoof.

At this, the bargeman said to Lamme and Ulenspiegl:

'Let's go to the kitchen.'

'War-kitchen,' said Lamme, uneasily.

'War-kitchen, but you can go down into it without any fear, my conqueror.'

'I have no fear and I follow you,' said Lamme.

The boy took the tiller.

As they went down they saw, everywhere, sacks of corn, beans, peas, carrots and other vegetables.

The bargeman then said to them, as he opened the door of a little forge:

'Since you are brave-hearted men and know the song of the lark, the bird of the free, and the warrior trumpet of the cock, and the bray of the ass, the gentle worker, I want to show you my war-kitchen. You will find a little forge like this in most of the barges on the Meuse. No one can suspect it, for it serves to repair the ironwork of the vessels. But what all of them do not have are lovely vegetables like those contained in these cupboards.'

Then, setting aside several stones that covered the bottom of the hold, he raised some planks and pulled out a fine sheaf of musket-barrels; and, lifting it up as he would have a feather, set it back in place and then showed them points for lances and halberds, sword-blades, bags of bullets and powder.

'Up with the Beggars!' said he; 'here are beans and sauce for them, the musket-stocks are the legs o' mutton, the salads are these halberd-points, and these musket-barrels are the ox-shins for the soup of Freedom. Up with the Beggars! Where must I carry this nourishment?' he asked of Ulenspiegl.

Ulenspiegl answered:

'To Nymwegen, where you will enter with your barge, still more heavily laden with real vegetables—brought to you by the peasants—which you will take on at Etsen, Stephansweert, and Ruremonde. And they also will sing like the lark, bird of the free, and you will answer with the warrior trumpet of the cock. You will go to the house of Doctor Pontus, near Nieuwe-Waal; you will tell him that you have come to town with vegetables, but that you fear the drought. During the time the peasants have gone to market to sell the vegetables, at a price too high for anyone to buy them, he will tell you what you must do with your weapons. I think, however, that he will order you to pass—not without danger—by the Waal, the Meuse or the Rhine, exchanging the vegetables for nets for sale, to wander with the fishing-boats of Harlingen, where there are many sailors who know the song of the lark; skirt the coast by the Waden, and get into Lauwer-Zee, exchange the nets for iron and lead, give the costumes of Marken, Vlieland or Ameland to your peasants, keep in by the coast, catching and salting your fish to keep and not to sell, for to drink cool and war saltily is a lawful thing.'

306

'Therefore, let us drink,' said the bargeman.

And they went up on deck.

But Lamme was steeped in melancholy:

'Mister Bargeman,' said he suddenly, 'you have here in your forge a little fire so bright that it could surely cook the suavest of hotchpots. My gullet thirsts for soup.'

'I'm going to refresh you,' said the man.

And soon he served him a thick soup wherein he had boiled a great hunk of salt ham.

When Lamme had swallowed a few spoonsful, he said to the bargeman:

'My throat's peeling, my tongue's burning: this is no hotchpot.'

'Drink cool and war saltily, it was written,' retorted Ulenspiegl.

The bargeman then filled up the tankards and said:

'I drink to the lark, the bird of Freedom.'

Ulenspiegl said:

'I drink to the cock, trumpeting the war.'

Lamme said:

'I drink to my wife; may she never be thirsty, the sweet darling.'

'You will go to Emden by the North Sea,' said Ulenspiegl to the bargeman. 'Emden is a refuge for us.'

'The sea is wide,' said the boatman.

'Wide for the battle,' said Ulenspiegl.

'God is for us,' said the boatman.

'Who then can be against us?' returned Ulenspiegl.

'When do you leave?' said the boatman.

'Right away,' replied Ulenspiegl.

'May you have a good journey and a wind at your backs. Here's powder and bullets.'

And, kissing them, he took them on land, after having carried like little lambs, on his neck and shoulders, the two donkeys.

Ulenspiegl and Lamme having mounted them, they started out for Liége.

'How is it, my boy,' said Lamme as they were going along, 'that that man who was so strong allowed himself to be so cruelly drubbed by me?'

'So that, everywhere we go, a terror of you may go before,' said Ulenspiegl. 'That will be a better escort for us than twenty *landsknechts*. Who, from now on, will dare to attack Lamme the mighty, the victorious; Lamme the peerless bull, who laid low with a blow of his head, and in full view of everybody, the Sterke Pier (the Strong Peter), the man who carries donkeys like lambs and lifts with his shoulder a whole wagonload of kegs of beer? Everybody here knows you already—you are

Lamme, the Redoubtable; Lamme, the Invincible, and I walk in the shadow of your protection. Everybody will know you on the road we are to take; no one will dare to cast unfriendly glances at you; and, considering the great courage of mankind, everywhere along your route you will find nothing but cap-raising, salutations, homage, and venerations, addressed to the strength of your redoubtable fist.'

'You speak well, my boy,' said Lamme, drawing himself up in his saddle.

'And I speak the truth,' retorted Ulenspiegl. 'Do you see these faces looking out so curiously from the first houses of the village? The owners are pointing out Lamme, the horrific conqueror. Do you see these men looking at you enviously, and these miserable cowards raising their hats? Answer their salutation, Lamme, my dear. Don't be disdainful of the poor weak people. See, the children know your name and repeat it with awe.'

And Lamme passed proudly on, saluting to the right and to the left, like a king. And the news of his bravery followed him from burg to burg and from town to town, right on to Liége, Chocquier, Neuville, Vesin, and Namur, which they avoided because of the three preachers.

They went on this way for a long time, following rivers, streams and canals. And everywhere to the song of the lark answered the crow of the cock. And everywhere, for freedom's cause, men forged, beat and furbished weapons that were taken away by the boats skirting the coast.

And they were passed through the tolls in casks, in cases, and in baskets.

And good folk were always found who would receive them and hide them in safe places, with the powder and bullets, until God's hour struck.

And Lamme, riding with Ulenspiegl, and still preceded by his victorious reputation, began himself to believe in his great strength and, becoming haughty and bellicose, let his hair grow long. And Ulenspiegl nick-named him Lamme the Lion.

But Lamme did not stick to his idea, because of the tickling of the four-days growth. And he passed the razor over his victorious face, which appeared once more to Ulenspiegl round and full like a sun lit up with the flame of good nourishment.

And so it was that they came to Stockém.

28 Towards night-fall, having left their donkeys at Stockem, they entered into the town of Antwerp. And Ulenspiegl said to Lamme: 'Here is the great city, here the whole world piles up its riches: gold, silver, spices, gilt leather, Gobelin tapestries, cloth,

stuffs of velvet, wool and silk; beans, peas, corn, meat and flour, salted hides; wines from Louvain, Namur, Luxemburg, Liége, Landtwyn of Brussels and Aerschot, wines of Buley whose vineyard is close by the Plante Gate at Namur, Rhine, Spanish and Portuguese wines; raisin-oil, known as Landolium, that comes from Aerschot; wines from Burgundy and Malvoisie, and many another. And the quays are encumbered with merchandise.

'These riches of the earth and human labour attract to this place the loveliest wenches there are.'

'You grow dreamy,' said Lamme.

Ulenspiegl answered:

'I will find among them the Seven. It was told me:

'In ruins, blood and tears, seek.'

'Who more than the wenches are the cause of ruin? Is it not in their company that poor maddened men lose their lovely carolus, shining and clinking, their jewels, chains, rings, and go off without their doublets, miserable and ragged, and even without their linen, while the wenches grow fat on their spoils? Where is the blood, red and limpid, that flowed in their veins? It's leek juice now. Or else, to enjoy the soft and darling bodies, do they not fight each other pitilessly with knife, dagger, sword? The corpses carried away pale and bleeding are those of poor men distraught with love. When the father scolds and remains forbidding on his seat, and his white hair seems more white and stiff, and from his dry eyes, wherein burns grief at the loss of a child, the tears will not flow; when the mother, silent and pale as death, weeps as though he saw before her all the sorrows of this world, who is it makes these tears to flow? The wenches, who only love themselves and money, and hold the thinking, working or philosophizing world attached to the end of their golden girdles. Yes, it is among them that the

309

Seven are, and we shall go, Lamme, among the wenches. Your wife may be there; that will be a double catch in the net.'

'I am willing,' said Lamme.

It was then the month of June, towards the end of the summer, when the sun already reddens the leaves of the chestnut trees, when the little birds sing in the trees and there is no mite so small that it does not murmur softly with the pleasure of being so warm in the grass.

Lamme trailed along beside Ulenspiegl in the streets of Antwerp, hanging his head and dragging his body along like a house.

'Lamme,' said Ulenspiegl, 'you seem steeped in melancholy; don't you know that there's nothing worse for the skin? If you persist in your grief, you'll lose it in strips. And that will be a fine thing to hear about you when your name is mentioned: "Lamme, the Peeled".'

'I'm hungry,' said Lamme.

'Come and eat,' said Ulenspiegl.

And they went together to the Old-Stairs, where they ate *choesels* and drank as much *dobble cuyt* as they were able to carry.

And Lamme wept no more.

And Ulenspiegl said:

'Blessed be the good beer that makes your soul all sunny! You laugh and you shake your belly. How I love to see you make your happy guts dance!'

'My boy,' said Lamme, 'they would dance much more if I had the luck to find my wife again.'

'Let's go and search for her,' said Ulenspiegl.

So they came to the Lower Scheldt quarter.

'Look,' said Ulenspiegl to Lamme, 'at that little house all made of wood, with fine windows well worked and glazed with little panes of glass; consider these yellow curtains and that red lantern. There, my boy, behind four casks of *bruinbier, uitzet, dobble cuyt* and Amboise wine, sits a lovely *baesinne* of fifty years or more. Each year she has lived has added a fresh layer of fat to her. On one of the casks burns a candle, and there is a lantern hung from the roof-beams. It is bright and dark; dark for love, bright for the paying.'

'But,' said Lamme, 'this is a convent for nuns of the devil, and that *baesinne* is its abbess.'

'Yes,' said Ulenspiegl, 'she's the one that leads in the ways of sin, in the name of Beelzebub, fifteen comely girls of amorous life, who find food and shelter with her but are forbidden to sleep there.'

'You know this convent?' asked Lamme.

'I'm going to search for your wife there. Come.'

'No,' said Lamme, 'I've thought it over and won't go in.'

310

'Are you going to let your friend expose himself alone amongst these Astartes?'

'Let him not go, then,' said Lamme.

'But if he must go to find the Seven and your wife?' asked Ulenspiegl.

'I would much rather sleep,' said Lamme.

'Come on, then,' said Ulenspiegl, opening the door and shoving Lamme before him. 'See, the *baesinne* sits behind the casks between two candles; the room is large, with roof of blackened oak whose beams are smoked. All about stand benches, shaky-legged tables, covered with glasses, steins, goblets, tankards, jugs, flasks, bottles and other implements of drunkenness. In the middle of the room are more tables and chairs over which are thrown all sorts of things; goodwives' capes, golden girdles, velvet slippers, bagpipes, fifes, shawms. In the corner is a ladder that leads to the first floor. A little, baldplate hunchback plays on a harpsichord set up on glass feet which make the instrument have a grating sound. Dance, fatty! Fifteen wild women are seated, some on the tables, some on the chairs, legs this way and legs that way, bending, upright, leaning on their elbows, thrown back, lying on their backs or sides, according to their fancies, dressed in white, red, with arms bare, and shoulders and breasts likewise, right down to their middles. There are all sorts of them; choose! For some of them the candle-light, caressing their fair hair, leaves in the shade their blue eyes whose liquid fire we can see shining. Others, gazing up to the roof, sigh, to the accompaniment of the viola, some German ballad. Some round, brunette, plump, shameless, drink down full tankards of Amboise wine, show off their rounded arms bare to the shoulder, their half-opened dresses from whence come out the nipples of their breasts, and without any modesty talk full-mouthed the one after the other or altogether. Listen to them!'

'A straw for money to-day! It's love we want, love of our own choosing,' said the lovely wenches. 'The love of a child, or a youth, or whoever pleases us, without paying.'—'Let those in whom Nature has put the virile strength that makes males come to us in this place, for the love of God and us.'—'Yesterday was the day for paying, to-day is the day for love!'—'Who wants to drink at our lips still wet from the bottle? Wine and kisses, a whole feast!' 'Away with widows who lie all alone.'—'We are young! It's Charity Day to-day. To the young, to the strong, to the handsome, we open wide our arms. Drinks!'—'Darling, is't for the battle of love that your heart beats the tabor within your breast? What a pendulum! It's the clock of kisses. When will they come with full hearts and empty pockets? Don't they scent out dainty adventures? What difference is there between a young beggar and Master the

Markgrave? The master pays in florins and the beggar in caresses. Up with the beggar! Who wants to go rouse the cemeteries?'

In this way spoke the good, ardent and gay among the wenches of the amorous life.

But there were others of them, with narrow faces and scrawny shoulders who made of their bodies shops for savings and, coin by coin, harvested the price of their meagre flesh. And these ones grumbled among themselves: 'It is very stupid for us to go without payment in this wearying trade for these absurd whims that run through the heads of wenches mad for men. If they are moon-struck, we are not; and we prefer, in our old age, not to drag about our rags in the gutters but to be paid now, since we are for sale. Away with free-giving! Men are ugly, stinking, growling, gutsy drunkards. They alone turn poor women to evil!'

But the young and good-looking ones heard not these words and, all at their pleasures and drinkings, said: 'Do you hear the bells of Our Lady toll for the dead? We are on fire! Who wants to go rouse the cemeteries?'

Lamme, seeing so many women all at once, brunettes and blondes, fresh and faded, was ashamed; lowering his eyes, he called out: 'Ulenspiegl, where are you?'

'He has passed on, my friend,' said a stout girl, taking him by the arm.

'Passed on?' said Lamme.

'Yes,' said she, 'three hundred years ago in the company of Jacobus de Coster van Maerlandt.'

'Let me be,' said Lamme, 'and don't pinch me so. Ulenspiegl, where are you? Come and save your friend! I'll go immediately if you don't let me be.'

'You won't go,' said the wenches.

'Ulenspiegl,' called Lamme again, piteously, 'where are you, my boy? Madame, don't pull my hair that way; it's *not* a wig, I assure you. Help! Don't you think my ears are red enough without you making the blood run to them? There's that other one that fillips me all the time. You're hurting me! La! what are they rubbing my face with now? A mirror! I'm black as an oven's mug. I'm going to get mad if you don't stop; it's wrong of you to maltreat a poor man this way. Let me be! When you have tugged me by my breeches to the right, to the left, backwards and forwards like a shuttle, will you be any the fatter for it? Yes, I'm certainly going to get mad.'

'He'll get mad,' said they, mocking him; 'he'll get mad, the old codger. Laugh, rather, and sing for us a love *lied*.'

312

'I'll sing one with blows, if you wish; but let me be.'

'Whom do you love here?'

'No one, neither you nor the others. I'll complain to the magistrate and he'll have you whipped.'

'Yes, indeed,' they said, 'whipped! And if we kiss you by force before the whipping?'

'Me?' said Lamme.

'You!' they all said.

And thereupon the fair and the ugly, the fresh and the faded, the blondes and brunettes threw themselves on Lamme, cast his bonnet in the air, in the air his cloak and, caressing him, kissed him on the cheek, the nose, the stomach, the back, with all their might.

The *baesinne* laughed between her candles.

'Help!' cried Lamme; 'help! Ulenspiegl. Sweep away all this rubbish for me. Let me be! I don't want your kisses. I'm married, God's blood! and keep all for my wife.'

'Married,' they said; 'but your wife has too much—a man of your girth. Give us a little. Faithful wife 'tis good and well, but faithful man's a capon. God keep you! you must take your choice or we'll take turn about in whipping you.'

'I won't do it,' said Lamme.

'Choose,' said they.

'No,' said he.

'Do you want me?' said a lovely blond girl; 'see, I'm gentle, and I love those who love me.'

'Leave me be,' said Lamme.

'Do you want me?' said a sweet wench with black hair, eyes and skin quite brown and for the rest extremely well turned out by the angels.

'I don't like gingerbread,' said Lamme.

'And me? Won't you take me?' said a tall wench whose brow was almost all covered with her hair, heavy eye-brows joined together, great drowned eyes, lips thick as eels and all red, and red also the face, the neck and shoulders.

'I don't like flaming bricks,' said Lamme.

'Take me,' said a young girl of sixteen, with a face like a squirrel.

'I don't like nut-crunchers,' said Lamme.

'He must be whipped,' said they. 'With what? Lovely whips with lashes of dried leather. Fine lashing. The thickest skin cannot resist them. Take ten of them. Carters' and donkeymen's whips.'

'Help! Ulenspiegl!' cried Lamme.

But Ulenspiegl made no answer.

'You're mean-hearted,' said Lamme, looking all about for his friend.

The whips were brought in; two of the girls took upon themselves the duty of removing Lamme's doublet.

'Alas!' said he, 'my poor fat that I had so much trouble making, they'll lift it off, no doubt, with their cracking whips. But, pitiless females, my fat won't be of any use to you, not even to put in your sauces.'

They answered:

'We'll make candles with it. Is it nothing to see clearly without paying? She who henceforth says "Out of the whip comes forth candles" will seem mad to her neighbours. We will uphold it unto death and win more than one wager on it. Steep the rods in vinegar. Now your doublet's off. The hour rings out at St. James. Nine o'clock. At the last stroke of nine we will strike, if you have not made your choice.'

Paralyzed, Lamme said:

'Have pity on me and be merciful; I swore fidelity to my poor wife and will keep the oath, although she was bad enough to leave me. Ulenspiegl, help me, my dear!'

But Ulenspiegl did not show himself.

'You see me,' said Lamme to the wild women, 'you see me at your knees. Is there a more humble posture? Is it not enough to say that I honour, as I do the saints, your great beauties? Happy he, being unmarried, who can enjoy your charms! It's paradise, no doubt. But don't beat me, please.'

Suddenly the *baesinne,* who remained between her two candles, spoke with a loud and menacing voice: 'Goodwives and girls,' said she, 'I swear to you by my great devil that if in a moment you have not by laughter and gentleness, brought this man to the right path—that is to say into your bed—I will go and call the night watch and have you all whipped here in his stead. You do not deserve to be called wenches if you have in vain the active mouth, the ranging hand, and the flaming eyes to excite the males, as do the females of the glow-worms who have but their light for that end. And you shall be whipped mercilessly for your silliness.'

At these words the girls trembled and Lamme became gay.

'How now, goodwives,' said he, 'what news do you bring from the land of the lashing whips? I am going myself to call the watch. They'll do their duty and I'll help them. That will be a great joy to me.'

But thereupon a sweet young girl of fifteen threw herself down at Lamme's knees.

'Messire,' she said, 'you see me here before you humbly resigned; if you do not deign to choose someone from among us, must I be beaten

314

for you, Sir? And the *baesinne* over there will put me in a nasty cellar, under the Scheldt, where the water drips from the walls and where I shall have only black bread to eat.'

'Will she really be beaten for me, Madame *Baesinne*?' asked Lamme.

'Until the blood flows,' she answered.

Lamme, looking at the girl then, said: 'I see you fresh, fragrant, your shoulder coming out of your dress like a great leaf of a white rose. I don't want this lovely skin, under which the youthful blood runs, to suffer under the whip, nor these clear flashing eyes of youth to weep because of the pain of the strokes, nor that the cold of the prison should make your love-fairy's body to shiver. Consequently I'd rather choose you than know that you were beaten.'

The young girl led him away. And so he sinned—as he had done all his life—through goodness of heart.

Meanwhile Ulenspiegl and a tall brunette, with crinkly hair, were standing facing each other. The girl, without saying a word, watched Ulenspiegl coquettishly, and seemed not to want him.

'Love me,' said he.

'Love you,' said she, 'fond lover who only wants to love when he feels like it?'

Ulenspiegl answered: 'The bird that flies over your head sings his song and is gone. So with me, sweetheart. Shall we sing together?'

'Yes,' said she, 'a song of laughter and tears.'

And the girl threw herself on Ulenspiegl's neck.

Suddenly, as the two men were transported with pleasure in the arms of their darlings, who should come into the house, to the sound of the fife and tabor, shoving each other, pressing, singing, crying, shouting, vociferating, but a jolly band of *meezevangers*—titmouse catchers of Antwerp. They carried bags and cages full of these little birds, and also the owls which had helped them with the catch and which opened wide their golden eyes at the light.

The *meezevangers* were ten, all red, flushed with wine and cervoise, with heads shaking and legs tottering, and shouting with voices so raucous and broken that it seemed to the frightened girls that they were listening to wild beasts in the jungle rather than to men in a house.

Meanwhile, as they had not ceased saying, speaking alone or all at once: 'I want the one I love.—We are for whoever pleases us. To-morrow to the rich in money; to-day for the rich in love!'—the *meezevangers* replied: 'Money we have, and likewise love. For us then the wild women. Whoever retreats is a capon. These are titmice; we are the hunters. Up at them! Brabant for the good duke!'

But the women said sneeringly: 'Fie! the ugly snouts that think to eat us! It's not to swine that sherberts are given. We take what pleases us and we don't want you. Barrels of oil, bags of lard, scrawny nails, rusty blades, you stink of sweat and filth! Clear out of here; you'll be well damned without any help from us.'

But the men: 'The *Galloises* are dainty to-day. Disgusted ladies, you might give us what you sell to everyone else.'

But they: 'To-morrow we shall be slave-dogs and take you; to-day we are free-women and reject you.'

The men: 'Enough of words. Who's thirsty? Let's pluck the apples!'

And, so saying, they threw themselves on the women, without distinction of age or beauty. The lovely ones, resolute in their project, threw at the men's heads chairs, steins, jugs, goblets, tankards, flagons, bottles, which rained down on them thick and fast like hail, wounding them, bruising them and knocking their eyes out.

Ulenspiegl and Lamme came out at the noise, leaving their trembling wenches at the top of the ladder. When Ulenspiegl saw these men striking the women, he took from the courtyard a broom whose twigs he tore away, another he gave to Lamme, and they struck out at the *meezevangers* without pity.

The game seeming a rough one to the drunkards, thus whacked, they stopped for an instant, whereat the thin girls, who wanted to sell and not give themselves, immediately profited by the calm spell. They slid like adders among the wounded, caressing them, binding up their wounds, drinking Amboise wine for them, and emptying so well their pouches of florins and other coins that there was not a single sou left them. Then, as the curfew rang, they showed them to the door, through which Ulenspiegl and Lamme had already taken their way.

29 ULENSPIEGL and Lamme journeyed towards Ghent and came at dawn to Lokeren. The earth in the distance dripped with dew; cool white mists floated over the fields. Ulenspiegl, passing before a smithy, whistled like the lark, the bird of freedom. And

316

straightway a head appeared, tousled and white, at the door, and a weak voice imitated the warrior trumpet of the cock.

Ulenspiegl said to Lamme:

'That's the *smid* Wasteele, who by day forges spades, picks, plough-shares, striking the iron while it is hot to fashion beautiful grills for the choirs of churches; and often at night making and furbishing weapons for the troops of Free Conscience. He hasn't won good looks for himself at this game, for he is pale as a ghost, sad as a damned one, and so scrawny that his bones poke holes in his skin. He is not yet in bed, having doubtless worked all night.'

'Come in, both of you,' said the *smid* Wasteele, 'and lead your donkeys to the meadow behind the house.'

This being done, and Lamme and Ulenspiegl being in the smithy, the *smid* Wasteele took down into the cellar of this house all that he had furbished of swords and cast of lance-heads during the night; then he prepared the daily task for his workmen.

Looking at Ulenspiegl with a lack-lustre eye, he said to him:

'What news do you bring me of the Silent One?'

Ulenspiegl answered:

'The prince has been driven out of the Netherlands with his army because of the cowardice of his mercenaries, who cry: *"Geld! Geld!"* (Money! Money!) when they ought to be fighting. He went towards France with the faithful troops, his brother Count Ludwig, and the Duke of Deux-Ponts, to succour the King of Navarre and the Huguenots; from there he passed into Germany, to Dillenburg, where many refugees from the Netherlands are with him. You must send him the arms and the money you have collected, while we shall ply on the sea the work of freemen.'

'I shall do what must be done,' said the *smid* Wasteele; 'I have the arms and nine thousand florins. But did you not come here on donkeys?'

'Yes,' said they.

'And didn't you hear, as you came along, news of three preachers who were killed, despoiled, and cast into a hole in the rocks of the Meuse?'

'Yes,' said Ulenspiegl, with great assurance. 'These three preachers were spies for the duke, murderers paid to kill the Prince of Freedom. Two of us, Lamme and I, made them pass from life to death. Their money is ours and their papers also. We shall take what is necessary for our journey; the rest we shall give to the prince.'

And Ulenspiegl, opening up his doublet and that of Lamme, withdrew the papers and parchments. The *smid* Wasteele, having read them, said:

317

'They contain plans of battle and conspiracy. I shall have them given to the prince, and he will be told that Ulenspiegl and Lamme Goedzak, his faithful vagabonds, saved his noble life. I am going to have your asses sold so that you may not be recognized by your mounts.'

Ulenspiegl asked *smid* Wasteele if the sheriffs' court of Namur had already sent out the catchpolls after them.

'I am going to tell you what I know,' answered Wasteele. 'A blacksmith from Namur, a brave Reformist, passed by here the other day under the pretext of asking my help with the railings, weather-cocks, and other iron-work of a castle that is going to be built near La Plante. The clerk of the sheriffs' court told him that his masters had already come together, and that a tavern-keeper had been called before them because he lived some few hundred fathoms away from the place of the murder. Questioned as to whether he had or had not seen the murderers or those whom he might suspect as being such, he answered: "I saw male and female country-folk riding along on their donkeys who asked for drinks while they remained seated on their mounts, or who dismounted to come and drink at my place, beer for the men and hydromel for the women and girls. I saw two brave rustics who spoke of shortening, by a foot, Messire Orange." And, saying this, the tavern-keeper whistled and imitated the passing of a knife over the throat. "By the steel-wind," said he, "I will speak to you of this secretly, being empowered so to do." He spoke and was released. Since that time the councils have doubtless addressed dispatches to their subsidiary councils. The host said that he had only seen male and female country-folk riding on donkeys; it follows that the chase will be given to all those who are found astride a donkey. And the prince has need of you, my children.'

'Sell the donkeys,' said Ulenspiegl, 'and keep the money for the prince's treasury.'

The donkeys were sold.

'It is necessary now,' said Wasteele, 'that each of you have a trade, free and independent of the corporations. Do you know how to make bird-cages and mouse-traps?'

'I used to make them,' said Ulenspiegl.

'And you?' asked Wasteele of Lamme.

'I shall sell *heete-koeken* and *olie-koeken* (French pancakes and doughnuts).'

'Follow me: here are cages and mouse-traps already made; the tools and the copper wire necessary to repair them and make others. They were brought to me by one of my spies. That's for you, Ulenspiegl. As for you, Lamme, here is a little stove and a bellows; I will give you

318

flour, butter and oil for the making of the *heete-koeken* and the *olie-koeken*.'

'He'll eat them,' said Ulenspiegl.

'When shall we make the first ones?' asked Lamme.

Wasteele answered:

'You will first help me for a night or two; I cannot finish my great task alone.'

'I'm hungry,' said Lamme, 'do we eat here?'

'There's bread and cheese,' said Wasteele.

'Without butter?' asked Lamme.

'Without butter,' said Wasteele.

'Have you beer or wine?' asked Lamme.

'I never drink,' he replied, 'but I will go to *in het Pelicaen* nearby, and get some for you if you want it.'

'Yes,' said Lamme, 'and bring us some ham.'

'I shall do as you wish,' said Wasteele, looking at Lamme with great disdain.

Just the same, he brought back *dobble clauwaert* and a ham. And Lamme gaily ate enough for five.

And he said:

'When do we begin working?'

'To-night,' said Wasteele; 'but stay in the smithy and do not be afraid of my workmen. They are Reformists like yourself.'

'Good!' said Lamme.

That night, after the curfew rang and the doors were shut, Wasteele, aided by Ulenspiegl and Lamme, went down and brought up heavy bundles of arms from his cellar to the smithy.

'Here,' said he, 'are twenty muskets which must be repaired, thirty lance-heads to furbish, and lead for fifteen hundred bullets to be melted; you are going to help me with all this.'

'With both hands,' said Ulenspiegl, 'and why haven't I four to help you?'

'Lamme will come and help us,' said Wasteele.

'Yes,' said Lamme piteously, falling asleep because of the excess of drink and nourishment he had taken.

'You shall melt the lead,' said Ulenspiegl.

'I shall melt the lead,' said Lamme.

Lamme, melting the lead and casting the bullets, looked with a sullen eye at the *smid* Wasteele, who forced him to wake up when he dozed off to sleep. He cast the bullets with silent rage, having a great desire to pour the molten lead over the head of the blacksmith Wasteele. Towards mid-night, the rage gaining on him at the same time as the excess of weariness, he addressed him in these words, with a hissing voice, while *smid* Wasteele and Ulenspiegl patiently furbished the musket-barrels, muskets, and lance-heads:

'There you are,' said Lamme, 'skinny, pale, and wretched, believing in the good faith of the princes and the great ones of the earth, and disdaining, through an excess of zeal, your body, your noble body that you allow to perish in misery and abjection. It was not for that end that God made it along with Dame Nature. Know you not that our soul, which is the breath of life, in order to breathe has need of beans, beef, beer, wine, ham, sausages, chitterlings and rest. You live on wafers, water and watching.'

'From whence comes this talkative fullness to you?' asked Ulenspiegl.

'He does not know what he's saying,' said Wasteele, sadly.

But Lamme, getting angry:

'I know better than you do. I say that we are mad, me, you and Ulenspiegl likewise, to put out our eyes for all these princes and great ones of the earth who would laugh loudly at us if they could see us dying with fatigue through lack of sleep in order to furbish their arms and melt the bullets for their service. While they drink French wine and eat German capons from golden tankards and English pewter plates, they will never enquire whether, if when we seek in the open for God—by whose grace they are all-powerful—their enemies cut off our legs with their scythes and throw us into the well of death. In the meantime they, who are neither Reformists nor Calvinists nor Lutherans nor Catholics, but sceptics and whole-hearted doubters, buying or conquering principalities, eating up the wealth of the monks, the abbeys, the convents, will have all: virgins, women and wild women. And they will drink from their golden tankards to their perpetual good-humour and to our everlasting silliness, foolishness and asininity, and to the seven deadly sins which they commit, O *smid* Wasteele, under the meagre nose of your enthusiasm. Look at the fields, the meadows; look at the harvest, the orchards, the cattle, the gold rising from the earth; look at the wild things of the forest, the birds in the air, the delicious ortolans, the delicate thrushes, the wild-boar's head, the haunches of venison: all is theirs; hunting, fishing, earth, sea, all. And you, you live on bread and water, and we, we are exterminating ourselves here for them, without sleeping, without eating, without drinking. And when we have died they'll land us a kick on our carrion and say to our mothers: "Make more, these are no longer any good!"'

Ulenspiegl laughed without saying a word; Lamme puffed with indignation; but Wasteele, speaking with a gentle voice, said:

'You speak lightly. I do not live for ham and beer, not for ortolans,

320

but for the victory of the free conscience. The Prince of Freedom does as I do. He sacrifices his wealth, his peace and his happiness to drive from the Netherlands the butchers and tyranny. Do as he does and try to thin down. It is not by the belly that people are saved, but by the proud courages and fatigues borne without a murmur, even unto death. And now go to bed if you are sleepy.'

But Lamme, being ashamed of himself, no longer wanted to go.

And they furbished the arms and cast bullets until morning. And this they did for three days.

Then they left for Ghent at night, and on the way there sold cages, mouse-traps and *olie-koekjes*.

And they stopped at Meulestee, the little town of the mills whose red roofs are seen from all around; here they agreed to carry on their trades separately and to meet in the evening before curfew at *in de Zwaen* (the Swan Inn).

Lamme wandered about the streets of Ghent selling his *olie-koekjes*, getting to like his trade, seeking for his wife, draining many steins, and eating endlessly. Ulenspiegl had delivered letters from the prince to Jacob Scoelap, licentiate in medicine; to Lieven Smet, cloth-cutter; to Jan de Wulfschaeger; to Gillis Coorne, dyer in scarlet; and to Jan de Roose, tile-maker. These all gave him money collected by them for the prince, and told him to wait several days longer at Ghent and they would give him much more.

These men having been hanged later for heresy on the New Gibbet, their bodies were buried in the Gallows-Field, near the Bruges Gate.

30 MEANWHILE THE PROVOST, Spelle le Roux, armed with his red baton, went from town to town on his lean horse, setting up scaffolds, lighting pyres, digging pits to bury poor women and girls alive. And the King inherited. Ulenspiegl, being with Lamme under a tree at Meulestee, felt overcome with weariness. It was cold, despite the fact that they were then in June. From the heavens, covered with grey clouds, fell a fine hail.

'My boy,' said Lamme to him, 'for four nights, now, you've been shamelessly gadding about with the wild women; you sleep at *in den Zoeten Inval* (The Sweet Fall Inn) and you'll be like the man on their signboard, falling head-first into a bee-hive. I await you in vain at *in den Zwaen*, and I predict to you that evil will come of this lecherous existence. Why don't you take yourself a wife, virtuously?'

'Lamme,' said Ulenspiegl, 'he to whom one woman is all of them,

322

and to whom all of them is one in this pretty combat called love, must not lightly precipitate his choise.'

'And Nele, don't you think of her?'

'Nele is in Damme, very far off,' said Ulenspiegl.

While he was in this pensive attitude and the hail was falling fast, a sweet young woman passed, running and covering her head with her petticoat.

'Hey, dreamer,' said she, 'what are you doing under that tree?'

'I'm dreaming,' said Ulenspiegl, 'of a woman who would make of her petticoat a roof to cover me from the hail.'

'You've found her,' said the woman, 'arise.'

Ulenspiegl arose and went towards her.

'Are you going to leave me alone?' said Lamme.

'Yes,' said Ulenspiegl. 'But go to *in den Zwaen*, eat a leg o' mutton, drink a dozen tankards of beer, and you'll sleep and not bore yourself.'

'I'll do so,' said Lamme.

Ulenspiegl approached the woman.

'Lift up my skirt at one side,' said she, 'and I'll lift up the other; and now let's run.'

'Why run?' asked Ulenspiegl.

'Because I want to flee from Meulestee,' she said. 'The provost Spelle is there with two catchpolls and he has sworn to have all the wenches whipped who do not pay him five florins. That's why I'm running; run too and stay with me to defend me.'

'Lamme,' cried Ulenspiegl. 'Spelle is at Meulestee. Go on to Destel-bergh, to "The Star of the Three Wise Men".'

And Lamme, rising up in fright, took his belly in both hands and began to run.

'Where's that fat hare going?' asked the wench.

'To a burrow where I'll find him,' answered Ulenspiegl.

323

'Let's run,' she said, striking the ground with her foot like an impatient filly.

'I would like to be virtuous without running,' said Ulenspiegl.

'What does that mean?' she asked.

Ulenspiegl answered:

'The fat hare wants me to renounce good wine, cervoise ale and the fresh skin of women.'

The wench looked at him with an ill-natured eye.

'You're short-winded, you must rest,' said she.

'Rest? I see no shelter,' replied Ulenspiegl.

'Your virtue will serve to cover you,' said the wench.

'I like your petticoat better,' said he.

'My petticoat,' said the wench, 'would be unworthy to cover a saint such as you want to be. Be off, so I can run alone.'

'Don't you know,' replied Ulenspiegl, 'that a dog runs faster on his four legs than a man on his two? That's why, having four legs, we'll run better.'

'You're quick-spoken for a virtuous man.'

'Yes,' said he.

'But,' she said, 'I have always noticed that virtue is a quality that's quiet, sleepy, thick, and chilly. It's a mask to hide growling faces, a velvet cloak on a man of stone. I like those who have in their breasts a stove well-lit with the flame of virility, which excites them to valiant and gay enterprises.'

'That's the way,' answered Ulenspiegl, 'the beautiful she-devil spoke to the glorious Saint Anthony.'

There was an inn at twenty paces along the road.

'You have spoken well,' said Ulenspiegl, 'now you must drink well.'

'My tongue's still fresh,' said the wench.

They entered. On a chest stood a great jug, nick-named 'Pot-belly' because of its large paunch.

Ulenspiegl said to the *baes*:

'Do you see this florin?'

'I see it,' said the *baes*.

'How many patards will you extract from it in order to fill up with *dobble clauwaert* the "Pot-belly" over there?'

The *baes* said to him:

'For *negen mannekens* (nine manekins) we'll call it quits.'

'That's six Flanders mites,' said Ulenspiegl, 'and overmuch by two mites. But fill it up just the same.'

Ulenspiegl poured out a goblet for the woman, then, rising proudly

324

and applying his mouth to the neck of the 'Pot-belly', he emptied its entire contents down his gullet. And it made a noise like a cataract.

The wench, astonished, said to him:

'How did you manage to put into your lean stomach such a great Belly?'

Ulenspiegl, without answering, said to the *baes*:

'Bring on a ham-knuckle and bread and another full "Pot-belly" so that we may eat and drink.'

And this was done.

While the wench nibbled at a morsel of rind, he took her so subtly that she was startled, charmed and submissive, all at once.

Then, questioning him:

'From whence are come to your virtue,' she said, 'this sponge-like thirst, that ravenous hunger, these amorous audacities?'

Ulenspiegl answered:

'Having sinned in a hundred ways, I swore, as you know, to do penance. That lasted a whole hour long. Thinking during that hour of my life to come, I saw myself nourished meagrely on bread; tastelessly refreshed with water; sadly fleeing from love; never daring to move or sneeze for fear of doing wrong; esteemed by all, feared by many; as solitary as a leper; sad as a dog bereaved of its master; and after fifty years of martyrdom ending by giving up the ghost on a pallet, most sadly. The penance was long enough; so kiss me, sweet, and let us leave purgatory together.'

'Ah,' said she, obeying willingly, 'but virtue's a lovely sign to stick on the end of a pole!'

Time passed with these amorous gambols; nevertheless they had to rise and go, for the wench dreaded to see, suddenly rising up in the midst of their pleasure, the provost Spelle and his catchpolls.

'Kilt your skirts, then,' said Ulenspiegl.

And they ran like stags towards Destelbergh, where they found Lamme eating at 'The Star of the Three Wise Men.'

325

31 ULENSPIEGL often saw Jacob Scoelap, Lieven Smet and Jan de Wulfschaeger in Ghent, and they gave him news of the good or bad fortunes of the Silent One. And each time that Ulenspiegl returned to Destelbergh, Lamme said to him:

'What do you bring? Good or bad luck?'

'La!' said Ulenspiegl, 'the Silent One, his brother Ludwig, the other chiefs, and the French, had resolved to go farther into France and join the Prince of Condé. They would thus have saved the poor Belgian fatherland and Free Conscience. God willed otherwise; the German *reiters* and *landsknechts* refused to go on, saying that their oath was to fight against the Duke of Alba and not against France. Having vainly beseeched them to do their duty, the Silent One was forced to lead them through Champagne and Lorraine as far as Strasbourg, whence they entered Germany. Everything fails through this sudden and obstinate departure: the King of France, despite his contract with the prince, refuses to turn over the money he promised; the Queen of England would have sent him some to recover the town and country of Calais; her letters were intercepted and handed over to the Cardinal of Lorraine, who forged a contrary answer to them.

'Thus we see this fine army, our hope, melt away like phantoms at the crowing of the cock; but God is with us and, if the earth fails us, the water shall do its work. Up with the Beggars!'

32 THE WENCH CAME one day, all in tears, to say to Lamme and Ulenspiegl: 'At Meulestee, Spelle is letting the murderers and the robbers escape in consideration for the money paid him. He's putting innocent people to death; my brother Michielkin among them! La, let me tell you of it—you will avenge him, being men. A filthy and infamous debauchee, Pieter de Roose, a regular seducer of children and girls, does all the harm. La! My poor brother Michielkin and Pieter de Roose were together one evening—though not at the same table—in the *Valck* tavern, where Pieter de Roose was shunned like the pest by everybody.

'My brother, not wishing to see him in the same room as himself, called him a lecherous blackguard and ordered him to clear out.

'Pieter de Roose answered:

' "The brother of a public slut shouldn't turn his snout up so high."

'He lied; I'm not public and only give myself to whoever pleases me.

'Michielkin then threw his stein of cervoise in his face, told him that he had lied like the filthy debauchee he was, and threatened to make him eat his fist right up to the elbow if he did not decamp.

'The other wanted to keep on talking, but Michielkin did as he said he would; he gave him two great blows on the jaw and dragged him by the teeth, with which he was biting, right on to the causeway, where he left him bruised and without pity.

'Pieter de Roose, being healed and not knowing how to live alone, went to *in 't Vagevuur*, a real purgatory and sad tavern where only poor people go. There also he was left to himself, even by all these rag-tags. And no one spoke to him, except several country folk to whom he was unknown, and a few rascally vagabonds or deserters from the army. He was even beaten up several times, for he was quarrelsome.

'The provost Spelle having come to Meulestee with his two catch-polls, Pieter de Roose followed them everywhere like a dog, glutting them at his expense with wine, meat and many other pleasures to be had with money. Thus he became their companion and comrade, and he began to act his nasty best to torment those whom he detested; that is to say, all the inhabitants of Meulestee and notably my poor brother.

'He started in on Michielkin first. False witnesses—gallows-birds avid for florins—declared that Michielkin was a heretic, that he had made filthy remarks about Our Lady, and many times had blasphemed the name of God and the Saints in the *Valck* tavern; that he certainly had, moreover, three hundred florins in a coffer.

'Despite the fact that the witnesses were not of good life and conduct, Michielkin was arrested and, proofs having been declared by Spelle and his catchpolls sufficient to warrant the torture, Michielkin was strung up by the arms to a pulley attached to the ceiling and on each one of his feet was placed fifty-pound weights.

'He denied the charge, saying that if there was in Meulestee a scoundrel, blackguard, blasphemer, lecher, it was surely Pieter de Roose and not he.

'But Spelle would not listen and told his catchpolls to hoist Michielkin up to the roof and then let him drop heavily with the weights on his feet. This they did, and so cruelly, that the skin and the muscles of the victim's ankle were torn and the foot was barely attached to the leg.

'Michielkin persisted in saying that he was innocent; Spelle had him tortured anew, giving him to understand that if he wanted to hand over a hundred florins he would be freed and acquitted.

'Michielkin said he would rather die.

'The Meulestee folk, having heard of the arrest and torture, desired to act as witnesses *par turbes*; that is, give the testimony of all the reputable inhabitants of the commune. "Michielkin," they said with one voice, "is in no wise a heretic; he goes each Sunday to mass, and on

327

high feasts to the holy table; he has never said any words about Our Lady except to call her to aid him in difficult circumstances; having never spoken ill even of an earthly woman, it's all the more reason that he never would have dared do it to the Heavenly Mother of God. As for the blasphemies that the false witnesses declared they had heard proffered in the *Valck* tavern, that was, from every point, false and lying."

'Michielkin having been released, the false witnesses were punished, and Spelle had Pieter de Roose brought before his Court, but freed him without examination or torture in return for one hundred florins paid down at once.

'Pieter de Roose, fearing that the money he still had would call the attention of Spelle to him a new, fled from Meulestee, while Michielkin, my poor brother, died of the gangrene in his feet.

'He who never wanted to see me had me called in, nevertheless, to tell me to beware of the fire within my body, which would lead me to that of hell. And I could only weep, for the fire is within me. And he gave up his soul in my arms.

'Ah,' said she, 'he who will avenge the death of my beloved and gentle Michielkin on Spelle shall be my master for ever; I would obey him like a dog.'

As she spoke, the ashes of Claes beat upon the breast of Ulenspiegl. And he resolved to hang Spelle, the murderer.

Boelkin—that was the girl's name—returned to Meulestee, quite safe in her house against the vengeance of Pieter de Roose, for a cattle dealer passing through Destelbergh warned him that the vicar and the burghers had declared that if Spelle laid hands on Michielkin's sister they would have him brought before the duke.

Ulenspiegl, having followed her to Meulestee, entered a low room in Michielkin's house and saw the portrait of a master-pastrycook, which he supposed was that of the poor defunct.

And Boelkin said to him:

'That's the picture of my brother.'

Ulenspiegl took the picture and, going away, said:

'Spelle shall be hanged!'

'How will you do it?' she asked.

'If you knew,' said he, 'you'd have no joy in seeing it done.'

Boelkin shook her head and said with a sad voice:

'You have no confidence in me.'

'Is it not,' said he, 'showing an extreme confidence to tell you: "Spelle shall be hanged!" for with that single phrase you could have me hanged before him.'

328

'You're right,' she said.

'Then go and find me some good clay,' retorted Ulenspiegl, 'a double stein of *bruinbier*, fresh water and several slices of beef. All separate.'

'The beef will be for me, the *bruinbier* for the beef, the water for the clay, and the clay for the portrait.'

Ulenspiegl ate and drank as he kneaded the clay, occasionally swallowing a morsel of it, but not worrying much and looking most attentively at the portrait of Michielkin. When the clay was kneaded he made a mask with a nose, mouth, eyes and ears, so like the picture of the dead man that Boelkin was dumfounded.

After this he set the mask in the oven, and when it was hard he painted it with the colour that corpses are, indicating the haggard eyes, the grave face and the divers contractions of a dying man. The girl then, ceasing to be amazed, watched the mask without being able to take her eyes off it; then, becoming pale and livid and covering up her face, she said, shuddering:

'It's he, my poor Michielkin!'

Ulenspiegl also made two bloody feet.

Having vanquished her first feeling of fright, she said:

'He shall be blessed who slays the murderer.'

Ulenspiegl, taking the mask and the feet, said:

'I need help.'

Boelkin answered:

'Go to *in de Blauwe Gans* (The Blue Goose Inn), to Joos Lansaem of Ypres, who keeps that tavern. He was the best comrade and friend of my brother. Tell him that Boelkin sent you.'

Ulenspiegl did as she requested.

After having worked for Death, Spelle went to drink a hot mixture of *dobble clauwaert* seasoned with cinnamon and Madeira sugar, at *in den Valck* (The Falcon Inn). At that inn they dared not refuse him anything, for fear of the rope.

Pieter de Roose, having summoned up courage, had returned to Meulestee. He followed Spelle and his catchpolls everywhere to be under their protection. Spelle sometimes paid for the drinks. And they gaily sucked in together the money of their victims.

The Falcon Inn was no longer filled as it was in the good old days when the village lived happily, serving God in the Catholic way and not being tormented because of religion. Now the village was as though in mourning, as might be seen from the innumerable houses empty or closed, from the deserted streets where several skinny dogs ran about seeking their rotten sustenance among the heaps of rubbish.

There was no place now in Meulestee except for the two evil ones.

329

The apprehensive inhabitants of the village saw them by day, insolently marking the houses of their future victims and making out the lists of the dead, and in the evening returning from the Falcon singing filthy refrains while the two catchpolls, as drunk as they, followed them, armed to the teeth, to act as escorts.

Ulenspiegl went to *in de Blauwe Gans*, to Joos Lansaem who was at his counter.

He took from his pocket a little flask of brandy and said to him: 'Boelkin has two casks for sale.'

'Come into my kitchen,' said the *baes*.

There, closing the door and looking him straight in the eye:

'You are no brandy-wine merchant; what do these eye-winkings mean? Who are you?'

Ulenspiegl replied:

'I am the son of Claes, burned at Damme; the ashes of the dead man beat upon my breast: I want to slay Spelle, the murderer.'

'Is it Boelkin who sends you?' asked the host.

'Boelkin sends me,' answered Ulenspiegl. 'I shall kill Spelle; you shall help me.'

'I will,' said the *baes*. 'What must be done?'

Ulenspiegl answered:

'Go to the vicar, the good pastor, enemy of Spelle. Bring together your friends and be with them to-morrow after the curfew, on the Everghem road beyond Spelle's house, between the Falcon and the aforesaid house. Place yourselves in the shade and don't have any white clothes on. At the stroke of ten, you'll see Spelle coming out of the tavern and a cart coming from the other direction. Don't tell your friends this evening; they sleep too near their wives' ears. Go and find them to-morrow. Come, listen well to everything, and remember well.'

'We shall remember,' said Joos. And, lifting up his goblet: 'I drink to the rope for Spelle.'

'To the rope,' said Ulenspiegl. Then with the *baes* he re-entered the tap-room of the tavern, where several Ghentish old-clothes merchants were drinking. They had returned from the Saturday market at Bruges, where they had sold the doublets for high prices, short mantles of cloth of gold and silver, bought for a few *sous* from nobles who had been ruined in trying to imitate the luxury of the Spaniards.

And they were indulging in drinking and feasting because of their great profits.

Ulenspiegl and Joos Lansaem, seated in a corner drinking, agreed, without being heard by anyone, that Joos should go to the vicar of the church, a good pastor and angry at Spelle the slayer of innocents. After that he should go to his friends.

The following day, Joos and the friends of Michielkin, being forewarned, left the *Blauwe Gans*, where they were drinking as was their custom, and, so as to conceal their plans, went out as the curfew rang and by different ways came to the Everghem road. There were seventeen of them.

At ten o'clock Spelle came out of the Falcon, followed by his two catchpolls and Pieter de Roose. Lansaem and his friends were hidden in the barn of Samson Boene, a friend of Michielkin. The door of the barn was open. Spelle did not see them.

They heard him pass, swaying drunkenly—as were Pieter de Roose and the two catchpolls—and saying with a voice made husky from much hiccuping:

'Provosts! Provosts! Life is good to them in this world; hold me up, gallows-birds who live off my leavings.'

Suddenly was heard, on the open country side of the road, the bray of an ass and the cracking of a whip.

'There's a stubborn donkey,' said Spelle, 'who refuses to get along in spite of that excellent warning.'

Suddenly they heard a great noise of wheels and a cart leaping down along the road.

'Stop it,' cried Spelle.

As the cart passed in front of them Spelle and his two catchpolls threw themselves at the donkey's head.

'The cart is empty,' said one of the catchpolls.

'Lout,' said Spelle, 'do empty carts run about at night all alone? There's someone hiding in that cart; light the lanterns, hold them up, I'm going to see.'

The lanterns were lit and Spelle climbed up on to the cart, holding his own lamp. But no sooner had he looked than he gave vent to a scream and fell back saying:

'Michielkin! Michielkin! Jesus, have pity on me!'

Then, from the bottom of the cart, there arose a man clothed in white like a pastry-cook, and holding in his hands two bleeding feet.

Pieter de Roose, seeing the man arise, lit up by the lanterns, cried out with the two catchpolls:

'Michielkin! Michielkin, the dead man! Lord have pity on us!'

The seventeen came out at the noise to look at the spectacle and were terrified to see, in the clear light of the moon, how much the image of Michielkin resembled the poor defunct.

And the ghost waved his bloody feet.

It was his same round, full face, but paled by death, threatening, livid, and gnawed away by worms under the chin.

The ghost, still waving his bloody feet, said to Spelle, who lay on his back groaning:

'Spelle, Provost Spelle, wake up!'

But Spelle did not budge.

'Spelle,' said the ghost again, 'Provost Spelle, wake up or I will make you go down with me into the gaping mouth of hell.'

Spelle rose up, his hair standing on end, crying dolorously:

'Michielkin! Michielkin, have mercy!'

Meanwhile the burghers had approached; but Spelle saw nothing save the lanterns, which he took for the eyes of devils. He confessed this later.

'Spelle,' said the ghost of Michielkin, 'are you ready to die?'

'No,' replied the provost, 'no Messire Michielkin, I am not at all ready, and I don't want to appear before God with my soul all black with sin.'

'You recognize me?' said the ghost.

'God help me,' said Spelle, 'yes, I recognize you; you are the ghost of Michielkin, the pastry-cook, who died in his bed, innocent, following his torture; and the two bloody feet are those to which I had fifty-pound weights attached. Ah, Michielkin, forgive me, that Pieter de Roose was so tempting; he offered me fifty florins, which I took, to put your name on the register.'

'Do you want to confess yourself?' said the ghost.

'Yes, Messire, I want to confess, tell everything, and do penance. But deign to disperse these demons who are ready to devour me. I will tell all. Take away these fiery eyes! I did the same at Tournai to five burghers; the same at Bruges to four. I don't know their names any more, but I will tell them if you insist; elsewhere also, I have sinned, Lord, and through me sixty-nine innocents are in the pit. Michielkin, it was necessary to get money for the king. They told me that; but I needed money also; it's at Ghent in the cellar, under the pavement, at the house of old Grovels, my real mother. I have told all, all, grace and mercy! Take away the devils. Lord God, Virgin Mary, Jesus, intercede for me; remove the fires of hell; I will sell all, I will give all to the poor, and I will do penance.'

Ulenspiegl, seeing that the crowd of burghers was ready to uphold him, leaped from the cart at the throat of Spelle and wanted to strangle him.

But the vicar came.

332

'Let him live,' said he; 'it were better that he should die with the hangman's rope than with the fingers of a ghost.'

'What are you going to do?' asked Ulenspiegl.

'Accuse him before the duke and have him hanged,' answered the vicar. 'But who are you?' he asked.

'I am,' replied Ulenspiegl, 'the mask of Michielkin in the person of a poor Flemish fox who is going back to his soil fearing the Spanish hunters.'

In the meantime Pieter de Roose flew off at full speed.

And, Spelle having been hanged, his wealth was confiscated.

And the King inherited.

33 THE FOLLOWING DAY Ulenspiegl went on to Courtrai, skirting the Lys, the clear river. Lamme walked along piteously. Ulenspiegl said to him: 'You moan, craven-heart, regretting the wife that made you wear the horned crown of cuckoldry.'

'My boy,' said Lamme, 'she was always faithful to me, loving me enough even as I loved her too much, my gentle Jesus. One day, having gone to Bruges, she came back changed. From that time on, when I begged her for love, she said to me:

' "I must live with you as a friend, not otherwise."

'Sad at heart then, I said:

' "Beloved darling, we were married before God. Have I not done everything for you that you wished? Did I not dress myself many times in a doublet of black cloth and a cloak of fustian so that I might see you, in spite of the royal decrees, dressed in silks and brocade? Won't you love me any more, darling?"

' "I love you," she said, "according to God and His laws, according to holy discipline and penance. Nevertheless I shall be a virtuous companion to you."

' "I'm not worrying about your virtue," I answered, "it's you I want, you, my wife."

' "I know you are kind," said she; "until to-day you were cook in the house to spare me the labour of making the fricassees; you ironed our sheets, ruffs and shirts, the irons being too heavy for me; you washed our linen, swept the house and the street in front of the house, in order to save me all fatigue. I wish to work now in your stead, but nothing more, my man."

' "That's all the same to me," I answered; "I shall be as in the past, your tiring-maid, your laundress, your cook, your washerwife, your own slave, submissive; but, wife, don't separate these two hearts and bodies

334

that were as one; don't break that gentle love-tie that bound us so tenderly."

' "It must be," she replied.

' "La," said I, "was it at Bruges that you took this unfeeling resolution?"

'She answered:

' "I swore before God and His saints."

' "Who then," I cried, "forced you to take an oath not to fulfil your wifely duties?"

' "He that has the spirit of God and placed me in the ranks of his penitents," she said.

'From that moment on she ceased being mine as much as though she were the faithful wife of another. I beseeched her, tormented her, threatened her, wept, prayed. But vainly. One evening, returning from Blankenberghe, where I had gone to receive the rent of one of my farms, I found the house empty. Weary, no doubt, of my prayers, angry and sad at my grief, my wife had flown. Where is she now?'

And Lamme sat down on the banks of the Lys, hanging his head and staring at the water.

'Ah!' said he, 'my dear, how plump you were, tender and sweet. Shall I ever find another lass like you? Daily dish of love, shall I eat you no more? Where are your kisses, fragrant as thyme; your sweet mouth where I gathered pleasure as the bee does the honey in the rose; your white arms that enlaced me caressingly? Where is your beating heart, your rounded breasts, and the pretty quiver of your fairy body all panting with love? But where are all your old waves, clear river that rolls your new ones along so gaily under the sun?'

34 PASSING BEFORE the woods of Peteghem, Lamme said to Ulenspiegl: 'I'm broiling; let's seek the shade.' 'Let's seek it,' answered Ulenspiegl. They sat down on the grass in the wood, and saw passing before them a herd of stags.

'Look well, Lamme,' said Ulenspiegl, arming his German musket. 'There are the great old stags that still have their dowcets and wear proudly their nine-point antlers; sweet brockets that are their squires, trotting alongside them ready to aid them with their pointed horns. They are going to their lair. Turn your musket lock as I do. Shoot! The old stag is wounded. A brocket is hit in the haunch; it flees. Let's follow it until it falls. Do as I do; run, jump, fly.'

'There's my mad friend,' said Lamme, 'trying to follow stags on the run. Don't fly without wings, 'tis labour lost. You'll never catch up with them. Ah, the cruel companion! Think you I'm as nimble as you are? I'm sweating, my boy; I'm sweating and I'm going to fall. If the forester catches you, you'll be hung. The stags are royal game; let them run, my boy, you'll never o'ertake them.'

'Come,' said Ulenspiegl. 'Do you hear the noise of his antlers in the foliage? Like the rush of a water-spout. Do you see the young branches broken and the leaves littering the ground? He has another bullet in the haunch, this time; we'll eat him.'

'He's not yet cooked,' said Lamme. 'Let these poor animals run along. Oh, how warm it is! Without any doubt I'm going to fall down here, never to get up again.'

Suddenly, from every side, the forest was filled with ragged and armed men. Dogs barked and dashed off in pursuit of the stags. Four fierce-looking men surrounded Lamme and Ulenspiegl and led them into a clearing in the middle of a thicket, where they saw, among the women and the children camped there, a great number of men armed variously with swords, cross-bows, muskets, lances, pikes and *reiter's* pistols. Ulenspiegl, seeing them, said:

'Are you the Leafers or the Brothers of the Woods, that you seem to live in common here to flee from persecution?'

'We are the Brothers of the Woods,' replied an old man, who sat beside the fire cooking some birds in a pan. 'But who are you?'

'I am from the fair land of Flanders,' answered Ulenspiegl; 'a painter, peasant, nobleman, sculptor, all in one. And I go thus about the world praising all good and lovely things and loudly mocking stupidity.'

'If you have seen so many countries,' said the old man, 'you know how to pronounce: *Schild ende Vriendt* (Shield and Friend) the way the Ghentish folk do; if you don't you are a false Fleming and shall die.'

Ulenspiegl pronounced: *Schild ende Vriendt*.

'And you, great pot-belly,' said the old man, speaking to Lamme, 'what is your trade?'

Lamme answered:

'To eat and drink my lands, farms, fees and revenues; to seek out my wife; and to follow everywhere my friend Ulenspiegl.'

'If you journey about so much,' said the old man, 'you cannot be ignorant of what they call the folk of Weert in Limburg.'

'I don't know,' answered Lamme; 'but won't you tell me the name of the scandalous rogue who drove my wife from the house? Tell it me and I'll go and kill him right away.'

The old man answered:

336

'In this world there are two things which never return once they have flown: spent money and a weary woman who has run away.'

Then, speaking to Ulenspiegl:

'Do you know what they call the folk of Weert in Limburg?'

'*De raekstekers* (exorcisers of rays),' answered Ulenspiegl. 'For one day, a live ray having fallen from the fishmonger's cart, the old women, seeing it jump about, took it for the devil. "Let's go and bring the vicar to exorcise the ray," they said. The vicar exorcised it and, having carried it away, made a good dish of it in honour of the Weert folk. So may God do with the king of the blood.'

In the meantime the barking of the dogs resounded through the forest. Armed men, running among the trees, shouted to frighten the beast.

'It's the stag and the brocket I set off,' said Ulenspiegl.

'We shall eat them,' said the old man. 'But what do they call the folk of Eindhoven in Limburg?'

'*De Pinnemakers* (bolt-makers),' answered Ulenspiegl. 'One day the enemy was at the city-gate; they bolted it with a carrot. Geese came and with great pecks of their greedy beaks they ate the carrot, and the enemy marched into Eindhoven. But it will be iron beaks that will eat the bolts of the prisons wherein they wish to shut up Free Conscience.'

'If God be with us, who shall be against us?' answered the old man.

Ulenspiegl said:

'Barking of dogs, shouting of men, and branches broken; it's a storm in the forest.'

'Is it good meat, stag flesh?' asked Lamme, watching the cooking.

'The cries of the trackers come nearer,' said Ulenspiegl to Lamme. 'The dogs are quite close. What a thundering noise! The stag! The stag! Beware, my boy. Fie, the ugly beast; he has knocked my bulky friend to the ground in the midst of frying-pans, sauce-pans, pots, stew-pots and fricassees. The women and girls are fleeing, terrified. Are you bleeding, my boy?'

'You're laughing, rascal,' said Lamme. 'Yes, I'm bleeding; he dug his antlers in my behind. There, see my breeches torn and my flesh also; and all these lovely fricassees cast to the ground. Here, I'm losing all my blood down my hose.'

'That stag is a provident surgeon; he's saved you from apoplexy,' replied Ulenspiegl.

'Fie, the heartless rascal!' said Lamme. 'But I'll follow you no more. I shall stay here with these goodmen and goodwives. How can you, without shame, be so hard on my troubles, when I walk at your heels

337

like a dog, in snow, frost, rain, hail, wind, and in warm weather when I sweat out my soul through my skin?'

'Your wound is nothing. Slap on an *olie-koekje,* that will be a fried plaster to it,' answered Ulenspiegl. 'But do you know what they call the Louvain folk? You don't know, my poor friend? Well, I'm going to tell you to keep you from moaning. They call them *koeye-schieters* (cow-shooters), for they were silly enough one day to fire on some cows which they took to be enemy troops. As for us, we shoot the Spanish he-goats; the flesh is stinking but the skin is good to stretch on drums. And the Tirlemont folk? Do you know? Not even that? They bear the glorious nick-name of *kirekers.* For with them, in the high church on Pentecost Day, a duck flies from the rood-screen on the altar, and that's the image of their Holy Ghost. Put a *koekebak* on your wound. You are silently picking up the pots and the fricassees knocked over by the stag. That's kitchen courage. You're re-lighting the fire, setting up the soup cauldron on the tripod; you're occupying yourself with the cooking, most attentively. Do you know why there are four wonders at Louvain? No? I am going to tell you. Firstly, because the living pass under the dead; for the church of Saint Michael is built near the town gate. Its grave-yard is therefore above it. Secondly, because the bells are outside the steeples, as can be seen in the church of Saint James, where there is a great bell and a little bell; being unable to place the little one inside the steeple, they placed it outside. Thirdly, because of the altar outside the church; for the façade of Saint James resembles an altar. Fourthly, because of the nailless tower; for the tower of the church of Saint Gertrude is constructed of stone instead of wood, and one cannot nail stone, except the heart of the king of the blood which I would like to nail above the great gate of Brussels. But you're not listening to me. Is there no salt in the sauces? Do you know why the folk of Termond are nick-named warming-pans (*de vierpannen*)? Because a young prince was going to come and sleep during winter at the Inn of the Arms of Flanders; the inn-keeper didn't know how to warm the sheets, for he had no warming-pan. He had the bed warmed by his young daughter who, hearing the young prince coming into the room, ran off; and the prince wanted to know why they had not left the warming-pan in the bed. May God make Philip, shut up in a box of red-hot iron, serve as a warming-pan in the bed of Madame Astarte.'

'Leave me in peace,' said Lamme; 'a lot I care for you, your *vierpannen,* your nailless tower, and all the rest of your fiddle-faddles. Leave me to my sauces.'

'Beware,' said Ulenspiegl to him. 'The barkings have not ceased to

338

re-echo; they have become much louder; the dogs howl, the trumpet sounds. Beware of the stag. You flee. The trumpet sounds.'

'It's the quarry,' said the old man; 'come back, Lamme, to your fricassees, the stag is dead.'

'It will be a good meal for us,' said Lamme. 'You will invite me to the feast because of the trouble I've taken for you. The birdsauce will be good; it crunches a little, though. That's the sand on which they fell when that great devil of a stag tore my doublet and flesh together. But don't you fear the foresters?'

'There are too many of us,' said the old man; 'they are afraid and so don't trouble us. It's the same with the catchpolls and the judges. The townsfolk like us because we do them no harm. We'll live yet awhile in peace unless the Spanish Army surrounds us. If that happens, old men and young, women, maidens, girls and boys, we'll sell our lives dearly and kill each other rather than suffer a thousand martyrdoms at the hands of the duke of the blood.'

Ulenspiegl said:

'The time is no longer when we must fight the butcher by land. It is on the sea that we must ruin his power. Go to the coast of the Isles of Zeeland, by Bruges, Heyst and Knocke.'

'We have no money,' they said.

Ulenspiegl replied:

'Here are a thousand carolus from the prince. Follow the water-ways, canals, streams or rivers; when you see boats bearing the sign I. H. S. one of you whistle like a lark. The crowing of the cock shall answer you. And you will be in friendly territory.'

'We shall do so,' said they.

Soon the hunters appeared followed by the dogs, dragging the dead stag with ropes.

All then sat in a circle about the fire. There were at least sixty of them —men, women, and children. Bread was brought out from the pouches, knives from their sheaths; the stag was cut up, skinned, cleaned out, spitted and roasted with some small game. And at the end of the meal, Lamme was seen snoring, with his head drooping on his breast, as he slept with his back to a tree.

At nightfall the Brothers of the Woods went to sleep in their huts dug out of the earth, and this Lamme and Ulenspiegl also did.

Armed men kept watch over the camp. And Ulenspiegl heard the dry leaves crackle under their feet.

The next day he went off with Lamme, as the camp folk said to him:

'Blessings on you; we shall go towards the sea.'

339

35 AT HARLEBEKE, Lamme renewed his stock of *olie-koekjes*, ate twenty-seven of them and put thirty in his basket. Ulenspiegl carried his cages in his hand. Towards evening they came to Courtrai and stopped at the *in de Bie* (The Bee Inn) kept by Gillis Van den Ende, who came to his door as soon as he heard the singing of the lark.

There everything was sugar and honey for them. The host, having seen the letters of the prince, handed Ulenspiegl fifty carolus for the prince and refused to accept payment for the turkey he served them, nor for the *dobble clauwaert* with which it was washed down. He also warned them that there were many spies of the Court of Blood in Courtrai and that was why he should hold his tongue and make his companion hold his.

'We shall be very careful,' said Ulenspiegl and Lamme.

And they left the inn.

The setting sun gilded the gables of the houses; the birds sang in the lime-trees; the goodwives gossiped by the sills of their doors, while the children rolled in the dust; and Ulenspiegl and Lamme wandered at hazard through the streets.

Suddenly Lamme said:

'Martin Van den Ende, questioned by me as to whether he had seen a woman like mine—I drew her darling portrait for him—told me that there was, at La Steve-nyne's Rainbow on the Bruges Road outside the town, a great number of women who met there every night. I am going there right now.'

'I shall see you anon,' said Ulen-spiegl. 'I want to see the town; if I meet your wife, I'll send her to you by and by. You know that the *baes* warned you to keep silent if you value your skin.'

'I shall keep silent,' said Lamme.

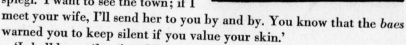

As Ulenspiegl wandered about at ease, the sun set; the night began to fall swiftly and he came to the *Pierpot-Straetje* (Stone Pot Lane).

There he heard a viola being played melodiously; coming nearer, he saw from afar a white form beckoning him, fleeing away, and play-

340

ing the viola. And she sang like a seraphim a sweet, slow song, stopped, turned round, beckoned him, then fled again.

But Ulenspiegl ran fast; he came up to her and was about to speak to her when she placed on his mouth a hand scented with benjamin.

'Are you a peasant or a nobleman?' she asked.

'I am Ulenspiegl.'

'Are you rich?'

'Enough to pay for a great pleasure, not enough to ransom my soul.'

'Have you no horse that you go on foot?'

'I had an ass,' said Ulenspiegl, 'but I left him in the stable.'

'Why are you alone and friendless in a strange town?'

'Because my friend wanders in his way, as I am doing in mine, curious sweet.'

'I am not curious,' she said. 'Is he rich, your friend?'

'In fat,' said Ulenspiegl. 'Will you be finished soon questioning me?'

'I have finished,' she said, 'leave me now.'

'Leave you?' said he. 'As well tell Lamme when he's hungry to leave a plate of ortolans. I want to eat you.'

'You have not seen me,' she said. And she opened a lantern that suddenly shone, lighting up her face.

'You are lovely,' said Ulenspiegl. 'Ho, the golden skin, the soft eyes, the red mouth, the sweet body! All shall be for me.'

'All,' said she.

And she led him to Stevenyne's on the Bruges Road, to the Rainbow (*in den Reghenboogh*). Ulenspiegl saw there a great number of girls wearing on their arms bands of a different colour from that of their fustian dresses.

His had an armlet of silver-cloth on a dress of cloth of gold. And all the wenches looked at her jealously. As she entered, she made a sign to the *baesinne*, but Ulenspiegl did not see this. They sat down together and drank.

'Do you know,' she said, 'that whoever has loved me is mine for ever?'

'Lovely fragrant wench,' said Ulenspiegl, 'what a delicious feast that will be for me, to have your flesh to eat always.'

Suddenly he saw Lamme in a corner, having before him a little table, with a candle, a ham, a pot of beer, and not knowing how to keep his ham and his beer from the two wenches who wanted at all costs to eat and drink with him.

When Lamme saw Ulenspiegl, he stood up and jumped three feet in the air, crying:

'Blessed be God who sends back my friend Ulenspiegl to me! Drinks, *baesinne*!'

Ulenspiegl, pulling out his purse, said:

'Drink until this is empty.'

And he jingled his carolus.

'Living God!' said Lamme, craftily taking the purse from his hands, 'it's I who pays and not you; that purse is mine.'

Ulenspiegl tried to take back the purse by force, but Lamme held on to it. As they fought with each other, the one to keep it, the other to re-take it, Lamme said in a whisper to Ulenspiegl, speaking in jerks.

'Listen: Catchpolls here. . . four. . . little room with three wenches. Two outside for you, for me. . . Wanted to get out. . . wouldn't let me. . . The wench in brocade's a spy. . . A spy, Stevenyne!'

As they fought together Ulenspiegl listened attentively, crying:

'Give me back my purse, rogue!'

'You shan't have it,' said Lamme.

And they caught each other by the neck, by the shoulders, while Lamme gave his good warning to Ulenspiegl.

Suddenly the *baes* of The Bee Inn entered, followed by seven men whom he did not seem to know. He crowed like a cock and Ulenspiegl whistled like a lark. Seeing Ulenspiegl and Lamme fighting each other, the *baes* spoke:

'Who are these two?' he asked La Stevenyne.

La Stevenyne replied:

'Two rogues that it would be better to separate rather than let them raise such a rumpus here before going to the stake.'

'If he dares to separate us,' said Ulenspiegl, 'we'll make him eat the paving stones.'

'Yes, we'll make him eat the paving stones,' said Lamme.

'The *baes* to save us,' said Ulenspiegl in Lamme's ear.

At this the *baes*, scenting some mystery, rushed headlong into the battle. Lamme poured these words in his ear:

'You save us? How?'

The *baes* made out he was shaking Ulenspiegl by the ear and whispered to him:

'Seven for you. . . strong men, butchers. . . I'm going. . . too well known in town. . . When I'm gone, 't is van te beven de klinkaert. . . Break everything. . .'

'Yes,' said Ulenspiegl, getting up and landing him a kick.

The *baes* struck Ulenspiegl in turn. And Ulenspiegl said:

'You strike hard, my hearty.'

'Like hail,' said the *baes*, as he quickly seized Lamme's purse and handed it to Ulenspiegl.

342

'Pay a drink for me, rogue,' said he, 'now that you have had your wealth returned to you.'

'You shall drink, scandalous rascal,' answered Ulenspiegl.

'See how insolent he is,' said La Stevenyne.

'As much as you are lovely darling,' answered Ulenspiegl.

Now La Stevenyne was over sixty years old and her face was like a medlar, but all yellow with bilious choler. In the midst of it was a nose like to an owl's beak. Her eyes were the eyes of a loveless miser. Two long tusks jutted out of her thin mouth. And she had a great purple birth-mark on her left cheek. The wenches laughed, jeering her and saying:

'Darling, darling, give him something to drink.— He'll kiss you.— Is it long since you had your first nuptials?— Take care, Ulenspiegl, she wants to eat you.— Look at her eyes, they are shining not with hate but with love.— One would say that she wanted to bite you until you died.— Don't be afraid.— That's the way all women in love are.— She only wishes for your good.— See what a good laughing humour she's in.'

And indeed La Stevenyne laughed and winked at Gilline, the wench in the brocade dress. The *baes* drank, paid, and went out. The seven butchers made knowing faces to the catchpolls and at La Stevenyne.

One of them indicated by a gesture that he held Ulenspiegl for a simpleton whom he would be able to do in very easily. He spoke in his ear, mockingly sticking out his tongue at La Stevenyne, who laughed and showed her tusks.

'*'T is van te beven de klinkaert!* ('Tis time to make the glasses clink!)'

Then louder, and pointing to the catchpolls:

'Nice Reformist, we are all on your side; treat us to food and drink.'

And La Stevenyne laughed with pleasure and also stuck out her tongue at Ulenspiegl, when his back was turned. And Gilline, of the brocade dress, did likewise.

And the other girls whispered, saying: 'There's the spy who, by her beauty, has brought to cruel torture, and to death more cruel, more than twenty-seven Reformists. Gilline is transported with pleasure dreaming of the recompense for her informing—the first hundred florins of the victim's estate. But she does not laugh in thinking that she must share the sum with La Stevenyne.'

And all of them were sticking out their tongues mockingly at Ulenspiegl. And Lamme, sweating great drops of perspiration, was red as a cock's comb with anger, but he did not want to speak.

'Treat us to food and drink,' said the butchers and the catchpolls.

343

'Very well,' said Ulenspiegl, making his carolus jingle anew, 'hand us out the wherewithal to eat and drink, oh, darling Stevenyne, drink in glasses that ring.'

At this the wenches began to laugh again and La Stevenyne to stick out her tusks.

Just the same she went to the kitchen and to the cellar and brought back ham, sausages, black-pudding omelettes, and ringing glasses which were so called because they were mounted on a stem and rang like a chime when knocked.

Ulenspiegl then said:

'Let him that is hungry eat and him that is thirsty drink!'

The catchpolls, the wenches, the butchers, Gilline, and La Stevenyne applauded this speech with their hands and feet. Then they all sat down as best they could; Ulenspiegl, Lamme and the seven butchers at the high table of honour; the catchpolls and the wenches at the two little tables. And they ate and drank with a great noise of jawing, even the two catchpolls who had been stationed outside and who were brought in by their comrades to take part in the feast. And these two were seen to bring out from their pouches the ropes and the chains.

La Stevenyne, sticking out her tongue and sniggering, said:

'No one shall leave here until he has paid me.'

And she went and locked all the doors, putting the keys in her pockets.

Gilline, lifting her glass, said:

'The bird is caged, let's drink.'

At this, two of the girls, named Gena and Margot, said to her:

'Is that still another one you are going to have put to death, wicked woman?'

'I know not,' said Gilline. 'Let us drink.'

But the three other wenches would not drink with her.

And Gilline took up the viola and sang in French:

344

Au son de la viole,
Je chante nuit et jour;
Je suis la fille-folle,
La vendeuse d'amour.

Astarte de mes hanches
Fit les lignes de feu;
J'ai les épaules blanches,
Et mon beau corps est Dieu.

Qu'on vide l'escarelle
Aux carolus brillants:
Que l'or fauve ruisselle
A flots sous mes pieds blancs.

Je suis la fille d'Eve
Et de Satan vainqueur:
Si beau que soit ton rêve,
Cherche-le dans mon cœur.

Je suis froide ou brûlante,
Tendre au doux nonchaloir;
Tiède, éperdue, ardente,
Mon homme, à ton vouloir.

Vois, je vends tout: mes charmes,
Mon âme et mes yeux bleus;
Bonheur, rires et larmes,
Et la Mort si tu veux.

Au son de la viole,
Je chante nuit et jour;
Je suis la fille-folle,
La vendeuse d'amour.

And, singing her song, Gilline was so lovely, so suave and sweet, that all the men, catchpolls, butchers, Lamme and Ulenspiegl, sat there silent, touched, smiling, captivated by her charm.

Suddenly, bursting out laughing, Gilline said, as she looked at Ulenspiegl:

'And that's the way birds are caged.'

And the spell was broken.

Ulenspiegl, Lamme and the butchers looked at each other.

'How now, are you going to pay me?' said La Stevenyne. 'Are you going to pay me, Messire Ulenspiegl, you who got such good fat from the flesh of the preachers?'

Lamme wanted to speak, but Ulenspiegl silenced him and, speaking to La Stevenyne, he said:

'We shall not pay in advance.'

'I shall pay myself then, afterwards, out of your inheritance,' said La Stevenyne.

'Ghouls live off corpses,' replied Ulenspiegl.

'Yes,' said one of the catchpolls, 'these two there took the money from the preachers; more than three hundred florins. That's a fine mite for Gilline.'

The latter sang:

> *Cherche ailleurs de tels charmes,*
> *Prends tout, mon amoureux,*
> *Plaisirs, baisers et larmes,*
> *Et la Mort si tu veux.*

Then, laughing maliciously, she said:

'Let us drink!'

'Let us drink!' said the catchpolls.

'Living God!' said La Stevenyne, 'let us drink! The doors are locked, the windows are strongly barred, the birds are caged; let us drink!'

'Let us drink!' said Ulenspiegl.

'Let us drink!' said Lamme.

'Let us drink!' said the seven.

'Let us drink!' said the catchpolls.

'Let us drink!' said Gilline, making her viola sing. 'I am lovely, let us drink! I could catch the archangel Gabriel in the nets of my song.'

'Let's have drinks, then,' said Ulenspiegl. 'Wine to crown the feast—and the best wine. I want a drop of liquid fire to be on every hair of our thirsty bodies.'

'Let us drink!' said Gilline. 'Twenty more gudgeons like you, and the pikes will cease to sing.'

La Stevenyne brought on wine. All were seated, guzzling and stuffing themselves, the catchpolls and the wenches together. The seven, seated at the table of Ulenspiegl and Lamme, threw from their table to that of the wenches hams, sausages, omelettes and bottles, which the girls caught in the air like carps snapping at flies above a pond. And La Stevenyne laughed, showing her tusks and pointing to packets of can-

346

dles, five to the pound, which were hanging up above the counter. These were the wenches' candles. Then she said to Ulenspiegl.

'When one goes to the stake one carries a tallow candle. Do you want one right away?'

'Let us drink!' said Ulenspiegl.

'Let us drink!' said the seven.

Gilline said:

'Ulenspiegl has shining eyes like a swan about to die.'

'Supposing they were given to the pigs to eat,' said La Stevenyne.

'That would be a feast of lanterns for them: let us drink!' said Ulenspiegl.

'Would you like,' said La Stevenyne, 'when you are on the scaffold, to have your tongue pierced with a red-hot iron?'

'It would be all the better for whistling: let us drink!' answered Ulenspiegl.

'You would have less to say if you were hanged,' said La Stevenyne, 'and your darling came to contemplate you.'

'Yes,' said Ulenspiegl, 'but I should weight myself down more and fall on your gracious snout: let us drink!'

'What would you say if you were flogged, and branded on the brow and the shoulder?'

'I should say that they had taken the wrong flesh,' said Ulenspiegl, 'and that instead of roasting the sow Stevenyne they had scalded the porker Ulenspiegl: let us drink!'

'Since you don't like any of these things,' said La Stevenyne, 'you shall be taken on the king's ships and there condemned to be drawn and quartered on four galleys.'

'Then,' said Ulenspiegl, 'the sharks shall have my four members, and you'll eat that which they don't want: let us drink!'

'Why don't you eat one of these candles,' said she; 'it will serve in Hell to light up your eternal damnation?'

'I see clearly enough to contemplate your luminous snout, oh badly-scalded sow: let us drink!' said Ulenspiegl.

Suddenly he struck the stem of his wine-glass on the table, and imitated with his hands the noise made by an upholsterer who beats rhythmically the wool of a mattress on a wooden frame, but this quietly, saying:

''T is (tijd) van te beven de klinkaert! ('Tis time to make the glasses clink!)'

In Flanders this is a signal for the drinkers' anger and the sacking of the houses with the red lantern.

Ulenspiegl drank, then made his glass tremble on the table, as he said:

347

' 'T is van te beven de klinkaert!'
And the seven imitated him.

Everybody kept still; Gilline became pale, La Stevenyne seemed astonished.

The catchpolls said:

'Are the seven with them?'

But the butchers reassured them with winks, while they continued saying, louder and louder with Ulenspiegl:

' 'T is van te beven de klinkaert! 'T is van te beven de klinkaert!'

La Stevenyne drank to give herself courage.

Ulenspiegl then struck the table with his fist in the rhythm of the upholsterers beating mattresses; the seven did as he did; glasses, jugs, dishes, steins, goblets, slowly entered into the dance, topping over, breaking, rising from one side to topple over on the other; and always resounded more menacing, grave, war-like, and monotonous: *' 'T is van te beven de klinkaert!'*

'Alas!' said La Stevenyne, 'they are going to break everything here.'

And, in fright, her two tusks stuck farther out of her mouth.

And blood, fury and anger were set aflame in the hearts of the seven and Lamme and Ulenspiegl.

Then, without stopping their monotonous and menacing song, all those at Ulenspiegl's table seized their glasses and broke them rhythmically on the table; then they strode their chairs and pulled out their knives. And they made such a noise with their song that all the windows of the house rattled. Then, like a round dance of maddened devils, they circled about the room and the tables, saying ceaselessly: *' 'T is van te beven de klinkaert!'*

The catchpolls got up then, trembling with fright, taking their chains and ropes. But the butchers, Ulenspiegl and Lamme, replacing their knives in their sheaths, seized their chairs, which they brandished like cudgels and ran alertly about the room striking to the right and the left, sparing only the wenches, breaking all the rest, furniture, windows, chests, dishes, steins, plates, glasses and flasks, striking at the catchpolls without mercy, and singing always to the rhythm of the upholsterer beating the mattress: *' 'T is van te beven de klinkaert! 'T is van te beven de klinkaert!'* while Ulenspiegl, having landed a blow of his fist on La Stevenyne's snout, took her keys from her pouch and was forcing her to eat her candles.

The lovely Gilline, scratching at doors, shutters, glass-panes and windows with her finger-nails, seemed to want to go through everything like a frightened cat. Then, all livid, she crouched in a corner, her eyes

348

haggard, her teeth showing, and holding her viola close to her as though she must protect it.

The seven and Lamme said to the wenches: 'We won't do you any harm,' and then with their help and the chains and ropes binding up the catchpolls, who were trembling in their boots and not daring to resist. They felt that the butchers, chosen among the strongest by the *baes* of The Bee Inn, would have cut them to bits with their knives. With each candle that he made La Stevenyne eat, Ulenspiegl said:

'This one's for the hanging; that one for the flogging; this other for the branding; this fourth for my pierced tongue; these two excellent, and most greasy, for the king's ships and the drawing and quartering by the galleys; this one for your lair of spies; that one for your wench with the brocade dress; and all the others for my pleasure.'

And the wenches laughed to see La Stevenyne sneezing with anger and wanting to spit out her candles. But in vain, for her mouth was too full.

Ulenspiegl, Lamme and the seven never ceased singing in rhythm: '*'T is van te beven de klinkaert!*'

Then Ulenspiegl stopped and made a sign to the others to murmur the refrain softly. This they did while he spoke these words to the catchpolls and the wenches:

'If any one of you calls for help, he'll be done for immediately.'

'Done for!' said the butchers.

'We'll be silent,' said the wenches, 'don't harm us, Ulenspiegl.'

But Gilline, crouching in her corner, her eyes starting out of her head, knew not what to say and hugged her viola close to her.

And the seven still murmured: '*'T is van te beven de klinkaert!*'

La Stevenyne, pointing to the candles she still had in her mouth, made a sign that she also would be silent. The catchpolls made the same promise as she did.

Ulenspiegl continued what he was saying:

'You are here in our power. The night has fallen black. We are here close to the Lys, where one drowns easily when one is pushed from behind. The gates of Courtrai are closed. If the night-watchmen have heard the rumpus they have not budged, being too lazy or thinking that it was made by good Flemings who, drinking, sang joyfully to the sound of steins and flasks. Therefore keep quiet before your masters.'

Then, speaking to the seven:

'Are you going to Peteghem to find the Beggars?'

'We prepared for this at the news of your coming.'

'From there are you going towards the sea?'

'Yes,' they said.

349

'Do you know one or two among these catchpolls who might be released to help us?'

'Two,' they said, 'Niklaes and Joos, who never pursued the poor Reformists.'

'We are faithful!' said Niklaes and Joos.

Ulenspiegl then said:

'Here's twenty florins for you, twice what you would have had if you had received the infamous price of informing.'

Suddenly the five others cried:

'Twenty florins! We'll serve the prince for twenty florins. The king pays badly. Give the half of that to each one of us and we'll say to the judge anything you want us to.'

The butchers and Lamme murmured indistinctly:

'*'T is van te beven de klinkaert! 'T is van te beven de klinkaert!*'

'So that you won't say too much,' said Ulenspiegl, 'the seven will lead you bound to Peteghem, to the Beggars. You will have ten florins when you are on the sea, for we shall be certain that until then the camp kitchen will have kept you faithful to bread and soup. If you are valiant men, you shall have your share of the plunder. If you try to desert, you shall be hung. If you escape, avoiding the rope that way, you shall find the knife.'

'We shall serve whoever pays us,' they said.

'*'T is van te beven de klinkaert! 'T is van te beven de klinkaert!*' said Lamme and the seven, knocking on the tables with the shards of broken pots and glasses.

'You shall also take with you,' said Ulenspiegl, 'Gilline, Stevenyne and the three wenches. If one of them tries to escape, sew her in a sack and cast her into the river.'

'He hasn't slain me,' said Gilline, leaping out from her corner, brandishing her viola in the air. And she sang:

> *Sanglant était mon rêve,*
> *La rêve de mon cœur :*
> *Je suis la fille d'Eve*
> *Et de Satan vainqueur.*

La Stevenyne and the others made faces as though they were going to cry.

'Fear not, my sweets,' said Ulenspiegl, 'you are so suave and gentle that you shall be loved, feasted and caressed everywhere. And from whatever war-spoils are captured, you shall have your share.'

'They'll give nothing to me, for I am old,' wept La Stevenyne.

'A cent a day, crocodile,' said Ulenspiegl, 'for you shall be the servant

350

of these four lovely wenches; you shall wash their petticoats, sheets and chemises.'

'Me, Lord God!' she said. Ulenspiegl replied:

'For a long time you have governed them, living off the profits of their bodies, leaving them poor and famished. You can moan and bray, it shall be as I have said.'

At this the four wenches laughed and jeered at La Stevenyne and stuck out their tongues at her, saying:

'Each one has her turn in this world. Who would have said it of Stevenyne, the miser? She shall work for us as a servant. Blessed be Lord Ulenspiegl!'

Ulenspiegl then said to the butchers and to Lamme:

'Empty the cellars of the wine, take the money; it will serve for the upkeep of La Stevenyne and the four wenches.'

'She's gnashing her teeth, Stevenyne, the miser,' said the wenches. 'You were harsh and now they are the same to you. Blessed be Lord Ulenspiegl!'

Then the three of them turned on Gilline:

'You were her daughter, her breadwinner, you shared with her the fruits of the infamous spying. Will you ever again dare to strike and insult us, you with your brocade dress? You scorned us because we wore only fustian. You are only so richly dressed through the blood of your victims. Let us take off her dress so that she may be like us.'

'I won't have it,' said Ulenspiegl.

And Gilline threw her arms about his neck, saying:

'May you be blessed, you who did not kill me and do not wish to see me look ugly!'

And the jealous wenches looked at Ulenspiegl and said:

'He's mad about her, like all of them.'

And Gilline sang to the accompaniment of her viola.

351

The seven departed towards Peteghem, leading the catchpolls and the wenches along the Lys. Walking along, they murmured:

''T is van te beven de klinkaert! 'T is van te beven de klinkaert!'

At sunrise they came to the camp, whistled like the lark, and were answered by the trumpeting of the cock. The wenches and the catchpolls were closely guarded. Nevertheless, the third day, at noon, Gilline was found dead, her heart pierced with a great needle. La Stevenyne was accused by the three wenches and taken before the captain of the troop, his *dizeniers* and sergeants, who sat as a court. There, without being put to torture, she confessed that she had killed Gilline through jealousy of her beauty and through rage at being mercilessly treated as a servant by the wench. And La Stevenyne was hanged and then buried in the wood.

Gilline was also buried, and they said the prayers for the dead over her sweet body.

In the meantime the two catchpolls, instructed by Ulenspiegl, had gone before the chatelain of Courtrai, for the noise, uproar and pillage, which took place in Stevenyne's house, had to be punished by the aforesaid chatelain, seeing that the house was within the castellany and outside the jurisdiction of the town of Courtrai. After having told the lord chatelain what had happened, they said to him, with great conviction and humble sincerity of speech:

'The slayers of the preachers were not at all Ulenspiegl and his trusty and well-beloved Lamme Goedzak, who had only gone to the Rainbow for their relaxation. They even had passes from the duke, which we saw. The real culprits are two Ghentish merchants, one thin, the other very fat, who went off towards the land of France—after having smashed up everything at Stevenyne's—carrying her and her four wenches off with them for their diversion. We would have tripped them up but there were seven of the strongest butchers in the town who stuck up for them. They tied us all up and only let us free when they were far into French soil. Here's the marks left by the ropes. The other four catchpolls are at their heels waiting for reinforcements in order to lay hands on them.'

The chatelain gave each of them two carolus and a new uniform for their loyal services.

He then wrote to the Flemish Council, to the sheriffs' court at Courtrai, and to the other courts of justice, to tell them that the real murderers had been discovered.

And he detailed the adventure to them at great length.

At which those of the Flemish Council and the other courts of justice shuddered.

And the chatelain was greatly praised for his perspicacity.

And Ulenspiegl and Lamme walked peacefully on the road from Peteghem to Ghent, along the Lys, wishing to arrive at Bruges where Lamme hoped to find his wife, and at Damme where Ulenspiegl, very pensive, would have wished to be already to see Nele, who lived dolefully with Katheline the distraught.

36 FOR A LONG TIME, in Damme and the surrounding countryside, many abominable crimes had been committed. Girls, young lads, old men, who had been known to go carrying money to Bruges, Ghent or some other town or village of Flanders, were found dead, naked as worms, and bitten in the neck by teeth so long and sharp that all of them had the bones in their neck broken.

The doctors and the surgeon-barbers declared that the teeth were those of a great wolf. 'Robbers,' they said, 'had doubtless come after the wolf and stripped the victims.'

In spite of all the searchings, no one could discover who the robbers were. Soon the wolf was forgotten.

Several notable burghers, who had haughtily set out on the road with no escort, disappeared without anyone's ever knowing what had become of them, save that sometimes a peasant, going in the morning to till the ground, would find a trace of the wolf in his field, while his dog, scratching with his paws in the furrows, would turn up a poor dead body bearing wolf's teeth-marks on the neck or under the ear, and often also on the leg, but always from behind. And always, too, the neck-bone or the bone of the leg was broken.

The terrified peasant would go off at once to give notice to the bailiff, who would come with the criminal clerk, two sheriffs and two surgeons to the place where the body of the slain person lay. Having looked at it diligently and carefully, having sometimes, when the face was not eaten by the worms, recognized its station, even its name and lineage, they would be astonished, nevertheless, that the wolf, which kills through hunger, had not carried off a piece of the dead body.

And the Damme folk were much afraid and did not dare go out at night without an escort.

Now it came to pass that several brave troopers were sent out to search for the wolf, with orders to seek night and day in the dunes and along the sea-shore.

They were then near Heyst, in the great dunes. Night had come. One of them, confident of his strength, wished to leave the others and go searching alone, armed with his musket. The others let him go, certain that, brave and armed as he was, he would kill the wolf if it should dare to show itself.

Their companion being gone, they lit a fire, threw dice, and even drank from their flasks of brandy.

And from time to time they shouted:

'How now, comrade, come on back; the wolf's frightened; come on and drink!'

But he did not answer.

Suddenly, hearing a great cry as though from a dying man, they ran to the place from whence came the cry, shouting:

'Hold on, we're coming to the rescue.'

But it was a long time before they found their comrade, for some of them said the cry came from the valley, while the others said from the highest dune.

Finally, having well scoured the dune and the valley by the light of their lanterns, they found their companion, bitten from behind in the leg and the arm, and with his neck broken like the other victims.

Lying flat on his back, he held his sword in his clenched fist; his musket lay in the sand. Beside him were three cut-off fingers which were not his and which they carried away. His pouch had been taken.

They hoisted the corpse of their poor companion on their shoulders, took his good sword and valiant musket and, grieved and angry, they bore these to the bailiff's house, where he received them in company with the criminal clerk, the two sheriffs and the two surgeons.

The cut-off fingers were examined and proved to be those of an old man who was not a worker at any trade, for the fingers were tapered and the nails were long like those of lawyers or churchmen.

The following day the bailiff, the sheriffs, the clerk, the surgeons and the troopers went to the place where the poor victim had been bitten. There they saw that there were drops of blood on the grass and footprints that went down as far as the sea and then stopped there.

37 IT WAS THE TIME of the ripe grapes, the month of the wine, the fourth day when, in the town of Brussels, they throw from the top of the tower of Saint Nicolas, after the high mass, sacks of walnuts to the people. At night Nele was awakened by cries coming from the street. She looked for Katheline in her room, but did not find her. She ran downstairs and opened the door, and Katheline came in, saying:

'Save me! Save me! The wolf! The wolf!'

And Nele heard howlings far off in the country-side. Trembling, she lighted the lamps and candles.

'What's happened, Katheline?' said she, folding her in her arms.

Katheline sat down, her eyes haggard, and said, looking at the candles: 'It's the sun that drives away evil spirits. The wolf, the wolf howls in the country.'

'But,' said Nele, 'why did you get out of your bed, where you were warm, to go and catch fever in the damp September nights?'

And Katheline said:

'Hanske screamed last night like a sea-eagle; and I opened the door for him. And he said to me: "Take the beverage of vision." And I drank of it. Hanske is handsome. Take away the fire. Then he took me near the canal and said to me: "Katheline, I shall give you back the seven hundred carolus and you shall give them back to Ulenspiegl, son of Claes. Here are two to buy yourself a dress; you shall have a thousand soon." "A thousand," said I, "my lover, I shall be rich then." "You shall have them," said he. "But is there not anyone in Damme, a woman or girl, who is now as rich as you shall be?" "I do not know," said I, for I would not tell him their names for fear that he'd love them. He said to me then: "Find out, and tell me their names when I return again."

'The air was chill, the mist rolled over the meadows, the dry twigs fell from the trees on to the road. And the moon shone and there were flames on the water of the canal. Hanske said to me: " 'Tis the night of the werwolves; all the guilty souls come from hell. You must make three signs of the cross with your left hand, and cry: 'Salt! Salt! Salt!' which is the emblem of immortality: and they will not harm you." And I said: "I will do what you ask me to, Hanske, my darling." And he kissed me, saying: "You are my wife." "Yes," said I. And at his gentle words a heavenly happiness went over my body like balm. And he crowned me with roses, and said to me: "You are lovely." And I said to him: "You are beautiful, too, Hanske, my darling, in your fine suit of green velvet trimmed with gold, with your long ostrich feather that floats from your bonnet, and your face pale as the fires under the waves of the sea. And if the Damme girls saw you, they would run right after you, begging for your heart; but you must not give it to any but me, Hanske." He said: "Try to find out who are the richest; their fortunes shall be for you." Then he went off, leaving me there, after having forbade me to follow him.

'I stayed there, jingling the two carolus in my hands, all shivering and frozen because of the mist, when I saw, coming up from the bluff, climbing the embankment, a wolf that had a green face and long reeds in its white hair. I cried: "Salt! Salt! Salt!" making the sign of the cross,

355

but it didn't seem to be frightened by this. And I turned and ran with all my strength; I cried, he howled, and I heard the sharp sound of his teeth close to me, and once so close that I thought he was about to seize me. But I ran faster than he did. By great good luck I met, at the corner of Heron Street, the night-watchman with his lantern. "The wolf! The wolf!" I cried. "Don't be afraid," said the night-watchman, "I will see you home, Katheline the madwife." And I felt that his hand, which supported me, trembled. And he was also afraid.'

'But he has taken courage,' said Nele. 'Do you hear him now singing out, drawlingly: *"De clock is tien; tien aen de clock"* (The clock strikes ten; 'tis ten o'clock) ? And he makes his rattle grate.'

'Take away the fire,' said Katheline, 'the head burns! Come back, Hanske, my dear.'

And Nele looked at Katheline; and she prayed our Lady the Virgin to take from her head the fire of folly; and she wept over her.

38 AT BELLEM, on the banks of the Bruges canal, Ulenspiegl and Lamme met a horseman wearing in his hat three cock-feathers, and riding full speed towards Ghent. Ulenspiegl sang like the lark, and the rider, stopping, answered with the clarion call of chanticleer.

'Do you bring news, impetuous rider?' said Ulenspiegl.

'Great news,' said the horseman. 'On the advice of M. de Chatillon, who is the Admiral of the Sea in the Land of France, the Prince of Freedom has given out commissions to equip ships of war over and above those already armed at Emden and East Frisia. The brave men who have received these commissions are Adrien de Berghes, Sieur of Dolhaim; his brother Louis de Hainaut; the Baron of Montfaucon; the Sieur Louis de Brederode; Albert of Egmont, son of the man who was beheaded and not a traitor like his brother; Berthel Enthens of Mentheda, the Frisian; Adrien Menningh; Hembyse the impetuous and proud Ghentois; and Jan Brock.

'The prince has given all he owns—more than fifty thousand florins.'

'I have five hundred for him,' said Ulenspiegl.

'Carry them to the sea,' said the horseman.

And off he went at a gallop.

'He gives all he has,' said Ulenspiegl. 'We give nothing but our skins.'

'Is that not something,' said Lamme, 'and will we never hear tell of anything else but sacks of massacre? The Orange has fallen.'

'Yes,' said Ulenspiegl, 'fallen, like the oak; but with the oak they build ships of freedom!'

356

'For his profit,' said Lamme. 'But since there is no longer any danger, let us buy asses. I like going along seated and not having ringing blisters on the soles of my feet.'

'We'll buy asses,' said Ulenspiegl; 'these animals are easy to re-sell.'

They went to the market and found there two fine donkeys all harnessed, which they bought.

39 As THEY straddled along, leg this way, leg that, they came to Oost-Camp, where there is a great wood whose fringe goes down to the canal. Seeking shade and sweet fragrance there, they entered and saw nothing but long alleys going off in every direction towards Bruges, Ghent; to South and North Flanders.

Suddenly Ulenspiegl jumped from his donkey.

'Do you see anything over there?'

Lamme said:

'Yes, I see.' And, trembling: 'My wife, my good wife! It's she, my boy. Ah! I cannot walk to her. To find her so!'

'What are you complaining about?' said Ulenspiegl. 'She is lovely, half-naked that way, in the doublet of muslin slashed to show the cool skin. That one is too young; she's not your wife.'

'My boy,' said Lamme, 'it's she, my boy; I recognize her. Carry me, I don't know how to walk any more. Who would have thought it of her? To dance this way, dressed as a gipsy, immodestly. Yes, it's she; see her shapely legs, her arms bare right to the shoulder, her round and golden breasts, half-out from her muslin doublet. See how she excites, with that red flag, the great dog that jumps up after her.'

'It's a gipsy dog,' said Ulenspiegl; 'the Netherlands have no breed like that.'

'Gipsy. . . I don't know. . . But it is she. Ah! my boy, I can't see any more. She's kilting her skirts higher to show more of her rounded legs. She laughs to show her white teeth, and loudly to let her sweet voice be heard. She opens the collar of her doublet and throws back her head. Ah! that neck of an amorous swan, these bare shoulders, these bright and bold eyes! I run to her.'

And he jumped down from his donkey.

But Ulenspiegl stopped him, saying:

'That girl is not your wife. We are near an encampment of gipsies. Beware. Do you see that smoke behind the trees? Do you hear the barking of the dogs? Here; there are several of them watching us, ready to bite, maybe. Let's hide ourselves better in the thicket.'

357

'I will not hide myself,' said Lamme. 'That woman is mine, as Flemish as we are.'

'Blind fool,' said Ulenspiegl.

'Blind, no! I can see her very well, dancing half-naked, laughing and worrying that great big dog. She has made out she doesn't see us. But she does see us, I assure you. Tyl! Tyl! There's the dog jumping on her and knocking her over to have the red flag. And she falls down, giving a plaintive cry.'

And Lamme very suddenly dashed off towards her, saying to her:

'My wife, my wife! Where have you hurt yourself, darling? Why are you laughing so loud? Your eyes are haggard.'

And he embraced her, caressing her, and said:

'That beauty spot which you had under your left breast. I don't see it. Where is it? You are not my wife. Great God in Heaven!'

And she kept on laughing.

Suddenly Ulenspiegl cried:

'Beware, Lamme.'

And Lamme, turning round, saw before him a great blackamoor of a gipsy, sour-phized, brown as *peper-koek* (gingerbread).

Lamme picked up his pike-staff and, putting himself in a defensive attitude, cried:

'To the rescue, Ulenspiegl!'

Ulenspiegl was there with his good sword.

The gipsy said to him in High German:

'*Gibt mi ghelt, ein Richsthaler ouf tsein*' (Give me money, a *Ricksdaelder*, or ten).

'See,' said Ulenspiegl, 'the girl goes off laughing loudly and turning round continually, asking to be followed.'

'*Gibt mi ghelt*,' said the man. 'Pay for your love. We are poor and wish you no harm.'

Lamme gave him a carolus.

'What is your trade?' asked Ulenspiegl.

'All of them,' replied the gipsy; 'being masters of the art of versatility, we do marvellous and magical tricks. We play the tambourine and dance Hungarian dances. There are those among us who make cages and gridirons for roasting fine carbonnades. But all people, Flemings and Walloons, are afraid of us and drive us away. Not being able to live from our profits, we live on the produce of our marauding, that is to say, on the vegetables, the flesh and the fowls which we take from the peasant, since he will neither sell nor give them to us.'

Lamme said to him:

'Where does that girl come from who looks so much like my wife?'

358

'She is the daughter of our chief,' said the blackamoor.

Then, speaking very low, like a timid man:

'She was smitten by God with love-folly and knows nothing of womanly modesty. As soon as she sees a man, she becomes gay and wild and laughs without ceasing. She speaks but little, and for a long time they thought her dumb. At night, doleful, she stays before the fire, weeping sometimes or laughing without reason, and showing her belly where it hurts her, she says. In summer, at mid-day, after the meal, her most vivid madness seizes her. Then she goes dancing almost nude on the outskirts of the camp. She will only wear clothes of tulle or muslin, and in winter we have the greatest difficulty in covering her with a goat's-hair cloak.'

'But,' said Lamme, 'has she no friend to stop her from abandoning herself like this to all comers?'

'She has not,' said the man, 'for the travellers, approaching her and seeing her distraught eyes, have more fear than love for her. That big man was daring,' he continued, pointing to Lamme.

'Let him speak on, my boy,' said Ulenspiegl. 'It's the stockfish speaking ill of the whale. Which of the two gives the most oil?'

'You have a sharp tongue this morning,' said Lamme.

But Ulenspiegl, without listening, said to the gipsy:

'What does she do when others are as daring as my friend Lamme?'

The gipsy answered sadly:

'Then she has pleasure and profit. Those who obtain it pay for their joy and the money serves to clothe her and cover the needs of the old people and the women.'

'She obeys no one then?' said Lamme.

The gipsy answered:

'Let us allow those whom God has smitten to do as they will. He marks His will in this way. And such is our law.'

Ulenspiegl and Lamme went off. And the gipsy, grave and proud, returned to the camp. And the girl, laughing loudly, danced in the clearing.

40 GOING ON THEIR WAY towards Bruges, Ulenspiegl said to Lamme: 'We have spent a great sum of money in enlisting troopers, paying the catchpolls, the gift to the gipsy-girl, and in these innumerable *olie-koekjes* that it pleased you to eat endlessly, rather than sell a single one. Now, in spite of your stomachal will, the time has come to live more honestly. Give me your money; I'll keep the common purse.'

'I am willing,' said Lamme. And he gave it to him. 'Just the same, you mustn't let me die of hunger. For think, big and powerful as I am, I must have substantial and abundant nourishment. It's all right for you, thin and miserable, to live from hand to mouth, eating or not eating what you can find, like the planks of the quay that live on air and rain. But I, whom the air hollows and the rain hungers, I have need of other feasts.'

'You shall have them,' said Ulenspiegl, 'feasts of virtuous Lent. The best stuffed paunches cannot resist them; deflating little by little, they render light the heaviest man. And we shall soon see, sufficiently thinned down, my darling Lamme running like a stag.'

'La,' said Lamme. 'What shall be my meagre fate henceforth? I'm hungry, my boy, and want to sup.'

Evening was falling. They arrived at Bruges by the Ghent gate. They showed their passes. Having had to pay a half-sol for themselves and two for their donkeys, they entered the town; Lamme, thinking of Ulenspiegl's words, seemed distressed.

'Shall we sup soon?' said he.

'Yes,' said Ulenspiegl.

They got down at the *in de Meermin* (The Siren Inn), whose signboard is a weathercock figure all in gold, set above the gable of the inn.

They placed their asses in the stable and Ulenspiegl ordered, for his supper and Lamme's, bread, beer and cheese.

The host sneered as he served this meagre repast; Lamme ate hungrily, watching with despair as Ulenspiegl worked with his jaws on the bread that was too old and the cheese that was too young, as though they were ortolans. Lamme drank his small beer with no pleasure. Ulenspiegl laughed to see him so down in the dumps. And there was also someone who laughed in the courtyard of the inn and came sometimes to show her nose at the window-pane. Ulenspiegl saw that it was a woman who hid her face. Taking it to be some sly servant, he thought no more about it and, seeing Lamme pale, sad and livid because of the gainsaying of his stomachal loves, he took pity and thought of ordering for his companion an omelette with black-puddings, a plate of beef and beans or some other hot dish, when the *baes* came in and, taking off his cap, said:

'If these travelling gentlemen would like a better supper, let them speak up and tell what they want.'

Lamme opened wide his eyes and wider still his mouth, and watched Ulenspiegl with an anxious inquietude.

The latter answered:

'Wandering workmen are not rich.'

'It sometimes happens,' said the *baes*, 'that they do not know all they

360

possess.' And pointing to Lamme: 'That goodly mug is worth two others. What will it please your lordships to eat and drink? An omelette with fat ham; *choesels,* just made to-day; *castrelins;* a capon that melts in the mouth; a fine carbonnade grilled, with a fourspice sauce; some *dobble knol* of Antwerp; some *dobble cuyt* of Bruges; some Louvain wine made in the Burgundy way? And without paying!'

'Bring on everything,' said Lamme.

The table was soon spread, and Ulenspiegl took pleasure in watching poor Lamme, more famished than ever, rush at the omelette, the *choesels,* the capon, the ham, the carbonnades, and pouring the *dobble knol* down his throat, the *dobble cuyt,* and the Louvain wine made in the Burgundy way.

When he could eat no more, he puffed with pleasure like a whale, and looked about the table to see if there was nothing else he could pop into his mouth. And he crunched the crumbs of the *castrelins.*

Neither Ulenspiegl nor he had seen the pretty face watching them smilingly through the window-panes, and passing and re-passing in the courtyard. The *baes* having brought on a hot punch seasoned with cinnamon and Madeira sugar, they continued drinking. And they sang.

At the curfew hour, he asked if they would like to retire each to his large and fine room. Ulenspiegl answered that one little one would be sufficient for both of them. The *baes* replied:

'I haven't any; you shall each have a lord's bedroom without paying.'

And in truth he led them to rooms richly garnished with furniture and carpets. In the one given to Lamme there was a large bed.

Ulenspiegl, who had had much to drink and was falling asleep, let him go to this bed and promptly went to his own.

The following day at noon he went to Lamme's room and saw him sleeping and snoring. Lying beside him was a dainty little wallet full of money. He opened it and saw there were golden carolus and silver patards.

He shook Lamme to awaken him; the latter started up, rubbed his eyes, looked about him, then said, anxiously:

'My wife, where is my wife?'

And, showing an empty place beside him in the bed:

'She was there a while ago,' said he.

Then, jumping from the bed, he again looked about him, hunted in all the corners of the room, the alcove, the press, and said, stamping his foot on the floor:

'My wife! Where is my wife?'

The *baes* came up at the noise.

'Scoundrel,' said Lamme, grabbing him by the throat, 'where is my wife? What have you done with my wife?'

'Impatient tramp,' said the *baes*, 'your wife? What wife? You came here alone. I know nothing about it.'

'Ha! He knows nothing about it,' said Lamme, ferreting about again in all the holes and corners of the room. 'La! She was here last night in my bed, just as in the days of our lovely love. Yes. Where are you, darling?'

And, throwing the purse on the floor:

'It's not your money I need, it's you, your sweet body, your kind heart. Oh, my beloved! Oh, heavenly joys! You'll never come back again. I had become accustomed to seeing you no more, to living without love, my sweet treasure. And here now, having taken me back again, you leave me. But I'd rather die. Ha! My wife! Where is my wife?'

And he wept burning tears on the floor where he had thrown himself down. Then suddenly opening the door, he began to run all over the inn and in the street, in his shirt-tails, crying:

'My wife? Where is my wife?'

But he soon came in again, for the mischievous boys had hooted him and thrown stones at him. And Ulenspiegl said, as he made him put on his clothes:

'Don't be so disconsolate, you'll see her again, since you have seen her. She still loves you, considering that she came back again to you, and that it was she who paid for the supper and the lordly rooms and who also left in your bed that full purse. The ashes tell me that these are not the doings of an unfaithful wife. Don't cry, and let us go forward for the defence of the land of our fathers.'

'Let us stay a while at Bruges,' said Lamme; 'I want to scour the whole town, and I shall find her.'

'You shan't find her, since she's hiding from you,' said Ulenspiegl.

Lamme asked for an explanation from the *baes*, but the latter would say nothing.

And they went off towards Damme. As they were going along, Ulenspiegl said to Lamme:

'Why won't you tell me how you came to find her at your side last night, and how she left you?'

'My boy,' answered Lamme, 'you know that we had feasted on meat, beer and wine, and that I could hardly breathe when we went up to our rooms. I held a wax-candle to light my way like a lord, and I had placed the candle-stick on a chest to go to sleep; the door was unlatched and the chest was right beside it. As I undressed I looked on my bed with loving eyes and a longing for sleep; the wax-candle went out sud-

362

denly. I heard breathing and the sound of light steps in my room; but being more sleepy than frightened I lay me down heavily. As I was about to fall asleep, a voice—her voice, oh my wife, my poor wife!— said to me: "Did you sup well, Lamme?" and her voice was close to me and her face too, and her sweet body.'

41   THAT DAY Philip the King, having eaten too much pastry, was more than usually melancholy. He had played on his living harpsichord, which was a case enclosing cats whose heads came through round holes above the keys. Each time that the King struck a note, the note in turn jabbed the cat with a dart; and the beast mewed and complained because of the pain.

But Philip did not laugh.

Endlessly he ransacked his brain to find out how he might conquer the great queen, Elizabeth, and set up Mary Stuart on the English throne. With this object in mind he had written to the Pope that he was needy and had many debts; the Pope had answered him that he would willingly sell, for this enterprise, the sacred vases of the temple and the treasures of the Vatican.

But Philip did not laugh.

Ridolfi, Queen Mary's favorite, who hoped by freeing her to marry her and become the King of England, came to see Philip to plot with him the murder of Elizabeth. But he was so *'Parlanchin,'* as the King wrote, that his designs were openly talked about in the Antwerp Exchange; and the murder was not committed.

Later, upon orders from the King, the duke sent to England two couples of assassins. They succeeded in getting hanged.

And Philip did not laugh.

And so God baffled the ambitions of this vampire, who really counted on carrying off the son of Mary Stuart and reigning in his stead, with the Pope, over England. And this murderer was exasperated, seeing that noble country great and powerful. Endlessly he turned his pale eyes on it, seeking to know how he could crush it and then reign over the world, exterminating the Reformists, especially the richer ones, and inheriting their wealth.

But he did not laugh.

And they brought to him mice and field-mice in an iron box, with high sides and open on one side; and he set the bottom of the box on a blazing fire and took his pleasure in watching and hearing the poor little beasts jump, cry, moan and die.

But he did not laugh.

Then pale, and with trembling hands, he went to the arms of Madame Eboli, to slake the lecherous fire lit at the torch of cruelty.

And he did not laugh.

And Madame Eboli received him through fear and not through love.

42 THE AIR WAS WARM. From the calm sea came not a breath of wind. The trees of the Damme canal barely quivered, the grasshoppers stayed still in the meadows, while in the fields the men from the churches and abbeys came to gather in a thirteenth part of the harvest for the vicars and abbots. From the ardent, deep blue sky, the sun poured warmth down and Nature slept under its rays like a lovely girl naked and swooning under the caresses of her lover. The carps in the canal cut capers above the surface of the water, to snatch at the flies that buzzed like a boiler; while the swallows, with their long bodies and great wide wings, disputed the prey with them. From the earth there arose a warm vapour, wavering and shimmering in the light. The beadle of Damme announced from the top of the steeple, by a cracked bell that rang like a cauldron, that it was noon and time for all the country-folk who worked at the haying to go and dine. Women shouted through their hands, closed funnel-wise, calling their men-folk, brothers or husbands, by their names: Hans, Pieter, Joos; and one could see above the hedges their red hooded-capes.

From afar, the tower of Our Lady rose high, square and massive, before the eyes of Ulenspiegl and Lamme, and the latter said:

'There, my boy, are your griefs and your loves.'

But Ulenspiegl made no reply.

'Soon,' said Lamme, 'I shall see my old home and perhaps my wife.'

But Ulenspiegl made no reply.

'Wooden man,' said Lamme, 'stony-heart, can nothing stir you, neither the nearness of the place where you passed your childhood, nor the dear shades of poor Claes and poor Soetkin, the two martyrs? What? You are neither sad nor gay? Who has so dried up your heart? Look at me, anxious, uneasy, bounding in my belly; look at me. . .'

Lamme turned to Ulenspiegl and saw his head hanging, his face livid, his lips trembling; and he was weeping silently. And Lamme also became silent.

And they walked this way without uttering a word until they came to Damme, which they entered by Heron Street, where they saw no one because of the heat. The dogs, lying on their sides with their tongues

365

hanging out, yawned before the sills of the doors. Lamme and Ulenspiegl passed by the Town Hall, before which Claes had been burned; Ulenspiegl's lips trembled more than ever, but his tears dried up. Finding himself before the house of Claes, now occupied by a master charcoal-burner, he said on entering:

'Do you recognize me? I would like to rest a while here.'

The master charcoal-burner said:

'I know you; you are the son of the victim. Go where you like in this house.'

Ulenspiegl went into the kitchen, then into the room of Claes and Soetkin, and there wept.

When he came down, the master charcoal-burner said to him:

'Here is bread, cheese and beer. if you are hungry, eat; if you are thirsty, drink.'

Ulenspiegl made a sign with his hand to say that he was neither thirsty nor hungry.

So he walked away with Lamme, who sat astride his donkey while Ulenspiegl held his by the halter.

They came to Katheline's cottage, tied up their asses and entered. It was meal-time. On the table there were string-beans mixed with large white beans. Katheline was eating; Nele was standing up and about to pour into Katheline's plate a vinegar sauce which she had just taken from the fire.

When Ulenspiegl entered she was so startled that she set the pot with all the sauce in Katheline's plate, who, wagging her head, began to spoon for the beans about the sauce-pan and, striking her brow, said like a madwife:

'Take away the fire! The head burns!'

The smell of the vinegar sauce made Lamme hungry.

Ulenspiegl remained standing, watching Nele, and smiling with love through his great sadness.

And Nele, without saying a word to him, threw her arms about his neck. She also seemed mad; she wept, laughed and blushed with a great and sweet pleasure, and could only say: 'Tyl! Tyl!' Ulenspiegl, happy,

366

looked at her; then she let go of him to stand farther off, where she joyfully contemplated him and then rushed at him anew, throwing her arms about his neck; and so several times. He held on to her, very happy, unable to let her go from him until she sank on to a chair, tired and as though out of her senses; and she said, without shame:

'Tyl! Tyl! My beloved, you have come back again!'

Lamme stood by the door; when Nele was calmed, she pointed to him, saying:

'Where have I seen that big man?'

'He's my friend,' said Ulenspiegl. 'He's seeking his wife in my company.'

'I know you,' said Nele, speaking to Lamme; 'you lived in Heron Street. You are seeking your wife. I saw her at Bruges living in all piety and devotion. I asked her why she had so cruelly fled from her husband; she answered me: "Such was the sacred will of God and the order of the holy penance that I cannot live with him hereafter."'

Lamme was saddened at these words and looked on the beans and vinegar. And the swallows, singing, rose in the heavens, and Nature, swooning, allowed herself to be caressed by the sun. And Katheline picked out with her spoon the white beans, the string-beans and the sauce.

43 AT THIS TIME a girl of fifteen went from Heyst to Knocke, alone in broad daylight, along the dunes. No one had any fear for her, for they knew that the werwolves and the wicked spirits of the damned bit only by night. She carried in a sachet forty-eight silver sols, worth four carolus florins, which her mother Toria Pieterson, who lived at Heyst, owed from a sale to her uncle Jan Rapen, who lived at Knocke. The girl, named Betkin, having dressed herself in all her best clothes, went off joyously.

In the evening the mother was uneasy at not seeing her return. Thinking, however, that she had stayed to sleep at her uncle's house, she reassured herself.

The following day fishermen, returning from the sea with a boatload of fish, pulled their boat up on the beach and unloaded their fish into carts, to sell them by the cartful at auction at Heyst. They climbed up the road strewn with sea-shells and found in the dune a girl stripped naked, even of her chemise, lying in blood. Coming closer, they saw on her poor broken neck the marks of long sharp teeth. She lay on her back and her open eyes looked up at the sky: her mouth was also open as though to cry out on death!

Covering the girl's body with an *opperst-kleed*, they bore it to Heyst to the Town Hall. There soon assembled the sheriffs and the surgeon-barber, who declared that the marks of the long teeth had not been made by a wolf's teeth, such as Nature knew, but were rather those of some wicked and infernal werwolf, and that they must pray God to deliver the land of Flanders from it.

And in all the county, and notably at Damme, Heyst and Knocke, prayers and orisons were ordered to be made.

And the populace, groaning, stayed in the churches.

And in the Heyst church, where the body of the girl was laid out, men and women wept, seeing her bleeding and broken neck. And the mother said, right out in the church:

'I want to go to the werwolf and kill it with my teeth.'

And the weeping women urged her to do this. And some said:

'You will never return.'

And she went off with her husband and her two brothers, well-armed, to seek for the wolf by beach, dune and valley; but could not find it. And her husband had to take her back to the house, for she caught a fever because of the nocturnal cold; and they watched over her, mending their nets for the next fishing time.

The bailiff of Damme, taking into consideration that the werwolf is an animal living off blood and not a despoiler of the dead, said that it was doubtless followed by robbers who wander about the dunes for their evil profit. Therefore he summoned all and sundry, by the ringing of the bell, to go about well-armed with weapons and sticks, seizing all beggars and vagabonds, arresting them, and searching them to see if they had not golden carolus or pieces of the victims' clothes in their pouches. And afterwards the able-bodied beggars and vagabonds would be taken to the king's galleys. And the old and infirm would be set free.

But nothing was found.

Ulenspiegl went to the bailiff and said:

'I want to kill the werwolf.'

'What gives you confidence?' asked the bailiff.

'The ashes beat upon my heart,' replied Ulenspiegl. 'Grant me permission to work in the town forge.'

'You may,' said the bailiff.

Ulenspiegl, without saying a word of his project to any man or woman in Damme, went to the forge and there, secretly, made a fine, large wild-beast trap.

The following day, Saturday, a day loved by the werwolf, Ulenspiegl, carrying a letter from the bailiff to the vicar of Heyst, and the trap

368

under his cloak, and armed besides with a good musket and a well-sharpened cutlass, went off, saying to the Damme folk:

'I'm going hunting sea-gulls and with their down I'll make pillows for the bailiff's wife.'

Going towards Heyst, he came on the beach, heard the angry sea rolling and unrolling, great waves rumbling like thunder, and the wind coming from England, whistling in the rigging of the beached boats. A fisherman said to him:

'This bad wind is ruination for us. Last night the sea was calm, but after sunrise she suddenly rose in a fury. We cannot go fishing.'

Ulenspiegl was happy, being thus assured of having help during the night if need be.

At Heyst he went to the vicar, to whom he gave the bailiff's letter. The vicar said to him:

'You are brave; know, however, that no one passes alone along the dunes on Saturday night who is not bitten and left dead on the sand. The workers, dykers and others only go in bands. Night falls. Do you hear the werwolf howl in the valley? Will it come again as it came last night, to howl dreadfully all night long in the cemetery? God be with you, my son, but do not go.'

And the vicar made the sign of the cross over him.

'The ashes beat upon my heart,' answered Ulenspiegl.

The vicar said:

'Since you have such a brave will, I wish to help you.'

'Messire Vicar,' said Ulenspiegl, 'you'll be doing me much good, and much good for the poor desolate country, if you go to Toria, the girl's mother and her two brothers also, to tell them that the wolf is at hand and that I want to await it and kill it.'

The vicar said:

'If you do not know yet on what road you must place yourself, stay

on the one that leads to the cemetery. It is between two broom hedges. Two men could not walk abreast on it.'

'I will stay there,' answered Ulenspiegl. 'And you, Messire brave Vicar, co-worker of deliverance, order and summon the mother of the girl and her husband and her two brothers to be in the church, all armed, before the curfew. If they hear me whistle like a sea-gull, it means that I have seen the werwolf. They must then sound the *wacharm* on the bell and come to my rescue. And if there are some other brave men. . .'

'There are none, my son,' replied the vicar. 'The fishermen fear the werwolf more than the plague or death. But do not go.'

Ulenspiegl answered:

'The ashes beat upon my heart.'

The vicar then said:

'I will do as you wish, bless you. Are you hungry or thirsty?'

'Both,' answered Ulenspiegl.

The vicar gave him beer, bread and cheese.

Ulenspiegl drank, ate and went off.

Walking along and lifting his eyes he saw his father, Claes, in glory beside God, in the sky where the bright moon shone. He looked on the sea and at the clouds, and he heard the tempestuous wind blowing out of England.

'Oh!' said he, 'dark clouds rushing rapidly, be as Vengeance on the traces of Murder. Grumbling sea, made dark like the mouth of hell by the sky; waves, with the fiery spume running over the sombre waters, shaking up impatient, angry, innumerable animals of fire—oxen, sheep, horses, serpents—which roll on the waters or rise in the air, spewing flamboyant rain; blackest sea, sky black with mourning, come with me and fight the werwolf, the wicked murderer of girls. And you, wind wailing plaintively in the gorse of the dunes and the rigging of the ships, you are the voice of the victims crying out for vengeance to God, who may help me in this enterprise.'

And he went down into the valley, tottering on his two natural props as though he had drunken dissolution in his head and in his stomach an indigestion from cabbage.

And he sang, hiccuping, zigzagging, yarning, spitting, and stopping to make believe he was vomiting, but in reality opening wide his eye to consider everything all about him; when suddenly he heard a sharp howling. He stopped spewing like a dog, and saw by the light of the moon the long shape of a wolf walking towards the cemetery. Tottering again, he entered the pathway between the broom hedges. There, feigning to fall down, he placed the trap at the side the wolf was coming

370

from. Then, loading his cross-bow, he went off ten paces, stood up in a drunken posture, continuing to stagger, hiccup, and retch, but really keeping his mind taut as a bow-string and his eyes and ears wide open.

And he saw nothing save the dark clouds rushing madly over the sky and a large, fat and short dark form coming towards him; and he heard nothing save the wind wailing plaintively, the sea rumbling like thunder, and the shell-strewn path crunching under a heavy stumbling step.

Feigning to want to sit down, he fell heavily on the ground like a drunkard. And he spat.

Then he heard the clink of iron at two paces from his ear, and the noise of the trap shutting and the cry of a man.

'The werwolf,' said he, 'has had his forefeet caught in the trap. He gets up howling, shaking the trap, trying to run. But he shan't escape.'

And he shot a cross-bow arrow at his legs.

'There, he falls wounded,' he said.

And he whistled like a sea-gull.

Suddenly the church bell rang out *wacharm* and a little boy's piercing voice cried through the village:

'Awake, sleeping folk, the werwolf is caught.'

'Glory be to God!' said Ulenspiegl.

Toria, mother of Betkin; Lansaem, her husband; Josse and Michiel, her two brothers, were the first to come with lanterns.

'He's caught?' said they.

'Look at him on the path,' answered Ulenspiegl.

'Glory be to God!' they said.

And they crossed themselves.

'Who's ringing?' asked Ulenspiegl.

Lansaem answered:

'My eldest; the youngest runs through the village knocking at the doors and crying that the wolf is caught. Glory be to you!'

'The ashes beat upon my heart,' answered Ulenspiegl.

Suddenly the werwolf spoke, and said:

'Have mercy on me, mercy, Ulenspiegl.'

'The wolf speaks,' they all said, crossing themselves. 'He's a devil and already knows Ulenspiegl's name.'

'Have mercy, mercy,' said the voice, 'order the bell to be stilled; it rings for the dead. Have mercy, I am no wolf. My wrists are pierced by the trap; I am old and I bleed, have mercy! What is that child's shrill voice waking up the village? Mercy!'

'I have heard you speak before,' said Ulenspiegl, vehemently. 'You are the fishmonger, murderer of Claes, you vampire of poor little girls. Goodmen and goodwives, don't be afraid. He's the dean who made Soetkin die of grief.'

And with one hand he grabbed the man by the throat under the chin and with the other he pulled out his cutlass.

But Toria, the mother of Betkin, stopped this gesture:

'Take him alive,' she cried.

And she pulled the man's white hair out by the handfuls and scratched his face with her nails.

And she howled with grievous fury.

The werwolf, his hands caught in the trap and stumbling along the road because of the keen suffering, said:

'Mercy, have mercy! Take away that woman. I will give two carolus. Break these bells! Where are these children who are shouting?'

'Hold him alive!' cried Toria, 'hold him alive that he may pay! The tolling bells, the tolling bells for you, murderer. By slow fire, by red-hot pincers. Hold him alive! Let him pay!'

Meanwhile Toria had picked up on the path a waffle-iron with long handles. Looking at it in the glare of the torches, she saw between the two iron plaques, deeply graved with lozenges in the Brabant fashion and armed besides like an iron mouth, two long pointed teeth. And when she opened it, it was like the mouth of a greyhound.

Toria, holding the waffle-iron, opening and shutting it, making the iron clink, seemed as though she were maddened with rage; and, gnashing her teeth, gurgling like a dying woman, groaning because of her grievously bitter thirst for revenge, she bit with the instrument on the prisoner's arms, legs, everywhere, but seeking above all the neck; and each time she bit him with it, she said:

'So he did to Betkin with the iron teeth. He pays. Do you bleed, murderer? God is just! The tolling bell! Betkin calls me to revenge. Do you feel the teeth, it's the mouth of God!'

And she snapped at him ceaselessly, mercilessly, striking him with

372

the waffle-iron, when she could not make it bite him. And because of her great impatience for revenge she did not kill him.

'Be merciful,' cried the prisoner. 'Ulenspiegl, strike me with your knife; I'll die quicker. Take away that woman. Break the tolling bells, kill the children who are crying through the village.'

And Toria still snapped at him until an old man, having pity, took from her hands the waffle-iron.

But Toria then spat in the face of the werwolf and tore out his hair, saying:

'You shall pay by slow fire, by the red-hot pincers; your eyes to my nails!'

In the meantime all the fishermen, peasants and women of Heyst had come out at the rumour that the werwolf was a man and not a devil. Some carried lanterns and flaming torches. And all shouted:

'Murdering robber, where have you hidden the gold stolen from the poor victims? Make him give up everything.'

'I have nothing; have mercy,' said the fishmonger.

And the women threw stones and sand at him.

'He pays! He pays!' cried Toria.

'Mercy!' he moaned. 'I am wet with my own blood that's flowing. Have mercy!'

'Your blood,' said Toria. 'You will keep enough to pay. Cover his wounds with balm. He shall pay with slow fire, the hand cut off, with red-hot pincers. He shall pay; he shall pay!'

And she tried to strike him; then, out of her mind, she fell on the sand like one dead; and she was left there until she came to herself again.

In the meantime Ulenspiegl, taking the trap from off the prisoner's hands, saw that three fingers were lacking from the right hand.

And he ordered him to be bound closely and placed in a fisher's basket. Men, women and children went off then, taking turns carrying the basket all the way to Damme, to seek justice there. And they carried torches and lanterns.

And the fishmonger kept on saying:

'Break the bells, kill the children who cry.'

And Toria said:

'Let him pay, by slow fire, by the red-hot pincers; let him pay!'

Then both became silent. And Ulenspiegl heard nothing more save the panting breath of Toria, the heavy footsteps of the men on the sand, and the sea rumbling like thunder.

And, sad at heart, he looked at the clouds rushing madly across the sky, at the sea where he saw the luminous foam-sheep and, in the light of the lanterns and torches, the livid face of the fishmonger, who looked at him with cruel eyes.

And the ashes beat upon his heart.

And they walked for four hours until they came to Damme, where the populace had assembled in a great mob, having already heard the news. All wanted to see the fishmonger and they followed the band of fishermen, crying, singing, dancing and saying:

'The werwolf is caught; he's caught, the murderer! Blessed be Ulenspiegl! Long live our brother Ulenspiegl! *Lange leve onse broeder Ulenspiegl!*'

And it was like a popular uprising.

When they came before the bailiff's house, he came out at the noise and said to Ulenspiegl:

'You are the conqueror! Glory be to you!'

'The ashes of Claes beat upon my heart,' answered Ulenspiegl. The bailiff then said:

'You shall receive half of the murderer's fortune.'

'Give it to the victims,' replied Ulenspiegl.

Lamme and Nele came; Nele, laughing and weeping with joy, kissed her lover Ulenspiegl. Lamme, jumping up and down heavily, slapped him on the belly, saying:

'He's brave, trusty and true; he's my beloved companion. You have not his like, you men of the lowlands.'

But the fishermen laughed mockingly at him.

44 THE BELL KNOWN as the *borgstorm* rang out on the morrow to summon the bailiff, sheriffs and clerks to the *Vierschare*, on the four grassy banks under the tree of justice, which was a splendid lime-tree. All about stood the common people. Being questioned, the fishmonger would confess nothing, even when they showed him the three fingers cut off by the trooper and which were lacking from his right hand. He kept on saying:

'I am poor and old; be merciful.'

But the common people booed him, saying:

'You're an old wolf, a slayer of children; have no mercy, master judges.'

The women said:

'Don't look at us with your cold eyes; you're a man and not a devil. We're not afraid of you. Cruel beast, more cowardly than a cat devouring a nest of birdlets, you slew the poor girls who only asked to live their sweet lives in all honesty.'

374

'Let him pay with the slow fire, the red-hot pincers,' cried Toria.

And, in spite of the town-sergeants, the wives and mothers egged the little boys on to throw stones at the fishmonger. And the lads did it willingly, booing him each time that he looked at them, and crying ceaselessly: '*Blood-zuyger!* (Blood-sucker!) *Sla dood!* (To the death!)'

And ceaselessly Toria cried:

'Let him pay with the slow fire, the red-hot pincers, let him pay!'

And the populace growled.

'See,' said the women to each other, 'see how cold he is under the bright sun, shining in the sky, warming his white hair and his face, torn by Toria.'

'And he trembles with pain.'

'It's the justice of God!'

'And he stands up there with a lamentable look.'

'See his murderer's hands tied in front of him and bleeding because of the cuts made by the trap.'

'Let him pay, let him pay!' cried Toria.

Lamentingly, he said:

'I am poor, let me go.'

And everybody, even the judges, jeered at him as they listened. He pretended to weep, trying to move them. And the women laughed.

Seeing that there was sufficient evidence to warrant torture, he was condemned to be placed on the torture bench until such time as he confessed how he killed, where he came from, where the spoils of the victims were, and in what place he had hidden the gold.

Being in the torture chamber, shod with foot-gear of new leather too small, and the bailiff having asked him how Satan had whispered to him such dark designs and so many abominable crimes, he replied:

'I myself am Satan, my natural being. Even when a child—but ugly looking, unfit for all bodily exercise—I was taken for a ninny by everybody and often beaten. Neither the boys nor the girls had any mercy. In my youth nobody wanted me, even when I paid. So I conceived a frigid hatred for everything born of woman. That was why I denounced Claes, beloved by everyone. And I only loved money, which was my white or golden darling; in having Claes killed, I found both profit and pleasure. After that it was necessary for me to live more than ever like a wolf, and I dreamed of tearing with my teeth. Passing through Brabant, I saw the waffle-irons of that country and thought that one of them would be a good iron mug. Why don't I have you all by the necks, you mean ones, tigers, who find diversion in the torture of an old man! I would snap into you with a greater joy than I did into the trooper and the girl. For her—when I saw her so sweet, sleeping on

375

the sands in the sun, holding in her hands the little bag of money—I had love and pity; but, feeling myself too old and not being able to take her, I bit her. . .'

The bailiff asked him where he lived, and the fishmonger replied:

'At Ramskapelle, from whence I went to Blankenberghe, to Heyst, even as far as Knocke. The Sundays and feast days I made waffles with that iron there in the Brabant way, in all the villages. It was always very clean and well-greased. And this novelty from a strange country was well received. If it pleases you to know more and how no one ever recognized me, I will tell you that in the daytime I painted my face and tinted my hair red. As for the wolf-skin which you point to with your cruel, questioning finger, I will tell you, in defiance, that it came from two wolves which I myself killed in the woods of Raveschoot and Maldeghem. I only had to sew their skins together to cover myself. I hid the skin in a case in the dunes at Heyst; there also are the clothes, stolen by me, awaiting a good occasion to sell them later on.'

'Take him away from before the fire,' said the bailiff.

The executioner obeyed.

'Where is your gold?' said the bailiff again.

'The king shall never know,' replied the fishmonger.

'Burn him closer with the flaming candles,' said the bailiff. 'Bring him closer to the fire.'

The executioner obeyed and the fishmonger screamed:

'I have nothing to say. I have said too much. You will burn me. I am not a sorcerer; why do you set me near the fire again? My feet are bleeding because of the burns. I will say nothing. Why closer now? They're bleeding, I tell you, they're bleeding; these boots are boots of red-hot iron. My gold? Ah, well, my only friend in this world is. . . Take away the fire . . . is in my cellar at Ramskapelle, in a box . . . leave it to me; grace and mercy, master judges; cursed executioner, take away the candles. . . He's burning me all the more. . . It is in a double-bottomed box wrapped about with wool so as to deaden the sound if the box is shaken; now I've told all; take me away.'

When he was taken away from before the fire, he smiled evilly.

The bailiff asked him why.

'With pleasure at being delivered,' he answered.

The bailiff said to him:

'Did no one ever ask to see your toothed waffle-iron?'

The fishmonger replied:

'They saw it was like all the others, except that there were holes wherein I screwed the iron teeth; at dawn I unscrewed them; the peasants preferred my waffles to those of the other merchants; and they

376

called them *"Waefels met brabansche knoopen"* (Waffles with Brabant buttons) because, the teeth being out, the empty holes formed little half-spheres like buttons.'

But the bailiff:

'When did you bite the poor victims?'

'Day and night. By day I wandered over the dunes and along the highways, carrying my waffle-iron, keeping watch, especially on Saturday, the day of the big market at Bruges. If I saw some rustic pass by, wandering melancholy, I left him alone, judging that his sadness came from his empty purse; but I walked alongside the man I saw marching on gaily. When he was least expecting it I snapped at his neck and took his pouch. And not only in the dunes but on all the paths and highways of the lowlands.'

The bailiff then said:

'Repent you, and pray God!'

But the fishmonger, blaspheming:

'It's the Lord God who has willed me to be as I am. I did everything in spite of myself, forced by Nature's will. Wicked tigers, you punish me unjustly. But do not burn me. . . I did everything in spite of myself; have mercy; I am poor and old. I shall die of my wounds; don't burn me.'

He was taken then to the *Vierschare*, under the lime-tree, to hear the sentence before the assembled populace.

And he was condemned, as a horrible murderer, robber and blasphemer, to have his tongue pierced with a red-hot iron, his right hand cut off, and to be burned by slow fire until death ensued, before the doors of the Town Hall.

And Toria cried:

'It is justice; he pays!'

And the people shouted:

'*Lang leven de Heeren van de wet!* (Long live the men of law!)'

And he was taken back to prison, where they gave him meat and wine. And he was gay, saying that he had never drunk nor eaten until then, but that the king, inheriting his wealth, could pay for that last meal.

And he laughed sourly.

The following morning, at early dawn, as they were leading him to the torture, he saw Ulenspiegl standing by the stake, and he cried aloud as he pointed at him:

'That one there, murderer of an old man, should likewise die. Ten years ago he threw me into the Damme canal because I had denounced his father. I acted in that as a faithful subject of His Catholic Majesty.'

377

The bells of Our Lady tolled for the dead.

'They are also tolling for you,' said he to Ulenspiegl; 'you shall be hanged, for you have killed.'

'The fishmonger lies,' cried all the folk in the crowd; 'he lies, the murdering butcher.'

And Toria, like one distraught, cried, as she threw a stone at him which cut his forehead:

'Had he drowned you, never would you have lived to bite my poor little girl like a vampirish blood-sucker.'

Ulenspiegl saying not a word, Lamme said:

'Did anyone see him throw the fishmonger into the water?'

Ulenspiegl made no answer.

'No! No!' shouted the populace; 'he lied, the butcher.'

'No, I have not lied,' cried the fishmonger; 'he threw me in while I implored his pardon, so much so that I only got out by the help of a launch that was anchored by the bank. All soaked and shivering I found my poor home with difficulty; there I had the fever and no one came to care for me, and I thought I would die.'

'You lie,' said Lamme; 'no one saw this.'

'No! no one saw this,' cried Toria. 'To the stake with the butcher! Before he dies he needs must have an innocent victim. To the stake; let him pay! If you did it, do not confess, Ulenspiegl. There are no witnesses. Let him pay with slow fire and red-hot pincers.'

'Did you commit the murder?' the bailiff asked Ulenspiegl.

Ulenspiegl replied:

'I threw into the water the murderous denouncer of Claes. The ashes of my father beat upon my heart.'

'He confesses,' said the fishmonger, 'he shall likewise die. Where is the stake that I may see it? Where is the executioner with the sword of justice? The bells are tolling for you, scoundrel, murderer of an old man.'

Ulenspiegl said:

'I threw you into the water to kill you; the ashes beat upon my heart.'

And among the people the women were saying:

'Why confess it, Ulenspiegl? No one saw it; you shall die now.'

And the prisoner laughed, bouncing with sour joy, agitating his tied arms, covered with bloody bandages.

'He shall die,' said he. 'He'll pass from earth to hell, the rope about his neck as a scoundrel, robber, rogue. He shall die; God is just.'

'He shall not die,' said the bailiff. 'After ten years, murder cannot be punished in the land of Flanders. Ulenspiegl did a wrong deed, but through filial love. Ulenspiegl shall not be made to answer for this deed.'

378

'Long live the law,' cried the people. *'Lang leve de wet.'*

The bells of Our Lady tolled for the dead. And the prisoner gnashed his teeth, hung his head, and wept his first tear.

And he had his hand cut off and his tongue pierced with a red-hot iron, and he was burned alive by slow fire before the doors of the Town Hall.

As he was about to die, he screamed:

'The king shall not get my gold; I lied. . . Wicked tigers, I shall return to bite you.'

And Toria cried:

'He pays, he pays! They writhe, the arms and legs that ran to murder; it smokes, the butcher's body; the white hair—hyena's hair—burns on his pallid snout. He pays! He pays!'

And the fishmonger died, howling like a wolf.

And the bells of Our Lady tolled for the dead.

And Lamme and Ulenspiegl re-mounted their donkeys.

And Nele, most sad, stayed with Katheline, who kept on saying:

'Take away the fire! The head burns. Come back, Hanske, my dear.'

Book Four

1 BEING AT HEYST, on the dunes, Ulenspiegl and Lamme saw coming from Ostend, Blankenberghe, Knocke, many fishing boats full of armed men, followers of the Beggars of Zeeland, who wear on their hats a silver crescent with this inscription: 'Rather serve the Turk than the Pope.'

Ulenspiegl was glad, he whistled like a lark; from every side came the answering warrior crow of the cock. The boats, sailing or fishing and selling their fish, went in, one after the other, to Emden. There William of Blois was detained who, by a commission from the Prince of Orange, was equipping a ship.

Ulenspiegl and Lamme went to Emden, while, on the orders of Tres-Long, the boats of the Beggars went out on the high seas.

Tres-Long, having been at Emden for eleven weeks, danced attendance bitterly. He went from boat to land and from land to boat like a chained bear.

Ulenspiegl and Lamme, wandering about the quays, saw a lord with a goodly face, rather melancholy, and trying to dig up one of the stones of the quay with a pike-staff. Not being able to do it, he continued in the same endeavour nevertheless, while behind him a dog gnawed at a bone.

Ulenspiegl came up to the dog and made as though he wanted to snatch the bone. The dog growled; Ulenspiegl kept on; the dog made a great uproar of puppy howls.

The lord, turning around at the noise, said to Ulenspiegl:

'What do you gain by tormenting that beast?'

'What do you gain, Messire, by tormenting that stone?'

'That is not the same thing,' said the lord.

'The difference is not great,' answered Ulenspiegl. 'If that dog likes his bone and wants to keep it, that stone likes its quay and wants to stay there. And it's very little for men like us to torment a dog, when men like you torment a paving stone.'

Lamme stood behind Ulenspiegl, not daring to speak.

'Who are you?' asked the lord.

'I am Tyl Ulenspiegl, son of Claes, who died in the flames for his faith.'

And he whistled like the lark, and the lord crowed like the cock.

'I am Admiral Tres-Long,' said he. 'What do you want with me?'

Ulenspiegl told him of his adventures and handed over five hundred carolus.

'Who is the big man?' asked Tres-Long, pointing to Lamme.

'My companion and friend,' replied Ulenspiegl. 'He wants, like me,

383

to sing on your boat, with the rare voice of the musket, the song of the deliverance of the land of our fathers.'

'You are both brave men,' said Tres-Long, 'and you shall sail on my ship.'

They were then in February. Sharp was the wind, keen the frost. After three weeks of grudging wait, Tres-Long left Emden with protestation. Thinking to enter Texel, he left from Vlie, but was forced to enter Wieringen, where his boat was ice-bound.

Soon there was a gay spectacle all about; sleighs and skaters all in velvet; women skaters with skirts and coats embroidered with gold, pearls, scarlet, azure; boys and girls going and coming, sliding, laughing, making a serpent, going two by two, in couples, singing the song of love on the ice, or going to eat and drink in the flag-decked booths, brandy, oranges, figs, *peper-koek*, *schols*, eggs, hot vegetables, *heetekoeken*, and vegetables in vinegar, while all about them sledges and ice-boats made the ice screech under their steel runners.

Lamme, looking for his wife, wandered about. skating like the goodmen and the goodwives; but he often fell down.

In the meantime Ulenspiegl went to quench his thirst and nourish himself at a little inn on the quay, where he did not have to pay too much for his food; and he willingly passed the time of day with the old *baesinne*.

One Sunday, about nine o'clock, he entered, asking to be given something to eat.

'But,' said he to the sweet-looking young woman who came forward to serve him, 'but, *baesinne* rejuvenated, what have you done with your old wrinkles? Your mouth has all its teeth, white and youthful, and the lips are red as cherries. Is that gentle and malicious smile for me?'

'Not at all,' she said; 'but what must I give you?'

'Yourself,' said he.

The woman answered:

'That would be too much for a skinny one like you; don't you want any other meat?'

Ulenspiegl said not a word.

'What have you done,' she asked, 'with that handsome man, well made and stout, that I often see with you?'

'Lamme?' said he.

'What have you done with him?' she asked.

Ulenspiegl answered:

'He eats in the booths; hard-boiled eggs, smoked eels, salt fish, *zuertjes*, and everything he can put in his mouth; and all to seek his

384

wife. Why aren't you mine, sweet? Do you want fifty florins? Do you want a necklace of gold?'

But she, crossing herself:

'I am not for the selling or the taking,' she said.

'Isn't there anything you like?' he asked.

'I love you as my neighbour; but I love above all else my Lord the Christ and Madame the Virgin, who command me to lead a modest life. Hard and heavy are its duties, but God helps us poor women. There are those, however, who fall down. Is your big friend happy?'

'He is happy eating, sad fasting, and always dreamy. But you, are you happy or sad?'

'We women,' said she, 'are slaves of that which rules us.'

'The moon?' said he.

'Yes,' said she.

'I am going to tell Lamme to come and see you.'

'Don't do that,' she said. 'He'll weep and I'll do the same.'

'Have you ever seen his wife?' asked Ulenspiegl.

She, sighing, replied:

'She sinned with him and was condemned to a cruel penance. She knows that he is going to sea for the triumph of heresy, and that's a hard thing for a Christian soul to think. Defend him if he's attacked; nurse him if he is wounded. His wife bade me make this request of you.'

'Lamme is my brother and friend,' said Ulenspiegl.

'Ah,' said she, 'why do you not return to the bosom of our Holy Mother, the Church?'

'She eats her children,' answered Ulenspiegl.

And off he went.

One March morning the wind, blowing sharp, thickening the ice, and the boat of Tres-Long being unable to leave, the sailors and the troopers were having feasts and parties with sleigh-riding and skating.

Ulenspiegl was at the inn, and the sweet-looking woman said to him, very sad and like one distraught:

'Poor Lamme! Poor Ulenspiegl!'

'Why are you complaining?' he asked.

'Alas! Alas!' she said, 'why do you not believe in the mass? You would doubtless go to paradise, and I could save you in this life.'

Seeing her go to the door to listen attentively, Ulenspiegl said to her:

'You are not listening to the snow falling?'

'No,' she said.

'It is not to the moaning wind that you're lending your ear?'

'No,' she said again.

386

'Nor to the jolly noise our brave sailors are making in the nearby tavern?'

'Death comes like a thief,' said she.

'Death!' said Ulenspiegl. 'I don't understand you. Come in and speak.'

'They are there,' said she.

'Who?'

'Who?' she replied. 'The soldiers of Simonen Bol, who are coming in the name of the duke to rush upon you all; if they treat you so well here, it is as they would the oxen they are about to kill. Ah, why,' she said, all in tears, 'did I only know of it a while ago?'

'Don't weep and don't cry out,' said Ulenspiegl, 'and stay!'

'Do not betray me,' she said.

Ulenspiegl ran out of the house and went to all the booths and taverns, whispering in the ear of all the sailors and troopers these words: 'The Spaniard's coming.'

All of them sped to the boat, getting ready in great haste all that was necessary for the battle, and they awaited the enemy. Ulenspiegl said to Lamme:

'Do you see that sweet-looking woman standing up there on the quay, with her black dress broidered with scarlet, and hiding her face in her white hood?'

'It's all one to me,' replied Lamme. 'I'm cold, I want to sleep.'

And he covered his head with his *opperst-kleed*. And in this way he was like a deaf man.

Ulenspiegl then recognized the woman and called to her from the ship:

'Do you want to follow us?'

'To the grave,' she said, 'but I cannot. . .'

'You will do well,' said Ulenspiegl. 'Think of this, however: when the nightingale stays in the forest it is happy and sings; but if it leaves and risks its little wings in the breezes of the open sea, it breaks them and dies.'

'I have sung at home,' she said, 'and I shall sing outside if I can.' Then, coming close to the ship: 'Take this balm for you and your friend who sleeps when he should be watching,' she said.

'Lamme! Lamme! God keep you from all ill; come back safe.'

And she uncovered her face.

'My wife, my wife!' cried Lamme.

And he tried to jump on the ice.

'Your faithful wife!' she said.

And she ran off swiftly.

Lamme wanted to jump on the ice but he was stopped by a trooper, who held him back by his *opperst-kleed*. He called, wept, begged them to let him go. But the provost said to him:

'You'll be hung if you leave the ship.'

Lamme wanted to throw himself on the ice right away, but an old Beggar held him back, saying:

'The floor's damp, you might get your feet wet.'

And Lamme fell on his behind, weeping and ceaselessly saying:

'My wife, my wife! Let me go to my wife!'

'You shall see her again,' said Ulenspiegl. 'She loves you, but she loves God more.'

'The rabid she-devil,' cried Lamme. 'If she loves God more than her man, why does she show herself to me so sweet and desirable? And if she loves me, why does she leave me?'

'Can you see clearly in a deep well?' asked Ulenspiegl.

'La!' said Lamme, 'I shall die soon.'

And he stayed up on deck, pale and distraught. In the meantime came Simonen Bol's men, with much artillery.

They fired at the ship, which returned their fire. And their cannon-balls broke the ice all about the vessel. Towards evening a warm rain fell. The wind blowing in from the west, the sea rose under the ice and lifted it up in huge blocks, which were seen to rise and fall and crash against each other, not without danger for the ship; which, when dawn broke through the nocturnal clouds, opened its canvas wings like a bird of freedom and sailed out to the open sea.

There it joined up with the fleet of Messire de Lumey de la Marck, Admiral of Holland and Zeeland and Chief and Captain-General, and, as such, bearing a lantern on the top-most mast of his ship.

'Look at him well, my boy,' said Ulenspiegl. 'He won't spare you at all if you want to quit the ship by force. Do you hear his voice booming like thunder? See how broad he is, and strong, with his great height! Look at his long hands with the hooked finger-nails! See his round eyes, eagle's eyes, and cold; and his long pointed beard that he will let grow until he has hanged all the monks and priests to avenge the deaths of the two counts. See how terrible and cruel he is; he'll string you up to the short-arm, if you continue to whine and cry eternally: "My wife!"'

'My boy,' said Lamme, 'the man who speaks of a rope for his neighbour has already a hempen ruff about his own neck.'

'You shall wear it first. Such is my friendly wish,' said Ulenspiegl.

'I shall see you at the gallows stick your venomous tongue a league's length out of your beak,' answered Lamme.

And they both jested.

That day the vessel of Tres-Long captured a Biscay boat, loaded with mercury, gold, powder, wines and spices. And the boat was drained of its marrow—men and booty—like a beef-bone in the mouth of a lion.

It was at this time also that the duke commanded the imposition of cruel and abominable taxes on the Netherlands, forcing all the inhabitants who sold real or personal estate to pay one thousand florins for every ten thousand they made. And that tax was permanent. All the merchants and salesmen whatsoever had to pay the king a tenth of their sale price, and it was said among the people that of merchandise sold ten times in one week the king had all.

And thus commerce and industry went towards ruin and death.

And the Beggars captured Briele, a maritime stronghold that was christened 'The Orchard of Freedom.'

2 IN THE FIRST DAYS of May, as the ship sailed proudly on the sea under a clear sky, Ulenspiegl sang:

> 'The ashes beat upon my heart.
> The butchers came, they smote
> With dagger, fire, might and sword.
> They paid the vilest espionage.
> Where once mild virtues were, Love and Faith,
> They set Denunciation and Distrust.
> Let us smite hard the butchers, then,
> And beat the drums of war!
>
> Up with the Beggars! Beat the drums!
> Briele now is in our hands,
> Flushing too, of Scheldt the key;
> Our God is good, Camp-Veere is ours
> Where Zeeland kept her cannon!
> We now have powder, bullets, balls;
> Bullets of iron, bullets of lead.
> Our God is with us, who then against?
>
> Beat the drums of war and glory!
> Up with the Beggars! Beat the drums!
> The sword is drawn, lift up our hearts,
> Strengthen our arms, the sword is drawn.
> Away with the tenth tithe, the total ruin,
> Death to the butcher; rope for the spoiler,
> For a perjuring king rebellious folk.

The sword is drawn now for our rights,
And for our homes, our wives and children.
The sword is drawn now, beat the drums!

Our hearts are high, and strong our arms.
Away with the tenth tithe; the infamous pardon.
Beat the drums of war, beat the drums!'

'Yes, good pals and friends,' said Ulenspiegl; 'yes, they have set up in Antwerp, before the Town Hall, a brilliant scaffold covered with red cloth; the duke is seated there like a king upon his throne, surrounded by his flunkies and troopers. Wishing to smile benevolently, he makes a sour grimace. Beat the drums of war!

'He has granted a pardon; silence, now; his gilded cuirass shines in the sun; the high provost sits on horseback beside the dais; here comes the herald with his drummers; he reads: It is a pardon for all those who have not sinned; the others will be cruelly punished.

'Hearken, good comrades, he reads the edict that orders, with the same penalties as for rebellion, the payment of tenth and twentieth tithes.'

And Ulenspiegl sang:

'Hear you the people's voice, oh Duke,
The mighty roar? It is the rising sea
When the raging storm rides high.
Enough of money, enough of blood,
Enough of ruins! Beat the drums!
The sword is drawn now. Beat the mourning drums!

It's the nail that claws the bleeding wound,
Theft after murder. And must you then
Mix all our gold with all our blood to drink?
We walked in duty, faithful, true
To His Royal Majesty. He having perjured,
We now are freed from our oaths. Beat the drums of war!

Duke of Alba, duke of the blood,
See these booths and shops shut down,
See these brewers, bakers, grocers,
Refusing to sell so as not to pay.
Who now salutes you as you pass by?
No man! Feel you not, like a pestilent mist,
The Hate and Scorn that cover you round?

The lovely land of Flanders
And Brabant's happy land
Are sad as any graveyard now,
There, where Freedom once did reign,
And viols sang and fifes were played,
Is naught but Silence now, and Death.
Beat the drums of war!

Instead of happy drinkers' faces
And those of singing lovers,
Only pale faces now are seen:
The faces of those who await, resigned,
The blow from the sword of Injustice.
Beat the drums of war!

No more in taverns is there heard
The happy clink of steins,
Nor the clear voices of bands of girls
That singing go along the streets.
And Brabant, Flanders, joyous lands,
Have now become the lands of tears.
Beat the mourning drums!

Land of our fathers, sufferer beloved,
Bend not your brow to the murderer's feet.
Laborious bees, rush in your swarms
Upon the idle Spanish drones.
The bodies, buried alive, of women and girls
Cry out to Christ for vengeance!

Wander by night in the fields, poor souls;
Cry unto God! The arm trembles to strike,
The sword is drawn now, Duke; we'll rip your guts,
And slap them in your face.
Beat the drums! The sword is drawn.
Beat the drums! Up with the Beggars!'

And all the sailors and troopers of Ulenspiegl's ship, and also those
of the other ships, likewise sang:

'The sword is drawn. Up with the Beggars!'

And their voices boomed like the thunder of deliverance.

IT WAS THE MONTH of January, the cruel month that freezes
the calf in the womb of the cow. It had snowed, and on top of
that had come the frost. With birdlime the boys snared the
swallows which sought meagre fare in the hardened snow and brought
their catches home. Against the grey and clear sky, the skeletons of
the trees were silhouetted immobile; their branches were covered with
snowy cushions, like those that covered the cottages and the wall-
copings whereon could be seen the foot-prints of cats that were also
hunting the sparrows in the snow. As far as one could see, the meadows
were hidden under the wonderful fleece which kept the earth warm
from the bitter winter cold. The smoke from the houses and cottages
rose darkly to the sky, and not a sound was heard.

And Katheline and Nele were alone in their home; and Katheline,
wagging her head, said:

'Hanske, my heart is drawn to you. You must return the seven hundred carolus to Ulenspiegl, Soetkin's son. If you are in need, come just
the same, that I may see your shining face. Take away the fire, the
head is burning. La! Where are your snowy kisses? Where is your icy
body, Hans, my beloved?'

And she stood by the window. Suddenly there passed, at a great
gallop, a *voet-looper*, a runner with bells at his girdle, crying:

'Here comes the bailiff, the high bailiff of Damme!'

And he ran thus, till he had reached the Town Hall, to call forth the
burgomasters and sheriffs to assembly.

And, in the heavy silence, Nele heard two trumpets sound. All the
Damme folk came to their doors, for they thought it was His Royal
Majesty who was being announced with such fanfares.

And Katheline also went to her door with Nele. Afar they saw a band
of shining horsemen and, riding before them, a person covered with
an *opperst-kleed* of black velvet, bordered with sable, and wearing a

392

doublet of velvet, broidered with fine gold, and calf-skin boots, furred with sable. And they knew him for the high bailiff.

Behind him rode young lords who, despite the command of his late Imperial Majesty, wore on their velvet accoutrement embroideries, trimmings, bands, edgings of gold, silver and silk. And their *opperst-kleederen*, under their outer garments, were edged with fur like those of the bailiff. They rode along gaily, shaking in the wind the long ostrich feathers pinned in their gold-garnished, buttoned bonnets.

They seemed all to be good friends and companions of the high bailiff, notably a lord with a sour face, dressed in green velvet ornamented with gold, whose cloak was of black velvet as was also his bonnet, decked with long plumes. And he had a nose the shape of a vulture's beak, a thin mouth, red hair, pale face and haughty bearing.

As the band of these lords passed in front of the house of Katheline, she suddenly rushed out at the bridle of the pale lord's horse, and with wild joy cried:

'Hans, my beloved, I knew it, you've returned. You are handsome, dressed this way, all in velvet and all in gold like a sun on the snow! Have you brought me the seven hundred carolus? Shall I hear you cry again like the sea-eagle?'

The bailiff stopped the band of gentlemen, and the pale lord said:

'What does this beggar want with me?'

But Katheline, still holding on to the bridle:

'Do not go away again,' said she. 'I have wept so much for you. Sweet nights, my beloved, snowy kisses, icy body. The child is here!'

And she pointed Nele out to him, who stood looking angry, for he had lifted his whip over Katheline; but Katheline, weeping:

'Ah,' said she, 'have you no memory of it? Have pity on your servant. Take her with you where you will. Take away the fire, Hans, mercy!'

'Get out of my way!' said he.

And he drove his horse so hard that Katheline, letting the bridle go, fell to the ground; and the horse stepped on her and made a bleeding wound on her brow.

The bailiff then said to the pale lord:

'Sir, do you know this woman?'

'I do not know her,' said he, 'she's doubtless some mad-woman.'

But Nele, having helped Katheline to her feet:

'If this woman is mad, I am not, my lord, and may I die here of this snow which I eat,' and here she took some snow with her fingers, 'if that man has not known my mother, if he has not borrowed all her money, if he did not kill Claes's dog so as to take from the well-wall of our house the seven hundred carolus belonging to the poor dead man.'

393

'Hans, my sweet,' wept Katheline, bleeding, and on her knees, 'Hans, my beloved, give me the kiss of peace. See the blood flowing; the soul has made a hole and would out. I shall soon be dead; do not leave me.' Then, speaking in a lower voice: 'Long ago you killed your companion through jealousy, by the dyke.' And she pointed her finger in the direction of Dudzeele. 'You loved me well in those days.'

And she placed her arms about the gentleman's knee and kissed his boot.

'Who is this murdered man?' asked the bailiff.

'I do not know, my lord,' said he. 'We should have no concern with the talk of this beggar, let us be on our way.'

The populace assembled about them; high and low burghers, workers and peasants, taking the part of Katheline, cried out:

'Justice, my lord bailiff, justice!'

And the bailiff said to Nele:

'Who is this slain man? Speak according to God and the truth.'

Nele spoke, and said, as she pointed to the pale gentleman:

'That man came every Saturday in the *keet* to see my mother and take her money from her! He killed one of his friends named Hilbert in the field of Servaes Van der Vichte, not through love, as this innocent mad one thinks, but to have for himself all the seven hundred carolus.'

And Nele told of Katheline's loves and of what she heard when she was hidden that night behind the dyke which runs through the field of Servaes Van der Vichte.

'Nele is wicked,' said Katheline. 'She speaks harshly to Hans, her father.'

'I swear that he screamed like a sea-eagle to announce his presence,' said Nele.

'You lie,' said the gentleman.

'Oh, no!' said Nele, 'and my lord the bailiff and all these noble lords here present can well see that. You are pale, not from hunger, but from fright. How comes it that your face no longer shines? Have you lost the magic mixture with which you rubbed it so that it would shine like the waves in summer when it thunders? But, cursed sorcerer, you shall be burned before the doors of the Town Hall. You it was who caused the death of Soetkin, you who reduced her orphan son to poverty. You are no doubt a nobleman, you came to us burghers, to bring money once to my mother and all the other times to take it from her.'

'Hans,' said Katheline, 'will you take me again to the Sabbath and rub me again with balm? Do not listen to Nele, she is wicked; do you

394

see the blood? The soul has made a hole and would out. I shall soon be dead, and I shall go to limbo where it does not burn.'

'Be silent, mad witch, I do not know you,' said the gentleman, 'and I know not what you mean.'

'And yet,' said Nele, 'you are the man who came with a friend, whom you wanted to give as husband to me; you know that I would have none of him; what did he do, your friend Hilbert, what did he do with his eyes after I had scratched them out with my nails?'

'Nele is wicked,' said Katheline, 'do not believe her, Hans, my sweet. She is angry with Hilbert, who wanted to take her by force, but he won't be able to do that any more; the worms have eaten him; and Hilbert was ugly, Hans, my sweet. You alone are beautiful; Nele is wicked.'

At this the bailiff said:

'Women, go in peace.'

But Katheline would not leave the place where her friend was. And she had to be taken by force to her house.

And all the people assembled there cried:

'Justice, my lord, justice!'

The sergeants of the town having come up on hearing the noise, the bailiff told them to stay, and said to the lords and gentlemen:

'My Lords and Sirs; notwithstanding all the privileges protecting the illustrious order of nobility in the Land of Flanders, I must, on the accusations and especially that of witchcraft which have been made against Messire Joos Damman, have him arrested until he can be judged according to the laws and ordinances of the Empire. Give up your sword, Messire Joos.'

'My Lord Bailiff,' said Joos Damman, with great haughtiness and aristocratic pride, 'in having me arrested you are transgressing the law of Flanders, for you are not a judge. Yet you know that it is not permitted to arrest without a judge's warrant any except coiners, highway robbers, firebrands, ravishers of women, men at arms deserting their captain, magicians making use of venom to poison water-sources, monks and nuns escaped from their convent, and the banished. How now, my good sirs and lords, defend me!'

Several seeming about to obey him, the bailiff said:

'My Lords and Sirs, as the representative here of our king, count, and lord, to whom is reserved the decision of difficult cases, I summon you and command you, under the penalty of being declared rebels, to replace your swords in their sheaths.'

The gentlemen having obeyed, and Messire Joos Damman still hesitating, the people cried out:

'Justice, my lord, justice! make him give up his sword.'

This he then did in spite of himself and, dismounting from his horse, he was led to the town prison by the two sergeants.

Nevertheless he was not shut up in the underground cells, but in a room with barred windows where, by paying, he had a fire, a good bed, and good nourishment—half of which the jailer took.

4 THE FOLLOWING DAY the bailiff, the two criminal clerks, two sheriffs and a surgeon-barber went to Dudzeele to see if they could find in the field of Servaes Van der Vichte the body of a man lying by the dyke that went through the field. Nele had said to Katheline: 'Hans, your darling, asks for the hand cut from Hilbert; to-night he'll scream like a sea-eagle, enter into the cottage and bring you the seven hundred carolus.'

Katheline had answered: 'I will cut it off.' And indeed she took a knife and went away, accompanied by Nele and followed by the officers of justice.

She walked quickly and proudly with Nele, whose sweet face had been made ruddy by the keen air.

The officers of justice, old and coughing, followed on, frozen; and they were all like dark shadows on the white plain; and Nele carried a spade.

When they had arrived in the field of Servaes Van der Vichte and at the dyke, Katheline, walking straight to the middle of it, said, pointing to the meadow on her right: 'Hans, you did not know that I was hidden there, quivering at the noise of the swords. And Hilbert cried: "This iron is cold." Hilbert was ugly; Hans is beautiful. You shall have his hand; leave me alone.'

Then she descended on the left side, knelt down in the snow and cried three times in the air to call forth the spirit.

Nele then gave her the spade, over which Katheline made three signs of the cross; then she traced on the ice the shape of a coffin and three reversed crosses, one on the east side, one on the west, and one on the north; and she said: 'Three is Mars by Saturn, and three is discovery under Venus, the bright star.' She then traced, about the coffin she had drawn, a large circle, saying the while: 'Begone, evil demon who guards the body.' Then, falling on her knees in prayer: 'Devil friend, Hilbert,' she said, 'Hans, my master and my lord, commands me to come here and cut off your hand, which I am to bring to him. I owe him obedience; do not make the earth-fire leap out against me because I disturb your noble grave; and pardon me through God and the Saints.'

396

Then she broke the ice within the tracing of the coffin. She came to damp turf, then to sand; and my lord the bailiff, his officers, Nele, and Katheline, saw the corpse of a young man, chalky-white because of the soil. He was dressed in a doublet of grey cloth, with a cloak of the same; his sword was lying beside him. At his belt he had a pouch of chain-mail, and there was a large poignard sticking out from under his heart; there were blood-stains on the cloak and the doublet; and the blood had flowed under his back. And the man was young.

Katheline cut off his hand and placed it in her pouch. This the bailiff let her do and then commanded her to strip the body of all its marks and vestments. Katheline having enquired if Hans had commanded this, the bailiff replied that he only acted on his orders. And Katheline then did all that they asked her to.

When the corpse was stripped it was seen to be dry as wood and not rotted; and the bailiff and the officers went off after having had it covered with sand; and the sergeants carried the things taken from the body.

Passing before the town prison, the bailiff said to Katheline that Hans awaited her there; and she entered gaily.

Nele tried to stop her, and Katheline kept on saying: 'I want to see Hans, my lord.'

And Nele wept on the threshold, knowing that Katheline was arrested as a witch for the conjurations and signs she had made in the snow.

And they said in Damme that there would be no pardon for her.

And Katheline was placed in the western underground cell of the prison.

5 THE FOLLOWING DAY, the wind blowing in from Brabant, the snow melted and the meadows were flooded. And the bell known as the *borgstorm* called the judges to the *Vierschare* court in the pent-house, because of the dampness of the grassy banks.

And the populace surrounded the court.

Joos Damman was brought in free from all bonds, in his aristocratic attire; Katheline was also brought in with her hands bound before her and dressed in a grey linen dress—the prison garment.

Joos Damman, being questioned, avowed that he had killed his friend Hilbert in single combat with the sword. When they said to him: 'He was struck with a poignard,' Joos Damman replied: 'I struck at him on the ground because he was a long time dying. I willingly confess to this murder, being under the protection of the Flemish laws, which forbids the prosecution of a murderer after ten years.'

The bailiff, speaking to him:

'Are you not a sorcerer?' said he.

'No,' replied Damman.

'Prove it,' said the bailiff.

'That I will do at the right time and place,' said Joos Damman, 'but it does not please me to do it now.'

The bailiff questioned Katheline, then; she did not hear him and kept looking at Hans:

'You are my green lord, beautiful as the sun. Take away the fire, my sweet!'

Nele then, speaking for Katheline, said:

'She cannot confess more than what you already know, my lord and sirs; she is not a witch, but only out of her wits.'

The bailiff then spoke and said:

'A witch is one who by diabolic means knowingly employed endeavours to arrive at a given end. Now these two, man and woman, are sorcerers in intent and deed; he for having given the ointment of the Sabbath and made his face to shine like Lucifer's, in order to obtain money and the satisfaction of his lechery; she for having submitted to him, taking him for a devil and abandoning herself to his desires; the one the worker of witchcrafts, the other his manifest accomplice. We must therefore have no mercy, and I must say this to you, for I notice that the sheriffs and the people are too indulgent towards the woman. She has not, it is true, killed nor stolen, nor cast a spell on man or beast, nor healed any sickness by extraordinary remedies, but only by known herbs and simples, as an honest and Christian healer; but she would have given her daughter to the devil, and if the girl in her youth had not resisted with such a frank and valiant bravery, she would have been ceded to Hilbert and become a witch like this one. Therefore I demand of these gentlemen of the court if they are not of the opinion that these should both be put to the torture?'

The sheriffs did not reply, showing clearly that this was not their wish as far as Katheline was concerned.

The bailiff then said, continuing his discourse:

'Like you, I too am moved by her to pity and compassion, but this witless sorceress, obeying a devil so well, might she not, if her lecherous co-defendant had so bidden her, have cut off the head of her daughter with a sickle, even as Catherine Daru, in the land of France, did to her two daughters on the invitation of the devil? Might she not have, if her dark husband had so commanded her, made cattle die; turned the butter in the churn by throwing sugar in it; assisted bodily at all the homages to the devil, dances, abominations, and copulations of sor-

398

cerers? Might she not eat human flesh, kill children to make pasties of them to sell, as did a pastry-cook in Paris; cut off the thighs of hanged men and carry them off in order to dig her teeth into them and be thus an infamous robber and sacrilegious person? And I ask the court that, in order to find out if Katheline and Joos Damman have not committed other crimes than those already known and discovered, they both be put to the torture. Joos Damman refusing to confess anything more than the murder, and Katheline not having told all, the laws of the empire command us to proceed as I have indicated to you.'

And the sheriffs pronounced the sentence of torture for Friday, which was the day after the following day.

And Nele cried: 'Pardon, my lords!' and the people cried with her. But in vain.

And Katheline, looking at Joos Damman, said:

'I have the hand of Hilbert, come and get it to-night, my beloved.'

And they were taken back to prison.

There, by order of the court, the jailer was commanded to give each of them two guardians who would beat them every time they tried to fall asleep; but Katheline's two guardians let her sleep at night, and those of Joos Damman beat him cruelly each time he closed his eyes or even lowered his head.

They had nothing to eat all day Wednesday, that night, and all day Thursday until evening, when they were given meat with salt and saltpetre to eat, and salt water, likewise saltpetered, to drink. That was the beginning of their torture. And in the morning, when they were crying with thirst, the sergeants led them to the torture chamber.

There they were seated facing each other and tied on benches covered with knotted ropes that made them suffer sorely.

And they had to drink, each one of them, a glass of salt and saltpetered water.

Joos Damman began to sleep on the bench and the sergeants struck him.

And Katheline said:

'Do not strike him, sirs, you will break his poor body. He only committed one crime, through love, when he killed Hilbert. I'm thirsty, and you also, Hans, my beloved. Give him a drink first. Water! Water! My body's burning. Save him; I shall soon die for him. Drink!'

Joos said to her:

'Ugly sorceress, die, and burst like a bitch. Throw her to the flames, master judges. I thirst!'

The clerks wrote down all his words.

The bailiff then said to him:

'Have you nothing to confess?'

'I have nothing to say,' replied Damman; 'you know all.'

'Since,' said the bailiff, 'he persists in his denials, he shall remain on that bench and these ropes until a new and complete confession comes from him, and he shall be left thirsting and prevented from sleeping.'

'I shall stay,' said Joos Damman, 'and I shall take my pleasure in watching that witch suffer on her bench. How do you find the marriage-bed, my love?'

And Katheline answered, groaning:

'Cold arms and warm heart, Hans, my beloved. I thirst, the head burns!'

'And you, woman,' said the bailiff, 'have you nothing more to say?'

'I hear,' she said, 'the chariot of death and the dry knocking of bones. I thirst! And it bears me away to a great stream where there is water —fresh water, and clear; but this water is of fire. Hans my love, untie these ropes about me. Yes, I am in purgatory, and I see on high my Lord Jesus in His paradise, and Madame the Virgin, so compassionate. Oh, our Dear Lady, give me a drop of water; do not bite alone into these lovely fruits.'

'That woman is smitten with cruel madness,' said one of the sheriffs. 'She must be taken from the torture bench.'

'She is not any more mad than I am,' said Joos Damman; 'it's pure play-acting and comedy.' Then, with a menacing voice: 'I shall send you to the flames,' said he to Katheline, 'you who act so well the distraught one.'

And, gnashing his teeth, he laughed at his cruel lie.

'I thirst,' said Katheline, 'have mercy, I thirst! Hans, my beloved, give me a drink. How white your face is! Let me go to him, master judges.' And, opening her mouth wide: 'Yes, yes, they are now placing the fire in my breast, and the devils tie me to this cruel bed. Hans, take your sword and kill them, you are so mighty. Water, to drink! To drink!'

'Burst, witch,' said Joos Damman. 'She should have a gag stuck in her mouth to prevent her, a peasant, from setting herself up against a noble-man.'

To these words a sheriff, enemy of the nobility, replied:

'Sir bailiff, it is contrary to the laws and customs of the empire to place gags in the mouths of those who are being questioned, for they are here to tell the truth, so that we may judge them after what they say. It is not permitted except when the accused, having been con-demned, might speak to the people from the scaffold, moving them and arousing popular feelings.'

'I thirst,' said Katheline, 'give me a drink, Hans, my sweet.'

400

'Ah, you suffer,' said he, 'cursed witch, sole cause of all the torments I am enduring; but in this torture chamber you shall submit to the torture of the candle, the *strappado,* the pieces of wood under the nails of your fingers and toes. They shall make you straddle a coffin whose raised lid shall be sharpened like a knife, and you shall confess that you are not mad but a nasty witch whom Satan has ordered to do ill to noblemen. A drink!'

'Hans, my beloved,' said Katheline, 'do not be angry with your servant! I suffer a thousand pains for you, my lord. Spare him, master judges. Give him to drink from a full goblet and save but a drop for me. Hans, is it not yet the hour of the sea-eagle?'

The bailiff then said to Joos Damman:

'When you killed Hilbert, what was the motive for the combat?'

'It was,' said Joos, 'for a girl of Heyst whom we both wanted.'

'A girl of Heyst,' cried Katheline, trying with all her strength to rise from her bench. 'You deceived me for another, traitor-devil! Did you know that I was listening to you behind the dyke when you said that you wanted to have all the money which belonged to Claes? No doubt to go and spend it with her in drinking and revelling! La! and I who would have given you my blood if gold could have been made out of it! And all for another! Be accursed!'

But suddenly weeping, and trying to turn about on her torture bench:

'No, Hans, say that you still love your poor servant, and I will scratch the earth with my fingers to find you a treasure; yes, there is one; and I shall go with a divining-rod that bends downwards where there is metal; and I shall find it and bring it to you; kiss me, sweet, and you shall be rich; and we shall eat meat and drink beer every day. Yes, yes, these people also drink beer, cool beer and foamy. Oh, sirs, give me but a drop, I am on fire; Hans, I know well where there are divining-rods; but you must wait for Spring.'

'Be silent, witch,' said Joos Damman, 'I know you not. You have mistaken me for Hilbert; it was he who came to see you. With your evil mind you called him Hans. Know that I am not called Hans, but Joos; we were the same height, Hilbert and I; I know you not; it was Hilbert, no doubt, who stole the seven hundred carolus; a drink; my father will pay a hundred florins for a little goblet of water; but I do not know that woman.'

'My lord and sirs,' exclaimed Katheline, 'he says he knows me not, but I know him well, and know that he has a hairy mark on his back, brown and large as a bean. Ah! you loved a girl of Heyst! Does a real lover blush for his dear? Hans, am I no longer lovely?'

'Lovely!' said he. 'You have a face like a medlar and a body like a

402

bundle of faggots. Look at the trumpery thing who would like to be loved by noblemen! A drink!'

'You did not speak this way, Hans, my gentle lord, when I was sixteen years younger than I am now,' she said. Then, striking her head and breast: 'It's the fire that's there,' she said, 'which dried my heart and my face. Do you reproach me for it. Do you remember when we ate salt, the better to drink, you said? Now the salt is within us, my beloved, and my lord the bailiff drinks Romagna wine. We want no wine; give us water. It runs through the grass, the trickling streamlet from the clear spring; the good water's cold. No, it's hot. It's water from hell.' And Katheline wept and said: 'I never harmed anyone and everybody casts me into the flames. A drink! They give water to stray dogs. I am a Christian, give me a drink. I never harmed anyone. A drink!'

A sheriff then spoke and said:

'That witch is only mad in that which concerns the fire that burns in her head; she is sane in other things, since she helped us with a lucid mind to discover the remains of the defunct. If the hairy mark is found on the body of Joos Damman, that sign is sufficient to establish his identity with the devil Hans, by whom Katheline was deprived of her wits. Executioner, show us the mark.'

The executioner, uncovering the neck and shoulder, showed the brown and hairy mark.

'Ah!' said Katheline, 'how white your skin is! One might say these were a girl's shoulders. You are beautiful, Hans, my beloved. A drink!'

The executioner then stuck a long needle in the mark. But no blood came.

And the sheriffs said among themselves:

'He's a devil who has killed Joos Damman and taken his face in order to deceive the poor world with more surety.'

And the bailiff and the sheriffs took fright.

'He's a devil and there's witchcraft in it all.'

And Joos Damman said:

'You know that this is no witchcraft and that there are fleshy excrescences which can be pricked without any blood coming from them. If Hilbert took the money from that witch, for she is a witch, having confessed to sleeping with the devil, he could only do it with the good and proper will of that foul one, and was thus, noble man, paid for his caresses, as the wenches are, every day. Are there not in this world wild fellows who, like the wild women, make their companions pay for their strength and beauty?'

The sheriffs said among themselves:

403

'Do you see his diabolic assurance? His hairy mark did not bleed; being an assassin, devil, magician, he wants to pass as a simple duellist, throwing all his other crimes on the devil-friend whom he killed in body but not in soul. . . And see how pale his face is! So appear all devils, red in hell, pale on earth, for they have not the fire of life which makes the visage ruddy, and they are ashes within. We must replace him in the flames so that he may be red and burn.'

Katheline then said:

'Yes, he is a devil, but a good devil, a kind devil. And my Lord James, his patron saint, allowed him to come from hell. He prays my Lord Jesus for him every day. He shall only have seven thousand years of purgatory. Madame the Virgin wishes it so but Satan opposes it. Madame has her way, just the same. Will you oppose her? If you consider him well, you will see that he has kept nothing of his devilish state, save the cold body, and also the face that shines as in August the waves do when there is going to be a thunderstorm.'

And Joos Damman said:

'Be silent, witch, you are having me burned.' Then, speaking to the bailiff and the sheriffs:

'Look at me, I am not a devil; I have flesh and bones, blood and water. I eat and drink, digest and expel like you; my skin is like unto yours and my foot also; executioner, take off my boots, for I cannot budge with my feet tied.'

The executioner did so, not without fear.

'Look,' said Joos, showing his white feet; 'are these cloven feet, devil's feet? As for my pallor, is there none among you as pale as I am? I see more than three in your midst. But the sinner is not I, but that ugly witch and her wicked, accusing daughter. Where did she get that money she loaned to Hilbert; where did these florins come from that she gave him? Was it not the devil who paid her to accuse, and send to their deaths, noble and innocent men? It is of these two women that you must ask who cut the dog's throat, who dug the hole and went off leaving it empty, to hide in another place, no doubt, the stolen treasure. Soetkin, the widow-woman, had no confidence in me, not having known me, but in these two whom she saw daily. They are the ones who stole what belonged to the Emperor.'

The clerk wrote, and the bailiff said to Katheline:

'Woman, have you nothing to say in your defence?'

Katheline, looking at Joos Damman, said most lovingly:

'It's the hour of the sea-eagle. I have Hilbert's hand, Hans, my beloved. They said you would return to me the seven hundred carolus.

404

Take away the fire! Take away the fire!' she then cried out. 'A drink! A drink! The head burns! God and his angels are eating apples in heaven.'

And she lost consciousness.

'Untie her from the torture bench,' said the bailiff.

The executioner and his helpers obeyed. She was seen staggering on swollen feet, for the executioner had drawn the ropes too tightly.

'Give her something to drink,' said the bailiff.

They gave her cold water, which she drank down avidly, holding the goblet in her teeth as a dog does a bone, and would not let it go. Then they gave her some more water, which she wanted to carry over to Joos Damman; but the executioner took the goblet from her hands. And she fell down asleep, like a mass of lead.

Joos Damman then cried out furiously:

'I, too, am thirsty and sleepy. Why do you give her a drink? Why do you allow her to sleep?'

'She is weak, a woman, and witless,' replied the bailiff.

'Her madness is feigned,' said Joos Damman, 'she is a witch. I want to drink, I want to sleep!'

And he closed his eyes, but the *knechts* of the executioner slapped him in the face.

'Give me a knife,' he shouted, 'that I may cut these rustics in pieces. I am a nobleman and have never been slapped in the face. Water; let me sleep; I'm innocent. I did not take the seven hundred carolus, it was Hilbert. A drink! I have never indulged in witchcraft nor incantations. I am innocent, leave me alone. A drink!'

The bailiff then said:

'What have you been doing since you left Katheline?'

'I know not Katheline, and I never left her,' said he. 'You are questioning me about things outside the case. I do not have to answer you. A drink; let me sleep, I tell you that it was Hilbert who did everything.'

'Unbind him,' said the bailiff. 'Take him back to the prison. But let him thirst and do not allow him to sleep until he has confessed his witchcrafts and incantations.'

And this was for Damman a cruel torture. He screamed in his prison: 'A drink! A drink!' so loudly that all the people heard him; but with no pity. And when he dozed off to sleep and his keepers slapped his face, he was like a tiger and shouted:

'I am a nobleman, and will kill you, peasants. I shall go to the king, our chief. A drink!'

But he confessed nothing and they left him alone.

405

6 THEY WERE THEN in the month of May. The lime-tree was green, and green also were the grassy banks whereon sat the judges.

Nele was called as a witness. On that day the sentence was to be pronounced. And the people, men, women, burghers and workers, all stood about the court; and the sun shone bright.

Katheline and Joos Damman were brought before the court; and Damman seemed more pallid because of the torture of thirst and the sleepless nights he had spent.

Katheline, who could not stand up on her shaking legs, pointed to the sun, saying:

'Take away the fire, the head burns!'

And she looked on Joos Damman with a tender love.

And he looked at her with hate and scorn.

And the lords and gentlemen, his friends, having been called to Damme, were all present before the court as witnesses.

The bailiff then spoke and said:

'Nele, the daughter who defends her mother Katheline with such a great and brave affection, has found in a stitched-up pocket in the mother's coat—her holiday coat—a letter signed Joos Damman. Among the things taken from the corpse of Hilbert Ryvish, I found in the pouch of the defunct another letter addressed by the said Joos Damman, the accused now present before us. I have kept both of these letters so that at the right moment, which has come, you might be able to judge the obstinacy of that man and absolve or condemn him according to law and justice. Here is the parchment found in the pouch; I have not touched it and know not whether it is legible or not.'

The judges were then greatly perplexed.

The bailiff tried to undo the parchment, rolled up in a ball, but in vain, and Joos Damman laughed.

A sheriff said:

'Place the ball in water and then set it before the fire. If there is any mysterious adhesion, the fire and the water will melt it.'

The water was brought in and the executioner lighted a great fire of logs in the field; the blue smoke rose up to the clear sky through the verdurous branches of the lime-tree of justice.

'Do not put that letter in the basin,' said a sheriff, 'for if it is written with sal ammoniac dipped in water, you will efface the writing.'

'No,' said the surgeon, who was there, 'the writing will not be effaced; the water will only soften the glue that keeps this magic ball from opening.'

The parchment was dipped in water, and, having softened, was straightened out.

406

'Now,' said the surgeon, 'place it before the fire.'

'Yes, yes,' said Nele, 'place the paper before the fire; Messire Surgeon is on the path of the truth, for the murderer pales and his legs tremble.'

At this, Messire Joos Damman said:

'I neither grow pale nor tremble, common little vixen striving for the death of a nobleman; you shall not succeed; that parchment must be rotten after sixteen years of lying in the earth.'

'The parchment is not rotten,' said the sheriff. 'The pouch was lined with silk; silk does not rot away in the earth, and the worms have not eaten through the parchment.'

The parchment was placed before the fire.

'My lord the bailiff, my lord the bailiff,' said Nele, 'the ink has become apparent here before the fire; order the letter to be read.'

As the surgeon was about to read it, Messire Joos Damman tried to thrust out his arm to seize the parchment; but Nele, fleet as the wind, rushed at his arm and said:

'You shall not touch it, for thereon is written your death or the death of Katheline. If your heart is bleeding now, murderer, ours have bled for fifteen years; fifteen years; fifteen years that Katheline has suf-fered; fifteen years since she has had her brain burning in her head for you; fifteen years since Soetkin died as a result of the torture; fifteen years that we have been in want, ragged and living in misery, but proudly. Read the paper, read the paper! The judges are God on earth, for they are justice. Read the paper!'

'Read the paper!' shouted the men and women who wept. 'Nele is honest! Read the paper! Katheline is not a witch!'

And the clerk read:

'To Hilbert, son of Willem Ryvish, Esquire, Joos Damman, Esquire, greeting.

'Fortunate friend, lose your money no more in gambling, dicing and other great miseries. I am going to tell you how to win it at one sure sweep. Let us make ourselves into devils, nice devils, loved by women and girls. Let us take the lovely and the rich, leaving aside the ugly and the poor; let them pay for their pleasure. I acquired at this game, five thousand rixdaelders in six months in Germany. The women will give their coats and shirts to their man when they love him; flee the misers with pinched noses who take their time in paying for their pleasure. For yourself, and in order to appear as a handsome and true devil in-cubus, if they accept you for the night, announce your coming with the cry of a night-bird. And to make yourself a real devil's face, a terrifying devil, rub phosphorus on your visage, which shines when it is damp. The odour is bad, but they think that it is the odour of hell. Kill anything that gets in your way—man, woman or beast.

'We shall go soon together to Katheline's; a fine, debonair wench; her daughter Nele—a child of mine if Katheline was faithful—is sweet and comely; you shall take her without any trouble. I give her to you, for I have had enough of these bastards that one cannot recognize with assurance as one's own offspring. Her mother has already given me more than twenty-three carolus—all she had. But she has hidden a treasure, which is, if I am not a fool, the heritage of Claes, who was burned as a heretic at Damme—seven hundred carolus subject to confiscation; but the good King Philip, who had so many of his subjects burned in order to inherit from them, cannot get his claws on that sweet treasure. It will weigh more in my pouch than in his. Katheline will tell where it is; we shall then share it. Only you will let me have the biggest share for having discovered it.

'As for the women, being our gentle servants and loving slaves, we will take them to Germany. There we shall teach them to become female devils and she-demons, making all the rich burghers and noblemen enamoured of them; there we shall live, they and we, on love paid for with lovely rixdaelders, velvets, silks, gold, pearls and jewels; we shall thus be rich without fatigue and, unknown to the she-demons, beloved by the fairest, whom we shall also make pay. All women are fools and ninnies to the men who can light the fire of love which God set under their girdles. Nele and Katheline shall be more so than the others and, believing us to be devils, they will obey us in all things. You shall keep your first name and never give the name of your father, Ryvish. If the judge arrests the women, we can clear out without their knowing us or being able to denounce us. To the rescue, my trusty. Fortune smiles on the young, as was wont to say His Late Sacred Majesty Charles V, past master in the ways of love and war.'

And the clerk of the court stopped reading and said:

'Such is the letter, and it is signed: Joos Damman, Esquire.'

And the people shouted:

'Death to the murderer! Death to the sorcerer! To the stake with the robber of women's wits! To the gallows with the thief!'

The bailiff then said:

'People, be silent, so that we may judge this man in all liberty!'

Then, speaking to the sheriffs:

'I wish,' said he, 'to read the second letter found by Nele in the sewn-up pocket of Katheline's holiday coat; it runs as follows:

'Sweet witch, here is the receipt for a mixture sent to me by Lucifer's wife, herself. With the help of this mixture, you will be able to transport yourself to the sun, the moon and the stars; converse with the elemental spirits who carry the prayers of men to God; and traverse all the towns, burghs, rivers, and fields of the whole world. You must bruise together in equal doses: stramonium, solanum somniferum, jusquiame, opium, fresh hemp-tips, belladonna and datura.

'If you wish, we shall go to-night to the witches' Sabbath; but you must love me more and not be so miserly as you were the other evening when you refused me ten florins, saying that you did not have them. I know that you have a hidden treasure and do not want to tell me of it. Do you not love me any more, my sweetheart?

'Your cold devil,

'Hanske'

'Death to the sorcerer!' shouted the populace.

The bailiff said:

'We must compare the two handwritings.'

This being done, they were found to be alike.

The bailiff then said to the lords and gentlemen present:

'Do you recognize this man here as Messire Joos Damman, son of the sheriff of the Keure of Ghent?'

'Yes,' they said.

'Did you know,' said he, 'Messire Hilbert, son of Willem Ryvish, Esquire?'

One of the gentlemen, named Van der Zickelen, spoke and said:

'I am from Ghent; my house is in St. Michel's Place. I know Willem Ryvish, Esquire, sheriff of the Keure of Ghent. He lost, about fifteen years ago, a son who was twenty-three years of age, debauchee, game-ster, idler; but forgiven all this by everyone because of his youth. No one since that time has had any news of him. I ask to see the sword, the poignard, and the pouch of the defunct.'

These having been laid before him, he said:

'The sword and the poignard bear on the button of the hilt the arms of Ryvish—three silver fish on a field of azure. I see the same arms reproduced on a golden shield between the meshes of the pouch of mail. What is that other poignard?'

The bailiff, speaking:

'That is the one which was found sticking in the body of Hilbert Ryvish, son of Willem.'

'I recognize,' said the lord, 'the arms of Damman—a tower gules on a silver field. So help me God and all His saints.'

The other gentlemen also said:

'We recognize the aforesaid arms as those of Ryvish and Damman. So help us God and all His saints.'

The bailiff then said:

'After all the proofs heard and read by the sheriffs' court, Messire Joos Damman is sorcerer, murderer, seducer of women, robber of the king's goods, and as such guilty of the crime of treason, both human and divine.'

'You say so, Messire Bailiff,' retorted Joos, 'but you will not condemn me for want of sufficient proofs. I am not, nor ever was, a sorcerer; I only played at being a devil. As for my shining face, you have the receipt for it and for that of the ointment which, while containing the poisonous plant, henbane, is merely soporific. When that woman, a real witch, took it, she fell fast asleep and thought she went to the Sabbath to dance in a ring face outwards, and worship the devil, in the shape of a goat set up on an altar. The dance being ended, she thought she went and kissed him under the tail, as witches do, to give herself up thereafter with me, her lover, to strange copulations which pleased her unreasonable mind. If I had, as she says, cold arms and cool body, it was a sign of youth, not of witchery. In the works of love coolness does not last. But Katheline believed what she wanted to believe and took me for a devil, notwithstanding the fact that I am a man of flesh and blood just like you who watch me. She alone is guilty; taking me for a demon and accepting me in her bed, she sinned, in intent and deed, against God and the Holy Ghost. She it was then, and not I, who committed the crime of witchcraft; she it is who should be burned as a wild and malicious witch, who feigns madness in order to hide her cunning.'

But Nele:

'Do you hear the murderer?' she said. 'He worked like a wench for sale, who bears the whore's sign on her arm, making a trade and a merchandise of love. Did you hear him? He wants to save himself by having burned the one who gave him her all.'

'Nele is wicked,' said Katheline, 'don't listen to her, Hans, my beloved.'

'No,' said Nele, 'no, you are not a man; you are a devil, cowardly and cruel.' And, taking Katheline in her arms: 'Master judges,' she exclaimed, 'do not listen to that evil, pallid one; he has but one desire— he wants to see my mother burned. She has committed no other crime than that of being smitten by God with madness and believing to be real the phantoms of her dreams. She has already suffered much in body and soul. Do not put her to death, master judges. Let the innocent one live her sad life in peace.'

And Katheline said:

'Nele is wicked, you must not believe her, Hans, my lord.'

410

And, among the people, the women wept, and the men said:
'Grace for Katheline.'

The bailiff and the sheriffs gave their sentence concerning Joos Damman on a confession which he made after renewed tortures. He was condemned to be degraded of his rank of nobleman and burned alive by slow fire until death ensued. And he suffered this torture the following day before the doors of the Town Hall, saying all the time: 'Put the witch to death, she alone is guilty! Cursed be God! My father shall slay the judges!' And he gave up the ghost.

And the people said: 'See him cursing and blaspheming. He dies like a dog.'

The following day the bailiff and the sheriffs delivered their sentence concerning Katheline. She was condemned to submit to the trial by water in the Bruges Canal. If her body floated, she would be burned as a witch; if she sank and so drowned, she would be considered to have died a Christian, and as such would be buried in the garden of the church—the cemetery.

The following day, carrying a candle, bare-footed, and dressed in a chemise of black cloth, Katheline was taken to the banks of the canal. They went along under the trees in a grand procession. Before her, chanting the prayers for the dead, walked the dean of Our Lady, his vicars, the beadle bearing the cross. Behind her came the bailiff of Damme, the sheriffs, clerks, sergeants of the town, provost, the executioner and his two helpers. On the banks was a great crowd of weeping women and growling men, full of pity for Katheline, who walked along like a lamb, allowing herself to be led she knew not where, and continually saying: 'Take away the fire, the head burns! Hans, where are you?'

From the midst of the women, where she was standing, Nele cried: 'I want to be thrown in with her.' But the women would not allow her to go near Katheline.

411

A bitter wind blew in from the sea; from the grey sky fine hail fell into the waters of the canal; a boat there was seized by the executioner and his helpers in the king's name. At their command Katheline got into it; the executioner was seen standing up, holding her; and, at the signal from the provost raising his rod of justice, casting Katheline into the canal. She struggled, but not for long, and sank to the bottom, having cried: 'Hans! Hans! Help!'

And the populace said: 'That woman is no witch.'

Some men jumped into the canal and brought out Katheline, senseless and rigid like one dead. Then she was taken to a tavern and placed before a great fire; Nele took off her clothes and wet linen to give her others; when she came to her senses, she said, trembling, and between her chattering teeth: 'Hans, give me a woollen cloak.'

And Katheline could not get warm. And she died the third day. And she was buried in the garden of the church.

And Nele, orphaned, went off to Holland, to Rosa van Auweghem.

7 ON THE HULLS of Zeeland, on *boyers* and *cromsteves*, off goes Tyl Claes Ulenspiegl. The free sea carries the valiant flyboats on which are eight, ten or twenty pieces all of iron; they belch forth death and massacre on the traitorous Spaniards.

He is an expert cannoneer, Tyl Ulenspiegl, son of Claes; you should see how he points right, arms straight, and pierces like a butter wall the carcases of the butchers.

He wears on his hat a silver crescent with this inscription: *'Liever den Turc als den Paus'* ('Rather serve the Turk than the Pope').

The sailors who see him climb aboard their ships, nimble as a cat, sharp as a squirrel, singing a song, ready with a jesting word, question him with curiosity:

'How comes it, little man, that you have such a youthful air when they say you were born such a long time ago in Damme.'

'I am not a body, but a spirit,' said he, 'and Nele, my beloved, resembles me. Spirit of Flanders, love of Flanders, we shall never die.'

'Just the same, when you're cut you bleed.'

'It only seems like that,' replied Ulenspiegl. 'It's wine and not blood.'

'We'll stick a spigot in your belly.'

'I'll be the only one to drain me,' replied Ulenspiegl.

'You're mocking us.'

'He that beats the drum hears it,' replied Ulenspiegl.

And the broidered banners of the Roman processions floated from the masts of the ships. And dressed in velvet, brocade, silk, gold and

412

silver cloth, such as the abbots wear at solemn mass, wearing mitres and carrying crosiers, the Beggars kept guard on their ships.

And it was a strange sight to see, coming from these rich vestments, rough hands carrying muskets or cross-bows, halberds of pikestaffs. And all of them were men of hard faces, with pistols strapped to them and cutlasses that shone in the sun, and they drank from golden chalices the wine from some abbey that had become the wine of freedom.

And they sang and they shouted: 'Up with the Beggars!' and thus they roamed the seas and the Scheldt.

8 AT THIS TIME the Beggars, among whom were Lamme and Ulenspiegl, captured Gorcum. And they were commanded by Captain Marin; this Marin, who was in other times a dyke-worker, bore himself with great haughtiness and sufficiency and signed with Gaspard Turc, defender of Gorcum, a capitulation whereby Turc, the monks, the burghers and the soldiers locked up in the citadel were to come forth freely with their bullets and muskets, and all that they could carry save the wealth of the churches, which belonged to the assailants.

But Captain Marin, on an order from Messire de Lumey, held thirteen monks prisoners and let the troopers and the burghers go.

And Ulenspiegl said:

'A soldier's word should be word of gold. Why does he fail to keep his?'

An old Beggar replied to Ulenspiegl:

'The monks are the sons of Satan, the canker of nations, the shame of the countries. Since the arrival of the Duke of Alba they have lifted up their noses in Gorcum. There is one among them, the priest Nicholas, prouder than a peacock and fiercer than a tiger. Each time that he passed along the street with his pyx, in which was the host made of dog's fat, he looked with furious eyes at the houses from whence no women came out to kneel, and denounced to the judge all those who did not bend their knees before his idol of paste and gilt brass. The other monks imitated him. This was the cause of many great miseries, burnings and cruel punishments in the town of Gorcum. Captain Marin does well to hold these monks as prisoners who, if free, would go with their kind in the villages, burghs, towns and townships, preaching against us, arousing the populace, and having the poor Reformists burned. Dogs are chained until they die; chain then the monks, chain the *bloed-honden*, the blood-hounds of the duke, cage the butchers. Up with the Beggars!'

414

'But,' said Ulenspiegl, 'my lord of Orange, our prince of freedom, wants us to respect, among those who surrender, personal wealth and free conscience.'

The old Beggar answered:

'The admiral does not wish it so for the monks. He is the master. He captured Brill. Cage the monks!'

'Soldier's word, word of gold! Why does he fail to keep his?' asked Ulenspiegl. 'The monks kept in prison suffer there a thousand insults.'

'The ashes beat no more upon your heart,' they said: 'a hundred thousand families, because of the edicts, have carried over there to the northwest, to the country of England, the trades, the industries, the riches of our country; commiserate those then who caused our ruin! Since the reign of the Emperor Charles the Fifth, Butcher the First; and under the reign of this King of the Blood, Butcher the Second, one hundred and eighteen thousand persons have perished by torture. Who bore the candles in the funeral procession in murder and in tears? The monks and the Spanish troopers. Do you not hear the souls of the dead complaining?'

'The ashes beat upon my heart,' said Ulenspiegl. 'Soldier's word is word of gold.'

'Who then,' they said, 'wished by excommunication to place the country outside the pale of nations? Who would have armed against us, if they could have, heaven and earth, God and the devil, and their serried ranks of saints? Who made the host to bleed with ox-blood and the wooden statues to weep? Who caused the *De Profundis* to be chanted in the land of our fathers, if not the cursed clergy, these hordes of lazy monks, in order to hold on to their riches, their influence over the worshippers of idols, and reign through ruin, blood and fire, over the poor . country? Cage the wolves that rush at men on earth, cage the hyenas! Up with the Beggars!'

'Soldier's word is word of gold,' replied Ulenspiegl.

The following day a message came from Messire de Lumey, containing an order to transport the nineteen monks, who were prisoners, from Gorcum to Brill, where the admiral was.

'They will be hanged,' said Captain Marin to Ulenspiegl.

'Not while I'm alive,' he answered.

'My boy,' said Lamme, 'don't speak this way to Messire de Lumey. He's fierce and will hang you with them, without mercy.'

'I shall speak according to the truth,' answered Ulenspiegl. 'Soldier's word is word of gold.'

'If you can save them,' said Marin, 'take their boat to Brill. Take with you Rochus, the pilot, and your friend, Lamme, if you wish.'

'I will,' answered Ulenspiegl.

The boat was moored at the Green Wharf; the nineteen monks entered it. Rochus, the timid, was set at the rudder, Ulenspiegl and Lamme, well-armed, went to the prow of the boat. Some rascally troopers, who had joined up with the Beggars for pillage, were beside the monks, who were hungry. Ulenspiegl gave the monks something to eat and drink. 'He's going to turn traitor!' said the rascally troopers. The nineteen monks, seated amidships, were all yawning and shivering, although it was July and there was a bright, warm sun and a gentle breeze that puffed out the sails of the boat, which glided along, massive and bulging, over the green waves.

Father Nicholas spoke then and said to the pilot:

'Rochus, are we being taken to the gallows field?' Then, turning towards Gorcum: 'Oh, Gorcum town!' said he, standing up and stretching out his hand, 'Gorcum town! How many woes have you to suffer! You shall be accursed among the cities, for you have allowed to spring up within your walls the seed of heresy! Oh, Gorcum town! And the angel of the Lord shall no longer keep watch over your gates. He shall no longer keep in his care the modesty of your virgins, the courage of your men, nor the fortune of your merchants! Oh, Gorcum town! You are accursed, unfortunate town!'

'Cursed, cursed,' replied Ulenspiegl, 'cursed like the comb that has passed and lifted out the Spanish lice; cursed like the dog breaking its chain; like the proud horse shaking out from under a cruel rider! Cursed yourself, silly preacher, who finds it wrong to break the rod, even of iron, on the backs of the tyrants!'

The monk was silent and, lowering his eyes, seemed preserved in devout hatred.

The rascally troopers, who had joined up with the Beggars for pillage, were close to the monks, who were hungry. Ulenspiegl asked for biscuits and herrings for them. The master of the boat replied:

'Let them be thrown into the Meuse, they'll eat fresh herring there.'

Ulenspiegl then gave to the monks all he had of bread and sausage belonging to himself and Lamme. The master of the boat and the worthless troopers said to each other:

'He's a traitor, he feeds the monks; we must denounce him.'

At Dordrecht the boat stopped in the harbour at Bloemen-Kaai (The Flower Wharf). Men, women, boys and girls ran in a crowd to see the monks and say to each other, as they pointed them out or threatened them with their fists:

'Look at these clowning makers of good gods that lead bodies to the

416

stake and souls to eternal fire! Look at these fattened tigers and these pot-bellied jackals!'

The monks lowered their heads and did not dare speak. Ulenspiegl saw them trembling anew.

'We are still hungry,' they said, 'compassionate trooper.'

But the master of the boat:

'What is always drinking? Dry sand. What is always eating? A monk.'

Ulenspiegl went to the town to find bread, ham, and a great pot of beer for them.

'Eat and drink,' said he. 'You are our prisoners, but I shall save you if I can. Soldier's word is word of gold.'

'Why do you give them all that? They won't pay for it,' said the rascally troopers; and they whispered into each other's ears these words: 'He has promised to save them, keep an eye on him.'

At dawn they came to Brill. The gates having been opened for them, a *voet-looper* (runner) went ahead to inform Messire de Lumey of their coming.

As soon as he heard the news, he came on horseback, hurriedly dressed, accompanied by several armed horsemen and footmen.

And Ulenspiegl saw again the fierce admiral dressed like a proud lord living in opulence.

'Greetings, messires monks,' said he. 'Lift up your hands. Where is the blood of Messires Egmont and Hoorn? You show me white paws and that is just like you.'

A monk named Leonard replied:

'Do with us what you will. We are monks, no one will claim us.'

'He has spoken well,' said Ulenspiegl. 'For the monk, having broken with the world, which is father and mother, sister and brother, spouse and lover, finds no one at the hour of God to claim him. Nevertheless, Your Excellency, I will do so. Captain Marin, when he signed the capitulation of Gorcum, stipulated that these monks should be freed like everybody taken in the citadel who surrendered. Just the same, they were kept prisoners without any reason; I have heard that they will be hanged. My lord, I address myself to you, humbly, speaking for them, for I know that a soldier's word is word of gold.'

'Who are you?' demanded Messire de Lumey.

'My lord,' answered Ulenspiegl, 'Fleming I am from the fair land of Flanders; peasant, nobleman, both together; and thus I go about the world, praising all good and lovely things and mocking loudly all stupidity. And I shall praise you if you keep the promise made by the captain. Soldier's word is word of gold.'

But the rascally troopers who were in the boat:

'My lord,' said they, 'he's a traitor; he promised to save them and gave them bread, ham, sausages and beer, and to us gave nothing.'

Messire de Lumey then said to Ulenspiegl:

'Perambulating Fleming and nourisher of monks, you shall be hanged with them.'

'I have no fears,' replied Ulenspiegl; 'soldier's word is word of gold.'

'You are very cocky!' said de Lumey.

'The ashes beat upon my heart,' said Ulenspiegl.

The monks were taken to a barn, and Ulenspiegl with them. There they tried to convert him with theological arguments, but he fell asleep as he listened to them.

Messire de Lumey being at table, which was spread with meats and wines, a messenger arrived from Gorcum, from Captain Marin, with copies of the letters of the silent one, Prince of Orange, 'commanding all the governors of towns and other places to hold the ecclesiastics in the same safety, surety and privileges, as the rest of the people.'

The messenger demanded to be taken to where de Lumey was, in order to place the copies of the letters into his proper hands.

'Where are the originals?' demanded de Lumey.

'In the keeping of my master, Marin,' said the messenger.

'And the peasant sends me copies!' said de Lumey. 'Where is your passport?'

'Here it is, my lord,' said the messenger.

Messire de Lumey read aloud:

'My lord and master, Marin Brandt, commands all ministers, governors and officers of the Republic, that they allow to pass safely, etc.'

De Lumey striking his fist on the table and tearing up the passport:

' 'Od's blood!' said he, 'What's he interfering for, this Marin, this trumpery knave, who had not before the capture of Brill the bone of a red-herring to stick in his mouth? He calls himself my lord and master, and he sends me orders! He commands and orders! Tell your master that since he is so "Captain" and so "my lord," since he orders and commands so well, the monks shall be hanged short and high immediately, and you with them, if you do not get out of here.'

And, landing him a kick, he sent him sprawling out of the room.

'Bring on drinks!' he shouted. 'Did you see the insolence of that Marin? I could throw up my food, I'm so furious. Let the monks be hanged immediately in the barn, and let the perambulating Fleming be brought before me after he has witnessed their torture. We shall see if he dares to tell me that I have done wrong. 'Od's blood! What use do we still have for these pots and glasses?'

And, with a great racket, he smashed the glasses and dishes, and no

418

one dared speak to him. The valets wanted to clear away the debris but he would not allow them; and drinking out of the flasks immoderately, he became more enraged, strode about the room crushing the bits of broken crockery, stamping on them furiously.

Ulenspiegl was brought before him.

'Well,' said he, 'what news do you bring from your friends, the monks?'

'They are hanged,' said Ulenspiegl; 'and a cowardly executioner, killing for hire, opened the belly and the sides of one of them after his death, like a disembowelled pig, in order to sell the fat to an apothecary. Soldier's word is no longer word of gold.'

De Lumey, stamping on the debris of the dishes:

'You defy me,' said he, 'four-footed rascal, but you also shall be hanged, not in a barn but ignominiously in the open place, before the world.'

'Shame on you,' said Ulenspiegl, 'shame on us: soldier's word is no longer word of gold.'

'Will you be silent, iron-head?' said Messire de Lumey.

'Shame on you,' said Ulenspiegl. 'Soldier's word is no longer word of gold. Punish rather the rascally merchants of human fat.'

Messire de Lumey then threw himself at him, raising his hand to strike him.

'Strike,' said Ulenspiegl; 'I am your prisoner, but I have no fear of you; soldier's word is no longer word of gold.'

Messire de Lumey then drew his sword and would certainly have killed Ulenspiegl if Messire de Tres-Long, catching his arms, had not said to him:

'Have mercy! He is honest and valiant; he has committed no crime!'

De Lumey, thinking better of it then, said:

'Let him demand pardon.'

But Ulenspiegl remained standing:

'I will not do so,' said he.

'Let him at least say that I am not wrong,' shouted de Lumey, growing furious.

Ulenspiegl replied:

'I do not lick the boots of lords; soldier's word is no longer word of gold.'

'Let the gallows be set up,' said de Lumey, 'and let him be taken there; that will be hempen word.'

'Yes,' said Ulenspiegl, 'and I shall shout it out before all the people; soldier's word is no longer word of gold!'

The gallows was set up in the market-square. The news soon spread through the town that they were going to hang Ulenspiegl the valiant Beggar. And the populace was moved to pity and compassion. And the people all crowded the market-place; Messire de Lumey also came there on horseback, wishing to give the signal for the execution himself.

Pitilessly he looked on Ulenspiegl, standing on the ladder, dressed for the execution, in his shirt, his arms bound to his body, his hands folded, the rope about his neck, and the executioner ready to do his work.

Tres-Long said to him:

'My lord, pardon him, he is not a traitor, and no one ever saw a man hanged because he was sincere and merciful.'

And the men and women of the people, hearing Tres-Long speak, shouted: 'Pity, my lord, pardon and pity for Ulenspiegl.'

'That iron-head defied me,' said de Lumey: 'let him repent and say that I did right.'

'Will you repent and say that he did right?' said Tres-Long to Ulenspiegl.

'Soldier's word is no longer word of gold,' replied Ulenspiegl.

'Draw the cord,' said de Lumey.

The executioner was about to obey; a young girl all dressed in white and crowned with flowers, ran like a madwoman up the steps of the gallows, threw her arms about Ulenspiegl's neck and said:

'This man is mine; I take him for husband!'

And the people applauded, and the women cried:

'Long live the girl who saved Ulenspiegl!'

'What's this?' demanded Messire de Lumey.

Tres-Long replied:

'According to the usages and customs of the town, it is right and law that a young girl, virgin or unmarried, can save a man from the rope by taking him for husband at the foot of the gallows.'

'God is with him,' said de Lumey. 'Untie him.'

Riding then close to the scaffold, he saw the girl prevented from cutting the ropes by the executioner, who stopped her, saying:

'If you cut them, who will pay for them?'

But the girl did not listen to him. Seeing her so hasty, loving and cunning, he was touched.

'Who are you?' said he.

'I am Nele, his sweetheart,' said she, 'and I came from Flanders seeking him.'

'You did well,' said de Lumey, in a roguish voice.

420

And he went off.

Tres-Long then came up to them.

'Little Fleming,' said he, 'once married, will you still be a soldier with our fleet?'

'Yes, Messire,' replied Ulenspiegl.

'And you, girl, what will you do without your man?'

Nele answered:

'If you wish, Messire, I shall be the fifer on his boat.'

'Very well,' said Tres-Long.

And he gave them two florins for their wedding-feast.

And Lamme, weeping and laughing with pleasure, said:

'Here's three florins more; we'll eat everything; I'm to pay. Let's go to the *Peigne-d'Or*. He's not dead, my friend. Up with the Beggar!'

And the people applauded, and they went off to the *Peigne-d'Or* where a great feast was ordered. And Lamme threw pennies out of the window to the people.

And Ulenspiegl said to Nele:

'Darling beloved, here you are beside me, then! Glory! She's here, flesh, heart and soul, my sweet love. Oh, the gentle eyes and the lovely red lips through which there never passes anything but kind words! She saved my life, the tender love! You shall play the fife of deliverance on our boats. Do you remember. . . no, no. For us the present house is full of gladness, and your face, sweet as the flowers in June, is mine. I am in paradise. But,' said he, 'you're crying. . .'

'They killed her,' said she.

And she told him the story of her mourning.

And, looking at each other, they wept the tears of love and grief.

And, at the feast, they ate and drank, and Lamme watched them, dolefully, saying to himself:

'La, my wife, where are you?'

And the priest came and married Nele and Ulenspiegl.

And the morning sun found them side by side in their marriage-bed.

And Nele rested her head on Ulenspiegl's shoulder. And when the sun awoke her, he said:

'Fresh visage and gentle heart, we shall be the avengers of Flanders.'

She, kissing him on the mouth, said:

'Wild head and strong arms, may God bless the fife and the sword.'

'I shall make you a soldier's costume.'

'Right away?' said she.

'Right away,' answered Ulenspiegl; 'but who said that berries are good in the morning? Your mouth is better far.'

422

9 ULENSPIEGL, Lamme and Nele, like their friends and companions, had taken from the convents the wealth begotten by these places from the people by the aid of processions, false miracles and other Roman mummeries. This was against the order of the silent one, the prince of freedom, but the money served to carry on the war. Lamme Goedzak, not content with taking money, pillaged the convents of their hams, sausages, flasks of beer and wine, and gladly came back to the ship with a shoulder belt, bearing poultry, geese, turkeys, capons, chickens and pullets, and dragging after him, by a rope, monastic calves and pigs. And all this by right of war, he said.

Happy at every capture, he brought them to the ship so that they all might feast; he complained nevertheless about the cooks being so ignorant in the science of sauces and fricassees.

Now on this day the Beggars, having downed the wine victoriously, said to Ulenspiegl:

'You have always the nose i' the wind to smell out news from land; you know all the adventures of war; sing them for us. And Lamme shall beat the tabor and the sweet fifer shall toot the rhythm of your song.'

And Ulenspiegl said:

'One May day, clear and cool, Ludwig of Nassau, thinking to enter Mons, cannot find his footmen nor his horsemen. A few faithful ones hold open a gate and let down a bridge so that he may take the town. But the burghers take the gate and the bridge. Where are the troops of Count Louis? The burghers are about to draw up the bridge. Count Louis sounds his horn.'

And Ulenspiegl sang:

'Where are your footmen or your horsemen?
They are lost in the woods, trampling all;
Dry twigs, flowering lilies of the valley.
Our Lord the Sun makes to shine

423

Their ruddy and warrior faces
And the glowing rumps of their coursing steeds:
Count Ludwig blows upon his horn;
They hear it. Softly beat the drum.

At full gallop, with bridle loose!
Lightning speed and speed of the cloud;
Cyclonic rush of rattling steel;
Come, flying on, the heavy horsemen!
In haste! In haste! to the rescue, haste!
The bridge goes up. . . Dig in the spur,
Into the charger's bleeding flanks.
The bridge goes up: the town is lost!

They are before it. Is't too late?
Ride at full speed with loosened reins!
Guitoy of Chaumont, on his Spanish steed,
Leaps on the bridge, that falls once more.
The town is won! And can you hear,
There on the paven streets of Mons,
The lightning speed, speed of the clouds,
Cyclonic rush of rattling steel?

Up with Chaumont and his Spanish steed!
Blow the trump of joy and beat the drum!
It's now the month of hay scenting the fields;
The rising lark sings in the sky!
Long live the bird that's free!
Beat the drums of glory!
Up with Chaumont and his Spanish steed!
The town is won! . . . Up with the Beggars!'

And the Beggars sang on their ships: 'Christ look down upon your soldiers. Furbish our arms, oh Lord! Up with the Beggars!'

And Nele, smiling, played upon the fife, and Lamme beat the drum; and on high, to the heavens, the temple of God, were lifted golden cups and hymns of freedom. And the waves, like sirens, clear and cool about the ship, murmured harmoniously.

10 ONE DAY IN the month of August—a heavy and hot day—Lamme was steeped in melancholy. His joyous tabor was silent and slept, while his drumsticks stuck out from his pouch. Ulenspiegl and Nele, smiling with amorous pleasure, warmed themselves in the sun; the look-outs up in the crow's-nest whistled and sang, searching the while to see if they could not spy some prey on the horizon. Tres-Long questioned them; they always replied: '*Niets*' ('Nothing').

And Lamme, pale and downcast, sighed piteously. And Nele said to him:

'Why is it, Lamme, that you are so doleful?'

And Ulenspiegl said to him:

'You're growing thin, my boy.'

'Yes,' said Lamme, 'I'm woeful and skinny. My heart loses its gaiety and my goodly phiz its freshness. Yes, laugh at me, you who have found each other after traversing a thousand dangers. Mock poor Lamme who lives like a widower, although married, while she,' said he, pointing to Nele, 'had to tear her man from the kiss of the cord that will be his last lover. She did well, God be praised; but let her not laugh at me. Yes, you must not laugh at poor Lamme, Nele my dear. My wife laughs for ten. La! you females are cruel towards another's woes. Yes, I have a woeful heart, pierced by the sword of abandon, and nothing will ever heal it, save my wife.'

'Or some fricassee,' said Ulenspiegl.

'Yes,' said Lamme, 'where is the meat on this sad ship? On the king's ships, they have it four times a week, if they are not fasting, and fish three times a week. As for the fish here, God damn me if that tow—I mean their flesh—does anything but warm up my blood with no consequence, my poor blood that will soon be running to water. They have beer, cheese, soup and good drinks. Yes! they have everything for their stomachal pleasure: biscuit, rye-bread, beer, butter, smoked meats; yes, everything; dried fish, cheese, mustard seed, salt, beans, peas, barley, vinegar, oil, tallow, wood and coal. As for us, they have just forbidden us to take cattle from no matter whom, burgher, abbot or gentleman. We eat herrings and drink small beer. La! I have nothing left: neither love of woman, nor good wine, nor *dobble bruinbier*, nor good nourishment. Where are our joys here?'

'I am going to tell you, Lamme,' answered Ulenspiegl. 'Eye for an eye, tooth for a tooth. On Saint Bartholomew's Night they slew ten thousand free hearts in the city of Paris alone; the king himself fired on his people. Awake, Fleming; seize the axe without mercy: there are our joys; smite the Spaniard enemy and Roman, where ever you may find him. Leave your edibles. They bore away their dead or living

425

victims to the river and there cast them in—whole cart-loads of them. Dead or living, do you hear, Lamme? The Seine ran red for nine days and clouds of ravens descended on the town. At La Charité, at Rouen, Toulouse, Lyons, Bordeaux, Bourges, Meaux, the massacre was horrible. Can you see the bands of satiated dogs lying beside the corpses? Their teeth are weary! The flight of the ravens is heavy, so full are their bellies with the flesh of the victims. Do you hear, Lamme, the voices of their souls crying vengeance and pity? Awake, Fleming! You speak of your wife. I do not think she is unfaithful, but merely distraught, and she still loves you, poor friend. She was not among these ladies of the court who, the very night of the massacre, stripped the corpses with their dainty hands, to see how big or small were their carnal virilities. And they laughed, these great lecherous ladies. Rejoice, my boy, in spite of your fish and your small beer. If the after-taste of herring is unsavoury, more unsavoury still is the smell of that nastiness. Those that did the slaying sat down to their repast, and with badly washed hands carved the fat geese to offer to the charming damozels of Paris, the wings, the legs, or the rump. They had lately felt other meat, cold meat.'

'I won't complain any more, my boy,' said Lamme, getting up. 'Herring is ortolan, and the small beer is malvoisy for free hearts.'

And Ulenspiegl said:

> 'Up with the Beggars! Weep not, my brothers.
> In ruins and in blood
> Flowers freedom's rose.
> If God be with us, who then can be against?
> When the hyena triumphs,
> There comes the lion's turn.
> With one paw-stroke he rips him wide.
> Eye for an eye; tooth for a tooth. Up with the Beggars!'

And the Beggars on the ships sang:

> 'The same fate holds the duke for us,
> Eye for an eye, tooth for a tooth,
> Wound for wound. Up with the Beggars!'

11 ONE DARK NIGHT, the tempest rumbling in the depths of the clouds, Ulenspiegl was on the deck of the ship with Nele, and he said: 'All our lights are out. We are foxes watching the passing of the Spanish poultry in the night; that is to say, their twenty-two *assabres,* rich vessels with lanterns burning, which are for them the stars of evil fortune. And we shall rush at them.'

Nele said:

'This night is a witches' night. The sky is black as the mouth of hell; these lightnings shine like the smile of Satan; the far-off storm rumbles dully; the seagulls scream as they pass; the sea rolls over its phosphorescent waves like silver serpents. Tyl, my love, come to the spirit world. Take the powder of vision . . .'

'Shall I see the Seven, my sweet?'

And they took the powder of vision.

And Nele closed Ulenspiegl's eyes and Ulenspiegl closed Nele's eyes. And they saw a cruel spectacle.

Heaven, earth and sea were full of men, women, children, labouring, drifting, wandering or dreaming. The sea held them up, the earth bore them. And they swarmed like eels in a creel.

Seven men and women in the midst of the heavens were seated on thrones, and their brows were girt with a shining star. But they were so vague that Nele and Ulenspiegl could only distinguish their stars.

The sea rose right up to the heavens, rolling in its foam, an innumerable multitude of ships whose masts and rigging clashed together, interlocking, breaking, crushing one another following the tempestuous movements of the sea. Then a ship appeared amidst all the others. Its careen was of flaming iron. The keel was of steel shaped like a knife. The waters cried and groaned as it passed. Death was seated in the stern of the boat, grinning, holding in one hand his scythe and in the other a whip with which he lashed the seven personages. One was a woeful man, thin, haughty, silent. He held in one hand a sceptre and in the other a sword. Beside him, riding a goat, was a ruddy girl with naked breasts, open dress, and lively eyes. She was lying back lasciviously beside an old Jew who picked his nails, and a great bloated man who fell down each time she set him up, while a skinny and furious woman struck at both of them. The fat man never avenged himself, nor did his ruddy companion. In the midst of these, a monk ate sausages. A woman lying on the ground crawled like a serpent among them all. She bit the Jew because of his old nails, the bloated man because he was too much at ease, the ruddy woman because of the watery brightness of her eyes, the monk because of his sausages, and the thin man because of his sceptre. And soon all of them were fighting.

When they passed, the battle was horrible on the sea, in the heavens, and on land. It rained blood. The ships were shattered with blows from axes, muskets, cannon. The fragments flew into the air amidst the smoke and powder. On land the armies clashed together like steel walls.

427

Towns, villages, harvests, burned up amid cries and tears. The high steeples, frozen lace, stood out from the flames with their proud silhouettes, then fell noisily down like oaks laid low. Black knights, numerous and serried like bands of ants, swords in hand, pistols likewise, struck the men, women and children. Some of them dug holes in the ice and buried old men alive there; others cut off the breasts of women and shook pepper on them; others hanged children in chimneys. Those who were weary of striking violated some girl or woman, or drank, diced, moved piles of gold, the fruit of their pillage, and dabbled their bloody fingers in the coins.

The seven crowned with stars cried: 'Pity for the poor world!'

And the phantoms laughed sneeringly. And their voices were as those of a thousand sea-eagles screaming together. And Death waved his scythe.

'Do you hear them?' said Ulenspiegl; 'these are the birds of prey of poor mankind. They live on the little birds—the simple and the good.'

The seven crowned with stars cried: 'Love, justice, mercy!'

And the seven phantoms laughed sneeringly. And their voices were as those of a thousand sea-eagles screaming together. And Death lashed them with his whip.

And the ship sailed over the sea, cutting through vessels, boats, men, women, children. From the sea resounded the plaints of the victims, crying: 'Pity!'

And the red ship passed over them while the laughing phantoms screamed like sea-eagles.

And grinning Death drank the water full of blood.

And, the ship having disappeared in the fog, the battle ceased, the seven crowned with stars faded away.

And Ulenspiegl and Nele could see nothing but the dark sky, the raging sea, the sombre clouds advancing over the phosphorescent waters, and, very close, red stars.

These were the lanterns of the twenty-two *assabres*. The sea and the thunder rumbled dully.

And Ulenspiegl rang the *wacharm* bell softly, and cried: 'The Spaniard! The Spaniard! He's headed for Flushing!' And this cry was repeated by all the fleet.

And Ulenspiegl said to Nele:

'A grey hue is spreading over the sky and the sea. The lanterns are now glowing but feebly, the dawn's coming up, the wind grows keen, the waves are throwing their foam over the decks of the ships, a heavy rain falls and immediately stops, the sun rises, radiant, gilding the

crest of the waves; it is your smile, Nele, cool as the morning, soft as the rays.'

The twenty-two *assabres* passed. On the Beggars' ships the drums beat, the fifes played; de Lumey shouted: 'In the prince's name, give chase!' Ewont Pietersen Wort, rear-admiral, shouted: 'In the name of my Lord of Orange and Messire the Admiral, give chase!' On all the ships—*The Johannah, The Swan, The Anne-Mie, The Beggar, The Compromise, The Egmont, The Hoorn, The William the Silent*—all the captains shouted: 'In the name of my Lord of Orange and Messire the Admiral, give chase!'

'Give chase! Up with the Beggars!' shouted the troops and the sailors.

Tres-Long's *houlque*, named *The Brill*, whereon are Lamme and Ulenspiegl, followed closely by *The Johannah, The Swan* and *The Beggar*, captures four *assabres*. The Beggars throw everything that is Spanish into the sea, take the inhabitants of the Netherlands prisoners, empty the boats like egg-shells and leave them to drift, without masts or sails, in the harbour. Then they pursue the other eighteen *assabres*. A violent wind blows in from Antwerp; the sides of the rapid ships lean over on the water under the weight of the sails that are puffed out like the cheeks of monks with kitchen breezes. The *assabres* sail swiftly; the Beggars pursue them right into the roadstead of Middleburg, under the fire from the forts. There the bloody battle takes place. The Beggars launch out with axes on the decks of the ships, soon strewn with cut-off arms and legs which must be thrown, after the battle, by baskets-full into the sea. The forts continue their fire; heedless to the cry of 'Up with the Beggars!' they take from the *assabres* powder, artillery, bullets, wheat, burn them after having emptied them, and sail off to Flushing, leaving these smoking and flaming in the roadstead.

From there they send out squads to pierce the dykes of Zeeland and Holland, help with the building of new ships, notably flyboats of a hundred and forty tons, capable of carrying up to twenty cannon of cast-iron.

12 IT SNOWS ON THE SHIPS. The air is all white, away in to the distance; endlessly the snow falls, falls on the dark waters, where it melts. On land it snows: all white are the roads, all white the dark silhouettes of the leafless trees. No noise save the far-off bells of Haarlem, sounding the hour, and the gay carillon, sending its muffled notes through the heavy air.

Bells, ring not; bells, play not your simple and sweet airs! Don

Frederic draws nigh, the dukeling of the blood. He marches on you, followed by thirty-five ensigns of Spaniards, your mortal enemies. Haarlem, oh freedom's town, twenty-two ensigns of Walloons, eighteen ensigns of Germans, eight hundred horses; a powerful artillery follow them. Do you hear, on the wagons, the noise of these murdering irons? Falconets, culverins, big-mugged mortars; all that is for you, Haarlem. Bells, ring not; carillon, throw not your happy notes out on the air heavy with snow!

Bells, we shall ring; I, the carillon, I shall sing, throwing out my bold notes on the air heavy with snow. Haarlem is the town of valiant hearts and courageous women. She watches without fear, from the tops of her steeples, the black masses of butchers winding like bands of hellish ants. Ulenspiegl, Lamme and a hundred Beggars from the sea are within her walls. Their fleet cruises in the lake.

'Let them come!' say the inhabitants; 'we are only burghers, fishers, sailors and women. The son of the Duke of Alba needs no other keys to enter our town, says he, than his cannon. Let him open if he can these weak gates, he shall find men behind them. Ring out, bells! Carillon, throw your happy notes out on the air heavy with snow.

'We have only weak walls and old-fashioned ditches. Fourteen cannon belch their forty-six pound balls out on the *Cruys-poort*. Place men where the stones are lacking. Night comes, every man works, as though never a cannon had passed through. On the *Cruys-poort* they have launched six hundred and eighty balls; on St. John's Gate, six hundred and seventy-five. These keys do not open, for behind there rises a new bulwark. Ring out, bells! Throw out, carillon, on the heavy air, your happy notes.

'The cannon beats, beats ever on the walls, the stones leap out, the walls crumble in large sections. The breach is large enough to let a company pass through. The assault! Kill! Kill! They shout. They mount; there are ten thousand of them. Let them pass over the ditches, with their bridges, with their ladders. Our cannon are ready. There's the troop of those who are about to die. Salute them, cannon of freedom! They salute; chain shot, circles of flaming tar fly, pierce, cut, flame, blinding a mass of assailants who fall back and flee in disorder. . . Fifteen hundred slain are piled up in the ditches. Ring out, bells! And you, carillon, throw your happy notes out on the heavy air.

'Return to the assault! They do not dare. They fall back on shooting and mining. We, too, know the art of laying mines. Under them, under them, light the train; run now, we shall see a fine sight. Four hundred Spaniards blown into the air. This is not the highway of eternal flames.

431

Oh, the rare dance to the silvery sound of our bells! To the happy music of our carillon!

'They do not suspect that the prince is watching over us, that every day, by well-guarded passages, there come to us sledges of corn and powder—corn for us, powder for them. Where are their six hundred Germans whom we slew and drowned in the woods of Haarlem? Where are the eleven ensigns we captured from them, the six artillery guns, and the fifty oxen? We had one wall about us, now we have two. Even the women go forth to battle, and Kennan leads the valiant band. Come on, butchers, march through our streets, the children will hamstring you with their little knives. Ring out, bells! And you, carillon, throw your happy notes out on the heavy air!

'But luck is not with us. The Beggars' fleet is beaten on the lake. Beaten are the troops sent by Orange to succour us. It freezes; it freezes bitterly. No more help. Then, for five months, one thousand against ten thousand, we hold firm. Now we must come to terms with the butchers. Will he listen to any terms, this dukeling of the blood who has sworn our destruction? Let us send out all the soldiers with their arms; they'll pierce the enemy bands. But the women are at the gates, fearing that they be left alone to guard the town. Ring out no more, bells! Carillon, throw out no more your happy notes.

'Here is June, the hay grows fragrant, the corn grows golden in the sun, the birds sing. We have hungered during five months; the town is in mourning; we shall all go forth from Haarlem, the musketeers leading, to open the way, the women, the children, the magistrates following, guarded by the infantry, which holds the breech. A letter, a letter from the dukeling of the blood! Is it death he announces? No, it is life to all within the town. Oh, unexpected clemency! Oh, lie, maybe! Sing you still, happy carillon? They enter into the town.'

Ulenspiegl, Lamme and Nele had dressed themselves in the uniforms of the German troopers locked up with them—to the number of six hundred—in the cloister of the Augustines.

'We shall die to-day,' whispered Ulenspiegl to Lamme.

And he clasped the darling body of Nele to his breast, all quivering with fear.

'La! I shan't see my wife any more,' said Lamme. 'But maybe our German soldiers' uniforms will save our lives.'

Ulenspiegl wagged his head, to show that he believed in no grace.

'I do not hear the sounds of pillage,' said Lamme. Ulenspiegl answered:

'According to the terms, the burghers have redeemed their lives and the town from pillage for the sum of two hundred and forty thousand

432

florins. They must pay one hundred thousand florins down within twelve days and the rest three months afterwards. The women have been ordered to retire within the churches. They are doubtless going to begin the massacre. Do you hear them nailing down the scaffolds and setting up the gallows?'

'Ah, we are going to die!' said Nele; 'I'm hungry.'

'Yes,' whispered Lamme to Ulenspiegl, 'the dukeling of the blood has said that, being famished, we will be more docile when we are led out to die.'

'I am so hungry!' said Nele.

In the evening the soldiers came to distribute bread for six men:

'Three hundred Walloon soldiers were hanged in the market-place,' they said. 'It will soon be your turn. There has always been the wedding of the Beggars to the gallows.'

The next night they came again, with their bread for six men:

'Four high burghers were beheaded,' they said. 'Two hundred soldiers were tied back to back and cast into the sea. The crabs will be fat this year. You do not look so well, you others who have been here since the seventh of July. They are gluttons and drunkards, these Netherland folk; we Spaniards have enough with two figs for our supper.'

'Is that the reason,' said Ulenspiegl, 'why you must have, everywhere, in the burghers' houses, four meals of meat, poultry, creams, wines and jellies; that you must have milk to lave the bodies of your *mustachios* and wine to bathe your horses' feet?'

The nineteenth of July. Nele said:

'My feet are wet; what is it?'

'Blood,' said Ulenspiegl.

In the evening the troopers came again, with their bread for six:

'Where the rope no longer suffices,' they said, 'the sword does the work. Three hundred troopers and twenty-seven burghers who thought to flee the town are now walking about in hell, with their heads in their hands.'

The next day the blood again entered the cloisters; the troopers brought no bread but merely came to look at the prisoners and say:

'The five hundred Walloons, English and Scots, beheaded yesterday, looked better. These here are hungry, no doubt; but who then should die of hunger if not the Beggars?'

And indeed all of them there were like phantoms, so pale, haggard, worn out, trembling with cold fevers.

The sixteenth of August, at five in the evening, the troopers entered laughing and gave them bread, cheese and beer. Lamme said:

433

'It's the feast of death.'

At ten o'clock four ensigns came; the captains had the doors of the cloister opened and ordered the prisoners to march four by four behind the fifes and tabors until they came to the place where they would be told to stop. Certain streets were red. And they marched towards the gallows-field.

Here and there, small pools of blood spotted the meadows; there was blood all about the walls. The ravens came in clouds from every side; the sun was hidden in a misty covering; the sky was still clear and in its depths stars timidly awoke. Suddenly they hear lamentable howlings.

The soldiers said:

'Those who scream there are the Beggars from the Fort Fuycke, outside the town; they are being left to die of hunger.'

'We, too,' said Nele, 'we are going to die.'

And she wept.

'The ashes beat upon my heart,' said Ulenspiegl.

'Ah,' said Lamme in Flemish—the escorting soldiers did not understand that proud language—'ah,' said Lamme, 'if I could only get hold of that duke of the blood and make him eat, until his skin burst, all the ropes, gallows, torture-benches, wooden-horses, weights and boots; if I could make him drink the blood he has spilt; and that there might come out through his torn skin and his open guts the wood-splinters, the bits of iron; and if even then he did not give up the ghost, I would tear his heart out from his breast and make him eat it raw and poisonous. Then surely he would pass from life to death, down to the sulphurous pit where the devil may make him eat it and eat it again with no cessation. And so on through the long eternity.'

'*Amen*,' said Ulenspiegl and Nele.

'But do you not see anything?' said she.

'No,' said he.

'I see in the west,' said she, 'five men and two women seated in a

434

circle. One is dressed in purple and bears a golden crown. He seems the chief of the others, all ragged and tattered. I see coming from the east another band of seven. Someone also commands them; he is dressed in purple but uncrowned. And they are coming against those of the west. And they are fighting together in the cloud; but I see nothing more.'

'The Seven,' said Ulenspiegl.

'I hear,' said Nele, 'near us in the foliage, a voice like a whisper, saying:

> "By war and by the fire,
> By pikes and by the sword,
> Seek;
> In death and in the blood,
> In ruins and in tears,
> Find." '

'Others than we shall deliver the land of Flanders,' answered Ulenspiegl. 'The night grows dark; the troopers light the torches. We are close to the gallows-field. Oh, sweet my love, why did you follow me? Do you hear nothing else, Nele?'

'Yes,' said she, 'a sound of arms in the corn. And there, above that ridge surmounting the road we are now entering on, do you see the red light of the torches gleaming on steel? I see sparks of fire in the locks of muskets. Are our keepers asleep, or are they blind? Do you hear that thunder stroke? Do you see the Spaniards fall down pierced with bullets? Do you hear "Up with the Beggars"? Running, they climb the path, the pike outstretched; all along the slope they descend with axes. Up with the Beggars!'

'Up with the Beggars!' shouted Lamme and Ulenspiegl.

'Look here,' said Nele, 'here are soldiers giving us weapons. Take them, Lamme; take them, my beloved. Up with the Beggars!'

'Up with the Beggars!' shouted all the band of prisoners.

'The muskets continue firing,' said Nele. 'The Spaniards are falling like flies, lit up as they are by the torches. Up with the Beggars!'

'Up with the Beggars!' cried the band of saviours.

'Up with the Beggars!' shouted Ulenspiegl and all the prisoners. 'The Spaniards are in a circle of fire. Kill! Kill! There is not one left standing. Kill! No pity; war without mercy. And now let us up and away to Enckhuysen. Who has the butchers' clothes of silk and cloth? Who has their arms?'

'All of us! All of us!' they shouted. 'Up with the Beggars!'

And so they went off by boat towards Enckhuysen, where the rescued Germans who were with them stayed to keep watch over the town.

And Lamme, Nele and Ulenspiegl found their ship again. And behold, they sing once more on the open sea: 'Up with the Beggars!'

And they cruise in the roadstead of Flushing.

13 THERE, ONCE MORE, Lamme was happy. He was always willing to go ashore to hunt oxen, sheep and poultry, as though they were hares, deer and ortolans. And he was not alone in this nourishing hunt. It was good then to see the return of the hunters, Lamme leading them, dragging the greater cattle by the horns, driving the lesser, directing the flock of geese by wands and carrying—in spite of their struggling, and slung from the end of their boat-hooks—hens, chickens and capons.

Then there was feasting and revelling on the ships. And Lamme said:

'The odour of the sauces mounts right up to heaven, delighting the angels, who say: "This is the best part of the meat." '

While they were cruising, there came a fleet of merchant-ships from Lisbon; their commander was unaware of the fact that Flushing had fallen into the hands of the Beggars. He gave the fleet the order to cast anchor; it was surrounded. Up with the Beggars! Fifes and tabors sound, the boarding signal; the merchants have cannon, pikes, axes, muskets.

Musket-shot and cannon balls rain on the Beggars' ships. Their musketeers, entrenched in the wooden fortress about the main-mast, aim with surety, without any danger. The merchants fall like flies.

'To the rescue!' said Ulenspiegl to Lamme and Nele. 'To the rescue! Here are spices, jewels, precious goods, sugar, nutmegs, cloves, ginger; reals, ducats, moutons d'or, all bright. There are more than five hundred thousand pieces. The Spaniards will pay the costs of the war. Let's drink! Let's sing the Beggars' Mass battlesong.'

And Ulenspiegl and Lamme ran about like lions. Nele played the fife in the shelter of one of the wooden fortresses. The whole merchant-fleet was taken.

The dead having been counted, there were a thousand on the Spanish side, and three hundred on the Beggars' side; among the latter was the chief cook of the flyboat *The Brill*.

Ulenspiegl demanded to be allowed to speak before Tres-Long and the sailors; this Tres-Long gladly gave him permission to do. And Ulenspiegl spoke to them as follows:

436

'Messire Captain, and you, comrades, we have just inherited a great many spices, and here is Lamme the old paunch, who thought that the poor defunct there—God keep him in joy—was not a great enough Doctor of Fricassees. Let us name Lamme in his place and he will prepare you heavenly stews and paradisical soups.'

'We will,' said Tres-Long and the others; 'Lamme shall be the chiefcook of the ship. He shall bear the great wooden spoon to skim off the froth from his sauces.'

'Messire Captain, comrades and friends,' said Lamme, 'you see me weeping with joy, for I do not merit such a great honour. Nevertheless, since you deign to have recourse to my unworthiness, I accept the noble functions of Master of Arts of Fricassees on the valiant flyboat *The Brill*; but I pray you humbly to invest me with the supreme command of the kitchen in such a fashion that your chief cook—myself—may by right, law and might prevent any one from coming in to the galley and eating part of what belongs to the others.'

Tres-Long and the Beggars shouted:

'Long live Lamme! You shall have right, law and might.'

'But I have another prayer to make to you, humbly. I am fat, big and robust, deep i' the paunch, profound i' the stomach. My poor wife—may God send her back to me—always gave me two portions instead of one; grant me also this favour.'

Tres-Long, Ulenspiegl and the sailors said:

'You shall have the two portions, Lamme.'

And Lamme, suddenly becoming melancholy, said:

'My wife! My sweet darling! If anything can console me for your absence, it will be to remember in my duties your heavenly cooking in our sweet home.'

'You must take the oath, my boy,' said Ulenspiegl. 'Let the great wooden spoon and the copper cauldron be brought on.'

'I swear by God,' said Lamme, 'who shall be my help, I swear fidelity to my lord, the Prince of Orange, called the Silent, who governs for the king the provinces of Holland and Zeeland; fidelity to Messire de Lumey, admiral commanding our noble fleet, and to Messire Tres-Long, vice-admiral and captain of the good ship *The Brill*; I swear to dish up at my poor best—according to the uses and customs of the great cooks of other times whose recipes have been handed down in the beautiful books with illustrations on the great art of cooking—the meats and poultry that fortune may bring our way. I swear to nourish the aforesaid Messire Tres-Long, Captain, his second, my friend Ulenspiegl, and you, master-mariner, pilot, boatswain, comrades, troopers, cannoneers, wine-keeper, captain's page, surgeon, bugler, sailors and

437

all others. If the roast is too underdone, the poultry not browned enough; if the soup exhales an unsavoury odour, against all good digestion; if the scent of the sauces does not make you all want to rush the kitchen; if I do not make you all sprightly and hearty-faced, I will resign my noble functions, considering myself unfitted to occupy any more the kitchen throne. So help me God in this life and in the other.'

'Long live the chief cook,' they shouted; 'the king of the kitchen, the emperor of fricassees. He shall have three portions on Sunday, instead of two.'

And Lamme became the chief cook of the ship, *The Brill*. And while the succulent soups were cooking in the pots, he stood by the galley door, most proud, holding his great wooden spoon like a sceptre.

And he had his three helpings on Sunday.

When the Beggars came to grips with the enemy, he willingly remained in his laboratory of sauces, but came out occasionally to go up on deck to fire a few musket-shots, then descend right away to watch over his sauces.

Being thus a faithful chef and valiant soldier, he was much loved by everyone.

But no one could penetrate his kitchen. For then he was like a devil and pitilessly smote them hip and thigh with his great wooden spoon.

And thereafter he was nick-named Lamme the Lion.

14 On the ocean, on the Scheldt, in sunshine, in rain, in snow, in hail, in winter and summer, glided the ships of the Beggars. All sails to the wind, like swans, swans of white freedom.

White for freedom, blue for grandeur, orange for the prince; that is the standard of the proud ships.

All sails to the wind! All sails to the wind, the valiant ships battered by the waters, foam-flecked by the waves.

They pass, they rush, they fly over the stream, the sails in the water, swift as the clouds before the north wind, the proud ships of the Beggars. Do you hear their prows cleave the waves? God of the free; Up with the Beggars!

Houlques, flyboats, *boyers, cromsteves,* swift as the wind bearing the tempest, as the thunder-bearing cloud. Up with the Beggars!

Boyers and *cromsteves,* flat-bottomed boats, glide over the stream. The waters groan as they cleave through them, going straight ahead, and having on their bow the deadly mouth of their long *culverin*. Up with the Beggars!

438

All sails to the wind! All sails to the wind, valiant ships, battered by the waters, foam-flecked by the waves.

On they go, day and night, under the rain, the snow, the hail! Christ smiles down upon them from the clouds, the sun and the stars. Up with the Beggars!

15 THE KING OF the blood learned news of their victories. Death was already gnawing at the butcher and his body was full of worms. He walked about the corridors of Valladolid, pitiful and sullen, dragging his swollen feet and his leaden legs along. He never sang, the cruel tyrant; at daybreak he never smiled and, when the sun lit up his empire as with the smile of God, he felt no joy in his heart.

But Ulenspiegl, Lamme and Nele, risking their skins, sang like birds. Lamme and Ulenspiegl, risking their white skins; Nele, living from day to day and rejoicing more in one stake-fire extinguished by the Beggars, than the darkling king rejoiced in the burning of a whole town.

And at this time, also, William the Silent, Prince of Orange, reduced, from his rank of admiral, Messire de Lumey de la Marck, because of his great cruelties. He promoted Messire Bouwen Ewoutsen Worst in his place. He also took counsel as to how to pay for the corn taken by the Beggars from the peasants, to return the forced contributions levied on them, and to grant to Roman Catholics, as to all others, the free exercise of their religion without persecution or insult.

16 ON THE SHIPS of the Beggars, under the shining sky, on the clear waters, sounded fifes, droned bagpipes, gurgled flasks, clinked glasses, shone the steel of weapons. 'How now,' said Ulenspiegl, 'let us beat the drum of glory, let us beat the drum of joy. Up with the Beggars! Spain is vanquished, tamed is the ghoul. Ours is the sea, Brill is taken. Ours is the coast from Nieuport in passing by Ostend, Blankenberghe; the island of Zeeland, mouths of the Scheldt, mouths of the Meuse, mouths of the Rhine, right up to Helder. Ours Texel, Vlieland, Terschelling, Ameland, Rottum, Borkum. Up with the Beggars!

'Ours Delft, Dordrecht. It's a trail of powder. God holds the linstock. The butchers abandon Rotterdam. The free conscience, like a lion with claws and teeth of justice, takes the county of Zutphen, the towns of Deutecom, Doesburg, Goor, Oldenzaal, and on the Welnuire, Hatten, Elburg, and Harderwyck. Up with the Beggars!

440

'It is the lightning, it is the thunder; Campen, Zwol, Hassel, Steen-wyck, fall into our hands with Oudewater, Gouda, Leyden. Up with the Beggars!

'Ours Bueren, Enckhuysen! We have Amsterdam, Schoonhoven, or Middleburg not yet. But all comes in time to patient blades. Up with the Beggars!

'Let us drink the Spanish wine. Let us drink from the chalices from which they drank the blood of the victims. We shall go by the Zuyder-zee, by streams, rivers and canals; we have North Holland, South Holland and Zeeland; we shall take East and West Frisia; Brill shall be the refuge for our ships, the nest of the setting hens of freedom. Up with the Beggars!

'Hear in Flanders, beloved land, how the cry for vengeance bursts out. They furbish the arms and whet the swords. All are stirring, vibrat-ing, like the strings of an Aeolian harp in a warm breath, the breath of those who arise from pits, from stakes; bleeding corpses of victims. All; Hainaut, Brabant, Luxemburg, Limburg, Namur, Liége, the free city; all. The blood flows and fecundates. The harvest is ripe for the reaper. Up with the Beggars!

'Ours the *Noord-Zee*, the wide North Sea. Ours all the good cannon, the proud ships, the daring band of redoubtable sailors, rogues, rob-bers, soldier-priests, gentlemen, burghers and workers, fleeing from persecution. Ours, all united for freedom's work. Up with the Beggars!

'Philip, king of the blood, where are you? Alba, where are you? You shout and blaspheme, coifed with the sacred hat, the gift of the Holy Father. Beat the drums of joy! Up with the Beggars! Let's drink!

'The wine flows in the golden chalices. Drink it down joyfully. The sacerdotal vestments covering the rough men are inundated with red liquor; the ecclesiastic and Roman banners float in the breeze. Eternal music! To you, fifes playing, bagpipes droning, rolling drums of glory! Up with the Beggars!'

17 THE WORLD WAS then in the wolf month—the month of De-cember. A bitter rain fell needle-like on the fleet. The Beg-gars cruised in the Zuyderzee. Messire the admiral summoned, on board his ship by trumpet, the captains of *houlques* and flyboats, and with them Ulenspiegl.

'Now,' said he, addressing himself first to Ulenspiegl, 'the prince wishes to recognize your good work and trusty services and promotes you to the captaincy of the good ship *The Brill*. I hereby hand you the commission on parchment.'

'All thanks be unto you, Messire Admiral,' said Ulenspiegl; 'I shall captain to the best of my little power, and so captaining I have high hopes, if God helps me, of uncaptaining Spain from the countries of Flanders and Holland: I mean to say from the South and North Netherlands.'

' 'Tis well,' said the admiral. 'And now,' he added, speaking to them all, 'I will tell you that the people of Catholic Amsterdam are going to lay siege to Enckhuysen. They have not yet come out of the canal, so let us cruise before it that they may remain there; and down with any or all of their boats that show their tyrannical carcasses in the Zuyderzee.'

They all answered:

'We'll knock holes in them. Up with the Beggars!'

Ulenspiegl, back again on his ship, had all his sailors and troops assembled on deck and told them what the admiral had decided.

They answered:

'We have wings—our sails! Skates—the keels of our ships! Gigantic hands—the grappling-irons for boarding. Up with the Beggars!'

The fleet set out and cruised before Amsterdam, a league out to sea, in such a way that no one could enter or leave without their willing it.

The fifth day the rain ceased; the wind blew bitterly in the clear sky; the Amsterdam people made no movement.

Suddenly Ulenspiegl saw Lamme come up on deck, chasing the *truxman* of the ship before him with his great wooden spoon, a young lad, expert in French and Flemish languages, but more expert still in gutsy science.

'Scoundrel,' said Lamme, striking at him, 'did you think you could prematurely eat my fricassees without any punishment? Get up to the mast-head and see if there isn't something stirring among the Amsterdam ships. Doing that, you'll be doing some good.'

But the *truxman* answered:

'What will you give me?'

'Do you think to be paid before you do the work? Robber's spawn, if you don't climb up there I'll have you flogged. And your French won't save you, either.'

'It's a beautiful tongue,' said the *truxman*, 'for the amorous and for the warrior.' And he climbed the rigging.

'Well, loafer?' asked Lamme.

The *truxman* answered:

'I see nothing in the town or on the ships.'

And, coming down:

'Pay me now,' said he.

442

'Keep what you stole,' replied Lamme; 'but it won't do you any good. You'll spew it up, no doubt.

The *truxman*, climbing to the top of the mast, shouted all of a sudden:

'Lamme! Lamme! There's a thief going into your galley.'

'I have the key in my pouch,' replied Lamme.

Ulenspiegl then, taking Lamme aside, said to him:

'This great tranquillity of Amsterdam frightens me, my boy. They have some secret project.'

'I thought of that,' said Lamme. 'The water freezes in the jugs in the cupboard; the poultry is like wood; hoar-frost whitens the sausages; the butter is like stone; the oil is all white; the salt is dry as the sand in the sun.'

'Frost is approaching,' said Ulenspiegl. 'They are going to come in great bands and attack us with artillery.'

Going to the admiral's ship, he spoke of his fears to the admiral, who replied:

'The wind blows in from England: there shall be snow, but no freezing: return to your ship.'

And Ulenspiegl went off.

That night a heavy snow fell; but soon the wind blew down from Norway, freezing the sea like a floor. The admiral looked on the sight.

Fearing then that the Amsterdam folk might come over the ice to burn the ships, he commanded the soldiers to get their skates ready in case they had to fight outside and round about the ships; he commanded the gunners to pile the balls up by the gun carriages, to load the cannon, and to keep the port fires always lighted.

But the Amsterdam folk never came.

And so it was for seven days.

Towards the eighth day Ulenspiegl commanded a good feast to be served to the sailors and the troops, so as to give them a protecting cuirass against the bitter wind that was blowing.

But Lamme said:

'There's nothing left but biscuits and small beer.'

'Up with the Beggars!' they said. 'That will be Lenten feasting, awaiting the hour of battle.'

'Which will not strike soon,' said Lamme. 'The Amsterdammers will come to burn our ships, but not to-night. They must first gather about the fire, and drink many stoups of mulled wine, cooked with Madeira sugar—which God grant you—then, having talked with patience, logic and full stoups, until midnight, they will decide that there are grounds for deciding the next day whether or not they are to attack the following week. Next day, drinking mulled wine with Madeira sugar again—

which God grant you—they will decide again, with calm, patience and full stoups, that they must come together another day to find out if the ice can bear a great band of men. And they will have it tried out by learned men who will set their conclusions down on parchment. Having received these conclusions, they will learn that the ice is half an ell thick and solid enough to hold several hundred men with cannon and field-artillery. Assembling again to deliberate with calm, patience and many stoups of mulled wine, they will calculate if, because of the treasure taken by us from the Lisbon merchants, it would better to assail or burn our ships. And so perplexed, but temporizing, they will nevertheless decide that they must take and not burn our ships, notwithstanding the great wrong they will thus do us.'

'You speak well,' replied Ulenspiegl. 'But do you not see these fires lit in the town and lantern-bearing folk running busily about?'

'That's because they are cold,' said Lamme.

And, sighing, he added:

'Everything is eaten. No more beef, pork or poultry; no more wine, alas! Nor good *dobble bier*. Nothing but biscuits and small beer. Who loves me, follows me!'

'Where are you going?' asked Ulenspiegl. 'No one can leave the ship.'

'My boy,' said Lamme, 'you are captain and master now. I will not leave if you do not wish it. But deign to consider, just the same, that the day before yesterday we ate the last sausage; and that, in these hard times, the kitchen fire is the sun of good companions. Who would not like to smell here the odour of sauces or sniff the perfumed bouquet of divine wine made of the joyful flowers which are gaiety, laughter and goodwill to everybody? How now, captain and faithful friend, if I dare say so; I'm eating my heart out, eating nothing. I, who love rest, never killing willingly save a tender goose, fat chicken or succulent turkey, am following you through weariness and battles. Look at the lights in that rich farm that's well-garnished with large and small cattle. Do you know who lives there? The Frisian boatman who betrayed Messire Dandelot and brought to Enckhuysen, then faithful to Alba, the eighteen poor lords and friends who were, because of him, beheaded in the horse-market in Brussels; it's the Petit Sablon. This traitor, who is named Slosse, received two thousand florins from the duke for his treachery. With this blood-money, true Judas, he bought a farm, which you see there, and his large cattle and the surrounding fields, which bore fruit and increased, have made him a rich man now.'

Ulenspiegl answered:

'The ashes beat upon my heart. You sound the hour of God.'

'And likewise,' said Lamme, 'the hour of nourishment. Give me

444

twenty men, valiant soldiers and sailors. I will go and seek out the traitor.'

'I want to lead them,' said Ulenspiegl. 'Who loves justice, follows me. Not all of you, dear and trusty; twenty only are needed, else who would guard the ship? Throw the dice to see who'll come. You are twenty, come. The dice spoke well. Put on your skates and glide towards the star of Venus shining above the traitor's farm.

'Guiding yourselves in the clear light, come on, you twenty, skating and sliding, axes on your shoulders.

'The wind whistles and drives the white whirls of snow before it on the ice. Come, worthy men!

'You do not sing, nor speak; you go straight on, silently towards the star; your skates make the ice screech.

'He who falls gets right up again. We're nearing the bank: not a human form on the white snow, not a bird in the icy air. Unbuckle your skates.

'Here we are on land, here are the fields, buckle on your skates again. We are about the farm, hold your breaths in.'

Ulenspiegl knocked at the door, the dogs barked. He knocked again; a window opened and the *baes* said, as he stuck out his head:

'Who are you?'

He saw no one but Ulenspiegl; the others were hidden behind the *keet*—the wash-house.

Ulenspiegl answered:

'Messire de Boussu bids you go to him at Amsterdam immediately.'

'Where is your safe-conduct?' said the man, coming down and opening the door.

'Here,' answered Ulenspiegl, showing him the twenty Beggars, who had rushed in behind him in the opening.

Ulenspiegl then said:

'You are Slosse, the treacherous boatman who made Messires Dan-

delot, Battembourg and other lords fall into an ambuscade. Where's the blood-money?'

Trembling, the farmer replied:

'You are the Beggars, grant me pardon; I knew not what I did. I have no money here; I will give all.'

Lamme said:

'It's dark; give us wax or tallow candles.'

The *baes* answered:

'The tallow candles are hanging there.'

A candle being lit, one of the Beggars, by the hearth, said:

'It's cold, let's light a fire. Here's good kindling.'

And he showed on a plank some flower-pots whose plants were all dried up. He took hold of one of the plants by the stalks and as he shook it the pot fell and with it fell, and scattered on the floor, ducats, florins and reals.

'The treasure's there,' said he, pointing to the other pots.

And, indeed, having emptied them, they found ten thousand florins. Seeing this, the *baes* cried out and wept.

The men and maid-servants of the farm came in, in their night-shirts, at the cries. The men, wishing to revenge their master, were tied up. Soon their goodwives, ashamed, and especially the younger ones, hid themselves behind the men.

Lamme advanced then and said:

'Traitorous farmer, where are the keys to the cellar, to the stable, the cow-barns, and the sheep-pen?'

'Infamous pillagers,' said the *baes*, 'you shall be hanged until you are dead."

'It is the hour of God; hand over the keys.'

'God shall avenge me,' said the *baes*, handing them over.

Having emptied the farm, the Beggars skated off towards the ships, the lighthouses of freedom.

'I am chief cook,' said Lamme, guiding them; 'I am chief cook. Push on the valiant sleds, filled with wines and beer; drive on before you, by their horns or otherwise, the horses, oxen, pigs, sheep and flocks, singing their natural songs. The doves are cooing in the baskets; the capons, stuffed up with bread-crumbs in wooden cages where they cannot move, are astonished. I am the chief cook. The ice screeches under the steel of the skates. We have reached the ships. To-morrow there shall be kitchen music. Send down the pulleys. Place the belly-bands about the horses, cows and oxen. It's a lovely sight to see them strung up by the belly like that; to-morrow our tongues shall be hanging on to rich fricassees. The crane hoists them up into the ship. These

446

are carbonnades. Throw them pell-mell into the hold for me; the hens, geese, ducks, capons. Who shall wring their necks? The chief cook. The door is locked, I have the key in my pouch. God be praised in the kitchen! Up with the Beggars!'

Then Ulenspiegl went to the admiral's ship, taking Dierick Slosse and the other prisoners with him; they were groaning and weeping for terror of the rope.

Messire Worst came out at the noise. Seeing Ulenspiegl and his companions lit up with the red glare of the torches, he said:

'What will you with us?'

Ulenspiegl replied:

'This night we captured on his farm the traitor Dierick Slosse, who caused the eighteen to fall into an ambush. This is he. The others are his innocent men and maid-servants.'

Then, handing over a pouch:

'These florins,' said he, 'flourished in flower-pots in the traitor's house; there are ten thousand of them.'

Messire Worst said to the Beggars:

'You did wrong to leave the ships; but because of your great success, you shall be pardoned. The prisoners and the pouch of florins are welcome, and you worthy men, to whom I give, according to the rights and customs of the sea, one-third of the capture. The second third shall be for the fleet and the other for my lord of Orange. Hang the traitor immediately.'

The Beggars having obeyed, they afterwards made a hole in the ice and threw the body of Dierick Slosse into it.

Messire Worst then said:

'Has the grass sprung up about the ships that I hear hens clucking, sheep baaing, oxen and cows lowing?'

'These are our belly prisoners,' said Ulenspiegl; 'they shall pay the ransom of fricassees. Messire the admiral shall have the best of them.

'As for these folk here, men and maid-servants, among whom are many sweet and comely goodwives, I am going to take them back to my ship.'

Having done this, he spoke to them as follows:

'Goodfellows and goodwives, you are here on the best ship that ever sailed. We pass our time in endless jollity, feasting and revelling. If you wish to leave, pay the ransom; if you wish to stay, you shall live as we do, working hard and eating well. As for these darling goodwives, I deliver to them, as captain, full freedom, telling them that it is all one to me if they wish to stick to their friends who shall come with

447

them on the ship, or choose some worthy Beggar here present to be their matrimonial companion.'

But all the charming maidens were faithful to their own lovers save one, who, smiling and looking at Lamme, asked him if he wanted her.

'Thank you, sweet,' said he, 'but I am bound elsewhere.'

'The goodfellow's married,' said the Beggars, seeing the maid vexed.

But she, turning her back on him, chose another who had, like Lamme, a fine belly and a happy countenance.

There were that day, and the following days, great feasts of wines, poultry and meats aboard the ships. And Ulenspiegl said:

'Up with the Beggars! Blow, bitter breeze, we shall warm the air with our breaths. Our heart is on fire for free conscience. Our stomachs are a fire for the enemies' meats. Let us drink wine, men's milk! Up with the Beggars!'

Nele also drank from a great golden tankard and, ruddy from the blowing breeze, played upon her fife. And, notwithstanding the cold, the Beggars ate and drank joyously on deck.

18 SUDDENLY THE WHOLE FLEET saw a dark troop on the shores, in whose midst shone torches and glistened weapons; then the torches were extinguished and a great obscurity reigned. The orders of the admiral being transmitted, the signal for the alert was given on the ships, and all lights were extinguished. The sailors and the soldiers, armed with axes, lay down flat on the decks. The valiant gunners, holding their linstocks, watched by their cannon, charged with bags of bullets and chain-shot. As soon as the admiral and the captains called out: 'A hundred paces'—thus indicating the distance of the enemy—they were to fire forward, or aft, or broadside, according to their positions on the ice.

And the voice of Messire Worst was heard saying:

'Penalty of death to whoever speaks loudly!'

And the captains repeated after him:

'Penalty of death to whoever speaks loudly!'

The night was starry, but moonless.

'Do you hear?' said Ulenspiegel to Lamme, speaking like the whisper of a ghost. 'Do you hear the voices of the Amsterdammers and the noise of their skates screeching on the ice? They are coming fast. One can hear them speak. They're saying: "The loafing Beggars are asleep. Ours the Lisbon treasure!" They're lighting torches. Do you see their ladders for the attack, and their ugly faces, and the long line of their attacking band? There are a thousand or more of them.'

'A hundred paces!' shouted Messire Worst.

'A hundred paces!' shouted the captains.

There was a great noise as of thunder, and lamentable howlings on the ice.

'Eighty cannon were shot off at once!' said Ulenspiegl. 'They are fleeing. Do you see the torches disappearing?'

'Pursue them!' said Admiral Worst.

'Pursue them!' said the captains.

But the pursuit did not last long, for the fugitives had the start of a hundred paces and the legs of frightened hares.

And, on the men who were calling out and dying on the ice, they found gold and jewels, and ropes for the Beggars.

And, after that victory, the Beggars said to each other: '*Als God met ons is, wie zal tegen ons zijn?* (If God be with us, who then can be against us?) Up with the Beggars!'

Now on the morning of the third day, Messire Worst, uneasy, awaited a new attack. Lamme leaped up on deck and said to Ulenspiegl:

'Take me before that admiral who would not listen to you when you prophesied the frost.'

'Go on without being taken!' said Ulenspiegl.

Lamme went off, locking the galley door. The admiral was on deck, looking to see if he could not discover some movement in the town.

Lamme, approaching him:

'My lord admiral,' said he, 'may a humble chief cook give you his opinion?'

'Speak, my son,' said the admiral.

'My lord,' said Lamme, 'the water is thawing in the jugs; the poultry are becoming tender; the sausage is losing its dew of hoar-frost; the butter is unctuous; the oil liquid; the salt weeps. It will soon rain, and we shall be saved, my lord.'

'Who are you?' asked Messire Worst.

449

'I am,' he replied, 'Lamme Goedzak, the chief cook of the good ship *The Brill*. And if all the great savants, pretending to be astronomers, could read the stars as well as I read my sauces, they might say that to-night there is to be a thaw with a great roaring tempest and hail. But the thaw will not last.'

Lamme returned to Ulenspiegl, to whom he said, towards noon:

'I am still a prophet; the sky darkens; the wind blows tempestuously; a warm rain falls; there is already a foot of water on the ice.'

In the evening he called out joyfully:

'The North Sea is swelling: it's the hour of the flood-tide, the high waves enter the Zuyderzee, breaking the ice which, by great lumps, breaks off and is thrown on the ships; it casts sparkles of light; here is the hail. The admiral asks us to retire from before Amsterdam, and that with as much water as our largest ship can draw. Here we are in the harbour of Enckhuysen. The sea freezes over again. I am a prophet and 'tis a miracle of God.'

And Ulenspiegl said:

'Let's drink to him, with blessings.'

And winter passed and summer came.

19 In mid-August, when the hens stuffed with grain remain deaf to the call of the cock who trumpets his love, Ulenspiegl said to his sailors and soldiers: 'The duke of the blood dares, being at Utrecht, to dictate a new edict which promises, among other gracious gifts, hunger, death, ruin to the inhabitants of the Netherlands who will not give in. All that remain intact shall be exterminated and his royal majesty shall people the country with foreigners. Bite, Duke, bite! The file can break the viper's tooth; we are files. Up with the Beggars!

'Alba, blood has intoxicated you! Think you that we fear your threats or believe in your clemency? Your illustrious regiments whose praises you hymned throughout the world—your *Invincibles,* your *Tels-Quels,* your *Immortals*—remained seven months gunning Haarlem, a weak town defended by its burghers. Like ordinary mortals, these famous soldiers danced in the air the dance of bursting mines. The burghers tarred them; but they ended by conquering gloriously, cutting the throats of the disarmed men. Do you hear, butcher, the hour of God ringing out?

'Haarlem lost its valiant defenders; its stones sweat blood. It lost and spent for its siege twelve hundred and eighty thousand florins. The bishop is reinstated there; he blesses the churches with a light hand

450

and a joyful face; Don Frederic is present at these benedictions; the bishop washes his hands for him, these hands which in the eyes of God are red, and he communicates in two kinds, which is not permitted to the poor populace. And the bells ring out and the carillon throws on the air its tranquil and harmonious notes; it is as an angelic hymn over a cemetery. Eye for an eye! Tooth for a tooth! Up with the Beggars!'

20 THE BEGGARS were then at Flushing, where Nele caught fever. Obliged to leave the ship, she was lodged in the house of Peeters, the Reformist, at Turven-Kaai. Although very sad, Ulenspiegl was yet happy in thinking that, in her bed, she would doubtless get well again and that the Spanish bullets would not be able to reach her.

And with Lamme he was continually at her side, caring for her well and loving her better. And there they talked together.

'Friend and trusty,' said Ulenspiegl one day, 'do you know the news?'

'No, my boy,' said Lamme.

'Did you notice the flyboat that recently came to join our fleet, and do you know who plays the viola every day?'

'Because of these last colds,' said Lamme, 'I am a little deaf in both ears. Why are you laughing, my boy?'

But Ulenspiegl, continuing what he was saying:

'Once I heard a Flemish *lied* being sung and I found the voice sweet.'

'La,' said Lamme, 'she also sang and played on the viola.'

'Do you know something else?' pursued Ulenspiegl.

'I know nothing, my boy,' answered Lamme.

'Orders have been given us to descend the Scheldt with our ships as far as Antwerp, there to find the enemy vessels and capture or burn them. As for their sailors; no quarter. What do you think of that, big-belly?'

'La,' said Lamme. 'Shall we never hear tell in this unfortunate country but of burnings, hangings, drownings, and other exterminations of poor men? When shall the blessed peace come then, so that we may, without turmoil, roast partridges, fricassee chickens, and make the black-puddings to sing in the middle of the omelettes in the pan?—I like the black ones better; the white ones are too rich.'

'That agreeable time will come,' replied Ulenspiegl, 'when in the Flemish orchards we shall see, on the apple-trees, the plum-trees, the cherry-trees, instead of apples, plums and cherries, a Spaniard hanging from every branch.'

'Ah,' said Lamme, 'if only I could find my wife, my so dear, dainty,

451

beloved, sweet darling, faithful wife! For mark you well, my boy, I never was nor ever will be a cuckold; she was too reserved and calm in her ways for that. She shunned the company of other men; and if she liked to dress well, that was only through feminine necessity. I was her cook, kitchen-man, scullion; quite freely I tell it. Why am I not all that again? But I was also her master and husband.'

'Let's stop this talk,' said Ulenspiegl. 'Do you hear the admiral shouting: "Up anchors!" and the captains repeating it after him, shouting as he does? We must be getting under weigh soon.'

'Why do you leave so quickly?' said Nele to Ulenspiegl.

'We are going to ship,' said he.

'Without me?' said she.

'Yes,' said Ulenspiegl.

'Don't you think that I am going to be very uneasy about you here?'

'Darling,' said Ulenspiegl, 'my skin's of steel.'

'You are joking,' said she. 'I only see your doublet, which is of cloth, not iron; under it is your body made of bones and flesh, even as mine. If you are wounded, who will bind up your wounds? Will you die alone in the midst of all the fighters? I will go with you.'

'La,' said he, 'if the lances, cannon-balls, swords, axes, hammers, sparing me, fall on your darling body, what shall I do, good-for-nothing that I am, without you in this evil world?'

But Nele said:

'I want to follow you, there will be no danger; I will hide me in the wooden forts where the musketeers are.'

'If you go, I stay, and they will call your friend Ulenspiegl traitor and coward; but listen to my song:

'My hair's of iron, like a casque.
Dame Nature forged it for my use;
Of leather is my first skin made,
My second skin of strongest steel.

In vain the ugly grinning Death
Has tried to catch me in his snare:
Of leather is my first skin made
My second skin of strongest steel.

My banner bears the words *Live On*,
Live on forever in the light:
Of leather is my first skin made,
My second skin of strongest steel.'

452

And off he went, singing, but not without having kissed the trembling mouth and the sweet eyes of the fevered Nele, smiling and weeping both at once.

The Beggars are at Antwerp, they take Alba's ships right in the port. Entering the town in broad daylight, they free prisoners and take others to serve as ransom. They force the burghers to get up and even make some follow them without uttering a word, on pain of death.

Ulenspiegl said to Lamme:

'The admiral's son is detained at the *Ecoutêtes*; we must free him.'

Going into the house of the *Ecoutête*, they saw the boy they sought, in the company of a great paunchy monk, who was preaching angrily to him, trying to make him return to the bosom of our Holy Mother the Church. But the young lad was not persuaded. He went off with Ulenspiegl. In the meantime Lamme, nabbing the monk by the cowl, made him walk before him through the streets of Antwerp, saying:

'You're worth a hundred florins of ransom; pick up your skirts and walk ahead. What's holding you back? Have you lead in your sandals? Walk on, lard-bag, victual-box, soup-belly.'

Most furious, the monk said:

'I'm walking, Master Beggar, I'm walking; but with all the respect I owe your musket, you are just the same as I am, a big-bellied, paunchy, fat man.'

But Lamme, pushing him on:

'Do you dare, vile monk,' said he, 'to compare your cloistral, useless, lazy fat, to my Flemish fat, nourished on labours, fatigues and battles? Run, or I'll make you go like a dog, and that with the spur of the toe of my boot.'

But the monk could not run, and he was all out of breath, and Lamme likewise. And in this fashion they came to the ship.

21 HAVING TAKEN Rammekens, Gertruydenberg, Alkmaar, the Beggars returned to Flushing. Nele, now better, awaited Ulenspiegl at the port. 'Tyl,' she said on seeing him, 'my love Tyl, aren't you wounded?'

Ulenspiegl sang out:

> 'My banner bears the words *Live On,*
> Live on forever in the light:
> Of leather is my first skin made,
> My second skin of strongest steel.'

'La,' said Lamme, dragging his leg along: 'the bullets, grenades, chain-shot rain about him and he only feels the wind of them. There is no doubt but that you're a spirit, Ulenspiegl, and you also, Nele, for I always see you both sprightly and young.'

'Why are you dragging your leg that way?' asked Nele of Lamme.

'I am not a spirit and I never will be,' said he. 'And so I got an axe stroke on the thigh—my wife's was so round and so white!—look, I'm bleeding. La, why don't I have her here to care for me!'

But Nele angrily replied:

'What need have you for a perjuring woman?'

'Don't speak badly of her,' answered Lamme.

'Here,' said Nele, 'here is balm; I was keeping it for Ulenspiegl; put it on the wound.'

Lamme, having dressed his wound, was gay, for the balm had soothed the stinging pain; and they went up, all three of them, to the ship.

Seeing the monk, who walked about with his hands tied:

'Who is that one?' said she. 'I have already seen him and seem to remember him.'

'He's worth a hundred florins of ransom,' replied Lamme.

22 THAT DAY THERE WAS a feast for the fleet. In spite of the bitter wind, in spite of the rain, in spite of the snow, all the Beggars of the fleet were on the decks of the ships. The silver crescents on the hats of the Zeelanders gleamed brightly. And Ulenspiegl sang:

'Leyden is freed: away from the Netherlands goes the duke:
     Ring out, resounding bells;
Carillons throw upon the air your songs;
     And tinkle glasses; bottles clink.

When the bull-dog slinks away from the blows
     His tail between his legs,
     With a bleeding eye
     He turns upon the stick
     And his torn jaws
     Quiver pantingly.
     He has gone, the duke of the blood.
So tinkle glasses; bottles clink, and up with the Beggars!

     He wished to bite himself,
     The truncheons broke his teeth.

455

Hanging his chub-jowled head,
He thinks of days of murder and of lust.
He has gone, the duke of the blood:
Beat then the drums of glory,
Beat then the drums of war!
   Up with the Beggars!

He cries to the devil: "I will sell
My canine soul for one hour of strength."
"Your soul, it means no more to me
Than does a herring!" said the devil.
His teeth no longer meet, and so
He must avoid the harder bits.
He has gone, the duke of the blood;
   Up with the Beggars!

The crook-shanked, one-eyed, mangy dogs i' the streets,
That live and die on rubbish heaps,
Lift up their hind legs, one by one,
On him that killed for love of murder . . .
   Up with the Beggars!

He loved not women, nor his friends,
Nor gaiety, sun, nor master,
No one save death, his lover,
Who broke his legs for him
As prelude to the betrothal,
For that she loved not:
Beat upon the drums of joy,
   Up with the Beggars!

And the dogs i' the street, crook-shanked,
And limping, mangy, one-eyed,
Lift their hind legs anew
In hot and salty fashion,
And likewise, greyhounds, mastiffs,
Hungarian dogs, and dogs of Brabant,
Namur, and Luxemburg.
   Up with the Beggars!

And sadly, foaming at the mouth,
He goes to die beside his lord,

Who lands a sounding kick at him
For not having bitten enough.
In hell he weds my lady death,
Who calls him "My Own Duke"
And he calls her "My Inquisition!"
   Up with the Beggars!

Ring out, resounding bells;
Carillons throw upon the air your songs;
And tinkle glasses; bottles clink.
   Up with the Beggars!'

Book Five

———

1 THE MONK CAPTURED by Lamme, perceiving that the Beggars did not want his death but rather his payment of ransom, began to stick up his nose on board ship. 'See,' said he, walking up and down and wagging his head furiously, 'see into what a pit of filthy, black and vile abominations I have fallen, in setting foot on this wooden tub. If I were not here, I whom the Lord anointed. . .'

'With dog's grease?' asked the Beggars.

'Dogs yourselves,' replied the monk, continuing his discourse, 'yes! dogs, mangy, stray, foul, half-starved dogs that have fled from the rich path of our Holy Mother the Roman Church to walk on the parched roads of your tattered Reformed Church. Yes, if I were not in your clog, your tub, the Lord would have swallowed it up in the profound depths of the sea, a long time ago, with you, your accursed arms, your cannons of the devil, your singing captain, your blasphemous crescents; yes, sent it down to the unfathomable bottom of Satan's kingdom, where you will not burn, no! but where you will freeze, tremble, die of cold throughout the long eternity. Yes! God in heaven shall extinguish in this way your impious hatred against our sweet Mother the Holy Roman Church, against the saints, messeigneurs the bishops, and the blessed edicts which were so sweetly and ripely thought out. Yes! I shall look down on you from paradise, purple as beetroots, white as turnips, so cold you'll be. 'T sy; 'T sy! 'T sy! So be, be, be, be it.'

The sailors, troopers and boys mocked at him, and pelted him with dried peas through pea-shooters. And he covered his face with his hands against this artillery.

2 THE DUKE OF THE BLOOD having left the country, Messires Medina-Celi and Requesens governed it with less cruelty. Then the States-General ruled in the name of the king. In the meantime the Holland and Zeeland folk, happily situated because of the sea and the dykes, which are their ramparts and natural fortresses, opened free temples to the God of the free. And the butchering Papists could sing their hymns beside them; and my lord of Orange, the Silent, refrained from founding a stadtholdery and royal dynasty.

The Belgian country was ravaged by the Walloons, who were dissatisfied by the Peace of Ghent, which was to quench all hatreds—or so it was said. And these Walloon *Paternoster knechten,* wearing about their necks great black rosaries, and of whom there were two thousand at Spienne in Hainaut, went about stealing oxen and horses by the twelve hundred and the two thousand, choosing the best; they went over fields and through marshes, carrying off women and girls, eating and never paying, and burning in their barns the armed men who would not let the fruits of their hard toil be carried off.

And the people said among themselves: 'Don Juan is going to come with his Spaniards, and his great highness will come with his Frenchmen, not Huguenots but Papists: and the Silent One wishing to reign in peace over Holland, Zeeland, Guelders, Utrecht, Overyssel, has ceded the Belgian countries by a secret treaty so that Monsieur of Anjou can make himself king over them.'

Some of the populace still had confidence. 'The States,' they said, 'have twenty thousand well-armed men, with many cannon and excellent cavalry. They will resist all foreign troops.'

But the very prudent ones said: 'The States have twenty thousand men on paper, but not in the field; they are lacking in cavalry and let the *Paternoster knechten* steal their horses within a league of the camp. They have no artillery, for, while having need of it here, they decided to send a hundred cannon and powder and balls to Don Sebastian of Portugal; and no one knows where the two million *ecus* have gone which we paid on four occasions with taxes and contributions. The burghers of Ghent and Brussels are arming themselves; Ghent for the reform, and Brussels like Ghent. At Brussels the women play the kettle-drums while their husbands work on the ramparts. And Ghent, the bold, sends to Brussels the gay powder and cannon which it lacks to defend itself against the malcontents and the Spaniards.

'And many, in the towns and the flat country, *in't plat landt,* see that they can have no confidence either in the lords or in many others. And we burghers and those of the common people are grieved in our hearts that, giving our money, and ready to give our blood, we see nothing going forward for the good of the land of our fathers. And Belgium is frightened and angry at having no faithful chiefs to give her the occasion for battle and grant her the victory, by a great effort of arms, all ready against the enemies of freedom.'

And the prudent ones said among themselves:

'In the Peace of Ghent, the lords of Holland and Belgium swore to quench all hatreds, swore reciprocal assistance between the Belgian States and the Netherland States; declared the edicts null and void, the confiscations lifted, and peace between the two religions; they promised to cast down all columns, trophies, inscriptions, effigies, set up by the Duke of Alba to our dishonour. But in the hearts of the chiefs, the hatreds are still aflame; the nobles and the clergy foment division between the States of the Union; they receive money to pay the soldiers and keep it for their own stuffing; fifteen thousand law-suits for the recovery of confiscated goods are in a state of suspension; the Lutherans

462

and the Romans are uniting against the Calvinists; the legitimate heirs cannot drive out the despoilers from their inheritances; the statue of the duke is thrown to the ground, but the image of the Inquisition is in their hearts.'

And the poor populace and the sad burghers still awaited the valiant and faithful chief who would lead them to the battle for freedom.

And they said among themselves: 'Where are the illustrious Signers of the Compromise, all united, they said, for the good of the fatherland? Why did these two-faced men make such a "holy alliance" if it was to be broken at once? Why assemble with such a bustle, excite the king's anger, only to break up afterwards like cowards and traitors? Five hundred as they were—lords, great and small, united as brothers —they saved us from the Spanish fury; but they sacrifice the good of the land of Belgium to their own interests as did Egmont and Hoorn.'

'La!' they said, 'now you will see Don Juan, the handsome, ambitious one, the enemy of Philip, but also the enemy of our country. He comes for the Pope and for himself. The nobles and the clergy betray us.'

And they began a semblance of war. On the walls of the large and small streets of Ghent and Brussels, even on the masts of ships, were seen posted up the names of the traitors, army chiefs, and commanders of fortresses; those of the Count of Liederkerke who did not defend his castle against Don Juan; of Messieurs Aerschot, Mansfeldt, Berlaymont, Rassenghien; those of the Council of State, of George de Lalaing, Governor of Frisia, of that of the army chief, the Lord of Rossignol, the emissary of Don Juan and *entrepreneur* of murder between Philip and the clumsy assassin of the Prince of Orange, Jaureguy; the name of the Archbishop of Cambrai who wanted to let the Spaniards into the town; the names of the Jesuits of Antwerp, offering three casks of gold to the States—that is two million florins—not to demolish the castle and hold it for Don Juan; of the Bishop of Liége; of the Roman preachers defaming the patriots; of the Bishop of Utrecht whom the burghers sent elsewhere to nibble the grass of treason; of the begging orders of friars plotting at Ghent in favour of Don Juan.

The people of Bois-le-Duc nailed on the pillory the name of the Carmelite, Peter, who, aided by their bishop and his clergy, tried hard to hand over the town to Don Juan. At Douai they did not yet hang the effigy of the Rector of the University, likewise Spaniardized; but on the ships of the Beggars might be seen on the breasts of mannikins— who were hanged by their necks—the names of monks, abbots, and prelates, those of the eighteen hundred rich women and girls of the convent of Malines who, by their contributions, sustained, gilded, and beplumed the butchers of the fatherland.

And on these mannikins, pillories of the traitors, could be read the names of the Marquis of Harrault, commander of the stronghold of Philippeville, who uselessly squandered the munitions of war and food in order to give up the town—under the pretext of lack of food—to the enemy; that of Belver who surrendered Limburg, when the town could have held out for eight months more; those of the president of the Council of Flanders, of the magistrate of Bruges, of the magistrate of Malines, holding their towns for Don Juan; of the gentlemen of the Chamber of Accounts of Guelder, closed because of treason; of those of the Council of Brabant, of the Chancellory of the Duchy, of the Privy Council and the Financial Council; of the High Bailiff and Burgomaster of Menin; and the wicked neighbours of the Artois region who allowed to pass, without any hindrance, two thousand Frenchmen en route for pillage.

'La!' said the burghers among themselves, 'here is the Duke of Anjou now with his foot in our country; he wants to be king over us. Did you see him enter Mons, small, with big hips, a great nose, a yellow snout with a sneering mouth? He's a great prince, having extraordinary loves; they call him—so that he may have in his name feminine grace and manly strength—*Monseigneur Monsieur Sa Grande Altesse d'Anjou.*'

Ulenspiegl was thoughtful. And he sang:

'The sky is blue, the sun shines bright;
Cover the banners all in crepe,
With crepe the hilts of all the swords;
Hide all the gems:
And turn the mirrors to the walls;
I sing the ballad of death,
The ballad of the traitors.

They set their foot on the belly
And on the breast of the proud lands

464

Of Brabant, Flanders, Hainaut,
Antwerp, Artois, Luxemburg.
The bait of recompense leads them on.
I sing the ballad of traitors.

When everywhere the enemy sacks,
When the Spaniard enters Antwerp's town,
Abbots, prelates, and army chiefs
Go walking up and down the streets
All clad in silk, bedecked with gold,
Their faces shining with good wine,
And showing thus their infamy.

And by them will the Inquisition
Awake again triumphantly,
  And new Titelmans
Arrest the deaf and dumb
  For heresy.
I sing the ballad of the traitors.

Oh, Signers of the Compromise,
  Cowardly signatories,
May your names be accursed!
Where were you at the hour of war?
You march like hungry vultures
  In the Spaniards' train;
  Beat the mourning drums.

Oh, Belgium's land, the years to come
Will judge you for that, being armed,
You let yourself be pillaged.
Oh, future be not quick to judge,
Look at the traitors labouring:
They are twenty; a thousand strong,
Occupying every post,
The great donating them to the small.

They have agreed together
On how to impede resistance
With discord and with laziness,
The motto of their treachery.
Cover with crepe the mirrors,

With crepe the hilts of all the swords.
This is the ballad of traitors.

They declare rebels,
The Spaniards and the Malcontents;
Forbidding any aid to them
Of bread or shelter,
Lead or powder.
If they are taken to be hanged,
    To be hanged,
They are set free right away.

"Stand up!" say those of Brussels;
"Stand up!" say those of Ghent
    And all the Belgian populace;
They want, poor men, to crush you
    Between the king
    And the Pope, who's launched
This crusade against your land.

They come, the mercenaries,
    At the smell of blood;
    Bands of dogs,
Of serpents and hyenas.
They hunger and they thirst.
Poor land of our fathers,
Ripe for ruin and for death.

It is not Don Juan
That makes the task right easy
For Farnese, the darling of the Pope,
But those you loaded down
With gold and eminence,
Who did the confessing of your wives,
Your daughters and your children!

They have cast you to the ground
And now the Spaniard holds
The knife against your throat;
They all were mocking you
When they feted at Brussels
The coming of the Prince of Orange.

When one saw on the canal,
So many fireworks and squibs
All crackling out their joy,
So many fine triumphant ships,
With paintings and with tapestries,
They were playing, Belgium, all for you
The ancient tale of Joseph
Sold by his brethren.'

3   SEEING THAT HE WAS allowed to talk, the monk lifted up his nose on the ship; and the sailors and soldiers, in order to hear him preach, spoke ill of Madame the Virgin, and of the Saints, and of the pious practices of the Holy Roman Church. Then, flying into a rage, he spewed out a thousand insults at them.

'Yes,' he screamed, 'yes, here I am right in the cave of the Beggars! Yes, here indeed are those cursed devourers of the country! Yes! and they say that the Inquisitor, the holy man, burned too many of them! No! there are still some of the filthy vermin left. Yes! on the fine and gallant ships of our lord, the king, so clean once and so well-scoured, may now be seen the Beggar vermin. Yes, the stinking vermin! Yes! they are all vermin, filthy, stinking, infamous vermin, the ballad-monger captain, the cook with his belly full of impiety, and all those others with their blasphemous crescents. When the king shall have his ships scoured down by the artillery it will be necessary to use more than a hundred thousand florins worth of balls and powder to clear away this filthy, vile, stinking infection. Yes! you were all born in the alcove of Madame Lucifer, condemned to live with Satanas between verminous walls, under verminous curtains, on verminous mattresses. Yes! there it was, out of their infamous love that the Beggars were born. Yes! and I spit on you.'

At these words the Beggars said:

'Why do we keep this loafer here, who only knows how to spew out insults? Let us rather hang him.'

And they set about getting ready to do this.

The monk, seeing the cord ready, the ladder against the mast, and that they were about to tie his hands, said mournfully:

'Have pity on me, Master Beggars, it was the demon of anger that spoke in my heart and not your humble captive, poor monk, that has but one neck in this world. Gracious lords, be merciful; gag me if you will with a choke-pear—a bitter fruit—but do not hang me.'

They, without paying any attention to him, and in spite of his furious

467

resistance, dragged him towards the ladder. He screamed then so shrilly that Lamme said to Ulenspiegl, who was with him, tending him in the galley:

'My boy! My boy! They have stolen a pig from the pen and they're cutting its throat. Oh, the robbers, if I could only get up!'

Ulenspiegl went up on deck and only saw the monk. The latter, perceiving him, fell on his knees, his hands outstretched towards him.

'Messire Captain,' said he, 'captain of the brave Beggars, dreaded on land and sea, your soldiers wish to hang me because I have sinned with my tongue; it's an unjust punishment, Messire Captain, for then you would have to rope with a hempen collar the necks of all the lawyers, procurators, preachers, and women, and the world would be depopulated. Messire, save me from the rope. I shall pray for you, and you will not be damned; grant me pardon. The wordy demon carries me away and makes me talk without ceasing; it is really a great misfortune. My poor bile becomes embittered and makes me say a thousand things I'd never think of otherwise. Grace, Messire Captain, and you all, sirs, pray for me.'

Suddenly Lamme appeared on deck in his shirt-tails, and said:

'Captain and friends, as it was not the pig but the monk that screamed, I am very happy. Ulenspiegl, my boy, I have conceived a great plan regarding His Paternity; let him live, but do not let him go free or he'll do some evil turn on the ship. Rather make for him, on the deck, a narrow cage, well-aired, wherein he can barely sit down and sleep, the sort of a cage they make for the capons. Let me nourish him and may he be hanged if he does not eat as much as I want him to.'

'Let him be hanged, if he does not eat,' said Ulenspiegl and the Beggars.

'What do you plan doing with me, fat man?' said the monk.

'You shall see,' replied Lamme.

And Ulenspiegl did as Lamme wished, and the monk was put in the cage, where everyone could easily see him.

Lamme having gone back to his galley, Ulenspiegl followed him and heard him arguing with Nele:

'I will not go to bed,' said he, 'no, I will not go to bed so that the others can come and stick their noses in my sauces; no, I will not stay in my bed, like a calf!'

'Do not get angry, Lamme,' said Nele, 'or your wound will re-open and you'll die.'

'Very well,' said he, 'I'll die. I am weary of living without my wife. Is it not enough for me to have lost her without your trying to prevent me, the chief cook of this ship, from looking after my own soup? Don't

468

you know that there is an innate health in the steam of sauces and fricassees? They even nourish my spirit and arm me against misfortune.'

'Lamme,' said Nele, 'you must take our advice and let yourself be healed by us.'

'I want to let myself be healed,' said Lamme; 'but that another should enter here—some ignorant rascal, scabby, ulcerous, bleary-eyed, snotty-nosed fellow—who would enthrone himself as chief cook in my stead, and puddle about with his filthy hands in my sauces, I'd rather kill myself with my great wooden spoon, which would be iron for the occasion.'

'Just the same,' said Ulenspiegl, 'you need a helper, you are ill.

'A helper for me?' said Lamme. 'For me, a helper? Are you stuffed with ingratitude, like a sausage with ground meat? A helper, my boy, and you're the one to say that to me, to me your friend, who has nourished you so long and so richly! Now my wound's going to re-open. Evil friend, who then is going to prepare the food as I do? What would you both do if I were not here to give you, Chief Captain, and you, Nele, some dainty stew?'

'We should work in the galley ourselves,' said Ulenspiegl.

'Ah, cooking,' said Lamme; 'you can eat it, sniff it, down it all right, but do it, no. Poor friend and Chief Captain, saving your respect, I could make you eat wallets cut up in ribbons and you'd take them for tripes —a little tough. Allow me, allow me, my boy, to be chief cook herein; if not I shall dry up like a lath.'

'Remain chief cook then,' said Ulenspiegl; 'if you do not get well I shall close up the galley and we'll eat nothing but biscuits.'

'Ah, my boy,' said Lamme, weeping with pleasure, 'you are as kind as Our Lady.'

4 NEVERTHELESS he seemed to be healing. Every Saturday the Beggars saw him measuring the monk's waist-line with a long leather strap. The first Saturday he said:

'Four feet.'

And, measuring himself, he said:

'Four feet and a half.'

And he seemed melancholy.

But, speaking to the monk, he was happy the eighth Saturday, and said:

'Four feet and three quarters.'

And the monk, angry when his measurement was taken, said to him: 'What do you want with me, fat man?'

469

But Lamme stuck out his tongue at him with never a word.

And seven times a day the sailors and soldiers saw him coming with some new dish, saying to the monk:

'Here are fat beans with Flemish butter. Did you ever eat the like in your monastery? You have an excellent phiz; one doesn't starve on this ship! Don't you feel cushions of fat sprouting on your back? Soon you'll have no need of a mattress to sleep on.'

At the second meal:

'Here,' said Lamme to the monk, 'here are *koekebakken* done in the Brussels style; the French folk call them *crêpes*, for they wear them on their head-dress in sign of mourning; these are not black but fair and made golden in the oven. Do you see the butter streaming from them? So will it stream from your belly.'

'I am not hungry,' said the monk.

'You must eat,' said Lamme: 'do you think that these are buckwheat cakes? They are of pure wheat, father, father in fat, fine wheaten flour, four-chinned father; I see a fifth one sprouting, and my heart is happy. Eat.'

'Leave me in peace, fat man,' said the monk.

Lamme, becoming angry, replied:

'I am the master of your life. Do you prefer the rope to a good dish of *purée* of peas with *croûtons* such as I'm going to bring you presently?'

And, returning with the dish:

'*Purée* of peas love to be eaten in company; and so I have German *knoedels*, fine little balls of Corinth flour, thrown quickly into boiling water; they are heavy but they make fat. Eat as much as you can; the more you eat the greater my happiness will be; don't act as though they disgusted you; don't puff so hard as though you had had enough; eat. Is it not better to eat than to be hanged? Let's see your thigh! It also is getting fat; two feet seven inches around. Where is the ham that measures as much?'

An hour later he came back again to the monk:

'Here,' he said, 'here are nine pigeons: they were shot down for you, these innocent beasties, who flew fearlessly over the ship. Don't turn up your nose at them, for I set in their stomachs a ball of butter, bread-crumbs, grated nutmeg, cloves pounded in a mortar of copper that shone like your skin. Our lord, the sun, is most happy to be able to reflect himself in a face as bright as yours, because of the fat, the good fat I have made you.'

At the fifth meal, he brought him a *waterzoey*.

'What do you think,' said he to him, 'of this hotchpot of fish? The sea bears you and feeds you; it couldn't do more for his royal majesty.

470

Yes, yes! I can plainly see the fifth chin sprouting, a little more to the left side than to the right. You must fatten up that side in disgrace, for God commands us "Be just in all things." And where would justice be if not in the equitable distribution of fat? I shall bring for your sixth meal some mussels—the poor folks' oysters—such as they never laid before you in your monastery. The ignorant boil them and eat them that way; but that is just the prologue to the dish; they should then be taken from their shells and their delicate bodies placed in a stew-pan, there to be gently stewed with celery, nutmeg, cloves, and then their sauce thickened with beer and flour; they should then be served on bread fried in butter. I have done them this way for you. Why do children owe their fathers and mothers such great gratitude? Because they gave them shelter, love, and, above all, nourishment. You should then love me like your father and mother, and even as to them, you owe me also belly-gratitude; don't roll your eyes so fiercely at me.

'I shall bring you soon a beer and flour soup, well-sugared, and with lots of cinnamon. Do you know why? So that your fat may become transparent and tremble on your skin. It can be seen thus when you move about. There, the curfew rings out now; sleep in peace without thought of the morrow, certain as you are to find your unctuous meals and your friend Lamme to hand them to you without fail.'

'Be off, and leave me to pray God,' said the monk.

'Pray,' said Lamme, 'pray with the gay music of snores: the beer and sleep shall make fat for you, excellent fat. And I am glad of it.'

And Lamme went off to go to bed.

And the sailors and soldiers said to him:

'Why do you feed so richly that monk who wishes you no good?'

'Let me alone,' said Lamme, 'I'm accomplishing a great work.'

5 DECEMBER HAVING COME, the month of long darknesses, Ulen-spiegl sang:

'Monseigneur Sa Grande Altesse
    Takes off the mask,
Wishing to reign over the Belgian lands.
    The States are Spaniardized
    But not yet Angevined
    And dispose of their own taxation.
    Beat the drums
    Of Angevine discomfiture.

They have at their discretion
Domains, excise, and funds,
The creation of the magistrates,
And other offices as well.
Monsieur Sa Grande Altesse,
Who passes as an atheist in France,
Is furious with the Reformists.
    (Oh, the Angevine discomfiture!)

For he would fain be king,
By force and by the sword,
An absolute king for evermore,
This Monseigneur and Grande Altesse;
He fain would traitorously seize
Many fine towns, even Antwerp too;
Signorkes, pagaders, rise in the morning.
    (Oh, the Angevine discomfiture!)

'Tis not 'gainst you, O France,
That these folk rush, all mad with rage;
These murderous armèd blows
Strike not your noble body;
These corpses rising in a mound
And blocking Kip-Dorp Gate
Are not those of your sons.
    (Oh, the Angevine discomfiture!)

No, these are not your sons
Thrown by the people from the ramparts, heights.
They are those of Anjou the Grande Altesse,
Of Anjou passive debauchee,
Living off your blood, Oh France,
And wishing to drink of ours;
But many's the slip 'twixt cup and lip.
    (Oh, the Angevine discomfiture!)

Monsieur Sa Grande Altesse—
In a defenceless town,
With all his lovely darling boys
Within whose eyes there burns
The shameless, restless, brazen fire
Of loveless lust—cried out:

"Kill! Kill! Long live the Mass!"
  (Oh, the Angevine discomfiture!)

'Tis them they smite, not you, poor folk,
Weighed down by heavy taxes,
Deflowering-tax, salt-tax, poll-tax;
Poor folk contemned and made to give
Your corn, your horses, and your carts,
You who are father to them.
  (Oh, the Angevine discomfiture!)

You who are mother to them
And giving suck to the evil deeds
Of all these parricides who soil
Your name abroad, Oh France you are repaid
With odours of their glory,
When they have added
By some savage deed. . .
  (Oh, the Angevine discomfiture!)

. . . A jewel to your military crown,
A province to your territory.
Leave to the stupid cock "Lust and Battle"
The foot on the neck,
People of France, manly race,
The foot that crushes them down,
And all the other folk will love you
    For Angevine discomfiture!'

6   In May, when the peasant women of Flanders, in the night,
    throw three black beans slowly backwards over their heads to
    keep them from sickness and from death, Lamme's wound re-
opened; he had a high fever and asked to be laid on the deck of the
ship facing the cage with the monk.

Ulenspiegl was quite willing; but, for fear that he might fall into
the sea in a fit of fever, he had him solidly attached to his bed.

In his reasonable moments, Lamme continually charged them not to
forget the monk; and he stuck out his tongue at him.

And the monk said:

'You're insulting me, fat man.'

'No,' said Lamme, 'I'm fattening you.'

A gentle breeze blew, the sun shone down warm; Lamme in his fever was well tied to his bed, so that in his delirious moments he would not leap out over the ship's deck; and, thinking he was still in his galley, he said:

'That fire is bright to-day. Soon it will rain down ortolans. Wife, set snares in our orchard. You look lovely like that with your sleeves rolled up to your elbows. Your arm is white; I want to bite it, bite it with my lips that are as velvet teeth. Whose is that lovely flesh; whose are these beautiful breasts showing through your bodice of fine linen? Mine, my sweet treasure. Who will make the fricassee of cock's combs and chicken rumps? Not too much nutmeg; it makes one feverish. A white sauce with thyme and bay-leaf. Where are the egg-yolks?'

Then, making a sign to Ulenspiegl to bring his ear closer to his mouth, he whispered to him:

'Soon it will rain venison; I shall hold for you four more ortolans than for the others. You are the captain, do not betray me.'

Then, hearing the waves lap gently at the side of the ship:

'The soup's boiling, my boy, the soup's boiling, but how slow this fire is to get going!'

As soon as he recovered his wits, he said, speaking of the monk:

'Where is he? Does he grow in fat?'

Seeing him then, he stuck his tongue out at him and said:

'The great work is being accomplished, and I am content.'

One day he asked to have the great scales set up on deck and that he be set on one side and the monk on the other: no sooner was the monk set on, than Lamme's side shot up like an arrow in the air, and, most happy, he said as he looked at him:

'He weighs it down! He weighs it down! I am a light spirit alongside him; I'm going to fly in the air like a bird. I have an idea. Take him off so that I can come down. Set the weights on; replace him in the scales. How much does he weigh? Three hundred and fourteen pounds. And I? Two hundred and twenty.'

7 THE NIGHT of the following day, in the grey dawn, Ulenspiegl was awakened by Lamme, shouting: 'Ulenspiegl! Ulenspiegl! to the rescue! Stop her from going! Cut the ropes! Cut the ropes!'

Ulenspiegl went up on the deck and said:

'What are you shouting for? I see nothing.'

'It's she,' replied Lamme, 'she, my wife, there, in that launch that

474

turns about that flyboat; yes, that flyboat whence came the sounds of singing and viola-playing.'

Nele had come up on deck:

'Cut the ropes, my dear,' said Lamme. 'Don't you see that my wound is healed? Her soft hand bound it up; she, yes, she. Do you see her standing up in the launch? Do you hear? She still sings. Come, my beloved, come, don't run from your poor Lamme, who was so lonely in the world without you.'

Nele took his hand, touched his face:

'He still has the fever,' said she.

'Cut the ropes,' said Lamme; 'give me a launch! I am living, I am happy, I am healed.'

Ulenspiegl cut the ropes: Lamme, leaping from his bed in breeches of white linen, with no doublet, started to let down the launch himself.

'Look at him,' said Nele to Ulenspiegl; 'his hands tremble with impatience as they work.'

The launch being ready, Ulenspiegl, Nele and Lamme got down into it with an oarsman and went off towards the flyboat anchored far out in the harbour.

'There's the fine flyboat,' said Lamme, helping the oarsman.

Under the cool morning sky, coloured like crystal, gilded by the rays of the new sun, the flyboat stood out with its hull and its elegant masts.

While Lamme rowed, Ulenspiegl asked him:

'Tell us now how you found her?'

Lamme answered, speaking in jerks:

'I was sleeping, feeling much better. Suddenly a dull noise. A piece of wood struck the ship. The launch. A sailor runs, hearing the noise: "Who goes there?" A gentle voice, hers, my boy, hers, her gentle voice: "Friends." Then a deeper voice: "Up with the Beggars! Commander of the flyboat *Johannah* to speak to Lamme Goedzak." The sailor threw over the ladder. The moon shone. I saw a man's form coming up the deck; big hips, round knees, wide pelvis; I said to myself: "False man." I felt as though a rose were opening and touching my cheek: her mouth, my boy, and I heard her say to me, she—do you understand?—she herself covering me with kisses and tears; it was like scented liquid fire falling over my body: "I know that I'm doing wrong; but I love you, my husband! I swore to God. I am breaking my oath, my husband, my poor husband! I often came without daring to approach you; the sailor finally gave me permission. I bound up your wound, and you did not recognize me; but I healed you; do not be angry, my man! I followed you, but I'm afraid he is on this ship: let me go; if he saw me he would curse me and I would burn in eternal fire!" She kissed me again, weep-

475

ing and happy, and went off in spite of me, in spite of my tears. You had bound me legs and arms, my boy, but now. . .'

And, so saying, he gave a vigorous pull on his oar; it was like the taut string of a bow that speeds the arrow straight onwards.

As they were approaching the flyboat, Lamme said:

'There she is, standing on the deck, playing the viola, my sweet wife with the golden brown hair, with the brown eyes, with her cheeks still fresh, her arms naked and round, her hands white. Fly, launch, over the waters!'

The captain of the flyboat, seeing the launch coming and Lamme rowing like the very devil, threw down a ladder from the deck. When Lamme was close to it, he leapt from the launch on to the ladder at the risk of falling into the sea, pushed the launch away about three fathoms; and, climbing up the ladder like a cat, ran on the deck to where his wife was. She, fainting away with pleasure, kissed and embraced him, saying:

'Lamme! Do not come to take me. I have sworn to God, but I love you. Ah! dear man!'

Nele cried:

'That's Calleken Huybrechts, the lovely Calleken.'

'The same,' said she, 'but, alas, the noonday hour is past for my beauty.'

And she seemed sad.

'What have you done?' asked Lamme. 'What had become of you? Why did you leave me? Why do you want to leave me now?'

'Listen,' she said, 'and don't be angry; I want to tell you everything. Knowing that all monks were men of God, I confided myself to the care of one of them; he was named Broer Cornelis Adriaensen.'

Hearing which Lamme said:

'What! That wicked hypocrite with the sewer-mouth full of filthiness and excrement, and speaking of nothing but shedding the blood of the Reformists? What! That panegyrist of the Inquisition and the edicts? Ah! it was that blackguardly scoundrel!'

476

Calleken said:

'Do not insult the man of God.'

'The man of God!' said Lamme, 'I know him: he was the man of filth and foulness. Unhappy fate! My lovely Calleken fallen into the hands of that lecherous monk! Don't come near me; I'll kill you. And I who loved you so! My poor wronged heart that was all hers! What did you come here for? Why did you take care of me? You should have let me die. Go away; I don't want to see you any more; go away, or I'll throw you into the sea. My knife! . . .'

She embraced him, saying:

'Lamme, my husband, do not weep. I am not what you think. I did not belong to that monk.'

'You lie,' said Lamme, weeping and gnashing his teeth at the same time. 'Ah! I was never jealous and now I am. Sad passion, anger and love; a need to kill and to embrace. Go away! No, stay! I was so good to her! Murder is master of me. My knife! Oh! this burns, devours, gnaws; you're laughing at me. . .'

She embraced him, weeping, gentle and submissive.

'Yes,' said he, 'I'm silly in my anger. Yes, you kept my honour, that honour which we pin foolishly on the skirts of a woman. So it was for this that you chose your sweetest smiles, to ask me to let you go to the sermon with your friends. . .'

'Let me speak,' said the woman, as she embraced him: 'may I drop dead this instant if I deceive you!'

'Die then,' said Lamme, 'for you are about to lie.'

'Listen to me,' said she.

'Speak, or don't speak,' said he, 'it's all the same to me.'

'Broer Adriaensen,' she said, 'passed for being a good preacher; I went to hear him; he set up the ecclesiastic state and the state of celibacy above all else, as being the most proper to win an entrance for the faithful into paradise. His eloquence was great and fiery: many honest women, including myself, and notably a great many widows and young maids, had their minds troubled. The state of celibacy being so perfect, he charged us to remain in it. We all swore not to allow ourselves to be espoused from that time on.'

'Save to him, doubtless,' said Lamme, weeping.

'Be quiet,' said she, angrily.

'Go on,' said he, 'finish; you have struck me a disagreeable blow; I shall never get over it.'

'Yes, my man,' she said, 'when I'm with you for ever.'

She wanted to embrace and kiss him, but he repulsed her.

'The widows,' she said, 'swore on his hands never to re-marry again.'

477

And Lamme listened, lost in his jealous reverie.

Calleken, ashamed, continued what she was saying:

'He would only take for his penitents,' she said, 'women and girls who were young and beautiful: the others he sent off to their vicars. He established an order of devotees, making everyone of us swear not to have any other confessor but him. I swore. My companions, more initiate than I was, asked me if I did not want to be instructed in the holy discipline and the holy penance. I said I did. There was at Bruges, on the Stone Cutters Wharf, near the monastery of the Minor Friars, a house inhabited by a woman named Calle de Najage, who gave to the girls instruction and nourishment for a golden carolus a month. Broer Cornelis could enter the house of Calle de Najage without seeming to go out of his cloister. It was into this house that I went, in a little room where he was alone. There he commanded me to tell him of all my natural and carnal inclinations; at first I did not dare; but I gave way finally, weeping, and telling him all.'

'La!' wept Lamme, 'and that swinish monk thus received your gentle confession.'

'He always said to me—and this is true, my man—that above earthly modesty there is heavenly modesty, through which we make to God the sacrifice of our worldly shames, and it was thus that we avowed to our confessor all our secret desires, and were worthy then to receive the holy discipline and the holy penance.

'Finally he forced me to strip myself naked before him, so as to receive on my body, that had sinned, the too light punishment for my faults. On the day he forced me to undress before him I fainted away when I had to let fall my chemise. He brought me to with salts and flasks. "That is all for this time, my girl," said he, "return in two days and bring a rod with you." That continued for a long time without ever. . . I swear before God and all his saints. . . my husband. . . understand me. . . look at me. . . see if I am lying. I remained pure and faithful. . . I loved you.'

'Poor sweet body,' said Lamme. 'Oh, stain of shame on your marriage robe!'

'Lamme,' said she, 'he spoke in the name of God and of our Holy Mother Church. Should not I have listened to him? I loved you still, but I had sworn to the Virgin by horrible oaths to refuse myself to you; yet I was weak, weak for you. Do you remember the hostelry of Bruges? I was at Calle de Najage's house when I saw you passing by on your donkey with Ulenspiegl. I followed you. I had a goodly sum of money, for I spent nothing on myself; I saw that you were hungry: my heart was drawn to you; I was filled with pity and love.'

478

'Where is he now?' asked Ulenspiegl.

Calleken answered:

'After an inquest ordered by the magistrate and an investigation of wicked people, Broer Adriaensen was forced to leave Bruges and take a refuge in Antwerp. They told me on the flyboat that my man had taken him prisoner.'

'What!' said Lamme, 'that monk, that I'm fattening, is. . .'

'He,' said Calleken, hiding her face.

'An axe! An axe!' cried Lamme, 'that I may kill him, that I may sell at auction his lascivious goat's fat! Quick! Let us go back to the ship. The launch! Where is the launch?'

Nele said to him:

'It is a vile cruelty to kill or wound a prisoner.'

'You look at me with a cruel eye; will you prevent me?' said he.

'Yes,' said she.

'Well,' said Lamme, 'I'll do him no harm: only let me make him come out of his cage. The launch! Where is the launch?'

They soon got into it; Lamme made haste to row, and wept as he did.

'Are you sad, my man?' said Calleken to him.

'No,' said he, 'I am happy; you'll doubtless never leave me again.'

'Never again!' said she.

'You were pure and faithful, you say; but, sweet darling, beloved Calleken, I only lived to find you, and here now, thanks to that monk, there shall be poison in all our joys, the poison of jealousy. As soon as I am sad, or merely weary, I shall see you naked, submitting your lovely body to that infamous flagellation. The spring of our love was mine, but the summer was to him; the autumn shall be grey and soon winter will come to bury my faithful love.'

'Are you weeping?' she asked.

'Yes,' said he, 'that which is past shall never come back again.'

Nele then said:

'If Calleken was faithful, she should leave you alone for the mean words you've said to her.'

'He does not know how I loved him,' said Calleken.

'Do you speak the truth?' cried Lamme. 'Come, darling; come, my wife; there is no more grey autumn nor grave-digging winter.'

And he seemed happy, and they arrived at the ship.

Ulenspiegl gave the keys of the cage to Lamme and he opened it. He wanted to pull the monk out on the deck by his ear, but he could not; he tried to drag him out sideways, but could not do that either.

'It must be broken down; the capon is fattened,' said he.

The monk then came forth, rolling his great besotted eyes, holding

479

his belly in his two hands, and he fell on his beam-ends because of a great wave that passed under the boat.

And Lamme, speaking to the monk, said:

'Will you still say "Fat man"? You are fatter than I am. Who gave you seven meals a day? I. How comes it, brayer, that you are now more calm, more gentle to the poor Beggars?'

And, continuing his discourse:

'If you remain one more year in the cage, you'll never be able to get out: your cheeks quiver like pig's-feet jelly when you move about. Already you don't shout any more; soon you'll not be able to breathe.'

'Be silent, fat man,' said the monk.

'Fat man!' said Lamme, flying into a rage: 'I am Lamme Goedzak, you are Broer Dikzak, Vetzak, Leugenzak, Slokkenzak, Wulpszak, Brother Big-sack, Fat-sack, Lie-sack, Stuffed-sack, Lust-sack: you have four inches of fat under your skin and your eyes can't be seen any more: Ulenspiegl and I could be lodged with ease in the cathedral of your belly! You call me a fat man; do you want a mirror to contemplate your bellyness? I'm the one that nourished you, monument of flesh and bone! I have sworn that you'll spit fat, that you'll sweat fat and leave behind you greasy traces like a candle melting in the sun. They say that apoplexy comes with the seventh chin; you have five and a half now.'

Then, speaking to the Beggars:

'Do you see this lecher! He's Broer Cornelis Adriaensen Scoundrelsen of Bruges; there he preached the new modesty. His fat is his punishment; his fat is my work. Now, hear you, all you sailors and soldiers: I am about to leave you; to leave you, Ulenspiegl; to leave you also, Nele; to go to Flushing where I have some property and live with my poor wife whom I have found again. You once swore an oath to grant me all that I might ask of you . . .'

'Beggars' word,' said they.

'Then,' said Lamme, 'look at that lecher, that Broer Adriaensen Scoundrelsen of Bruges; I swore to make him die of fat like a hog; construct a larger cage, force him to take twelve meals a day instead of seven; hand him starchy and sugary food: already he is like an ox, feed him so that he'll be like an elephant, and you'll soon see him filling up the cage.'

'We'll fatten him up,' said they.

'And now,' continued Lamme, speaking to the monk, 'I say goodbye to you also, scoundrel, whom I nourished monkishly instead of having you hanged; grow in fat and apoplexy.'

Then, taking his wife Calleken in his arms:

480

'Look, growl, or bellow, I carry her off from you, you'll never be able to flagellate her any more.'

But the monk, flying into a rage and speaking to Calleken:

'You are going then, carnal woman, to the bed of lust. Yes, you are going off without pity for the poor martyr of the Word of God who taught you the holy, suave, and heavenly discipline. May you be cursed! May no priest ever pardon you; may the earth be as fire under your feet; may sugar seem as salt to you; may beef be as dead dog to you; may your bread be as ashes; may the sun be of ice and the snow as the fires of hell; may your fruitfulness be accursed; may your children be detestable; may they have apes' bodies and hogs' heads bigger than their bellies; may you suffer, weep, groan, in this world and in the next, in the hell that awaits you, the hell of sulphur and bitumen, lit for such females as you. You refused my paternal love; be thrice accursed by the Holy Trinity, seven times by the candelabra of the ark; may the confession be as damnation to you; may the Host be as mortal poison to you, and in church each paving-stone rise up to crush you and to say: "This woman is the fornicatress, the accursed, the damned!"'

And Lamme, most gay, jumping about with pleasure, said: 'She was faithful; he said it, the monk. Long live Calleken!'

But she, weeping and trembling:

'Remove,' said she, 'remove that curse from me, my man. I see hell! remove the curse!'

'Remove the curse!' said Lamme.

'I will not remove it, fat man,' retorted the monk.

And the woman remained all pale and swooning, and on her knees she implored Broer Adriaensen with clasped hands.

And Lamme said to the monk:

'Remove your curse, or you'll be hanged, and if the rope breaks because of your weight you'll be re-hanged until death ensues.

'Hanged and re-hanged,' said the Beggars.

'Then go, wanton,' said the monk, speaking to Calleken, 'go with that fat man; go, I lift the malediction; but God and all His Saints will have their eyes on you; go with that fat man, go.'

And he was silent, sweating and puffing.

Suddenly Lamme shouted:

'He's swelling! He's swelling! I see the sixth chin; the seventh is apoplexy! And now,' said he, addressing the Beggars:

'I commend you to God, you, Ulenspiegl; to God, you, all my good friends; to God, you, Nele; to God and the holy cause of freedom. I can do no more for it.'

481

Then having given to all and received in turn the accolade, he said to his wife, Calleken:

'Come, it is the hour for lawful loves.'

While the little boat glided over the waters, bearing away Lamme and his beloved, he in the stern, all the sailors, soldiers and ship-boys shouted as they waved their caps: 'Good-bye, brother; good-bye, Lamme; good-bye, brother, brother and friend!'

And Nele said to Ulenspiegl, as she wiped with the tip of her dainty finger a tear from the corner of his eye: 'Are you sad, my love?'

'He was good,' said he.

'Ah,' said she, 'will this war never cease? Shall we be forced for ever to live in blood and in tears?'

'Let us seek the Seven,' said Ulenspiegl. 'The hour of deliverance approaches.'

Following Lamme's wish, the Beggars fattened the monk in his cage. When he was freed, in return for a ransom, he weighed three hundred and seventeen pounds and five ounces, Flemish weight.

And he died prior of his monastery.

8 AT THIS TIME the gentlemen of the States-General assembled at the Hague to judge Philip, King of Spain, Count of Flanders, of Holland, etc., according to the charters and privileges, consented to by him. And the clerk spoke as follows:

'It is well known to all men that a prince of a country is set up by God to be sovereign and chief of his subjects and preserve them from all wrongs, oppressions, and violences, even as a shepherd is ordered to defend and guard his flocks. It is well known also that the subjects are not created by God for the prince's use, to be obedient to him in everything that he commands, be it pious or impious, just or unjust; nor to serve him as slaves. But the prince is a prince for his subjects, without whom he could not be, so as to govern them in accordance with right and logic; to uphold and love them as a father his children, as a pastor his flock, risking his life to defend them; if he does not do this he must be held not for a prince but for a tyrant. Philip the king launched against us, through appeals to soldiers, papal bulls of crusade and excommunication, four armies of foreigners. What shall his punishment be by virtue of the laws and customs of the country?'

'Let him be deposed,' replied the gentlemen of the States.

'Philip has been false to his oaths; he has forgotten the services we rendered him, the victories we helped him win. Seeing that we were

482

rich, he allowed us to be ransomed and pillaged by those of the council of Spain.'

'Let him be deposed for his ingratitude and robbery,' replied the gentlemen of the States.

'Philip,' continued the clerk, 'set up new bishops, in the most powerful towns of the country, endowing and making them the beneficiaries of the wealth of the largest abbeys; with their aid he introduced the Spanish Inquisition.'

'Let him be deposed as a butcher and squanderer of the wealth of others,' replied the gentlemen of the States.

'The nobles of the country, seeing this tyranny, presented a request in the year 1566 wherein they beseeched the sovereign to moderate his rigorous edicts and notably those concerning the Inquisition; but he always refused to do this.'

'Let him be deposed as a tiger, obstinate in his cruelty,' replied the gentlemen of the States.

The clerk continued:

'Philip is strongly suspected of having, by those of his council of Spain, secretly provoked the breaking of the images and the sacking of the churches so as to be able, under the pretext of crime and disorder, to send foreign armies against us.'

'Let him be deposed as an underling of death,' replied the gentlemen of the States.

'At Antwerp, Philip massacred the inhabitants, ruined the Flemish merchants and the foreign merchants. He and his council of Spain gave to a certain Rhoda, notorious scoundrel, secret instructions, enabling him to set himself up as chief of the pillagers, to gather in the booty, use the name of Philip the king to counterfeit the seals, and counterseals, and act as his governor and lieutenant. The royal letters which were intercepted and are now in our hands prove this fact. Everything happened with his consent and after deliberation by the council of Spain. Read these letters, they praise the doings in Antwerp, acknowledge having received a signal service, promise to reward it, and charge Rhoda and the other Spaniards to continue along that glorious path.'

'Let him be deposed as robber, pillager, murderer,' replied the gentlemen of the States.

'We wish for naught save the maintenance of our privileges, a loyal and assured peace, a moderate freedom, especially inasfar as religion is concerned, which touches God and conscience. We have had nothing from Philip save lying treaties serving to sow discord among the provinces, to subjugate them one after the other, and treat them as the Indians are treated, with pillage, confiscation, executions and the Inquisition.'

'Let him be deposed as an assassin, having premeditated the murder of the country,' replied the gentlemen of the States.

'He bled the country by the Duke of Alba and his catchpolls, by Medina-Celi, Requesens, the traitors of the councils of State and the provinces; he enjoined Don Juan and Alexander Farnese, Prince of Parma—as you may see from the intercepted letters—to practise a rigorous and bloody severity; he set the ban of the Empire on my lord of Orange, paid three assassins—awaiting the payment of a fourth; set up castles and fortresses here; burned men alive, buried alive women and girls, to inherit their goods; strangled Montigny, de Berghes, and other lords, notwithstanding his royal word; killed his son Carlos; poisoned the prince of Ascoli, whom he had made to marry Dona Eufrasia, heavy with his child, so that the bastard-to-be might be enriched by the prince's wealth; launched against us an edict which declared us all traitors having lost bodies and wealth, and committed this crime, unheard of in a Christian country, of confounding the innocent and the guilty.'

'By all laws, rights and privileges, let him be deposed,' replied the gentlemen of the States.

And the seals of the king were broken.

And the sun shone down on the earth and the sea, making golden the ears of corn, ripening the grapes, throwing on each wave pearls to adorn the bride of the Netherlands—freedom.

Then the Prince of Orange, being at Delft, was struck down by a fourth assassin, receiving three bullets in his breast. And he died following his device: 'Calm amid the cruel waves.'

His enemies said of him that, to thwart King Philip and never hoping to reign over the southern and Catholic low countries, he had offered them to Monseigneur Monsieur Sa Grande Altesse d'Anjou by a secret treaty. But that prince was not born to procreate with freedom the infant Belgium, which loves not perverse loves.

And Ulenspiegl, with Nele, left the fleet.

And the Belgian country groaned under the yoke, garrotted by the traitors.

9 IT WAS THEN the month of the ripened grains; the air was heavy, the breeze warm; the reapers could gather in the harvest—which they had sown—at their ease under a free sky, on a freed soil. Frisia, Drenthe, Overyssel, Guelder, Utrecht, North Brabant, North and South Holland; Walcheren, North and South Beve-

484

land; Duiveland and Schouwen, which form Zeeland; all the coasts of the North Sea from Knokke to Helder; the isles of Texel, Vlieland, Ameland, Schiermonnik-Oog, were, from the eastern Scheldt to the western Ems, to be delivered from the Spanish yoke. Maurice, the son of the Silent One, continued the war.

Ulenspiegl and Nele, having their youth, their strength, and their beauty—for the love and the spirit of Flanders never grow old—lived quietly in the tower of Neere, waiting till they might come and breathe on Belgium, after many cruel ordeals, the breath of freedom.

Ulenspiegl had asked to be appointed commander and keeper of the tower, saying that, having the eyes of an eagle and the ears of a hare, he would be able to see if the Spanish ever dared to show up again in the freed countries. Then he would sound the *wacharm,* which is the alarm in the Flemish language.

The magistrate granted Ulenspiegl's request and, because of his good service, they gave him a florin a day, two quarts of beer, beans, cheese, biscuits, and three pounds of meat a week.

Ulenspiegl and Nele both lived very well; they saw with joy the free islands of Zeeland, away in the distance; meadows, woods, castles and fortresses, and the armed ships of the Beggars guarding the coast.

In the evening they often climbed up into the tower and there, sitting out on the platform, they talked together of hard battles, of loves past and to come. From where they sat, they could see the ocean, which during the warm weather rolled and unrolled on the shore its phosphorescent waves, throwing them on the isles like wraiths of fire. And Nele was frightened seeking the will-o'-the-wisps in the polders—they were the souls of the poor dead folk, she said. And all these places had been battle-fields.

The will-o'-the-wisps would spring out from the polders, run along the dykes, then return to the polders as though they did not wish to abandon the corpses from whence they had come.

One night Nele said to Ulenspiegl:

486

'See how numerous they are in Duiveland and how high they fly; it is on the side of the Birds' Isle that I see the most of them. Will you come with me there, Tyl? We shall take the balm that shows invisible things to mortal eyes.'

Ulenspiegl answered:

'If it is the same balm that made me go to that great Sabbath, I have no more confidence in it than in an empty dream.'

'You must not,' said Nele, 'deny the power of charms. Come, Ulenspiegl.'

'I will.'

The following day he asked the magistrate to send a clear-sighted and faithful soldier to replace him, so that the tower would be guarded and watch kept over the country.

And off he went with Nele to the Birds' Isle.

Walking along by fields and dykes, they came to little verdant islets, between which runs the sea water; and on grassy hillocks, running right down to the dunes, a great crowd of plovers, sea-gulls, and sea-swallows, all perfectly immobile, made the islets seem all white with their bodies; above them flew thousands of other birds. The earth was covered with nests; Ulenspiegl, bending over to pick up an egg from the path, saw a sea-gull coming at him, flying and screaming. At this appeal there came more than a hundred others, all screaming with anguish, skimming over the head of Ulenspiegl and the near-by nests, but not daring to approach him.

'Ulenspiegl,' said Nele, 'these birds are demanding grace for their eggs.'

Then, beginning to tremble, she said:

'I am afraid. Now the sun is setting, the sky is white, the stars awake; it is the hour of the spirits. See, gliding over the earth, these red exhalations. Tyl, my love, what monster of hell is this, opening its fiery mouth in the mist in this way? See the will-o'-the-wisps dancing over there by Philipsland, where the butcher-king, for his cruel ambition, twice killed so many poor men. Now is the night when the souls of the poor men killed in battle leave the cold limbo of purgatory to come and warm themselves in the tepid air of the earth. Now is the hour when you can ask anything you will of Christ, who is the God of good sorcerers.'

'The ashes beat upon my heart,' said Ulenspiegl. 'If Christ would only show me the Seven whose ashes, thrown to the winds, were to make Flanders and the whole world happy!'

'Oh man without faith,' said Nele, 'you shall see them by virtue of the balm.'

487

'Maybe,' said Ulenspiegl, pointing to Sirius, 'if some spirit descends from that cold star.'

As he pointed, a will-o'-the-wisp, flying about, landed on his finger, and, the more he tried to shake it off, the more it clung.

Nele, trying to deliver Ulenspiegl, also had a will-o'-the-wisp at her finger-tips.

Ulenspiegl, striking his, said:

'Answer me! Are you the soul of a Beggar or a Spaniard? If you are the soul of a Beggar, go to paradise; if you are the soul of a Spaniard, return to the hell from whence you've come.'

Nele said to him:

'Do not insult the souls, even though they be the souls of the executioners.'

And, making her will-o'-the-wisp dance on the end of her finger:

'Will-o'-the-wisp,' said she, 'gentle wisp, what news do you bring from the land of the souls? What are they busy doing there? Do they eat, do they drink, having no mouths? For you have none, sweet wisp! Or do they not take on human form save in some blessed paradise?'

'How can you waste your time talking to that fretful flame that has neither ears to hear nor a mouth to answer with?'

But, without heeding him:

'Wisp,' said Nele, 'answer by dancing, for I am going to question you three times; once in the name of God; once in the name of Madame the Virgin; and once in the name of the elemental spirits who are the messengers between God and man.'

This she did, and the will-o'-the-wisp danced three times. Then Nele said to Ulenspiegl:

'Take off your clothes, I will do the same; here is the silver box with the balm of vision.'

'As you wish,' answered Ulenspiegl.

When they had both undressed and anointed themselves with the balm of vision, they lay down naked side by side on the grass.

The sea-gulls screamed; the thunder rumbled dully in the clouds and the lightning flashed.

The moon barely showed between two cloud-banks the golden horns of its crescent; and Ulenspiegl's and Nele's will-o'-the-wisp went dancing off with the others in the meadows.

Suddenly Nele and her friend were seized by a giant's great hand, which cast them into the air like children's balloons, caught them back again, rolled them one over the other, kneaded them in his hands, threw them in the pools of water between the hillocks, and drew them out again covered with sea-grass. Then, carrying them through space

488

thus, he sang, with a voice that awoke all the terrified sea-gulls of the
islands:

> 'They wished with squinting eyes,
> These miserable lice,
> To read the divine symbol
> That we hold captive.
> Read the mystery, flea,
> Read the sacred word, louse,
> Which in the air, sky, and earth
> By seven nails is held down.'

And, indeed, Ulenspiegl and Nele saw, on the grassy sward, in the
air and in the heavens, seven tablets of shining brass which were attached by seven flamboyant nails. On the tablets there was written:

> 'Upon the dung-heaps flowers the seed;
> Seven is bad but seven is good;
> Diamonds come from out the coal;
> From foolish teachers, pupils wise;
> Seven is bad but seven is good.'

And the giant walked, followed by all the will-o'-the-wisps, who
chirped like grasshoppers, saying:

> 'Look well, it is their great master.
> Pope of the Popes, King of Kings,
> 'Tis he leads Caesar forth to grass,
> Look well at him, he's made of wood.'

Suddenly his features changed, and he seemed more thin, sad and
tall. He held in one hand a sceptre and in the other a sword. His name
was Pride.

And, throwing Nele and Ulenspiegl down to the ground, he said:

'I am God.'

Then alongside him, seated on a goat, appeared a ruddy-faced girl,
with naked breasts, her dress all open, and her eyes sparkling; her name
was Lust; came then an old Jewess gathering up sea-gulls' egg-shells;
her name was Avarice. Then a gusty monk eating chitterlings, stuffing
himself with sausages, and chewing endlessly like the sow on which he
was mounted; this was Gluttony. Came then Idleness, dragging her legs,
pale and puffy, and dull-eyed; she was chased by Anger, who jabbed
her with a needle. Woebegone Idleness lamented and burst into tears,
and fell down on her knees. Then came thin Envy with the viper's head
and pike's teeth, biting Idleness because she was too much at ease, bit-

489

ing Anger because she was too quick, Gluttony because she was too well-filled, Lust because she was too ruddy, Avarice because of the egg-shells, Pride because of his purple robe and crown. And the will-o'-the-wisps danced about them.

And, speaking with the voices of men, of women, of girls and plain-tive children, they said, as they groaned:

'Pride, father of Ambition, Anger, well-spring of cruelty, you killed us on the battle-fields, in prisons and torture-chambers, in order to hold fast to your sceptres and crowns! Envy, you destroyed in their seed many noble and useful thoughts; we are the souls of persecuted in-ventors. Avarice, you changed into gold the blood of the poor populace; we are the spirits of your victims. Lust, companion and sister of Murder, who begot Nero, Messalina, and Philip, King of Spain, you bought virtue and paid for corruption; we are the souls of the dead. Idleness and Gluttony, you defile the world, you must be swept from it; we are the souls of the dead.'

And a voice was heard, saying:

> 'Upon the dung-heaps flowers the seed;
> Seven is bad and seven is good.
> From foolish teachers, pupils wise;
> To have the ashes and the coal also
> What will the wandering louse do?'

And the will-o'-the-wisps said:

'We are the fire, the revenge for the old tears, the griefs of the people; the revenge on the nobles who hunted the human game over their lands; revenge for useless battles, of blood spilled in prisons, men burned, women and girls buried alive; revenge for the past, bound and bleed-ing. We are the fire; we are the souls of the dead.'

At these words the Seven were changed into wooden statues without losing anything of their original forms.

And a voice said:

'Ulenspiegl, burn the wood.'

And Ulenspiegl, turning to the wisps:

'You who are of fire,' said he, 'fulfil your office.'

And the will-o'-the-wisps crowded about the Seven, who were burned and reduced to ashes.

And a stream of blood flowed.

From these ashes came seven other figures; the first said:

'I was called Pride, now I am called Nobility.' The others also spoke, and Ulenspiegl and Nele saw Economy come forth from Avarice; from

490

Anger, Vivacity; from Gluttony, Appetite; from Envy, Emulation; from Idleness, the Reverie of Poets and Sages. And Lust, on her goat, was transformed into a lovely woman called Love.

And the wisps danced a happy round about them.

Ulenspiegl and Nele then heard a thousand voices of hidden men and women singing sonorously, chucklingly, like the sound of castanets:

> 'When on the earth and on the sea
> These Seven transformed shall reign,
> Lift high your heads then, men,
> For that will be the world's felicity.'

And Ulenspiegl said:

'The spirits are mocking us.'

And a powerful hand seized Nele by the arm and cast her into space.

And the spirits sang:

> 'When the north
> Shall kiss the west,
> Then shall ruin end:
> The girdle seek.'

'La!' said Ulenspiegl: 'north, west, girdle. You speak in riddles, Spirits.'

And they sang chucklingly:

> 'The north is Holland;
> Belgium is the west;
> The girdle is alliance;
> The girdle is amity.'

'You are most wise, Spirits,' said Ulenspiegl.

And they sang chucklingly again:

> 'The girdle, poor man,
> Binding Holland and Belgium,
> Shall be good amity
> And fair alliance.'

> *Met raedt*
> *En daedt:*
> *Met doodt*
> *En bloodt.*

> 'Alliance of council
>   And of action,
>   Of death
>   And of blood
>   If necessary,
> Were it not for the Scheldt
> Poor man, were it not for the Scheldt.'

'Alas!' said Ulenspiegl, 'such is our tormented life, then: tears of man and laughter of Fate.'

> 'Alliance of blood
>   And of death,
> Were it not for the Scheldt.'

chuckled the spirits.

And a powerful hand seized Ulenspiegl and cast him into space.

10 NELE, FALLING DOWN, rubbed her eyes and saw nothing but the rising sun surrounded by golden mists, the tips of the grass all golden too, and the rays yellowing the plumage of the sleeping seabirds that soon awoke. Then Nele looked at herself and, seeing that she was naked, dressed herself in haste; then she saw Ulenspiegl likewise naked and covered him up; thinking that he slept, she shook him, but he budged no more than one dead. She was terrified. 'Have I,' she said, 'killed my love with that balm of vision? I would fain die, too. Ah, Tyl, wake up! He's as cold as marble!'

Ulenspiegl never awoke. Two nights and a day passed and Nele, feverish with anguish, watched over her lover.

At the beginning of the second day Nele heard the sound of a bell, and saw a peasant coming along carrying a spade; behind, carrying candles in their hands, walked a burgomaster, two sheriffs, the vicar of Stavenisse; the latter was followed by a beadle, who held a parasol over him.

They were going, they said, to administer the holy sacrament of extreme unction to the brave Jacobsen who was a Beggar through fear, but now, the danger past, was re-entering the bosom of the Holy Roman Church before he died.

Soon they came face to face with Nele, who was weeping, and they saw the body of Ulenspiegl lying on the grass, covered with his garments. Nele went down on her knees.

'Daughter,' said the burgomaster, 'what are you doing here with this dead person?'

Not daring to raise her eyes, she replied:

'I am praying for my friend, fallen here as though struck by lightning; I am alone now and wish to die too.'

The vicar then, puffing with pleasure:

'Ulenspiegl, the Beggar, is dead,' said he, 'praised be God! Peasant, haste you to dig a pit; take off his clothes before we bury him.'

'No,' said Nele, rising to her feet, 'they shall not be taken off; he'll be cold in the earth.'

'Dig the pit,' said the vicar to the peasant who carried the spade.

'You may,' said Nele, all in tears; 'there are no worms in that sand full of chalk, and he will remain whole and handsome, my love.'

And all distraught she bent over the body of Ulenspiegl and kissed him, weeping and sobbing the while.

The burgomaster, sheriffs and the peasant were filled with pity, but the vicar kept on saying joyfully: 'The Great Beggar is dead! God be praised!'

Then the peasant dug the grave, placed Ulenspiegl therein, and covered him with sand.

And the vicar said over the grave the prayers for the dead. All knelt about it. Suddenly there was a great movement under the sand and Ulenspiegl, sneezing and shaking the sand out of his hair, seized the vicar by the throat:

'Inquisitor!' said he, 'you lay me i' the earth alive while I sleep? Where is Nele? Have you also buried her? Who are you?'

The vicar screamed:

'The Great Beggar has returned to this world. Lord God! Receive my soul!'

And off he flew like a stag before the hounds.

Nele came to Ulenspiegl:

'Kiss me, sweet,' said he.

Then he looked about him again; the two peasants had fled like the vicar, throwing first to the ground, the better to run, the spade, the candle and the parasol; the burgomaster and the sheriffs, holding their ears with fright, lay groaning on the grass. Ulenspiegl went towards them and shook them, saying:

'Can you bury Ulenspiegl, the spirit, and Nele, the heart, of our mother Flanders? She also can sleep, but die, never! Come, Nele.'

And off he went with her, singing his sixth song. But no man knows where he sang his last.

Chronological Table

1519   Charles I of Spain elected Emperor (Charles V): Netherlands part of Spain

1527   Sack of Rome (May 6); Philip, son of Charles V, born (May 21)

1531   Charles V prohibits Reformation doctrines in Netherlands

1539   Rebellion of Ghent

1553   Charles V fails to take Metz

1554   Philip marries Mary, Queen of England

1555   Charles V resigns Netherlands to Philip

1556   Charles V resigns Spain to Philip (Philip II, 1556-1598)

1558   Charles V dies

1563   Organization of Calvinism in Netherlands

1564   Philip recalls Cardinal Granvela from Netherlands

1565   'Religious Edict'; opposed by William of Orange, Egmont and Admiral Hoorn

1566   The *'Compromise'* of the 'Beggars' refused by Margaret, Duchess of Parma

1567   Alba arrives in Brussels (August 8)

1568   Egmont and Hoorn beheaded (June 5)

1572   Dutch War of Liberation begins. William of Orange elected Stadtholder

1573   Alba recalled from Netherlands, succeeded by Requesnes

1576   Spaniards sack Antwerp (November 4). All Dutch provinces united against Spain

1577   'Perpetual Edict', refused by William of Orange

1578   Duke of Anjou Defender of Dutch liberties. Alexander Farnese, Duke of Parma, Governor of Netherlands

1579   Union of Utrecht of the seven Northern provinces. Peace of Arras: Southern Netherlands recognize Philip II

1581   Northern Netherlands renounce allegiance to Spain

1583 Anjou sacks Antwerp, leaves Netherlands
1584 William of Orange assassinated (July 10) ; succeeded by his son, Maurice. Ghent surrenders to Spaniards. Parma besieges Antwerp
1585 Parma takes Antwerp, regains Flanders and Brabant. English auxiliary corps under Leicester supports the Dutch
1587 Leicester fails, returns to England
1592 Alexander of Parma dies
1596 England, France and Netherlands ally against Spain
1598 Philip II dies (September 13)
1601 Spaniards begin siege of Ostend
1604 Spaniards capture Ostend
1609 Twelve Years' Truce between Spain and Netherlands

10ᵐ